WOMEN OF FAITH®
FICTION COLLECTION

WOMEN OF FAITH®

FICTION COLLECTION

PATRICIA HICKMAN
LORI COPELAND
AND ANGELA HUNT

WESTBOW
PRESS

A Division of Thomas Nelson Publishers
Since 1798

visit us at www.westbowpress.com

Westbow books may be purchased in bulk for educational, business, fundraising, or sales promotional use. For information, please email SpecialMarkets@ThomasNelson.com.

ISBN 1-5955-4071-7 (hc)

Printed in the United States of America

05 06 07 08 09 RRD 9 8 7 6 5 4 3 2 1

Sandpebbles

BY PATRICIA HICKMAN

WESTBOW
PRESS
A Division of Thomas Nelson Publishers
Since 1798

visit us at www.westbowpress.com

Library of Congress Cataloging-in-Publication Data

Hickman, Patricia.

   Sandpebbles / by Patricia Hickman.

      p. cm.

   ISBN 0-8499-4300-0

   I. Title: Sand pebbles. II. Title: At head of title: Woman of Faith fiction club presents. III. Women of Faith (Organization) IV. Title.

PS3558.12296 S36 2002

813'.54—dc21   2002016722

Printed in the United States of America

To Jessica Nicole Hickman
who loved dance, music, butterflies, and daisies.

9-21-1980
4-27-2001

While my memories of you, my angel girl, are rent by the pain of separation, I know that we are only a whisper apart until the day our Savior reunites us. I found this scripture written by your own hand on your nightstand, and I know you really meant it: *"Do nothing out of selfish ambition or vain conceit, but in humility consider others better than yourselves. Each of you should look not only to your own interests, but also to the interest of others."* (Philippians 2:3–4) This was your beacon, and it is still shining today.

One

NOT LETTING GO IS MY DOWNFALL. I CAN THINK OF
at least three lives I saved because of it and at least two lives I wrecked.
Case in point: Whenever my husband Joe and I saw an accident, I
leaped from the car, checked the victims' vitals, and directed traffic
until the local cops and EMS team arrived.

Be that as it may, succumbing to this same inner mechanism is
why I held a gun on two thugs and rescued my baby-sitter, Yolanda,
from what would have been possible torture. It was not a real gun.

A year and a half after Joe's death I drove home from Gum's Food
Mart loaded down with ears of corn and shrimp for a seafood boil near
the ocean. My boy, Mason, expected me to punctually pick him up
from his Grandpa's and chauffeur him to his baseball game. My late
habits at the newspaper office triggered occasional tardiness. He
tended to get miffed about my weak timekeeping. So I almost missed
seeing Yolanda at the Hep-Ur-Sef coin-op car wash because I exceeded
the speed limit. But in an oblique sort of manner, I saw the spray wand
lift and lower above Yolanda's VW Beetle. Then the whole hose con-
traption went haywire. Suds fountained in the air as the hose spewed
in circles and made cobralike gyrations that caught my eye and caused
my foot to hit the brake.

That is when I saw the thugs. One wielded a terrorizing blade. According to the ten o'clock news that night, the wayward boys had escaped from a jail in New Jersey, stolen a car, and made it all the way to our town of Candle Cove, North Carolina—a mistake they will most surely never make again. We are tight here. Whatever they intended to do with Yolanda never came to light. Before they could wrestle her away from the Beetle, my tires squealed to a dead stop right in front of them. Grenades of corn pitched throughout my SUV and I remember whisking away husk hairs for a solid month from the upholstery and carpet, a fact that irked me for the longest time. Mason had dropped his black water pistol onto the floor of the car. With both hands, I gripped it tight through the open window. I hid the plastic cap that holds in the water with my thumbs. "Put up your hands! I'm the police!"

Yolanda whitened and tried to speak even though one of the brutes had his filthy hand clamped over her sweet teenage mouth.

Both of the men were so surprised they froze, and the one with a knife threw it down. I called May at the police station on my cellular and she sent our two cops, Harold Gleason and Bobby White, over right away. (They were having jalapeño bagels at the nearby Lighthouse Java Mill.) I ordered the criminals to lie facedown on the pavement and Yolanda ran shrieking out into the street to flag down Harold and Bobby. Harold held them at bay while Bobby cuffed them and read them their rights. Harold said he wanted to swear at me for succumbing to my mechanism only to endanger the life of two helpless women, one being myself. But I had already stepped aside to retch into the Hep-Ur-Sef trash container.

Yolanda cried and ran up the bill on her parents' cellular phone, calling first her mother, her father who was away in Pittsburgh on business, her orthodontist, and her best friend in the whole eleventh grade. She hugged me and bawled on my shoulder so hard I had to tear myself away to run and fetch Mason, who by that time paced in front of his grandfather's house, tapping the tip of his bat against the walk, irate as mad bees. Even though I had rescued his lifelong baby-sitter, he was angry enough that he spilled out disconnected phrases that seemed to combust at the end with incensed grunts. The slightest infraction on my part, in his ten-year-old estimation, was worthy of castigation.

That is why I took him to Virginia every spring to visit his father's grave, to leave flowers, and to help Mason forgive me.

Six months later, the second anniversary of Joe's death rolled around, and Mason and I drove all the way up to northern Virginia to visit his daddy's grave. Neither of us wanted to stay behind in Virginia, or return to North Carolina. The trees along I-95 were not greening yet, and that disappointed Mason. Ten-year-old boys like him see sunsets and blooming trees and grow up to be men who can cry. Mason's daddy could not cry, and I believed that was what caused his death.

I thought that Joe's death would end my life. Even when Bobby and Harold showed up at my door stiff as soldiers with the news of Joe's passing, I had said just that very thing—"Dear God, my life is over!" But instead of ending me, Joe's accident left me opened up and walking around. Yet if I attempted the most menial tasks, I felt a paralysis slip over my mind. The most insignificant incidents reminded me of my Joe, like the time I opened a tool drawer out in the garage and found it stuffed with bank slips and gas receipts. I thought I had cleared away all of the clutter that reminded me of his pack rat tendencies, but right next to a ratchet and a box of matches lay more of his addiction to disorder. I cried for days. For hours every night after I sent Mason to bed, I cleared out every possible cranny in the house where Joe might have tossed a piece of this or that, even poring through his shoeboxes filled with tax returns until his clutter was eradicated and every inch of our house cleared of the-history-of-us. After the Nights of Eradication, I worked to close the windows of my soul and bar the attic of my mind.

It was the very worst thing I could do.

During our summer, we are the sun children of the Sound Country, not a long distance from the ferry that tools tourists out to Ocracoke Island or from any number of the fishing villages that dot the decaying womb of upper coastal North Carolina. Candle Cove draws beachcombers and business opportunities but not always both trades at once. Winter does not kiss us with heated passion the way it plays to its mistresses of the low country and Florida. Damp winters sluice the Sound people with blankets of firmament so thick the sky is one with the fog beneath our feet.

Summer is where we prefer to live. Mason wanted to cross the threshold to the inland with its thickets of live oak and find it green, not plain—not allowing the wind to howl through the naked tree limbs, brittle beggars undressed in the fields. Winter makes its home up north, but it plants its feet in the Carolinas, enough to chill the field and to blow snow across the upper decks of the mountains and leave a tinsel of cold upon the Atlantic side. Mentally I had painted our little piece of heaven green, just as I painted my mother alive. "Soon, Mason, we'll have us a good spring."

We saw the "Welcome to North Carolina" sign as we left Virginia behind, but the crossing of thresholds had lost its sheen. When too much change comes to your door, you grow anxious around thresholds.

I had learned to watch Mason without him knowing it. He sat with the passenger shoulder safety belt twisted behind him. Mason complained of seat straps too high for short kids. He never minded the height issue until fifth grade. But now he attached all of his worth to it, as though it were his defining trait. Within every comment from a grade-school imbecile—and every class has one—he found hidden meaning between what was said and what was implied.

My observances of Mason were as covert as all of the things that kept me a step ahead of him, like the furtive ways that a mother watches her boy so he won't complain she's smothering him. I cata-

logued a mental collection of a mother's snapshots into little significant files like "Mason when he is angry with me" and "Mason when
he daydreams." I thirsted for the tender and rare moments right now,
the sight of things that stole my breath and gave me pause. You learn
to look for beauty in the fragile lace of life when other things in your
world come unthreaded.

Mason remained transfixed on the ebbing color that stained the
horizon, as though he were sucking the color out of the sky himself.
A mélange of orange and cinnamon firmament floated just above the
mountains, a marker for where the sun had just kissed the sky before
bed. He traced the cloud shape onto the surface of the car window.
Or perhaps he drew something else. I don't know why I give every
action a meaning. It's just the thing a writer does when she sees something mysterious.

"This is North Carolina," he said, "not South."

"Right, Professor. North comes before South."

"Not if you're coming from Florida."

"Let's stop here tonight. Then tomorrow morning we'll have only
three hours left until we reach Candle Cove."

"Grandpa's looking for us."

"I told him it might be tomorrow."

A LaQuinta sign the color of orange and cinnamon floated above
the interstate. It advertised a special for families.

"Free breakfast. Let's stop here." I braked.

"Continental. That's not real breakfast."

"We have continental every morning: cold cereal, frozen waffles,
toast."

"Ask if we can check the pillows first. I hate pillows that are overpuffed," he said

"*Overpuffed* isn't a word. Unless you're saying it as two words." We
drove over a speed bump and past the flashing vacancy sign.

Mason slid his finger up and down the bridge of his nose in a
manner that followed the inward curve of the bridge to the upturned

and rounded curves that housed his trademark Longfellow nostrils. Whenever anger shot up his spine, those same nostrils flared and he looked pug-nosed.

"I hope the dog and cat are all right. Hercules always acts psychotic after he's been at the Pet Spa," I said.

"Johnson acts psychotic every day. Cats are all psychotic."

But none as off-the-wall as Johnson who had feline phobias such as a fear of walking on sand—he would mince onto the sand, shake his paw, and turn and run back up to the cottage. Only he didn't like the cottage either, and I swore he had agoraphobia or whatever you call that thing when you just want to stay in all of the time. "You know you love Johnson, Mason. You ought to. He's gotten too old to give away."

"A needy family still might take him. For a rug."

"This LaQuinta looks new. Maybe we'll get a new room. Toss my shoes over here, will you?"

"I'd rather pick up Hercules tonight. He's nervous without me." Mason slid my sneakers toward me with the side of his foot.

"He'll be fine one more night. Anyway, the Pet Spa closes at seven, I think. We have to wait until tomorrow to check him out anyway. This is like a three-day weekend for me. If Gloria keeps her word about it, that is." Gloria Hammer, my assistant at the Candle Cove *Sentinel,* had promised to keep the presses rolling in my absence from the weekly newspaper. I had never used my degree until after Joe died so I chose a business that seemed to line up with my journalism major, forgetting I might have needed a few courses on small business administration. I purchased the *Sentinel* as a safety net after Joe's death. Instead, it consumed our money as if we had carved a hole beneath the little downtown bank and plugged it with a vacuum. "Your last day of spring break. No cooking, no making the beds."

"We don't make the beds now. This place looks Mexican. See if they have a Taco Bell, Mom."

"You wait here, Mason. I'll get a key to check a room."

"And don't forget to check the pillows." He yelled "overpuffed" through the glass.

I crossed the asphalt beneath the registration overhang and glanced at Mason, but he stared down at the floor, stared as though he needed to count how many caramel corns had dropped to the floor between northern Virginia and North Carolina. He had grown more argumentative over the last few weeks, more as we packed away the office where Joe had kept his law files. And even more so when we swept away the veil of snow from the grave site where two years ago we had laid Joe to rest.

The night clerk was a Southerner who had developed a sonorous Midwestern elocution. I knew that because I could still hear the mountains in his vowels whenever he said, "Please take advantage of our free breakfast that starts at dawn."

"I notice a large bus parked out back. Is that a seniors' tour or a youth group?" I wanted peace all night.

"Neither. It's a basketball team from Florida."

I held the key card a foot away.

"They're a good bunch of young ladies."

"Oh, ladies' basketball." I always thought it strange to call those young girls "ladies," and imagined them with enormous handkerchief-stuffed black leather handbags with brass latches. I remembered Mason's request but felt too silly to ask about the pillows. "I need to check out the room first. But I'm sure it's fine. If I don't come back, it means I took the room."

The clerk picked up the phone but answered me tacitly, lifted his head and pinched his forehead until both eyebrows beetled, black antennae spreading over dark insect eyes.

I steered the car around the lot, slowly ascending the hills of speed bumps and following the red arrows the clerk had scrawled on a hotel map. "You can check out the pillows yourself, Mason."

"I wish I was already home. It was dumb to plant Daddy so far away."

"His family comes from Virginia, Mason. Your dad grew up there." Mason followed me up the little rear porch dimly illumined by the muted yellow courtesy light, and then tramped ahead to be the first inside.

"Virginia is too cold. My fingers almost froze up and cracked off."

"I think we enter through that doorway. Then down the hall is the elevator."

"You don't listen to anything I say."

"Mason, I'm tired."

"You look it."

We rode the elevator up to the second floor without a word exchanged between us. The door opened to a hallway decorated with quiet red carpet. Electric candlesticks cast a soft ambiance. I fiddled with a luggage strap and then said to him, "I know for a fact I haven't said anything to make you mad at me. I think you're tired."

Mason turned his rounded koala face from me, as if to keep me from studying the way his eyes lilted, slumberous at the corners. "You don't miss him as much as I do. If you did—"

An older man, his years frozen around his eyes, stopped to look at us two doors down. We vanished from the stranger's reproving stare and locked the door behind us.

"Mason, I just took a road trip halfway up a nation just so we could visit your daddy's grave."

"You didn't cry."

"Maybe I'm cried out. Folks get cried out. Tear ducts empty. It's not unnatural." A weird bareness rose up inside of me. I felt naked, my insides twisted open by a ten-year-old corkscrew.

"Why does his name on the grave thingy look so cold anyway? I feel like I want to cry, or I'm supposed to but it's not coming out. I waited for you to start, right when you put those plastic daisies in the stone vase. But you never cried, Momma."

"I see what you mean. I need a soda. You fill the ice bucket and I'll get the drinks."

I swore that Mason and I had talked out Joe's boating accident. Heaven knew the rest of Candle Cove had talked it to death. Mason's gut-thundering honesty shined up nice on some days but on others left me without any energy.

When Joe died, he had left enough of the aroma of manhood on Mason to make him wish for it, but the scent had faded. Mason ran in dogged circles in search of his dad, in search of a face that would tell him what God looked like.

Mason handed me the overnight case and then gutted his duffel bag, a bombed-out explosion of boy's underwear and game cartridges. He dumped both bags near the bathroom door and then scuttled downstairs to lock up the car, marching almost in cadence, the chivalrous male. On some days, he faked it so well, so near ultimate maleness that I believed Mason needed no more than just me. Just us; that was all we needed. I pressed a tissue against my eyes. The cold made them moist.

Sunrise had come too early, especially since I had allowed Mason to rent an in-room movie at nine the night before and break open the microwave popcorn deposited onto a tray by the maid. After an hour or so of driving, I initiated conversation to suppress the sleep demons that turned my eyelids to lead.

"For lunch, let's have a root beer float and toast it just like when your daddy did on that day up at Ocean City. It was your birthday, I believe. I'll bet your daddy would like that."

"Should we wait until we get home and invite Grandpa? Will we be home by then or did you mean along the way?" Mason had encircled the calendar day in red crayon and scribbled three initials— DDD—for the "day Dad died." He laid the calendar on the seat between us open to the month of March, the tenth day.

I might have noticed an important calendar notation made earlier on my way out of town, but I didn't even give it a glance. That is what caused all of the trouble. "We might be home by then but I have work waiting at home. I have to stop and pick up some extras for the cottage, too. Grandpa's invited a pastor to preach either next week or the week after. Or, I guess he's an evangelist. But for the life of me I can't remember if it was next Sunday or not. Whatever. Dad acts like he needs the break, anyway." My father had pastored Candle Cove Presbyterian for twenty-seven years without a real vacation.

"Grandpa wants to go fishing, like he thinks I like it."

"If you don't want to fish, tell him."

"I'd hurt his feelings."

"Grandpa's been told worse things than that, Mason. Pastors hear everything." I felt as though I were slipping back into my old flannel bathrobe as we passed by the familiar towns such as Brinkleyville and Glenview.

"When we go away and then go home, I'm glad to get away, but gladder to get back home," I said.

A rabbit raced alongside the SUV, slightly ahead of us, its legs stretching behind it so extreme in gait, it seemed to fly. Mason eyed it and squinted like a wishful huntsman. He drew an invisible gun, made a cocking sound with his tongue, and then yelled, "Blam, blam!"

"I'll bet you're ready to get back in school after a break."

"I hate school." He blurted it out as though he knew it would annoy me.

"Boys like to say that, right? It's something you're supposed to say when you're a guy. I wonder if you really mean it, though."

"Of course I mean it." He fired his invisible bullets again. A satisfaction spread across his face as though he didn't see the long legs split a sea of grass and vanish, but rather lurch in a moment of surprise, a stain of red forming at the heart, a jerk, and then a collapse.

"When I kept up with my school work, I mean, when I was your age, I liked school. I never hated it when I had it all together, had my GPA up."

"We don't call it a GPA. Just grades. I make the grades, but I still hate it."

"Hating it has to be a male thing."

"All my friends hate it." He scanned the passing field for more wildlife.

A rotary movement caught my eye, a twenty-something-foot-tall mug that rotated above a hamburger stand. "It's a sign, Mason."

"I'll get my shoes on." He said it like a television jingle.

"Good. I'll make the list for Dad." I parked us right outside the takeout window. "Dad's secretary forgets so many little things, especially since Mother died. I don't know why that is. He should pay me a salary for all I have to do to keep Thelma straight."

Mason carried the tray of cheeseburgers, onion rings, and root beer to a red Formica table with chrome legs. "We never take this long to get home."

"I don't know what you mean." I emptied the tray, arranged the food, and then handed the tray to a passing waitress.

"You were in a hurry to get to the cemetery, to Daddy's grave. But you're taking longer to get home."

"I hadn't noticed."

"We've been in the car like forever."

"Drat, they put ketchup on my burger," I said.

"I need to sign up for baseball season this weekend. Tomorrow morning."

I drew in a breath and sighed. "You didn't tell me."

He broke our communal glare with an irritating retort. "I did. Mom, you forgot. Again."

"So we'll get up in the morning and do it. Mason, you exaggerate about me as though you have to parade all of my flaws out in front of the world. I'm not a bad mother."

"I need new pads, cleats, pants. Everything's too small. If I have to wear those pants another year, maybe I won't play. "

"We'll get the baseball gear. Don't make me feel like a louse, as

11

though I'm going to make you go to practice with your rear end hanging out."

"If you don't want to go, Grandpa can take me."

"I said I'd take you. I'll be right back. I can't eat this with ketchup." I returned the burger to the front-counter attendant, who sighed and ferried the sandwich into a suspiciously hidden-from-sight kitchen. Mason sat with his back to me. When he wanted something, he always made me feel inadequate, a loose thread on his shoulder.

We finished lunch without sharing many more words. I made a list of things, certain Dad had forgotten them.

The sky clouded an iron gray painted with winter shades that darkened the nimbostratus layer and its ragged skirts. But the quiet aroma of spring left a far hint of complaint in the air, as though winter had stayed beyond its welcome. I shifted and it caused Mason to stand and clear away the litter. He shuffled the trash into a rubber bin and walked alone to the SUV.

He crawled into the middle seat behind me. The rest of the trip, he slept. A tinny rhythm emanated from his earphones. They curved around his neck like a stethoscope. I turned off his cassette player. As we drew nearer to Candle Cove, to Pamlico's teeming universe, I felt something slipping from me. The cemetery visit left me feeling as though I swam the journey home with anchors tied to both feet.

I once believed that North Carolina offered a comfortable lap for errant souls like Joe. But the ocean beyond the estuaries and further, on past the archipelago of islands adorning the eastern shores like a bridal tiara, was unforgiving. It swallowed up too much. You can only be swallowed once by water if you don't pull yourself out fast enough. It was no way for Joe to leave the world, in my opinion. I wanted significance in my marriage—banners I could wave around and say, "Joe and me, we made it." But he left all hope on the bottom of the sea with the fish and the sand. Sand pebbles make for weak touchstones, shifting, hiding, and changing places until the world forgets you once made footprints.

Joe left little behind in the way of a legacy, except a disputed piece of land and a cat. I hate cats, although I am cautious to never make mention of it in the *Sentinel.* I could lose subscriptions. My loathing for cats had more to do with the acquiring of my last name, a stylish name for a writer, according to some of my writer friends. When I said my vows to Joe, I acquired a cat and a good literary name. Once I considered the name a lucky amulet for a writer, although my prose never bubbled close to the abilities of the writer's circle I admire— the Candle Cove Inksters. It is believed that genius flourishes in remote pockets of the Carolinas, but seldom in Candle Cove. I know of at least one irritating genius who ran with the Inksters, but I wanted nothing to do with her. Sarai Gillman was a Wilmington grad who poured coffee up at the Lighthouse Java Mill by day. The girl's wand-shaped shadow flickered against a stained window shade every evening as she fashioned plots that she never shared, even with the Inksters. But also perched in the window were cats. Cattails sashayed back and forth in the girl's window, little metronomes keeping time to the ticking of the keys, the cadence of thought shaped into words by her. The very idea of the creatures jumbled in a mass around that writer's feet repulsed me; all that thrumming those animals do annoys me, as though their motor is forever idling. I know that Inkster has an overage of cats by the silky filaments that cling to her T-shirts and the jagged claw marks along the hem of her uniform: Caucasian-pink knit slacks tattooed with an embroidered lighthouse on the front pocket. But since Joe died, I've wanted nothing to do with cats—especially the aged family tomcat, Johnson, that coils around my feet every evening when I water the potted geraniums that droop along the three sage-green shelves above my kitchen sink. But that doesn't mean I neglect him. My antipathy for cat lovers I acquired much earlier. But as I said, I'll sell them a newspaper.

Joe adopted Johnson when we dated. Johnson hated my golden retriever, Hercules, the puppy I bought for Mason when he turned three. After Mason's birthday party that year, we relegated Hercules to

a backyard pen simply as a means of quelling the constant feud between cat and dog. It is mysterious the way the animals mirrored their
owners. I argued with Joe at the slightest provocation in hopes I could
help him grow. I was always honorable in my motives.

It was all my fault for falling for lawyerly charisma in the first place.

Joe Longfellow had hooked me from the start. My initial hunch
that he would ultimately draw me in by his devices against my better
judgment came when I first took notice of the sound of his voice. I
kept myself from men like him by cataloguing male voices into a
secret system I shared with no one, save my best friend, Dinah
Buckworth, who hosts a local radio show called "In the Kitchen with
Dinah." I was proofing a college paper I had just roughed out while
at the study of my parents' beach cottage. Stumped by one elusive
fact, I had phoned the venerable law offices of Blakely and Chase in
Wilmington for one loaded detail, only to wind up with the after-
hours answering machine. Joe Longfellow had just passed his bar and
made use of his afternoons by researching cases for Blakely and Chase.
Blakely had asked Joe to provide the message for their answering
machine. I phoned in for a meager thread of research for a postbacc
paper. Joe Longfellow's dazzling pitch explained the firm's law specialty, that thing they did for the banking industry as transactional
attorneys. Immediately, I placed him on the farthest spectrum of my
male voice scale, a scarlet ten with conjuring, albeit, troublesome tendencies that marked his deep vibrato with a subtle trace of jagged
machismo—a slight touch of it, but nonetheless, enough to sound the
siren. I possessed in my midtwenties a weak splinter of craving that
seldom hooked me with the wrong man, but on occasion pricked me
in all of my vulnerable places. It was a dreadful chink in my ideology;
a gene for which neither of my parents accepted blame.

Joe's voice had had such an effect on me. Instantly pricked, I had
left a brief message, but called back ten minutes later to inform "the
voice" that I would pick up the information the following day. In
person.

My mother, Julia Norville, had a premonition about him, even though she took no store in premonitions. She called those shudders of portent that afflict maternal instinct her "discerning quakes"—a slight tremor that stole her breath and nothing more. Mother quaked only twice for my sake—once when through a dot-com Web site I bought a used Tercel that gave out after one year and, second, when I met Joe Longfellow.

"He's not of your moral fiber," she had said, but how she knew that I never knew.

"Mason, we're home."

Candle Cove sat as a breath along the Atlantic, a phosphorescent crescent of light at the end of the day. A pallid shard of daylight flickered, engulfed by the curtain of rain that followed us home.

"Don't forget the dog, Mom."

As if I would. "After we unpack, we'll pick him up. And Johnson." I remembered the root beer stand again. We had wandered into and back out of the roadside stand without ever acknowledging the anniversary of Joe's death, without toasting root beers, as though numbed by the calendar date. Mason dragged his gear to the house, put his key into the twenty-year-old keyhole, and vanished into the dusky entry. The sky let go of the rain and it washed the dust from the SUV, ran into the gutters, flushed down into the waterway, and out into the ocean.

The untoasted moment left me feeling unpardoned and unfinished. I would step inside and ask Mason's forgiveness if he even so much as hinted at the infraction. If he forgot, then I would pick up the dog and cat, and go to bed tacit and incomplete. That is what you do when your life is a wreck.

Two

MASON PULLED A QUILT OUT OF THE FAMILY TRUNK that masqueraded as a coffee table and tented up a cozy hiding place on top of the sofa where he curled up with Hercules. The cat paced out on the deck, done with his business and whining miserably to get back inside. His tail was ringed with charcoal and bent like the flagpole of a defeated foe.

I cradled chlorine cleanser under one arm like the Princess of Hygiene. "You stay here and relax, Mason, and I'll be right back."

I drove to Dad's seaside place where I would make a checklist for the cottage. I could clean it on Monday. That would be soon enough to prepare the place for any guests.

I passed Dad's house on the way to the cottage. His home, lit low like the whispered blush of a monastery, was tucked into a copse of trees. A tangle of hardwoods and yellowed palms, a product of Florida transplants that clashed with native trees, cosseted the pale green bungalow. Every Friday since I could remember, James Norville shut himself away from the fray of committees and hospital visits to lay the finishing touches to the Sunday morning message. His preaching books encircled his comfortable chair: a *Strong's Concordance*, a newsmagazine or two, and a handbook of biblical history. A dim study light illuminated the soft veil of window sheers that rustled whenever the floor vent warmed the room. Later, I would call and tell him we made it back all right. But for now I imagined him with an afghan draping his lap, planted next to his mother's old upright radio that had not played a single hymn since the days of "The Old Time Gospel Hour." My mother's miniature dachshund, Arnie, would lie on the braided rug with its chin and face pressed against Dad's woolly house slippers. The dachshund developed white chin whiskers in its later years, a phenomenon Dad called "Arnie's beard." I would not transgress to disturb such a scene. I drove to the cottage a mile away.

The cottage windows revealed an illumined kitchen. A movement inside the cottage startled me. A shadow crossed the lace curtains hung one summer by my mother and me in the old place. Twice I glanced down at the calendar day circled by Mason. It occurred to me that Mason's broad red strokes might be hiding other things, such as a note about a visiting pastor, and yet I plowed into the sandy back garden without so much as an inspection of my own orderly records.

Three additional human shapes appeared inside behind the lacy sheers, smaller bodies wildly moving through the kitchen, nymphlike shadows dancing against my mother's sacred window. I elevated myself from the red leather seat of the Mustang once driven by Joe. The sounds muffled by the closed-up nature of the house in its winter state had a natural quality; not like the noise of intruders, but the abiding familiarity of ownership.

I approached the house from the kitchen side, a rear entrance with a yawning two-level deck. The ocean roared and slapped at the shore, digging saltwater talons into the sand as the tide shrank and flexed into frilled gills of spray and grasping waves. I entered the rear deck from the wooden steps that Dad and I had stained blue-gray to accent the ocean hues of the cottage. Through the windows, I saw her: a blond-haired woman scoured the twin sinks and chattered with several children, one of which clung to her shirttail. Dad never hired a housekeeper, never would have paid hired help to clean the cottage when he could call me.

My trip away with Mason must have convinced him I needed a break. I tapped on the rear-door window as I hid the cleanser inside the deepest pocket of my Windbreaker.

I startled the woman. A young girl sidled behind the woman's hips, a kittenish yelp emanating from her soft triangular mouth. The blonde looked to be in her late twenties, the gleam of youth melding with the chic of maturity. I returned her faint smile, but felt the woman intercepted my concern. She opened the door with one hand. In the other, she clutched one of my mother's old aprons.

"May I help you?"

Her question annoyed me. "This is my father's cottage. I've been out of town and dropped by to check on the place."

"Oh, are you Marcia?"

"March. Like this month, the month of March."

"I like that name. Charlotte, go and bring your brothers and sister in here to meet Ms. Norville."

Charlotte flew, her arms and fingertips draped with wings made of felt, gold braid, and a translucent fabric, wings that fluttered behind her, primitive and fashioned by an unrestrained imagination.

"March Longfellow. Norville was my maiden name." I followed the blonde goddess into the kitchen, careful to close the door to keep out the chill of the ocean wind.

"I'm pleased to meet you. I'm Ruth Arnett. Your father told you Pastor Colin Arnett was coming, I hope."

"That's this weekend, then?" I felt my mother's opinions alight all over me, scrutinizing my tone and intent. I reconstructed the sentence. "Welcome to Candle Cove. I'll do everything I can to make you comfortable." I sounded mechanical, like a flight attendant droning her spiel over the intercom. But the unparalleled scrutiny of Julia Norville lived inside of me, eliciting the proper response.

"I feel as though we've made you uncomfortable. I don't believe you were told about us. I know Colin. He won't want to be a bother, but sometimes when the men do all of the planning, well, not all of the details get ironed out. Please, all I have are some cold drinks until Colin returns from the store. Let me fix you something."

"No, I don't need a thing. My father doesn't usually handle the details of visitors. I've always done that. I usually ask the ladies at church to bring meals by for visiting ministers. I must have written down the wrong date, is all. I hope you know it isn't like me at all." I changed directions, not wanting to sound grasping. "Reverend Arnett doesn't need to stock the pantry. I can make a few phone calls tonight and you'll have dinners on the way by tomorrow night, home cooked. Our ladies are really good cooks too. Breakfast items we leave here in the cottage for you, if that's all right. Or we can set up an account for you at Millie's if you prefer a hot cooked breakfast. Millie's pancakes are popular."

"No, goodness no. I already feel as though we've imposed enough. Your father was kind enough to consent to our joining Colin at the last minute. That's why he volunteered to run for groceries. I do all of the cooking, so I'm used to that, although Charlotte here is turning out to be quite the kitchen helper herself."

The winged child smiled, her hair white and poking out of a ponytail holder in damp spikes.

"Colin called Reverend Norville last night, thought the kids and myself would like a seaside visit. It's been a hectic year. I've been working on my dissertation."

"I'm just thinking of finishing my master's myself," I said, although it sounded down the ladder from Ruth Arnett's dissertation. "I write, though. I guess I don't have much use for a doctorate unless I decide to teach college.

"I didn't know you wrote, Ms. Norville."

I didn't correct her this time. "I own a small newspaper here in Candle Cove. Sometimes I write travel articles for the *Charlotte Observer*, too. But that's just a little freelance work on the side I do for a friend. Helps to pay the bills." The newspaper had yet to meet budget or clear a profit, but I kept that bit of sour news to myself.

"It's so pretty here. We drove here in the rain. But we arrived in time to see the sunset and it's beyond what the postcards around here can portray. If ever we have the time, I want to visit the Outer Banks. But I don't know how you get out to those islands. By plane, I guess."

"Or ferry. Roanoke Island has festivals; you might try Roanoke first. Or Ocracoke Island."

"But I don't like a lot of tourists. I'm looking for solace." Ruth lightened her tone as though she longed for peace at this very instant.

"Pamlico Sound is perfect, then."

Two little boys made the flight down the staircase in only six steps.

"Troy and Luke, mind yourselves and come in here and meet Reverend Norville's daughter."

"Nice to meet you boys." I waved at them knowing how children in this day and age are less prone to shake a hand.

Ruth Arnett rinsed out the sinks and wiped down the tiled counter-tops as she spoke. It made me uneasy.

"I actually carried over some cleaning supplies," I told her and half-turned as though I might go back out to the car to fetch them. "If you all want to go to dinner, I'll have the place dusted and ready before you return. I don't know how Dad and I crossed wires, but I'd like to make it up to you."

"The cottage is already in really nice shape, and you weren't expecting the whole Arnett clan, so I insist—you don't need to do a thing. I've had my mind so buried in books; really, a little domestic duty is a welcome change. Colin's bringing back barbecue. I hope I sent him to a good place. We found this little dive as we drove down this road that parallels the beach. Dives have the best food, we've found."

"JoJo's Barbecue, I'll bet. Plenty enough of a dive, if that's what you like."

"You should join us."

"I can't. I left my ten-year-old asleep on the sofa with the dog."

"You have a child, March. Maybe he can come play with the kids this weekend."

"He would like that. I have to get him signed up for baseball practice tomorrow morning. We'll see how tomorrow goes."

"And don't worry about breakfast. Colin's picking up milk and cereal for the kids. We'll be just fine with that."

"I should go, then. Glad we could meet. Maybe I'll meet Reverend Arnett tomorrow. You all have a good night's rest."

"Thank you, Ms. Norville."

Two headlights flooded the kitchen, then dimmed next to the Mustang. Ruth waved through the window to Colin Arnett.

"Daddy's back with the food," said Charlotte. "Luke, you and Troy go wash your faces and hands right this minute."

Troy grimaced, unwilling to bend to his sister's dictates.

"That's a good idea," said Ruth. "I haven't seen Rachel. Ms. Norville, I'll be right back. Seems like the youngest is always the last one down."

"Four children." I counted them.

Ruth bounded up the stairs, her long legs wrapped in black knit and punctuated at her narrow feet by Nikes. She sprinted like a runner. I tried to imagine my mother in clingy knit but couldn't. Ruth Arnett had failed to adopt the wrappings of a clergyman's family. No floral frocks off the KMart blue-light-specials bin, no Payless Shoes enclosing her delicate toes. Just the lightly girded style that makes the few size-two women in the world look to-the-nines when scarcely wearing a thing.

Colin Arnett banged the rear door with his knee.

"I'll get it!" Charlotte ran past and nearly tripped on a loose ruffle around her hem. She twisted the brass knob with both hands. "I hope you got me chicken, Daddy!"

"Charlotte, grab this bag under my arm. I'm just about to drop it, honey," Colin said.

The girl, who looked to be an eight-year-old, hefted the bag of milk but swaggered under the weight of the gallon jug.

I reached for the milk. "I can help."

"I have it." Charlotte lifted her wings and thrust the milk carton onto the countertop.

"Charlotte lives under the mistaken impression she's in charge." Colin set the other bags next to the milk. "Just like her mother. Hi, I'm Colin Arnett." He held up his hand crooked to one side with his thumb pointing up at the ceiling as though he felt comfortable holding a calligrapher's pen.

He had long fingers, curved at the tips. He seemed well practiced in ordinariness. My father's poise when he introduced himself held a mystery about it. I remember how awestruck I'd felt as a girl about the word *Reverend* carefully placed in front of James Norville's name. It was the way he said it, with careful enunciation, plummy with a bit of starch. Colin Arnett said his name insouciantly, like a bohemian in Greenwich Village.

"I'm Reverend Norville's daughter. I've been away or else I would have stocked the pantry for you. I hope you're not inconvenienced."

"Your father told me you were gone away on a trip. I'm here a day early and bringing five more than he expected. I'm glad to pick up a few things. Hope this barbecue place has food as good as it smells."

"I can put all of that away for you," I said.

"No, please. Ruth will manage and she doesn't mind. Charlotte, you and your brothers go pick up your toys. You left them all over the downstairs parlor."

"We haven't entertained an evangelist in a while. I've made friends over the years with evangelists and their families. The road can be wearying with all of those motels. When my mother and dad bought this place, they wanted it to be a refuge for traveling ministers. I hope you find it peaceful here."

"Actually, I'm a pastor. I haven't had to dwell for long summers in the caves of Motel 6s. Your father and I met at a ministers' meeting last year and we've corresponded ever since."

"Dad loves to write letters."

"Almost a thing of the past, I'm afraid. It's unique to find a fellow minister who is willing to pen a letter. You find out more about a person when he writes than if you're having a telephone conversation. Or e-mail."

"I guess that's true."

The boys ran through the kitchen and disappeared into the downstairs bedroom. Ruth had dressed them in robes and slippers.

"Your tribe is hungry," I said.

Colin left his jacket atop a table where my mother once cultivated violets. When he turned his back to me, I placed it on the hall tree.

"They've been restless. I've been careful not to share the purpose of our visit here. It's too early. But it's as though they sense a change. Children are more insightful than we give them credit for." When he moved, it was with balance, like a man practiced at tennis or any sport that required agility in a small quadrangle of space.

I transported the gallon of milk to the refrigerator. "I'm not altogether following you, but as I said, I've been away."

"I can't imagine moving away from our home near Lake Norman. My wife spent so many hours decorating the place. It has her touch all over it."

I lifted a pint of slaw from one of the brown bags. Then I stood with it pressed against my stomach, forgetting my domestic obligations in order to try and decipher the coded language of this city minister.

"When your father's steering committee first called, well, it just didn't seem plausible. But they were so persistent. I have a lot of admiration for tenacity in a church committee."

"I don't know anything about a steering committee, Reverend Arnett. I'm close to my father and he would tell me about any changes. Does he know why you're here? I certainly don't."

"Your father is a thorough planner, Ms. Longfellow. He explained to me his desire to retire a year ago. But I never saw myself as the one to take his place."

"My father isn't old enough to retire. He's in his prime and his congregation would never stand for it."

"He hasn't told you." He leaned against the countertop. He had gray eyes, studious, and they studied me. "Then I have no business telling you. This is terrible."

"My mother and father built this church from nothing, gave birth to it as though it were their own child. They spent up all of their savings just so the new church would not founder under the weight of a salary." I felt my nostrils flare, just like Mason's.

Ruth waited at the foot of the stairs. "Colin?"

"I've made a mess of things, Ruth," he told her.

"What did you do?"

"Reverend Norville hasn't shared the news of his retirement with his daughter."

"Colin, no. Ms. Norville, I'm afraid we've intruded on your life tonight. You must think of us as awful people. Charlotte, go back into the parlor with Rachel and the boys." She rushed them out of the room much the way my mother used to send me out of my father's study.

"Dad would not retire without telling me. Reverend Arnett, you don't understand how it is between us."

"I do. Your father speaks highly of you, Marcia."

"March."

"Like the month, Colin." Ruth gathered up four small drinking cups.

"I feel I should call him tonight," said Colin. "If he doesn't mind, perhaps you and I can pay him a visit together, Ms. Longfellow."

"I'll drop by on my way home. I should leave anyway. My son is at home alone. I'm sorry if I've messed up your evening. You all seem to have misunderstood about this matter with the church. But I'll get to the bottom of it. I do look forward to hearing your message on Sunday, Reverend. And I will send the ladies over tomorrow with hot meals."

"That isn't necessary, March," said Colin.

"It's what I do here."

I hurried to Dad's place. I lingered out on the porch and rehearsed what to say. All of his hints about retirement, if they were hints, lined up, but somehow I had never connected the dots. He had invited me to bring Mason over the day before we left for Virginia. Mason and I dropped by, but I cleaned his bathroom floors while he ground peppercorns for a salad. When he talked about fatigue, I suggested he give his secretary, Thelma, more hours or hire her an assistant. I insisted I would drop by his house on Fridays and do his deep cleaning. On Monday, I said, I could fax a list of tasks to Thelma just as my mother once made up the Monday list. He sat in his chair and read the rest of the day.

Reverend James Norville opened his door. "You're home. I was just about to phone you and see if you all made it back all right. You've picked up your dog, I guess." He never asked about the cat, but I knew why. Dad hated hearing about money spent on family pets, and caring for Johnson equaled what it would cost to finance a small island.

I put my arms around him and kissed the side of his face. "I just came from the cottage. It's full of people." I walked past him. "But you already know that, I guess. I'm sorry I wasn't here to let them in. Did I misunderstand you about the date or, well, it doesn't matter now."

"You met Colin Arnett, then."

"And his wife. Is she a young thing or what? I guess those four kids keep her skinny and anorexic looking."

"Ruth is not his wife."

"Sure, she's his wife. Ruth Arnett. She introduced herself. Caters to her husband like nobody I've ever seen. Kind of poured into that little knit thing she wore, but if I were a size two . . . you were making ham and eggs for dinner?" The carton of eggs lay open on the kitchen island, an efficient package of cholesterol. The vacuum-packed ham lay beside it. "You should come to my place, Dad. I'll make us both something else, something substantial. Pasta, maybe, or lentil soup and French bread."

"I don't call lentil soup substantial. Colin Arnett's wife, Eva, died four years ago of cancer."

"Then who is Ruth Arnett?"

"Colin's sister. She moved in with them after Eva died. Being the only two old widow men at the ministers' state council last year, he and I became friends. We've written back and forth some."

"He told me. I wouldn't call him an old widow man."

"Just me."

"Not you either." I closed up the eggs and put them back in the refrigerator.

"I plan to eat that."

"Soup and salad. That's what we need tonight."

"I'm glad you came by." He retrieved the eggs. "If you want to go back and get Mason, I'll cook for all of us tonight. But you make the biscuits. Mine taste like plaster of Paris."

"Mason won't eat pork, Dad. Kids are funny these days."

"They'd rather eat pulverized chicken fried in a vat and served by a clown."

"I should call Mason, wake him."

"Let me go and bring him back. That way you could start the biscuits." Dad reached for his hat.

"No, Dad." I put down the phone. "I don't want Mason to hear us talking about Colin Arnett."

He let out a breath. "I tried to get together with you and tell you. Kind of like stopping a runaway train."

"All this time I thought it was a misunderstanding. You can't retire. What a silly notion! You'll have no income and the church people, well, they'd not allow it."

"I have a small retirement saved, March. Your mother and I planned for this."

"Not enough. In five years you'd have a good retirement. And there's the school project. Half the congregation didn't want that school but you convinced them we needed one. They'll shut it down if you leave."

"The school is stable. Phil is adding a sixth grade next year. Just in time for Mason."

"Colin Arnett has different ways than you."

"Make those cheese biscuits. It's been a good bit since I had cheese biscuits."

"He doesn't go by a title, just says, 'Call me Colin,' and you know what the board will do when they hear that. They'll not want this man. He's not conservative enough."

"You've known him five minutes and already he's a liberal."

"Not a liberal. His ways are not as conservative as yours."

"March, I know your whole life is wrapped up in the church. I haven't made any decisions, though, and neither has Colin. He doesn't want the job and we've set no date."

"I'm glad to hear that." I foraged for biscuit mix.

"The only reason he came was to get away. He's taken a little country church of fifty people and grown it to more than a thousand. He thought a trip to the ocean would do him good, give him time to think."

"Candle Cove Presbyterian is large enough for the size of the town." I felt as though it shrank as I spoke. I sprayed diluted bleach along the top of the countertop to counteract the faint smell of bacon grease.

"He's a go-getter, a real man of vision."

"He wears Nikes, for heaven's sakes."

"I've been thinking of switching, myself." He stared at his own two feet.

"Nikes don't go with polyester."

"Oh, before I forget, your mother-in-law called while you were gone. I guess you haven't had time to check your answering machine."

The silence between us was close to tangible. Dad turned his back to me and swayed as though he mentally sang a hymn.

"She's such a greedy woman, Dad. You know I don't want to talk to her."

"I take it you didn't visit her in Virginia."

"She has no business contacting me."

"Anyway, I've done my bit by telling you she called. Don't shoot the messenger."

I pilfered through the pantry. "You're out of biscuit mix, Dad."

"No, you're looking in the wrong place. It's under the kitchen sink."

"You shouldn't put food products next to cleansers and mop buckets." I dragged out a bottle of mop detergent, two scouring pads, and a soap pad and organized them into a plastic pail.

"I moved the mop bucket to the back on purpose. It was in the way."

"You're turning this house into a bunker." My mother had once said it would happen if she were to land in heaven ahead of my father.

"You treat me like a visitor in my own house. I feel as though I'm conversing with a drill sergeant. Not my daughter."

I pulled out a pen and paper to add to Monday's list the need to reorganize Dad's kitchen.

"Mrs. Longfellow sounds so dismal, March. To hear her talk, you're just not listening to her side of things."

"As usual, she said too much. Someone needs to hang a sign on Joan Longfellow that says 'Warning—she overshares.'"

"She's really worried about the family estate."

"Dad, Joe wanted Mason to have that five acres in Virginia. To hear Joan babble on you'd think I was breaking up a set of museum crystal or something. Mason is a Longfellow too."

"The land has family buried in it."

"I'm not having them dug up, for Pete's sake! My husband is buried there, too, but she doesn't seem to distinguish the connection."

"Family burial plots are sacred. You know how the old families in our church feel about that little church cemetery."

"You want to tell Mason he has to give up his inheritance from his father, you do it, then."

"You're jumping to conclusions, March. I just think you should be easier with this woman, more sensitive. Coddle her, maybe. Assure her that Joe's part of the estate hasn't fallen into enemy territory."

"I'll not coddle a greedy, grasping woman. She acts as though I sank Joe's boat myself."

"Grief makes you act like someone you're not sometimes."

"Will wonders never cease? I found the biscuit mix, Dad."

A set of heavy knuckles pounded the door frame. "Someone's at the door, March. You want to get it, or should I?"

"Oh, I hope it's not that Colin Arnett. I'm not in the mood for him."

"It's him." Dad squinted to see the top of a man's head through the small window above the peephole in the sash door.

I scooped up my purse, in no mood to iron things out. Colin Arnett was probably one of those smooth take-charge types who envisioned setting me down and calming my brow just before he coaxed me into his way of thinking. Men like him could not fathom people like me who quietly held together the works for years without intrusive help from outsiders. "You talk to him, then. And be sure you tell him you haven't made up your mind, that you might have been hasty in calling him in the first place."

"You should write it all down. I can just read it to him, like a script."

"I'm going upstairs to call Mason." Aggressive tactics called for evasive measures. I stepped over Mother's rug in the entry, but kept my back to the door. When Dad opened it, I didn't want to make eye contact with Colin Arnett. My eyes would give away the fact that I had talked about him. Eyes always give away our secrets. He would jump to conclusions and believe I had disparaged him, which I had not.

The porch slats out front squeaked beneath male weight.

"March," Dad yelled from the entry. "It isn't Colin at all. It's Jerry Brevity. I think he saw your car in the driveway."

Jerry Brevity exterminated rats for the families that lived near the water, especially those families who lived near the Intracoastal Waterway.

"Keep your voice down. I can see how you confused Jerry's giant rat truck for the Arnett SUV." I tried to become one with the ficus tree at the foot of the stairs.

"Jerry's been asking around about you."

"Tell him I don't have time to talk, Dad."

"Why don't you like him?"

"His bulb's a little dim, that's all." I whispered now and waved my hands at Dad to release me.

I heard the door open but turned the circular corner on the staircase. Jerry Brevity had asked me last week to join him for pie and coffee at the Lighthouse. I took Mason bowling instead. Jerry gave off a chemical tang that reminded me of citronella.

Jerry had parked his truck behind the Mustang. The rat atop his truck advertised his trade. The giant rat curled on its back with *X*s for eyes appeared to be placed at the curb for me, a rodent offering much like Johnson leaves at the back door when I scold him.

I took the stairs two at a time and entered my father's bedroom. He still had not removed Mother's fussy Priscilla curtains, but the lace comforter was folded and placed in a corner of the room. Mother's quilts lay folded in not-so-tidy angles at the foot of the bed. Stacks of books rose like columns on the nightstands that flanked the headboard. The old books and Dad's rubbing ointment made the room smell like the lobby of the Airfresh Inn, the local retirement home. I would come Wednesday after I finished the weekly edition, clean this room, and restore it to its natural condition.

It is what I do.

Three

GOOD MORNING, CANDLE COVE, AND WAKE UP TO THE
*Saturday journal of "In the Kitchen with Dinah," a weekend edition of
this week's highlights. Dinah reveals her secret recipe for hummingbird
cake that will tickle your rib cage with only half the calories.* . . .

The radio alarm next to my bed blared, the town trumpet ruling
over Saturday, insensate to the fact that I had not had a day off in at
least twelve months. Dinah's drawling and catarrhal voice oozed from
the taped version of her daily weekday show.

"Mom, I can't find my glove." Mason clattered outside my bedroom door.

"This can't be Saturday." My legs stuck straight out, stiff. The flat
sheet enshrouded my right calf.

"Here it is. I found it." Mason appeared in the doorway. "You're
not dressed."

"It won't take long. I can't see. By George, I knew it would happen! I've gone stark blind." I groped around me.

"You have your Lone Ranger on your face."

I pulled the sleep mask down beneath my chin. "I don't smell coffee. Shouldn't I smell coffee?"

"I think you forgot to set the timer. We have to leave in fifteen
minutes. I can call Grandpa if you can't move any faster."

"I'm up, Mason, for crying out loud!" Dinah Buckworth sounded overly cheery. I hit the off button on the radio. "You go and fish out all of your gear while I dress."

"I put it in the car already."

"You can make me some coffee then." He walked out of the room. I whispered, "Please."

The phone rang. Mason answered it in the kitchen. He said, "sure thing" a few times and then hung up. "Mom, it was a lady named Ruth. She has kids and they want me to come play with them this afternoon. They're at Grandpa's cottage."

"Mason, you should have called me to the phone."

"She said she wanted to talk to me."

"I think we have plans this afternoon. We're doing something with Dinah and her girls."

"The Buckworths are mean. Come on, let's go!" His hands quivered like springs. "Want me to call a cab?"

I sat on the edge of the bed. The night before, I had arranged the meals for the Arnetts and mentally qualified that act as the end of my obligation. On Sunday, I would greet them, duty fulfilled and obligation discharged. Then I would bid them farewell. The thought of Ruth Arnett percolating about the cottage as though she feathered the little Arnett nest sent me into a quasi-neurosis. Mason could visit with the Arnett brood for half an hour and then I would offer up an excuse to cut us free.

I turned the spindle to open the wooden blinds. The trees budded outside my window, a yellow-green pattern against gray bark and the fading gray of morning. I wanted spring to come, to pass through my walls, a little splendor without so much change. Joe had given me a life's worth of adjustments. Today I only needed a splash of color and the sight of a baseball diamond studded with little boys. Tomorrow I would like to manage a quiet Sunday the color of faded grass. Let God lavish his brush strokes with deeper hues elsewhere on the planet. I only needed a watercolor wash and a whisper of his attention. Even a late spring would not bother me one iota. Winter lingered as a quiet guest.

"Mason, let's throw together a picnic lunch. Later, I mean. Once we're finished at the park."

"And take it to the cottage. I hope this lady has boys. All of the best boys have moved away from our neighborhood. We never move. We just let everyone else move away from us and leave us at the mercy of the Buckworth girls. I'm glad we got invited. You'd be glad too if you'd just think about us not having enough boys around."

He ran out and climbed into the Mustang. He never heard me raise a note of complaint or say I only intended to include just the two of us in our afternoon agenda. I scrunched into a pair of faded denims and joined my boy who had obligated me with the very family I had intended to avoid. I did not know how to train him in the fine craft of putting up defensive little walls.

A ring of people surrounded the baseball park, Southern men who wore ball caps and mothers engaged in baby chat and diaper dialogue. We parked in the only empty space next to an SUV so large I couldn't see around it. I would not let Mason step out until the dust settled. I slipped the car keys into a cloth bag and handed Mason a bottle of chilled water.

"We don't need bottled water today. Just to be on time with pants that fit." Mason's eyes could not be seen at all. He hid the upper half of his face beneath the brim of his cap.

"We're not late, Mason. So you can stop pouting. And don't worry about your trousers. You're not playing until next week so blue jeans are fine today, so don't make me out to be the guilty party in all of this."

He pulled the cap down further over his eyes.

"Let's go, then." I said it above my emotions to show him that I remained in charge.

The assemblage of automobiles acted as coals in the sun. The park air already felt warm, a distant hint of the Southern heat that, by April's end, would gather the parents into the few shaded areas that bordered the baseball diamond.

"March, over here!"

Dinah Buckworth waved from the metal bleachers.

"Mason, here's your money. Go join Dinah's girls in the T-shirt line."

"I don't want the Buckworths on my team. Dinah's girls fight all the time and give knuckle bruises. Nobody wants to admit they've been knuckle-bruised by a Buckworth."

I unscrewed the lid on my Diet Coke and waved at Dinah. "We made it!" Even though Dinah sat two feet away, I yelled due to the fact that getting a ten-year-old boy off to baseball practice on time seemed worthy of at least a brief outburst of euphoria. "Looks like they're just getting started. I overslept." I clambered up onto the bleacher. It was hot against my posterior and caused me to lift and sit lightly.

"You should wear your hat, March. Too much sun messes up your smile." Dinah moved over a space.

"I don't know what the sun has to do with my smile."

"If you take a good look at Rena Foley's senior picture you'll see what I mean. She had that drop-dead-on-the-ground-I'm-beautiful smile back then. Now she's spent so much time tanning, her smile just sort of freezes. There's no brilliance in that." Rena had been the high-school prom queen. Not all of them keep their bloom.

"That's not the sun, Dinah. That's plastic surgery."

"Have you noticed anything else different about her lately?"

"Not especially."

"It's as though, and I'm not a shrink, mind you, but I'd say Rena is a little shy a bulb in her attic and not at all the together little cheerleader she once seemed cut out to be. Not altogether whacked out, mind you. More like—eccentric." Dinah rubbed sunblock on her elbow.

"Eccentric? Angst-ridden. But not eccentric."

"You and your words. Can I say eccentric if I want? You sound like some English teacher."

"Dinah, I'm not correcting your grammar. It's about the right choice of the word. Like you pick the right garlic for the right pasta. *Angst-ridden*. Drama, you want drama. I always say that's what's lacking in radio."

"Angst-ridden. Say, you know I woke up this morning with one of those epiphanies."

"There you have it. *Epiphany*. A perfectly good word."

"Dinah, old girl, I thought, you have to step up to home plate and take a few swings at life yourself. Then, I thought to myself, we need to take a road trip."

I filed down a splintered thumbnail.

"Like you hear women do at our time of life." Dinah kept ruminating on her epiphany and saying "our time of life" as though she delivered a eulogy. "First we map out our points of interest, but it's not like we're just wasting gas for antiques. We look up ancient Indian burial grounds, map the constellations and such. I couldn't find Orion if you held a gun on me and told me to do it or else. It's high time I explored the planet and figured out my existence and stuff like that."

"I can't see wasting a vacation milling around a burial place. I just did that, and it's no vacation."

"It's a spiritual trek. We just go to them, for whatever reason. A soul journey, but we pick who gets to go. But not Rena. Too eccentric."

I listened to Dinah's epiphanies at least once a month.

"I guess you and Mason must have gotten back last night. Janie said she saw the lights on down at your father's cottage. Your daddy must have company."

I scooted closer to Dinah to allow another mother some room. Her twins whispered to one another and waited in the shirt line behind Mason.

"Dad invited a minister to come up from Lake Norman. He's speaking tomorrow morning at church. He brought his family with him."

"Your daddy hasn't asked anyone to speak in a long time. I imagine he's ready for the break. You reckon he's playing around with the idea of retiring? My father waited too long and didn't get to enjoy his time on earth."

"Dad's fine. He enjoys his time on earth by working for the Lord, Dinah. He's been corresponding with this minister for a while. They're friends."

"Geraldine, you stay in line next to your sister," Dinah shouted from the bleachers. Dinah and her ex, Gerald, had disputed over the girl's name and then went round two when he pitched for the second daughter to be named after his father. "Claudia, stop tying up your shirt like that so the whole world can see your navel!"

"I have to go see them today. Pastor Arnett's sister invited Mason to drop by and play with the kids."

"He even brought his sister. I'd like to see where they're stuffing all of those people."

"He's a widower. His sister bunks with his two daughters. At the cottage, anyway. I don't know about their arrangements at home." I yelled at Mason, "Mason, get your shirt a size too large! They shrink."

"The minister's a widower."

"Right. Colin Arnett. You ought to come and hear him speak."

"Does he look preacherly?"

I thought of his tennis player's posture and the comfortable way he wore his own skin. "I don't know what you mean."

"Don't act like I'm insulting every minister on the planet. I mean, does he, well, have those provincial habits and J. C. Penney wardrobe and such?"

"I don't remember. I should have marched in and picked through his clothes, Dinah."

"So, you didn't get a good look at him?"

"I didn't have a reason to get a good look at him. I was only at the cottage to clean it up. I met him for an instant. Geraldine is punching that Aimes boy, Dinah. If Lucy Aimes sees that, she'll breathe fire."

"Geraldine, don't fight with the boys! I swear, March, if ever these girls marry off it'll be the day I walk on water."

"Who says they have to *marry off?*" Dinah made pawning off her girls to the first available man sound like an auction.

"I tried to get Gerald to spend a lot of time with them when they were small so they'd get along with men, not become like them."

"You've done right by them, Dinah. They need to stand on their own." I never told her what the hometown boys thought of her darling twins.

"After you spoke with this minister, I guess you decided you'd be better off with the rat man, Jerry Brevity."

"You just come right out of nowhere, Dinah, with your wild imaginings."

"Jerry's not so bad. At least we thought he wasn't so bad in high school."

I momentarily leave behind the image of Jerry in the industrial-green jumpsuit. "Rat Man. We never thought we'd be calling him that, not when he was the star quarterback for the CCHS Stingrays. Back then Candle Cove had so few stars."

"Jerry's a fine match, don't get me wrong. His house is paid for and it has this wonderful loft room upstairs. A body could set up a nice place to write and never come out again. Maybe he wouldn't mind if you seldom saw him."

"Maybe you need to set your sights on Jerry Brevity's loft. With the right equipment up there, you could broadcast your cooking show all the way to Raleigh."

"Dinah and the Rat Man. Sounds like a rock group."

"I hate it when you get off on talking about men, Dinah. You're too becoming to engage in desperate talk."

"I can't believe *you're* calling *me* desperate." When she was perturbed with me, she stared flatly ahead.

"I don't know why you would bring up Jerry Brevity or this Colin Arnett as though I were out hunting with my man net."

"March, your good looks have your brain all confuddled. One day you'll look in the mirror and see those little smile lines and there won't be a smile, just the lines."

"I'm not lonely, Dinah. I have Mason. Then there's Dad and the church."

"And Europe."

"Europe was Joe's dream."

Someone handed me the team's snack roster. I signed the parent rotation and handed it off to Dinah. A mother with a baby in a frontal sling turned to face Dinah and tell her that she tried her hummingbird cake and really liked it.

"I'm sorry, March. I'm an idiot and I can prove it. You're right. I've never seen you so happy. You were happy before marriage and you're happy once again. Not every woman has to have a man, and if anyone fits that category, it's you. I told you I'd stop trying to make you a match and here I am at it again."

"The kids are finished." I rose up and moved around the stooped back of the mother with the frontal sling. "I have to go pick up deli food. We're taking it to the cottage. Mason and I decided to take a picnic lunch over to the Arnetts."

"Cozy."

I saw the Buckworth twins approaching Mason from the rear so I yelled, "Mason, grab your gear." I cleared my throat to resume a certain amount of decorum. "Dinah, you have a good Saturday. Maybe we'll see you and the girls at church tomorrow."

"When I walk that church aisle next, I'll be carrying a bouquet."

"On the arm of the rat man," I said.

"You just like to meddle."

When my folks, James and Julia Norville, bought the cottage, some of the neighbors thought the young minister and his wife were being frivolous. James had inherited a little money from his father. He knew that he could send it off to a foreign mission or a shelter for young mothers. But it was only five thousand dollars, and he wanted to see the money used to encourage others. After he hit on the idea of providing a cottage for weary pastors and their wives, Mother worried that the purchase of a beach house might be misconstrued as self-serving, although it was their money, fair and square. When the money didn't cover the monthly mortgage payment, she took on extra baby-sitting just to pay the added expense.

One summer a minister lived at the cottage for a month after an overzealous church board had ousted him from a church he had founded. The division had started over the selection of new carpet and ended with the purchase of new baptismal curtains. I never met the minister but was aware that my mother carted hot meals out to him in the early evening, little trays of crab salsa and grilled salmon and cheese bread. Dad stayed at the cottage well into the night, climbing into bed with Mother after I had fallen asleep.

I never crossed paths with most of the clergy and only sometimes with the wives whose hearts mended at the Norville cottage. I served because I always did, because my father needed me. That is important.

After Mason slid his seat belt into place, the phone rang inside my purse. Dad called to see if Mason and I were dropping by the cottage this afternoon. I told him we were.

"So you're visiting the Arnetts. That's a bit of a surprise," he said.

"Mason and I are taking a picnic out to the Arnetts, Dad. It's a polite gesture. You're welcome to join us."

Dad declined. I heard him draw in a breath and then confess the real reason he called. "Joan called again. I'm becoming less adept at knowing what I should say to her."

"I didn't return her call because she's making a nuisance of herself. Eighty acres isn't enough for her, Dad."

Mason stared out the window. His silence proved his invisibility to the conversation.

"March, tell me what you want me to say to her." His voice sounded tinny over the phone.

"Even if she comes, I won't see her. The last time I saw her, she blamed me for things, well, you know what things, and tried to pressure me into giving up Joe's tract. It doesn't surprise me, Dad, but I don't care if she's headed for my house. Mason and I are visiting the Arnetts, so Joan can wait all alone. She should have called first."

"She's holed up in that ritzy hotel spending who knows what kind of money and she seems to be reaching out to you, March."

"I know she called, but she didn't connect like polite people connect. You know, like to say, I'm dropping by for a visit on such-and-such a day. How does this sound to you, yada-yada-yada. You don't just drop in uninvited. If she calls back, tell her we're gone for the day. Maybe she'll take the hint."

"What if she shoots the messenger?"

I ended the conversation.

"Mason, please do something for your mother. Here, take the phone. You call the cottage and ask Ruth Arnett if it's all right if we bring over the picnic." I pulled up to the curb at Ruby's Deli and Box Lunch Haven. Ruby had sewn new curtains from red-checkered tablecloths. Her high-school-age boys, Dillon and Frank, teetered on ladders tall enough to allow them to clean the windows top to bottom. A flock of sea gulls squawked at the guests gathered at the outdoor picnic tables.

"Hello, Mrs. Arnett, my mom wants to know if we can bring a picnic lunch when I come over." Mason cupped the receiver. "She says that would be great."

"Tell her we'll be at the cottage shortly, right after our order is ready."

Mason passed along the message and hung up.

"I'll just order at the takeout window," I said.

"If Grandma doesn't want us to have that land, I don't want it, Mom."

"Don't ever say things like that, Mason. Suppose a person decides he doesn't want you to have an education. You don't just lie down and throw away your education."

"You say Daddy left it to me. If the land in Virginia is mine and Grandma wants it, then I'll just give it back and stop all the fighting. You're always upset. Before Daddy died, you and Grandma never fought."

"Mason, at your age, you don't know everything. For your father's sake, I seldom said the things to your grandmother I wanted to say. It's really hard to explain. After your daddy died, it was like opening a wound too soon. All of your grandmother's anger came spilling out. Things I never even knew that she thought about me, now I'm hearing for the first time." I did not want him to know any of that. I opened the door hoping to close my mouth. Mason joined me at the takeout window. "I didn't want you to know any of this."

Mason looked like his daddy, the backward leaning stance with one foot poised toe-down behind the other heel. But he was less of Joe when it came to Longfellow philosophies. Joe, like the rest of the family, had always employed an overly thin-skinned approach in regard to his mother. I went along with him for a while. But the way she always had her hooks in Joe made me think less of him.

"Grandma must have bad feelings about me too, then."

"She loves you, Mason."

"But she doesn't want me to have my daddy's land, like, I'd never live in Virginia anyway."

"Maybe she knows that, and if we ever sell the land, well, then this hundred-year-old estate will lose a little part of the past. That's her fear. The past is very important to the Longfellows. But it's also a part of your daddy I want to preserve for you. When you're grown, you'll be glad I saved this tract for you." I felt as though less of what I said was actual reality. I wanted to say the right thing to a boy who warred on the side of conciliation but who might grow up to remember a mother that fought for his future. I wondered if this was less about Mason and more about what he might eventually think of me. The purity of my motives troubled me. "By the time you're a grown man you'll know what you want."

"I want a triple club with American cheese," said Mason.

Ruby, her big red hair glinting in the sun, smiled through the window.

"You ought not to have gone to all of this trouble," said Ruth Arnett. "I've never seen pickles so big, and this potato salad doesn't look store-bought, not at all."

"All the locals here frequent Ruby's Deli. Ruby and her sister make everything fresh in the morning. I've never been able to match her potato salad," I said.

Beyond the cottage, the Arnett children ran on the sand a few feet from the tide's edge. They all wore red department-store parkas as they flung rocks into the ocean and waited as if to see what the chilly waves would swap in return.

Ruth knelt and faced Mason with a look that said he was the only person in the room. "You must be Mason. If you want, you can join the kids. Charlotte is probably closest to your age."

"It looks like you have a lot of kids," said Mason.

"I don't have any. But I treat them like my own. My brother, Colin, and his wife wanted a large family." Ruth lifted herself without effort and addressed me. "It really disappointed Eva when she couldn't have any more children. But it didn't make sense to take any more risks after she found out about the cancer. Did I mention it was ovarian?"

Mason watched the Arnett children and fixedly stared after them as though he willed them to look over toward the cottage and see him.

I helped him out. "Mason, you go introduce yourself to the Arnett children. Invite them to join us for lunch. We can feed you kids on the deck. Plenty of seating out there if you think it's warm enough, Ruth." I opened a sack of paper plates.

"This is a treat for us. Colin's kids have always grown up around the mountains. After we saw how quickly we arrived right here at the ocean, we felt silly for not having come sooner. I don't guess you ever tire of the ocean."

"Never have."

"That's the best part about living in the Carolinas, people say. Mountains to the west and ocean to the east," Ruth said.

"And the nation's Capitol just to the north."

"I've been to Washington, D.C. Ever visited the Capitol during the cherry blossom festival, March?"

"No, I made the mistake of visiting D.C. in the middle of a protest. Some group upset about ecology. Streets blocked everywhere by police." Mason and I had traveled to the District of Columbia to see the Space Flight Museum. The Capitol was grayed over that day by a nasty spring rain, while the streets, in a heightened state of security, filled with D.C. police.

"Your father mentioned you've done some travel as a food critic."

"It gets me good deals when I travel. But I also run a small newspaper here in Candle Cove, the *Sentinel.* All the goings-on around Candle Cove can be summed up in a day; the Thursday edition. Everything else I do is freelance, food articles and travel pieces."

"After I'm finished with school, I want to know more about preparing food beyond the mundane. Our mother cooked meat and potatoes every night, meat loaf and such. When I see those cooking shows on television, I admit it intimidates me. I understand your mother was somewhat of an expert on cuisine." Her focus connected briefly with the shoreline.

"Julia Norville. My mother could have written her own cookbooks but she only cooked for us and the visitors to our cottage."

"Such a shame we missed out on that. I know you miss her."

"I guess your mother and father are still around."

"They are. Getting on in years, but still a little involved in their church. Mother and Daddy retired in Texas, near Galveston."

"Then you've seen your share of the ocean."

"Yes, but not as pretty as here, obviously. But I'm glad Colin's children can be here. Colin's so busy at the church, our parents usually have to come to see us." Ruth inhaled as though she could still smell the Gulf of Mexico. "When Eva was alive she made certain they all had at least one little trip a year just to get away. Colin tends to work himself to death. I don't know if he works smart, necessarily. But he certainly works hard."

"My father takes his vacations inside of a book."

"Colin loves that about your father. Reverend Norville recommended so many books, Colin can't read them all. He loves collecting them, I think just to swap them out with other ministers."

I had not come to the cottage to grow to like Ruth Arnett. I opened the kitchen door. "Mason, you all come to lunch."

He ran out ahead of the pack, the noon sun burnishing his crown as though someone had dipped him in butter.

"I guess Reverend Arnett is at the church," I said.

"Colin found an open-air restaurant down the beach on his morning run. Said they had these grass huts covering the tables and chairs. No one was about, so he took his Bible down along with his notes to prepare for tomorrow. I find him studying outdoors quite a lot, so he's apt to disappear into the landscape here as well."

"I hope you like these sandwiches, Ruth." I plucked each sandwich from the bag and peeled away the butcher paper. "I had them made up plain—no lettuce, no tomato—for your children. But ours are loaded. Ruby makes her own bread. Be sure and take home some of her foccacia."

"I hear a phone ringing. Oh, you must have one in your purse." Ruth pointed gently at my handbag.

I took the call out on the front porch.

Dad's tone was flat. "March, I told your mother-in-law you were away for the afternoon. Joan has checked in at the Concord Suites, but she insisted on finding out when you'll be back home. If you call her, it might give me some peace for a good little bit." His smooth, lacustrine pitch punctuated the sentence with a ripple of worry.

"She's a vulture."

"I have her number at the Concord."

"I'll meet her there. But don't tell her, please, Dad. Mason can stay here and visit for a while with the Arnetts."

"So you're having a picnic. That's nice of you, March."

"Nothing more than I always do for you and your guests."

"Colin, he's a nice man."

"When you say that, like you keep saying that to me, I'm sure you aren't implying anything by it."

"I wouldn't do that, you're right. I think you should know that Colin is sensitive about his Eva. He talks about her in present tense. Death is something that some people get over. Others don't. Colin's never gotten over Eva." His television made intermittent sounds as he rummaged for entertainment. "In other words, you're safe from human intrusion," he said.

I did not tell him how annoying I found his comment. "I should go, Dad."

"Bring me by one of those sandwiches from Ruby's, if you have the time."

"I'll drop one by on the way back from the hotel."

We divided the large poor boys each into three sandwiches and passed them out to the children. Charlotte rested her hands on the tabletop. After she nudged her brothers and sisters to bow for grace, I noticed her left hand held no symmetry with her right hand. The thumb was a rounded stump, her fingers small and malformed like tiny baby carrots harvested too early. Mason introduced Charlotte to me.

"Charlotte's eight," he said. "She might move here. She likes baseball."

I overheard a gentle sigh from Ruth's direction. She did not look Charlotte's way.

Four

JOAN LONGFELLOW TORE THE TOP OFF THE SWEETENER packet as though she saw through it or past it. Somehow her hands finished the task without her full attention. I waited in the Concord's lobby behind a potted palm, a tall tropical tree encircled at the roots by bromeliads with centers so red they seemed to lay open, wounded. Joan sat right next to the plate-glass window. Her manner at the Concord Grille drew eyes. I knew without a doubt that the way she wore her money on her face had less to do with money and more with the fact that she was a Barton—not the Oklahoma Bartons but the Virginia Bartons, the Clara Barton of the Red Cross Bartons. And somewhere in there were General Lee and Turkey Trot, but Joan never wanted to be associated with Indians. She often pointed out that Turkey Trot, the big park near the Potomac, changed hands several times. Her family purchased it from the Indians, she would always say. I would not say that her family outright donated the land as a park, but sometime before the charitable donation, they farmed on it. Joe never understood it completely. When Joan dies, most of what is the truth will die with her.

She nested in front of the Concord Grille window, I felt, so that no one passing by might miss her. From the corner of Lantern Street and Fourth, I saw that hat, stiff felt with a wide brim that tilted to one side. The color fizzled somewhere between hibiscus red and crimson. It contrasted with her Lanzoni pumps and the knee-length sport jacket. While another woman might appear uncomfortable seated alone in a restaurant, Joan exuded a broker's air about her, as though she anticipated at any moment that an important coterie of polished chums would appear. Her movements became a pattern. She checked her watch, turned over the wine list to see the choices, and then examined the appetizers on the menu. I witnessed her ritual three times before I collected enough courage to approach her.

Joan's hat tilted back and then up, which caused the attached plume to wave hypnotically; it drew me into her magic web as if she understood her own power while I fell helpless to it. I stopped behind her in order to form an opening line.

"I apologize I didn't call first before coming into town," said Joan.

I saw her eyes looking at me in the glass in front of her.

"No need to apologize," I said. My intent was to say, "You should have called first, of course."

Joan maintained her focal point through the vitreous wall that secured her like a protected egg. The fine hotel, the doting waiter, and polished windows—all of it encompassed her security and her power.

"If you try the crab canapés, have them made up fresh," said Joan. "You have to watch the crab in North Carolina. It isn't like the Maryland crab. They don't know how to season it here, either."

"I had a sandwich from Ruby's." I pretended to enjoy being common around Joan.

"I've come all this way. You may as well join me."

I pulled out a chair at the farthest arc of the circular table. My fingers rested atop the chair back. I sighed and then politely took a seat.

"How's my grandson? He isn't with you, I see."

"Mason is playing with friends. Dad invited a minister in for the weekend. He brought his family along. They're all at the cottage."

The waiter filled my water glass and delivered an iced tea to me on a paper doily. "I can bring Mason by tomorrow afternoon, if he wants to come."

"He can swim in the pool here at the hotel."

I pretended to like her idea. "Mason might like that."

"I went by Joe's grave. Someone's redecorated it." Her voice lowered and thickened but she made her comment while looking past me into the street. I squeezed lemon into my tea.

Joan tapped at the tabletop, quiet for a moment as though she mentally took aim with her arrow. "You'd think that if someone were going to decorate the grave, they'd tell me about it. Or ask me if I'd like to come and help. It's our custom to attend the decorations as a family."

"You have some purpose for visiting us, Joan. I'd like to hear what that might be."

"Joe used to tell me when you all dated, 'that March is a really direct girl.' He thought I'd like that about you."

"If this is about Mason's inheritance—"

"Sometimes, it's as though Joe is still alive. Just like our land lives inside us."

"Mason's a Longfellow, too."

"You always hated Virginia. If I thought we could keep it all together, like a family, I'd not worry about it."

"When Mason's an adult he'll decide, then, on his own. I've told him about the family legacy. I can't do any more than that with a ten-year-old boy." *And,* I thought, *I won't allow you to hang that land around his neck like a weight, like being a Longfellow was a noose around his daddy's neck.* "Joe didn't do everything right, but he left the land to Mason."

"I won't hear anything disparaging about Joe."

"Don't presume you will." I pushed away the water glass, not wanting any part of this luncheon.

"He was a tender young man. I always knew he cared about me. He didn't hide his feelings like his daddy, Ronald. I think Ronald thought it wasn't manly, but he never understood Joe like I did."

"But Joe had his flaws, Joan." I muted my words. I lived in this town. "I didn't see them at first, either. He had his way of making me believe what I wanted to believe about him. But I fell in love with someone that didn't exist. The last morning I saw him, I didn't even know him anymore."

"He knew you didn't love him. That became his insecurity." She heightened her tone and spoke in an ingratiating manner as though Joe might overhear and be proud of her. "And the downright end of him."

I looked at my watch. "Don't be ridiculous! You didn't know him any better than me. And you stop all of this critical blame laying, accusing me of sending Joe out into that storm or the same as!"

"It didn't come out of *my* mouth."

"I won't let you tie me into one of your corners. Not with lies. Reality is what exists in spite of what we believe." At least that is what Julia said into my mind right then.

"You use it to bite people, March." Her slender fingers lifted and made a clenched fist that she used to lightly rap the tabletop, once for each overly enunciated word.

What that woman could cause to run through my head I could never repeat! The way she tried to tie me up in her despotic bag and throw me onto the highway of her twisted opinions as though I would mewl for mercy made me physically ill. She obviously underestimated how fast on my feet I could be. "You irk me, that's what!"

"The thought of him going into that ocean alone, like a man devoid of love, depresses me." She pulled out a bottle of pills and demonstrated her need for prescription medications. She popped a couple and downed them with wine.

"Joe knew I loved him. His insecurity consumed him long before I ever met him." I crooned "long" and then realized I sounded just like her. I put my face in my hands. Either I was morphing into a Longfellow or some distant gene encoded with bellicose insanity had finally reared its ugly head.

"Any woman with her head on straight could have helped Joe find his way."

The waiter appeared again, although he stood three feet away.

A vise around her vocal chords could not have silenced her. Not an ounce of energy remained in me. I felt my little rubber raft deflating right smack in the middle of her tumultuous diatribe. "Joan, I think you've come a long way for nothing. I'll not sit here and allow you to tie my heart in knots and leave me feeling guilty because it makes you feel better about yourself." I hate myself when I cry.

She laid a finishing touch of gentility to her reply. "I promised Ronald I'd not feud with you and here we are at it."

"Assure Ronald that it only lasted for a moment." I rose and left the Concord Grille. Without glancing up, I minced past the polished plate glass. I pulled away when the doting waiter attempted to accommodate me, and turned my back to the red felt hat that hid a woman and her cold plate of insecurities.

It rankled me to know that if it were not for me and the procession of notorious faces from his daughter's past my father might be sitting in his red easy chair having an otherwise quiet Saturday afternoon.

"Can we not talk about this—say, save it for a day we want to fully ruin?" I asked him.

"Remember Ruth and Naomi." When Dad used his Bible analogies, it deflated me.

"I can't be Ruth to Joan, Dad."

"Let me finish. Ruth's humility is the example I'm trying to unearth. I'm not blind to Joan. I'm only suggesting you emulate Ruth. We all should emulate Ruth."

"Women like Joan dominate, like she dominated Joe. Like she would dominate Mason and me if I allowed it. You just can't play the humility card around Joan, Dad. She's a usurper. If I give in, then Mason loses all rights to his inheritance. I can't let her win."

"It's about winning, then," he said.

"Rights. It's about rights, but not mine. Joe wanted it this way." I pasted a cardboard frame around a photograph of Dad and Mother. "This church album is almost finished. I made it sort of like a pictorial diary from the day you and Mother started the church until now."

A lone man stood as a ghost in one photo, an old black-and-white snapshot I rescued from one of the many shoe boxes in the attic. The man, Avery Woodard, had a broom in one hand and a box that said "kick in" in the other. His mother was a Lumbee Indian; the Lumbees descended from the Cheraw that inhabited North Carolina for more than two hundred years. Avery's father was a drunkard. Some said Avery's father beat his wife during her pregnancy and that caused Avery's deformity. Others said his father beat Avery before he was big enough to stand up for himself and that ruined him and bowed his back. Young boys teased Avery whenever he walked downtown with his cane. Local men had fun with Avery, playing tricks on him at the only barbershop in Candle Cove back before the first salon took over all of the local haircuts. One man told Avery to lie back in the barber chair so that he could give him a shampoo. Avery hobbled around town for months with red hair. The red color accentuated the spike of cowlick at his forehead. For the longest time, the flat-faced boys along Brindle Street called him Rooster.

Dad paid him five dollars every time he swept the walks around the church. He fashioned a shoebox with a leather strap that Avery hung around his neck. Avery used the box to beg for money. "Kick in," he would say.

Dad smiled when he saw Avery's crooked frame, his gaunt face staring out from the album page. "Old Avery. Sometimes when I go for a cup of coffee or a haircut, I expect to see him all over again pushing that broom up Main Street."

"Rona Guggenheim, one of the Inksters, says she knows for a fact

Avery's ghost chased some kids down Brindle Street last October. But her writing is so mystical I think it's made her weird."

Dad made an *L* around Avery's photograph with his right hand.

I held up a sepia photograph, the edges slightly curled and scalloped. "Here's Collette Russell. I scarcely remember her; kind of a stick-looking woman with poppy-seed eyes. She started the first baby nursery." I snipped the white edges from the photo to fit it into a smaller mat.

"She's passed on too," said Dad.

"Lot of memories from church. If I get this finished tonight, I'll display it tomorrow at the church social."

"You want Colin Arnett to see it, I guess."

I closed up the album. "Not Colin especially. I don't know what he has to do with our church album."

"Nothing. That's your point, I guess."

"I don't have a point. I started this album a year ago, long before I ever met the Arnetts. You look flushed."

"I feel fine. I believe I'll go visit the cottage. I can bring Mason home, if you want," he said.

"Sure. I'll make some pasta before I go. Or if you want, you can eat with us."

"Pasta here sounds fine. I plan to read a little tonight, maybe watch an old movie, go to bed early. Don't need company for that." Dad had placed the soup cans and tomato sauce cans inside three different cabinets. I stacked them into two rows while I searched for the pasta and garlic.

"I guess you haven't met Arnett's children," I said.

"Not yet. He picked up the keys here while they waited at the seafoam-green cottage."

"Colin's daughter, Charlotte, she's a special girl," I said.

"Her hand was deformed from birth."

"I meant special, like she has a creative nature. That's all."

"I can't help but notice how children like that have great buckets of wisdom, something innate, as though before they were born they basked in the presence of God." Dad's words almost smelled of thunder when he talked about God.

"For crying out loud; linguini's in the broom closet!"

"It's all right. I moved the broom to the garage. It's my new system."

"So the garlic must be in the attic."

"That wouldn't make sense at all, March."

Phyllis Murray canceled her Saturday hot meal for the Arnetts. Her youngest, Gregory, came down ill. She apologized three times after she finally reached me at Dad's place as I was making spaghetti sauce. Mason and I made up a basket of chicken-salad sandwiches, macaroni salad, and brownies including extra helpings for ourselves since I had no inclination to eat the spaghetti I had cooked for Dad. I took M&Ms and put them on top of the brownies for Colin's children. It was such a nurturing gesture, but his kids were beginning to have that effect on me. Especially that little doll, Charlotte.

We pulled up to the cottage with the afternoon sky as blue as larkspurs. "We're here," I said. The cottage's architecture was from the Arts and Crafts era. I knew about its architecture only because my mother would say that to the pastors' wives who flounced through the cottage on one of Mother's tours. She had asked my father to paint it sea green six years ago, to match the ocean, she had said. But Dad never could squeeze in the time. He drove up one day to see Mother hefting a large can of seafoam-green paint onto a ladder. The white trim matched the sea gulls, she had told him, knowing he might not realize the why of the color, while the "algae-blue" shutters contrasted with the deep furls in the ocean waves. I kept geraniums in her flower boxes for several years until travel assignments ate up my summers.

Mason and I gathered up all of the Rubbermaid containers too large for the picnic basket. We balanced them, our arms loaded, all the way up to the deck.

"Your teacher called today," I said.

"I'll carry in the sweet iced tea." Mason pressed down the screen door latch. Then he stepped back onto the deck with no intention of sharing the facts of his lackadaisical work habits with strangers.

"I'd appreciate it, Mason, if you'd give me an explanation."

"Tell me what she said, first."

"Mrs. Wagner's message mentioned 'concerns about Mason's grades.'"

His bony shoulders lifted, then ebbed along with a sigh. He carried the iced tea back around to the cottage deck.

Ruth had opened all of the blinds, lifted them up as high as blinds would go. The windows on the west side of the house reflected the late afternoon sun while the east side emitted shadows from the ephemeral day. Mounds of Mexican heather sprouted leaves as green as watermelon rind along a brick border that wound from the front walk to the rear of the house. A group of empty clay pots lay heaped near the deck, yawning for lack of attention, pining for a departed mistress to return and fill them.

Ruth met Mason at the door. Her arms wrapped around him, slender long fingers cupping the back of his head like an old friend. Mason lifted the pitcher up to her. At once, Charlotte appeared and grasped Mason's forearm with her good hand. They leaped from the third step onto the sand and raced to meet the tide.

"March, you must be weary of all of this running back and forth," said Ruth. Her feet moved across the wood deck in Birkenstocks and thick, oatmeal-colored socks.

"Phyllis Murray's son is sick. I'm afraid it's chicken salad tonight. Phyllis is a much better cook, too."

"Then I insist you join us. No need to run back home and cook all over again. Besides, chicken salad is perfect for this time of year. Time to put away sweaters and heavy foods."

"Don't worry about us. I made enough for us too. It's at the house, though. I'm putting Mason to bed early. He's a difficult one to get up on Sunday."

"All kids are like that. Imagine four heads to comb on Sunday."

I couldn't imagine. "Here's the macaroni salad in this tub. I'll bring in the rest if you can take the salad." I retrieved the picnic basket and met her in the kitchen.

Colin finally made an appearance from the sanctum of his studies and took the basket from me. "All of the meal carting has given Ruth a nice break," he said.

Ruth filled four plastic cups with milk.

"We look forward to your message. Several from the congregation have called to ask me about you," I said. It was true, one call setting off the curiosity of another probing member, to another, and then another. I could scarcely tell them everything. It was not my place. But neither could I lie. That would not have been Christian.

Colin averted his gaze. When he crossed his arms, he mulled over my words and injected an ambiguous silence between us.

I had spoken with several women who consoled me by saying that no man could replace James Norville, and the thought of any man so much as standing in my father's shadow was just a big farce. But Colin did not need to be privy to any of our private affairs. "A little variety is good for them," I said. I think I inserted a little laugh.

Troy and Luke plowed through the kitchen with sand buckets for helmets. They bore a starfish in each hand, beach tokens their aunt must have picked up for them at a tourist shop. Starfish seldom make an appearance on our shores. When they do, early-to-rise vacationers snatch them at once.

"Colin filled me in on your situation," said Ruth.

I stepped out of her way so that she could arrange the food on the plates according to the dictates of a nitpicking brood.

"Your father explained about your husband's boating accident. God has really strengthened you, I can tell. After the death of a spouse, we know, it's so hard to rebound."

"Mason helps me to be strong." I realized how that sounded. "And God, of course."

"And I've been calling you Ms. Norville and you've been so patient with me, not correcting me. Longfellow is such an interesting name. And you're a writer. It must be a fascinating life to spend your summers traveling the coast and then writing about it." Ruth scooped her chicken salad onto a lettuce bed instead of bread.

"I mostly run my paper. But when I do pick up a travel piece, Mason travels pretty well. It gives me a chance to get him out of here, but at someone else's expense. Dad says you've built a thriving community church, Pastor Arnett."

"Colin is fine. "Pastor" sounds too formal."

"Some congregations really like it when you take their small flock and increase it several levels."

"I'm no magician. It's a spiritual matter, a matter of hungry hearts."

"That, I guess, and a growing populace. Take Candle Cove. We have a large influx of tourists, but our growth is seasonal. We can barely keep a coffee shop in business." He had a right to know the demographics of the matter. The least I could do was to tell him the facts of the matter.

"But you've become an offshoot of New Bern's growth. You have an untapped college population. The business community needs spiritual leadership injected into it." He counted it all off, tapping each perfectly curved fingertip. "That ethnic grocery store across the street from the deli is thriving. That's another unreached group. Growth is not always about numbers. It's about touching your community."

I felt as though he were trying to lure me into his classroom for dunce laymen.

"Colin, you can call in the children," said Ruth.

"The Latinos come to our bake sale every year," I said, and then wished to goodness it had not popped into my head. "I think we touch our community."

"Of course you do." Ruth had such a desire to be the bridge between any obvious divide. "All this church talk makes me dizzy."

Beyond the cottage, Charlotte held her pant legs up around her knees while the waves dampened her cotton hand-sewn top and pants. Colin threw open the door and yelled for her to back away from the water. The wind and sea absorbed his words. I watched him cup his hands to his mouth and yell twice more. Colin loved all of his children, but I imagined the thread that attached him to Charlotte trussed his words with pain. He was besotted with her, forever trying to keep her under his injured wing. I imagined Eva on her final breath handing him the duty of taking over her watch of Charlotte, anxious about her only alternative—that a solitary man had to fill the post of a multitasking mother.

"I'll send them back in. Mason and I need to go. If you want, Ruth, you can return the picnic basket to church in the morning."

"We'll see you then," said Ruth.

Mason finally looked up and noticed me waving my sweater amid the lilting heads of swaying oat grass. We waited while Charlotte skipped up the steps and twirled all the way into the cottage, a graceful pod returning to her protective tree.

I felt then that Colin would worry less over her if he would take her home where she belonged. Pain is best conciliated in the entrails of its own cave.

I was not sure if Mother had said that or I.

Five

COLIN WALKED INTO CHURCH WITH HIS SISTER ON his arm as though he escorted her to the prom. Ruth Arnett was too sexy to stand beside her minister brother. I don't mean that she dressed indecently or exposed things that should not be exposed. While she lived all week in knit items appropriate for either vacuuming or a run on the beach, her Sunday ensemble could have come out of the Jackie Onassis museum. Not many women wear the colors of the sun well, but the fiery red radiated from Ruth.

Colin wore a navy turtleneck with a classic jacket, dark gray with thin slivers of blue thread that matched his turtleneck tastefully enough to say "I don't wear ties." My worries faded. If this turtleneck-clad offshoot from the casual nineties was my father's only excuse for retiring too early, I had no cause for alarm.

Ruth and Colin's children took up most of the front left pew. Rachel wore a necklace made from string and plastic beads that did not match her dress, and colored socks with white sandals. It looked as though the boys had dressed themselves. They both wore faded jeans. No self-respecting pastoral family sent their offspring to church in faded denim.

"Mrs. Longfellow, I made this for you," said Charlotte.

She was the first Arnett to call me by my real name.

She crossed the aisle to the right front pew where I sat with Mason every Sunday. Mason helped his grandfather distribute church bulletins in the lobby. We had no official children's program. All of the older people thought it best to teach the young ones to sit respectfully through the minister's message. Charlotte held up one of her origami creations, an elaborate white angel.

"Charlotte, this is beautiful. Maybe you should save it, though. I don't want to take your best work, and this looks like your very best," I said.

"Hang him in your kitchen window above your plants and he'll be with you through the storms." She placed the paper angel in my hand. She whispered on a breath as sweet as a cherry Lifesaver, "The ocean makes the storms around here, and this angel will blow them back. He told me that himself, but it's a secret."

I felt the limp flesh of her fingers against my wrist. The warmth of her skin against mine surprised me, although I don't know why I expected her misshapen hand to be cold. "I do have plants in my window. Mason must have told you."

"Boys don't talk about such things, Mrs. Longfellow," she said. "You just have that look about you of a plant lady like my mother." I was surprised again when she held her smallish nose close to my white sweater. "You have her same smell."

I felt Charlotte's arms go around me. The little girl held on to me as though both hands were whole. I've heard of accident victims who sensed a limb as whole again even after an amputation. It was as though I could close my eyes and count ten little appendages hooked around my upper arms. Before I could thank her, she pressed her cheek against my lips. Without a thought, I kissed her. "Thank you," I said.

"But you have to remember that angels just work for the man upstairs. Not us."

I laughed.

She joined Rachel on the front left pew. Before she sat down, she lifted herself up on her knees to smile at Mr. and Mrs. Caudle. Ruth leaned over to whisper something to all of Colin's children. Charlotte turned and seated herself. All of them sat up straight and looked up at their father. Colin opened his Bible and lifted a laptop to the podium. By the use of a remote control, he flashed a sermon outline onto the white screen, regarded it for a brief satisfied instant, and then turned it off. Behind me, Lorraine Bedinsky emitted a faint gasp. Whether she thought it a sacrilege to use computers in the church, or was satisfactorily impressed, I could not say. I read the elders' minds, though.

Later when the sanctuary grew warm right in the hot center of Colin's Sunday morning message, Ruth peeled off the blazing orange-red jacket and laid it across her lap. This innocent action exposed her tanned shoulders and I thought Mrs. Caudle would elbow her husband's rib cage sore. The Caudles occupied the second pew to the left every Sunday, a pew they had paid for during the pew drive of the eighties. That accounted for the polished brass plaque on one end engraved with the name CAUDLE. But this vantage point gave Mr. Caudle a birds-eye view of Ruth Arnett's perfect shoulders. Dad stepped gingerly up the steps to the platform, made a half-turn, and gazed appraisingly over the congregation. For the entire life of his pulpit ministry, he had ascended the stage with the assurance of a wizened old college professor. I remember a candlelight Thanksgiving service when he had not noticed a loose button as he dressed that morning, two buttons down on his suit coat. It dangled from two threads like a loose eye. My mother noticed it first. She could look more perceivably appalled than any woman in the church. As he opened his spiral notepad, his right hand traveled up the breadth of his coat, moved up and down on the button as though he plucked the strings of a cello, and then quickly laid hold of the offending member. Those who saw it craned their heads, turkeys in a lineup. With one hand, he plucked the loose button from the coat, held it up for all to see, and made an object lesson of it, some sort of analogy how one unattended sin could distract from the fabric of our lives. Every person in attendance but my mother and myself praised his wit and courage for showing up for a holiday observance ready to sacrifice his appearance for a point well-driven.

Mother knew the truth, the way my father awoke on Thanksgiving morning, his thoughts riveted to one crystal revelation that he fiercely harbored until he released it from his notes and delivered it to the congregants. He had no more noticed that button than he would acknowledge the agony on my mother's face.

A seasonal storm had settled all up and down the East Coast and, while our Carolina brethren up in the mountains woke up to six inches of snow, Candle Cove braced for the chilly rain. Our numbers were down in spite of the announcement about the visiting speaker and the rumors that Reverend Norville was hinting at finding his own replacement. Dad looked out over the sparsely filled pews and said, "In spite of the gloomy weather, Candle Cove Presbyterian has a spark of sunshine this morning." He read a list of Colin's accomplishments to the chilled congregates. Colin crossed his legs first one way and then the next.

I pulled out a pair of eyeglasses I use only for reading and opened my Bible as though somehow I had previewed and endorsed the sermon's text from Colin's notes.

Mr. Caudle spread himself against the pew while his wife whispered something to him. If Ruth heard Mrs. Caudle's nasal, asthmatic idioms, she made absolutely no indication but kept her eyes on her brother.

Lorraine Bedinsky sighed again.

Several more families entered from the rear wearing dark raincoats that shimmered with the effects of the East Coast storm front. A woman, dressed slatternly, entered from the rear. None of us had seen her before, not around the New Bern mission when we dropped off our clothing bundles, nor around the soup kitchen where we flocked every Thanksgiving Eve. While Dad capped off his introduction,

Colin lifted his crossed leg to plant both feet against the crimson car-pet. I do not know if leaving the platform followed proper etiquette, but he left the platform. Dad's gaze lifted above his spectacles. A mod-est sprinkle of serenity dimpled the corners of his eyes. Instead of introducing Colin, he lengthened his preface and explained how he and Colin had first met. But, with transparent stares aplenty, all of us followed Colin to the rear of the church.

The woman had a stooped posture. Some condition had left the right side of her face in a contorted smile, although her eyes had ceased to smile in juxtaposition to the rest of her.

"Welcome," was all that Colin said. He placed a soft grip on her wrist and pointed toward his sister. The visitor allowed him to escort her to the front.

Lorraine leaned toward me to ask if Colin knew this woman.

I shrugged. All I knew of Colin Arnett was what Dad had shared over the last twenty-four hours.

Ruth and the children lifted in unison, as though moving to the pew's end was part of the morning's orchestration.

The sky hurled rain against all the windows as though it had waited for this one bent-in-two woman to enter the sanctuary.

As for Colin, he seated the woman next to Charlotte and took his place again on one of the platform thrones.

Dad, his usual polite baritone drawing every eye, announced, "It is my pleasure to introduce Pastor Colin Arnett."

I have heard of congregations that applaud but we at Candle Cove Presbyterian do not assemble to applaud any more than we gather to sway as some are given to do during the offertory. Some feel that if we so much as tap a toe, by the very act of music combined with move-ment we lead the children into outward displays inappropriate for a solemn assembly.

If Colin noticed the hushed welcome, the hint of polite smile that peppered the sanctuary, he returned nothing in the way of a gesture. I expected him to launch the colored computer thingy he had put

together for his sermon outline. Instead, he bowed his head and whatever he prayed, he shared only with God and none of us. That elicited
another sigh from Lorraine, although the Caudles kept their heads
bowed without so much as a flutter of an eyelash.

Colin concluded his prayer and then introduced his sister and his
children. While Rachel, Troy, and Luke turned their heads to only
peep at the people behind them, Charlotte turned effusively around
in her seat and waved her undersized hand.

The Caudles' fixed stares took on a domino effect. Eyes flew open
from the front to the rear of the sanctuary. I could sense the fascination with the child's hand from the farthest pew as if she had hypno-
tized them. Mrs. Caudle pulled out a stick of spearmint gum,
unwrapped it, and handed it to Charlotte as though the child had the
pew jitters that seize children on occasion.

Colin thanked my father for inviting him to speak. But every perfectly timed polite gesture from this city preacher sent pangs of
annoyance through me. And every anxious posture shift I made in my
pew elicited a harrumph from Fern Michaels. I returned my attention
to my open Bible.

Colin, more succinct than when he spoke in casual conversation,
said, "In keeping with my promise to my own children not to bore
them to death, I'd like to invite all of the children to come to the front
of the sanctuary."

Charlotte slid from her seat while her brothers and sister inched
to the seat's edge without truly committing.

"If you like stories, I'll tell you all a story." Colin knelt at the platform's edge as though all of the children from our church had already
responded. He obviously did not realize the tenacious discipline
exacted from every exhausted parent to train offspring to sit like little
soldiers upon the pews.

I did have enough sympathy for the man to finally nudge Mason
out of his seat. From every pew, the children fell into a procession down
the aisle to the area in front of the communion table. Colin glanced

toward me and I nodded my head ever so slightly as though I held the release code over all of the offspring of our esteemed families. I had never counted the heads of all of the children, so it surprised me to see thirty heads lined up across the front. Colin drew them in closer, more in a cluster in front of him, and from that point on it was as though his cognizance of every present adult disappeared from his mind. Mason moved toward the front of the pack and sat cross-legged next to Charlotte.

Colin led them in a song accompanied by hand motions. His singing voice differed from his everyday talking voice, a rich, stentorian baritone that settled into a euphonious miracle of a sound as he led them into the chorus. But I did not give Dad the satisfaction of a glance. After the song, he brought out a gold pocket watch. He told a story of his grandfather's watch and how his grandfather passed it on to him. Somehow he tied all of that in with how our faith is like gold passed on from the grownup to the child. After another sort of finale song, Colin sent them back to their seats.

The woman with the bowed back pulled a tissue from her purse and dabbed her eyes, although I did not sense the need for tears.

Behind me, Lorraine sniffed.

Mrs. Caudle uncrossed her arms and fiddled with an offering envelope.

Lightning carved barbed blue fire across the sky and the sanctuary cooled a degree or two.

Nothing that followed could be blamed on me, although I felt my father shoot one too many of his glances my way after the morning service. If two women had made egg salad that morning for the church social to follow, then six more followed suit. Under the cabinet that housed fifty pounds or more of coffee and sugar, I pulled out the large metal bowl that had served no less than five hundred pounds of egg salad over the last twenty-five years. I was up to my elbows in egg salad, consolidating it, topping it off with parsley and paprika. It had not been my job to escort the royal family around to the dining hall. All they had to do was follow the crowd from the sanctuary to the fellowship hall. As Colin called for the final prayer, I slipped out along with the other ladies who led the food committee and prepared for the hungry. By the time my father led them to the back of the building, the line outside the doorway was already three deep. Dad led the Arnetts to a circular table and gestured for Wanda Albemarle to serve them all iced tea and lemonade. "March," he said in front of everyone, "if you and several of the ladies could prepare a plate of food for the Arnetts first, it would help them on their way."

I had duly escorted every visiting minister through the buffet line more times than I could count, but making eye contact with Colin Arnett agitated me. So I removed my apron embroidered by the Tea and Scriptures club, folded it over one arm, and breezed past him to mutter, "Pastor Arnett, if you all will follow me, then you can fill your plates as you desire." I had noticed the way that Ruth, out at the cottage, had pecked around her food, ignoring the meat and going straight for the potatoes and corn. In my estimation, she was a polite vegetarian. It was a simple fact that I did not know how to feed the woman. Dad glared at me.

Colin watched his family fill their plates. He put a few items on his plate but never really looked at his food.

"Good day to be inside," said Fern Michaels.

"Indeed," I said.

She winked at me. Somehow I failed to understand the nature of it. Yesterday, during a phone call, she had mentioned her loyalty to my father as pastor. I thanked her. It was innocent.

After first routing the seniors through the line followed by the families and then the singles, I handed my apron to Wanda. "I'll go and see if the Arnetts want seconds," I said. *Before my father blows a gasket*, I thought.

"Oh, they're already gone," said Wanda, and then she added with a degree of indignation, "The pastor ate almost nothing and then had that sister of his round up the whole kit-and-kaboodle and off they went. Maybe they don't like our food."

"Wanda, you keep the line moving. I'll be back in a minute."

Several people told me that Dad had retired to the pastor's study. I found him at his desk with a plate of partially eaten chicken wings. His chair back faced me and he sat looking out at the rain. Thelma laid the offering report on his desk and excused herself.

"I feel as though I'm part of some conspiracy," I said.

"And you've come to confess," he said.

"I mean, against me. Not that I've instigated one."

A row of tightly closed hyacinth and daffodils, little embryonic orbs, banged against the glass like windshield wiper blades.

"Dad, I fail to see how you can be mad at me. All weekend I've run loosey-goosey to cater to the Arnett family, mind you, in spite of the fact that you forgot to clue me in on their arrival. I assume you had me arrange this whole social today to benefit them. Then they up and disappear as though we've insulted them."

"And you, of course, warmed them with your charm."

"Like always."

The clock ticked in syncopation to his steady breathing.

"We have a hundred people to feed, Dad. Surely Pastor Arnett understands that I have other duties to fulfill and can't tend to his every whim."

"He does. For the record, he said nothing about your lack of attention. I've never met a more gracious guest."

Lightning brightened the office. I closed the drapes.

"Some of the families are under the impression that Colin came to—how did they put it—steal my job. That wording wouldn't have originated with you, I guess."

"Of course not. At least, if some of them said that, I would have just said nothing at all. It isn't my place to discuss church matters." The one or two phone calls I made on Saturday night in no way should have been misconstrued as divisive. I only answered truthfully the few things I knew about the man. Innocent, innocent words, in my estimation.

"March, you know this church needs you and I've needed you. But with a stronger man at the helm—"

"There is no stronger man, Dad, than you."

"I've always loved to see myself through your eyes. But I think you should know, I like Colin because he reminds me of myself twenty years ago. I've faded a bit."

"Mother wouldn't allow such talk." All of this nilly-natter about fading left me feeling unsettled, as though the ground eroded beneath me while the church walls creaked, threatening to collapse.

"She'd agree with me."

"And you should have let me fill your plate. I'll get rid of these chicken wings and bring you some salad."

"March, will you please just sit and listen? Forget what's on the menu for once and listen to me."

Suffice it to say I hated it when he sat me down as though I were twelve all over again.

"Colin Arnett received some horrible news this morning. In spite of it, he managed to deliver a timely message that we all needed to hear—at least, I needed to hear it."

"I haven't criticized his message."

"When he took over that little church in Lake Norman, he had one man on his side, a man who accepted the position as his first board member and his best friend. Through all of the changes Colin brought, he never left Colin's side. That friend died this morning. Some heart condition, to hear Colin tell it. But Colin took the platform in spite of the weight around his neck. He's got more character in his little finger than most people have head to toe, March."

"Dad, I didn't know about his friend."

"I know. But you need to know something else. Colin turned down our pastorate. To tell you the truth, I'm heartsick over the whole thing. I've seen steering committees search for three years and not come across a single candidate of Colin Arnett's caliber."

"You think I ran him off."

"Wild horses couldn't run him off if he felt this was the right place. But you certainly didn't welcome the man, either. I've never seen so many steely-eyed stares coming from a congregation. A godly love, that's what the whole place lacked this morning."

We sat, both of us, listening to the clock and the thunder.

"We showed that out-of-towner where to hit the road, I guess," said Fern.

She and three other women wiped out casserole dishes near the pass-through to the kitchen.

"There's our dear March," said Grace Caudle. "We'll not let a Charlotte man come in here and tell us how to run our church."

It sounded like a line from a fifties sitcom.

"Grace, I don't think Pastor Arnett came here to tell us anything. Dad invited him. They've known one another for a year. Could it be you're all imagining things about him?"

"I only know what you told me," said Fern to me.

"This whole business of me telling things around the church is getting out of hand. I don't know anything about Colin. He's a decent enough man, I guess." I helped Fern set out the clean dishes so the owners could claim them.

"It's how you say it, March," said Grace. "Like how you just said he was decent, but you had a sort of question in your voice about the whole thing, like you didn't really believe what your own mouth said."

"Grace, you're imagining things."

"I heard it too, that questioning," said Fern. Her lips had a beak-ish look, pursed and ready to peck. "March, is this man trying to take your father's place or not?"

"Fern, I'm not at liberty to discuss my father's business."

"There's that dubious tone again." Grace stacked the twentieth foam plate on her tower and asked a deacon to come and tote the leftovers to the garbage pail. "March, Fern and I, we've been around a long time. Don't think we don't know a pushover when we see one. And you're just that sweet pushover. This Arnett fellow might blind you, but he can't blind us."

I could not tell them my father had searched for over a year for his own replacement. "If Reverend James Norville trusts the man, perhaps you should offer the same trust."

Fern harrumphed all the way to the kitchen.

"I just want to know if anyone in particular, certainly not either of you, but are you aware of anyone making anything in the way of a rude comment to Pastor Arnett?" I asked.

Grace spoke first. "We're the pillars of the Presbyterians, Hal and I. We offered our kind and gracious appreciation of his message."

"And told him how no man would ever replace our own Reverend Norville," said Fern. Both of them all but turned up at the toes and laughed.

"But we weren't the only ones." Grace changed aprons. After she tossed the soiled one in the laundry bin, she said, "Everyone showed support. Reverend Norville should feel very secure in his position."

Fern adjusted the rabbit brooch at her shoulder, a rhinestone hare with ruby eyes that appeared to bleed whenever she moved. She looked leporine herself the way her eyes twitched. "All done. Time for choir rehearsal."

It occurred to me that Colin Arnett must have felt that he sat among vultures. Several groups had formed around the dining hall, husbands and wives, elder members who joined the quiet talk, wide-eyed and shaking their heads as though they had all weathered a larger storm than the one moving up the coast.

Bill Simmons, a board member, approached me. "March, we're so sorry we couldn't attract this Colin Arnett to our church. We'll form an official steering committee and take the weight of the search off of your father. He was so hopeful of finding his own replacement."

The church organist struck up a progression of chords out in the sanctuary that sounded like a spirit song at a baseball park. Choir rehearsal started at two o' clock on Sunday afternoons. Several stragglers left the dining hall clutching a hymnal against their chests. The thunder became distant, a far-off clanging of pots in heaven.

Showers of blessing, Showers of blessing we need;
Mercy drops round us are falling, But for the showers we plead.

Before I went to bed that night, I finally rounded up a pen and wrote in my long-neglected journal:

Even as I write, I cannot recall the meaning of mercy, its dictionary meaning. If I find a place for it in my journal, first of all, I shall have to look it up. I am a stickler for just the right word with just the right meaning. The word "mercy" is misunderstood because it is so overused in church circles. Like other words such as "grace" and "love."

I want to compose a letter to Colin Arnett and his family and thank them for the gracious love they showed to us this weekend. It will cover a multitude of sins if I choose just the right words. I want to find a place for "mercy." It seems so appropriate.

Six

THE TWO-SIDED COTTAGE-STYLE BUILDING THAT housed the *Sentinel* was also Julia–Norville green. My business neighbor, Eric's Tropical Pets, had signed the lease only six months ago to take over when Bette's Doggie Treats had gone belly up. (Little canine snacks in the shape of Bette Midler from her pre–Divine Madness days had little impact on Candle Cove, even though we do love dogs here.) Eric left a sticky note on my door that read: *I have a missing iguana. Eric*

My assistant, Gloria Hammer, had arrived ahead of me. I could see her blouse pressed against the upper portion of the plate-glass door, her arms over her head. Since her body had a fourteen-year-old's trunk, she looked adolescent in the glass, a teenage girl lightly balanced on the ladder, small-chested in a T-shirt designed for a boy. I tapped the glass.

"Hold on. I'm installing the bell." She said it as though I was waiting for an answer. She graduated from high school seven years ago, but still had the look of one of those olive-skinned seniors who never has to wear makeup. Gloria repaired small appliances for laughs, a skill she had picked up from her Ecuadoran grandfather. Our coffeepot had seen two repairs, the last of which, she declared, would make it a lifer. On our slowest day, Thursday, Gloria would compile a list of gadgets we needed to make our workdays easier, and then she would proceed to invent the most economical plan for implementing the new widget. Every Monday, I edited the obituaries, prepared for the city council meeting, and listened to the pinging chorus of Gloria's thrumming cosmos.

Her feet moved down the stepladder like a firefighter's, toned calves leading her on to her next experience. "Welcome home," she said through the glass. "Your mother-in-law is in town." She opened the door as though she were handing me the trapeze bar. Most of her hair was pulled back into a ponytail, but little stubborn ringlets the color of auburn and fire made a halo around her forehead.

"If she came by here, I don't want to know."

"No, I saw her at the Lighthouse Java Mill this morning."

"This is important, Gloria. If her car looked all packed down, like, packed to leave, that is a good thing. But if she looked more like 'Hey, I'm just grabbing some coffee before I plot ways to stay and haunt my ex-daughter-in-law,' well, that is something different entirely."

"But if she is only here for the weekend, her car wouldn't look packed down, but might have a bag or two in the trunk. And I couldn't just say, 'Hey, Mrs. Longfellow, looks like a two-bag weekend.'"

"Joan never has a two-bagger weekend."

"Then I haven't a clue as to how to check the woman's vitals."

"Joan likes to get an early start when she travels. If she's staying to shop, you won't catch sight of her until the mall opens."

"Then, you're safe. She was at the Java Mill at six."

I breathed a sigh of relief and penciled in Mason's baseball practice on the calendar.

"Coffee's ready."

Gloria had already filled my ceramic mug and left it next to my keyboard.

"You forgot the cardboard," I said.

"I don't think cardboard placed where you put your lips is sanitary."

"Cardboard is good, Gloria. It keeps my coffee hot. They make cardboard from trees. It's organic so it can touch where my lips touch."

"Mrs. Pickles left her daughter's wedding announcement in the night drop."

"It's about time someone gave Eleanor a reprieve from that hideous name."

"Bad enough Mrs. Pickles is known for her prize-winning canned pickles and tomatoes." Gloria erased last week's edition from the white grease board. "We need to make Thursday's paper seem like the Spring Edition, as though we were thinking about the season in advance. I could take some shots of the fashion show at Bernie's. All of the families who have high-school daughters parading down Bernie's runway will buy us out."

"Good idea. Oh, Eric's missing an iguana," I said.

"Life was calmer when the doggie treat lady was next door."

"Once the little lizard sees that we don't leave food lying around, it will go back home to Eric. If it's here, that is. By now, it could be in the causeway."

"I think they eat cardboard," said Gloria.

The bill sorter pinged.

"I didn't know anything was due today," I said.

"Eric owes you rent. I set the bill minder to do both—remind you of paying and billing. Oh, and that editor friend of yours from Charlotte left a message. Something about a new seafood place in Gastonia."

"That's code for catfish house," I said. "If it's not near the ocean, it can't be seafood."

"Gastonia. That must be in the mountains."

"No. Other side of Charlotte. I told Brady I don't do catfish houses. The Carolinas are full of these perfect bed-and-breakfast places—you eat, you go to bed in another century, you wake up with breakfast at your door. Catfish is so eighties. Women read my articles. They don't want something from a deep-fryer vat."

Gloria roughed out the front page on the white board. "I guess Mason had some qualms about going back to Virginia."

"When I promised we wouldn't go out to the Longfellow estate, he was okay with it, really."

"If ever I have kids, I want them to like visiting their grandparents."

"So Phil isn't ready yet, I guess?"

"Neither of us is ready. It would be like kids having kids." She never liked to talk about the fact that she and Phil had been trying to get pregnant for four years.

One of Gloria's gadgets flashed a tiny red light, meaning low battery or some such. "Having you for a mom and Phil for a dad would be kind of like having the Disneys for parents. That's not so bad, Gloria."

"We're not mature enough."

Eric waved at us through the door. Gloria beckoned him in. Eric Weinstein looked like a long, deflated balloon, a thin frame curved at the spine. His nervous hands appeared homeless if he did not have something to hold. He handed Gloria the rent and then relit his cigarette. The envelope had ashy residue around the seal.

"Always on time," said Gloria. She did not mean to make a dimple on one cheek when she smiled at Eric. But I always suspected she knew of his crush on her. "Find your iguana?"

"I've looked every place an iguana might hide. Fritz will look for the warmest place and just stay there and wait for the flies to come to him. He isn't aggressive or anything. Sort of a lazy iguana. I think that's why I haven't sold him."

"Eric, I don't think people know if the iguana is lazy unless you tell them," said Gloria.

Eric paused. He always fished for ways to elongate the conversation with Gloria.

"Thanks for bringing by the rent," I said. "We'll keep a lookout for Fritz."

"'Bye, then." Eric strolled out, moving light as air, as if the weak indoor currents propelled him.

"I think you torture him on purpose," I said.

"Finally, he leaves. If I torture him, March, it's by my very presence. Not one single thing do I say to lead him on."

"Of course—it's your breathtaking presence."

"It's a curse."

"Or that hint of twinkle in your brown eyes, that look that says, 'go ahead and salivate, Eric, but I'm far beyond your grasp.'"

"Look, the man can see I'm married. Men like him levitate to women like me because we're safe. With me, he never has to face rejection just because he's, well, Eric Weinstein."

"Gravitate. I think I'll turn up the heater in the bathroom." The weather idled between the dead end of winter and the mouth of spring. The circulation room, the place where our three hired retirees bundled the papers before delivery, smelled earthy, as though Gloria had just watered all of the potted plants. I figured Gloria must have moved the plant cart out and away because it angled several inches away from the wall near the bathroom. Wylie and Brendan Poe, the brothers who manned the print shop, never showed up before nine on Monday. A pile of soil caught my eye. One of the large clay pots lay on its side with jagged triangular tears in the begonia leaves.

"Gloria, maybe you should call Eric," I said. I looked inside the bathroom. The big dragon opened its mouth and hissed. Its saurian tail wrapped around the base of the toilet. The pea-colored hide hung loose around its stomach. I closed the door.

A camera dangled from one of Gloria's hands as she phoned Eric.

Eric and two high-school boys entered with a length of rope. While Eric looped the rope over the iguana's head, the boys wrestled with its trunk.

Gloria took a photo of all of us standing around the beast. It made page two of the upcoming *Sentinel,* right between the city pound's pet-of-the-week column and Doris Idlewild's recipe for corn relish.

By the lunch hour, we had written the copy for the stories that had trickled in over the weekend, typeset them, and set up the obits, the weddings, the divorces, and, of course, ended with Eric's iguana. By two, Gloria and I shared a submarine sandwich and watched the downtowners, other small business owners who milled around the square during the lunch hour. Every Monday, several women from the bakery held a paperback swap under the large oak in the dead center of town. Leon and Edward Seam, two brothers who run a small law office, conversed with a carpenter. It was rumored they planned a facelift on the law office.

"So I guess you and Mason will be off on another beach excursion soon."

"We have only three miniature bottles in our sand collection," I said. "High time we added another." Mason and I schemed to collect sand from almost every beach in the world. Joe called it ambitious. We collected our first bottle of sand from nearby Myrtle Beach, the second from Candle Cove, and then the last one from Ocean City. Mason picked up several catalogues from the Travel Hut at our small beachside mall. He found a lagoon in Cancún he wanted to visit, deep-blue water, scuba diving, and white sand. We had yet to collect truly white sand. To the Ocean City bottle, Mason had added three small pebbles that sat atop the bottled sand until three months ago when one of them disappeared. I jostled the sand around but never found the third black pebble. "I think Mason is going through some things," I said.

"He's missing his dad."

"Always that. He acts mad at me a lot of the time. Lately, anyway."

"They probably sent you some grief material after Joe died, I guess."

"So he might still be going through the anger phase. Is that what you mean?"

"Joe died so abruptly. Maybe Mason's still trying to pull all of it together."

"Makes two of us."

She gave me one of those piteous sympathy gazes I had grown to dislike. "I guess visiting the cemetery left you feeling a little melancholy, too."

"You know how that crazy lunatic from Georgia drove up here just to shoot someone because he was mad at his girlfriend?"

"That loon from Macon?"

"Yes, the Macon loon. He killed that poor old man who lived his whole life just to open an ice cream shop in Myrtle Beach. That old guy got up that morning thinking that all he had to do was heat up the fudge and chop the walnuts. It was a lousy way to go. But I'd like to get a phone call from the police one day, a call from the chief of police to let me know that they finally got a confession from Joe's killer, that Joe didn't just veer into the high seas and dump himself overboard. But that a loon from Macon who was mad at his girlfriend hijacked Joe's boat. That Joe died fighting. I just want to know that Joe died fighting. You know that shooter had a bandage over his nose when they led him up the steps to the jail. That old man died fighting. Took a crowbar to that gunman."

"Joe's boat dumped over during high winds. What are the chances some loon from Macon would find Joe, mug him, and dump him into the ocean?"

"It's not even plausible, Gloria. I just said, 'I wish,' that's all."

"Mason believes it was an accident, March. Can't you just leave it at that?"

"I hope Mason believes it. But he hasn't been himself. He was too eager to help pack away Joe's office at the house. I wanted to put the rest of his dad's stuff up in the attic with his other things. But I had to stop Mason from carting it all out to the curb. Just lately, he acts as though he's mad at Joe."

"That doesn't mean he suspects anything other than the truth—it was an accident. He's just mad at his father for leaving. And you don't have any proof of anything other than an accident either."

"Just that he left me broke. That the insurance company took a long time to settle. That Joe's firm went belly up three months after his funeral."

"They say that auction was fabulous." Gloria said it gently, as though she was not sure I wanted to hear it. "Those attorneys must have had high tastes. All we need is just one of those mahogany desks to give this place the sprucing up it needs. I wish they would've had the decency to offer you a piece of it or a part of the auction revenues."

"Not possible. The bank got it all. I carted a box of Joe's stuff out one day, the stuff I really wanted for sentimental purposes. Pictures and bookends I had bought for his office myself. I stopped and asked a security guard what he thought happened. He said to me, 'Too many chiefs. Not enough Indians.' I think Joe and his partners wanted too much too fast. But Joe never listened to me. He always wanted to prove to his family he could measure up. He made me feel as though they were his real family."

Doris Idlewild opened the front door. In one hand she carried a brown bag from the deli. In the other, she toted her large purse that always looked weighted down with a bowling ball. "Don't tell me you two were really attacked by a vicious animal—" she whispered the remainder of her sentence, "from next door?"

"Sorry, Doris. You'll have to buy the weekly to get the full story," said Gloria.

"I have to wait until Thursday?" She looked disappointed.

Gloria nodded.

Doris glanced ahead as though overtaken by an afterthought. "You got my corn relish recipe?"

"We did and it's already on page two," I said.

"Oh, fine, then. Got to run, girls."

"Gloria, you're so hard, making poor Doris wait until Thursday. By then she'll have us taming Godzilla."

"What a nice idea. Eric's lizard was kind of a Godzilla. Maybe we should change the headline."

"We'll look silly. It was bad enough I agreed to stand next to that scaly Fritz, but now it will look as though I had some part in wrestling it out of my bathroom."

"How is that silly?" Gloria gathered up our deli wrappers, but saved the leftover lettuce—the loose part untouched by mayo—for her compost bin.

"Silly as in we don't have anything better to do around the *Sentinel* than to wrestle iguanas. Like we're not a serious newspaper."

"Of course, we're a serious newspaper. Didn't we give Doris Idlewild's corn relish recipe second page? A frivolous newspaper would have given it front page news along with the iguana story."

"But if we nix the whole iguana story and use an AP clip of the president overseas, well, that's what a serious newspaper would do on page two. We need more world news."

"Not so. Don't you remember when the snapping turtle stopped traffic across that bridge in New Orleans? The *New York Times* picked it up. To outscoop the big guys, you have to be in the right place at the right time."

"An alligator, Gloria, not a snapping turtle. If we had wrestled an alligator, well, that is newsworthy—two domesticated suburbanites face off with an alligator. That's not a pet-store lizard story."

"March, that iguana is all of six feet long. He's no gecko."

I put the cup to my lips but pulled it away when the now frigid coffee touched my mouth. "I think I'll make a fresh pot."

"If you want to pull the story, March, then pull it. It's your newspaper." Gloria heaved the sigh of a martyr. She swiveled her chair all the way around and, after hand-pressing the wrinkles from her cotton skirt, she took our deli trash around to the small kitchenette in the corner of the newsroom. I heard the sound she makes when she digs through her tool drawer.

"Okay, I won't pull the story." I yelled it so she could not later say that I never said it. "Maybe it is good human interest for us after all."

The clink-clank drawer-shuffle noise stopped.

On my desk, a group shot of me and a few friends from Chapel Hill including Brady Gallagher, the travel editor for the *Charlotte Observer*, had faded. Brady was the only member of our little group with whom I had kept close communicado.

Next to the college snapshot, Joe stared at me from the framed wooden photo just above my desk pad. Behind him, the mast of his boat furled against the wind. I snapped the photo the day he christened it with a bottle of champagne. Both he and Mason had taken the maiden voyage of the *Sparticus* around the beach and up to Wilmington.

I tipped the frame forward and lay the photo facedown. Sometimes when I looked straight into his eyes, soft orbs of dark green that looked free from care, I relived the worst of times.

Like the worst day of our marriage.

If the bank had not called that morning about the overdue car payment we might not have had such a terrible fight. Someone had called Joe from the office when I returned that morning from taking Mason to school. Otherwise, when I sauntered into the kitchen with a sack of Lighthouse bagels, he might have already been on his way to the office. I sliced the bagels, toasted them, and buttered his on one side since he'd never developed a taste for cream cheese. Before I could hand it to him on a plate, the phone rang again. I answered it that time. The woman from the bank had a punctilious manner, as well she should, but had it been one of the girls I went to high school with, I might have really wanted to bean Joe for not mailing the payment. I had specifically remembered the way he had asked me for my share of the house payment a week early, as though he were ahead of things. A year before, I had opened a separate bank account due to the fact that he had a bad habit of laying his little automatic teller machine slips all over the place until he got a pink slip in the mail telling him he was overdrawn. Since the pink slips made me feel as though his bad banking habits were a reflection on my character, I opened my own account so that I would never get a pink slip with my name on it. When I paid him early for the house payment, I thought he was paying all of it early, the house, the car, the electric bill. But here was the bank woman asking why the car payment was ninety days past due.

That is what caused the fight between us. I railed on and on about his responsibility to Mason and to me. He swore that he thought he had made the payment, but could not cough up the proof. Then he grew peaceful. Joe never finished his buttered bagel, but left the house. We had not kissed in several days and perhaps that was the very thing that clouded the whole reel of my memory with guilt. His secretary told the police that he had come in to work happier than she had seen him in days. When he left for lunch, he never returned. The office staff thought he had met with the firm's biggest client, United Nations Bank. None of the staff knew that Joe had lost the account a week prior and spent his days carrying on as though he still possessed a good lawyer-client relationship with them. Only his partners knew. Joe had taken cash for one bill to pay another bill, believing the large check to be imminent from United Nations. But I never thought that he had stopped kissing me, or making love, just that I had not initiated it myself as a punishment for his incompetence.

Never did I mean for him to think that I would never kiss him again. But as the reality of our bankruptcy surfaced, my desire to solidify our relationship with an alm of affection drowned under swells of anger. Joe's happy gaze mocked me. He knew things that he did not bother to share with me.

But realizing he had not touched me, when he knew it would be the last time, really lit my fuse. Big time.

Maybe tomorrow I would move the photo to my top drawer. By week's end, to the bottom drawer.

Gloria walked in. She clutched the newly developed picture of us and Eric's iguana. Her gaze took an oblique dive left of where she stood and she saw Joe's photo facedown. "You need a new picture for your desk? I have a nice one for you."

My shoulders rolled forward. I reached for Joe's framed snapshot and sat it back up again. I couldn't replace him with a lizard. Joe still lived among us and made me feel as culpable as ever.

Seven

I SHOULD HAVE SENSED SOMETHING SOUR IN THE
Monday afternoon air when I pulled up to the baseball park with
Mason. We parked next to the truck with the upside-down rat
attached to the top. Jerry Brevity gathered Mason's team around the
bleachers left of the concession stand. The Salamanders gathered into
a huddle while he passed out team shirts and caps.

"The rat man is our coach—no way! He drives that stupid truck.
All the other teams will make fun. And he smells like Grandpa's
closet." Mason slapped his glove against his leg to make either a small
cloud of dust or a statement.

"I had nothing to do with it, Mason."

"Grandpa should have coached. I told him, but he never did nothing about it."

"*Anything* about it. Grandpa can't keep up with you boys, Mason,
and run the church. Don't you go and make Dad feel guilty. If Jerry's
the coach, then I want you to respect him as such." Jerry waved at us.
"Besides, Jerry doesn't have anything better to do. Grandpa has
church matters to think about."

"'Salamanders' is a stupid name, anyway. They don't have teeth or
claws. You can't win if you're an amphibian."

"People used to think salamanders were magical."

"But they're not. They have those stupid little legs and you can't tell if they're a lizard or a fish. It's like they can't make up their minds."

"You kids voted on the name."

"It was the Buckworth twins that did it. They had just enough pull with some of the wimps, like, if they didn't vote for their name, then later they might get a fist in the face. No guy wants to be known as the kid beat up by a Buckworth girl."

"If you want to play ball this year, then don't walk—run! Get up to those bleachers, Mason. Run, now, or I'll march you back to the parking lot and we'll go home! You run!"

Mason ran. His head bobbed part of the way, an agitated jerk that somehow, in his mind, gave him the final say. When he reached Jerry Brevity, he tossed me a glance as though he wanted to let me in on the fact that he plotted his moment of vengeance.

Finally, the row of Bradford pear trees that surrounded the field had turned a milky pink and shed petals around the boundary of the playing field in a soft snowy trail of strewn blooms. Visitors to North Carolina sometimes mistake the trees for cherry trees or some other fruit tree when the truth is that the trees produce no fruit at all. Not pears, not anything; just blossoms that fall away to reveal the perfectly pear-shaped foliage that looks as though an elfin arborist slipped into the fields at night to create paper-doll symmetry.

Jerry had a standard coach's posture: always arms akimbo with his right thumb tucked into his front pocket. Even when he traveled house-to-house, he carried himself like a coach, knit slacks tight against his derriere with a crisp white shirt tucked just so the curve of the tail made a smile on his backside. To hear Mason describe Jerry Brevity, one would imagine the rodent exterminator with poison canister in hand, a smarmy lurker with missing teeth. But Jerry managed his life with such precision, his first imperfect wife left him in search of a less exacting paradigm.

"March, I missed you at your dad's place the other evening," he said.

"Oh, you were there?"

"I saw your Mustang. You must have been upstairs, or some such. Say, I noticed those—what do you call those little road signs?—bandit signs, stuck in the ground out along the roadside and saw your son's league needed a coach. Thought you all might use a little help."

Mason lifted his glove and placed it on his head. He emitted a deep sigh, just loud enough to make Jerry glance and then look back at me.

"Can never get enough good coaches," I said.

"Your Mason, your little guy here's a sharp player. We'll have us a good time, won't we, little buddy?" He rubbed Mason's head, but Mason moved away from him.

I heard a trill from inside my handbag. "Pardon me. Phone call."

Jerry called the Salamanders into a huddle.

I seated myself next to Gladys Martin, who must have carpooled with Dinah. I saw no sign of my best friend— just the Buckworth girls spinning near first base and grinding their heels into the dirt.

Brady Gallagher phoned to remind me that I forgot to return his phone call. Gloria had left the note from him right atop my desk with *Charlotte Observer* underlined as though I could not remember.

I did not remember.

"I'm sorry, Brady. You wouldn't believe what happened today," I said.

"One guess. You trapped a dragon in your bathroom and it's making headlines."

"Gloria."

"You work her too many hours. I like that."

"I told her to go home."

"And you think we only have catfish houses in Charlotte. We have real seafood."

"As usual, Gloria keeps no secrets."

"But you were right. It was a catfish house. That's what I like about you, March. You're pure class. You want seafood—I'll give you good seafood. Write down 'LaVecchia's.'" He waited, somehow knowing that I scribbled it down.

"With a *k?*"

Brady spelled it for me. "I'd like this piece by next Monday."

"Mason and I could take a trip down Friday night."

"You're a pro."

"Anything else?"

"That piece you did last year on Ocean City—Fred liked it."

"I'm pretty sure it was over two years ago."

"He thinks you should do more travel pieces. Fred's outlined a new column concept called 'The Barefoot Traveler'."

"Sounds big, Brady. Like something you'd save for yourself."

"I've got bigger fish to fry. Maybe I'll tell you about it when I don't have so many ears around. Besides, you know I'm a soft touch for friends." He hesitated. When I did not respond with wild appreciation, he said, "Fred wants to give the customer a wider travel scope. Not just North Carolina and catfish houses, but more of the South— from D.C. to Florida."

It sounded like a more rigorous schedule, but a temptation. "Brady, I genuinely love the idea, but I have a son, and a newspaper to run."

"You'll have a budget, an expense account. Maybe an expense account. We'll grow into that stuff, you know. You'll fly. If this column takes off, say in three months, you'd get a raise. You could do it on weekends at first—take the boy with you. We'd use your lovely face in some touristy pose, say with a nice pair of shades, you sort of glancing over the rims. If you're good enough, we're talking syndication. I thought since you could use the money, you'd want to have first shot."

"We're fine with money." I moved away from the team moms. None of them needed to know I was nearly destitute.

"But you could be better."

Mason swung at air. He choked the bat and pounded home plate with it a couple of times. I could tell he was preoccupied with Jerry Brevity. The dust on the plate rose like steam.

"I'll let you know, " I said.

"Monday. I need to know by then."

"Maybe a little more time than that."

"Fred wants to move on it. You know how he can be."

"Okay, Monday."

Gladys Martin and two other mothers raised their brows and smiled at me, sort of a deliberate invitation to join them, I assumed. I ambled up the metal bleachers. Gladys moved to one side and offered me the awkward middle position between them.

"March, I was just saying, well, all of us are talking about you. Hope your ears aren't burning. We've watched you with Mason, with your business, well, everything. Not every woman could hold up as well as you have."

"We're doing fine, Gladys." Except for the town *Sentinel* that managed to pay its managing editor/owner a mere subsidy of a salary, but why go into that?

"We just want you to know that you're admired. That's all," said Gladys.

"I've had good moral support. My dad's been, well, pretty unbelievable."

"But you're strong, March, you little warrior-mother, you." Gladys could have stood her words atop a white picket fence and they would have been no less saccharine or less obvious to those seated around us. Several other mothers shifted and turned to look at me, the warrior princess. My mouth felt dry inside, unable to press a credible smile into my resistant cheeks.

Joan Cramden handed me a rice cereal marshmallow treat.

Flattery caused me to falter over my words. "Look, I really don't think I warrant accolades." I finally pieced together a cognizant thought. "Things happen and you either get up the next day and face whatever life throws you, or you just stay in bed." *Some days, I'd rather stay in bed.* But I didn't say that, any more than I would blurt out the details about the nights I lay with my head on the pillow softly moistening the linen fabric I once shared with Joe. No one wants to know the real truth about how suddenly pain can enter a person's life, knife through her heart, and leave her bleeding without a single visible scar.

"Still, you are just a dream of a trooper." Joan brushed lint off of my shoulder.

She did not want to know the truth, believe me. Once a soccer mom had commented about the flower bed in front of our house that was bountiful with blooms, and I mechanically pointed out how the perennials sent to us for Joe's funeral had become the flower bed. She fell silent and I realized no one could take facts like that in quick pill form. *It's a lovely flower bed. Yes, they're straight from the funeral parlor.*

Mason bunted. I knew he hated to bunt. His scowl could be seen from space.

The baseball moms continued in their misconstrued worship of March Longfellow. I remained staid, saying little in return. It isn't that I try to prove anything to these friends of mine, or be falsely strong. It's just that when the facts of your life have gone from normal to dark, no one wants to hear about the dark. So you fall silent about the painful things and talk about the things that are more palatable to the general populace.

That is how you keep your friends.

Doris opened an orange soda and gave it to me.

A salt breeze floated past and it cooled our skin.

"Nice of Jerry Brevity to coach for our kids," said Joan.

"It seems to me that if he'd stop tooling around Candle Cove with that dead rat on top of his truck, he'd do better for himself," said Gladys.

"That's how he picks up extra business." Doris acted informed about Jerry, as though she had picked through his underwear drawer or something.

"I don't mean more rodent business. More—other kinds of business. Like, he's eligible and all, but who wants to be seen riding around with a hundred-pound rat?" Gladys stared after Jerry as though he were a wasted container of man.

Doris said, "I don't guess you should care, Gladys. You're fifteen years with number two."

I think Gladys mouthed, "Not me."

"Jerry just blew his whistle. Water break, girls," I said, ready to put a period on the chatter.

Two of the moms carted chilled bottled waters down to home plate.

"Thanks, ladies, for the rice treat and the orange drink." I sidled between the two of them and melded into the throng of parents.

We watched the boys polish off the cold bottled waters. Doris passed out the rest of the marshmallow snacks to them, but Mason turned his down. He and Jerry conversed a few feet away from the parents. Mason smiled at me, direct, like he sent me some son-to-mother signal. Jerry nodded and patted Mason's head. Jerry turned around and caught my eye. I met them along the baseline between home and first.

"Mason here has a fine idea," said Jerry.

Mason and I exchanged glances. I thought he smirked, but I could not be certain.

"He said that we should all go out for dinner and then an ice cream cone. I suggested Dooley's. They have those great outdoor tables, little umbrellas like you women like. It's a nice warm evening."

Several excuses flew through my mind. But because Mason had set up this whole evening with Jerry Brevity he would never back me up. "Mason, you have homework. And you know we have that teacher meeting tomorrow." I thought the hint of revealing his scholastic indiscretions might deter him.

"She didn't give us homework, Mom. We can go." Mason's sappy buoyancy as he leaned against his bat typified some little con artist.

"We'll make it an early dinner, March. They have the Early-Bird specials, too."

"And ice cream," Mason kept interjecting until I wanted to throttle him. "You know how you like ice cream, Mom." In spite of Mason's self-proclaimed loathing for the town exterminator, he managed a sentimental smile that warmed just like the glimmer of sunlight in Jerry's eyes seemed manipulated.

"I have a good idea, too," I said, being certain to avoid Mason's gaze. "I'll follow you there, Jerry. But Mason here can ride with you in your truck. Jerry, Mason's been saying for the longest how he would like a ride in Brevity's rat truck." Instead of waiting for an answer, I made my way toward the Mustang. "See you there." It would take a day to scrub the exterminator's scent off Mason. It would be worth it.

Sybil Ettering started the Inksters, and if she never published a line of prose in her life, she would go to her grave with one byline—as the founder. Her gravestone might say—"Founder of the Inksters"—and anyone who read it might look at it and wonder about it. Sybil sat with Sue Bonadett and Glenda Wiggins in the far corner of Dooley's. The three of them sipped beers and tossed peanut hulls onto the floor (which was not only allowed but recommended because the oils enriched the wood floor's finish).

If I could have stopped Mason and Jerry at the door, I would have steered them over to Sonnet's for fish and chips. I had not seen the Inksters in two months. The thought that I might be seen on what appeared to be a date with the rodent man who walked so familiarly beside my son, and both of them wearing matching peach Salamanders T-shirts, made me feel as though something inched the floor from under my sneakers. I told myself that dragging behind in Jerry's shadow was my only hesitation and not the fact that I had not written a thing in several weeks. The shining glass windows that encircled the dining room mirrored the three of us, bugs under a microscope. I wanted to pay Jerry to walk a few steps ahead of us and then sit two tables away, but Sybil already bore a hole through us. Sue stopped her glass at her lips. A smile formed and I saw her hand pat Glenda's leg. Jerry approached them first.

"Must be ladies' night out, and a finer group of ladies I've never seen!" said Jerry. Everyone in town knew that he and Sybil's husband, Bernie, played side by side on the same bowling league.

"Look at the three of you. Jerry, you must be coaching Mason's team." Sybil never looked at Jerry the whole time she spoke, but kept staring at me. She had glued on her sort of splayed-looking lashes that parted like starfish prongs. Sybil's fingers, adorned with her ring collection, made her fingers look like little sausages wrapped and stuffed with pawn-shop jewelry.

I wanted to explain the platonic nature of my dinner with Jerry, but the translation was vague and lost in my anxiety. "Mason just finished baseball practice. Jerry's joining us for a bite to eat."

"We've been missing you, March, at group critique. Sue here has just finished her twentieth poem," said Sybil.

"Why, Sue, I never knew you to be a poem writer," said Jerry.

I heard Mason whisper "poet." I could not invent a punishment to equal the misery on his face.

Sue's timidity was her aura. "I finally got the nerve to write about my divorce. It's been a very cleansing experience." She always looked back at Sybil when she spoke, for approval or some other such affirmation to let her know she had made a valuable contribution to the conversation.

"March, I hope you've been practicing your creative webs. We'll get that little creative flow of yours going before you know it," said Sybil.

"I've come up with a few ideas," I flat out lied. "Mason and I have been so busy with just life, I haven't much time for development."

"March, your mind paints life in such grand strokes," said Glenda, making graceful swirls in the air with both hands. "You think in ways that sort of just—your ideas make money. For instance, I can't think of a thing that anybody would want to buy. But you come up with this little newspaper, and, next thing you know, everyone in town is reading your *Sentinel.*"

The *Sentinel's* profit margin could be scraped off the bottom of Glenda's shoe, but I did not bother to tell her that.

Sherry Dooley offered us a table. I asked Sybil about the next critique group and then tried to act interested.

"We've switched it back to my house," Sybil told us. "Glenda's having her floors relacquered. The fumes nearly killed us. Say, I don't know if you've heard about Sarai Gillman—you know the girl that pours coffee down at the Lighthouse ? She got her first nibble from a New York editor. It's the big time for her, I'd venture to say."

"Sarai Gillman heard from an actual editor, she did," said Glenda.

"She's a gifted girl," I said, not showing jealousy. "I never thought she would stay long here in Candle Cove. Sarai is so—I don't know—sophisticated in her thinking. She can just walk into a room and everyone knows she's not from around here."

"Now before you go, tell me the name of your new idea," said Sybil.

"It's a story about—angels," I said.

"She's going to be rich, Jerry. Better get her while she's poor," said Glenda.

Mason pulled at my hand.

I knew it would do no good to say, "Jerry and I are just friends." Not with this group.

Sherry Dooley led us outside to the red tablecloth-draped tables on the veranda. The tide ebbed into mirrored sheets that reflected the rose-and-yellow strips of sky strung out like a clothesline. Mason dropped his hat onto the seat and ran to climb onto the thick rail that overlooked the beach. I wondered how he might react to Brady's phone call from the *Charlotte Observer.* We would have to spend most weekends flying. I tried to imagine him at home with Dad or hefting his duffel bag through airport terminals. Before Mason climbed into his bed, I would tell him of Brady's offer but not admit that it was a temptation for me. Nevertheless,

I could not get the thought out of my head of how carefree I would feel sitting at a desk writing about places I had visited. "This is my favorite table, Sherry," said Jerry. He handed her a dollar.

"My pleasure. Janet will take your order, folks."

Four high-school boys sporting green-and-gold letter jackets collected around a corner table. Jerry returned a nod. Some summer past he had most likely coached their baseball team or played referee for the community soccer league.

"Jerry, you never coached full time. I'll bet you would have been a good coach," I said, speaking aloud what I had always privately wondered.

"My folks never encouraged me to go on to college. I guess that's the only reason. Never was much of a student, but I got good business sense. You know my ex always called me "the perfectionist." I do well for myself, March. Spend my summers coaching Little League. Work on my house some. Everything I want, I have." The last few words of his sentence wilted. A trace of melancholy rose in his eyes and he looked at me with a question in his face, as though he had asked me something and then waited for my reply.

"Mason, come take a look at the menu. You still have school in the morning and I don't want you up too late." I drew the conversation away to other things.

"I tell you, son, you just get anything you want, steak, what have you. I seldom get to pick up the tab for a hungry boy." Jerry pushed a menu toward him.

Mason and I had not had a steak since before Joe's death. Joe was the family carnivore. Mason sat on the edge of his chair with his eyes planted on me as though he awaited a mother's verdict.

"Mason usually orders off the children's menu. Really, he can't eat a whole steak."

"Nonsense." Jerry flipped open the menu and pointed to Dooley's steak list. "Can't be hitting them out of the ballpark on French fries and chicken nuggets."

"Filet mignon," said Mason.

"There you go!" Jerry helped him select a loaded potato caked over with all sorts of Dooley toppings.

"Mason, let's split it, then," I said.

Jerry ordered two filets for the both of us and a porterhouse for himself. "Tell me about your little news operation, March. I guess I've seen your *Sentinel* in Wilmington, New Bern, and even along those little gas stations up around Raleigh."

"Still too early to say. I've picked up a new advertiser. Bill Hayden's Chevrolet." It sounded insignificant compared to the news Joe once came home boasting about.

Mason rolled his eyes and sort of deflated onto the tabletop.

"Seems like I've seen your office light on late at night. You burning the candle at both ends, I guess?"

"Tuesday nights. Mason sleeps at Grandpa's unless Yolanda is available to baby-sit. You remember her, don't you? Cute face, braces? Almost got kidnapped?"

"You almost got yourself killed," said Jerry.

"Anyway, we have to finalize our stories and make sure we're not leaving out Ed Finneman's special on dog food. He keeps threatening to take his business to Wilmington. Other nights Gloria stays late if the printer's acting like it does when it goes on the fritz. Our printer gives the guys fits. But Gloria has her way with the machinery. Liona's good enough to take notes for me on Mondays sometimes for the city council meeting, especially if Mason has Little-League practice."

"Ever play tennis up at the country club anymore?" He seemed to remember every small detail about my past, but I did not let on that it bothered me.

"Tennis? Not in a year." Three gulls flapped into the landing and collected near our feet. "Mason, don't feed them. It makes them aggressive," I said.

"You used to be pretty good at tennis, from what I remember."

"They have these funny ideas about dues at Randolph's Country

Club. Gee, do they have courts—the best. But you know, I don't miss all of the country club goings-on. You know, all of that who's-wearing-what and who's divorcing. Joe loved the club. So it's good I don't go. It would remind me too much of him. I don't even know how I got ushered into all of that—hoopla. Well, this all sounds pretentious. Club blather—it's not really what I'm into." I hoped Jerry would take the hint that I did not intend to go prancing into Randolph's all tennis skirted up and hanging on his arm as if we were the new couple.

"The city built those new courts up near the ballpark. If you want, I can swing a racket. Maybe this weekend we could meet for tennis."

"Jerry, thanks. But I just have too much going on with us, with Dad, work, my church. And since you are, in a manner, bringing it up—not that you are calling this an official date—but, sort of, you know, I just can't see myself in the dating circle again. Besides, Mason and I are going out of town this weekend. It's a travel assignment from a friend in Charlotte."

Mason sat up.

"I didn't know until just a while ago," I said to Mason. "Brady called while you were at practice."

"Is it a beach?" asked Mason.

"No, up around Charlotte," I said.

Mason pressed his face into his hands again on the table.

"It's a seafood place. So, it's not really a travel assignment, per se. More of a food critic's assignment. But freelancing for me can take on many forms. Maybe I'll have my plans all under one roof one day, be organized enough to have more help at the *Sentinel* so I have more time to write. Who knows? Is it getting chilly?"

"March, you sound as if you think you have to make up excuses for what you do. If you're a writer, just say it out like that—'I'm March Longfellow, the writer.' You don't have to chase rabbits all over creation trying to explain it."

Now he was advising me. Cute.

"I am a writer. But I don't know why I'm bothered about saying it. Maybe because I feel more like a Little League mom or the preacher's kid. Or Joe's wife. Or if I say I'm a writer, maybe someone will actually ask me to show them, say, something in writing. I feel like a fraud. Then all I have to show them is, sort of, a few odds and ends, here and there, the city council meeting or the report from the school board. And some people don't think you're a real writer unless you have your name on the front of a book. You take whatser-face, Sarai Gillman. When all of the Inksters are yammering on about what we all write in our various ways, you just see the level of interest go up when someone says her name. She's, to them, a real writer. But, say 'March Longfellow' and all of them, well, wink and elbow one another. They don't understand that running a newspaper takes a lot of time." All of my creative juices glug down with the bubble bath at night.

"Get out the gun. March Longfellow's hunting for wabbits."

"Jerry, don't try and do imitations. You sound Iranian."

"Your steaks will be right out, folks," said the waitress.

"The phone's ringing, Mom," said Mason.

The quick, almost emotionless voice on the other end of the line had to repeat the statement twice. "I'm sorry to inform you," was all that I understood.

"Mom, you look funny," said Mason.

"I'm sorry, Jerry. We have to go. Mason, honey, your grandpa's had a heart attack."

Jerry sighed, offered his sympathy, and ordered a beer.

Mason followed me out of the restaurant. I tried not to show watery eyes to him. "I knew his eating was going to get the better of him." I pressed a tissue against both eyes.

The drive to the hospital, past the hot dog stands, Leon's ABC store, and the ebbing tide along the Candle Bay faded into a listless horizon. I could not remember saying my good-byes to Jerry or somehow letting Mason know that everything would turn out, well, fine. I don't remember how we made it to the emergency room at Holy

Mary by the Sea Hospital with two foam boxes packed with steak and potato.

I had never seen my father hooked up to monitors and IVs. "Daddy, we're here," I said.

Before they had taken his wallet and belongings, he had pulled out a photo of my mother. He held it against his chest with his one free hand. It was an old picture of her standing out on the deck of the cottage as she painted it the color of the sea. "It's Julia, March. I think she misses me," he whispered.

"No, Dad. Not yet. It's a slow tide tonight."

Eight

OUR LITTLE HOSPITAL, HOLY MARY BY THE SEA, cared conscientiously for the bruised and those afflicted by infection. But by the first kiss of day, the local doctor issued the order that Dad should ride by ambulance to Raleigh. Dinah Buckworth drove behind the ambulance with Mason so that I could ride shotgun with Dad. Bill and Irene Simmons called those who could get away and ferried them by church van to Raleigh. Dinah weaved in and around the jarring host of motorists full throttle until the highways thinned of school buses and commuters idling toward New Bern or Jacksonville. The Presbyterians were no bigger than a filament of lint in her rearview mirror.

Dad's doctor proclaimed the surgery a success although Dad lay in his bed sluiced of color, a soldier winged by his own bullet. Three bypasses issued through his arteries to unclog all of the routes to a more agreeable tomorrow.

Since Tuesdays required so much of my attention at the newspaper office, my phone did not stop ringing the whole morning. I took Gloria's calls out in the hallway. She held together the weekly like the glue I knew her to be.

Fern and Leon Michaels doled out magazines to the church members gathered out in the lobby. Lorraine Bedinsky, engrossed in soap operas, knitted coasters beneath the overhead television. Grace Caudle dropped Hershey's Kisses in silver heaps around the lobby tables, as though by doing so she prevented fainting spells between breakfast and the lunch hour. The act caused a surge in aluminum foil wrappers balled up and dropped in all of the planters.

I stayed beside Dad, acting as custodian of the floral arrangement cards and the get-well greeting cards. The doctor taught him to place a pillow against his chest whenever he laughed. Only Bill Simmons elicited a flutter of laughter from Dad in his postoperative slouched-and-drained-of-life posture. It was the same old dialogue that older men all said to one another after a heart attack—"Some people will do anything for a vacation."

By the second day, the doctor told him he might find his appetite. He more than found it and gave us a shameless list of foods he wanted brought in.

"Dad, they just cleaned your pipes. Should you be clogging all the works back up again?" I asked.

"March, you know better than to try and convert me to that taste-less soup-o-mania lifestyle you call healthy eating. None of it appeals to me. If you have to live life in misery, then you may as well cave in and eat rocks. Now go and bring me a box of vanilla wafers."

"It's on the list, Dad. Mason's back at school today. I have to leave around noon in order to pick him up on time. Before I leave, I'll bring you a few things."

"Fine. If you don't wind your way back down to that paper office, Gloria will find 102 ways to take up the remaining office space with her gizmos."

Bill Simmons opened up a chess board. "I thought we could get caught up on my beating you again at chess, James." Bill had gained a lot of seniority as a systems analyst and took advantage of some time off with Dad.

"Bill, you always liked punishment. Set her up," said Dad. He cleared a *Moody* magazine off his tray. "I'm glad it's not raining today.

We've had such a parade of people driving back and forth, I'd feel terrible if they had to drive in bad weather. Bill, I want you to take over the midweek service, of course. March can get you a good book of devotions off my bookcase. Steal one by Oswald Chambers. Just don't read it verbatim. Too boring. At least try and, well, if you can teach—how are you at summarizing?"

I hoped Bill did not overhear my sigh. His penchant for leading board meetings overshadowed his ability to stir the hearts of spectators.

"You want me to try and preach?" Bill said with a near squeak in his voice.

"I'm well aware that you can't preach, Bill. But give it a go, if you can."

"James, I'll do my dead-level best."

"If you call the state office, they might have a young intern that can fill in Sunday. I'll be back week after next."

The head board member slid the chess pieces into place. He offered no more than a half nod. But then he emitted a sigh and arched one brow. "Week after next. I don't know, James, if that is wise."

"Dad, you just had triple bypass surgery. Maybe you should ask the doctor how soon you should be back in the pulpit," I said.

"Harry Weising up at Kannapolis had his quadruple bypass and in two weeks conducted a wedding, two funerals, and stepped back into the pulpit without so much as a blink. I'm in better shape than Harry. Let's flip to see who goes first." Dad faced his king and queen toward Bill.

"James, you go first."

"I don't need your sympathy, Bill. You go first."

"Dad, I don't know Harry Weising but I do know how stories circulate. I think I should call Colin Arnett. He knows our church now and considers you a friend. I'll bet he'd come if we ask," I said.

"Whose going to ask Colin Arnett? You?"

"Perhaps I should be the one." I still had not penned a letter to Colin with my grace-and-mercy speech and could now kick myself for the delay. So I mentally fashioned conciliatory speeches that might warm him up to visiting Candle Cove Presbyterian again.

"Colin is done with us, March. It would be in poor taste to call him back now."

"You say that as though something bad has passed between us. But Colin lost a friend Sunday. It distracted him, that's all. If I call and tell him you've just had triple bypass surgery, he'll come back."

"March, we've formed a steering committee. Don't trouble yourself about the matter. We'll find a candidate," said Bill.

"I'm not talking about a candidate. Only a fill-in guy."

"You don't ask a man who pastors a congregation of 1,005 and counting to fill in at a church of 110." Dad grunted. He lost a pawn to Bill.

"Although if you could get him to reconsider, March, well, we'd be the happiest church around," said Bill. "We have people willing to start a building fund, for once. Man like Arnett, he could steer us in ways we can only imagine." He moved another pawn forward.

"March is too busy, Bill. She's got this Charlotte paper after her now for a new travel column."

"Be sure and speak for me, Dad," I said. "I can't think for myself."

Bill had grown accustomed to our gentle sparring, but I made certain I punctuated each sentence with a wooden smile.

"Neither can I, March. That's why you always think for me." Dad placed his pawn in Bill's square and shoved the black pawn aside. "It's just the way we Norvilles are, Bill."

"I believe I'll hunt us down a cold drink. Don't touch that board, James. I have eyes in the back of my head," said Bill. He tiptoed out of the room.

"Colin Arnett lives in Lake Norman, Dad. This weekend I agreed to do a piece about a seafood restaurant in Charlotte. Not too far from Lake Norman. I'll just drop by. Piece of cake."

"So you plan to pay him a visit and, what, tell him things have warmed up in Candle Cove?"

"No. Here's what—first I'll request a meeting with him. I'll tell him our congregation might have felt a little blindsided this weekend. We didn't have a chance to show him our best side. I'll ask him will he simply give us another go." It sounded levelheaded to me.

"So we ask this man to whom we gave the cold shoulder this weekend to please reconsider coming here for a cut in pay and a congregation that is easily blindsided. My friendship with the man is the only reason he considered Candle Cove in the first place, March. We don't have much to offer Colin Arnett or anyone of his caliber."

"I beg to differ." Bill appeared with a canned drink in each hand.

"Bill, you know what I mean. We just tend to run a little behind here." Dad popped the top on his drink.

"March traipsing off to Lake Norman is like sending the ant off to bring back the whole banana farm." Bill moved another chess piece. He studied Dad's reaction, which was nothing at all.

"You can be negative about it or you can at the very least let me give it a try," I said.

"Maybe she's just the ant we need, James. Check." Bill stared right at my father.

"Check?" Dad seldom lost at chess. "Maybe we should have started with checkers. Next thing you know, I'll be keeping up with the soaps." Dad picked up the remote control. "Hand me a *TV Guide*, will you, March?"

Never did I intend to approach Colin Arnett with the pastorate of Candle Cove Presbyterian. I did not know him well enough to do that. Had I given the idea more thought, I might have returned to Bill Simmons and told him our scheme was a pretentious front for my worry that I was still being blamed for Colin's rejecting us. But as Dad lay attached to bleeping monitors, the urge to patch the hole that sucked life from James Norville's world hissed at me.

The night before, thoughts had trickled in as I tossed in bed nervous about Dad's heart. When I finally drifted off, I dreamed about saving my father. In the past year I had had this recurring dream, an emotional flight through a dreamscape of ocean hues. This was the same dream, although in the midst of it, nonsensical elements weaved through the main elements. Always, though, I flew in the dreams, but not as an angel. I had brittle translucent wings, fluttering dragonfly wings that were too small for my body. My weight pulled at the insect wings. I had moments I thought I would separate from them, and I could feel them fraying at the small hinge that attached them to my back. Instead of lifting above the arc of ocean that wrapped our cove, I struggled to stay above the tide and not plunge into the roiling bath of salt water. The sand pebbles appeared as boulders that dissolved into the water and allowed the tide to swallow up our cottage. The seafoam-green paint made oily splotches on the surface of the sea, and I could see my mother floating away on the surface while Joe's hand disappeared into the darkest middle of its raging torrent. But this time, my father sat atop the church roof with his Bible, held it close to his chest, and quoted Psalms. He seemed bothered by my attempts to lift him from the swirling church, but even more so when I left him atop it. When I could not raise him and felt my wings crumble into the tide, he looked at me and I understood his wordless assessment of me. His mantle of disenchantment cloaked me, and I fell to the shore beneath its saturated weight.

Brady Gallagher phoned me on my drive back to Candle Cove. His wife had left him two years ago when his long nights at the office offered her too much time on her hands to make fast friends with a neighbor who rescued her one too many times from her dysfunctional lawn mower. Brady persisted on coffee and doughnuts and vociferous meetings. When I ran into him again face to face as a journalist— three years after our graduation from Chapel Hill—the dark sunken spaces beneath his eyes prognosticated his pitted road ahead. Once a year he disappeared into the Rocky Mountains for a two-week stretch of fly fishing, only to return and allow the newspaper business to hook up to his tank of inventiveness and readily drain him of it.

"Brady, some things have changed," I said.

"You aren't coming. If I scared you away with that column, don't let that keep you from this one piece." He sipped coffee. I could hear the slight breeze he made as he breathed across the top of it and then allowed it to slip between his lips.

"My father just suffered a heart attack. But I am coming. I just don't know if I can give you an answer so quickly about the column now. Dad met a pastor from Lake Norman. If I can convince this minister to return to Candle Cove, it will be a weight off Dad. But I need to be around for Dad's recuperation from the surgery for a couple of weeks. The biggest chore will be to get him to stay in bed and rest."

"That's bad news about your father, March. If I can do anything at all, you let me know."

"We have a good support system at the church. This health matter with my father has thrown me a curve, that's all."

"If you need to be released from this weekend, I understand."

"Trust me. I'm coming. Colin Arnett's church is in Lake Norman somewhere; Cornelius, I think."

"LaVecchia's has a location in Cornelius. I don't know Colin Arnett, but then, I don't know many preachers, as a rule."

I pulled up Bill's notes that I scrawled inside my Palm Pilot. "Arnett pastors Church on the Lake on Catawba Street. Sounds like a yuppie church."

"I guess they have to have their own churches now. To each his own."

Dinah met me at the cottage. Whenever I begged, she would take time off from the caterer's business she operated out of her house to help me clean the beach house. She always said it was because she knew if she helped me she could have the use of it whenever she wanted. It could not have possibly been because we had seen one another through the worst of female disasters and lived to tell about it. We washed and folded linens and prepared the downstairs bedroom as though Colin Arnett might soon return. Mason ran with Hercules along a crisp row of shells washed ashore overnight.

"I made us a big old pitcher of sweet tea, March. Let's fix ourselves a cold glass and take it outside. The sun is so bright today," said Dinah. Twin heads bobbed down the shoreline. Dinah's girls carried seashells inside the tails of their shirts. They dumped them at Mason's feet and all of them knelt and picked through the pile to ferret out the good shells and toss away the broken or chipped ones.

Dinah arranged a few store-bought cookies on a platter, balanced our tea glasses in the center, and carried it all out onto the deck. "I don't guess I ever had a chance to meet this Colin Arnett. You seem different about him now, is all I know."

"I think that my father believes I ran him off."

"Is he right?"

"No. Not entirely so. But in a manner of speaking, I'm still guilty. Because in my heart I was cold to him, even if I didn't say everything I was thinking. At one point, I may have sounded defensive. My memory's a little fuzzy. The man caught me so off guard I didn't know what to say. Dad should have warned me about all of it. But maybe that's the whole point—maybe Dad did try to tell me and I wasn't willing to hear him out."

"You can leave Mason with me and I'll take him to the game on Saturday."

"The game. Oh, Dinah, here I just spilled all of this stuff about going to Lake Norman onto Mason and then wondered why he was so silent on the way over here. He thinks I treat him like everything is important except what he wants to do. He probably tried to tell me about his game and I just talked right over him."

"I do believe I've never met anyone busier than you, March."

"No one else will do what I do, Dinah. If I don't take care of us, no one will. I have to run the newspaper. And since Mom died, if I don't keep all of these volunteers organized at church, well, then, who else will do it?"

"If the ladies spring bazaar is canceled, then what? The end of civilization as we know it?" Dinah scraped away the chocolate cookie icing with her teeth.

"It's not specifically the bazaar, Dinah, or the newspaper deadlines, or the town council meetings. All of it is held together in so fragile a way by such few people."

"Delegate. Hand it off."

"I've tried. But no one seems to care about the inner workings of the church or the newspaper as much I do. So the work is only halfway done, as though the person trying to take my place is just going through the motions."

"If you're the only one who cares, then maybe what you're doing isn't so important."

"Tell that to my father."

"The long and short of it, then, is that you do it for your father."

I broke my cookie in two and laid one piece on the plate. "Dad had depended so much on my mother to keep their busy nest comfy and stocked, to maintain all of her organizational charts she kept so well in her head. When she died, I stepped into her shoes without so much as a 'hold it' or 'let me think about it.'"

"I guess your father asked you to take her place then."

"Not in so many words." I pretended to look for the children. Finally, I saw movement on the shore.

They shook the sand from their clothes and chased after the tide in their bare feet.

"I could never take Julia Norville's place," I said.

"Just all of her obligations."

Dinah irritated the truth out of me, the sand in my oyster shell. "What are you implying—that maybe I'm just trying to keep her alive?"

"I always said you were sharp as a tack, March Longfellow." She handed me a cardboard box. "Take a gander at this. You'll never guess what's inside."

"Mason, when I told you about this weekend, you didn't say anything at all about your game. I think we should talk about it."

"You wouldn't have listened, I figured, so why mention it." He had used silence to make his point and make me feel guilty.

"I care about your games, your practices, everything about you, Mason. In the same way my father has to be reminded about his obligations, it wouldn't hurt if you reminded me. I don't get angry with my father when I have to remind him that he is having dinner with us on a specific night or that he is picking you up from school when I have to stay late on Tuesdays."

He shrugged. "So Grandpa's coming home Friday from the hospital. That seems kind of quick."

"They send patients home sooner nowadays, and don't get off the subject. I think you prefer to pout instead of talking things out. That isn't a mature way to do things, Son."

"I don't pout. That's a baby thing."

"Mason, if you would have mentioned your game to me on the trip over, well, we might have had the chance to talk it out. I know you realize that this trip to Lake Norman is important for Grandpa's sake. But your game is just as important to me."

"Are you farming me out to the Buckworths?"

"What if I am?"

"If Grandpa's coming home, I'd rather stay with him. Maybe I could help him out, you know, bring him things when he needs it."

"I like that idea. Then you could ride with the Buckworths to your game. Don't sigh like that, it's only a ride. Once you arrive, you run off with your friends, your teammates. No harm in that. Unless you want Jerry Brevity to pick you up."

"I'll ride with the Buckworths."

"Just don't go off trying to fix me up with Coach Jerry again. I still have to take my revenge for that last maneuver of yours."

"Is Pastor Arnett taking Grandpa's place?"

"If Dad wants that to happen, I pray it happens. Mason, we have to trust Grandpa on a few issues and this is going to have to be one of them. I don't know if Pastor Arnett wants to come to Candle Cove. We're a small church. But if he agrees to come, then maybe it's high time Grandpa took more time for himself, did a little fishing." I felt a pang when I said it.

The phone rang. Gloria was doing battle with the printer.

I sighed and knew how Mason would react. "Let's swing by the office. Gloria needs my help."

Mason rolled the back of his head against the seat. He emitted a faint moan. I understood the meaning of it. He never got to go directly home from school, from baseball practice, from a trip to the beach. While the other children filed from church with their parents only to head out for Sunday dinner, we stayed behind to collect litter around the sanctuary and to visit with committee members who needed advice. When I was not at work, I was still at work because the *Sentinel* clasped onto me like a newborn. "I think I'll just call her back and ask if she and the fellows can handle the printer without me."

"I can play outside, then," said Mason.

"What a good idea. I'll throw you a few balls. Don't roll your eyes again. I know I throw like a girl."

The phone rang again.

"I won't answer it. Probably nothing."

After two more rings, I picked it up.

"March, you need to get down here. The whole computer system just crashed," said Gloria. She never had a frantic edge to her tone, but she did this time.

I apologized to Mason several times on the way to the *Sentinel.* Mason never said a word, but stared out of the window and shot at invisible rabbits. I wanted to shout at Joe for not being around to see it.

Nine

WHEN DINAH HAD FOUND THE BOXED DIARY, SHE held it out nine inches from her face, closed but with her thumb stroking the edges of the pages. Both of us had agreed we should not read it, that it would be unfair to trip without consent across the strings of a man's private soul. Dinah, had she found it while alone, might have allowed temptation to rule.

The journal lay undisturbed on the passenger's seat for over an hour on the way to Lake Norman until I stopped to buy gas and a soda. I opened to the latest entry while gasoline glugged rhythmically into the car tank. I surmised Colin must have penned it the day he disappeared down the beach to study.

Colin's diary read like a photographer's journal.

I prefer the westbound road at early morning. The sun at my back has not yet dominated the sky and the horizon bleeds only a little color, a whisper of the day. All is pale. Swallows are busy in the trees, little creatures with darkened wings that sing and sing into the quiet of my pale morning. It is a pure song, one as quiet as a dimple made by one sky-cooled raindrop upon a pond. Some rush into the day with blaring horns, all moments penciled into the minutes as though they had already happened, as though handed to us already spent. But I sip the morning when

I travel, at least the virgin part of day before I am overtaken by my will. Until I become like everyone else.

I closed it up and continued down the winding rural snake of road thinking about what else he must have tucked into the journal. Thoughts about death. And Eva.

Halfway between Candle Cove and Lake Norman a lonesome stillness settled over me. I stopped to buy peanuts at a farmer's stand on Andrew Jackson Highway only to load up on honey and pecans. A girl clad in a dress too old for her young frame, the farmer's daughter, poured me a cold cup of apple cider and invited me to sample her pecans. I sat on a barrel to sip the cider, and that is when the insatiable urge to read Colin Arnett's diary again overtook me. It was a shameful urge but one that adhered to me. I returned to the Mustang and retrieved the diary.

Not even the darkest tide of guilt could pull me away. I flipped through the often-touched pages until I found an entry he wrote about Eva.

It is my first night curling up against your pillow without you, the wretched lone spoon. Your smell upon the linens is like a bed of narcissus after rain, a common flower until it is placed upon your gentle wrist and turns to nectar. I beg that smell to stay, but feel desperate, as though it is fading from me as quickly as my last moment with you. I keep whispering your name hoping the angels might deliver my frantic message to heaven's portals to tell you I have died without you. Surely God will finish me so that I may leave earth's ragged, spinning orb and join you in a dance among the stars. Hateful bounds! I am the blackest soul given by God's own hand the kindest treasure, a shining beam of womanly daylight for too brief a moment. To me the blackest soul, undeserving of your sacred attentions, God granted this cherubic gift and then revoked it. . . .

His words took my breath, his love for Eva suffused with self-contempt. He finished out the page with two lines of poetry.

For oh, my soul found a Sunday wife. In the coal-black sky, and she bore angels! Dylan Thomas

My throat tightened and I thought I smelled narcissus. I snapped the book closed, and glanced around feeling as though the farmer's daughter minced by me, stared with accusing little bullet eyes, and shook her finger at me to shame me for intruding on a grieving man's private musings.

I had not earned the privilege of peering into Colin Arnett's quiet moments, but there I sat swallowing whole his inner voice, doused with a drink of farmer's cider.

I read some more until shame seized me and then I put it away and continued eastward toward Mecklenburg County and the buzzing hive of Charlotte.

I practiced looking at Colin without revealing my culpability.

For all my love of the ocean with its procession of gulls embroidering the sky like starched origami, I could as easily make my bed in the city, and especially the Queen City of Charlotte. If I had not fallen in love with the Sound, I might have hitched my star to Charlotte. She offered so much to those who could no more bear to leave the South than to go without air. All of the designer companies had flocked from the hub of Charlotte out to her suburbs in Lake Norman and Concord— Starbucks, Banana Republic, Ann Taylor—along with various chain restaurants like Spaghetti Warehouse with its period indoor trolley and, of course, Joe's Crab Shack. If I had not accepted the assignment, I might have been fickle in determining where I would eat dinner. For lunch, I would ask Brady's suggestion in hopes he might spring for the midday meal. I had mooched from Brady since college; cadged jobs from him, lunches, and anything I could get without officially calling it a date. It would have been like dating a brother.

I drove into the parking deck and ferried the stub inside to be sure he stamped it "paid." My mother would have disapproved of my power over Brady, although I never shared such things back then. I considered it senseless to add to her censure list.

Whenever Brady and I met up again, he and I chatted about everything from frat houses to the old weekend beach parties as openly as my mother once chatted over the fence about Tupperware. I kept pictures from college in a shoebox, three specifically with Brady stuck between all of us six girls on the same floor who ran amok on weekends. Over the years his ginger-jar shape had expanded, with the bottom half as round and encompassing as the moon. In the grainy photograph, you could still see his inhibited grin thinly stretching into his cheeks and his eyes gallivanting obliquely—a bashful soul's refusal to look straight into the camera lens.

Since he had signed on with the *Observer* after our little gang all graduated, over time I noticed that whenever I departed his office, he had a habit of loosening his tie. Then he hesitated as though his heart stood on end for an instant. That is when I walked away as if on cue. I could not give him a moment of eye contact or indicate I ever knew of his ancient infatuation with me. My fondness for Brady and his geekish inclinations never crossed the threshold to fulfill his Walter Mitty-ish fantasies.

The secretary ushered me into his office, a shared space cluttered along the walls with posters of food award winners and travel pieces for which Brady held an eclectic fondness. The *Charlotte Observer* was not of the size to have a true travel column but instead tossed a few dollars toward the Sunday travel section, Brady's first twenty hours of weekly commitment. He referred to his other twenty hours as the "other things" he wrote for the paper.

I found him seated at his desk; several paper cups sat like bumpers on a snooker table, each cup filled in varying degrees with cold coffee— the first coffee of the day interrupted during the morning meetings and accompanied by the editorial doughnut, the coffee he brought back from the meeting, and the just-before-lunch coffee, still warm. Yet, Brady might have balked if any secretary had attempted to wrest any of them away before the noon hour.

He kept stacks of articles situated around his desk categorized into the edited-pieces stack and the not-yet-jelled-pieces heap—usually mailed-in articles by freelancers that required such wide snatches of editorial attention that he sometimes left them to morph into fodder for the circular file.

"Good for you; you made it. Hope the traffic didn't tie you up. March, you look great. You've lost weight and I must have found it for you," he said.

"Interstate 277 was stacked all the way into town." I peeled off the kiwi-colored sweater and draped it on a chair back. "Your secretary said they've closed the café here in the building. You must be brown-bagging it." Brady and I always started out our conversations in a desultory fashion, leaping from one trifling topic to the next.

"Some of us guys around the office eat at Showmar's. They make the best gyros I've had. Too, I have a friend at the Duke Power building and sometimes he gets me in at their eatery. You have to know someone."

"Gyros. I haven't had a real one since Joe and I took Mason to Ocean City."

He gathered three foam cups from his desk and dropped them into his waste can.

"Here's a pen and paper. If you want, just give me the directions. I can find—what did you call it—Showmar's? I realize I'm here early. If I can reach Colin Arnett, maybe he can meet me at LaVecchia's tonight for dinner. "

"Kill two frogs with one wheel."

"In a manner of speaking."

"Melanie, I'm taking Ms. Longfellow out for a business lunch-eon," he said.

The secretary shrugged. Her pouf of bangs billowed in a frayed sort of flight against what curl she had tried to hot iron into place that morning.

"I can pay," I said.

"These tightwads can front me a lunch. Forget about it."

"Any more details about this, what you call it, Barefoot Traveler column?"

"No up-front budget. That's the bad news. But you live in beach city, so I figured if anyone could make it work, you could. We're a Knight Ridder paper, so we dig up all the syndicated stuff, the exotic, for nothing. But it's the pieces on regional places we lack because there is no actual budget per se. And we get a lot of garbage from the guys who take a buggy ride in South Carolina and send us what they think is the definitive Charleston story. But they're not writers. They'll never be writers. Not like you. They just want to have written. Sure, they're cheap, but I have to completely rewrite the mess they send to me. I might as well do it myself. With you living between Pamlico Sound and Myrtle Beach, you're the perfect candidate for 'The Barefoot Traveler.' The money comes in when you build an advertising base. Folks all up and down the coast need someone like you to plug their place—but not just any place. We want the unique, the quaint, the quirky, and lots of local color."

"So I really wouldn't be away from Mason."

"Not right away. Depends upon how fast you build a budget and your own travel stash. How far you travel is up to you. The way I figure it, you have enough material in your neck of the woods to launch this thing."

It intrigued me.

The dining room at Showmar's was a cross between old people who eat applesauce in Florida restaurants, and an East-Coast deli. Every table displayed plastic red-and-white flowers inside empty olive-oil bottles as ordinary as laboratory vials. Brady cajoled a waitress he knew into fitting us in ahead of the line of noonday office dwellers that waited in the lobby and out onto the sidewalk next to Tryon and First. She led us to a window table, and that suited Brady fine.

"You staying in Cornelius, I guess," he said.

"I didn't make reservations. It's Lake Norman. How busy can they be?"

"Depends. Lake Norman has its own traffic jams now. All those New Yorkers and New Jersey types have invaded, bringing traffic jams and New York pizza with them."

"I'll bet the old-line rural families like that, the farmers and locals."

"They hate it. You'll see these stretches of rural, undeveloped land squeezed between two major commercial zones, and lo and behold, Old Farmer Jones has stuck little homemade signs in the ground near the road that say NO MORE LAND GRABBING! But the developers land on them with a bag of money, and out goes the family legacy and in goes a new subdivision."

"And a LaVecchia's."

"Say, that's a good piece of news. You have to drive four and a half hours in your direction to get real seafood otherwise. Only other reason I know someone would drive that far is for love."

A few seconds passed. If I stared at his coffee cup long enough, perhaps he would stop sniffing around imaginary holes. "My father's had a heart attack. He wants this Colin Arnett to take his place. I . . . when he first came to town, I didn't realize what transpired between him and my father, and I sort of, well, I wasn't expecting him and I misunderstood the situation is all."

Brady laughed. "You ran him off."

"Not at all." The waitress took our order. "But the whole church was caught unaware and no one rolled out the red carpet. Candle Cove Presbyterian knows how to welcome a newcomer if given a proper introduction. I just want to invite Pastor Arnett back to give us a second chance."

"Tell me how Mason's doing."

"Great. Or good, I should say. Maybe on some days lousy. Missing a dad around the house, but we make do."

"Mason's a good kid. Boys like him rebound amazingly enough. It's the widow who worries me."

"I'm fine, Brady. First a month and then a year after the accident, I hit a slump. Joe's family had such odd ways of managing grief, and

I felt as though I had to run around propping everyone up the week of the funeral. They all thought I was a barracuda because I didn't shed a tear that week. But I felt as though weakening for even a moment would make me a target. You'd have to know the Longfellows intimately to understand."

"I'll pass. You mentioned her once, that mother-in-law person. I had one once, but don't get me started."

"One night, four weeks later, I fell apart. I was in my bedroom—our bedroom—alone. Then the gloom sort of passed, and I thought I'd be back on the path to sanity. A year later it hit again. I thought I was losing my mind."

"March, you never call me even though I tell you to call me if you need me. I've told you at least a thousand times to call. But you never do."

"Even you wouldn't want to see me in such a mess, Brady."

"Pastor Father couldn't console you." He said it with sympathy.

"Dad was his usual bowl of compassion. But I needed to express some things to Joe, and without an audience."

"It's best to get it out. Keeps them from having to throw the net over you. But all of that propping up isn't good either. What else are you propping up?"

"That's a good question." I hated it when Brady started digging up all of my emotions. But I never let on to the way he annoyed me like a finagling little brother.

"That's what your trip here is all about. More propping."

"Maybe it isn't propping. What if I say that I'm doctoring? That isn't the same thing."

"It could be."

"I just know that I have to try and repair something I loused up. Do you ever do that, Brady, just open your mouth fully believing the right thing is coming out? You think you're a crusader but instead you wind up the village idiot."

"My ex-wife might like to answer that for me."

"I'm haunted by my own words, Brady. It's as though I watch myself going through the motions of setting things straight, but it's all in slo-mo, and I have this sort of deep satisfaction that I've just conquered another mountain. Days later, or maybe a week passes, and I wake up to realize that instead I've set fire to the whole thing."

"Pyro March."

"This conversation isn't helping, Brady." After my confessional to "Father Brady," he knew more about me than I knew about myself. Brady had that affect on me, like when he used to drag me in front of the cheap beveled mirror nailed to my dorm-room wall and make me look. "March, this is you," he would say. "*You*, meet March." He forever accused me of holding my feelings inside. He was wrong, I would tell him. But he just kept standing behind me making me look. The waitress placed a warm ceramic plate in front of me loaded with the gyro, tomatoes, and a white sauce.

"You know a little lamb had to die for that, don't you?" Brady shook salt all over his burger and fries.

I stared at my own hands and then nodded. I was glad I had my back to the window. I wasn't in the mood for reading my reflection.

"Pass the ketchup, will you?" Brady inhaled his food, the human vacuum.

I checked into a hotel in quaint Cornelius, a Best Western with all the usual appurtenances of a Lake Norman village-chic look. The desk clerk told me I was only a block or two from LaVecchia's. Mason would be setting out a hot meal for himself and Dad, some casserole and dessert brought over by Phyllis Murray. I called Dad's place. Mason answered.

"Mason, it's me. Phyllis brought you dinner, I hope."

"She did. Something with macaroni. Grandpa hates macaroni."

"Dad's more than likely going to be grumpy, Mason. Do you know who is taking the pulpit tomorrow?"

"Someone's taking the pulpit?" A second or two passed before he responded. "Some man from South Carolina. Grandpa says he knows him."

"That is a relief. You staying home with Grandpa in the morning?"

"We're going to watch videos. Mrs. Murray brought over a whole sack of them from Video Mac's. But Grandpa can't laugh too hard. It makes his chest hurt. He's making us do a devotional. 'I'm the preacher,' he says, 'so I get to give it.'"

"Can Grandpa talk on the phone? I mean, does he feel up to it?" Mason asked him. I heard a long sigh, as deep as the ocean ebbing only to recede and then muster a weak wave onto the shore. Dad took the phone. He said he had allowed Mason to bring Hercules, but Johnson remained at the house with his weekend supply dish over-flowing. We spoke for a few moments until he tired of talking. I let him go, but sat with my hand wrapped around the receiver.

When I called the Arnetts, first the answering machine engaged. But Ruth Arnett swooped up the phone. I could almost see her blond ponytail and knit Capri pants.

"Ruth, guess who? It's me, March Longfellow."

There was a pause and I listened to the awkwardness of silence.

"Oh, Pastor Norville's daughter. Say, we felt so horrible about rushing off that Sunday, but Colin's closest friend had a sudden heart attack. I've not seen Colin so devastated. Not since Eva died, anyway."

"I understand. My father's just had a heart attack, too." I heard her take in air.

"I'll bet Colin doesn't even know," she said.

"I told Dad I'd tell him myself. The surgery went great, Ruth. Dad is back home. Mason is tending to him. They're like two old bache-lors eating all the wrong things and watching television. But I'm in town doing a food piece for a local restaurant. I was hoping to have a chance to speak with Pastor Arnett, if he's around."

"He's out on the lake with Troy and Luke. They're trying to learn how to sail. I hope they don't wreck the thing. Boats make me nervous."

"Me too."

She gasped again.

"Don't give it a second thought," I said.

"Colin has the same thing happen to him. People make comments about death all the time without thinking about it. You don't think about loose words, do you, until it visits your own house?"

"I know I'm calling last minute, but if he could meet me to-night . . . You know about a restaurant called LaVecchia's?"

She breathed out an accommodating, "Uh huh."

"Maybe ask him if he could meet me around seven or so. That is, if you all don't mind parting with him an hour or two. I need to discuss a matter with him."

"I'll leave a note here on his note board. He always checks it when he comes home. I'm taking Charlotte and Rachel for haircuts. But I'll be back later, so it's no problem for me to stay with the kids. LaVecchia's just took the place of that other restaurant. I can't remember the name. But Colin has eaten there before. I've heard good things about their food. Where are you staying?"

"At a Best Western in the Cornelius area."

"You aren't far from us. You and your church were so hospitable. If you want, I could just fix dinner here. Why don't I do that?"

"I can't. I'm here on a food critic's assignment. The *Observer* is expecting something on LaVecchia's."

"You have such creative sources for your vocation. I can't write a letter. Better at math."

"I can't do math. See, it takes all kinds." I thanked her and hung up. I placed my knit tops on wooden hangers to allow the wrinkles to fall out and then decided to take a drive around the lake.

Although a manmade lake with five hundred miles of shoreline, Lake Norman has such a busy-harbor look about it, you can sit out on a pier with your feet in the water and dream of the ocean. Dog owners ran with their pets along the shoreline. The warm day brought out the Jet Skiers. Their spray shot up from the glittering horizon, tooling against the wind with the sound of a lawn mower beneath the rider. Sailboats dominated the lake; white, red, and blue sails winding across the water's surface, pleasure carriers skating on a mirror. A yellow sail billowed, tilted aft, and then led the small craft away from shore. A father assisted his children with the boom, but the distance prevented me from determining if it was Colin and the boys. I watched until they disappeared around the curving line of suburban beach.

I left only a small amount of time to shower and change. The *maitre d'* seated me at a round table near a wall of glass that looked out over a garden. A pianist played soft jazz.

I waited until the waiter visited my table three times.

I had not warned Colin that I was coming and knew it was silly to fume about being stood up. I tried to imagine what magnanimous event kept him from a simple courtesy call to me, the person who had used up two tanks of gas getting here. I fumed over that thought until the waiter bent over and asked, "Is there anything I can do to help?"

"I'm fine." My face reddened.

The sky darkened as it always does when the sun exits to leave the moon alone to monitor the night. I ordered the sesame seed-clustered tuna and ate alone.

Ten

IT WASN'T UNTIL I RETURNED TO THE BEST WESTERN
that I finally got an explanation about Colin's awkward absence. The
concierge forwarded a message to the phone in the room: an endless
message by Colin explaining a long evening on the lake with the boys
and how immeasurably terrible it was to hear about Dad's heart
attack. He invited me to join Ruth and the children for the morning
service with a promise to meet with me afterward.

If it had not been for the promise to Dad, I would have never
made the drive to Colin's church.

At ten the next morning, I followed the Yellow Pages directions
to Colin's church, Church on the Lake, and found the entry drive a
bedded-down-the-center floral island, a fusion of perennials such as
not-quite-open day lilies and candytuft. A velvet border of purple
pansies ringed the curbed island flanked by spikes of snapdragon with
yellow dew-filled mouths lifted to the sun.

I parked and followed a chattering group of couples and children
through the glass door entry, a perfectly high wall of glass that set off
the church entrance like the gates of heaven. Two couples greeted me,
effusive and smiling, and stuffed a church bulletin into my hand
along with a brochure that pictorially led the reader through the amal-
gam of activities offered throughout the week.

I wandered through the lobby and stood antlike in what Bill Simmons had branded the "banana tree grove." Everywhere my eye fell, signs of Colin's and Eva's diligence shone, especially in the animated clusters of people gathered outside the doors that led to the main sanctuary. Colin Arnett had never intended to pastor our church, I realized. His kindness was the pure cause of his coming; a pastorly gesture of the ministerial brotherhood, the code of consideration held among clergy.

I fingered the set of keys to the Mustang.

"March, you came. We feel so privileged," said Ruth. She wore an Ann Taylor pantsuit, a chic algae color with a silk blouse woven from a bright lime fabric. Next to her, my cream polyester suit seemed ordinary, a blue-light special, the peach blouse now more like a splayed salmon hue under the fluorescent lights.

"I was in town already. It isn't my intention to be any bother to you all, so please, I'll just take a seat in the back," I said. More than anything I wanted to avoid meaningless banter about being left to eat alone.

"You'll do no such thing. Colin's given me specifics about you, March. You're joining us for Sunday dinner after the morning service. We're all going out to the Mid-Town Café. It's a bar-and-grill sort of place right on the lake. They'll seat us outside right near the water if we ask. Ride with me and I'll bring you back here to your car later. Are you headed home today?"

"Yes. Mason has school tomorrow, and I really have to get back and take care of Dad. He has a lot of people checking on him, but I worry about Mason being there alone with him. Like what if something happened and Mason didn't know what to do?"

"Then I insist you join us for a bite to eat. Besides, last night you sounded as though you needed to speak with Colin."

I had changed my mind. "I did?"

"I already told him you indicated some purpose about this visit. Colin, he's so approachable, really. You should always feel you can talk to him about anything."

"Your church is so, well, big, and it has such elaborate flower beds."

"Eva designed all of the landscape islands and the beds around the church. Her fanaticism for perennials lives on. I want to show you her shade gardens out back. The elders' wives held some rummage sales and raised enough to turn that area into a prayer-and-meditation garden. It's a memorial to her."

"Eva sounds so much like my mother." Except for the fact that Eva did not reside in my thoughts, still trying to correct my mistakes.

"If you want to see Eva, Colin says, just look into Charlotte's eyes."

Ruth led me around the lobby that encircled the entire sanctuary. I might have wandered like a rodent in an endless maze on my own. We passed through two exit doors and walked out onto a stone walk, red stones embedded in the manicured lawn. Apple trees flanked the walk all the way to the shade garden. But someone knelt inside so we stopped. Wisteria vines covered an arbor and allowed a gentle effusion of sunlight to bathe the garden in a holy, weightless illumination.

"It's Colin," I whispered. A sound as still as a robin on a branch, and barely discernible as a man's stifled sob, caused Ruth to take my arm. We left the garden and found our way back into the sanctuary.

Pastor Colin Arnett took the platform ten minutes later. No one but me saw the damp piece of shredded grass tumble from the part of his pant leg where his knees had bent only a few moments before.

Colin had a subtle teaching manner, a commanding presence that kept all eyes glued to him. He had the gentle touch of a Southern accent that wrapped the perfectly selected phrases like soft butter warming his words before he fed them to us. He taught a message about Mary and Martha, two sisters who served Christ—one with her works and one with her heart.

"We can so intellectualize our faith until we feel as though our mission is that of a good-works club," he said. "But until we find that intimacy with him, that quiet place of uninterrupted passion and communion, we will never know him, but only about him. The travesty is in only knowing about him. For then we can convince our dry, parched souls that he is our friend, when instead, our relationship with him is no deeper than that of a once-met acquaintance. Compare an ocean to a rain puddle and you will find juxtaposed the depth of these two sisters' commitments to their Lord, and the vast chasm between them."

Ruth pressed a soft handkerchief into my hand. I dabbed my eyes. The pollen is unbearable this time of year.

In spite of the crowded lobby in the Mid-Town Café, Ruth led us past all of the waiting groups to the rear of the restaurant and out into a screened-in patio. A girl in white shorts and a knit top that revealed her tanned stomach chatted with Colin. She was the hostess. He patted her shoulder and called her by her first name. The scantily clad hostess guided us to a table that overlooked a dock on the lake.

"How's this?" Her gum popped in time to the eighties rock vibrating through the sound system.

"Perfect," said Ruth.

The Arnett children clambered for a seat near the window while the hostess placed coloring menus in front of each child.

Large sailing masts rose up, white canvasses that spread a table for colored red banners and flags that showed off family crests. Girls in bikini tops and shorts sunbathed on the yacht decks.

"The people fortunate enough to live on the lake like to drive their boats right up to this dock and lunch here," said Colin.

"Dressed like that?" I said. He and Ruth exchanged a glance.

"I live near the beach. We have the tourists who pop into the restaurants dressed as-is. But not in church. It seems disrespectful to come to church dressed like you're going to a clambake." I remembered young girls dressed exactly like this hostess—a sea of long, bare legs milling outside in the lobby of his church. "How do you handle that?"

"We can't clean them up first, make them look like us, and then lead them to the Lord. If we do that, we negate the entire grace message. Jesus showed the seeking heart love and acceptance and then told them to go and sin no more. We have to trust God to complete his work inside of them. That is why we have small group studies, to help them on their journey."

"March, here's your menu," said Ruth. "Share an appetizer with me. The potato skins are especially good."

Colin had been especially chummy with the young hostess, probably one of those methods to establish a relationship with her. I tried to imagine Phyllis Murray's reaction if I led Miss Tanned Stomach up our church aisle. "Let's get the potato skins, Ruth. What else is good?" I said.

She recommended several choices.

"Ruth, you order for me, please. I'd like to show March the dock," said Colin.

Ruth quelled the children's protests and their tinny pleas to accompany their father.

Colin walked toward the exit to the dock as though he knew I would follow.

"I guess order for me too, then," I said.

Colin waited against a rail atop a sort of bridge that led out to where the boat owners tied up their crafts. A school of two-foot-long carp, speckled orange and brown, shimmied beneath the dock to the other side where children tossed fish pellets into the water. The fish competed aggressively with the Canada geese that floated on the warm lake water. Colin dropped twenty-five cents into a coin-operated fish food dispenser and funneled the pellets into my hands. I managed to draw the attention of an otherwise lethargic catfish.

"I'm sorry we had to leave your church social so abruptly. You all had worked so hard to lay out such a nice meal for us." Colin took a few pellets out of my hand and dropped them onto the surface of the water.

"No, please. You had more important matters to attend to."

"Jonathan Henshaw helped me start this church. If the Lord had not sent him along, I might have given up at the starting gate."

That would be a rare sight, I thought.

"Eva and I tried to start Church on the Lake in a motel meeting room. Our first four weeks, not a soul showed up. Finally, Jonathan and his wife just walked in one day. He encouraged me and prayed for me continuously. He found us a better location. Just when we would be down to our last penny, he would throw another check in the offering plate and it would be just enough to pay the expenses. He and Martha were older than us. I know they had to grow accustomed to our young ways, but they helped us build the mature core we needed."

"Early on, my dad and mother experienced the same struggles. I suppose that's one of the zillions of things you and Dad have in common. I sometimes wonder if the folks who wander in and out of churches every Sunday ever stop to think that their privileges were paid by another's sacrifice?"

"Willingly paid. I spoke with your father this morning. Sounds like he's having a relaxing morning with Mason. And Hercules. Charlotte speaks of your dog as though he were human."

"Did he mention anything else?"

"Your father? He asked about you. I had to tell him I left you to eat alone. I'm sorry about the no-show last night. It was nice of you to offer dinner out. It would have been nice for a change."

I dropped the remaining pellets into the lake water. They separated and floated away, uneaten.

Charlotte wandered up to the door of the patio to watch us converse. She pressed her most delicate hand against the screen of the patio as though it would give her a better view of us.

I waved at her. "You have such a way with your children. Between you and Ruth, it's as though their mother's death has left no ill effect."

"Children tend to minimize grief. Then one day, when they are older, say in their teens, something small, like an aroma of perfume or a face that reminds them of their lost family member, will surface. They experience a delayed grief. But I've found Charlotte several times out in Eva's rose garden collecting fallen rose petals and grieving over her mother."

"And what about you?" I remembered the soft curve of his posture bent over a kneeling bench.

"You, of all people, must know," he said.

"I have a troubled sort of grief."

"There is another kind?"

"Joe's death was questionable."

"I guess your father has spared me such things."

"Joe's family helped him obtain his law degree, kept him in law school. I never fully understood all of his struggles until later. He started drinking. And confessing when he drank."

His interest in what I had to say softened his eyes. "You don't believe the accident story, then?"

"Honestly, I never know what I believe. Only what I want to believe for Mason's sake."

"Mason needs a positive image of his father worse than he needs the truth, then?"

I was not sure how he had backed me into this time of confession. I kept my answers short. "It's second best when I don't know the truth."

"Joe's family believes it was an accident, I guess."

I nodded. The carp appeared out of nowhere and sucked my fish pellets into their mouths like scaly vacuums skimming along the pollen-coated surface.

"Ruth is under the impression that you came here for a purpose other than a food critic's assignment."

I kept watching the carp, weighing whether or not to continue. "It wasn't an excuse, if that's what you mean. I take freelance assignments from time to time from Brady Gallagher. He's the travel editor for the *Charlotte Observer*. When I attended the University of North Carolina at Chapel Hill, he and I worked together on the campus paper. We've stayed in touch over the years. He's a good friend. We've seen one another through bad marriages." I had never said "bad marriages" aloud until now. Not in reference to my own, at any rate. This man was better than my father at digging all the rocks out of my ledges.

Colin humanely allowed the comment to pass.

The sun warmed the tops of my forearms and I felt them reddening although they appeared white as porcelain in the incandescent sunlight.

"You were here strictly here on business then. I do like that about you. You tend to business without getting so sidetracked." His whole face brightened, like he had found something about me he really liked.

I knew that Ruth must have had her fair share of corralling four children alone inside a restaurant, but his words calmed me and left me wanting to hear him speak again.

"You have to leave today, Ruth said."

"Dad needs me." I sounded like a recording I had played so many times, the tape frayed.

Colin never blurted out anything, but formed every word deliberately. "You aren't upset that I didn't accept your church's pastorate? I suppose I know the answer to that question. Strike that comment altogether."

"I'm sorry you didn't accept it. I believed it was my fault that you turned them down. But now I can see why you would never leave Church on the Lake. You belong to these people. Candle Cove Presbyterian was lucky to have someone of your caliber come and speak, let alone consider us as your future church. We are small-minded people, Colin, and I don't mean that to sound so critical. If it is, then I criticize myself with the rest of them. You are vision-minded. When you started Church on the Lake, you started with nothing. But you built the church with this vision of yours in mind. Your people grew with that vision. Just look at us, so ingrained in the past that any hint of change seems like a sacrilege. We sing from books that look like Bibles. So to remove them to free up minds for worship is like removing a sacred emblem of the past."

"I can make a recommendation. A man I've met on several occasions. Solid and likable. Someone a little less turbulent than me."

"You aren't turbulent. Inventive and turbulent are two different things entirely."

"He's a little older than me. Seminary trained and hymnal ingrained."

I dusted the fish-food particles from my palms.

"We better get back to Ruth and the kids," he said.

Now all four Arnett-shaped faces peered from the screened-in patio.

"You're certain you didn't want to speak to me about something? Eva used to tell me all the time I plowed ahead like a steamroller. I hope I come across as agreeable. That is my intent."

We exchanged smiles.

I felt more relaxed. "More than you know, Colin." I refused to expose my own steamroller nature a second time.

"Thanks for calling me Colin."

Colin delivered the children back home, certain that Rachel and Luke needed an afternoon nap. Ruth waited while I changed into traveling clothes inside the church's ladies room. She hugged me in typical Ruth fashion.

That is when I saw the diary tucked beneath a peanut bag on the front passenger seat. I retrieved it and handed it to her. "I almost forgot, Ruth. Colin left this in the cottage."

"He's torn up the house looking for it. He'll be happy to see it. I'll have to resist the temptation not to peek. Diaries are such a lure, aren't they?"

My smile felt wooden, but it was the best I could do. "Thank you for a wonderful lunch, Ruth. Maybe we can get together again sometime."

"I would not be surprised. Better run."

My telephone rang. Brady called to see how the meal at LaVecchia's turned out.

"A pleasing presentation with a surprise hint of cinnamon in the salmon coating."

"Not the food. Did you wrangle the minister? You know, did you have your way with him?"

"Brady, it wasn't like that at all. Colin Arnett is not about to leave a church he's sweated into being. My father had a brief mental lapse and that is all this crazy scheme amounted to. Colin Arnett is not going to leave here and move to Candle Cove."

"You didn't ask him. I can tell."

"I'm not going to ask him. He lives here in happiness with the ghost of his wife literally entombed in the wallpaper and landscaping."

"That troubles you more than anything, I'll bet."

Did it? "What if it does?"

"After all this time, March is smitten."

"Not smitten at all, Brady. Don't jump to conclusions. I'm tired. Don't make me say something I don't mean. I have this long drive ahead of me."

"Come stay at my place. You could get some shuteye and drive home early in the morning. In my guest room, of course. Everything above board, I promise."

"I'm ready for the solitude, if you catch my drift. I crave aloneness, Brady. Maybe that's why I'm a writer. I want an early start, before dark."

"It's almost three. Did you know that church has been over for hours in most places? Doesn't seem like an early start was in the plan." He was still implying things not because he believed them but possibly because he might have the slightest hint of hope that I would deny them altogether.

"I joined the Arnetts for lunch."

"This Colin Arnett, he invited you to lunch?"

"Only in a manner of speaking. Through his sister, Ruth, really."

"Something's in the air, March. I think you should have given this Arnett fellow more encouragement. Another invitation, perhaps, to visit your little church again."

"It's between him and my father. I have to get out of all of this church business. It's not my problem anymore. How I get myself all caught up in Dad's affairs, I'll never know."

"It's the Norville way."

"Have I ever said that?"

"You be safe."

"Thanks for the work, Brady."

He hung up.

The security guard circled the church parking lot in a squad car and watched me for a moment. Figuring I posed no immediate threat, I suppose, he disappeared to the other side of the church parking lot. Except for a few teacher-training classes and a gathering of youths, the church would remain quiet. Colin had never initiated the traditional evening service, another reason he would not fit into my father's provincial oxfords at Candle Cove Presbyterian.

A group of teenagers squealed past, scraped the curb with their tires, and then parked at a slant in a parking place. A youth leader dressed in shorts stepped out from the building and waved them all inside. One of them carried a pouch of drumsticks. They whooped and followed him into the building and disappeared. The lights illuminated the windows one at a time all along their path.

I sank into the quiet leather of the Mustang and turned on a classical station. Some disc jockey played Beethoven softly, a quiet prayer between artist and maker.

Road trips offer the best time to pray. God listened to me complain quietly. He is always good at listening, even when I am not exactly where he wants me. But when you don't know exactly where you are supposed to be, the difficulty is offering him a silent elongated moment to fill you in on the details. His plans are never what you expect.

Eleven

I CANNOT EXPLAIN WHY THE NORVILLE HOUSE, A bungalow that roared with femininity, potted geraniums and impatiens, a place that existed for a lover of both Maker and his earth, now embodied only half its soul. It is as though a house knows and understands loss and mourns it with a cavernous ache. The front porch had grayed a lamentable shade of pewter and anticipated never again the pad of Julia Norville's canvas-topped soles upon its weathered boards at the evening hour. She never believed in ghosts, so it took an act of my will to imagine her final momentary garden vigil before nightfall, the manner in which she surveyed her fulsome, triangle-shaped acre with a gardener's approval. I counted three cars, one parked along the curbless road my mother once complained lacked definition, and the other two parked side by side along the curving driveway that disappeared behind the bungalow.

I left all of my things in the Mustang except a crinkled brown paper bag, a bakery bag I hefted beneath one arm. Before the drive home, I'd run in at a grocery store bakery at the Cornelius end of Lake Norman and purchased a half-dozen French pastries.

A mahogany cane occupied the end table in the corner of Dad's living room, a reminder of the surgery and the new, solemn change upon his life. The doctor had borrowed veins from Dad's leg for the bypass, and the incisions left Dad hobbling around, unbearably sore, and unable to drive for three weeks. I heard the quiet intercourse between Dad and Mason in the small downstairs room, the old guest room into which Dinah and I had moved Dad's things before I left.

"Anyone home?" I yelled. "I'm back with the goods."

"Mom!" Mason hopped out into the living room missing a shoe. He wore a faded yellow shirt, no socks, and a Tar Heels cap turned backwards on his head.

Gloria slid out behind Mason holding a comb. "I found this under the bed." She held a thermometer in her other hand between her fingers like an orchestra baton.

"Dinah must have called," I said to Gloria. "I've never known you to play nursemaid."

"Her girls are at their dad's and she had to pick them up tonight. She slept over last night, though. I think Pastor Norville believes no one can take care of him except his darling daughter. Bandage check is done, and your father is so cranky about his chest dressing. Doesn't want me to touch anything, so I'll leave all that to Miss Ellie. I cleaned out the bathroom sink and the john, needless to say, in spite of his complaining."

Mason used his arms to lift himself up utilizing Mother's kitchen tabletop. "We haven't even combed our hair, and we've watched at least six videos and two old movies on TV—they stunk, but the videos were good. Grandpa and I have so much food in the refrigerator, you won't believe." Mason sidled up next to me to whisper, "I found out I hate John Wayne."

Phyllis Murray stirred a pot of missionary stew. "The meal's all done. Nothing too spicy, but everything more than filling."

"That nurse you got for Grandpa makes him take his pills," said Mason.

"Ellie." I set a few extra plates around the kitchen table.

"That's her. She's got bad breath and one gray tooth."

Dad called out. He sounded relieved to hear my voice.

"Don't set a place for me," Gloria whispered. "Phil made a pasta dinner for us tonight and besides, I think your father's had enough company for the day. The good reverend is a little on the cranky end of the continuum." She held open the creaky front door and allowed Phyllis to hurry past.

"If you've never tried them, I brought home six of those tube-looking pastries filled with cream—I forgot what they're called—you have to try at least one."

"Don't even let me see one." Gloria held the bag to her nose. "Too divine. Better hide them from your dad, or did you forget about his appetite for breaking the dietary rules? Nurse Ellie left a list of your dad's marching orders, when the next pill is due, and all of that. She told him he could have angel food cake when he badgered her about his sweets list. Does that sound right? Oh, and your pastor friend, Arnett, left a message on the answering machine."

"A message for me?"

"No, for your father." Gloria poised her face as she often did when she treaded softly—her skin erased of lines and her eyelids half-closed. "If you have anything to tell me about, you know, the Arnett guy coming to take your dad's place, well, it can wait if you're too tired. Or maybe it's too sensitive to discuss right at this moment. If so, I understand completely."

"No news. The trip was a water haul." The fact that Colin called surprised me.

"Guess I'll go. See you later. Mason, be sure you put to use that comb I found."

Out in the street, Phyllis beeped delicately on her horn and pulled away.

"See you in the morning, unless you need to stay home with your dad," said Gloria through a crack in the door. The neighbor's outside light came on.

"I'll be in. Be certain Avery knows he has doughnut duty in the morning."

Dad yelled out again.

"See you at seven-thirty, then." Gloria lit down the front-porch steps. Her heels never touched the concrete.

The flour canister, devoid of flour for six months, made the best stash for the cream horns or whatever they were that I should have known better than to buy. The entire kitchen smelled of cream cheese and powdered sugar. I fanned the oven door to hide the smell of pastry with the aroma of warmed pita bread.

Dad sat next to the bed in the wingback chair, the one reupholstered by my mother in a feminine featherstitched texture of royal blue and violet. My mother once nurtured a fondness for this room, the first always to point out the flush of early day and hue of warmth upon the sill. Dad sat trapped in the late afternoon shadows of my mother's morning room, a purple afghan over his knees. Several books lay perched on top of the guest bed's blue coverlet, books by Richard Foster, C. S. Lewis, and Dostoyevsky. Three different times he had started reading *The Brothers Karamazov* in the last six years. The book lay closed but with the bookmark moved halfway through the thick mass of pages.

"March, you're home. That nurse is annoying. I'd rather you do the bandages. And let's do keep Gloria at the newspaper office. She's happier in her own surroundings."

Hercules crept from the blue dusk of the darkest side of the room, a whisper of sentry in his gaze. He lowered his head and widened his cola-painted eyes until I could see the red rims, a sorrowful question in his face that asked if I could possibly assume his nervous post. Arnie lifted his prickly chin although he kept his back in the curved shape of Hercules' torso, as though the Golden still lay curled around him, protective and warming his cold Doxie bones.

"Gloria never does this. You're a privileged man."

"She doesn't do it because she's better off with those coffeepot projects. If I had a broken coffeepot, that's when I'd call Gloria."

"Colin Arnett's church is sizable."

Dad pressed his chest pillow against the stitches. "I don't feel human. God, help me to feel human again."

"I couldn't ask him, Dad. You were right. It was a useless trip."

His needle-bruised hand caressed Hercules's crown. "The Arnetts are good people. Can't say I've met a nicer family. So I had a stupid pipe dream. It didn't work and I can move on. I don't always know the ways of the Lord." The next part he said with no degree of delicacy, as though he said it just for me. "Letting go of what I don't know is the hardest part."

"It bothers me that Colin suspected I was there with an ulterior motive."

"I can't imagine him saying that. He would have been right, of course, but he'd never say it."

After playing Colin's words through my mind again, I could not say for certain that he had even implied such a thing.

"I heard Gloria say that he called," said Dad.

"First, then, we'll have a listen to what Pastor Arnett has to say. Phyllis made missionary stew. I'll fix us each a bowl and we can all eat on trays in here together. Mason, you take Hercules and Arnie for their walk and we'll eat right afterward."

Hercules slid around me to beat Mason to the door. Mason appeared small in the wide cavity of the bungalow's entry; boy-denim blue, yellow torn shirt, and hair-thin minutes having ticked by this weekend that ripened him in my absence. He rounded his shoulders before he set off at a dead run, rounded his knobby arm sockets as Joe used to do and, in an instant, filled the doorway with the tactile likeness of his father.

"Missionary stew. Haven't had a good bowl of that since Julia and I stopped at that little place on Ocracoke Island. Missionary stew and Ocracoke fig cake. Can you cook fig cake, March?"

"No fig cake, no missionary stew. I'll be right back, Dad." I left the door open so he could hear Colin's message. Hercules and Mason thundered out onto the grinning porch followed closely by Arnie the yapper. I always called it a grinning porch as a child—the smiling upper landing, the porch-step lower jaw, and the window eyes.

"We should go over your homework," I told him, but Mason would have to hear it later. He was leaping off the porch, followed by Hercules, while Arnie minced down the steps to dodder off behind them.

Colin said so little in his message that I found I listened and heard nothing at all. I replayed it. *"James, Colin, you old dog, you need a rest. I'll call you later about it."*

Dad coughed and then let out a tenuous moan.

"Coming with that missionary stew and angel food cake," I said.

"Angel food cake is for wimps."

"That's what we are, Dad. Wimps." I set his food on a TV tray next to his chair.

The sky darkened. A few stars appeared, the first of the evening's orchestral players to warm up the night sky with the cosmic purple of twilight. Mason returned with the dogs and the faint light of perspiration on his upper lip. He pulled his school satchel from behind the door and ran with it upstairs only to emerge with his face washed of most all of the dirt except the ring around his jaw that made him look like the man in the moon.

We ate the stew and the pita and even the creamy pastries that I never should have bought. After I helped Dad back into the guest bed, I closed his door. Mason headed upstairs with his torn shirt, happy to sleep with me one night in Grandpa's room.

I insisted he shower.

I tapped the small knob of the answering machine to lower the volume. Once more, I listened to Colin's message. He had a pleasing voice that raised no red flags, no dangerous levels of tide that could draw me under except for one small, battered flag that insisted that I had grown happy alone. It waved raggedly above the shipwreck of my heart as I worked maddeningly to keep my life nailed together. March, the happy wreck. My finger hovered above the erase button for a moment. I left the message on my father's recording after a deliberate inspection of my ability to let go. James Norville, a grown man, could decide on his own what to do with the man.

Ellie showed up at six the next morning, just as I pushed Arnie and Hercules through the doorway and out onto the lawn to do their business. She set to work on Dad, first making him stand and then coercing him into taking the first minute steps of the day. I turned my face so that he would not see my lips stretched down the corners of my jaw. The drill sergeant tactics pained him as they pained me.

"Feels like fire shooting from my thigh down to my ankle. This isn't necessary," he said.

Many patients loaned veins from both legs, the doctor had told him, and did he realize his fortunate situation of rehabilitating just the one leg? Reverend James Norville held to the bedpost, his forehead pressed against the womanly shape of the wood, and asked Ellie if they could wait a few days. When she made him take another slow step, I turned away.

Then it hit me—a strategy. I needed to use the same tactics to pull the paper out of the nonprofit bog. I wrote down a note or two between flipping flapjacks and pouring juice. I rarely had epiphanies. I brainstormed some more.

"Mason, you'll never believe this! I made pancakes." I yelled twice up the staircase until I heard the thud of sneakers on carpet. He started down the steps, ran back for his satchel and the lunchbox in desperate need of fumigation, and ran up to me with a red folder full of school work. "Monday folder. Sign please."

I pulled out the "keeper" side first. "Spelling is all right. Mason, you can spell anything; how could you miss 'abbreviate' and then get 'raucous' right?"

"Assessment tests start today. I need a good breakfast and two number two pencils. Sharpened," he said.

"I'll sharpen your pencils if you'll go back and clean that patch behind your ear. You could grow corn." I pulled out two pencils from the satchel and took them out into the garage where Dad had bolted a hand-cranked pencil sharpener to a workbench.

By the time Ellie got Dad to the breakfast table, it was time for Mason and me to leave. Ellie read my face. "Don't you worry about your father, March. Every day he'll get better and better. It takes time, and sometimes it comes by the inches."

Dad massaged the lines in his forehead. "Pick me up some of that good orange juice, will you, March? Gloria bought that pulp-free kind. It tastes like kerosene."

"Ellie, you have plenty of food. Just warm it and he'll eat it." I let Hercules and Arnie back inside. Hercules balanced a ham bone in his mouth, one he must have nursed all weekend; nothing remained of it except the shape of a Stone Age cylinder.

"Bring me a pad and pen, Ellie. I need to make my calls," said Dad. I heard the nurse sigh.

Mornings were warmer now. Mason leaped from the car before I could pull him up to the dead center of the car line where the mother Nazi insisted we stop each morning. He did not kiss me and had not kissed me in the car line since the second week of school. With his back to me, he yelled "good-bye" and ran to catch up with a young boy I only knew as Tony.

Six cars filled the gravel lot in front of the *Sentinel.* Gloria paced back and forth in front of the door and passed out her signature collated-and-stapled notes to everyone. She waved through the window glass at me and then stepped away to let Lindle open the door for me.

"Here's the lady of leisure back from the big city," said Lindle. He scratched deep inside his ear with his right pinky finger and then vibrated it, as though he tried to soothe one of those exasperating allergy itches.

"I hope you don't mind working late, Lindle. We need every person on deck if we're going to try and outdo the Raleigh *Thrifty Nickel.* They're pitching a big gardening issue to all the retailers." I walked past Lindle and into the middle of Gloria's womb-shaped circle of employees. "Hardware stores, gardening centers, nurseries, even grocery stores are being hit up by that *Thrifty Nickel* sales guy." I snapped my fingers at Lindle. "What's his name?"

"Garth Allen. But I think it's a pseudonym to gain customers," answered Lindle.

"If we're going to match the competition, we have to stay a jump ahead with new ideas." I pulled out my notes and flicked away a dried glob of pancake batter.

All of them stared at me as though I had walked through the door with smallpox.

"Anybody got any new ideas?" Gloria whimpered.

"I'm tired just thinking about it." Shaunda yawned.

I picked up an agenda and started redlining the points Gloria had made that needed a finer edge and then crossed out the discussions that took away from productivity. My mind ticked like a racing stopwatch.

"What are you doing, March?" Gloria whispered.

"Frankly, I don't see the need for discussing why we need a better system for collecting dimes for every cup of coffee. To me, it's like discussing whether or not we need more sugar on the powdered doughnuts." I paid her the respect of whispering it back, although it seemed everyone was privy anyway. I seated myself in the only empty chair.

"No need to be snippity," said Gloria. Her Latino accent took over whenever she was perturbed, making her consonants spit.

"I think a dime a cup is more than reasonable, March," said Lindle.

Everyone agreed except Shaunda who kept checking inside her purse for gum.

"Visibility is everything, people. If we're going to sell more papers, we have to think like the big guys. Expand our market."

Gloria sighed.

Lindle scribbled some notes onto a spiral pad.

"So does this mean we have to pay for the coffee in the old coffee can or do we pay Gloria directly?" Shaunda asked.

"I think the system is fine just the way it is," said Brendan.

"You would," said Wylie. He flicked his brother in the back of the head with a finger-and-thumb maneuver.

Brendan took off his baseball cap and flogged Wylie's thin, anemic-looking arm.

"Guys, can we get serious?" I wanted to flog them myself.

Gloria spoke. "Come on, everybody. March is trying to rally us. Get us pumped up. You know, this reminds me of a movie. There were all these little paperboys trying to make a living, but the big newspaper guys wanted them to work harder, to squeeze more out of their pitiful, starved lives. It's like that. March is trying to stretch us." Gloria ended her speech with a flourish of her hand and gave the floor back to me.

"Thanks, Gloria," I said, miserable.

"Are we going to be big, like a real paper, because if we are, I'm in!" Shaunda radiated ambition.

I recollected less significant Monday meetings. We accomplished more the Monday before Christmas than we did on this day. "Coffee break, everyone."

Brendan and Wylie beat the women to the coffeepot while Shaunda kept saying, "I'm just so confused."

Gloria watched me slink over to my desk chair. "I'll get your coffee. Cardboard on the top just like you like it."

"Wait, don't get me anything, Gloria." I patted the chair next to my desk, the one usually sat in by little old ladies setting up yard-sale ads.

Gloria accommodated me. Her dark brows made crescents above her eyes, as though she could ever hide the concern from her face.

"I'm no good at this, this hard-nosed boss business. The *Sentinel* needs K rations and the lean-mean-fighting-machine bluster and I'm just serving up biscuits and gravy and patting everyone on the head."

"I don't know who told you all that nonsense, but you are good just the way you are. We don't want you to change. What would be the fun of that?" Gloria rested an olive-brown hand on top of mine.

"The bottom line tells me, Gloria. We're not making it. I practically live here and it's not helping. Nothing I do is helping."

Shaunda appeared with a cup of coffee. "This is for you, March. Brendan and Wylie paid for it and said it was their treat." She set the cup in front of me and walked away.

"It takes five years for a new business to see a profit. You told me that once. Why you would start being so hard on yourself now is beyond me," said Gloria.

"Starting over isn't easy, is it?"

"My grandfather, he came to this country and had to start over. He was thirty-five, not much younger than you."

"I've never told you my age."

"Now he owns three restaurants and a dry-cleaning business."

"I know this speech. You got this off of a movie, didn't you?" I stirred a packet of sweetener into my coffee.

"March, you are doing all the right things. Look at all of these people."

I did as she said and stared while the girls pushed the Poe brothers away from the coffee machine.

"You got this many people on payroll, and none of us have missed a paycheck."

Except me, I thought. "I need to apologize to everyone before they quit."

"No one is going to quit. We all love our jobs. We sort of like you. On most days." Gloria kissed me on the right side of my face.

Brendan tried to kiss Wylie, to mimic us, but got slapped.

I thanked Gloria and disappeared into the bathroom. I had to freshen up, put on my better countenance, as my mother once told me, so that I wouldn't look so much the wreck that I really was.

Twelve

DAD AND COLIN CHATTED AT LEAST ONCE A WEEK until Dad had wrangled a commitment from him to come and visit. Dad called to tell me I'd better make the cottage ready for company again. The anticipation in his voice even made me excited.

On the way to school, Mason made me swear that I would pick him up at the first bell. He never said that he wanted to see Charlotte, which would be like saying he wanted to play with a girl. But he made it clear he wanted to be at the cottage as soon as the Arnetts arrived.

Gloria took over the proofreading while I ran to check on Dad. Dad watched old Andy Griffith episodes and held his chest with a pillow when he laughed. Ellie tried to coax him up from the bed to take his walk but he groaned until I could not stand it anymore. She asked me if I wanted to help. As each day passed, the killer instinct inside of me receded exponentially. I could never be a physical therapist, no more than I could make the Poes act their age. I left Ellie to fend for herself.

I listened to the radio as I drove to the cottage. Dinah's daily show was on. She'd invited the high-school home-economics teacher as a visitor. They discussed flan and other things I happened to know that Dinah never cooked. I flipped to a Top 40s station and listened to a male voice crooning about something up on the roof. *Is that Neil Diamond?* I thought. I could not remember, and it annoyed me to no end.

I opened all of the cottage windows to allow in a salt breeze. The aroma of an impending summer filled the musty cottage with fresh airy breezes. Overhead the skies floated lazily like lace doilies on a table of blue. I inspected the tabletops for dust and then bounded upstairs to change out all of the linens. In one corner I saw what looked to be a doll so I scooped it up. She had tiny wings on the back; Charlotte's angel made by her own hands with twine and cardboard. The angel was left against the wall as though in the midst of a teddy-bear tea party. Turning it over, I thought about Charlotte's fascination with angels and realized that she must have deliberated often about heaven when her mind wandered to thoughts of her mother.

Suddenly the cottage looked aged. I must have freeze-framed it some time ago to make it always look as new and fresh as when Mother potted geraniums in all of the window boxes and watered the nodding caladiums along the walk. But walking into the cottage now had the same effect as if I had pulled an old postcard from an attic trunk. The Julia–Norville green had taken on a faded hue. Her pronounce-ments—in her genteel estimation, therapeutic—were forever embed-ded in my thoughts, but fading too. I recalled how she once boasted to another mother about the easy A's I made in all of my English courses. She had an approving smile at that moment. I'd frozen it in place.

The phone rang. "Hello, Gloria."

"You remember, I gather, that Tuesdays are all-nighters at the *Sentinel*," she said. I could almost see the dimple of sarcasm.

"I'm almost finished here." The name came to me. "James Taylor." I blurted it out and was met with a wrinkle of silence.

"Who?" she finally responded.

"The guy who sang 'Up on the Roof.' It was James Taylor, wasn't it?"

"That's old stuff. I get all them old guys mixed up. Does this have anything to do with Tuesday nights?"

"Or was it Cat Stevens? No, I'm right. It's James Taylor."

"Is this some sort of new therapy, or have I called the wrong number?"

"A flight of fancy, that's all. Seventy's throwback nostalgia silliness." I ended the conversation in a delicate manner wondering why the gentle music of the past was surfacing along with happier memories. It was like the good stuff popping above the surface after a shipwreck, large barrels filled with expensive commodities and free for the taking. I gathered up the guest linens before I closed up all the cottage windows again, just as the sun moved once more to turn the sky the color of the cottage walls.

Sea gulls squawked at me on the deck as I intruded on their day.

A couple walked along the shoreline while a Labrador retriever, brindled and aging, ran ahead of them. This couple had walked the beach most days since before I sharpened number-two pencils for my father on Sunday morning to leave in the pencil slots in the pews. Two matching candlesticks, they were, two faces glowing from the shoreline in infinite splendor. The sun upon their backs caused their images to shimmer. They appeared to dance in the froth and looked like James and Julia Norville. Although dancing had never been a part of their courtship, it offered a lively image.

I thought about Joe's death, leaned against the deck and tried to remember him as I remembered us on the good days. I drew a frame around us, without the negatives or the reproving way I judged him as I had been taught to disapprove of irresponsible behavior. It was how we Norvilles elicited a positive outcome. It is a strange thing to dialogue with a ghost. But if I say things to Joe in private that I never said in life, I find a grain of completion. I longed for a fine finishing point to us, one not thrust upon me by a man who picked a poor choice of days to sail out on a stormy ocean. I wanted to know, "Joe, why did you go away so quickly and leave me to breathe without you, to be both mother and dad to our boy when you know I am a wreck? You saw me at those club tennis matches pretending to be a woman on top, while earlier I sat out in the parking lot wondering how I fit into the elite mix of the life you wanted for us." I cried my private tears, ones I do not share, even with Mason. Not even with my father. It is a different flavor of pain even compared to my mother's passing. It is a bond of the gold band, the bond of vows.

The couple disappeared behind the curve of shoreline that dissolves into ocean. The shoreline that is ours became nothing but the pulse of the tide, the whisper of laughter from the past. The warm breeze that had filled our sound with a comfortable kiss upon our skin called like a siren, making me long for endless stretches of summer. But with each passing year I had become less and less of who I once was, as though parts of me were carried away by the tide. Earthly summers were never meant to linger eternal any more than the same exact sand pebbles were meant to linger on the shore.

At once, something hard and ancient knocked against my soul a deep, creaking thump against my heart. I looked beyond the deck to where my father once kept the old Ford, the doors locked fast with a rusted padlock, the lock that banged in the wind. The lock that forever entombed my pain. It came to me then. I had kept things locked up for too long.

Gloria, Shaunda, Lindle, the Poes and I had one of those eat-in choke-it-down box lunches from Ruby's. Lindle finalized all the ads while Shaunda polished up her stories. Gloria had all the proofreading completed by two o'clock, which gave me the time to help Lindle position the ads. Half an hour later Gloria shuffled me out the door to pick up Mason from school. Something in Gloria's gaze indicated a deeper motive although I could not always read her as well as she read me.

Mason waited by the curb, his mouth turned up at both corners as distinct as a slice of melon rind. He jumped into the car, his breath seemingly stolen. "I made an A!" He waved a spelling quiz under my nose.

We cheered.

"We're headed for the cottage, right?" he said.

"Nope. Tuesday crunch day."

"Could you drop me by? Are they here?'

"I don't know. No time to see, either. I'll bet your teacher is happy about your spelling grade."

"I'm happy, you're happy. Who cares about her? I want to see the Arnetts."

"Mason, let's go this weekend to Neuse River Days. You know how everyone in New Bern builds those crazy rafts and races them. So funny when one of them falls apart right in the middle of the race. We could go Friday right after I pick you up from school."

"And take the Arnetts?"

I turned on the left signal and headed toward the office.

He constructed a perfectly aimed sentence. "Does that mean we'll be eating at the office again tonight? You know those people who work for you are completely bonkers."

"I can drop you by Grandpa's."

"Or drop me by the cottage. I can fix it up and get it ready for company."

"Done already."

"You don't like him. I can always tell when you don't like some-one. It's kind of obvious."

"I don't like who?"

"Pastor Arnett." Mason was digging.

"Must be a problem. Gloria's standing at the door waiting for me."

"Ruth Arnett likes you. She says it all the time, but not in just what she says. I can just tell."

One of us sighed. Or maybe both of us.

"I like her, too. I like Pastor Arnett. I like all of them, but I have a job, Mason. Lindle's getting takeout from Dooley's. Do you want to eat with us or with Grandpa?"

He did not answer.

Right as we walked in, we heard a sort of shrill yelp, like a piglet caught in the gate.

"What's wrong, Shaunda?" I asked.

"It's the waxer. It bit it again!" She spoke of the temperamental machine the galleys of copy are rolled through before they're placed on the layout page. When the gizmo does happen to work, it applies a thin layer of wax that adheres to the layout pages. But when it doesn't—which is most of the time—it globs a thick coat of wax on the entire sheet of copy. "It's ruined!" she exclaimed.

"Did you use the foot pedal?" Lindle asked.

"Of course!" She shrieked again.

Mason settled his book satchel and homework against a desk. I joined Shaunda in the back.

We both stared at the waxy hunk of paper as though we expected it to somehow draw breath and repair itself.

"It would have been ruined anyway," I said.

"I waxed it on the wrong side. Now I have to do it all over again. I hate this job! I hate it!" said Shaunda.

"Shaunda, you say that every Tuesday."

"I do hate it!"

"Has anyone seen my Exacto knife?" Gloria, who never lost a thing, was perpetually territorial about her desk and her tools: her Exacto knife, her rollers, her pica ruler. None of those things could be touched without threat of penalty. Gloria had marked them all with her name. Yet every Tuesday one piece disappeared, then just as mysteriously reappeared the next day.

"Real journalists don't have to do their own layout or fight with a waxer," muttered Shaunda.

"When you are, as you say, a "real journalist," Shaunda, you can hire someone else to do your layout. But for now, just redo the ad, please." I coaxed her back to the computer.

"March, did you return Jerry Brevity's call yesterday?" asked Gloria.

"I did not. Why do you ask?"

"He called again this morning." She said it flatly, as though she brushed crumbs from her fingertips.

"Tell him anything, that it's Tuesday. Say 'crunch day.' That's a power phrase, isn't it?"

"He wants to bring by dinner for everyone." Gloria helped Shaunda guide her story into position.

"If he's paying, I'll have a steak," said Lindle.

"I didn't know what to tell him," said Gloria.

"He's coming, then," I said.

Gloria's brows came together to answer for her in a wordless way while she stared at Shaunda's page.

Mason slapped his forehead.

The phone rang in a sequence of calls. Gloria placed three callers on hold. "Line two's for you. I'll get the others."

I mouthed "Jerry Brevity" to her in the form of a question.

"It's your dad."

The Poes made a chortling noise from the print shop like cowboys too long away from women.

"What's up?" I could hear Dad's breathing on the line.

"March, I'm not sure what I've just done. You know I'm muddled up with all of these pharmaceuticals and it's just got me all in a twinge. Colin Arnett just called and we, or at least, he discussed the *Sparticus* with me."

"Joe's boat? I don't get it."

"I thought he had already discussed the matter with you and it got all tipped over in my mind until I got off the phone. That is, I think I gave him permission to take her out of the garage. The more I think of it, the more I think I really did just that."

"Dad, no one's taken the *Sparticus* out since the accident."

"I thought he was asking to take you out in it, you know, as though he were running it by me."

"Not take her out *and* put her in the water. We don't even know if she's seaworthy."

"You've not heard a word from Colin Arnett about the *Sparticus*, then, I gather?"

"None whatsoever."

He was silent.

"Is he at the cottage now?" It irked me to no measure that Colin would ask Dad about the boat and not me.

"You know he's a good seaman himself. He wouldn't take her out if she weren't good for the trip."

"I'm going there right now."

"You'll be miffed at me, then."

"We'll discuss it later. Let's blame it on your medication for now." I hung up.

Gloria and Shaunda stared up at me.

"So I guess you'll be leaving," said Gloria.

"Can you finish up without me?"

"Problems back at the ranch?" Gloria's smile did not match her glazed-over look.

"Someone's trying to take the *Sparticus* out for a ride."

"Let's call the cops, Mom! Harold and Bobby will cuff them just like they did Yolanda's crooks." Mason looked as though he shifted back and forth waiting to get into the little boy's room.

"Woe to that poor slob," said Shaunda.

"He's not a crook. He's a friend of Dad's. Can you handle the waxer, Shaunda?" I asked.

"I know what I'm doing, I've started all over. It's the pedal that gets stuck. I have the hang of things," said Shaunda.

"And what do we tell Jerry Brevity?" asked Gloria.

"Enjoy dinner," I said.

"I'll set out the china," said Gloria.

Mason leaped out of the car when we arrived at the cottage and beat a path down to the garage.

We found the garage door standing open. Inside, we saw the sandaled intruder who sashayed into my past without so much as a blink or Mother-may-I. He inspected the sail cloth.

"What are you doing? Or should I say, welcome back, and then what are you doing?" I stayed in the doorway until our eyes met.

"March, you're here. I tried to call you at your place, but no answer. Your father gave us the thumbs-up, though. I found your family's boat. Nice vessel. Really nice. How long has your father had her?"

"I stored the boat here. After Joe's accident. It is my boat, that is, it was Joe's."

We stared for the space of time that lapses between ocean waves.

"March, I apologize. Here I am scrambling all over your sacred ground. Had I any idea, I would have never called in the first place."

"I don't think the *Sparticus* is seaworthy."

"She looks fit," said Colin.

"We could put her in the water. See what happens," said Mason.

I thought that by touching Mason's shoulder he would read my thoughts. Instead he looked at Colin, hopeful.

"We could wet her, but not unless your mother approves, my man."

"Please," said Mason.

"I don't think it's safe," I said.

Colin's girls appeared.

"We changed into our swimsuits, Daddy. Ready for a boat ride," said Charlotte.

If I didn't give in, I'd be a louse in Mason's eyes and the Arnett children's to boot. "I guess it's all right."

The way we had left the vessel lodged between two stacks of tires, Colin had to drag her out with his car hitch at an angle.

Colin stuck his head out the window and watched Mason's gestures. "Turn the wheel right," said Mason.

Colin had to pull up and back several times before hauling her out completely. He jumped out and crawled beneath the trailer to inspect the hull. He rubbed the surface from stern to aft with the wide expanse of his hands as though he rubbed down a wet mare. Along one long side, he examined a bruised-looking scratch. "Here's some damage. But it isn't deep," he said.

"Actually we did that putting her away. The boat went over in a storm. Joe didn't have on a life jacket. It was a weird accident. Joe went over, but the boat survived."

Colin went over the bruised scratch with a chamois. "Not bad at all. But I'll take her out by myself the first time."

"I think I should go with you," said Mason.

Charlotte looked disappointed.

"Maybe later. Mason, I'll come back for you if she behaves herself." Colin ran his fingers across Mason's straight row of bangs.

If Colin agitated him, Mason hid it well.

Colin hitched up the *Sparticus* and drove her out to the boat slip. We watched the vessel plop down into the water and slide into place as though it pleased her to be out of the dungeon. He caught my eyes lingering over the boat as though I willed it to sink.

"This is a bad idea," he said. "Isn't it?"

"You've already wet the hull. Go ahead and take her around the cove. If you sink, we'll call the Coast Guard."

We watched him push away and troll past the buoys. The sail snapped and then furled. Colin looked like cast bronze leaning out from the mast, following the direction of the masthead as it turned with his body.

"My daddy knows what he's doing," said Charlotte.

"We have a boat too," said Troy.

"See, Mom. It's working and not sinking," said Mason.

"I could have done it. I can sail, too," said Troy.

"No, you're not, Troy. You're not big enough," said Charlotte.

Her words stirred a brother's spite and it glowed from the rims of his basil-green eyes.

151

Colin disappeared around the curve of the shore, past the neighbor cottage. The neighbors waved at him from shore. He sailed around the cove and then turned back toward us.

I will always remember the painful "firsts" after Joe's death. The first time I went alone to the Lighthouse Java Mill. The first trip to the mall Christmas shopping without him. With every "first" came a new bath of tears that plunged me back into my cave to hide from everyone I knew and to hide my tears from Mason. To see the *Sparticus* floating again without Joe's guidance sent me teetering.

As the boat lapped toward us, I stood on the dock and from behind me felt Mason's arms go around my waist. I remember when Joe passed from us, Mason could hug me right around my hips. I turned and looked down at him, then bent near him, but not so far this time as in the past. He kissed my face.

"Are you all right?" I asked.

He nodded as though by trying to speak his lower lip might quiver or those strong male feelings he worked so hard to hold inside might tumble out.

"We'll put her up. Maybe this isn't the right time," I said.

"No, I want this, Mom. I want to ride in the *Sparticus* again and feel the wind, like I might feel Dad again."

"You are the wise one. If you want Pastor Arnett to take you out, then I think you should go," I said. I turned away from the lapping ocean.

"Dad taught me to sail. I know how, too," he said it to me but looked at Troy.

Colin returned to the dock and all of the children spilled into the boat. Mason passed out the life jackets and helped the boys strap on the vests.

Colin held out his hand to me.

"Not this time," I said.

Mason looked at Colin and then at me.

"I have to get back to the office. Today's a long day for the *Sentinel*," I said.

"Maybe next time then." Colin gave me a sort of hokey salute. "Mason can stay with us for a bit, I hope?"

"I'll come by for him later." I gave a little tilt of the head at Mason, a signal that said that everything was all right between us.

Joe's boy took charge of the vessel, telling the Arnett brood where to sit and how to act. I realized I had taken too long to bring the *Sparticus* out into the daylight again. But the farther I moved from the date of the accident, the more I wanted to deny time to anything that brought back its memory. Mason pulled out the captain's hat, the one Joe had worn the day we christened the boat. He tipped it back so the bill wouldn't hide his eyes.

"Careful now," I said.

They sailed away. For every wave that lifted them up and then down, the children squealed like baby seals. The sea played gently against the hull and toyed with the vessel like a father bouncing a child on his knee. With every lap of water that kissed the hull, I felt the beat of my own heart. I turned away, not wanting Mason to see my tears. Not because I wanted him to think I was burly, a bastion of motherhood, but because lately we had shared too many tears. When I cried he looked as though he were to blame. I loved him too much to allow my inherited cloak of guilt to fall upon his small boy shoulders. I wanted us to share something else instead. A launching of our hearts, a putting to sea the things of the past.

He waved from the bay until he became a glistening twinkle in a mother's eye.

Thirteen

DINAH IS THE QUEEN OF SPONTANEITY. SHE CALLED with her latest epiphany, a clambake she would host at the cottage on the very evening the *Sparticus* had been planted back in the sea.

"This is rather abrupt," I said.

"You know me."

"So your first location didn't pan out."

"I would have had to get permits, and you know how I despise red tape. At your cottage we have all those cooking pots of your mother's, which is as close to a clambake as Candle Cove gets anyway."

I tried to think like Dinah. "You need a guinea pig. I understand."

"Guests. I just need guests, and you have plenty. I'll bring lanterns, lots of paper lanterns and Frankie Avalon music. If I do this fifties style, then I could really pull in some new listeners. You know how you're always talking about spark and drama. This could send me into syndication. I'll cook clams, lobsters—hot-and-spicy red potatoes and corn cobettes. Lots of French bread."

"Heavenly. I'll bring the watermelon," I said.

"Plus homemade ice cream. I'll add that to the list. The girls can pull the ice cream maker out of the attic."

"You always pull a party out of the hat just when I need it," I said.

"You'll help me hang the lanterns then?"

I could see Gloria's half-guarded stare. "Can't. We're right on top of pub day. But Ruth can help. I'll join you both as soon as I can get away."

Ruth and Dinah spent the rest of the afternoon hanging Dinah's lanterns. Mason and I joined them at the end of the workday. Ruth helped Dinah dig out Mom's old steamer pot. I called Dad and promised to bring him a plate of Dinah's delectables if he promised to behave for Ellie. He had few questions as though he crept cautiously around the *Sparticus* issue. I decided to let him simmer in the brew of his own making for a while. Before hanging up, he made certain I had properly invited the Arnetts to Dinah's little shindig—as though we would party under their Lake Norman noses and toss protocol to the sea.

Before the sun set above the ocean, Ruth and I set the steam pot to boiling and shucked corn on the deck. Charlotte joined us. She cradled the corn next to her with her small hand while her good hand pulled down the husks. After we made a good pile of husks, Charlotte tore them into shreds and braided them. She formed a basket the size of an apple with a miniature handle.

Dinah arrived with her station wagon loaded with baskets of food, the ice cream freezer, and the twins. Colin, Mason, and Troy carted her things to the picnic table while the twins joined Charlotte on the deck. Troy chased Hercules out onto the beach. Mason soon followed. Charlotte continued weaving the husks, mesmerizing Dinah's girls with her magic.

"You won't even guess what I made, not in a million," said Dinah.

We all stared blankly.

"Ginger ale. Have you ever known anyone who could make homemade ginger ale? Not too many people, I'll bet." She wielded the bottle with a kitchen towel as though she held out fine wine.

Charlotte cheered, nakedly impressed, and then ran to flash her handmade wares at Dinah.

I pondered the small cost of a bottle of ginger ale against a person's time, but I kept it to myself.

Ruth broke up the corn, washed it, and placed it all in a large bowl. "The corn and potatoes are ready. Tell us what to do, Dinah. We are your clay."

"First place the potatoes in the steamer, put on a good tight-fitting lid. I'll let you know when to add the corn. Someone needs to help me wash these clams. They still have some sand in them. Then we'll clean the lobsters."

"They're alive!" Charlotte stared, squeamish, and twisted her face into a grimace.

Dinah held up a large container with the lobsters inside.

"I can't eat them. They look like huge bugs," said Charlotte.

"I'll eat yours," said Colin.

That satisfied her.

Ruth followed Dinah back into the kitchen. They set aside the corn and started to work on the clams.

"We have some table covers around here somewhere," I said. I ran upstairs and rummaged around the linen closet. I felt my heel tap against something. It was Charlotte's angel. I picked it up and bounded downstairs with tablecloths and the doll in my arms.

"You found her. I left her for you," said Charlotte.

"Thank you kindly, madam." I lifted the doll by the string attached to its back. It swung below my waist, a pendulum.

Dinah reappeared with a large bowl of clams. Ruth brought the lobster and helped Dinah find a nearby table.

I disappeared into the kitchen to make sweet tea for any person with no affinity for ginger ale.

Colin followed. "I visited your father this afternoon. He's on the mend."

"He's complaining more. He's better. Trying to rule the world from his bed, though. Ellie wants him to walk around more, but it makes him cross."

"I could take him some of this good food," he said.

"No need. I have to go by his place on the way home."

"Quick! Time to add the corn." Dinah stuck her head inside.

"Should we place the bread in the oven?" asked Ruth.

Colin passed them the corn while I dipped a few more slices of bread into the garlic butter.

Charlotte helped me toss the tablecloths over the wooden tables. She placed plastic plates and flatware along the table edge and spaced each place setting so equally apart, it gave the tabletop a measured appearance. We watched in awe while Dinah added the clams and lobsters to the boiling mix.

"What do you ladies do for fun in the winter?" asked Colin.

"Cook indoors?" Dinah shrugged.

"Sounds like church people," said Colin.

We joined hands around the table while Colin offered thanks. Dinah stepped away from the scene and used the boiling pot as her excuse to turn her back to us. After Colin's "amen," she dished up the lobster and clams like a New England chef. All of us salivated. Dinah set hot pepper sauces and seasonings around the tables. Then she pulled out a large container of her own coleslaw and set it at the end. "It's buffet. Dig in," she said.

Frankie Avalon crooned "Venus."

Dinah and Colin talked sports. She told him about the girls' athletic prowess, but not in a disparaging way as she did around the other team moms who all had sons. I saw a pride in her eyes, and felt amazed at Colin's adeptness at drawing her out.

"So you once lived in Maine?" he asked her.

Dinah typically took longer to settle down around new people. But Colin had a way with her. He invited to her attend the midweek service with the girls.

I knew she would decline.

"That's kind of you to ask," she said.

"Why don't you come?" he asked again, as though he asked her for the salt and pepper.

I turned away and pretended to check on my ten-year-old.

"Maybe I'll come," she said.

My lashes batted several times. I reached for the margarine without looking up at either of them. I avoided staring at her open-mouthed. She always had some humorous way of avoiding my invitations to darken the door of the church. If I looked at her even once, she would jinx the moment. Of that, I felt certain.

"All right, I will come," she finally said.

I saw Mason elbow one of the twins.

"What's wrong with that?" She looked straight at me.

I did not know whether to feel grateful or resentful that Colin had coaxed her into the portals of our sanctimonious halls with such ease. Dinah and Ruth set to work to collect the dishes and pass warm cloths to the children to wash their hands and faces.

I stood and offered to take the dishes from Ruth so she could focus on the dirty faces. Colin followed me into the kitchen. Before I could pull the watermelon from the refrigerator, Colin knelt, and brought it out as though it were the size of a baseball. He found a knife and sliced it open.

"It's best if you slice it up into the smaller pieces. Not my gift," he said.

"Colin, I have asked Dinah to church so many times but she's never wanted to hear such things."

"Eternity is written on the heart of every man."

"Not Dinah's. Or if it is, she hasn't broken the code. We'll see tomorrow night if she really comes."

"But you want her to come, March, don't you?"

"Of course I do. I'm just doubtful. That's all I'm saying."

"After we pass these out to the kids, you want to take a walk on the beach?" he asked.

"You don't like watermelon?" I asked.

"I just need a walk."

After we distributed the sliced melon, he placed a hand on my shoulder and gave me an odd sort of nod.

At once Dinah, Ruth, Charlotte, and Mason looked up at us.

I followed him off the deck like Hercules did when he galloped after Mason. Colin removed his sandals so that he could walk closer to water. He allowed the water to lap over his feet, sloshing through it, his pants rolled up to his knees. He walked several paces ahead of me, enough to cause me to have to speed up to catch up with him. I felt awkward, aware of at least a dozen eyes on my back. I refused to look back at them.

A shrimp boat made a serpentine path not many miles out. The crew lifted the nets as they prepared to bring it in for the day. Colin watched the vessel out in the harbor. He turned to me and said, "I made a mistake today. It haunts me. Once you told me that the *Sparticus* was Joe's boat, the one that took his life, I should have turned it all around. For you, especially. I get trapped within my own zeal sometimes."

"It happened too far away from shore. It's not as though I have to pass the same corner every day where the accident happened. But seeing the *Sparticus* again, I suppose it had the same effect as passing the dreaded corner. It is something I've been needing to do. Mason needed today to happen."

He apologized again.

"Colin, you shouldn't apologize. When I saw Mason's face as he climbed aboard, I knew that it was right. I've been selfish about my grief, as though it belonged only to me. Mason has to deal with Joe's death in his way, his boy way. I've never been adept at sharing pain. I say I'm doing that to protect him."

Colin hurled a shell into the ocean. It skipped once before the ocean swallowed it.

"Do you find that you play mind games with yourself?" I asked.

"I do, when missing Eva is unbearable." he said.

"I've blamed myself a lot. This is all different from what you go through, I realize, since we're facing different issues and all. I felt blind to what was going on inside of Joe. He wasn't one to tell me, you know, man thoughts."

"Ha-ha! What are man thoughts?"

"That's what I call them. Man thoughts. Men keep the thoughts to themselves that drag the life out of them, only it poisons their souls like a tainted well."

"This afternoon, when I looked at you looking at that boat, I replayed the times I used to pass by the hospital and finally started driving different routes just to not have to look at that place anymore. Then I would forget and drive past and weep, until the day I drove past and the pain just stayed inside without a tear to shed. Which is worse—well, I haven't decided. I don't know what I imagined about your husband's boat. Maybe I thought it was on the ocean floor and you were safe from seeing it." He processed that thought. "That sounded lame."

"You turned the day into a celebration. What's wrong with that? Do you know how long it's been since we opened the garage door and drove the pain away from the cottage and allowed ourselves to celebrate the world of the living again? Consider what you did today as a gift to my son. We conquered—something."

"It felt good. I like to see Mason smile. I like to see you smile."

"How were the nights for you? What I mean is, when the day was over and everything was quiet, and all of the well-wishers disappeared, were the nights hard?" I asked.

"Evil. Dark, although it got better to get through the evenings. Less dread as time passed. How about you?"

I remembered his diary. "It's difficult to put it into words, how when the night comes the pain flounces in and sits on your chest, no smaller than an elephant. Nights were the worst time to me."

He watched the lapping waves, soundless while the ocean resonated a song for eventide, and then said, "Oh, hateful night. I wrote about it."

"You are such poet at heart, Colin." I pretended to look far up the shoreline. If I looked at him directly, he would know for certain I had read his secret writings. The wind blew through his hair and made the sleeves of his chambray shirt billow. I didn't know if chambray had a smell, but I swore I could smell Colin's chambray and his man scent in the ocean breeze. It was not my right to do that, but I did it anyway.

"The night comes and you pull it over your head like a hateful blanket. And you lie in your uncomfortable solitude and aloneness while all of the splendor and joy and wonder of life have abandoned you, leaving you with an extra pillow on your bed and no head to lay on it. You want to hide away." Some days I craved the aloneness, but I even craved being alone sometimes when Joe was alive, and that was another reason to feel guilty. I was afraid someone would notice my insanity, my little bouts with neurosis, and turn me in. But I did not tell him that.

"I made the mistake of trying to date. It hadn't been a year since Eva's death. I was trying to fill up the void with another person as though I could fill up an Eva-sized hole in my heart. No one could measure up. I tended to romanticize her." While Colin had painted Eva more lovely, I had mornings when I had to look at Joe's picture until I recognized his face again.

Colin waved at the couple who lived in the next-door cottage.

I waved too and then confessed, "I tried to fill up my void with busyness. Still do. But when the quiet returns, I have to face the pictures and words that filled up that awful day. Over and over I hear that policeman say, 'He didn't make it.'"

"I once thought it was awful to think about Eva's flaws. It made me feel as though I desecrated her holy memory. Then I realized it was her flaws that made me love her."

Colin peeled away two years' worth of guilt off of my plastic façade with that one statement.

"All of it is sacred. Everything she touched."

"Colin, that's it! I know exactly what you mean." I started to remember. "I couldn't empty Joe's trash can and couldn't stop digging through it as though I'd find some part of him in it. Even the litter in his trash basket was sacred to me." It felt good to say that about Joe. Maybe I didn't hate him, just the way he had left me.

"It's better not to play the saint, to remember the bad along with all of the good, because it was the bad times that strengthened you as a couple."

Now he sounded like a pastor again.

We stopped and looked back at Mason and the other children who looked only an inch high in the sand.

"You have no idea how much this has helped me," I said. I felt downright dizzy with relief, baptized by Colin's confessions.

"You know what they're all thinking back there, don't you?" Colin said and I bit my lip into submission to suppress a silly smile. He finished his announcement. "That I've started something between us. They don't understand our mutual pain."

"Colin, no one can understand it but us. I'm glad we took this walk." Until now I had not found as much goodness in the soil of Joe's life as he had in Eva's. Too much of me clung to his flaws. "Sometimes I feel bitter, like I'm going to grow old a bitter old prune."

"Before the accident were you mad at him?"

Maybe a little more confession would lighten the load. "We fought and it was awful. His firm was on the brink of bankruptcy, but he never shared it with me. When he came home from work in a state of unsettling quietness, he would shrug off my questions. That left me mad at him. So much unresolved. Too much revealed after the fact. Then when our two cops showed up to tell me about the accident, I wanted to shout at Joe and then hold him again and tell him we could work anything out if he would just stay around long enough to let the sun come up again.

"Every day after that when the phone rang, more bad news would come and that would compound the pain of his death. But being kept in the dark about his problems was the deepest well of my grief."

I could not share any of this with Colin without feeling sucked back in time. It was my descent into the definitive valley; in that whistling moment when thoughts fly like gulls against the heart, the pain had spilled in, the beating of the tide against our protected cove, the leveling of my soul. The reason I was a wreck.

I found my bearing and continued. "And then there was the problem of his family. His mother, Joan, knew enough about us to take her little digs at me. I didn't handle it as well as I should. She's always implied I caused his death even though she doesn't admit he may have taken his own life." It was as though she had been looking her whole life to find someone to blame for Joe's problems and happily found me. We always had this friction between us, so when he died, what little good we had between us fell apart after the accident. She acted as though I drove Joe out into the storm. "Neither Mason nor I knew Joe had taken the *Sparticus* out that day. He always invited at least Mason. It was the last time he would push me out of his life. But no one could prove he took his own life. That remains the million-dollar question."

"Did the insurance company investigate?"

"They might have but Joe's partner had neglected to pay the premium for several months. No insurance, no investigation. I'm convinced Joe thought Mason and I would have that policy for security, but his partner was in deep trouble too. Seems nobody talked much around the firm about problems."

"I'm sorry. Did he keep a journal?"

"It was always business as usual with Joe."

Colin looked at me, and I felt transparent and fragile, a piece of broken glass washed ashore that he had found and turned over and over to examine. My father as a pastor could always see into my soul, but Colin stripped me of all my armor.

"Shall we go back? The cottage has become a pin dot," he said.

I saw that he was right. "Here comes Hercules." The dog bounded toward us at a maniacal pace. Fast on his tail were the Buckworth twins. They squealed, their fondness for pursuit turning their mouths red. One had a kite, and they looked intent on tying the string to Hercules's tail.

"Dinah has her hands full with those two," said Colin.

"She does well. Dinah has made many friends in the community and established this cooking show out of a small catering business."

"You seem to be close friends."

"We grew up together. Her family moved here from Maine when she was thirteen years old. From that point on, we were like sisters. We're both as much a part of Candle Cove as the sand is the shoreline."

Colin picked up a handful of sand. "You know what is so amazing about this stuff?" He stooped and allowed the water to wash away all but a few translucent particles on the ball of his hand. He held up the granule to what little remained of the sun before the sky closed up its shop. "Who would have thought that God would use such small things to hold back the tide?"

We watched the Buckworths continue on their spree. Mason ran past, one hand brushing against me. He yelled for the girls to leave his dog alone. Colin laughed, and it sounded like rain on cracked ground.

Fourteen

WITH PUB DAY AHEAD OF US, I DRAGGED MYSELF INTO the bathroom as fast as my numb little feet would carry me the next morning, which was Wednesday—pub day, church night, but with a nice little caveat—Colin would be preaching, or as he called it, "teaching."

Before I roused Mason, I examined our sand bottle collection on the small stand in the bathroom. The bottle that had once held three small onyx stones now only held two. It reminded me of the unsaid words between Joe and me and all I had divulged to Colin. Maybe it was just my imagination and I was barking up the wrong tree, but if Mason had removed the third stone from our memory bottle, I might be able to get him to talk about it. If we, Mason and I, were going to be better than his father and me at talking things out, maybe bringing up the memory bottle would help.

I rapped at Mason's door again. "I hope you're up. I made your lunch." I heard the whispery, early groans of just-waking boy. "I want to talk to you," I said.

He invited me into the room, stumbled across the rag rug made by my mother, and breathed out a mumbled question that not even the U.S. Naval Intelligence could decipher.

I stood over his empty bed, baffled at how a tucked-in boy could awaken with his sheets twisted into ropes that barely covered his chunky frame.

"What did I do?" He yawned and balanced his not-yet-awake body against his bookcase.

"You're not in trouble, Mason. It's nothing, really. I know it's early and all. You'll think this is stupid. But do you know what happened to the third stone in our bottle?"

He leaned against his bookcase and backhandedly twirled the propeller on a model plane.

"Am I losing my mind, or did we have three stones in here?"

"Is this a trick question?" he asked.

"So you don't know about the stone? Not that it's a big issue. Let's don't make this a big issue. I'm going somewhere with all of this. Bear with me."

He shrugged and crashed the plane into his coverlet.

"Okay, I'll say it like this. We made this memory bottle in Ocean City. Sand from the beach, right?"

He nodded, but with his head lowered he stared up at me as though I were stupid.

"Then you, not me, dropped three little black stones into the bottle with the sand. One for Mason, you said. One for Daddy and one for Mommy."

"I need to get ready for school, okay?"

"Now, someone removed a stone. Let's say it's the Daddy stone. Would that be right?"

"I guess." He shrugged and took a step toward his closet door.

"It's supposed to be okay or something if we talk about your dad's death. Just like it was all right for you to take a ride in the *Sparticus*."

He took the bottle from my hand. "A memory bottle was a stupid idea. Daddy even said it was a bad idea."

"I believe he called it 'ambitious.' But it was our idea and therefore good. Just a memory. Nothing more," I said.

"It isn't a good memory anymore." He tossed the bottle into his waste can.

"For me it is." I retrieved it.

"You didn't even want us to take a ride in the *Sparticus*. It made you mad."

"Not mad. Sad and mad are two different things entirely. Everyone deals with grief differently."

"I wanted to get in the boat yesterday. But when you stayed behind, I felt bad."

"You shouldn't, Mason."

"I hate the way I feel sometimes," he said. He lifted the model plane by the body, gently this time, and placed it on his bookcase. Then he dragged out his bag of marbles, held the velvet pouch by the bottom, and shook them out onto the bed. He picked through them until he found a small black onyx stone. He held it out to me. "I couldn't throw it away."

I saw tears form around the rims of his eyes. I cried with him and we allowed the tears. "I knew we could talk about this, Son. It's okay to be mad, I swear it. I get mad too. We don't know whether to toss out all our memories of Daddy or put them on display." I was just as confused about my feelings as Mason, but we sat ourselves down and had the finest of talks. I helped him find socks, and then we fixed his lunch for school and somehow made it before the late bell.

He ran past the Nazi car-line mother and then twirled like a quarterback faking a right, then going for the pass. "Mom, wait!" he shouted and I hit the brake.

My automatic window came down in maternal obedience. "What did you forget, love?"

He yanked open the passenger door and clambered to my side of the car. With his most extravagant embrace, he grabbed my face and sloshed me with the most wonderful and joyous kiss a boy could ever give his mother. "I love you, Mom!" He scrambled out past the bewildered Nazi mother and into the school building founded by his grandfather.

"Did you see that?" I said it to the bewildered Nazi as I grabbed for the Kleenex box.

She waved me on, but managed a smile.

Hal Caudle rang the church bell that evening as he had done on so many Wednesday nights, and many more Sunday mornings, and every New Year's Eve. I remember those New Years when he set a chair beneath the rope of the bell. One by one we children were each allowed to ring the bell. Grace Caudle said it was our way of telling the village "Jesus loves you; Jesus loves you." I always remember her standing beside Hal in navy polyester, the hornet brooch at her breast, and the earrings that matched exactly. I remember the glisten of love in her eyes for Hal. To her and Hal and their friends at the church, tradition was their way of touching God, even if at a safe distance.

Mason and I took our place up front. We heard a breath of whispers around us, but more heightened than usual. The sound seemed to come from the back to the front. That is when I saw Dinah and the girls taking a seat on the back pew for the first time. Dinah caught my eye for a moment and then dug through her purse as if she looked for something lost.

Change comes slowly in Candle Cove. Something as small as seeing a new face in church threw every little planet off its orbit. Cobwebs could form in the window just above where my father stood for so many years, but it was so subtle that it might go unnoticed until the web formed a pattern. There was a crack in the window's wood that now ran from the top of the window frame to the bottom, but since it happened over time no one noticed. I thought about the platform that would not hold my father's notes on this night or the old worn Bible, but the notes of a younger man. All at once, every particle in the building seemed to deteriorate in front of me, shifting as slowly as the orbit of the earth. I felt as though I deteriorated, slowly dissolving into the pew, but what was incremental had become exponential. I complained about my bad feet, my receding gums, and the twinges in my right shoulder. But I accepted it as a natural part of life.

The old air conditioner revived and blew the cobwebs, but not away.

It reminded me of the verse in the scriptures that says that even though outwardly we are wasting away, yet inwardly we are being renewed day by day. I wondered if anyone around me was aware of the renewal thing or just going for the wasting away aspect of it. Or if the deterioration had become so commonplace perhaps the thought of inward change was more unsettling than the idea of wasting away.

Hal and Grace dispensed with the ringing of the bell and marched up the aisle with Bill and Irene Simmons and the Michaels. They paraded up the aisle, penguins that never noticed the crack in the window, the cobwebs, or my bad feet. They did not see the age spots that appeared upon the hands of the bell ringers. Their expectations were small—that this night would mirror the church services of Wednesdays past.

Grace placed her handbag next to Lorraine Bedinsky and said, "I don't like the new gardener they hired to clip the church hedges. He has a bleary-eyed look about him."

"I'm glad you brought it up. I wasn't going to say anything," said Lorraine.

"He doesn't look old enough to be trimming the church hedges. That's the long and short of it," said Hal.

"How old does he have to be?" asked Lorraine.

"Old enough to reach." Hal adjusted his wallet in his back pocket. Then he stretched his hands over his head and made a clipping motion with his hands.

The women laughed.

All of them set to talking about the next church social and egg salad.

I felt as though I had been here before, as if aliens had picked me up and forced me to live the same day over and over. All at once, I wanted to step into the future or the past or anywhere but here and any time but now. I had spent too much time thinking about time travel and Joe's accident. I had to lay it down, put aside the fear of change invading my cloistered little universe, and stop deteriorating in front of the ones who loved me.

Lorraine Bedinsky pointed at Colin with her nose and whispered to Grace, "He thinks we're sort of clubby, doesn't he?"

Fern tapped me on the shoulder. "I went to see your father today. He's looking perky again. Got that rose bloom in his cheeks. Would not surprise me *at all* to see him back in the pulpit in two shakes."

Bill Simmons took his place next to Hal. "Let's not rush things, Fern. Pastor Norville has to mend. Things like this can't be hurried along."

Lorraine turned back to Fern and in her desultory manner launched into her egg-salad diatribe.

Hal sat back in his seat so only Bill could hear. His eyes had a dim color that reminded me of a fish that sat on the bottom of the ocean growing old and fat while the plankton fell into its mouth. The top of his head had lost all of its bald-man's sheen and looked like an old peacock that had lost its plumes. "Are we going to lose our pastor, Bill?" Old people like him do not know how well practiced they are in loud whispering.

The women glanced up and then looked away, looked at me.

I turned away from them and nodded toward the front so that I could avert Mason's curious gaze.

Colin ascended the platform. He delivered a message that lasted no longer than twenty-five minutes, yet was weighty with content. Even Lorraine later alluded to the "fine, fine message."

As every person gathered in the rear of the church, Mason tugged at my blouse.

"What is it?" I asked.

"Go talk to him before he leaves." Mason had combed the front of his hair up in a straight swoop that looked exactly like a young shock of wheat.

"Whom should I talk to?"

"Pastor Arnett."

"We have plenty of time to talk to them."

"Charlotte told me they're leaving tonight."

"They don't want to stay another night?"

"They're already packed. Pastor Arnett has a lot of work to do back in Lake Norman. The car is loaded."

"We'll go and say good-bye to them then."

"I don't want to say good-bye. You can talk to them and ask them to stay. Grandpa's sick. He told me about his retirement. They can move here and you can ask them to come."

We stood in line and it almost looked like a receiving line, as though we were accepting the new pastor and his family. I overheard Bill and Colin talking. A piece of paper was pressed into Bill's hand. He did not wait to open it. I peered around Grace and Hal and caught a glimpse of a name and phone number. Colin had made his recommendation to Bill.

Mason and I finally shook Colin and Ruth's hand.

"March, I want to thank you and Mason for your hospitality. You've learned well from your mother," said Colin.

"We have really grown to love your family," said Ruth.

While we continued to exchange pleasantries, I felt Mason's occasional tug at my blouse. Colin and Ruth led the children out across the dark parking lot. It was as if Mason, by the act of his will, tried to propel me toward them.

I stood glued to the asphalt and waved.

Colin strapped the last child into the backseat, turned, and walked toward me.

"Here's your chance!" Mason ran back up the steps and disappeared into the church.

Colin and I stood under the Wednesday moon. He shook my hand but held it a little longer.

"If you don't mind my asking, where were you when they told you about Joe?"

I didn't know what to say. Nothing came to mind. He turned away, embarrassed.

"In the bathroom cleaning out the sink." I blurted it out. I wish that I had made up something such as I was in the hospital visiting the sick. Or I was at the church. Anything but cleaning the sink. Now he would have this anemic image all the way back to Lake Norman of me shaking chlorine cleanser out into the sink. I had heard of women who had had premonitions about the loss of a loved one just as my mother had once had them. But nothing about the day had warned me what was about to happen. It was raining. Lightning flashed, and I imagined Joe seated at his desk working another Saturday to build his practice, then dragging home another briefcase of work and sitting with his back to me. Nothing told me in advance the day was over before the sun set.

Colin must have noticed my embarrassment. "Ha-ha." It was a nervous laugh, not cruel.

"Is that funny?" I asked.

"I think you're funny. The way you say things. That's all."

He shook my hand again and headed for his tank-sized SUV.

I thought of Colin's journal and how he gleaned moments and thoughts into a collective assessment of who he and Eva were as a couple. I stood out under the glow of the yellow parking-lot lights that looked like antique lamps and imagined. I visualized a little cloud hovering above my seldom-touched diary. It made me wonder in a hopeful way what good I might pull from the story of Joe and me. I had tried to erase us, but it only hurt worse, like flogging the air and hitting myself. Because I could still see us in Mason's eyes and we looked handsome and hopeful, all intelligence and freckles in the package of a boy.

Colin had molded each morsel of pain and shaped it into a metaphor that would help those around him consume it and be encouraged by it. While my life was forever on troll mode, Colin always moved with the wind at his back, never in the doldrums. He sailed off in splendor while the rest of us waved and cheered from shore effusively praising the magnificence of his courage.

To his poetic query, I had nothing more to say than I was cleaning the sink. "Ha ha, hoo boy, what a laugh!" I thought I was alone. (But what would be the chances of that?)

"Mom, are you okay?" Mason peeked out of the church doorway.

"I'm good, Son. Really."

He rested against the doorway and it seemed to me my mother had even painted the doorjamb.

I dredged up my thoughts about Joe's last day. We had pancakes. We had not had pancakes since the Christmas before, and I put blueberries in them just the way he liked them. He thanked me and there was this moment when he kissed my face, and then I turned toward him and we really kissed. He tasted like blueberries and both of us thought that was funny.

We had touched. I saw it and knew it was true.

The taillights of the Arnett SUV flashed red. The vehicle came to an abrupt halt. The side door flew open. Out flew the loveliest butterfly, her blond hair flying behind her, gold tresses falling around her shoulders in the sweetest aroma of little girl.

"Wait, we forgot, we forgot!" said Charlotte. She threw her arms around me, and I felt the presence of her hands wrapping around me.

"What did we forget?"

"Our angel hug," she said.

"You never told me about an angel hug," I said.

"Are they back?" Mason was fully outside now, under the exposed yellow light bulb above the door.

"Just for angel hugs," I said.

"Oh," he said it as though our girlish demonstration of emotion disgusted him.

I bent down and Charlotte kissed me right on the mouth.

"You be good and don't forget to pray," said Charlotte. She ran and disappeared into the car with her wings fluttering behind her.

They pulled out of the parking lot, their bumper a quarter-inch from scraping the sloped exit of the church parking lot. I watched until the taillights became distant, like a rescue flare at sea.

I said good-bye to Bill and Irene Simmons.

"Sounds like a good one." Bill held up the paper given to him by Colin.

"I want nothing to do with it," I said, and both of us laughed. I stepped back in to the church to turn off all the lights, a job my father had commandeered for years. The cobwebs disappeared with the dimming of the lights, and yet there was that scent of desuetude that settles on old churches. It is a sweet scent, like old bee boxes out in the field that have ripened with the aroma of honeycomb and the renewal of life every spring. Yet the musty ache of old pews cried for something new.

"Ready to go, Mom? I have practice tomorrow. Can you remember this time?"

"I'll remember, Mason. Let's go see your grandpa."

On the way home, Mason sang an unfamiliar song.

"What is that?" I asked.

"A song I learned."

"Then sing it."

He did.

"Interesting rhythm," I said.

He swayed back and forth and turned the dashboard into a set of drums.

"Where did you learn it?"

"Pastor Arnett."

"He is a good one to know new songs."

Fifteen

GLORIA BOLTED THROUGH THE POES AND STOOD IN the middle of the floor. "The test was blue!"

Shaunda lifted up a rounded fist and cheered, "We have liftoff, people!"

"What test? Did Gloria have to take her driver's test again?" asked Lindle.

I had read it all for the past few days in Gloria's face. The tired eyes, the pasty complexion. "Are we pregnant?"

"We are!" She hugged me.

The Poes bought her morning coffee and doughnuts. Shaunda left little pink and blue candies in a dish for her.

Thursday was slack day at the *Sentinel*.

Shaunda took a call from her friend at the courthouse. "News on Yolanda's criminals, March. Their attorney took a waiver of speedy trial, so there's a continuum."

"Continuance?" I asked.

"That's right. The trial is delayed." Shaunda typed up the story.

"I'm just ready for it to be over and done with," I said.

Gloria pulled out the layout pages and stripped them so that we could use them again. Lindle gathered up the waxed ads, filed the ones that we would use again the following week, and stuck the rest in a scratch-paper file. Nothing was ever thrown away. I sat at my desk and issued paychecks, as always semimonthly, and caught up on the bookkeeping I neglected all week.

"Gloria, would you mind if I check on my father? He seemed a little down last night."

"We're all under control," she said.

If anything had a pulse in Candle Cove, it was the *Sentinel*. While Monday through Tuesday led up to Wednesday's pub day, Thursday began the process all over again. Wylie and Brendan puttered around the print room and swept paper from the floor to prepare for the next print run, while Shaunda made appointments with school board members and the local schoolteacher, Tyler Klutts, who had decided to run for mayor—a fact that annoyed the incumbent, Fred Joiner.

Gloria took over the bookkeeping in a proprietary fashion, and I stepped away feeling incongruous with the day. I turned and left.

I found Dad out on the porch. He ate eggs and toast but complained raggedly. His hair, once clipped to the scalp, now grew in wisps that touched his collar with points of gray. Even with a warmer May, he buttoned long sleeves at his wrist, I assumed to hide the bruises from the intravenous tubes. His laugh pillow lay behind him against the wall as though he had not needed it for days.

"These aren't real eggs, you know. She thinks I don't know that this isn't genuine food. They'll find it causes cancer, and then the hens will be back in production again working double-time."

"Dad, can you never have eggs again?"

"I will if I want."

"If you don't mind, I'd like to go through those boxes I put up in your attic a couple of years ago. Joe's boxes."

He shrugged and tamped the noneggs into an empty soup can.

The attic had a window at one end, a circular pane of glass that allowed light to flood the otherwise darkened rafters. Beneath it was my grandmother's trunk graced at one end by three cardbaord boxes. On the cardboard side Dinah and I had marked it simply "Joe."

On the other side of the trunk, I saw a wooden pallet my father had fashioned with castors. In the early ministry years, he'd taught himself to repair our old Oldsmobile. He used the pallet to slide under the Oldsmobile to examine the underbelly.

It made a perfect dolly for one of Joe's heavier boxes, so I dragged it down and ferried it over to the attic opening and then slid the box down the ladder.

Dad was staring beyond the rail when I pushed the box over the threshold and out onto the porch.

Ellie held up the soup can with two fingers as though she held up a dirty sock and dropped it into a trash bag.

"I'd like two eggs over easy and toast with butter. And bacon if we have any," he said.

She argued with him.

"Please, Warden," he argued back, "just a simple breakfast with real butter and salt. That's all I ask."

"Go ahead, Ellie. But no salt, no butter, certainly no bacon," I said.

After she disappeared, he waved his cane at the neighbor's yard. "Clyde Janway's let his grass grow up. Must be off at his fishing cabin in Asheville. We once cut each other's grass when the other took a vacation."

"I don't remember Clyde ever cutting our grass," I said.

"Good people, the Janways."

"I think I'll go through this box."

"Looking for anything in particular?"

"If I were, it'd be a miracle to find it. At the time, just looking at his things all the time sent me into a nosedive, so Dinah and Mason helped me box it all up. We packed away all of Joe's junk like mad-women tossing every little piece down to his paper clips into boxes. I thought I might find a few things of his that would be more personal. You know, like a journal."

Dad drifted back to his world, a trait more common since his surgery. He was self-absorbed with any facet steered by James Norville: the church, his diet, his provincial circle of friends. "Bill Simmons called this morning. The board is contacting the minister that Colin suggested, " he said.

"Aha! This is the stuff Joe'd kept in his desk. You can tell the secretary boxed up this one."

"I forget where this minister graduated, but he's highly credentialed and open to the idea of living near the ocean. At least that is what Colin told Bill. He's writing his dissertation."

I pulled out Joe's leather desk calendar and a pen set. Mason might want the pen set unless he thought it looked too old-mannish. I remembered when all of the attorneys gave pen sets to one another at Christmas. Joe's set appeared brand-new, a brown faux marble sort of finish with a gold brass clip and a velvet lining in the box the color of egg yolk. It clashed with his gray desk set, or at least he might have said that at some point. For the life of me I could not remember.

"Everyone, all of the ministers, make videos now. Bill says this minister, Matthew Vandiver, is overnighting his video. What do you make of it?"

"I suppose he is sending a video of himself preaching or teaching, Dad."

"It doesn't seem natural. You aim a camera in my face and I go as wooden as a hobby horse." He disappeared inside his thoughts for a moment, his eyes wide like a doll's eyes and his mouth frozen in a smile.

"I wonder if this means something. All of Joe's desk thingamabobs look new."

"Excuse me, brothers, but we need to do another take for the video. We know you won't mind." Dad mimicked a broadcaster's voice, although he was lousy at it. He sounded more like Norman Vincent Peale on valium.

"Colin's church has a video camera in the balcony. They give videos to visitors. You just take a little ticket to the information booth after the service and they give you a free video of one of the services."

"Not Colin. He never sent us a video."

"Not to keep getting off the subject, but does it seem odd that all of Joe's office supplies are brand new? Look at this package of paper clips. Never opened. A letter opener that is still in the case. Is this a clue, or am I making something out of nothing?"

Ellie set Dad's eggs on the TV tray next to him. "Eggs over easy, toast with something on it, but I won't say exactly what it is or you'll start in on me again."

Dad thanked her in his most strained it-pains-me-to-say-this tone.

"I'll be back later with some dinner, Reverend Norville. Have a good day, March," she said.

After she pulled away, Dad said, "It's a shame she and I have to assume such an adversarial role. She is an otherwise nice woman."

"Back to me and my world. You've counseled people for years, Dad. The fact that Joe did not use his office supplies, would that be a red flag?"

"March, you've never practiced letting go of the past." He ate his eggs.

"I liked it better when you ignored me."

"You can't make God cough up all of the answers, line them all out just to please human curiosity. When God seems silent, it's possible he is trying to coax us into trusting him."

"I wouldn't call what I want to know human curiosity, Dad. Mom died too soon, but at least you knew the day was inevitable. When death pounces suddenly, it's like the aftermath of a bomb. You have to lift up stones and look underneath to find answers. I am not trying to find all of life's answers—just this one."

"Assume the worst; commit it to God." He sighed over his eggs and then placed a napkin on top of them.

"Admit it. You're crabby because it's hard to let go of your pulpit. So there you have it. The nut doesn't fall far from the tree."

A teenage boy motored up dragging a gleaming green trailer behind him. He backed a riding mower off the trailer and cut Clyde Janway's grass.

Dad studied his technique with a critical eye. The entire lawn was cut and edged in ten minutes.

"His blade is too low. Clyde won't like that chopped off-to-the-cuticle look. He should have hired a man with a push mower."

Arnie slumped around from the side of the house dragging his belly in the grass. Every step the low-slung pooch leaped to make the climb up to the porch punctuated his age, just as my father's inching gait accented his injured carriage. Dad yanked off the napkin, set the plate of remaining egg yolk on the porch, and allowed the dachshund to lick the surface clean. "Gloria tells me you've had some travel opportunities. You didn't tell me you have more travel assignments in the wings. What else don't I know?" he asked with a hint of pity, a man pulled out of the fight of life and told to sit in a corner.

I scooted the china dish from under Arnie's gluttonous tongue to rescue the Blue Willow heirloom.

"I'd hate to think you were turning down job prospects because of me." He drew up his lips like he did when he grew introspective. "Not that you did it because of me, but I'd hate to think you might."

"The timing isn't right, but I do have an offer of sorts. I could make the job as big as I want it to be or just let nothing happen. I never seem to have definitive offers, you know the kind that change everything, and your neighbors suddenly see you moving into the swanky end of town."

"You've held down the fort since your mother passed. It's time you had a life separate from mine. Maybe you could let this thing enlarge, as you say. You deserve a little swank, March. Nothing says you have to settle for the crumbs. I chose to make the church my life. I didn't choose that for you."

"The church is my life, too. Mason is my life. You, Mason, the

Sentinel. Period. And don't act like I've lost who I am just because I'm looking out after you."

"See! I knew it was because of me."

"Okay, maybe it's about you. You and everybody else. I can't just start hopping planes and leaving Mason or the newspaper behind. I've got people depending on me."

"I ask God every day, don't let me become a burden to my daughter. I can get along without you, in spite of what you may think."

"Would you look at this! Here's an entry in Joe's calendar. He always had nice handwriting. Did I ever tell him that, I wonder? He penciled in a few lunch appointments set up for the week after the accident."

"That would be a good sign."

"No, I'm afraid not. Not one business meeting. No court dates. In other words, if someone called him for lunch, he accepted it. But he didn't pursue anything legal or lawyerly. Not that it's any great surprise. I don't know why I did all this digging through his stuff. I keep holding out for a little grain of something I can give to Mason when he grows up and pieces his Dad's accident together."

"Maybe he won't. Not everyone wants to know the hard facts." Dad cupped his hands over his knees. He did that his whole life as a way of saying this conversation is beginning to bore me.

"Or maybe I just did all of this for me." *Mothers do that,* I thought. Make decisions out of selfish motives and then try and attach our motives to something as noble as *I'm doing this for the child.*

"Mason told me you and Colin took a walk on the beach."

"We talked about Joe and Eva, if that's what you want to know. We knew everyone gawking from the cottage would make something of it, but there was nothing to it. Believe me when I say that Colin is long gone. But it has nothing to do with me this time. Not that I was the cause of him not coming for good to Candle Cove the first time. Or returning. He didn't come because of me, Dad, but because of his friendship with you. You already know that, I gather, so don't look so smug. But I was hospitable, that's all I'm trying to say. So my hands are, as you say, clean in regard to Colin Arnett."

"You know why I like him? His faith has clarity," said Dad.

"I agree with that. Colin is everything I would like to be as a person of faith. While I lollygag along complaining as I go, he sprints ahead. You're right. He has clarity. Good choice of words. But I don't know what the big difference is between us. You know, like the *big* difference, the part of his armor that makes him so all-fired victorious."

Dad removed his spectacles and cleaned them. If he knew the answer, he did not say. "That little Charlotte has a way of winding her way into your heart," he said.

"She's a charmer."

"Bill Simmons would give away the church treasury to get that family in our midst. I somehow missed the mark in bringing them here. But who isn't glad they didn't get the chance to know them? They make everyone they meet feel refreshed. He may not be our new pastor, but somehow he touched all of our lives even if God didn't give him to us fully."

"He has his flaws. He fears death. Not that he's said anything. But he dotes on his family as though he is always spreading his large eagle wings to keep them close to the nest. Especially Charlotte."

"You don't fear death?"

"It's not death I fear, but the valley. You know as in the Twenty-third Psalm. When someone falls ill, or finances sag, or if you lose your job, you simply struggle to climb out. But when death comes this close, you move into the valley but you never see the moving van come back to take you out. You wonder if God still hears you when you speak to him or if he is tuned in to the pounding of your heart. You wonder if you will gather strength to take the next breath or the next step. Literally take the next step and walk into the next day. That's my biggest fear. Making it each day through the valley. We don't walk alone. But when I watch Colin, I envy his joy. He says it is not his own. But how does that translate to me?"

"You, Colin, and me, we've all walked through the same valley, March. But the reason the shadows are so deeply dark is that the light behind it is so joyously brilliant." His brows lifted. He was proud of the metaphor.

"I'm going to take this box and put it back upstairs. I don't know what I was thinking."

"Fine. Clutter up my house."

"If you don't mind, that is. There are no answers in this box. Maybe I need to have another talk with Colin. After we speak, I feel better." I pressed the old pieces of packing tape back onto the seams of the box and hefted it back down the hall and up the attic ladder. I stood in the light of the circular window and watched the sun caress Joe's boxes with a soft light.

"I really loved you, Joe. We never held one another long enough when we embraced. In our final year together, we didn't kiss in that lingering way. We never had the chance to say how we felt because we were always so busy. I'm listening now." Two wrens fought outside the window, causing the fruit-tree branch to lift and quiver. Joe and I had battled like those birds, fighting for turf, instead of for our love for one another. Twin tears spilled out, streaked down my face, and dampened my blouse. "If I've held on to you too tightly these last two empty years, it is because I am still waiting to hear what you never felt you could say. Maybe it's time I left those silent wishes up here in the attic." I now understood why some believed in the myth of ghosts in the rafters. "Good-bye, Joe. You've taught me a lot."

I left to pick up Mason from school.

We stopped at Ginger's for a quick meal of Cantonese chicken and rice. Thelma, Dad's secretary, phoned me on the cellular.

"March, I hate to phone you in the middle of all of your work, but we received a request for a hospital visit and Bill Simmons is off at a bowling tournament."

I could not for the life of me remember who might be in the local hospital.

"She's a cancer patient. I wouldn't take her a food basket although her family might appreciate it. Her name is Victoria Lane."

"I don't know any Lanes."

"Her dear sweet hubby picked us out of the Yellow Pages."

"She might be expecting a pastor, Thelma."

"Her husband says she wants to talk to someone about God."

"Mason is with me. Hospitals are a bore to children."

I was drowned out by the sound of preschoolers parading past Thelma's desk for afternoon recess and cookie break.

"You'll find her at Holy Mary by the Sea in that little pigeonhole of a cancer ward." She gave me the room number and paused as though I wrote it down on the steering wheel.

"Might she prefer the Baptists? They have a whole mime skit thingy for the sick." Channel 6 once came out and filmed them. It was a big production.

"Your daddy's done this so much, I figured you'd probably know by heart what to say. Ask Jennifer Cantalona at the volunteer's front desk for a Gideon's Bible if you don't have a spare on you."

Mason sighed when I told him where we were going. We debated about him being dropped off at a friend's house until I saw his school satchel exploding with assignments.

"I guess you know my answer," I said.

Mason did his math out in the waiting room. I sat outside the cancer ward in the hall and waited for the words to come to me, not recalling a single cognizant thing my father ever said to a dying person. *Why me, God? I'm as useless as a gnat.*

Sixteen

THE LANE FAMILY ACTUALLY CONSISTED OF THREE families. As many times as Mr. Lane defined his family to me, his ex-wife's portion—three teenagers with hair the color of corn—and Victoria's family, I never shuffled the deck in exactly the same manner every time. Two sisters, freckled and running their fingers through long tangles of hair that blazed into natural red curls, took frequent nicotine trips to the stairwell to light up. Victoria's skin tone indicated she might have once possessed the family red mane too, but all that remained were burnished filaments of sparse brows above her lashless eyes.

"Do I know you?" she asked.

Herb Lane stepped away from his wife's bedside and tramped toward me double-time with his hand extended.

"I'm March. One of you must have called Thelma at Candle Cove Presbyterian."

"You don't look like a preacher," said Victoria. She looked me over with blue eyes, intense as gas flames.

"I'm Herb, Vicki's husband. We only called an hour ago. You must have a sound dispatch system."

"Thelma. She's all we have," I said.

Herb dusted off the chair beside her bed and stepped away in hopes I decoded his gangly body language.

"I didn't know about your diet, Mrs. Lane," I explained. "Or I might have brought a fruit basket."

Behind me was a shuffling of feet, and the room emptied.

"I want to talk about Jesus, church, and my cancer," she said.

"My father is actually our pastor. He's recuperating from surgery. You can call me March."

She invited me to call her Vicki.

"I wrote down all of my questions. You should know I am dying, and this is all new to me. Dying and Jesus are new, I mean."

"What do you know about him? Jesus, that is."

Two Baptists at work had prayed with her and led her in prayer after her collapse from a brain tumor. I knew the Baptists in town to be fairly thorough.

"Maybe we should start with your questions, then," I said.

Vicki smoothed the paper in front of her that looked to be written on a grocery-list pad. "How do I know if I'm going to heaven?"

I knew that one by heart. Vicki had a Bible on her nightstand, placed in the room by the Gideons. I fumbled through the crisp pages and was greatly relieved when I opened to Romans. "That if thou shalt confess with thy mouth the Lord Jesus and shall believe in thine heart that God hath raised him from the dead, thou shalt be saved."

She scribbled on the pad.

Some kind person had left a bookmark in the back of the Bible printed with scripture references. God had sent in reinforcements. I turned to the book of John and read: "Let not your heart be troubled: ye believe in God, believe also in me. In my Father's house are many mansions: if it were not so, I would have told you. I go to prepare a place for you. And if I go and prepare a place for you, I will come again and receive you unto myself; that where I am, there ye may be also."

Right about now, James Norville would have pulled some really crisp and neat apologetics out of his knapsack of spirituality. I hoped she didn't see me fidgeting. Standing for years in my father's shadow did not qualify me for evangelism. I took another glance at the bookmark and then read: "If we confess our sins, he is faithful and just to forgive us our sins, and to cleanse us from all unrighteousness."

Vicki's fingers stopped moving. She rested her chin on her chest with eyes shut tight. Her monitor beeped steadily. My heart bumped against my chest to see if I was still alive.

She opened one eye. "I'm ready, then. Tell me what to say," she whispered as though we stood in the lighted bowels of a cathedral.

I leaned against the side of her bed with my elbows planted in the linens and my forehead against my clasped fingers. "Repeat after me, Vicki." I prayed a silent prayer. *God, I feel like an idiot. I'm so inadequate it's laughable. Could you please fill in the blanks for this woman?*

Gloria and Shaunda left a message. They photographed the fungus in the school gym, an incomprehensible photo, Shaunda said, of the janitor pointing at what looked to be scattered potting soil. Gloria's note said she would use a lot of adjectives for the piece, but the photo was nixed. The two of them went off to Dooley's for fish and chips and near beer, Gloria's pregnant-person substitute for her favorite summer beverage.

Lindle was at the Pontiac dealership selling the owner, Freddy Lydel (accent on the "LIE") on a full-page ad, Shaunda's note said.

Mason had finished his homework at the hospital. He and Dad sat out on the front porch straightening out the contents of Dad's tackle box while I ran back to the office to edit the LaVecchia's piece.

I had overused the words *delectable* and *satisfying* so I described the fish as "a phenomenal yet understated dish with a nutty kick and a heavenly cloud of garlic potatoes." The phone rang.

"Colin." I may have said it with a sort of animal-in-the-headlights astonishment.

His words possessed a discomfited nuance. His secretary, or some office clerk, spoke in the background. He answered her with a dismissive tone.

"How are you?" I asked.

"I've been thinking that perhaps we should try and hook up again."

"Hook up?"

"Meet."

"As in?"

"Meet."

"Mason loves playing with your kids. We'd love to have you all down again. Should I call Bill for you and arrange another service?"

"No Bill. No kids. No church. Just us. What I'm trying to say is, will you consider seeing me, but not with our families present?"

I did not know that Colin had room for such thoughts. "Colin, is this what it sounds like?"

"I'm trying to ask you out. But then there's the distance equation to figure out. We have a guest house at the church. Really, it's the old parsonage, but a nice cottage sort of house. Quaint, some say." He muttered something about not being well practiced at courtship.

"I am without a thing to say. We're just so different. You're like brass and jazz. I'm like old dusty organ keys." I don't think I said what I intended, but he caught me so off guard with his *let's get together* discourse.

"Oh, no, I disagree. You're really innovative."

I felt as though I was fishing for words of approval, so I opted for comedy. "Are you sure you have the right number?"

He had a laugh that pealed clear and concise all the way from Lake Norman.

Before I could answer with any sort of intelligibility, I argued with myself about my current situation. I had found my rhythm finally, I told myself. I knew what to do when I awoke and what to plan for the next day. In the big picture all I could see was distance and tension thrown into the mix if we tried to merge Longfellows and Arnetts. And then there was the matter of Eva. I could never live up to her perfect persona.

Someone tapped at the plate-glass door. It was locked, a practice of mine when I worked alone. If I answered it, I could stall. "Colin, hold on a teeny moment. Someone's at the door." I left the phone off the cradle and the line open.

Jerry Brevity smiled at me through the plate glass. He looked freshly showered and he had ditched the rat-man uniform for a nice polo and a pair of khaki slacks. I opened the door to him. He looked like a nicely aged version of the strapping high school quarterback.

"March, let's go get a burger. The yacht club is having a parade out near the pier. We can take chairs and buy a sack of burgers and have us a picnic while the boats parade by. Supposed to be a nice sunset. I know how you like sunsets."

It was true about me. Jerry was so observant of my every move, of every whim. He knew my flaws but saw them as (how did he put it?) sparks in the embers.

"I would love to go, Jerry. How nice that you thought of it." I said it overly loud.

"I'll put the top down on the Jeep." He strode back outside with almost leaping steps.

"Colin, are you there?"

There was an undeniable pause. "Yes, I'm here."

"I have a date. Well, it's nothing really. There is this boat parade. Our equivalent of the Disney parade, only with dime sparklers instead of a fireworks display."

"You don't have to explain. I realize you have a busy social life, March."

His diplomacy unsettled me. Not even a spark of antipathy. I felt guilty and conflicted. I tried to convince myself I would have joined Jerry anyway.

Colin apologized for disturbing my evening and then hung up.

"What was that all about?" Gloria and Shaunda had slipped in through the side entrance. They stood grinning at me.

"You've been standing there a while, I gather," I said.

"Colin called you again?" Gloria put away the camera case.

"Was that preacher asking you out? You know you'd make a good preacher's wife, March. You know the ropes. Me, I'd be lousing things up, getting into trouble," said Shaunda.

"Don't look now, but Jerry Brevity's waiting right outside with the top down on that bright red fancy Jeep of his. And that look in his eye says he's got his net out," said Gloria.

"I don't blame you, March. That Arnett, he has too many kids for my tastes." Shaunda locked up her desk drawer.

"Tell me you don't have a date with Jerry." Gloria sat backwards in the chair next to my desk to face me.

"Jerry's a respected business owner. Practical man," I said. "He's solvent."

"Safe," said Gloria.

"We're going to the yacht club's parade. Burgers and fries and nothing more." I closed up my purse with a rapid snap and stood to leave.

"Maybe you passed up good wine for near beer," said Gloria.

"I think you're making the right decision, March. Tell that preacher he needs to go find hisself a nursemaid." Shaunda stacked her notes into a tray.

"I thought you two were gone for the day," I said.

"Long-distance relationships never work anyway." Shaunda nudged Gloria out the door. They greeted Jerry and then left for the night.

I locked up my desk and the front door.

"We better hurry if we're going to catch the sunset," said Jerry.

He smelled of clean laundry and deodorant soap. His back sank against the seat and melded with the comfortable curve of leather. The lines of tanned skin around his eyes and mouth blended well with his surroundings, a comfy sofa of a guy you could never toss out for sentimental reasons.

But when I slunk into the Jeep, I felt lousy, like that left-out feeling when I'd been home for a week with the flu. Or like I'd just thrown out brisket for egg salad. Jerry smiled at me, crinkling the corners of his eyes, but all I could return was a musteline grin. I was climbing into the carriage of the town exterminator, not that his profession wasn't keenly needed in a township near the ocean. But when I sat next to him, I had no curiosity about the man, whether he smelled like chambray or wrote like Dylan Thomas. Jerry was Jerry, six feet of former athlete strung together by a past eminence. Jerry was no more than who he once was, and even minus that. His own existence was eclipsed by a few years of illustriousness. A legend who had faded with less importance than an old set of encyclopedias. His only claim to fame now was that he could say he knew me.

We motored away from the *Sentinel* toward the pier and the glow of sky along the horizon. Gulls lulled in the breeze as though drawn onto the fabric of gold-and-pink sky with gray *conte* crayons.

The office phone rang again, a distant chirring muffled by plate glass.

"You want to answer it?" he asked.

I could see the yellow light of the phone line blinking through the window, a wounded lightning bug.

"No. If it's important enough, anyone who knows me knows my mobile number." Whether or not Colin possessed the other phone number, I could not remember.

Jerry chauffeured us away and I felt a deep and sickening panic. My head felt as though it were swelling with the ether of anxiety. I gripped the seat and donned a pair of black sunglasses while my hair blew around my face in unbecoming tentacles. The visor in front of me was down and I saw my own face in its mirror, a reckless Medusa. Jerry rattled through the cove all the way to the pier while I turned stone silent.

Someone had erected a lemonade stand next to the Kiwanis Club's burger-and-dog shack. Jerry ordered a sack of burgers and fries with two lemonades. We set up our chairs and a camp table close to the shoreline. I bought grilled ears of corn including an extra to take home to Mason who always ran to the corn stand at the county fair each fall.

"I forgot to mail my article to Brady Gallagher," I said.

"For the *Charlotte Observer?* We can swing by the post office on the way back to your car," he said.

"Not to worry. I'll just fax it to him. It will be waiting for him when he comes in tomorrow morning."

"I wish my secretary, Adele, had your efficiency," he said.

A boat horn sounded on the bay. Children assembled along the ebbing water. Their sparklers made neon squiggles in the air.

"Someone like you could sure increase effectiveness at Brevity's Exterminating. You could drop that newspaper business, all of the pinching pennies, and have yourself a steady little income working for old Jerry. There's a lot to be said for security, March."

"I'm not a secretary, Jerry. I employ one, though."

The sun melted away, a big lemon drop.

He doled out the paper-wrapped burgers.

I waved with exaggeration toward the string of boats. "Oh, will you look at Harry and Clara Monoghan's *Miss Ursula!* They've decorated her sort of Calypso style with stuffed parrots. Surely they got them from some party supply. I mean, they wouldn't use dead birds, would they?" The lemonade circulated over my tongue in swirls of undissolved sugar granules.

Miss Ursula led the boat parade. Harry Monoghan wore a grass skirt over Bermuda shorts. He swung around the mast and shouted at the land-bound spectators.

"Harry's been nipping down at Dooley's," said Jerry.

"Look who we found, Sue!" Sybil Ettering juggled a lawn chair and a miniature ice chest.

Jerry sat forward but did not stand to greet them. "Well, it's our writers-in-residence in the flesh! Ladies, take a load off. Join us."

I acknowledged Sybil and Sue but glanced away when they paired us up with their gazes.

"March, it surprises me to find you among the landlubbers this year," said Sybil. The way she said "landlubbers" sounded unnatural.

"I heard you took the *Sparticus* out for a trip or some such." Sybil handed a ten to Sue and sent her for food and drink.

"March, you should have told me. I would have helped you decorate her and enter her in the parade," said Jerry.

"I don't belong to the yacht club anymore," I said.

"You're a veteran, March. Wing Bester would have let you in for old times' sake." Jerry pulled out a second burger.

Sybil had an epiphany. "Think how much that would encourage everyone to see you floating along all dolled up in your boat. Reminiscent of the days when you were voted in as Queen Pamlico."

"Did you take her out alone?" Jerry asked.

"I still remember that paddle-boat ferry with all of you girls in Southern belle gowns and parasols. You looked like crocuses blooming along the harbor. Bernie and I were still young marrieds in those days," Sybil gushed.

"I didn't know you could sail the *Sparticus*. Will wonders never cease?" Jerry found the large sack of fries.

"I was never Queen Pamlico, Sybil. You're confusing me with Dinah."

"You and Mason must have had a good time putting her back into the water," said Jerry.

"It was a whole group that went. Right, March?" Sybil set up two chairs and squeezed into one of them.

I was still trying to figure out how Sybil knew about the *Sparticus*. While Jerry zoned in on the bit of news about Colin and the *Sparticus*, Sybil spilled my private life out like a gossip scout for the *National Enquirer*.

"Couldn't have been more than seven or eight or she'd be over the limit. You have to watch your body limits or the Coast Guard will nab you quick," said Jerry.

Sue yelled at Sybil to find out her condiment preferences.

"Excuse me." Sybil lifted herself out of the chair and traveled labo-riously across the sand, her sheer floral blouse billowing like a per-fumed scarf.

"I didn't take her out, Jerry."

"Mason, then?"

"My father invited a visiting pastor into his pulpit. He and his fam-ily stayed in the cottage. They sort of found her out in the garage."

He pulled back the wrapper on burger number two, but then froze. "I hope they were sensitive to your feelings."

"Mason took to the sailing right off, like we should have tried it sooner. So I'm glad it happened. He's been a different boy ever since, like we're talking about things more openly now."

Jerry choked down a bite and looked sophomoric doing it. He rushed to interject himself into the conversation. "I'm glad you told me. I've been thinking you and I need to be more open about a few things."

I felt a swell of things I didn't want to hear billowing toward me.

"Ms. Longfellow, is that you?"

Two red-haired women stood blocking the evening sun.

"You're Vicki's sisters," I said.

"It is her," said one of the sisters.

"We don't know what to say, but you did a lot for our sister," said the other. "I'm Carla and this is Simone."

We shook hands. Simone flicked a cigarette butt into the sand next to her and ground it into the sand with her heel. I introduced them to Jerry.

"Nice to meet you, Jerry." Simone gripped his hand, an athletic handshake for such a petite female.

"Your wife came to visit our sister today at Holy Mary by the Sea, and she just was the best person anyone could have sent. Here we don't know you all from Adam, but she just came anyway," said Carla.

"Jerry and I are friends. We're not married," I said.

"For now." He placed his hand atop mine on the lawn-chair arm, curled his fingers around mine, and squeezed out some vague Morse code as though he cued me to counter his obscure proposal with girl-ish wild abandon.

"Do you mind telling me how long Vicki has to live?" I asked.

"A week. Maybe two. She's already hung around two months longer than the doctor predicted." Simone dabbed her eyes with the back of her hand.

"She's only two years older than me, and I'm thirty-nine," said Carla.

"It just goes to show you. I guess we better run. We saw the lights from the hospital window and thought we'd take a break." Simone pressed a light-up button on her watch face.

"This is such a small world. Thank you for stopping to say hello. And I was really glad I helped your sister." I decided not to divulge how worried I was that I would botch up things between Vicki and Almighty God. Somehow, in spite of my inadequacies, God reached through and reeled her in.

"Candle Cove is the most darling place. I can see why Herb and Vicki bought a house here on the water. It's like the end of the map, the last place you stand just before the climb to heaven." Carla's voice broke.

Simone lit two cigarettes and handed one to Carla.

"She just won't stop talking about God and all that stuff you told her. I hope you can come back. Bye, now," said Simone.

They walked away from us.

Jerry and I stared at the boat parade that was halfway finished by the time we looked up.

"The last stop before heaven. I never thought of Candle Cove like that," said Jerry. He turned away to listen to baseball scores on another man's radio.

"Jerry, are you familiar with Dylan Thomas?" I asked.

"Didn't he play for the Dodgers in the sixties? Nah, I'm mixing him up with another guy."

Sybil and Sue joined us and handed us each a funnel cake.

"Oh, we almost missed the whole thing standing in those awful lines," said Sue.

"You'd think there was nothing else to do here." Sybil laughed, her bottom lip coated in powdered sugar.

I watched Vicki's sisters walk, sandals in hand, all the way down the shore. I thanked God for filling in the places I may have left out.

Jerry chatted up my counseling skills and other things he really knew nothing about. I could feel him trying to draw me in as his good points ebbed from sight. The way he slipped in that little bit about marriage irked me to no end.

Someone set off Roman candles and a small fireworks display on the peninsula's shore. Fireballs erupted like blazing spheres lifting above the harbor, drawing a line from our cove to the sky as though it connected our lives to things not seen.

The phone vibrated inside my purse. I fished it out and walked away from our little banquet to find a quiet patch of sand.

"I've had the most goshawful day, March." Dinah was breathless.

"Are you at home?" I asked.

"I've brought the girls down to your daddy's pier to fish."

"You all missed the best yacht parade. Someone even sprang for a fireworks display."

"That's just the kind of crowd I need to avoid right now. How can I show my face after the worst show ever? Tell me you didn't hear the broadcast today?"

"The crab thingy. I'm sorry. I forgot."

"Clambake. The show was terrible, and I just can't go out in public. Syndication is a laugh where I'm concerned. I'm going to hurl the master tape out into the ocean and pray it's eaten by something with a slow digestive system."

"You want me to come out to the pier, I guess."

"I could use a shoulder to cry on," she said.

"I have to go," I whispered to Jerry.

He dropped me off at the *Sentinel* although he lingered at the door for something as encouraging as a kiss from me.

"Thanks for the picnic," I said.

He held my hand, lingered over it, his eyes a flicker of puerile hope in the yawning moonlight. The calloused fingers, sticky from a night out on the harbor, would not let go.

"If I don't hurry, I won't have time to fax my article. I have a friend in need or we could go for coffee. Besides, I've got to pick up Mason before he completely wears out my father." I kissed Jerry on the side of his face and disappeared inside my office.

I felt his eyes examine me through the window, begging for me to look at him and offer him the wee glance of hope he had been attempting to dredge out of me for all these past months. If I did so, it would be a lie. I kept my face from the window, turning it to the soft glow of Gloria's blinking nightlights decorating the wall near my desk.

It appeared Brady Gallagher had left his fax machine on all night. The article flowed in and out without a hitch. I drove as fast as possible and picked up Mason. We joined Dinah and the girls down on Dad's pier.

The twins coerced Mason into dragging out his grandfather's choice fishing gear. He led them to the edge of the small dock prattling like an old fishing pro about his treasury of lures newly acquired from Dad. They imagined sharks and manatees in the dark opal of the cove and how they would capture one and wrangle it to shore.

Dinah and I walked along the shoreline. Couples who had gathered earlier to ritually observe the sun sizzling into the ocean looked cloaked and dark in the twilight.

"I think you're being too hard on yourself. Shaunda said she caught your broadcast today and it sounded chic and eclectic. Those were her exact words," I said.

"She's being kind, March. It's the worst one I've ever done. I sounded like a complete fraud. I've never been to real cooking school, you know, just sort of fly by the seat of my pants. I sounded like some single mother trying to invent a job for herself. I can't say it enough how I just don't like being me today."

"I like you, Dinah, and I think you're just the best cooking-show host, and the best mother, single or not."

"If I could figure out exactly what makes me tick, I'd not go after a whale with the butter sauce and wind up looking like the biggest fool ever. Only I have to pick a career that magnifies all of my flaws and parades them out in front of the whole entire world."

"Candle Cove is not the entire world, and a hometown cooking show does not put you on parade."

"It's my entire world."

"I know. I know. I live in the same world, and know what it feels like to be scrutinized. That's when we turn on the song and dance, right, Di? Just so we feel accepted? We spend half our life spinning our wheels and asking open-ended questions to which none of us knows the answer. Like 'why am I here?' Maybe we've all gotten good at faking it just because we can't answer those hard questions."

"Are we really good at faking it, March?'

Suddenly every couple barely visible along the shoreline looked pink and still, as though each person had matched up with a star in a constellation and formed a parallel universe.

"See the corner where that dock used to be, March?"

I saw a corner post, dark and lifted above the wake where a dock had once been. I nodded.

"That's me on that corner. I used to hold up my life just like that post before the elements washed away the whole upper dock. Now it's as though I'm still standing alone with the tide beating against me. I stand there strong, as though anyone is going to notice. But all the while I'm wondering what happened to the meaning of me. I can't remember why I'm still standing in the harbor while the tide turns my insides into soggy splinters."

"See that other corner, Dinah? Well, that one is me, and there we both stand holding up nothing. You, the former Queen of Pamlico, and me the queen of nil. Our lives have worn away from us somehow. But we are still standing, and there is a lot to be said for a monument."

"Do people see us as a monument or do we just look abandoned, two fools standing in the fray while the world beats against us?"

"Well, that's something, Dinah!"

"I always thought I would account for something, March. Tell me what to do."

I didn't know what to tell myself, let alone Dinah. Here I had wrapped up all of my life in church and work and family but possessed not a single answer for my friend, my sister.

The moon appeared and cast a net of green across the lifting froth.

"Colin called today."

"Is he coming back?"

"He asked me to visit him in Lake Norman. All of the wrong things paraded through my mind, such as "What if he's just feeling sympathy for me?" What if when I get there, he just wants to set me on his pastoral couch and pick my brain apart? But he didn't say any of that, and I just sounded like a ninny, that's what."

"And you went out with Jerry Brevity instead?"

"I used Jerry. I swear to goodness, Dinah, it was the worst thing I've ever done."

"You make every change that comes your way sound like a disaster."

"I do, don't I?" I said.

"Call him back. Plead a brief moment of insanity."

"If I do, what if I realize it was the worst mistake in the world and then our children have gotten, well, accustomed to the idea of maybe, well, a family forming between us?"

"He only invited you to dinner."

"You're right. I'm making this the Titanic."

We heard a squeal from the dock. Mason and one of the twins tugged at the line while the bow bent toward the water.

Dinah and I ran toward them.

"We've caught something huge!" Mason yelled, then grunted as he lifted the rod. He inched the nylon thread back into the reel.

"It's a whale!" one of the twins shrieked.

"I wish I had my camera," said Dinah.

"Grab the net, people!" Mason yelled again, the man in charge of Moby Dick.

One of the girls grabbed the fishing net and scooted next to him on her stomach. She scooped the hideous-looking fish into the net. Dinah helped her lift it to the dock.

"It's a catfish." Mason was not impressed. Sea catfish were not considered game fish by the locals.

"But a really big one," I said.

"I'd rather catch a stingray," he said.

The fish's gills undulated out as the creature gasped for water.

I suggested that Mason throw it back.

He and the girls flopped it over on its back, careful to watch out for the sharp fins and whiskers.

Dinah and I returned to the cottage to make tea.

"Is there something you're hanging onto, March?" she asked.

"That's an odd thing to say."

"You just always seem to be blowing off perfectly good invitations."

"Does it seem like that? Or am I just taking longer to weigh things? When I first met Joe, he left me thunderstruck. He was a man without imperfections. But that was my perception of him. I was wrong. When I look at Colin and I don't see any flaws, I'm paralyzed. Trust me, I lie awake thinking about the unseen dark side of a perfect man."

"You won't unearth any flaws sitting here in Candle Cove. You know he has them, though."

"Don't you think men are better at hiding them than we are?" Dinah cackled.

"Then I see how he's taken over his family. Colin's such a good father. He's good to his sister."

"You know we've had our victories, March, and without the aid of a man. Maybe Colin's just one of those people who genuinely has his act together. I have my days like that. But explain why I grapple with this empty pang inside of me even when I've had a good day."

"It's the God space, Dinah. Every human has one, my father says."

"You know I don't like religious talk. Besides, you never shove your ideas down my throat. That's what I love about you."

She grinned, but I did not feel like acting inane, blowing off the moment.

"I'm not talking about religion. But I've had this workaholic mind-set about church and God, as though by filling up every minute of every day with toil and effort I'm earning points with my Maker." I suddenly felt a need to find a still place.

"But, March, you're the most religious person I know, besides your dad, and he's ready for sainthood."

So was the Apostle Paul, I thought. But God struck him down with a blinding light long before he qualified for sainthood.

"Let's don't ruin the night with our single-woman blues." She held up her tea glass. "A toast to us."

We toasted and then walked out onto the deck to wave the kids back up to the cottage. The moon had taken over the sky and given it a melancholy cast. No fireworks pointed toward the heavens to give us answers.

I would find a quiet place, I told myself, somewhere at the edge of the earth where the only distractions were the whispers of marsh grass and the sand pebbles washing from the shore. God is unambiguous in those quiet coves.

Seventeen

"IF WE COULD JUST HAVE IT A LITTLE QUIET IN HERE,
everybody!" In a blinding flash of cowardice, I cut my eyes down at the
office linoleum. On Monday Gloria and I had spent an hour before
everyone else arrived deciding that the *Sentinel's* second-quarter earn-
ings were redder than Mrs. Pickle's tomato preserves.

"When will I breathe life into this dead body of a newspaper,
Gloria? Tell me I'm doing the right thing."

Her face softened with Job's patience as she cut out a fresh new
cardboard cover for my coffee cup. "You know you're doing the right
thing. Candle Cove needs its own paper."

We heard the sound of slamming doors. Some of the staff had
arrived, but with every nimble body that sashayed through the door I
felt another weight tossed into the scale.

The Poes' humming annoyed me. Shaunda, with her gum-smacking,
drove me over the edge, and even Lindle's nervous fluttering back and
forth to fill my coffee cup made me wish for a sedative.

"I'm sorry. Just go do what you do and I'll be fine," I said to them.

Gloria and I pored over the stories that had potential for the
front page. A swarm of bees had invaded the mayor's office, a fact that
had triple significance in an election year, and had the incumbent

and his opponent parlaying accusations back in forth in veiled figures of speech as though the plague of bees had apocalyptic significance.

The New Bern Chamber of Commerce had faxed the data for the Neuse River Days: the homemade raft races, New Bern's version of Junkyard Wars—nail together the most disorderly jumble of scrap lumber, discarded tires, anything that floats, and enter it in a race. Then there were the petting zoos, moon walks, a couple of craft stands, and a mishmash of games set up beneath the spreading oaks along the river to take your mind off of the heat. Gloria streamlined the facts into a two-column piece.

"You work miracles, Gloria," I said, but she did not radiate as usual.

Shaunda interjected her weekend story about the winners of the tennis tournament. "Also six seniors received state scholarships. I'm out of here," she said. She grabbed a cup of coffee to go and headed for the high school to take photos of the scholars.

I phoned Dad and described the weekend pulpit substitute: an aging Presbyterian army chaplain with a nervous hand and a tendency to misplace his eyeglasses in the middle of his sermon.

"That is a good thing, March. It will encourage the church to be swift about finding a new man," he said.

"Line two. It's Brady. Can you take it?" Gloria refilled my now-empty cup and hers with dark Jamaican coffee.

I finished church business with Dad and took the call.

"March, this is the best piece we've ever printed. I can't say enough about your style. Well, you actually have one. Bill says there is no shadow of doubt you could find syndication as a travel columnist."

I sprinkled sugar into my cup.

"I have the perfect piece for you, and you won't travel far from home. A two-page spread on the Pamlico Sound, but the hook is the pirate history. You'll sample food, visit the B&B's, the inns and cottages along the islands, the boat tours, but play up the history about Blackbeard, the sunken ships, so forth and so on."

The need to get away and find a quiet place to think enticed me. "I'll do it."

"Good. That was easy."

"I'm needing some time to be by myself, like when you do the trout-fishing disappearing act."

"How soon?"

"As soon as we're ready to go to press here, I'll leave it with Gloria and head for Ocracoke Island. Expenses paid, I hope."

"Covered. But try and work out a few deals from the locals in exchange for your mentioning their business."

"I'm no good at that, Brady. No one ever catches my vision for swap-outs until it's too late."

"You'll try."

I hung up the phone and called Gloria aside. "Would it make sense to take a travel story assignment in the midst of our sinking ship?" I whispered it to her.

"Stop saying that. You know once we get the paper to bed, you're a free woman. You need the money. Go, go."

Between the hysteria of Tuesday's news day and Lindle's paranoia that he might lose the Gum's Food Mart account, I could not gather facts for the trip until Wednesday afternoon.

"Gloria, do you remember the ghost story piece out of Raleigh? Were there any pirate ghosts, or are they all strictly out of colonial America?"

"We have a paranormal file. I'll riffle through it and see if I find any pirates floating around." Gloria devoured deviled eggs from Ruby's and chocolate macadamia nuts from Beach's Nut House, her first visible craving.

"I want you to be in charge while I'm away," I told her.

Gloria kept her eyes on the notepad in front of her and left wide gaps of silence between her sentences. She stepped away from her desk and moved past me to straighten clutter around the copier and to clear away empty Frito bags left behind by the Poe brothers. If she saw me watching her, it might have accounted for the way she kept her back to me.

I had juggled the workload so long, it did not occur to me that dumping my juggling act on her might feel as though I was laying a pregnant elephant in her already pregnant lap. "You don't want to be in charge, I understand."

"No, you believe in me. I can do it."

"I shouldn't go to Ocracoke right now. The timing is bad," I said.

"You're the owner. You can do whatever you want."

"If I go, I'll be putting pressure on you, and you're having morning sickness and this is just wrong on my part."

She turned and leaned against the painted credenza. To see her straight on made her look thin, instead of the sideways silhouette with the slight hint of a bowling ball emerging from her abdomen.

"You're trying to tell me something."

Gloria burst into tears.

"Let's go for pastries at the Lighthouse. You ride with me." I guided her out away from everyone else.

The Poes stared at her from the doorway of the print room, their mouths two *o*'s.

"Back in a minute. Hold down the fort," I said to Shaunda.

Sarai had lit vanilla candles on every table, an aroma that blended with the fresh hot bagels. We bought the bagels and coffee and picked a secluded table far from the ears of the elderly newspaper readers.

"Gloria, if you're stressed over the responsibilities or maybe it's the numbers, you know it's only our second year," I said.

"We made payroll by a thin hair." She blew her nose and spoke, her words trembling between hiccups. "I keep wanting to encourage you, but this is my first time to know so much about the place I work for. I'm no good at this." She scraped an overabundance of cream cheese from her bagel with a plastic knife.

"Of course you're good at this. You're great! You're the downright queen of great. If this job is a burden to you, I just wish you'd told me sooner. This isn't fair, and what with you in your motherly condition and all. I swear I'm blind to all of these maternal hormonal things. It's been a while since I had my baby. I'm not insensitive,

Gloria. Just distracted. I'm the most distracted person you know. Now you know the truth about me. Can you still like me?"

Her laughed sounded gurgly, coated with phlegm. "Look at me blubbering like a hormonal weakling. I know we can do this, March. We'll have to juggle a few things. If it doesn't make you nervous, then far be it from me to worry for both of us."

"Who said it didn't make me nervous?"

"No arguments about this either—I'm buying your lunch today for all of this nonsense I've put you through. And I think you should take your trip, and I'll manage for you. Poe brothers and all. I don't want you to worry about us. I'm just feeling pregnant. That's all."

"It's my job to worry for the both of us, Gloria. You take care of you, Phil, and the baby."

"When you leave, it's as though things slow down. No one wants to listen to me."

"You're hereby promoted as my official assistant. I'll announce it to everyone so they'll know that what you say goes."

The color came back into her face.

"If my travel is affecting you, I want to know. I realize my job at the *Sentinel* is a twenty-four-seven job," I said.

"You have to pay the bills too," she said.

Sarai filled our cups again.

"I can't fathom what we'll do when I go into labor."

"You better call me. I'll be right there with you."

"That's not what I mean. Shaunda has her head all in the clouds about New York; Lindle is no manager. Too disorganized. The Poe brothers are out of the question."

"I won't travel the whole month of your due date."

She looked relieved.

By afternoon Gloria gathered all of the pirate history from the files into a tickler file and placed it all on my desk.

"You're the queen," I said.

Gloria sighed so loudly it made us all look. Lindle's desk looked like the grounds after the county fair.

"Think of this clutter as ideas coming to life." Lindle's brows made *v*'s above his eyes.

I called a meeting and announced Gloria's promotion. The Poe brothers, with faces as pallid as a fish's underbelly, peered at Gloria curiously but offered no comments. Lindle shook Gloria's hand and asked to be excused. Shaunda sighed but tried not to show jealousy. When they all disappeared into their cubicles, Gloria cleaned off the table where the men had shelled boiled peanuts.

"They don't like the idea," she said.

"Give them time to get used to it. Once they see you're as fair as I am, they'll relax. Their respect for you is more important than friendship right now."

"This is all my fault."

"It was the right decision and that's why we did it."

"You keep your cellular phone with you at all times in case of a mutiny," she said.

By Thursday we could all take a breath again. Shaunda took to the idea of Gloria's promotion first and invited her to lunch to celebrate.

But the Mustang was making a funny noise. Just to be sure, Gloria had a rental car delivered to the office for my trip. She left a few numbers on my desk with the names of recommended inns and motels on Nags Head. She also printed off an Internet map. I told her to pick a hotel and secure the reservation.

"The entire trip from here to Nags Head will be about three and a half hours. You'll take the ferry from Cedar Island. Wait, you told me you've done this before when you were young. Don't you think it is the longest stretch of nothing but water? Unless you see a boat or two. Oh, and pelicans. You'll see a lot of birds and such flapping around not being so far from the—what is it you call that—a bird sanctuary? But you nearly always have to show up with reservations for the Cedar Island ferry or you might get left behind. I took the liberty of making your ferry reservations. The ferry to Hatteras is shorter, no reservations needed whatsoever. Then just travel the highway up to Nags Head. Shaunda's taking me to lunch. Will you be gone when we get back?"

"The car is loaded down. Mason is staying over tonight with Dinah and the weekend with Dad. I'd take him with me, but he didn't want to miss a game. Maybe I'll journal. I'll grab a sandwich from Ruby's to go and see you all next week when I get back. You feel ready for the Tuesday crunch, I guess?"

"We can do this. I just have a feeling about it like it's a step for us in the right direction, you know, like with responsibility we grow and all that," said Shaunda.

Gloria gave me a hug.

I turned on my cellular phone right in front of her.

I took off for Cedar Island and allowed myself a chance to vent. I had waited for this quiet time and now would have it without interruption.

If anyone walked into my mind and joined me in the middle of what winds through my neural paths on road trips, they would call me certifiably nuts and start analyzing whether or not I hated my mother, or did I even realize I exhausted the topic of Joe's suicide with every person I ever knew. But if I spoke my thoughts aloud, I'd always be the one dampening the lively conversations with talk of death.

No one wants to hear it. I know it for a fact. Not the ones you like to run around with, anyway. It is the odd person, the woman you scarcely know who gets right in your face and say things like, "How are you doing? No, I mean, how are you *really* doing? Come, dear, now you can really tell me. I'm worried that you're holding it all in," although I was never certain what the "it" of the matter might actually be that I was nutting away. She wants to make you believe you've grown up knowing her your whole life, Great-aunt Henny Penny suddenly back in your life and brilliant. She treats you as if you've suddenly been put out for adoption and here she stands, this merciful angel with her twenty-two-liter urn of womanly balm ready to scoop you up in a basket with pink blankets and rescue you off the curb. "Tell me; I want to know," is code for "I see a person in pain and want to experiment with her hot buttons," as though she were the latest video game.

Truth be told, I don't hold in anything. I just organize pain, visiting with her in increments. "Oh, hello pain, so it's you! Well, come in and have a seat and we'll have a cup of tea." It is true I don't invite the neighbors in to watch. It is a private conversation, not one most civil people want to observe. I likened the moment to inviting your friends over to watch while you have your spleen removed. Now really! Who would want to come?

But as I meandered down past the least populated lanes of East Coast highway, I could not get the painful matter of the cross off my chest. Not the jewelry, the crucifixes that people wear for luck or tradition. But the splintered wood nailed together by men who did not consider the human suffering that would be laid upon its crossbeam. Pain. The kind that proper society would not consider polite dinner-table conversation. Pain as heavy as the world sinking into a man's chest until he became it—the cries of hungry, sick, angry, and hurting people needing an emergency bridge to God. Christ became the cries. The pain. The death. While He hung in vertical humiliation, He lifted His face to say my name as He swallowed my bitter pill, and said He was done so that I could cross over His lifeless body, clean.

Pain. I finally got it. The necessity for suffering, so that from the pyre of misery, eyes would be lifted up to see God's Son and emulate in a smaller worm-sized way His price.

I entered the harbor village of Beaufort, crying and undone. The town smelled of grilled fish and salt water. I set off for the ferry landing. The road made its crook to the left to wind ferry riders onto Highway 70. Within only a few miles the entire topography turned from rural trees to marsh grass. The stress ebbed away as the land narrowed on either side of the road to become wetland and a fusion of inward sea and fresh water known as Pamlico Sound.

I rolled down the windows to smell the sea water and hear the intermittent cry of gulls.

I called back amid the song of birds and sea, "You are God even when it hurts!"

The marsh grass was dark and thick and made underwater islands where fish nested and spawned. The highway became a winding high wire between motorists and Cedar Island, a crooked pencil line of artery. I wondered what exactly might hold up the roadway to keep it from floating out to sea, but something told me I knew. Then the land widened again and became rural neighborhoods in towns named Otway and Bettie and Stacy and Sealevel. Picket fences smiled in front of cottages with kitchen-garden patches, houses painted the color of grapes and daffodil next to tired-looking trailer homes with neglected lawns. A woman wearing her husband's shirt lifted an over-sized watering can above her head and offered a drink to the potted geraniums that hung on rusted nails all along her covered porch. The floral baskets swayed like red petticoats hung out to dry. She was the only human I saw along the way.

But everywhere I looked was God.

Someone had taken scrap lumber and paint and nailed signs to trees all the way down Highway 70, or else many people had the same idea. The signs all said the same thing: JESUS LOVES YOU. I must have counted a dozen of them all the way out to Cedar Island.

Every time I read another one, the words sank deeper inside of me. Just the way I was without holding together anybody else's world, Jesus loved me.

I pulled onto the parking lot at Cedar Island. A line of cars had already formed a procession. A carload of adults and children pulled into line behind the Mustang. A young child with blond ringlets poked her head out of the minivan window and squealed when she saw a heron take flight. She made eye contact with anyone who looked at her and waved as though we were all about to embark on a great adventure.

I waved back at her and she laughed at what Mason sometimes called my silliest of grins.

The Island attendants finally allowed the cars to drive onto the ferry. After we parked on deck, the captain made ready and set us out across the sound. I locked up the Mustang and found a bench where I could journal. I wrote about everything that touched my senses, the stretches of ocean on either side of the ferry that cried how wide God is. The brown waters of the sound slapped lazily against the vessel, holding up the boat the way God holds up the universe.

I photographed an interesting-looking older man whose skin was browned by years spent in long stretches of daylight. His face told a story, but I could only guess it. I imagined he had spent his life aboard a shrimp boat. He watched fishermen dropping nets and spoke to another man next to him as though he possessed all of their thoughts. He chatted up the marine life that circulated in and around the estuaries and spawning grounds that emptied into the sound; fish like striped bass, carp, bream, and puppy drum. He spoke of how the tarpon returned to Oriental's shores in July to spawn, and the giant red drum that spawned on the lower Neuse and Pamlico Rivers.

After the first hour, the sun emerged from behind a cloud. It peeked out enough to scatter shimmering lights atop the surface of the water. Another hour passed and the white obelisk of Ocracoke's lighthouse came into sight. The ferry entered the channel called Teach's Hole, the place where Blackbeard lost his bragging rights when he died in a sea battle. The captain invited us to step back into our vehicles as the ferry entered the narrow passageway to the Silver Lake Harbor of Ocracoke Island.

I checked Gloria's notes. For lunch places, she wrote "check out the Pony Island Restaurant." A local who stood out on the park service dock gave it the thumbs-up although you cannot always trust locals in small villages. The lack of choices can broaden a discriminating palate.

None of the roads was marked with street signs, so I relied on a local map that invited visitors to look for landmarks. I passed the Anchorage Inn, the Ragpicker Too, the Jolly Roger, and the Pirate's Chest before I spotted the sign for the Pony Island Restaurant. The restaurant, an older building that preceded a motel by the same name, had only one vacant table. Several couples conversed across the tables near where the waitress seated me. Two women discussed the striped bass they had all caught and fried the night before and gave the impression they all camped along the water and bonded like tykes at a slumber party. *Campers who frequent Ocracoke congregate in packs and tend to meet year after year,* I wrote.

I observed them too long, unwilling to interact and spoil the reverie. One of the bass fisherwomen poked a camera in my face and asked if I would mind taking a photograph of the group. They collected around the table and primped for the first time all week.

"You, sir, to the right. Yes, you. If you could skooch in just a tad," I said. He misunderstood and tried to suck in a stomach that had stretched his T-shirt beyond its tailoring. I took two steps back, snapped the photo, and took a second one to satisfy them.

The waitress placed a sandwich platter atop my paper place mat. She filled my iced-tea glass again and dropped two more sweetener packets next to my plate.

Joe and I had never visited Ocracoke together. While I was taken in by the village architecture he would have liked the banter of the fishermen, the quiet coded language of the locals. I myself had not seen Ocracoke since a trip one weekend before Easter when my mother insisted my father escape from a cantata run amok. An organist who passed away some years past, Faith Justin, had decided the church needed an Easter cantata. She found just enough men to take the major biblical roles except for the part of Christ, who was played by a cousin of hers who had flaming red ears and a terrible case of acne. But the players all decided Faith was too domineering and that she favored the cousin who put in a poor showing as Christ. They called in Reverend Norville to quell the feud and soothe the afflicted emotions. We never heard anyone speak of cantatas again after that year.

The sky darkened outside the Pony Island. I phoned ahead to confirm my reservation at the First Colony Inn on Nags Head. Rain pattered against the windows, but only intermittently.

"You must have brought a storm with you," said the waitress.

"What time does Teach's Hole close?" I asked.

"Six this evening if that college student they hired doesn't take off early to tie one on."

The sign read TEACH'S HOLE—THE PIRATE SHOP. I picked up a history of pirates book, an eye patch for Mason, and a small bottle for collecting sand. A newlywed couple asked me to take their picture by the tall fake pirate.

The rain kept me from tripping through the woods where Blackbeard hid out. It didn't matter anyway because not even the faint aroma of history's cannons remained; nothing remained but trees.

But I found the wild mustangs herded onto a beach where they grazed. I scribbled notes about them that made little sense, except for a few metaphors that seemed to resonate.

The ferry trip to Hatteras was only a half-hour, and the sight of the candy-striped lighthouse made me long for Mason's eyes through which to see it. I passed right through Hatteras through the villages of Frisco and Buxton and up to Avon where the locals gathered at the Mad Crabber. Highway 12 into Nags Head was a coastal wonder of sand dunes and sea oats. The sun broke through during the twenty-minute drive through a feral landscape. The dunes, no longer the massive camel humps of sand and grass that blocked the view through Buxton, compressed to form gentler slopes. The Atlantic shined and tossed to the east while Pamlico Sound calmed and ebbed to the west.

Gloria's directions led me to the next highway and then I located the store called The Farmer's Daughter. The next turn down a two-lane road took me straight in to the First Colony Inn. She had found a quaint inn, lovely and historic. But I felt a need for a vast expanse of water out my window. I found a place called The Sea Oatel, a sea-side inn recommended by the newlywed couple. I checked in and dragged my own luggage into the room.

While Ocracoke lured campers, Nags Head attracted shoppers. I fished a camera from the overnight bag along with an empty canvas bag with *The Charlotte Observer* imprinted on the side. A package of photos fell out. I did not pack them but had a feeling Mason stuck them into my toiletries case the night before. Placed inside the gold drugstore processing envelope, Mason had handpicked photos of himself with Hercules, one of him with his grandfather, and a dozen of him and the Arnetts in various ham-face poses. I remembered how he tucked reminders of himself into Joe's luggage whenever he would take the occasional business trip. Once Mason had taken a tea bag and written on the tag HERE'S A PICTURE OF ME AND HAVE A CUP OF TEA. He had taped a wallet-sized photo of himself to the tea bag. Joe had found the gesture cute, but it made me ache and smile all at once. Finding these photographs in my overnight bag made me wish I had taken him out of school and brought him along against his will.

A room attendant appeared and opened the sliding glass door to allow in the ocean breeze. She placed extra towels in the bathroom and departed without allowing me to tip her.

One of the photos left me curious. I did not remember when Mason and Colin had posed in front of the *Sparticus,* but recalled Ruth snapping photos at every turn that week, taking photographs of Colin and the children posed outside the boat, inside the boat, and sailing away. Mason's thick shock of boy bangs blew off his forehead and made him look all the more masculine, like the handsome man he would soon become. Colin, dressed in faded denims and a white cotton shirt, had placed his hand on Mason's shoulder, a gentle grip; not overly familiar but convivial.

When I saw Colin in the photo it made me wonder why I had not thrown my arms around his neck, pulled his big strapping self toward me, and kissed him right on the mouth. But Colin's preacherly posture made me think of my father, and that was such a hard thing to kiss in any way other than a polite peck on the cheek. Yet I thought of Colin a lot and how it would feel to just drop all of the decorum kneaded into me by Julia Norville and blow all caution to the wind. Colin had broken into our circle in his mellifluous way but not because his intent was to intrude, but to quietly appear and mend whomever he touched. He touched Mason, my father, even Dinah.

He might have touched me and I imagined in what way. First he tried to find the connection between Christ and me, and that seemed to be a priority, and well it should be. But I had to figure out the Christ equation on my own. At Candle Cove Presbyterian, my father had reluctantly married couples who in his estimation were spiritually out of sync. One led the other down the road to God while the other pedaled along pacifying the wishes of the spiritual mate just to get the hook set. I had done that with Joe—strung him along on what I thought was a spiritual journey while he pretended to go. But I felt like the spiritual lesser of Colin and me. Now I understood why.

Thunder rolled distantly, like a bear waking. According to the clock, ten minutes had passed since I had opened that packet of photographs. I laid aside the camera and the shopping bag. Everyone had evacuated the beach from the first storm. I passed through the open door and left my shoes on the patio. The air was a cocktail of oxygen and mist and distant salt. My feet bare, I walked in a slow progression down the shore. The water had finally warmed. The clouds were still tall boulders stacked above the Atlantic, but they separated into islands. I saw sky.

The thought came to me that some need a cause and it helps them over and through the dark places. At first glance, it occurred to me that Colin plowed into causes to ease the loss of his Eva. After all, everything that rose up around him had her touch on it as though she breathed it into being. But now I realized Colin's only cause seemed to be in making himself invisible. By doing that, it doubled who he was and what he was about, and suddenly it became very clear to me: Invisibility gave him his potency. Visibility had taken me down.

I bent one knee and then the other. Salt water flushed around my calves. I felt broken in two, a twig washed on shore. God helped me with our conversation. He took his time with me. We had our time together. Our hands locked. He washed my confessions from the shore and left nothing behind but the clean sheen of new tide.

Surrender is delicious.

Eighteen

THE SUNRISE ENCAPSULATED ALL THINGS GLORIOUS about the Atlantic. If America embodied one address, we occupied the country's eastern window, the keepers of dawn, the wardens of the first minute of day. To bask in that light before the rest of the country awoke tasted like a warm secret.

Just off the sandy porch of shoreline the bottle-nosed dolphins fed early. I took a mile run.

Gloria phoned to say she awoke at four with major acid so she figured she may as well make the most of it and work. She wrote an article for pregnant women who want to increase the intelligence of their unborn children.

"Perfect for you," I said.

"All the women in my Lamaze class will buy us out. Who doesn't want to birth, say, the next Albert Einstein?"

"Good idea! But I read to Mason from the womb, and he's no Einstein."

"It's something in certain foods called *choline*. Anyway, I want to fax it to you first so you can help me knock out the benign words and make it, how do you say, concise."

I gave her the hotel fax number.

"Oh, and I found a place called John's Drive-In and it's close to you, March. You have to try it for lunch. John's specialty is tuna boats, fried okra, and peanut butter shakes. I would donate a kidney to meet you for lunch."

"Can't wait," I said. I paused as if I wrote down everything she said.

I drove to the Grits and Grill for breakfast and made notes for the future. Brady did not make mention of restaurant facts for the pirate piece. An idea cooked in my mind: *The Haunted Lanes of Pamlico Sound.* I found an entire book full of the ghost stories of the area at a gift shop. We could offer a map of famous coastal ghosts, haunted accommodations, and places to eat for Halloween. I would pitch it to Brady.

The proprietor served me the house grits with biscuits, a side of the smokehouse meats, and homemade jam. It tasted like a meal fresh off a grandmother's cookstove, the strawberry jam still warm and glistening inside the open-mouthed biscuits.

I could never wind down on Fridays, an anomaly that had somehow been encoded into my psyche. Friday had always been *finesse* day for my father, the day he laid the finishing touch to his Sunday message. While the rest of the community prepared for leisure, Dad prepared for the flock. My mother and I rubbed Parson's Wood Soap over the historical wood at the church. Thelma ran overages of the church bulletin. We all turned the hymnals face out and stuffed offering envelopes into the wooden slots on the pew backs.

I could see my father's face, but somehow it turned into Colin. I imagined him in his study. Or crouched in Eva's prayer garden. I wondered if all the members of his flock assumed he had gotten on with life, unaware of the ache that does not pass. A grief that deep opens hollows too wide to fill. As far away as I tried to pull myself from him, I could not deny the connection we made when we looked into each other's eyes. A knowing. A blending of two pains I knew only served to deepen the crater.

Angst swept over me. If ever I embraced another love, I feared loss would come to call again. All of it became a stony, shingled shore in my dreams. It loomed in front of me, and I could not reach it. If I tried to run to Colin, I'd risk all new wounds. That is why I called myself a wreck, after all. Because of how I had to live in order to save myself. Alone, the island of March. The lonely savior of me disconnected from the shore. But desire wooed me into the tidal pool.

Colin had not allowed himself to become the poster child for grief. Instead he remained as a calm beacon. The more he helped others, the more it seemed to lift him out of the place that consumed me.

Instinctively, my fingers hovered over the directory in my palm mechanism. Colin Arnett's number blinked onto the screen. I mentally apologized to him for turning down a kind dinner invitation. I dialed his number, closed up the phone, and laid it aside. "Don't, March," I whispered.

The phone rang and my nerves coiled. It was Gloria with an idea.

"March, Ocracoke is sponsoring a kite festival in the morning and we thought how convenient that you happen to be in the vicinity. You want to get some shots in the morning before you leave? Closeups of the sky full of kites, the kid-and-dog shots?"

"Gloria, I need you to talk me out of something," I said.

"Don't say it. You met someone."

"It's crossed my mind that maybe I should drive on up to Raleigh. Catch a flight to Charlotte, maybe as soon as this weekend."

Background noise crackled through. The Poe brothers laughed wickedly over something that was between just the two of them.

"It's so unlike you, March."

"That's good. Keep talking like that."

"That's why I like it."

"You need me at the office."

"Shaunda and I are managing splendissimo in spite of what you might imagine."

"Mason hates staying with the Buckworths, though," I said.

"I took him to your dad's. They're out at the cottage. Fishing."

"Dad can't go fishing. It's too soon."

"Ellie the nurse got it in her head."

"I've been away too much."

"True, but I need the hours. Does this mean you can't do the kite shoot? Festivities begin in the morning. If I can get you a flight out Sunday, you can still catch the kite festival. Unless you think it's a bad idea."

"Or I could leave Saturday afternoon. I'd arrive in Charlotte in less than an hour," I said.

"I'll call you back." The phone went dead.

The flight from Raleigh on Saturday afternoon got delayed on the runway, and we sat for forty-five minutes while a shrieking infant tortured her adolescent-looking mother in the last seat. I stayed in the rest room up front as long as possible to nurse a throbbing headache. I checked my mascara twice, as though someone waited for me in Charlotte.

I checked Gloria's travel preparations. She'd arranged for a rental car to be waiting for me in Charlotte and threatened the man with her ancestor's ghost if he didn't find for me a nonsmoker's vehicle. She would be happy to see two rolls of film used up completely at the morning's kite festival.

Finally the jet taxied forward and I felt the lurch, the lift, and the squealing vacuum in my ears as the ground disappeared from under us.

Some of the clouds looked like charcoal etchings. We flew completely through them and left them behind at the state capitol.

I sat next to a woman, her body padded as soft as a marshmallow. She swathed herself in a polyester caftan that hung to the floor whenever she sat. Around her stack of black curls she wrapped a turban that matched the caftan exactly. She smiled and her whole face bloomed cherry red. I decided that if a seat remained empty, I should move and allow her to spread her luxury over two seats.

"I notice you use a palm gadget. Lately, they seem to be lower in cost, and I've been thinking perhaps I should invest in one," she said.

I handed it to her and showed her how it worked.

"All of my grands are on the Internet. They say you can take photos and zoom them up or whatever you call it and show off your pictures right then and there to your family and friends."

"How many grandchildren do you have?" The headache subsided slightly. Normally I sought out a nonverbal passenger, one who allowed me to sleep or read without commenting about every small nuance in the air. But I liked the sound of her voice, low like water burbling gently over a rock ledge.

"Six in all. Three here in Raleigh. I spend half my summer here, and we go to the beach. The other half I spend in Colorado and the mountains with my other grands."

She handed me the palm device and squeezed a canvas bag up from the floor.

I hoped she had it filled with traveling curiosities that would hold her attention. She fished around the bag and pulled out a half-eaten cinnamon roll wrapped carefully in wax paper. "I have all of the best magazines if you want something to read," she said. The cinnamon roll did not hold her interest so she pulled out a roll of hard candies. She had maintained dexterity in spite of her long acrylic nails dotted with daisies. With the middle of her upper finger and thumb she pinched the candies in just a way to lift them out, her other three fingers fanned daintily away from her.

"You live in Charlotte, then?" I said.

"Yes. Do you?" The thought enlivened her as though she had found a new friend.

"I live in Candle Cove. March Longfellow. I'm going to Charlotte on business." I stumbled on "business," as if it were a lie.

She sighed and her eyes looked as though someone had dabbed away the sheen. "I said I had three grands in Raleigh. But it isn't true anymore. It just seems unfair to leave Lula out and just say two. Let me show you the children's pictures."

I took the small album and turned the pages. Two little boys with stout bodies that looked as though their knit shirts would burst at the seams smiled from a blanket on the ground. The next photo showed a young girl attempting to cradle them in her lap. The third photo was of a grave decorated with so many flowers the town florist must have locked up and gone home that day because they all but ran out of flowers.

"That's Lula when she was only eight. Leukemia took her, but not until she was seventeen." She lowered her voice.

It occurred to me that the screaming infant had calmed in the rear of the plane. Some of the passengers had begun to fall asleep. I had never taken photos of Joe's grave, and it seemed distasteful to do so. Grandmother-of-Lula seemed bent on reliving her last memory of this child in the worst place a child should be.

"She held on for four years. Thought we might get to keep her, but that last bone-marrow transplant failed."

I dug a traveler's packet of tissues from my purse and handed it to her. For my sake, I flipped to the next photograph. A young woman with a youthful face and a prim nose sat next to a fountain. "Is this Lula?" I asked.

"Lula's mother. My daughter-in-law, Nancy. She and my son James met at Chapel Hill."

"No way! That's my old alma mater." It was a polite way to change the subject.

"Doesn't seem fair that a mother would outlive her child," she said.

"I lost my husband two years ago. Seems like the pain might soon ease, but you just learn to live with it."

"That's why you have to embrace it. It's been six years since we lost Lula."

From the way she spoke, I had assumed the child had died only months ago.

"It's forever fresh. But so is the good Lord's grace. It's new every day."

"I had hoped for a respite from the pain," I said. *Six years.*

"This is new for me, too. You know you fall into valleys in life, little problems in marriage, on the job, what have you. But when you lose a grandchild, the valley becomes your permanent abode. You don't climb out. Valleys have sunshine too, green grass, and growing things. It's not a walk in the park, mind you. But I've found an abundance of peace. Dear, do you know God?" she asked.

I nodded. Her hand slid on top of mine on the armrest. I had known him better in the last twenty-four hours than in my whole life put together.

"It's hard to imagine that God gives us pain as a gift. Doesn't seem the least bit fathomable at first. But it's like getting a new pair of glasses. You see life a little more clearly. Certainly you feel a lot closer to heaven," she said.

"You do. It's true. It's as though I once thought of heaven as far away. When I lost Joe, I spent more time thinking about things I can't see and certainly can't explain. It's as though I've decided I need to be ready, like I've got my passport stamped and ready for the trip."

The flight attendant appeared with the drink cart.

I asked my seatmate about her daughter-in-law.

"Lula was such a big part of Nancy's life. She was a bubbly kid, all denim and dirt bikes, who really loved God. Sometimes it seems as though that makes it harder to let her go."

"I suppose she tries to stay busy, keep her mind occupied with other things," I said.

"Actually, Nancy finds comfort in solitude and looks for quiet ways to remember Lula. She and James go away on Lula's birthday and take photos that remind them of the way she laughed. Lula was a regular comedienne. Never let us have a serious day. I didn't mean to get off on all of that. Tell me what you do for a living. I notice you've been holding that journal the whole trip."

I told her about the *Sentinel* and my work for the *Observer*.

"I've always wanted to own a little newspaper outfit. I was a journalist when I met Alfred. You must be on your way downtown, then," she said.

"Not actually."

"I'm almost positive I've seen your name then. Not that I eat out as much since my husband passed. I hate to eat alone."

I turned her attention to the cirrus clouds that had formed wisps outside the airplane window. The flight attendant almost sprinted back up the aisle to retrieve the litter while the other one announced that we should buckle our seat belts again.

"Such a short flight. I'm glad we met. By the way, I'm Geraldine Montague."

"Not Senator Alfred Montague's Geraldine?" I was shocked.

"God rest his soul." She stuffed magazines and candies back into her bag.

My face flushed.

"We're flying over his interstate right now." She pointed to a busy artery of throughway.

I craned to see it.

"Seems like they'd run out of bridges and interstates to dedicate. Alfred never knew he had an interstate named after him. I don't think he would have liked it. Maybe early in his young campaign years, but not later. He would have thought it ostentatious."

"I'm so glad we met," I said.

The landing gear dropped beneath us.

She snapped a business card out of her wide canvas purse and handed it to me. "I had these made up just for fun. Helps people remember me."

I wondered how anyone could forget Geraldine and her exotic turban.

May had blown its billows across the South and opened the door to the warm garden of summer. I stepped out into the heat with my bag and found the rental-car lot. Gloria's nagging had not produced a completely smoke-free car, but it was better than some I had rented.

Rush-hour traffic bunged the Charlotte highways like bumper cars at the county fair.

After forty-five minutes, I inched my way to the Cornelius exit, the middle village on Lake Norman. My stomach growled although the flight had stolen my appetite. I imagined Ruth scrambling around the kitchen preparing for the evening meal. Instead of interrupting their Saturday-night ritual, I stopped and had a sandwich at a Honey Baked Ham, stalled another hour at a home-decorating store called The Black Lion, and then drove up and down the stretch of lake near Colin's house. He lived on the peninsula, code for where elitists moved old lake houses off half-acre lots to build four-story walk-ups. Over coffee, Ruth had told me that Colin and Eva had snatched up the modest lake house when everyone else identified the lake as swamp living, before New Yorkers had spotted Lake Norman as a little slice of suburbia and developed it as a haven for millionaires. Eva found ways to stretch small living quarters into wide open spaces including a billiard and game room in the basement.

I toyed with an alibi.

If by chance Brady lingered in his office, I could connect with him about the pirate article, thereby giving me the proper business angle so that I could legitimately tell Colin I had breezed into town on business rather than let on that I wanted to beg another invitation from him. Several times I rehearsed the telling of it: *Hi, Colin. I'm in town on business with the* Charlotte Observer. *No. I'm meeting with Mr. Gallagher tomorrow about developing a column for possible syndication. . . .*

Brady's phone rang until it switched over to the operator who offered to forward me to his voice mail. I hung up.

From the rounded and curbed corner, Colin's house blended with the years-old trees, an emerald-green house that looked deceptively small from the street.

The airline ticket stub hung out of the front zippered pocket of my handbag. Though wrangled by Gloria on a budget ticket Web site, it was still treacherously expensive. I imagined writing it off my taxes come January and recalling the night I sat outside Colin's house to watch the sun slide into Lake Norman before I skulked home undetected.

Out of the foliage, a jeep appeared. Lights blazed in the dim glow of a young evening. I saw Ruth heading away from Colin's house, loaded down with Arnett children. I felt idiotic parked three blocks away; a stalker who waited for the sun to dissolve like sugar on the lake. Alibis raced through my mind. I dove for the recesses of the passenger-side floor and excavated through absolutely nothing. Ruth never saw me, and I realized that the car I sat in was completely foreign to her.

Colin was home alone. My bowels knotted around my throat.

I must say there are moments when imagination is a woman's darling friend. You can, as a writer, sit with your mind floating on a placid stream of consciousness and conjure scenes that come to life. Vivid only to you, they feed you with enough audacity to help you take paths you might otherwise avoid. I might do well to avoid them, but what I imagined sat upon the plate of my mind's eye, pleasing. Alluring but unsullied and enticing, I felt as comfortable speaking with him as I did my own father and saw the whole thing played out as plain as my own hands in front of me: The two of us conversed on his sofa an unsafe distance from one another. But the very idea, the danger of failure elicited in my thoughts caused me to pull right into the drive, pull back out, park, walk through the neighbor's backyard and stand a safe distance from Colin's rear patio. The only thing I had to catch sight of, I decided, was Colin himself moving about the house. After that, I assured myself, I would sidle back around to the front landing and ring his doorbell.

Through a set of tall windows, a candelabrum flickered on the dining table. I moved in closer because white window sheers obstructed a clear view. But for certain, Colin seated himself with his back to the window. He ate alone.

Not more than a half-minute passed when I caught sight of another person. She placed a water glass in front of Colin and another near the place setting next to him. Ruth had never mentioned a cook or a maid, but we did not discuss every detail of our everyday lives.

The woman lit candles, for Pete's sake! Her face radiated a confidence, a rare shade of self-assurance that shone through the window sheers. Tranquillity was her beauty as well as an auburn hair color she had purchased, in my estimation, at great cost. Colin entertained a dinner guest. Or from this distance it appeared she entertained him.

The airline ticket stub flapped against my leg. I shoved it deep into the purse pocket. My knees turned gelatinous. When I looked up again the woman had stopped halfway without completely taking her seat. She said something to Colin and both of them turned to look out the window toward me. I stepped sideways to hide my face, but twisted my ankle and toppled onto the lawn. Years ago, Eva must have gotten the idea in her head to install an automatic lawn sprinkler. It came on.

By the time I dug my shoe out of the bog that had formed near the window bed, Colin and his date disappeared to see what was the matter with the woman who swam about the back yard. But they found no one for I had already sprinted up the side yard and leaped into the rental car to speed toward the airport, and back to Candle Cove. Where I belonged.

The sky, black and ugly, overshadowed my six-hour drive back to the coast. Several times I attempted to call Gloria with the intent that I would bribe her into telling no one about my mad flight to Charlotte. I would pay her whatever she asked.

Nineteen

FIVE WEEKS PASSED SINCE I HAD TAKEN A ROLL
through Colin Arnett's backyard lawn. The long gap in days that had
passed since then had to equal the pure embarrassment I felt for having traipsed off to Lake Norman after a man. Julia Norville would
have turned green around her feminine little gills if she had been privy
to such things in Glory.

Gloria managed to pull snatches of information out of me until she
had the humiliating whole. The fact that Colin never bothered to pursue me any further with phone calls annoyed her, but I never agreed
with her outwardly. I pretended to only care about the newspaper business and in her estimable opinion that morphed me into a calculating
machine incapable of feelings, while inwardly I fumed that Colin had
not pursued me or at least called to find out if he was blind or if he
had indeed witnessed my undoing in his very own backyard.

"So you aren't in the least bit put out?" asked Gloria.

I shook my head.

Gloria's stomach expanded seemingly with heliumlike velocity. By
the end of June, her short frame heaved the extra weight around like
an ant hefting an M&M. Eric the pet man's capacity to love a married woman amplified by the time Gloria crossed the doorstep to her

second trimester. He brought by imported pickles and chocolate spoons to be stirred into the gourmet coffees left at night upon our doormat.

Phil Hammer, who enjoyed Eric's extravagant gifts lavished upon his wife, phoned her in the afternoon on some days to see what Eric had dropped secretly through the night drop or placed in the driver's seat of Gloria's Carman Ghia.

Summer once again visited our cove. I developed my journal entries about the island mustangs into a short piece. I slipped it through the fax machine one night so that it would be waiting on Brady's office floor when he came in the next morning.

Mason and Jerry Brevity took to sailing the *Sparticus* around the inlet every Friday in the early evenings while I came to a decision. I rehearsed gentle ways to ease Jerry on down the river. Jerry arrived with his usual bag of burgers that he passed out to me, invisibly stamped with obligation although his hints were becoming more blatant attempts to seal a commitment. I joined him on the shore for a ceremonial send-off, but grew weary of the way he tried to hold my hand or hook his arm through mine. "Jerry, we need to talk. I just don't know how we could ever be anything more than friends."

"It's that minister guy that's come between us," he said to me.

I held a finger over my lips, stepped toward the boat where Mason had already clambered aboard, and told my son to snap on his life jacket. I stopped Jerry before he boarded. "If you're spending time with Mason to be a nice man, I appreciate it. But, Jerry, whatever you hoped might happen, it just isn't happening for me."

It was Jerry's last voyage aboard the *Sparticus*. But that did not stop Mason from wanting to go out in her.

I took the dog for a walk on the beach one day. Mason was untying the boat alone. I threatened him with floggings and made him promise to never attempt to sail single-handedly no matter how calm the water.

"I'm not a little kid, and I know how to sail!" Mason battled with me once again.

"The *Sparticus* isn't a toy, and you know how I feel about taking it out again anyway. I wish we'd just left her in your grandfather's shed."

"It's not my fault Dad took her into a storm. You're punishing me for what he did, and I know it."

"Mason, don't make me say it."

"Say what?"

"That I'll sell her if you keep pushing me like this."

"You can't sell this boat! It's really mine anyway. You don't want it but you don't want me to have it." Mason charged down the shore kicking at seashells and jellyfish carcasses that had washed ashore.

Brady Gallagher accepted my pirate piece but rejected my mustang story ideas twice before I figured out he wanted no slices of island life, just the history. I could no more interest him in a story about the mustangs than I could entice him away from the trout in the spring. He did show an interest in the Pamlico ghosts. I developed it from two different angles and promised that I would personally visit the site of the headless lantern ghost at the railroad crossing at whatever place it happened, if indeed it happened. I would report it accordingly, in spite of my reservations.

I sat out on my father's dock and by lantern light read the meanderings of my journal while Mason night fished. Until he had the Buckworth twins to compete with, he had complained at the very mention of fishing. Now they headed for his grandfather's dock at least twice a week.

One evening off Nags Head, I had sloughed around the bog and listened to the spatter of sound fish upon the water's surface. I identified nothing, not even a long-legged bird that fed on fish in the shallows. But I had used the phrase *clean tide* every so often. I had truly encountered God at Nags Head. What came of it altered my perception of Christ, and now I served Him beyond words. I had written down a sentence taken from scripture. "This people honors me with their lips. But their heart is far from me." God was teaching me a better way. I honored Him now in my heart with more than tradition and talk.

Mason snagged three striped bass.

"You'll be wanting me to cook them, I gather," I said.

From a cord, he dangled them in front of me.

"Bass are supposed to be, what, broiled?"

He shrugged. "All's I can do is clean them. I know how. Grandpa taught me the best way to do it."

Five children who visited their grandparents up the shore ran along the sand with flashlights, searching for crab.

"Summer is too short," said Mason.

"We still have more summer left. Don't shortchange it with worry."

"Jerry says he has this special ingredient for bass."

I sighed. "Mason, I told you not to expect to see Jerry so often."

"I don't want to share these fishes anyway. Except with Grandpa," he said. He saw that pleased me.

I dug my phone out of my purse and hit the speed-dial button, Brady Gallagher's home phone number. I had manipulated it from him after my debacle in Charlotte. He answered as though he were waiting for my call.

"I got your pirate piece. Everyone has read it. You've got a star with your name on it in newspaper heaven."

I interrupted him while I had the nerve. "Brady, I've come to a decision."

"You'll marry me."

"I don't want to write travel pieces, or ghost stories."

He waited as though he felt I had more to say. I did.

"For the life of me, I don't know what it is that is churning up inside of me. But it smacks faintly of something deeper than what I've been doing."

"But does it smack of filthy lucre?"

"Everything doesn't have to be about money."

"Bite your tongue."

"When you go away to the mountains, you have time to reflect on your life. This doesn't move you in some way?" I asked.

"Oh, you're talking deep. Well, I've never confessed this to anyone, but when I'm standing out in the middle of that clear stream with nothing but me and the fish, it gives me pause. Like, someday they'll walk into my office and find me gone. A note will be taped to my chair."

"Sakes alive! What kind of note?"

"Don't be morbid. It will say, 'Brady's gone fishing.'"

"That's deep."

"Maybe I'll go so far as to say I've set aside a little money. I've had my eye on this mountain cabin for a while. Any day that owner's going to come down on his price and I'll scoop it up with my bag of money. It would be a shame not to share it with someone."

"Brady, some really lucky woman is going to think you've handed her the chance of a lifetime."

"Just not you." He read my silence. "Thank you for not saying something cliché."

He deserved better.

"So you're not interested in the column." His voice sounded flat.

"You'd think that I would at least figure out what I do want first before I go off the porch clubbing all of the things I don't want."

He did that breathing thing editors do when they don't know how to agree or disagree.

"I knew you'd understand." I promised we would get together soon for lunch. He hung up.

The tide was coming in and subtracting the shoreline from the walkers. *I hope I've done the right thing, God. You know what happens next, and I don't. And that is just fine with me.*

Gloria watched me appraisingly. Two mornings in a row, I had slipped into the office at dawn. Both times she found me sitting at my desk, writing in my journal.

"Here's your fan mail from yesterday. I don't know if you meant to overlook it, but one piece appears to be a check from the *Charlotte Observer*."

"For the pirate piece. Oh good! It should be just enough to cover the new pair of shoes I ruined in Colin's backyard. Of course, the travel expense was a wash. One flight to Charlotte, two rental cars, a fairly decent ham sandwich, and a new pair of stockings."

I opened my journal and sat it next to my monitor. I typed some of it onto the screen to see how it looked in print.

"Let's see what else is in here. The rest are what looks to be the light bill and a letter from the President of the United States. He wants to do lunch with you next week, say Friday," she said.

"I realize you think I'm not listening to you, but I heard every word. I'll take the check." I turned around and snapped it out of her fingers.

She tightened the screws on the bill reminder with a Phillips screwdriver.

"You did a good job on your pregnancy series. The hospital bought extra copies to slip into their new mother gift package," I said.

"My feet are so swollen I had to wear sandals today. I hope you don't mind."

"I don't know. Might upset the dress code around here."

"If you don't want to tell me what you're doing here so early, March, you don't have to."

"Thank you."

She walked away, her face sullen.

"Oh, look," I waved and spoke with a strange jaded innocence. "This one's for you," I said. I stuck her envelope in the air.

We exchanged smiles.

She took it and opened it at her desk. Twice she blinked, then ran back to throw her arms around my neck.

"You're welcome. I figured you were the one who brought in the extra business. You deserve a bonus. But hide it. I don't want Lindle sniffing around for his bonus, like it's bonus day or something. I can't just toss out bonuses whenever I please."

"This will pay for a new crib," she said.

Later I called Phil and told him to stall her off on the crib. Shaunda had taken up a collection around the office. Instead of a baby shower, everyone opted for a new crib for Gloria and Phil. Not to be outdone, Eric filled a basket with stuffed pets and baby linens.

By the next day, my early mornings caught up with me.

"Subscriptions are down. Please, I need ideas, people," I said.

Shaunda raked sand in the wooden box on her desk, a Zen garden, though she wasn't a Buddhist. "I don't know how this reduces stress, but I'll give it a try."

Lindle lifted just high enough to show sleepy eyes over the top of his cubicle. "Don't look at me. I'm the ad guy," he said.

Gloria pressed cucumbers against her puffy eyes. "I need a massage. Do they do that for pregnant women?"

Wylie and Brendan ducked into the printing room.

"While you're in there, guys, please collect all those dirty coffee mugs. You could fill the pantry again with ceramics."

Gloria lifted my coffee mug and sniffed it. "You take a bossy pill or something?"

I just looked at her.

She watched the Poes skulk across the office with a box of clanking dishes.

"Just leave them by the sink, Wylie. I'll wash them for you," she said. She printed off the subscription list and handed it to me rather defensively.

Eric flounced in. He sported a completely new haircut although it was nothing more than a change of the part in his hair that made him look less like Opie Taylor and more like Andy.

"We're really busy, Eric," I said. Both of them ignored me, which made me feel more impatient.

Gloria blew out a breath.

He disregarded me and directed all of his attention on Gloria. "If you want me to stop by Saturday and paint the nursery, I checked my calendar and I am free. I still think lemon yellow is the best color since you want the baby's sex to remain a mystery until it's born."

"If you could discuss personal matters later, we might actually get some real work accomplished," I said.

Gloria fished a handful of paint samples out of her desk drawer. "You pick out the color then and just bring me the receipt."

Eric had already headed for the door and did not see the paint samples. "Frankly, I'm rooting for a girl and I hope she looks just like her mother," said Eric.

We watched him go.

"Gloria, a handful of female collegiates are home for the summer and while Eric moons over what will never be, and I say that with kindest concern, the parade passes him by. This doesn't bother you?"

"March, he's painting my nursery. Friends do nice things for one another," said Gloria. She yelled after him through the window. Like a happy sentinel, he stuck his head back through the doorway. She met him at the door, handed him the paint chips, and scooted him off to the animal farm.

"I have to head for Wharton's Pond. The Jaycees' summer duck races are today," said Shaunda.

"They train them to race?" Lindle asked, surprised.

"Rubber duckies, Lindle. As in, your mother put those little yellow toys in your bubble bath. You know, like a fund-raiser for the hospital children's fund?" Shaunda rubbed her finger over the painted daisy embedded in her manicure.

"I smell business people afoot. I'll go with you," Lindle said. He followed her out to her car.

"I need carbs. For the baby. I'll be right back." Gloria grabbed her knapsack of a purse and sauntered out behind them. The Poes tinkered around the sink. They commented about the amazing collection of mold and the awful shame of watching it glug down the drain. I held up the subscription list to the empty room. "So, any ideas, people, for increasing subscriptions?" Each of them scattered to the wind, confetti in a parade. *Okay, Lord, I'm still waiting on what's next. You're stretching me, right?*

Another silent answer.

Learning to wait was not an active image, but somehow I could feel God in it.

Gloria returned within the hour toting two bag lunches from Ruby's and a liter of soft drink.

"You didn't abandon me after all," I said.

"I got you the Reuben on rye, tortilla chips, and a sweet iced tea, extra ice."

"Are you mad at me for acting like the boss?"

"I like my job, March. The reason I like it is because you don't act like one."

"But if I don't take charge of the business it eats me alive."

"People are your business. The reason you do well is because everyone trusts you, they know you won't publish some left-wing propaganda mumbo jumbo, but that you will be fair and paint the world in living color."

"Am I fair?"

She set a paper plate in front of me and dropped a napkin onto my lap.

"Gloria, I'm sorry if I was rude to Eric."

"Eric eats Sunday dinner every weekend at my house after mass. Do you think Phil is worried? He and Eric are painting the nursery together."

"I should be taken out and shot, that's what."

"You take my salsa. It sends me to the throne room in a nanosecond."

"The Poes cleaned up the print room. I feel guilty about it."

"You shouldn't. Like you said, you're the boss."

"But I was harsh."

"That is true. But it was beginning to smell like my Uncle José's undershirts."

"I must have left my diplomacy at home this morning. When they get back from lunch I'll give them the afternoon off."

"I think you can't stop thinking about that preacher fellow."

"Nonsense." I used the remote to turn on the radio.

Dinah's otherwise live show had gone into reruns she called "The Best of Dinah." She introduced the show live, though. "Today's show teaches you how to make Valentine Cake, a dessert that is sure to please the main attraction in your life. I dedicate this show to a friend who shall remain anonymous, but who is as miserably in love as anyone I know."

I choked on my tea.

"Maybe she wasn't talking about you, March. You know, the whole world doesn't revolve around you. She knows you better than that anyway, that you have your head on straight and don't walk around in a stupor over some guy who is too lacking in persistence for you to care about."

"I find this is an exhausting conversation."

"But you do think about him. I wouldn't go so far as to say you're in love. That is just low for her to say it like that. If she's even talking about you. Do you want your pickle?"

"For all we know, the man is engaged and I am thankful and relieved to have my life uncomplicated by a long-distance relationship."

"I wonder if tuna contains choline. Or is it mercury? I can't remember anything today."

"But my attitude today has nothing to do with Colin. I'm writing a novel, if you have to know everything. It's beyond me how to start it, so I just began typing and it seems I have an opening to a chapter."

Gloria giggled.

"I shouldn't have told you."

"I'm happy as a clam for you. Finally, you're doing something for yourself for a change."

"I didn't think of it like that."

Gloria fished emeralds of pickle out of the tuna salad with a fork and ate them separate from the sandwich.

Dad called from the cottage to tell me the news: Bill Simmons invited a pastoral candidate in for a speaking engagement. He was from Pennsylvania. Colin's candidate had fizzled. He showed no interest in a small-town congregation.

Yolanda had picked up Mason and taken him to a movie. Dad said that before she came Mason had made them both turkey-and-lettuce sandwiches. He requested that I stock the cottage pantry with finer delicacies such as canned ham, cheddar, and bologna.

The Poes returned but would not hear of leaving for the day. They could not fathom at what moment I had offended them.

Brendan stepped out of the bathroom and pointed imperiously. "Help! The toilet is squealing again."

Gloria got out her wrench and worked her stomach between the toilet and the tight space of cabinet.

I handed her tools while she executed her magic.

"I've been thinking. If we know for certain that we are only going to attract a certain percentage of Candle Cove, then we need to expand our circulation all the way out to Cedar Island," she said.

"Why didn't I think of that? And I just came from there too. Lindle could approach the few stores along the way with an ad that targets the tourists, but include coupons for the locals who have to shop in those mom-and-pops along Highway 70 and in Beaufort." I ran for my pen and pad and wrote while Gloria and I brainstormed.

Shaunda returned with photographs from the duck race.

"Hop and shop at the mom-and-pop," said Gloria.

"They don't know we call them that, Gloria." I kept writing. "It isn't a compliment."

She gave her lyrics a melody.

"If anybody wants to know, I just sold a story to a newspaper in New York," said Shaunda.

"The *Times?* No way," said Gloria.

"Not the *Times*. But it isn't far from the Big Apple, and it wouldn't surprise me at all if this didn't lead to bigger things." Shaunda covered her egg roll from Ginger's with paper and placed it in the refrigerator.

"The phone again! Shaunda, will you please get it this time?" Gloria turned sideways to make more room for her stomach, but it did not help.

"March, it's for you. Someone by the name of Simone," said Shaunda.

I had visited Victoria Lane only once more since our first encounter before my trip to Ocracoke. "Simone? Is something wrong?"

"The family has been called in. Vicki is in a coma, and they don't expect her to last through the night." Simone sounded short of breath.

A nurse had placed several vases of flowers on a table outside Victoria Lane's window in ICU. I found Carla and Simone holding on to one another. An RN closed the curtain.

"I didn't make it," I said.

"Vicki just took a breath and was gone." Carla pulled a sweater about her shoulders.

I stepped into Vicki's room.

Herb had both hands clasped behind his neck. Both of us observed the stillness of a life just crossed over. He pulled the Gideon Bible out of his wife's hands. "I don't think they would mind if I kept this."

We left the room. I gave him my father's number and told him that Dad would like to speak with him. Together they could discuss the funeral arrangements.

I waited until I returned to the car. Then I pulled out a box of tissues and cried.

Before I picked up Mason, I dropped by the *Sentinel* to help Gloria lock up.

"I'm sorry about your friend." Gloria fastened the tool chest.

"Vicki's just not here anymore, that's all. Heaven is just another country." I waited until she left and then allowed myself to cry again. God had somehow used me to point the way to Him when I was just coming alive in my soul myself.

"You are a mystery sometimes, Father. You reveal yourself in ways that surprise me." I wondered what other mysteries and surprises lay beyond the valley.

Twenty

HERB LANE FOUND CHRIST. NO ONE HAILED IT AS AN overnight conversion. I compared it more to dawn. The light sends the night away and then incrementally reveals the source. Either you stay in bed or you embrace the sun. Herb embraced the Son.

First he showed up one Sunday and sat on the back pew. Bill Simmons joined him and invited him to stay for the church social. We did not see him again for two weeks. After that, he never missed a Sunday.

Herb could not keep quiet about his transformation. That made a few veterans of the faith green-eyed, but they painted their envy with condescension. He set to work carving little praying hands out of wood and passing them out to people so that each of us might remember the carpenter who set men free. Although not a soul seemed aware of the difference in their take on God and Herb's, I was grateful I finally did.

I placed the carving he gave to me on the kitchen windowsill beneath Charlotte's origami angels.

His sister-in-law Simone came into town for a visit, to help Herb box up Vicki's things. She brought her sons for a visit with their Uncle Herb on the weekend they didn't have to go and see their father.

Simone found a mouse in the attic and screamed until the next-door neighbor ran out into the yard. Herb did what everyone in Candle Cove did. He called Jerry. I am almost positive I saw the rat truck parked outside Herb's door for three nights in a row. Jerry must have been tending to other things besides rodents.

It was his time.

The pulpit committee settled on a candidate for the pastorate, the gentleman from Pennsylvania. From a video, the Reverend Frederick Tuck, a thin minister with a shoehorn-shaped posture, crooned the offertory with his wife, Lilly, while she played the organ. The Caudles and the Michaels forgave him the necessity of modern media techniques and applauded his time-honored views and oral execution of the sacraments. My father questioned the validity of offertory songs but agreed the sacraments and Tuck's immaculate views outweighed his one divergent practice. Bill and Irene Simmons lived for the day the telephone on their kitchen wall stopped resonating with impatient callers from the congregation. They found not even the teensiest flaw. Even as the candidate clambered into the rigors of the credentials committee and the meetings on the presbytery floor, we met and asked grace and guidance from above.

The fall sky appeared hard as glass to me, and I imagined our prayers hitting the ceiling of the earth and ricocheting off like tennis balls. When Reverend Tuck sermonized, a restless wind blew into my heart. It seemed a man could master the song and dance of church doctrine and still miss the calling. Every pastor, my mother said, was a watering hole, to some a crystal stream and others a neglectful algae pool. Not that Pastor Tuck with his simpering glances at his wife fell into any sour extreme. But some men lead while others just manage. Tuck was a maintainer if ever I saw one. I withheld my opinions, having found solace in quiet observance.

Bill and Irene Simmons hosted a dinner party for Dad in the fellowship hall Sunday evening after the service. But no one dared call it a going-away party. The children's club decorated the hall with crepe paper and a computer banner that said WE LOVE PASTOR NORVILLE surrounded by a border of hearts and cupids. Lorraine Bedinsky designed arrangements of diminutive potted mums with imaginative miniature spades and artsy-craftsy potter's tools. A youth with calligraphy ability designed small placards according to Lorraine's specifications. She placed the cards around the clay pots in such a way to indicate my father had gardened or tended the souls of men, the master cultivator, or some such metaphor that not everyone got, though Dad did. I saw him dab his eyes.

The only matter that kept me from the total enjoyment of the festivities, aside from the nagging worries about candidate Tuck, was the fact that early Monday I had to attend the trial of the two convicts that had held Yolanda at knife point. Since I was the key witness, the prosecuting attorney, Judd Neisen, placed my testimony at the crux of the trial. He called it open-and-shut, but I was well aware that the examination gave the New Jersey inmates another good gander at my face. In a town the size of Candle Cove, a good hiding place was nowhere to be found. But the boys' criminal trail stretched across four state lines, including a robbery spree all the way through the Chesapeake Bay that implicated them in four counties. Judd said the yellow Yanks faced a city full of witnesses for the next three years. By the time they peeked into the free light of day, their revenge list would be tethered to a foggy history.

Two little girls from the M&Ms, the Sunday night Memorization and More club, dragged my long-handled handbag across the floor.

"Your purse is chirping, Mrs. Longfellow," said one.

"My phone. Thanks, girls."

On the phone I heard a young woman sniff. She cleared her throat.

"May I help?" I asked.

"I'm Brady Gallagher's daughter, Jenny Owens. I just flew in from Dallas. It's Daddy. He's had a heart attack. They put him in intensive care here at Mercy Hospital. I know you're supposed to call people in instances like this, but I don't live here and he's not in a position to tell me whom I should call. I found his Christmas-card list and your name is at the top." Her voice had the sound of a young woman on her own for too long against her will. Her personality was not as well defined as her father's. She could not have been as educated or worldly-wise. I remember her small childhood portrait on his credenza, a plump girl whose deportment left uncomfortable inches between herself and her father with her round arms crossed in front of her.

"I'm Brady's friend. You did the right thing. How long is the list?"

"Five names long."

"Where is Brady?"

"At the Heart Center at Mercy."

"I don't suppose they've given you a prognosis."

"It's serious. My little brother, Will, just walked in. He lives in Kansas. I have to go."

Dad sat at the center of a ring of admirers. He sipped punch from a crystal mug kept full by Lorraine Bedinsky. If he ever noticed her admiration he did not indicate so. Her lack of loveliness would not have been the deterrent. My mother was a beautiful woman, but even women like her fade with years. Though even with cancer, Mother had never lost her splendor. Lorraine fluttered around my father while he acknowledged her with the same nod he might offer to a domestic.

He caught my eye and read the gloom in my thoughts.

"Pardon me." He dismissed himself from the well-wishers and joined me next to the punch bowl. "My daughter has a problem?"

"My newspaper friend, Brady Gallagher, Dad. He's had a heart attack."

"He's too young to join that club."

"Brady's forty-three. His eating habits would make you the king of health food. They've placed him in ICU in downtown Charlotte."

"Maybe you should go to Charlotte."

"I have to testify at that trial Monday. That's tomorrow morning. Judd said we could be tied up for days."

Dad clasped his hands around mine. "You'll have to send someone in your place. If you think about it for a bit, I'm sure you'll come up with a name." He joined the circle again.

Colin Arnett and I had not spoken for the length of the summer. Pastors could find admittance to ICU when even relatives could not. I felt desperate. I dialed his number.

It rang twice. He answered himself.

I hesitated. His voice sounded warm, expectant.

"Anyone there?"

"Colin, it's me, March. I have a problem. If I could handle it myself, believe me I would."

"March, I've been thinking about you. How are you?"

I was surprised. "I'm good. But I have a friend in need."

"What can I do to help?"

"Brady Gallagher, at the *Charlotte Observer*, he's had a heart attack. They rushed him by ambulance to Mercy Hospital. Near you, I think." My breath sucked in while I stifled a tear.

"He must mean a lot to you." Colin turned from the phone and scolded Troy and Luke for not taking their baths.

"Brady and I, we've been friends for years. Like Dinah and me."

"It's after eight. I'll call first and see if they'll allow me in. I know someone at Mercy. Does he have a pastor or a priest I should call?"

"No one."

"I'll go right away."

I expected him to hang up. But I heard him still breathing. Then a pause.

"I'd like to ask a favor of you, too," he said.

"Anything. I'm so appreciative of this, Colin. I know it's late. I know I haven't contacted you in a while."

"Thursday evening, I have to attend a banquet in Wilmington. It's an annual event. Your father and I first met at this ministers' banquet, two old widowed bachelors. The wife of one of our deacons is pressuring me to take her niece. I'd like to tell her I've made other arrangements. If you'd rather not go, I understand."

"Thursday night in Wilmington." I pretended to check my calendar. "Is it a formal affair?"

"Semiformal. But you look nice in anything. In my opinion."

I refrained from asking him if he saw me that night flitting around in his sprinkler system, wearing his lawn. "I believe I can go."

The next morning I climbed the stone steps to the courthouse. Fall trickled into the cove dropping summer temperatures to a bearable blister. Our fall provided its own tonic for the vacation weary, our shores a comfortable pillow for strangers, our streets a welcome mat. But climbing the steps to participate in a highly publicized trial made me feel anything but welcome. Photographers from newspapers and magazines snapped pictures of every person who entered the courthouse down to the hefty tax assessor who wiped jam from his bottom lip.

Judd Niesen met me at the door.

If Colin met with Brady or any of his family, he did not call later Sunday night to inform me of it. After the first court recess, I would call Mercy Hospital and see how Brady had fared through the night.

Judge Bernard Joiner presided over the trial, brother of the mayor whose heated mayoral race had dominated the front page of the *Sentinel* the entire summer. A news crew from a Raleigh television station pulled up at the base of the steps just as Judd whisked me inside.

Yolanda's excitement spilled over when she heard the TV news crew had arrived.

"March, my savior!" She hugged me and then stepped aside to allow her mother, Toni Goya, to shake my hand.

Toni never made eye contact, distracted by the camera crew. "We have not slept in a week, March. Worse than that is the absolute nightmare of this trial. Ever since these hideous men tried to abduct our baby girl, well, I can't tell you how it has disrupted our entire lives. I hope they put them away so far they can't find themselves, that's what. I'm just glad my Frank is in Washington State this week or I don't know what he would do the minute he saw them."

"I might need therapy," Yolanda said. The thought made her smile.

"He's not one to contend with." Toni Goya checked her face in the mirror of a powder compact. The whites of her eyes were pink, most likely from the neglected rest. Her teeth appeared a stark white, a product of expensive bleach trays.

Yolanda met the news crew at the door. Her attorney blew out a breath, stepped ahead of her to give the crew a "no comment until after the trial" statement, and led her down the hall and into a room. Toni followed them. I took a seat inside the courtroom.

If the accused man who had held the knife recognized me, he did not show it on his face. The only reaction I saw was when Yolanda and her mother entered the room. He shifted uncomfortably in his chair and leaned sideways to receive counsel from his attorney.

Yolanda's counselor must have scolded her for her candidness with the paparazzi. She seated herself somberly, her skirt falling prettily over her knees. Once or twice she allowed her eyes to regard the convict with disdain, careful that Judge Joiner failed to observe the reaction.

At exactly twelve, Joiner called for a recess for lunch. Yolanda met me out in the hall, asked if I carried a compact, and checked her rubescent cheeks thrice. I slipped away and ate alone in the courthouse cafeteria, exhausted by Yolanda's bubbly discourse on courtroom procedure and how she felt just every ounce of support from the jury issuing toward her like petals off a cherry tree, or some such. After several attempts to call Mercy, I finally reached a nurse who told me Brady was resting well, but she knew nothing about a visit from a pastor.

By the time Judd called me to the stand, it was thirty minutes after we had returned from lunch. Bill and Irene Simmons's daughter, Darlene, swore me in. She had a sweet demeanor that said she had been loved to death, but a pursy voice due to her size. Her squash-shaped frame filled up the straight-legged police trousers like bratwurst. She spoke to me in a manner that let everyone know we were acquaintances. That put me at ease somewhat.

Judd exercised precision in setting up the entire scenario of my part in the confrontation. "Would you point to the victim?"

I pointed to Yolanda, who allowed a small smile to dimple her cheek.

"Mrs. Longfellow, would you describe what you saw, please?" said Judd.

"Yolanda Goya has been my baby-sitter for many years. I was on the way home from the grocery store loaded down with corn and shrimp, and that's when I saw this hideous man put his hands on Yolanda."

Judd asked me to point out the criminal.

"Let the record show that the witness, March Longfellow, is pointing to the accused, Sam Jackson," said Judd. He asked me to continue.

"For the life of me, I could not think straight. If I called the police and just waited, well, then they might get away and take Yolanda with them. They say that once a person is kidnapped, her chances of making it home safely again are slight. So I told them they better stop what they were doing or something like that."

Jackson's attorney objected. Judge Joiner ordered me to say exactly what I said that day.

"I told them I was the police and to drop their weapon. I asked them to lay on the parking lot until our two cops, Harold and Bobby, arrived."

"Did you use a weapon, Mrs. Longfellow?"

"Not exactly."

"Describe how you apprehended the accused man, Samuel Jackson, and his partner, Eddy Fallon."

"With my son's water pistol."

Everyone laughed, and that really upset Judge Joiner. He had observed enough land-border arguments and sow-odor disputes to last his whole life. This trial was big publicity for our county, and he wanted it treated with importance.

"Were you questioned about the use of a weapon by the arresting officers, Mrs. Longfellow?" asked Judd.

"I gave it to them. Mason would really like it back." Bobby winked and gave me a thumbs-up as though he would handle the matter later.

Judd held up the water pistol. A tag dangled from it marked Exhibit B.

Joiner rapped the bench to quell the laughter again. "Mrs. Longfellow, I ask that you simply answer the prosecutor with a simple yes or no."

I tried.

The accused, Sam Jackson, stared at the tabletop the whole time. That helped settle my nerves.

After I finished my testimony, the judge called a recess until the next day.

I approached Judd. "I have to leave town early Thursday afternoon. Is that a problem?

"I'll let you know by Wednesday for certain, March. You did great today."

I had a headache. I hated the uncertainty of Judd's comment. I disappeared from the hall and down the courthouse steps before the news crew crowded around the victim and her family. Next door to the courthouse, a wedding party collected and waited for the bride and groom to appear from the old Methodist church. White wreaths with enormous satin bows hung on the centuries-old double doors of the church. I passed through the throng, a woman on a mission.

Madame Fergie's Boutique was having a sale. If heaven was in my favor, by Thursday I'd need a dress, semiformal.

On Thursday morning, Judd dismissed me entirely. At first, relief washed through me. But as soon as I descended the courthouse steps, I was nearly giddy. Then I thought about being alone with Colin and saying the stupidest things. So, by reason of insecurity, fear replaced giddiness. I was without any excuse for turning down Colin's invitation and glad about it.

Also petrified.

Yolanda stayed with Mason after school, and I gave them money for pizza and a rental movie.

Dad, if he formed any opinion at all about the meeting with Colin Arnett (I called it a meeting), offered none of it, and I did not share so much as a glimmer of the elation that was slowly overtaking me. I knew he would just stare at me smug, self-satisfied, and all at once the seer to this whole evening out.

The only route to Wilmington was the scenic coastal route. I traveled past Cape Carteret and Sneads Ferry until I connected with High-way 17. It was a picturesque route that allowed me to slip in Wilmington's back door, so to speak, and avoid the traffic that pa-raded in from Interstate 40.

I followed Colin's directions to the Hilton Riverside. A concierge directed me to a powder room where I changed for the evening and freshened up. A young woman just in town from Raleigh for a smaller dinner event wandered in to find a quiet place to take a prescription drug. She shook out two pills with her manicured fingers. Then she helped me with my dress zipper and with the hook and eye that is never easy to do alone.

She wore a shimmering teal calf-length sequined dress that had slits from calf to thigh. Her blond hair was upswept and then cascaded all around the back of her head in curls. She looked like a mermaid.

"I can never find a good black dress," she said to me.

If she was complimenting my own black creation from Madame Fergie's I could not tell.

"They all look the same, as though the buyers all think we women are in too big of a hurry to shop so we'll just take whatever. As if!"

"I actually took my time with this one," I said.

"That's what I'm trying to say. Always with the foot-in-mouth, my ex would say. Yours is so appealing with those sheer shoulders and sleeves. You have the shoulders for it. Well formed, like you don't have to do tricep weights or nothing. Not many girls could wear your dress. Nice choice."

What a relief! I had the mermaid's blessing.

The Hilton connected with an enormous floating dock. I left my day-wear and makeup kit in the Mustang and then took a walk near the ocean. The Ministerial Alliance banquet did not start for another hour, just enough time to have a full-blown anxiety attack. I wondered what Julia might say to her daughter right now. Might she offer me advice on table etiquette or how to sit, feet together, never crossing my legs? Or would she say how lovely I looked in black? Or disapprove of my moving on, away from Joe? Or with her new heavenly mind-set, somehow approve of Colin? Or approve of me?

A small orchestra rehearsed underneath snapping flags. The music soothed and wafted along the stream of early-evening breezes. I found a table and sat for a while to watch the tourists pad away only to emerge dressed for dancing and evening dinner parties. An older gentleman walked a younger lady half his age onto a yacht the size of a house. The moon appeared even though the daylight would dominate the harbor until well past eight o'clock. I followed the older yacht man and that giggling woman with my eyes and thought how mismatched the two of them looked. Colin was taller than Joe by at least three inches. People once commented how well matched Joe and I were. Until the walk on the beach I had not compared our heights. I wondered if people would look at Colin and me together and declare us mismatched.

I saw a flash of black coat. A gentleman seated himself at the table next to mine but I felt mesmerized by the yacht people.

I pulled out a stick of gum and chewed it.

Colin had asked me to meet him in the hotel lobby by seven. Thirty minutes to go. I felt awkward about that now. I imagined walking through the doors with a self-conscious smile to give the room a once-over only to find he was late. I would stand in the lobby, my high-heeled shoes gnawing at my feet while people I did not know swam around me as though I were a post in the shallows.

"I hate walking into parties too early. But here I am, too early. I must be nervous." The gentleman at the nearby table spoke. He sat alone with his back to me and it occurred to me that bewilderment seized this poor fellow enough to cause him to talk to himself. He turned around and smiled at me.

"Colin!" I think I swallowed my gum. "You should have joined me. I hope I didn't appear rude."

"You looked peaceful. I couldn't bring myself to disturb you."

Couples gathered around the orchestra to dance, men dressed in military dress uniforms and women in formals. The mermaid joined her lieutenant in a slow waltz.

"Your friend, Brady, he's going to be fine," he said casually, almost as though he assumed I knew.

"I keep missing him when I call. He's either sleeping or they've got him up and walking. They do that so fast nowadays." My eyes followed the progression of his movement, back relaxed against the chair, right foot and left hand tapping to the orchestral strains. "Thank you for coming to the aid of my friend. He knows nothing about God. I just thought you might help."

"We talked about God. Brady attended Sunday school as a kid."

"I never knew that."

"He might call me later." He turned slowly around in his chair, his leg crossed over his other knee. "The banquet inside will last a good two hours. I'll bet no one ordered an orchestra, either."

"One never knows. It's an interdenominational crowd."

"Have a go with me, March. The sun is going down."

"This isn't our party, Colin. Should we?"

He took my hand and led me onto the floating dock. We danced through the next three songs.

The sun disappeared and we could see the banquet hall filled with ministers and wives.

"We don't have to go inside." He said it while he looked right into my anxiety-laced eyes. "I'd rather not, come to think of it."

"But you came all this way for it," I answered, hoping he wouldn't listen to me.

"March, you can lay down your walls now. We don't have to play polite games."

Is that what I was doing? I felt his hand brush what the mermaid had termed my well-formed shoulder.

"We have to eat, I suppose. Wouldn't want to send you home hungry." He extended one hand as though he intended to lead me toward the hotel lobby.

First I laid my hand inside his. Then I screeched to a stop. "Colin, I want to finish what you just said to me. I have laid aside some walls since we spoke last. Some between God and me and some I had in place to ward off pain. You have to know that my timetable for healing is set at a different pace that yours."

I wanted to be next to him again, to dance. It is beyond me why I could not have said that instead.

"I know you came to Lake Norman that evening when I had a guest."

Oh, just great! "So you know I'm a fool." I said it matter-of-factly, as though I commented on the weather.

"I didn't want to see that woman. You have to understand the friends who badger me with eligible women friends. But I don't apologize for wanting a social life again."

"You weren't expecting me. I deserved to feel like an idiot." I hoped he would disagree with me as swiftly as possible.

"Please don't give excuses for me, March. Not that I did anything wrong. You know it and so do I. I didn't know you were coming and you—surprised me."

He didn't have to take it that far. "I wanted to surprise you. Are you saying that's wrong?"

"It isn't always a good idea. Not until you know someone better."

"It was a mistake." I felt a knot in my throat grow bigger than the one I got worrying over saying something stupid.

"So we both agree and that's that." He clasped his hands together as though he were in charge of punctuation, putting the big period at the end of our conversation.

"I feel as though we're having a fight, but we couldn't be because we don't know one another well enough and a quarrel would ruin the night. We have a moon out. Could we just dance again?" I asked. Marriage had its seesaws, but all of these undefined parameters spinning around Colin and me were complicated

The orchestra played "How Can I Remember?"

"I've made you uncomfortable. Let's start over. How about dinner? If I had stayed with the plan, we'd be inside cutting up our pâté and exchanging pleasantries right now."

He obviously didn't know what pâté was. I liked that in a man.

"Join me for dinner, please, March," he said, looking self-injected with regret.

I took his hand. Perhaps I was right about the bewildered man seated next to me.

"You're lovelier than I remember," he said. He kissed me. I felt his arms lift me, my toes pointed at the dock.

I tried to push away, to tell him I wasn't Eva, that I couldn't be as good as the angel he had lucked upon. He kissed me again while a tear ran down the side of my face.

"Do you want me to let you go, March?" He lowered me to the dock. When he saw the tear, he touched it and looked at his finger as though he had broken something.

"Colin, you don't know me or how easily I say the wrong things to the wrong people at the wrong time. I still live with my mother in my head telling me what to do. I can't be who you need."

"Will you listen to me for once? No one's asking you to be anyone but you. You don't have to step into Eva's shoes or your mother's or hold together anyone else's life. Just hold me, March. Hold me now. That's all I want."

We held each other, mismatched, while the moon cast spells upon the ocean.

Twenty-one

BRADY GALLAGHER CONVALESCED IN HIS CHARLOTTE apartment. The day nurse from Mercy Hospital promised to check on him since he lacked local family support. She dropped by every evening and brought him a meal. Then Brady suggested she stay and dine with him. He phoned me one evening early after she left for home.

"Tell me what to say, what to do, March. I don't want to blow it with this angel."

"You're smitten, Brady."

"Smitten, bitten. I'm supposed to go back to work Monday. But if I get well, she might disappear."

"Why do you think it's one-sided?"

"I have a history."

"Brady, you can count on one finger the relationships you've had since your divorce. If this nurse, this Elaine, is coming by every evening of her own free will, it is safe to assume there's the possibility of a spark between you. What is she saying to you? Is it all medical mumbo jumbo or has she asked you about yourself?"

"Elaine knows my life history. She knows more about me than I know about myself. She seems interested."

"Give it a chance to happen, Brady."

"See, that is exactly what I mean, that I won't give it the chance to just happen. That I'll rush her or wait too long. The timing thing is what turns me into Jell-O. I never had timing as a kid, not with girls. That is why I married Janelle from college. She wafted in from a wrong turn in Burlington and wound up working at the campus bookstore. She wasn't even a student, for Pete's sake! But she was available. That's all it took for me, availability."

"Trust Elaine. Be transparent. If it's meant to be, the slightest blunder on your part shouldn't scare her away. Get well. Ask her out on a real date, the kind where you pick up the tab."

"But what if the attraction is that she's one of those Florence Nightingales and once she realizes I'm healed, the magic is gone?"

"Then you admit you imagined it and move on."

"I like the fantasy better."

"You asked my advice."

"So how are things going with you and Billy Graham?"

"Colin would consider that a compliment, Brady. The Arnetts are coming into town tonight." I had counted down the days and even set the alarm on my Palm Pilot as though I might forget.

"I can joke, can't I? The good Reverend did me good that night. It just seems he lives the provincial life and you fancy a hint of danger." Brady had always put me on some glamorous pedestal.

"You've got it backwards. Colin isn't provincial. You don't know him."

"And you call me smitten."

Johnson walked crooked for a week before I took him to the vet. I found him leaning against a potted plant, an odd stance even for a cat with multiple phobias. The vet ran all sorts of tests, one where he aimed his tubby front portion toward a tabletop. Any cat, the vet said, would stretch its front paws toward the table to guard its body. Johnson only held out one paw. After accruing a two-hundred-dollar vet bill, the vet informed me our cat had a brain tumor.

From that point on, Johnson was treated with such newborn attention, it changed Hercules's behavior. He grew nervous and insecure, and every time I would pass him, he would clutch my feet in a strange scissors move as though he were trying to make me stay by his side. The dog had to either stay in a part of the house where he could not taunt the tabby or remain outdoors. Every time I drove the Mustang, Hercules stretched his long limbs across the back seat, the wind blowing the blond tufts around his ears and throat, just to meet his daily golden retriever quota of human contact.

But Colin and the Arnetts were coming to town. I met Colin and Ruth at the cottage with Hercules in tow.

"You've all had dinner, I presume," I said.

"I packed a picnic and we stopped at a rest stop along the highway," said Ruth.

Charlotte stroked Hercules along his back and pulled wads of hair from his shedding coat. "Where's Mason?"

"Here he comes." Mason ran dragging his book satchel behind. "If he doesn't finish his homework Friday night, it haunts him all weekend," I said.

"Charlotte and the boys have homework, too. But I'm too tired to care," said Ruth. "We'll do it in the morning before our swim."

"I'll help you all in with your things. Then I'm taking the dog for a run on the beach. He's been cooped up all day in our study. Our cat has a brain tumor of all things, and I have to keep them separated."

"My mother had a cat but we gave it to my aunt," said Troy.

"You boys run upstairs and take your bath together," said Colin.

"Your poor kitty. I'll walk your dog, Mrs. Longfellow." Charlotte slid her slight fingers through the leash handle and allowed it to slip over her forearm. She gripped the handle with her strong hand.

"We can go together if your father doesn't care." I waited for Colin's approval.

"You look pretty tousled, sister. Wouldn't you rather crawl into bed and get an early start?" He endeavored to coax Charlotte toward the cottage. She sidled toward me.

"We can all take the walk then," he said.

Rachel leaned against her Aunt Ruth, drowsy.

"The rest of us are going to bed," said Ruth.

We helped them in with the luggage and bags of food and toys.

A waxing moon drew out the tide. The lunar magnetism charmed us out onto the beach.

Mason invited Charlotte to take a run with him. I hurried to the Mustang and dug through the emergency bag in the trunk. I dug out two flashlights and brought along two foldable chairs. "Take this flashlight, will you, Charlotte? Your father will be less nervous." I encouraged her to unleash Hercules and allow him to run off his pent-up energy. She charged off after him and Mason. I aimed the other flashlight toward them. The gentle flow of low tidewater failed to wash her flip-flop imprints from the sand.

Colin tried to call after her.

"Let her go, Colin. She can keep up with Mason. Hercules will wear them both out and we can bed them down more easily tonight," I said, but in a ginger manner, not wanting Colin to think I tended to interfere. "Charlotte is so athletic."

"Athletic, artistic, tender, and rowdy. She's an anomaly."

"Or a gift. You realize, Colin, you can't keep her cooped up like I have to keep Johnson inside now. Charlotte is one of those girls bursting with health, her little motor on high speed. Somehow she'll find the way outside."

"Eva was better with Charlotte. She knew when to rein her in and when to let her go."

"Colin, you're a good father. I didn't mean to imply you aren't."

"Just overprotective." When he confessed it, it was the first time he had ever looked old, worn out by the lapping pangs of parenthood.

"It's our prerogative to feel guilty about our parenting."

"Yes, but you women have that nurturing mechanism. I'm blind to it. Don't they have 'Nurturing 101' in Braille for blind fathers?" He closed his eyes and felt around in the dark.

I handed Colin one of the chairs and we set them up. "Joe said one time that fathers teach their offspring to lead while mothers teach them how to live."

"I once taught them to lead, I think. But when Eva left me, I floundered. Charlotte is part Colin, part Eva. She is independent by nature. But I try and mold that nature and all I wind up doing is suffocating her."

"I just try to notice what draws Mason. He is drawn by baseball but he didn't want to try fishing. But he finally tried fishing and liked it. If I pushed him into fishing with his Grandpa, he might have resented it and hated it. But I'm not so balanced otherwise." I expected him to interrupt, but he just listened. "I can be a mother bear but with me it's not a noble thing, you know, where all of my friends sit on the sidelines cheering. You seem to have this magnetism about you that makes everyone who knows you admire you."

He laughed, of course.

"If I feel like my turf is being threatened, or Mason's for that matter, my fangs come out. It's not attractive at all."

"You don't look all that threatening."

"My mother-in-law would disagree."

"This is Joe's family that makes you feel this way—animalistic?"

"Joan Longfellow can bring out the worst in me, the way that woman drives her family. Case in point: Joe never felt comfortable in law. But Joe had one of those evenings where he started with a glass of wine but then finished off the whole bottle. I didn't know what was going wrong at the firm, but whatever the problem, it weighed on him. He didn't cry. I never saw him cry, but when he spoke, he had this deep anguish. He was trapped. It made me cry. He started confessing things, things such as he never wanted to be an attorney anyway. He wanted to be a social worker, help humanity, but Joan wouldn't hear of it. I told him to quit the practice. I never wanted the big house and the fancy cars. But Joan had this sick control over him. It made me resent her."

"She knows you know all of this?"

"That's why she hates me. I called her the next morning when he went to work. Before I called I had rehearsed it all in my head, you know, painted it all up with daisies and such, so I had it in my mind that Joan would really listen to me—another woman. I told her everything he said and she accused me of lying, of trying to manipulate Joe into quitting the practice."

Colin slid his fingers on top of mine. "Sounds as though Joe was never who he wanted to be."

"That's why we fought. The last thing I said to him was not the last thing I would have wanted to say. But I thought he was being weak. I hate that in anyone, but it made me the adversary. I was afraid he was going to pass all of this on to Mason, so I played the parent card all the time. Stand up to your mother, for Mason's sake, Joe. Not two weeks later the call came from the bank, the one that sent Joe running out of the house. But all I could think about was the bill collectors. I was more worried about humiliation or security than the pressure on Joe."

"You have a right to want to feel secure."

"My father struggled through much of my life to make our little church grow. He and my mother sacrificed a lot for the church. But somehow they always managed to pay the bills. So I feel maybe I was too hard on Joe about the phone call that morning about the unpaid bills."

"March, Joe put all of his eggs with that one big bank. Transactional attorneys can't do that, they have to take in enough clients to allow for a loss. Then he overspent. At least, that is what you have told me. He got in over his head. But he could have changed everything with one decision. He never took matters to God."

"Keep talking, Colin." His words lifted me away from the pulse of my emotions. The night was not so dark with Colin close by. He spoke with a soothing cadence, a poet imbued with the power to show me the better part of me, and how to forgive myself.

"Here I am now in charge of our money, and I'm not such a financial wizard myself," I said.

"You're faithful, March."

"Good old dependable March."

"I don't think it's out of style."

I turned my hand palm up so we could clasp hands. His middle finger slowly stroked my palm. "Have you always been a wise man?" I asked.

"It would have saved us a lot of pain, but, no, I haven't. It had to sort of develop. I became a minister later in life. I was in business, trying to live in both worlds—Eva's church world and my business crowd. I almost lost her."

"I can't imagine it."

"Eva's prayers and her patience were my salvation."

Charlotte and Hercules bounded toward us. Mason thundered behind them, panting.

"The call to the pulpit followed my surrender to the Lord. You know what I mean by surrender, I'm sure."

It was new, but I nodded.

"I fell in love with Christ and my wife fell in love with me again."

"Lots of jellyfish washed up on the shore, Daddy! They looked like bell jars," said Charlotte. She was out of breath. Hercules tried to use his weight against her. She shoved him back, picked up a thin piece of driftwood and hurled it. He scrambled across the sand to sniff it out in the dark.

"How do you know what a bell jar is?" Colin asked her.

"Read a book about it." She ran off after the dog and Mason.

"So that is why you're so good at bringing in the worldly set, Colin."

"We're all worldly, March. Who doesn't have the stench of the past on them?"

"So for the sake of your church crowd, you make it easy to come to Christ. Come as you are. That's the way it should be," I said.

Colin leaned toward me. "I'm not as good as you make me out to be, but I sure like seeing myself in your eyes, March." He kissed me, a quick brush of lips against mine just before the troops invaded.

"Mason taught Hercules to sit, but he won't do it for me," Charlotte reported back to her father.

"He knows whom to obey, Charlotte. His master." Colin put his left hand around her waist, but kept the other hand clasped firmly to mine. "Really, Charlotte, you've stayed up much later than your brothers and sister. Say 'goodnight' to Hercules and Mrs. Longfellow."

Charlotte threw her arms around me and held on to me for several minutes. It was a low tide and we had oceans of time.

Colin and I returned to the shore after we bedded down Charlotte and Mason. He told me he had to see me again, and I told him that it seemed crazy to move ahead but that I would if I could feel as though I was not being pulled into the tidewater of decision. He promised me there was no hurry, but as they left a few days later, I had to keep from running after them, tying my body to the bumper with a hyperactive golden retriever, a phobic cat, and Mason, and forgetting the life I had built here.

But something fashioned out of a storm has a way of becoming an anchor. So I let Colin pack up the children and Ruth believing all of what I said to him to be true. I swallowed the lump in my throat caused by my own uncertain declarations and quietly whispered while the Arnetts pulled away, *"Don't listen to me. I don't know what I'm saying."*

Colin and I took turns visiting the other's town in our long-distance romance. It was proving to be more and more difficult to be away from him. But I kept my nose to the church and the *Sentinel* and did what I always did—my job.

Baseball season faded and gave rise to soccer moms, all of us loaded down with kneepads and bottles of cold water iced down in summer coolers.

Dinah popped open a beach umbrella over our camp chairs. We lugged an ice chest to the players' side of the field and left it next to the coach's bench.

Mason played for his school, the CCCA Hawks. But this game was known locally simply as The Presbyterians against The Baptists.

Dinah's mother-in-law had placed the twins in Mason's school and the scent of blood was in the air. The Hawks warred in a slow simmer, though, their attack skills numbed by summer vacation. Mason took a defensive stance, the color of red defining his posture.

"Make me swear, Dinah, on my honor that I won't be the loudest soccer mom on the sidelines."

"I can promise you won't." She shrieked at Geraldine to hustle to her position.

The ref blew the whistle.

"Did I tell you I saw Ruth Arnett at Ruby's Saturday?" Dinah opened two bottles of water and handed one to me.

"She brought us all back lunch," I said.

"Ruth told me she is almost finished with her dissertation. What is she, a doctor or something?"

"It's a doctorate in math. She plans to teach college. Davidson is interviewing her."

"Don't you wish we had the sense to use our God-given abilities at that age? Now that I've wizened in my old age, I realize I've short-changed myself. Who said I had to settle here in Candle Cove? I might have liked Los Angeles."

"You got two talented girls in the swap, Dinah. Nothing is stopping you from completing your degree, what with all of the online courses available, what have you."

"I've hemmed myself in, so to speak, March."

"It's all in your mind."

Her finely tweaked brows lifted, soft brown pencil lines making a curve above the sheen on her face. "You ever think about starting over?"

Mason nailed the ball with his head and drove it straight toward the net. The Baptist stopped it in midair and punted it back into the game. A corporate sigh reverberated up and down the row of Hawk parents.

"You didn't answer me," she said.

"I'm sorry, could you please repeat the question?"

"You ever considered starting over again?"

"A month ago I might have said 'no.'"

Dinah shot forward on her chair. Geraldine rammed the ball toward the net but the goalie leaped in the air and stopped it. The row of parents groaned again.

"You've seen Colin, what, twice in four weeks?" Dinah asked.

"I don't belong in Lake Norman and he doesn't belong here."

"I knew it. By that, I mean that you're in love."

"If I so much as stepped a foot into Eva Arnett's shoes, you'd hear hissing all the way from Charlotte."

"His children seem to have taken a shine to you."

"It's not his children. It isn't even Mason who worries me. Eva was the Queen Mother at that church."

"You do seem to have your own little kingdom at Candle Cove Presbyterian, on a much smaller scale, of course."

The Baptists scored.

"I don't need a throne. That isn't what I meant at all. I just can't step into the shoes of perfection."

"You do a pretty mean job of it here."

I knew Dinah was blinded by friendship. "Nobody at his church, short of Ruth and Colin's children, is aware we're dating. Every matron in that place is trying to fix him up with her single niece or daughter. I act like it doesn't bother me, like this is all just an experiment." I hesitated and she looked at me. "But it bothers me. I'm starting to wish for things that will never be, like Colin taking over our little church, an act he says will never happen. So then I imagine what it would be like to live in his world and I start worrying about leaving Dad."

"You have given this some thought. Has Colin actually asked for a commitment?"

"We've not discussed anything but our past lives and child rearing. I think we're avoiding the subject altogether."

"But you love him."

"I never thought this would happen. He wants me to bring Mason up this weekend. He wants to introduce me to some of his church friends."

"Geraldine just kicked a goal!" Dinah leaped out of her chair and pranced up and down the sidelines.

I offered a thumbs-up to Mason who appeared dumbfounded.

Dinah settled back into her chair.

"Colin took me to Sonnets Saturday night. We shared fish and chips. And oysters. Did I tell you that? A jazz band played outdoors on the veranda. I don't know if I told you, but Colin's a good dancer."

"You told me about Wilmington. Do they allow pastors to do that sort of thing?"

"Who is *they?*"

"My mother's pastor would get excommunicated for dancing."

"I never saw my father and mother dance. Such a shame. But I don't know if it's, you know, church legal or not for pastors to dance these days. I'll ask Dad about it."

"Do they have good jazz in Lake Norman? Maybe it isn't an issue."

"See, even you are putting me in Lake Norman and not vice versa."

One of the boys on the Presbyterian team wildly kicked the ball out of bounds.

"Both teams are lousy. Geraldine, you get in the game or get out!" Dinah shouted so loud her drill sergeant demonstration raised the brows of the starchy booster club.

"Mason is so red-faced. They are desperate for shade on their side.

Maybe I'll put a bug in the ear of the Hammonds that the team needs an overhang. Marie Hammond and I once played tennis." I glanced toward the Hammonds at the end of the parents' row.

"Geraldine and Claudia are always red-faced. It's in our family tree."

The other team scored again.

"I'm sorry I've rattled on about all of this Colin business, Dinah. Here I am worrying about matters that haven't come up and most likely won't. Colin has only invited me to visit his church. That's all I'm going to do. I'll put on a visitor's badge and that will be the end of it."

She took my hand. "Look at you. You have a little pink hive on the palm of your hand. It's only Monday and you're having nerves. By Sunday you'll be coated in calamine lotion. But that's all right because you look good in pink," said Dinah.

I held up my right hand. In the center of my palm was a perfectly formed welt. "I never wanted to be my mother, Dinah. As the good reverend's daughter, I have slightly more license to be frank, to speak my mind. Those people will hang me out to dry."

"These aren't the fifties or the sixties or even the seventies, March. Who says you have to fit into some polyester mold?"

"Convention."

"If I were you, I'd just stay out of those conventions, that's what," said Dinah.

"Thanks, Dinah. You've solved everything." Here I kept telling myself that I would not show up at Lake Norman a bundle of nerves, that I would just be myself and not worry about whether or not I struck out or scored with the who's who of Colin's church. I wasn't trying to win any awards, I reminded myself; it wasn't about winning or being compared to Eva, or measuring up. If I just kept my thoughts on Colin, being supportive of him, I'd come out a winner in his eyes.

The Hawks lost, but only by a point. I hoped it wouldn't be a trend for my life in the upcoming days.

Twenty-two

DAD CARRIED ARNIE UNDER HIS RIGHT ARM LIKE A rolled-up rug and stroked the white whiskers on his chin. "I can't just go off and leave him, March. Arnie's never known the inside of a kennel. He might think I've abandoned him. They keep them in cages, don't they?"

"Crates. Doggie crates. Like a den. The lady at the Pet Spa is always good to Hercules. It's a home away from home when I have to leave town," I said.

"Seems like it's been a while since I went out of town. Things are so unsettled at the church. What use am I to you all in Lake Norman anyway?"

"Colin invited you. He wants to return your kindnesses for allowing him so many stays at the cottage. The polite thing to do is accept."

"Or politely decline."

"Your doctor says you can travel. It would do you good to get out of here. You act as though the whole village will float away if you aren't here to anchor it to land."

"What about your cancerous cat?"

"Dinah is keeping Johnson. The vet has him on medication and she's going to keep an eye on him for me."

"Can't send Arnie to the Buckworths," Dad continued ruminating. "Forget that idea then. Those girls would make him nervous."

"I can ask Gloria if she'd mind taking the dachshund. He's no trouble, Dad."

He dropped Arnie onto the carpet and walked into the kitchen without the cane.

"You don't even show signs of a heart attack, Dad. Look at you. You're your old self. Take advantage of this time. Go somewhere with us."

"What do you do in Lake Norman, anyway?"

"Colin has a room, an atrium where he reads. It's shaded with a garden outside the glass."

"No one will try and make me get on a boat."

"I swear you won't be coerced to try anything new."

Dad had never learned to swim. He was an enigma to some. A man who hated the water yet lived by the sea.

"We'll go with the top down. Road trip," I said.

"I can't find the vanilla wafers. You had something to do with it, March. May as well confess."

"The laundry room, next to the grits."

I dreamed that Joe and I sat on the sofa, only I was sleeping while he watched me. The peaceful glow of morning gilded his lashes. He awakened me and two people were walking into our living room. The woman had red hair and was astoundingly beautiful. The man was round and dressed like Mafioso. But he stood back at a distance while she perched herself on the arm of our sofa with an air of propriety She said nothing to me but spoke to Joe and greeted him. He laughed nervously.

Angered that Joe had not allowed me to run upstairs to hide my pajama state, I asked him why he had let them in.

"I didn't," was all he said.

I looked up at the young woman. She pulled out a pistol, silver and feminine, and aimed it at Joe. They had come to rob us.

I could not bear to lose him, willing to die myself instead. I fought her and tried to ram her head against the kitchen bar. Joe said nothing. He watched like a man watching the minutes pass. Somehow I knew it was not a cowardly act. He could not lift a finger to hurt her.

I did not have the strength to knock her out and finally managed to wrest the gun from her manicured hands. She was as weak as me. Feeling that the pinstriped accomplice might jump me, I stepped back and fired. The girl died instantly and the fat guy ran off. At first I drank in the swell of triumph until the reality of this human death overtook my heart. Then I fell on the floor and sobbed deeply and hopelessly, just like I did when the policemen, Harold and Bobby, had told me my husband was gone.

When I woke up, the morning sun freckled my pillowcase with atoms of autumn gold. I could not understand if I had killed someone in my dreams or slain myself. It was odd the way my mind had painted me beautiful and Joe as a fat crook. And him as the guy who couldn't lift a finger to hurt me while we both robbed ourselves of a good life.

Dad had trouble deciding what hat to wear. Mason finally convinced him a baseball cap possessed the engineering to withstand the gusty streams of a convertible ride. Between the two of them, they added a whole duffle bag full of things easily left behind. But Dad would leave behind every bit of it to make room for Arnie. The dachshund wanted nothing to do with his travel crate, a pet accessory bought years ago by my mother and used once when she first brought him home. Twice I placed him in it, re-adjusted the soft doggie bed, and twice I took him out unable to bear the lugubrious cries he made. He sounded like an infant.

Mason settled him on the back car seat next to him and fed him gourmet liver snacks, five dollars for every quarter-pint.

Dad studied the map. He wanted to be certain that all of us who had traveled back and forth between the same two destinations for several months had not somehow missed a secret path.

Neighbors had gathered out on the lawns and waved at us as we drove past.

"Your neighbors are awfully friendly today, Dad. That's kind of odd, as though they've rolled out the red carpet. What did you do?"

"I've always said we have a good neighborhood," said Dad.

A carload of teenagers screeched to a halt and waved wildly out the open windows of someone's parent's Ford. A girl with braces blew me kisses and then held up both fists in a sanguine salute.

"Do we know them?" asked Mason.

"They look like some friends of Yolanda's. Maybe they're happy the trial is over and those New Jersey thugs were shipped up the river. I'll bet that's it," I said.

Dad watched Mason in the rearview mirror of his visor until we connected with I-40 south of Raleigh.

"Bringing along the dog was a good idea. Arnie keeps Mason company," he said.

By the time we reached the molasses-slow traffic of Greensboro it was lunch time.

"I wish we would have flown," I said.

"What, and miss the fall color?" Dad pulled out a paperback Tom Clancy novel.

"I forgot that you can sit for an hour alone just fifteen minutes outside of Greensboro. May as well stop here for lunch."

"My legs are tingling. I need to give them a stretch."

The leaves were mostly green along the coast. The closer we got to the Piedmont the more the trees turned to autumn bouquets. The brightness of the day made the leaves look translucent and membranous.

We found a hamburger hamlet with an outdoor patio. Arnie sat on Dad's feet and waited for munificent bites from his master's hand. Mason ordered a round of root beers for all, and we toasted to cooler weather.

"Bill Simmons said the new minister is jumping through all of the hoops. He has a bit of a tic, though. No, not a tic. I forget what you call his idiosyncrasy. It disturbs Grace and Hal Caudle, though. He cannot say his *s*'s without whistling. I've heard of men who whistle out of their nostrils, but this man distinctly does it with any word containing the letter *s*. I wish to goodness it wasn't pointed out to me, now. I feel like a dog hearing one of those dog whistles and no one around me can hear it. Just me. I can't even converse with the poor fellow without hearing it. Maybe if it isn't pointed out, everyone will be none the wiser. The elders should keep it among themselves. It's a dreadful thing to reveal about a man who is about to oversee a congregation."

"Mason, pass me that bowl of lemons, will you," I said.

"Don't tell me you've heard it too." The age spots along Dad's forehead made his face look like a speckled bean.

"It's best I don't have an opinion about the man. If this is his only flaw, then what's a small-town church to do but to hire him? He sent videos from Pennsylvania. Goodness knows everyone had the chance to listen for whistling consonants."

"Anything else?"

"I told you, I don't have an opinion."

"You said it's best you don't have an opinion, March."

"He's not of your caliber, Dad."

"Or Colin's." Dad handed Mason a straw.

"He's not even in the same boat as Colin. It's as though they're on completely different rivers with completely different maps."

"Not exactly. They both point to Christ."

"That's the objective anyway."

"But you don't have an opinion."

"No."

Leaves had begun to fall but only early loose foliage; it fell upon the Arnett lawn like yellow coasters. Colin had both garage doors open. He wore khaki Bermudas and a gray flannel sweatshirt with doeskin hiking boots. He might have looked like an advertisement for L. L.

Bean but his calves were too thick. If he had ever made it into films, his thick calves would be too distracting. I stared at his legs for the first time. I wanted to see how far my fingers would reach around them. I said a quick prayer for restraint.

He carried flattened boxes and overstuffed garbage bags out to the curb. All of the boxes had once held cling peaches. I imagined them standing in kitchen-help-high stacks in his church's pantry. Cling peaches exist for church socials crowning scoops of cottage cheese, the perfect cross between a dessert and a salad.

"We're taking the sailboat out to sail around the peninsula," he said. He opened my door and leaned forward with both arms becoming the gate between me and his lawn.

Dad sighed.

"Is it all right if Dad stays here?" I asked Colin.

"Ruth isn't going, either. You can keep her company, James. Or watch us from the shore at Jetton Park. We can help you set up a lawn chair. Jetton has a small beach."

Dad picked up his paperback and looked at me. "Where is that little glass room you were telling me about?"

Troy, the oldest and most agile of the boys at age seven, lugged a box of broken toys down the driveway and dropped them next to his father's heap. He had small knobby knees and an Adam's apple that protruded like a farm boy's. "She's here! We finally know someone famous."

Dad and I just looked at one another and blinked.

Ruth sat on a windowsill upstairs, buttocks out, and ran a squeegee down the window. When she saw us, her elegant knees lifted and she pulled herself inside. The window was only half washed.

"Troy, please show Reverend Norville into the house. He'd like to relax in the atrium," Colin told him.

"Are you all spending the night here?" Troy took my father's hand as though it were his duty to physically lead the decrepit old guy.

"We're staying at the old parsonage," I said.

Luke appeared in the doorway, sucking the life out of a blue Popsicle.

"My sister Charlotte was almost born right in the parsonage, right on the braided rug. You know, like having puppies." Luke waited as if he wanted to see whether or not I had already heard the story. When I did not respond, he said, "But my dad finally got up and drove Mom to the hospital."

"Wait until you're older, Luke. You'll find we men try to stick together," said Dad. He obliged Troy by allowing him to lead him all the way up the walk.

"Mrs. Longfellow, may I have your autograph?" asked Luke.

Mason compressed Arnie into the shape of a gherkin and followed them inside where Charlotte's shrill, eager greeting spilled out of the open doorway.

I returned to the car and fished out my purse.

"I didn't know I was courting a celebrity," said Colin. He met me at the car.

I picked crumbs of Cheetos off of my knit slacks.

Colin clasped both of my hands and pulled me out of the car. "Don't tell me you haven't seen a copy of *LIFE* magazine?"

I had not.

He retrieved his magazine off the top of a cling peaches box as though he had been reading it. He held it up. The cover story was "Hero Moms." Three women's faces, one of which was mine, were captured in a still-life frieze, our photographs forming a triangular ring. I had a pair of kiwi-colored sunglasses perched on the crown of my head. I remembered wearing them the day of Yolanda's trial. My expression read like a woman determined to lasso the villains of the world. I was pretty certain I was trying to mentally gather my grocery list, that pinch between the eyebrows simply a sign of my scattered memory trying to recall the inside of the pantry—iodized salt, Cheerios, brown sugar (or was it white?), and juice boxes for Mason's lunch. One of the other women was a Detroit mom who had donated a kidney to a child overseas, while the other lady had rescued an entire family from a burning car hit by a train in Toad Suck Ferry, Arkansas.

"I never saw this," I said.

"They didn't tell you?"

"A lot of cameras were popping all around me. I thought they were after Yolanda. I was trying to get out of the way, let her have her little moment in the limelight."

"*LIFE* just hit the stands this morning. I'll bet the local press is on a manhunt to find you. They'll want to interview you, too." Colin handed me the magazine.

"They'll find me gone, then. Good thing we brought Dad with us. This is embarrassing." I thumbed through the article and found adjectives like "heroic widow" and "courageous mother" next to my name. "This Detroit woman, Georgia Wallace, she donated a kidney to an orphan in Zimbabwe. This other lady, Flo Minirth, she rescued an entire family from a burning car with her own hands. Look at the bandages on her poor little parched hands. Mine should read 'March Longfellow pulled a water gun on two dweebs.'"

"You rush in where angels fear to tread. People want to admire you for it," said Colin before he added, "Some people are just admiration magnets."

"I'm an idiot and I can prove it. I'm not the hero type. It's just that somehow my gene pool has tanked me up with an overage of adrenaline. It gets the best of me. In my opinion, if you think heroically, you act heroically. You can't prove by me that I think at all. Mostly, I react."

We stood between the car and its open door, hands still clasped. Colin's eyes were two moons settling upon the gentle dunes of his face as he looked down at me.

"You left your socks at the cottage. I washed them. Want me to get them for you?" I asked.

"How kind of you. I think I'd rather kiss you."

"Your neighbor is out walking the dog. Is this a good idea? I mean, my father never kissed Mother out on the lawn like this." Surely he wouldn't listen to me.

Colin stooped like a crane getting at its fish and we kissed. I felt my powers slipping away, as though I were losing control of my monarchy.

Charlotte and I held hands on the shore at Jetton Park and waved at the sailors. My heart followed the fellows and Rachel around the waving line of peninsula while my feet remained on the sand. I don't believe they saw how I split in two on shore, frail and dichotomous, wanting to leap astern and grab a rope while panache nautical phrases spilled off of my tongue. When Charlotte heard that I don't do boats, she stayed on shore with me.

"Aunt Ruth is fixing a sandwich party for us tonight. At the parsonage," said Charlotte.

"We'll go back and help her then." I pulled a sweater around my shoulders.

"Everything is done. She's taking a nap. I cubed the cheese." When she said it, a blush reddened her entire face, like a girl who is not well-practiced at boasting.

We sat down together in the foldout camp chairs Colin had dragged out of his SUV. Charlotte pulled zippy plastic bags of sliced apples out of a small cooler and handed me a bag. "I dreamed last night that the angels took my mother to heaven, sort of like I got to watch the whole thing. I know why I dreamed it. Sometimes I worry about the walk from here to heaven, like, did my mother get lonely walking by herself to God. I think Jesus let me watch it all so that I wouldn't worry about her. Kind of like he pulled out the video of the whole thing and loaned it to me. Mother actually flew. I always wondered about, you know, will we fly because she told me that angels were different from humans, that we would not have angel's wings. She just lifted." Charlotte lifted her arms and pointed to the sky with one good hand and one disabled. It came to me that her flaw was what made her so perfect.

"I believe in angels too, Charlotte."

"Is your husband in heaven?"

"I don't know. He knew what it took to get there." Only because I had told him once. "I'd like to think that in those last few minutes when he realized he wasn't going to make it back that he took care of business, so to speak."

"My mother was very friendly. I'll bet she's already made your Joe feel right at home." Charlotte laid aside the apples and took off her shoes. She ran one big toe along the sand. "Usually, we do not have good sand for angels. Today it's soft." Then she lay down flat on the sand and spread her arms and legs back and forth just like Mason had done in Virginia in the cemetery snow.

"Making sand angels?" I asked.

"Have you ever made angels in the sand, Mrs. Longfellow? If we make them everywhere then more people will know."

"Know what, Charlotte?"

"That God cares for them and watches over them."

I joined her on the soggy shore of Lake Norman where we created whole families of celestials. As far as we knew the sand angels remained until the sun had set, turning the earthen impressions to gilded immortals.

Back in the eighties, a carpenter from Colin's church had assembled a large deck along the entire rear of the parsonage.

Ruth burned tiki torches around the perimeter of the deck and left all of the windows open to justify a fire in the fireplace of the old great room. Colin floated medallions of oranges in apple cider and warmed the batch over the fire until the whole room smelled like an orchard.

He and Ruth seated all the children around the kitchen table, mounding sandwiches and chips with dip in front of them, to keep them occupied. Troy made a moat with his potato chips and chocolate pudding. Ruth ate an anorexic portion of something she called vegetable jumble. Then she harnessed Arnie and coaxed him out the front door for a jog down Rio Oro.

"James, join me on the deck. It's a clear night," said Colin to Dad.

Dad threw on his corduroy jacket and then followed Colin out under the shadow of night and the stars.

Charlotte and I gathered up the paper plates smudged with mustard and other garnitures. Rachel nudged her way in between the open dishwasher door and her older sister, demanding a woman's share of the kitchen duties. I obliged her with the task of scooping up the plastic cups and dumping them into the almond porcelain sink.

Colin and I had spent all of twenty minutes together and even then it was in front of the next-door neighbor and his neurotic boxer. In the glow of the lawn lanterns Dad stretched out his arms like a clothesline cord. He heaved a sort of old-man sigh that said he was ready to turn in for the night. I pretended to gather the afghans up around the fireplace and then folded up on the recliner with my back to the men. Colin must not have noticed my antsy glance toward him. He kept talking to Dad, lowering his voice and filling the silence with a somber guys-only dialogue.

"It isn't easy to let go of a church," Dad told Colin. "Not when you've nurtured it from its inception. I worry that Candle Cove Presbyterian has such a limited outlook. It's hard to see beyond our own front porch when all you see are the same faces every week. I dreamed of a man who would take the church to the next level. I feel this new man needs more time with me. He needs a mentor."

"Speaking of letting go, James, I'd like to know how you feel about letting go of March and Mason."

I stared into the embers and felt like a spy curled beneath the mound of knitted throws. If Dad answered Colin, it tumbled out as a breathy whisper. Colin had not asked me about any sort of commitment but he must have known my worries about my father.

Their voices grew as soft as the glow of heat from the fireplace. I fell asleep and dreamed of tumbling into a cavern. I lay on the precipice of a cliff and stared into jagged bowels so deep and dark the bottom was fathomless. Below me was my father who clung to one of my hands. Above me was Colin who climbed out and wanted me to follow. I stretched to reach out to them both, but felt nothing between us but space. The one candle that lit the entire cavern dimmed and I felt the suffocating sense of gasping like a fish on the bank.

Colin dug me out of the afghans and awakened me. "You sounded like you were having a bad dream."

"Where's Dad?"

"He's gone upstairs to sleep. Mason's in bed too."

"Ruth? Your kids?" I climbed out of the recliner and saw my tangled reflection in a decorative mirror.

"Gone home. Except Charlotte. She's in your bed. I told her, okay, as long as she shares the blanket. We're all alone. Finally. But I won't stay long."

"You can if you want," I said while he pulled me to my feet.

"The kids have a fall break in three weeks. They want to come to Candle Cove again, and I told them we would. But the distance between us is . . ." He stopped so that I could fill in the blanks.

"Frustrating." I knew it was coming. "We discussed this already, that the distance would become a problem."

"March, you're all I think about. I'm looking for solutions here. That wasn't a complaint," Colin told me and then held me next to him, with both arms around my waist.

I could have thrown myself at him right at that moment and been done with it. "Colin, you don't have to feel as though this has to work out. There's no pressure from me." I had grown good at lying.

I heard Dad gargling in the upstairs bathroom.

"Over the next few weeks, March, I want you to think about us. How this could work out for both of us. For my family and yours." He stopped and looked toward the stairwell. Charlotte hovered at the top of the staircase in a white gown, all flannel and satin ribbon. The light above her head gave her crown an aura. She rubbed her eyes and floated back to her room as though she sleepwalked.

"She's checking on us." I moved my hands up both of his arms.

"Charlotte loves you, March. They all love you."

"I've never been good at starting at the beginning. It makes me feel impatient with myself." Somehow I knew this wasn't new to him, but I kept piecing together sentences hoping I would eventually make sense without chasing him out of my arms. "These people here at Church on the Lake have expectations of who you are and who Eva was. I just don't have any sort of way of turning myself into Eva. Socially, I'm not adept, and I can't keep my opinions to myself."

"And I'm not Joe, March. I'm not going to leave you stranded. Or emotionally bankrupt."

"Who said I was emotionally bankrupt? I'll admit, I've had to reshuffle my priorities." I tried hard not to sound defensive. "I was the epitome of a church lady, but not, as you say sometimes from your pulpit, so fully yielded in my heart to Christ. It was hard for me to admit I needed the Lord and easier to think that he needed me. Sometimes I was slow to admit I needed anyone for that matter." But "emotionally bankrupt" was just, well, severe. Said aloud, anyway.

"I think the question is, do you need me?"

"Only when I breathe, Colin. Or when it's storming. Or if the sky is completely clear and void of clouds, then I need you. Other than that, no."

"I don't want you to go home. Stay here in Lake Norman. Stay with me."

I buried my face against his chest and felt his breath against my neck.

He finally left without my answer.

The next morning, Colin did not embarrass us by asking us to stand in the middle of the service. Instead, after the dismissal, he led us himself to a church dinner in the large fellowship hall. It was catered by some barbecue catering group, and no one had to cook, not even Ruth. The youth group served and the older women stood behind them offering direction. Colin introduced me to members of his advisory board.

A younger woman who held an infant with cheeks as red as vermilion stuck out her hand and made an overboard effort to welcome me. She introduced herself as Laura Feines, the wife of Jack on Colin's board. She asked me a lot about myself and told me how she had been a college student staying in an apartment with two guys and three girls when Colin and Eva knocked on her door and invited her to a barbecue. "They didn't even try and get me to church, but just come and eat they said. And here I am now married to a board member. It's just the oddest way that God works."

I did not flinch at all when she mentioned Eva's name and she seemed to do so several times.

"Why don't you and your son join my family at our table?" she asked.

Mason had run off with Charlotte to the dessert table or some such so I picked up a plate of food and headed her way until Colin stopped me. "I have another person I want to introduce you to. He's special." He took me through the crowd of denim-clad people and led me right up to a young man who helped his young wife calm a newborn. "Ralph here is the son of the man who was with me from the beginning, Jonathan Henshaw. We lost Jon to a heart attack. Ralph, this is a friend, March Longfellow."

Ralph glanced up red-faced, apologetic that he could not quell the newborn mewl. "Nice to meet you, March. We go way back with the Arnetts. Colin and Eva were like second parents to me and my sister. Did you ever know Eva?"

"I never had the privilege," I said.

"If it wasn't for her, I don't even know if this church would exist." Ralph turned his back to us and lifted the infant out of the carriage. "Excuse me."

We politely dismissed ourselves.

"March, I'm sorry. Eva meant a lot to Ralph. He got into drugs and she coaxed him into rehab."

I could feel the ghost of Eva arising, but I didn't want to act defensive, as though I was just waiting for someone to breathe her name.

"Before I could tell him about you he was off into talk of Eva. That wasn't what I intended at all."

The more Colin apologized, the more I wanted to shrink up the size of a snail and slink away.

"Don't apologize. I wouldn't want everyone at Dad's church to just sweep the memory of my mother out with the newspaper."

An older woman with silver strands of hair glistening through her bangs interrupted. "Pastor Colin, I don't mean to be a tattletale, but your Charlotte has skipped the meal altogether and gone for the dessert." She pointed at the far corner of the hall.

Charlotte and Mason stacked towers of giant cookies onto their trays, no sight of a green salad or entrée between them both.

"Sakes, if she doesn't look just like that Eva leading that little boy around like she owns the place," said the lady who seemed to disappear into her memories.

Instead of waiting for Colin to explain that Eva had sat by this woman's bedside and breathed life back into her pneumonia-racked body, I simply said, "I'll go and get Mason and Charlotte and lead them back toward the real food line. Don't feel you have to introduce me to another person, Colin. I'll see those two get fed and then I'll just mingle."

His chest lifted and I could see flickers of anxiety in his face.

"Just watch. I'm quite the mingler." I turned away and began mentally packing up our luggage, Dad's new collection of books from Colin, and the dog's things. I wouldn't want to leave anything behind where it didn't belong.

Twenty-three

"IF YOU AND PASTOR ARNETT GET MARRIED, WILL my last name change?" Mason asked in a rush, his words spilling out before he sneezed.

"Bless you, and use a tissue, Mason." I handed him a Kleenex. "No one said anything about marriage. Eat your Froot Loops." He grew less and less interested in breakfast each morning.

"I saw you kiss him. Do you miss Dad?"

"Are you going to eat your cereal, Mason?"

"I don't think Grandpa wants to move. We can't leave him here."

"We're not leaving Grandpa, we're not getting married. I can't remember if I gave Johnson his meds this morning."

"You did. He hacks every time you do. Do you love Pastor Arnett, Mom? I want to know, so stop beating out the bush." He dropped to the floor and began shoving pencils and dog-eared textbooks into his book satchel.

"Beating *around* the bush." I removed the bowl of colored sludge that was once his cereal. "I might love him, Mason. Is that a bad thing?"

"It's not. I just think it's going to be a big mess if you are. He calls a lot. The phone bill will be big, but you're nicer now."

"So I'm nicer. Don't forget your lunch." The phone rang. "Colin. I'm glad you called."

"I need to see you again," he said.

"When can you come?"

Mason lifted like a tortoise, his back straining to hold up the satchel. He craned his neck and stretched out his arms to adjust the straps. He studied my face and then lifted to kiss me. "You're a wreck, Mom, but a nicer wreck."

Colin read two calendar dates to me and we settled on one while I fretted over how this trip might be the one that scattered us in opposite directions.

The night the Arnetts arrived, an autumn cold had settled upon the cove, plunging temperatures to near freezing by bedtime. Mason emptied the Mustang's trunk of his belongings at the same time Ruth handed luggage and bagged possessions to Charlotte and the others to carry inside.

Our church school that Mason attended scheduled a fall break every October to make up for the long, tenuous stretch of school that ebbed into the first week of everyone else's summer. He seized the time off to spend the night in the cottage where he and Colin's boys stretched out sheets around the furniture and shoved flannel sleeping bags beneath their town of linen tents as near to the brick fireplace as Ruth would allow.

Colin and I stood against the cold wind and inspected the *Sparticus.*

"First thing in the morning I'll haul her back up to the shed after one last run around the harbor," said Colin. His words carried a weighty finality, as though he were resigning himself to the task. He watched the last Arnett drag a duffel bag into the house and close the door.

"I took the day off tomorrow. Gloria is helping me out," I said.

"I've missed you, March." He opened his navy pea jacket and wrapped it around me so that it swallowed up the both of us.

I laid my head against his chest until the warmth soothed the chill in my bones. "Colin, the new pastor is being installed. Dad is in such a gloom."

"Look at me, March."

I lifted my face out of the dark folds of his jacket.

He kissed me and I wanted to live forever curled inside the warm sanctuary of his arms.

"Colin, you're all I can think about. Gloria is near to killing me because I just start something, some PTA piece that screams to be written or somebody's aunt's obituary, and then I drift away and it's all on account of you." I felt ruined, with parts of me scattered along the sand.

"Walk with me," he said.

"No, I'd rather stand here with you like this."

"Let's walk." He led me a mile past the cottage and up an embankment where he seated himself in the cleft of a large rock. With one arm he pulled me up and drew me against him. "It's warmer here out of the wind."

"So this is where you hide when Ruth says she hasn't seen you all day." My back molded with the curve of his chest. "Colin, I've been thinking about what you asked me to think about." I pulled my head beneath his chin not wanting to see straight into the eyes that saw over pulpits into men's hearts.

"So have I and I wasn't being fair to you. I've realized, March, you never asked to be pursued, but that made me want to pursue you all the more. Your whole world is here and I've asked you to leave it, everything you call home. Then I expect you to live in a place filled with Eva, around people who have romanticized her memory."

I turned sideways and looked at him, my right hand against his chest. "You don't have to sound so apologetic. I don't know that you've officially asked me to leave it." I waited to see if he would.

"I want you to know that you don't have to answer anything, or do anything that makes you uncomfortable. Stand firm on that account, March. Never let anyone coerce you into choices that make you lose who you are."

I felt the pounding of his heart against my hand.

Colin turned his head and leaned toward me. We kissed, his breath warming me.

"If I ask you to leave everything that is you, that you've worked so hard to preserve and make your own, I'm asking you to leave behind who you are and become someone else. It's wrong. I don't want you to become someone else."

"So you're saying you don't want me to think about a life with you," I said.

"You're off the hook, March."

He thought I wanted to be released. "Is this how it ends then? You just cut me loose and I walk away?"

"I think you're one of those people who likes to set up hurdles and jump them when all you have to do is run."

I kept my eyes ahead on the dark ocean. "It's getting colder."

"Tell me what to say, March. I thought you'd want it this way. Can you imagine a life with me?"

"If I had known what would happen with Joe, would I have married him anyway? If you factor Mason into the equation, I have to say I would." I laid my head against his shoulder. "But it's like I have this ability now to see ahead and I hate it." I sat up and looked at him. "Is that caused by enduring the hard things?" He hesitated so I thought he probably knew the answer but waited. "I wish I couldn't predict what would happen to us."

"What makes you think you can?"

"Without a second thought, I could just take the life you seem willing to share with me. But when I stepped foot in your church, Colin, I knew they couldn't accept me."

"When I asked Eva to marry me, it seemed natural that she would say yes and that we would have a happy life. If I'd known about her cancer in advance, would I have avoided her just to avoid the pain?"

"I don't know. Would you have asked her, with the full knowledge of what you know now?"

"We aren't meant to know about pain in advance, any more than we can anticipate the thrilling moments like the one I just had when I kissed you. How else can we grow if we make choices knowing that all will be well and perfect? Look at all I acquired in the process: Rachel, Luke, Troy, and Charlotte. Without them I don't think I would have had the will to get out of bed the day after I buried my wife. By myself, I'm one grain of sand. But with my family, we are a shoreline built by the hand of Almighty God. That is how we hold back the tides, March. Not by escaping the storms, but by staying together through them. If we scatter, we are lost."

"Have I lost you?" The wind caught my words. Colin and I bowed our heads until the blustery cold died down.

"What did you say?" He tempered his words.

"I made hot chocolate. Let's go back to the cottage and I'll pour you a cup." I said it as brightly as possible. I had just lost all of my resolve to spill the hard things out in the open. But I would try and muster my thoughts again in the morning when the day's luminosity painted me objective and clever.

I would have tomorrow to say what I should say.

My phone rang sometime after six o' clock, just after the dawn arose with a storm on its back. Ruth sounded ill, her insides twisted around her heart.

"March, Rachel just woke me to tell me the boys, Luke and Mason, plus Charlotte took off in the *Sparticus*. A storm has moved in and they're all out in the middle of it. Sweet Jesus, have mercy!"

"Where is Colin?" I fumbled for my reading glasses.

"He's getting dressed. I've already called the Coast Guard but Colin says he's going out after them." She yelled something down the hall. "A neighbor has offered his boat, Colin says."

"Tell Colin I'm coming with him." I prayed all the way into the bathroom, started to brush my teeth, but then in my stupor came to myself and reconstructed my morning ritual so that I would be out the front door in five minutes. All I could see was Mason's face, his eyes the only shard of color in a black storm at sea. My motherly intuition concluded that Mason, on his own, might have never come up with the idea of sailing off in the *Sparticus* before dawn. Troy wouldn't, either. The culpability rested on the two of them jointly conspiring. I imagined them staying up past midnight daring one another, and then hatching the whole scheme to sail before dawn.

I then imagined Mason taking the helm and heading them back to the little dock by Sonnet's Fish and Chips, as though by willing him to do the right thing he would do it. I knew the owners who came early to start the salad bar would run out to them and wrap the kids in blankets and seat them around the table near the fireplace inside, laughing at how silly they had all been. Then the fantasy faded and Mason became Joe, and he fought the sea and wrestled the slapping waves refusing to turn back because he sought a more meaningful battle than the one that waited back home. He never cried out once, and I wondered how I knew that about him.

Several times I spoke Mason's name aloud in a fragile, ragged pleading to God to not let him slip from me or else I might not recover this time. Colin might not recover. We would have nothing between us but loss, and that is too much space between two people. I bargained all the way out to the beach, offering up my life for Mason's if the ocean had to be so hungry as to tear another piece from me, the one that gave me a reason to breathe.

A squad car flew past, all squealing tires and glaring lights.

A white, fragile paper angel tossed back and forth on a string, dangling from my rearview mirror. Upon the penciled-on angel toes were the initials "CA." Charlotte had made it for me along with a whole battalion of celestials that twirled comically in my kitchen window, down from my bathroom light fixture, and from the pull cord on a bedroom shade. Charlotte had surrounded me with angels and little-girl prayers. I knew why she had followed the boys onto the boat. She had gone off on her own crusade, the delicate sentry to her brother and my son. Through the kitchen window I saw that the cottage was filled with milling souls. Ruth traipsed back and forth cradling a pot of coffee while Rachel clung to her blouse.

I do not remember running up the rain-soaked path past the broken clay pots and across the deck stained by my mother.

"Colin, March is here!" Ruth handed the coffeepot to Dinah who had shown up barefaced, her hair pulled back in a ponytail.

Dinah's girls lay on the living-room floor cradling their pillows brought from home.

"I heard it on the police band, March. The whole town knows," said Dinah. She poured Bobby and Harold a cup of coffee.

"Have you heard anything?" I asked Ruth.

"Nothing from the Coast Guard. The neighbor is coming with the boat but I'd rather you all didn't go. Just look at that storm. It isn't safe, not for anyone!" Ruth said it to her brother.

"March, I don't know what to say." He grabbed me and held me. "The boys slipped out while we slept." Colin's eyes were red.

"Let's go, Colin. We'll find them."

"You on a boat, that's a laugh. You don't have to go, March. Maybe it's best you don't, that you wait here and answer the phone." Colin tied the hood of his rain slicker at his throat.

"Ruth and Dinah can take the calls. We're wasting time, Colin!"

Bobby took Ruth aside to gather facts and insert significance into the wait.

I felt Colin slip his hand into mine. He asked us all to bow for prayer. Harold and Bobby took off their caps and Dinah's daughters stopped their banter.

"We need you, God, need your guidance. Out of our weakness we lean on you. Please keep our children safe in your care. In Christ's name, amen," he said.

Colin and I barreled across the deck and ran for the dock. Dad's old neighbor, Vern Hottinger, clambered onto the dock and held the rope while we climbed aboard.

"She's a twenty-seven-footer, closed-bow, Reverend. She'll be fast and slice through the brine well enough, but the weather service is warning of ten- and twelve-foot swells in this torrent. Do you know how to operate a VHF radio?" Vern asked.

"I have one myself. Our thanks, Mr. Hottinger. We'd best shove off," said Colin. He helped me into the cabin.

Colin departed the banks at an angle. The craft nosed through the swells just as Vern said it would do, slamming the bow against the backs of the curls.

"None of this makes any sense, Colin. Mason has never taken the *Sparticus* without asking first. Then there's Charlotte who is just so well mannered and an obedient girl."

"Troy says they were up last night having popcorn wars and daring one another. They all thought Rachel was asleep but she heard the whole thing. When she woke up Charlotte was gone too."

The sky lowered all around us shrieking and roaring territorially around the misplaced humans.

"I didn't know you had experience driving a boat like this one," I said.

"Not exactly like this one." His thoughts seemed to disappear into the clamoring ocean ahead. "It's dark as coal out here. Times like this you realize the importance of knowing your coordinates."

"But you do know how to drive it?"

His mouth stretched into one of those superior smiles that men toss to women when they ask simple questions about plumbing parts. Only this was not a leaky toilet.

"I keep thinking that I didn't push Mason enough in his swim lessons. You know they start out as minnows and then progress up to trout, then dolphins, and then sharks. I can't even remember if he was a dolphin or a trout. But he stopped and started up his baseball again as though it didn't bother him that he never got his shark badge."

"Even a shark would have a hard time in this mess," he said.

"I read about experts who say you should sit down with your children and teach them, well, things about coping with real life. But it sounds like theory to me, you know, like how does that translate to something that prepares your child for danger? I don't know how to train him for disaster."

Colin kept staring into the storm and the waves while I babbled nervously.

"I mean, for gosh sakes! Does that mean we send them off to commando school? I can see him out in the middle of all of this scared and not knowing what to do and wondering why my voice is not breaking through and telling him 'Mason, do this' or 'Mason, do that.'"

"Mason is a good boy, March. You've done well by him."

The boat nosed up and smacked down so hard on the swell, it felt as though we were toppling. I grabbed tight and held on to the seat. The water never calmed for any space of time.

"Please God, help me see them!" said Colin.

The weather service broke through with another storm warning counseling all sea vessels to return to land.

I assumed Colin would ignore the warning. I proceeded to analyze my input in Mason's life, what would drive him out into this mess and how he might react in a crisis. It helped me to focus and not fall into the dark cavern of insanity. "I'm just worried. Mason has the ability to think, but he doesn't always practice it." I always saw those moms who came out of parent-teacher conferences smiling and hugging. But I always had this little twinge of anxiety about conferences. I knew the teacher would use words like *capable* and *potential,* which is code for he just doesn't try hard enough. I never heard that I did a good job as a mother and that all of my efforts shone through so clearly in the life of my child. I never understood why the teacher couldn't just validate me. I needed to be validated. "Somehow I missed out on all of these signals with Mason. I never saw this coming."

"Our kids made a mistake, March. We can't blame ourselves for this, although it wouldn't have hurt for me to put away the *Sparticus* last night. All the while I was teaching them to sail I never thought they would try this. But Mason is a good sailor. He knows what to do under normal circumstances." His words wilted.

"Colin, I see a light ahead."

"I see it." He changed gears and headed us toward the lights.

A large wave scooped us up and pushed us back, but Colin kept bearing down on the gas until we lurched ahead. "Thank God, it's the Coast Guard." He sounded the horn.

"That's the *Sparticus;* look!" I stood and clambered to see through the glass.

We pulled alongside the Coast Guard boat and saw Troy lifted from the *Sparticus.* He was rain-drenched and crying hysterically.

Colin dropped anchor.

"I don't see Mason and Charlotte, Colin. Where are they?" My knees felt weak and my hands trembled. I looked hard at the faces of the men who tried to calm Troy and question him. Colin leaped across the Coast Guard's vessel and grabbed his son. He pulled a blanket around him and shouted something at me. His words were snatched away by the wind. He pulled another soaked boy from the cabin and I saw that Mason was already safe inside. I cried and climbed out of Vern's vessel and allowed the crew to help me aboard.

Mason fell into my arms. "Mom, Charlotte tried to hang on, but she just couldn't! I tried, Troy and me tried really hard to help her, but it was her small hand that slipped. She lost her grip and we can't find her!" Mason wailed. "I'm so sorry. It's my fault!"

The Coast Guard searched the waters, their lights hovering over the ocean, motor trolling gently so as not to miss the smallest place a girl might be found.

Colin asked me to take the boys into the Coast Guard's cabin. He joined the crew in watching the searchlight. "Charlotte, angel! Charlotte, answer Daddy!"

I cried and held the boys. Troy buried his face in my shoulder. We held one another close and wept while Colin shouted at the storm.

Twenty-four

I KNOW NOTHING MORE COMFORTING THAN HOLDING my son next to me, but nothing more agonizing than watching a father look over the bow of a ship for a lost child. Colin looked flat in the dark next to the rescuers, all of them swaying in union like a row of paper dolls. The searchlights passed in front of them reflecting in the rain, which at times blew horizontally.

"How come they can't find Charlotte?" asked Troy. His whole body trembled, and it seemed I would never dry all of the rain and salt water from his hair.

"I don't know. It's such a big ocean, Troy," I told him, knowing I sounded like a lame adult.

Two of the men set up a commotion on deck. Three divers leaped into the water while two men held on to Colin to keep him from climbing overboard.

"Mason and Troy, I want you both to stay right here in your seats while I check on things out front." The wind blew me back and so I crouched and almost crawled up to the bow.

"I saw something, March, next to that buoy!" Colin pointed until the searchlight locked onto the buoy.

The divers fought the swells and bobbed in and out of sight until one of them grabbed onto the buoy. Another man broke the surface and waved wildly until he coaxed the searchlight his way.

"It's Charlotte," I whispered. They found her.

We watched them move her toward the boat against the wind and waves. She was strapped in a life vest, her eyes closed. They brought her aboard, a small doll-child wrapped in angel white. And still.

One of the Coast Guard crew members wrapped Charlotte in blankets. She never spoke or opened her eyes. Harold and Bobby had the ambulances waiting on shore. All three of the children were rushed to Holy Mary by the Sea Hospital.

I rode with Mason. He whispered the entire way as we drove past the beach cottages and the hundred-year-old homes along Durning Lane. Rain fell over the town, gray and pattering against the glass of the ambulance windows. The noontime lunch crowd had dis-appeared into the delis and coffee shops but I saw faces against the windows that turned into blurs of color and then flashed from sight.

Dinah stood with Dad just inside the emergency-room entrance. After we phoned home she had left immediately to fetch him and meet us at the hospital.

Charlotte was wheeled in first, but we could not see her for the flurry of attendants that surrounded her, lifted up her gurney, and literally ran with her through the open doors. The doors behind us were opened. I followed the parade through the doors, up the hall, and into the emergency room where each bed was divided by curtains.

A physician introduced himself to Colin then politely moved him aside, out of the way of the emergency-room nurses and a doctor who looked as young as Mason to me.

"Colin, let's wait here," I said. I gestured toward a group of three blue plastic chairs against the wall.

Colin hovered outside the flurry of movement around his daughter for a moment and then acquiesced to take a seat. Dad joined me on the other side.

"March, I just sat there next to her in the ambulance feeling as though I had nothing to offer her while the attendant intubated her. They called it aspiration pneumonia. I overheard the doctor say she has hypothermia, too," said Colin.

The young doctor moved down to Mason's bed while the older one took over Charlotte's care. I wanted to hover, but stayed next to Colin. "Mason looks so pale. When will they let me go to him?"

"Please, Lord, touch my little girl," Colin breathed out a prayer.

Dinah showed up with coffee.

"Thelma set the prayer chain in motion," said Dad. His fingers slid around my right hand.

"Mrs. Longfellow, we're ready for you," said the young child-of-a-physician.

"Finally. Come on, Dad. You come too." Dad followed me behind the curtain.

"We're treating Mason for shock. He's going to be fine but we'll keep him overnight just to make certain he doesn't develop pneumonia," said the doctor.

"What about Troy and Charlotte?" asked Mason.

"Troy is fine." Colin stopped there.

I kissed Mason first on his forehead and then directly on the mouth. When I stepped out from behind the curtain to tell Colin the good news, I saw him following the nurses out of the emergency room with Charlotte. He turned to me and his movements were mechanical, powered by rote rather than by reason. "They're moving her to ICU," he said and disappeared.

Dad and I opened the curtain between Troy and Mason so that they could see one another and know they were protected and safe.

The quiet humming outside of Intensive Care was like a large clock ticking, with each tick or tock carrying someone ahead into the next minute or carrying someone away. Holy Mary by the Sea Hospital, in its smallness, provided stoic efficiency with two nurses on duty. The reception desk was decorated with paper mobiles of orange-and-black Halloween motifs, hissing cats, and doe-eyed ghosts.

Colin paced outside of ICU calculating all of the things about him that were the sum total of a horrible father.

He had a stoop-shouldered posture, and I did not know whether I should touch him or leave him to himself. "If you get some food inside you, you'll feel better this afternoon," I said.

"I don't know about this place. If they could just get her stabilized and then get her back to a Charlotte hospital." Colin said it in a whisper. Then he signed another form the nurse handed to him.

"Did the doctor say what they think is wrong?"

"It's a concussion. Her breathing isn't right, either, and now she has a fever. It isn't good, and I have to get back down to Troy."

"Troy is fine. He and Mason are in the children's ward, maybe eating a little something by now."

"There is a children's ward here?"

"It's not fancy, but it isn't Dogpatch, either."

"March, I'm sorry. I don't mean to sound like your hospital is substandard, not big city enough or whatever. I'm not in my right mind. Where is James?"

"Dinah took him home. I told him he could come back tomorrow, but they're releasing Mason and Troy in the morning. Ruth took Luke and Rachel to the cafeteria for lunch. I think it finally stopped raining."

"Oh, I didn't realize it was lunchtime."

A nurse adjusted the oxygen mask over Charlotte's mouth. Her face looked oyster white with two bands of dark lashes that underlined her closed eyelids.

A candy striper clattered past and a nurse hushed her.

"Ms. March, is that you?" Yolanda whirled around with her hat barely pinned to a tousled half-ponytail. She wore a striped pinafore straight out of the fifties and a little white underblouse.

"Yolanda, I didn't expect to see you," I said.

"I'm a candy striper now. That whole kidnapping attempt thing changed my life. I've decided to dedicate my life to helping others. It's the least I can do considering, like, you know, I've been given a second chance and all. I would not be the least bit surprised if I didn't end up working with hungry children in a Third World country."

"You were almost kidnapped? You must be the girl March rescued in the story that they wrote about in *LIFE* magazine." Colin accepted a cup of coffee from the desk nurse.

"You saw it too?" Yolanda said it breathlessly, threw back her head, and declared, "Is there anyone who didn't see that piece? The whole town is forever changed, and it's all due to March."

I offered to add cream to Colin's coffee.

"But why are you here, Ms. March?" She looked at Colin. "Don't tell me you're the father of the little girl they rescued. Oh my word! Did you rescue that sweet precious little girl too?" Yolanda fiddled with the cap and poked more hair beneath it while she said to Colin, "I just would not put it past her at all."

"Yolanda, this is Reverend Arnett. Our children took an unexpected sailing trip and fell into some trouble. The Coast Guard actually rescued them," I said.

Colin clasped his hand around her trembling white fingers and greeted her, his words washed of any life.

"Mason—not Mason too?" Yolanda screeched.

"Mason's fine," I answered as quickly as was possible with Yolanda.

"Did he tell you how it happened?"

I nodded. He and Troy had argued over the fine points, but we came to something of a consensus. "Mason confessed some of it. He had gathered up the life vests but Troy denounced the need for them. Mason could not remember whether or not he had tossed them into the bow of the ship or if they just ended up there in a jumble." Charlotte had startled the boys with her appearance, still clothed in her angel-white gown but wearing a coat Ruth had purchased for her at the

Kmart. "Charlotte tried to talk them out of going, but machismo ruled the morning. Troy decided she had to go with them or risk being found out. That is how she wound up on board, sleepy-eyed and vulnerable."

A salmon-red sky had lured the trio out into deep waters. The raging storm was upon them before the first light appeared in the cottage window, when the darkening sky to the land dwellers was nothing more than a reason to lie in bed a few minutes more.

"But is Mason hurt?" asked Yolanda.

"No, Mason is going to be fine. He'll be released in the morning along with the pastor's son, Troy, and it wouldn't surprise me if they didn't let them go home tonight. Are you working in ICU? Because if you are, it would do a world of good if you could keep a watch out for little Charlotte here so Reverend Arnett can grab some lunch."

"I don't know if I should," said Colin.

"Little Charlotte! What a sweet name. Now you go get some food, Pastor, and I swear I'll send for you straightaway if there is any change. I practically raised Mason, so I am really a good one to sit with your angel." Yolanda trounced off toward Charlotte's bed.

Colin followed me, taking gangly reluctant strides backward with his back to the door.

When the elevator door opened, Jerry Brevity walked out with a basket of fruit piled a foot high. "Oh, thank goodness, I found you, March. They won't let you send flowers to ICU so I brought fruit. When my uncle was burned over forty percent of his body, the one thing my aunt appreciated was fruit and cheese. Ellen threw in a box of crackers too. How is Mason?" he asked.

"Oh. Fruit. How nice of you. Mason will get to go home tomorrow. He isn't in ICU. Jerry, this is Reverend Arnett. His little girl Charlotte is the one in ICU. Reverend Arnett, this is Jerry Brevity," I said. I couldn't remember if Colin knew about my sporadic life with Jerry, but Jerry most assuredly knew about Colin. It had seemed so simple to just drift, come-what-may, and not go into lengthy explanations either way.

"So you're the minister." Jerry stuck the fruit basket in my hands and turned and walked back into the elevator. "Going down?" He would not look at either of us, and his polite offer to hold the elevator door was sprinkled with a sharp tinny whine in his voice.

We stepped on and rode down with him, none of us speaking. After the old Holy Mary elevator lurched to a stop, the doors hesitated before opening, like always. Jerry sighed in a disgruntled groan twice before the doors finally jerked open. Jerry stepped off without saying another word to me and marched across the lobby and through the automatic doors at the entrance.

"I take it you're friends with Mr. Brevity." Colin held out his hands awkwardly, as though he wanted to relieve me of the weight of the basket but unsure if he was meddling.

"Jerry and I saw each other off and on."

"He knows about me?"

"The whole town knows about you, Colin. I don't have the luxury of privacy."

"I don't believe you've mentioned him." He hefted the basket. "Or was this the guy who took you to the sparkler boat parade? That's him, right?" It was the first time I had ever read sparks of jealousy on Colin's face. It was lovely to behold.

"I didn't think it was all that important."

"He had a rat embroidered on his lapel," he said flatly.

"They're having chicken fajitas in the cafeteria today. Would you prefer that or a burger?"

"If this Mr. Brevity is an issue with you, you should say so rather than letting me run around in circles wondering if I've done something wrong by moving toward an actual commitment."

"Jerry is not an issue." I wasn't sure if I wanted to calm his concern completely or give him food for thought.

"Fine."

"The cafeteria is this way," I said. I reeled in a smirk.

"But then everything else is of no consequence now anyway."

I don't believe he intended to sound harsh. Anger was the flagship for worry, I told myself. He wasn't angry with me, just the situation.

"I just want Charlotte back. I want her home where she belongs and everything back as it was."

He was taking too many jabs. I stepped back and allowed him to walk past and into the cafeteria.

He stopped and we looked at one another until I dropped my head, unable to retort with any womanly intelligence.

"I just can't muster an appetite, Colin. Please go ahead and join Ruth and Luke for lunch. I've got something I need to do." I tottered down the hallway and took a left into the gift shop. Colin might misinterpret my tears.

In one window, the shop attendant assembled an early Christmas display. I stared at the angels with feathered wings for so long the clerk asked if she could help me. "How much for the feathery angel whatnots?" I asked.

"Thirty-nine ninety-five, plus tax and you get a free Christmas wrap with that today." She wore a red gingham apron to usher in a little Yuletide spirit, but also had clasped on a Halloween pin, a battery-operated spider with a light-up orange nose that spread its spider legs every time the pull-string was yanked.

"I'll keep looking," I said. In an umbrella stand, someone had placed several packages. I pulled one out and saw it was a kite. The label displayed the full view of an angel. "How much are these?"

"Ten dollars. They're really left over from March. But the owner thought they might sell, what with the angel business picking up this time of year."

"I'll take one and the gift wrap."

"Gift wrap is three dollars and fifty cents. It's only free with one of those ceramic angels."

"I'll wrap it myself. Just bag it up then, if you will." I added a laptop checker game and two all-day suckers for the boys and a stuffed kitten with tufted ears for Charlotte when she woke up. The clerk clicked off the amounts on a computer. In the center of the Christmas display, a wig form had been transformed into a garish sequined hat display. Atop it was a plumed hat, and for a moment the wig form seemed to nag me like Joan. I could almost see the feathers waving in the little windowed cove at the hotel restaurant.

The clerk gave me the total and wrapped each piece with tissue paper even though I had not bought the ceramic thingy. I turned my back on Joan and her sequined eyelids and felt my soul turn into gelatin. She was Mason's grandmother, no matter what we thought of one another. Whatever the woman's transgressions, I had to make things right. I felt a Godlike thawing going on inside of me.

I found the boys perched in their beds behind hospital dinner trays. Troy was trying to engage Mason in a war with corn kernels from his lunch plate. But Mason stared straight ahead, his cheeks still pale.

"How about a checkers game?" I held up the bag, but both of the guys deflated. "I realize you were expecting a video game, but I swear you'll like this." I laid the suckers on each tray.

"Thanks, Mom," said Mason.

Troy reciprocated and then allowed the pillow to swallow his head. "This food is for people in jail."

"Mason, I want to ask you something. You know that big fight between Grandma and me? I think it's time we settled it."

"Just let her have the land?" His brows arched into pup tents above his eyes.

"Let's shake on it." We did.

"I'm in trouble, I guess." Mason rolled the sucker back and forth with one finger.

"I guess. We'll talk about it at home."

"Great. I'll look forward to that." He looked past me.

Colin appeared. His eyes conveyed resolve, as though he had been thinking things through again.

I turned my attention on Mason.

"Dad! Where have you been? Is Charlotte okay?" Troy tried to crawl out of his bed but Colin lifted him right back up into it.

"She's going to be fine." The circles under Colin's eyes made dark crescents like blue canoes, and I realized he was terrible at lying, which made him treacherously fascinating.

"I should have asked you if you have any candy issues, Colin," I said without a glance in his direction.

"Not at all." He kissed Troy. "I need to step out for just a minute, son, to talk with Ms. Longfellow."

"Don't think you have to, Colin. You need this time with your son. Anyone want to play checkers?"

Colin ambled around the foot of Mason's bed. "Please, March?"

"You go ahead and set up the checkers and I'll be back in a jiff," I told Mason.

Colin hesitated until a group of senior women in pink smocks walked past with salad trays. "March, sometimes you make me say things I don't mean."

"I make you?"

"You know I'm distracted right now. I just need to clear my head and then I'll say all of the right things. But just now when you walked away, I felt as though you were walking away from me, leaving me, not just without words, but leaving me period. I felt empty."

"I apologize for that," I said.

"Don't apologize! Just let me talk without a comment, if you don't mind."

I stared at him.

"Do you feel a part of my life, right now? Of the life that's up on the second floor and here in this room next to us?"

I opened my mouth, but all that came out was a whimper. I wiped the tears from my eyes and knew exactly, for once, what I had to say.

"March, Reverend Arnett, sir!" Yolanda skidded across the hall ahead and then ran toward us. "I am so glad I found you. This is awful! You've just got to come right this minute back up to ICU!"

Colin lost his breath.

"Yolanda, what on earth is wrong?" I asked.

"It's your little Charlotte, sir! She's gone into respiratory arrest." Yolanda burst into tears.

"We're coming, Yolanda," I said. I grasped Colin's hand. "Colin, let's get you upstairs."

A medical team surrounded Charlotte's pediatric bed. A doctor yelled at one of the nurses for her fumbling hands. The monitor beeped sporadically.

I waited several feet behind Colin. His shoulders were stooped. Whatever color had been in his face left him. He sobbed and all at once I could see him standing over Eva's bed. But I was not repelled by the image. I moved closer to him, took his hand, and pressed the side of my face against his arm. "Colin," I said, almost afraid to speak, to draw a father's attention from his little girl's bedside.

"March. I'm helpless to help her."

"I'm here, Colin."

He brought his arm around my shoulders and I cried with him. "To answer you earlier, of course I'm part of this, Colin." How could I not be? I was the least important person in the world now.

Twenty-five

NAGS HEAD IS A QUIET PLACE BETWEEN WINTER AND spring with plenty of places for children to run. Colin jogged along the water's edge holding the back of a kite while Mason, Troy, and Luke ran ahead to get the ten-dollar thing up in the air. The boys did not seem to mind the girlish smiling angel on the kite, only that it flew. Rachel ran behind them, galloping and tossing her hair like a mane. The angel soared and made loopy curls and zigs and zags at the ocean, but never did it nosedive altogether. It lifted and eventually folded out fully against the wind as though it would never come down. The kite reminded me of when Charlotte and I made sand angels along a bank that did not threaten to wash them away, only time. So different from the shoreline of an ocean.

We had spent the day before at Ocracoke, watching the local horsemen round up the wild mustangs that somehow had escaped their controlled areas and ventured into the village neighborhoods where they did not belong. I wrote about the ponies when I had first visited the Outer Banks alone, my spiritual trek back to the heart of God. I wrote until the words turned into pages of musings and then stories. Colin called it my "first novel", but I believed him to be too ambitious. But he knows that I know that about him.

The tide drew back and slapped against an outcropping of rocks beyond where the kids played. I know the ocean can swallow up things against your will, but it did not swallow up Troy, or Mason; nor did it swallow up Charlotte. Colin and I had gathered in the hospital chapel and breathed a prayer of gratitude for all of our many blessings and especially for our own little miracle girl the morning she woke up and asked for, of all things, water.

A squeal I likened to that of a wild ocean bird came from behind me and Charlotte leaped over our blanket and ran at the boys. "You put my kite back, you thieves, you! Get your grimy, boy hands off my angel!"

Colin accepted his defeat as a gentleman should and returned the ball of twine to its rightful owner. Charlotte lifted both hands high, her fingers fanning the wind, and she guided the kite in the beatific perfection that only a girl can give an object that dwells between the earth and the sky.

Colin walked toward me with his back to the shoreline and his face toward his miracle He settled beside me.

"Colin, this paragraph sounds terrible. Here, let me read it to you," I said.

"You've already read it to me and I like it. Stop trying to correct it as you write, March, and just let the words sing. You can't create perfection. Perfection arrives in thin layers, one atop another. It's like God remaking us until we take on the shape he intended."

"Why are you so wise?" I asked.

He rolled over on his stomach and faced me as I sat cross-legged. He touched my hand that rested on my knee. "Marry me, March."

"I already told you I would."

"You are lovely, lovely to look at." He ran his fingers along my nails as though he touched porcelain.

"If you're trying to flatter me, you cannot have another ice cream cone. I can't abide a fat husband."

"I don't know if I told you, but the minister just called. The chapel we wanted just came open. We won't have to marry at the hotel reception room after all."

"Colin, you don't say? I can't believe it. That is such a, well, an unbelievable place for a wedding. I'll call the photographer, the florist, and Dad. I hope he remembers to bring the wedding vows. First I'll call Dinah and ask her to meet him early and make certain he has everything. I'll bet he hasn't married anyone in a year. I know I'm forgetting so many things. But that isn't so awful, I guess."

"I'll call Mom and Dad. They should be here anytime. I'm glad Ruth is meeting them. I'm needing a little nap right about now." Colin checked his watch and flicked sand off of the face. "The realtor says we should meet him Monday morning." He rolled onto his back to follow the path of the angel kite overhead.

"But should we do that? You won't know if you want to pastor that church in Rocky Mount until after Sunday. Will Monday give you enough time to know for sure?"

"Have a little faith and then walk out on it. What have we here? A new bottle." He picked up the small, clear bottle with a tag around the neck that said "Nags Head."

"Mason made it."

"What are these inside it?"

"Seven stones. One for each of us. Enough for a whole shore."

Mason plopped down between Colin and me. "Save me from those crazy women!"

"Excuse me, sir. You're invading my space." Colin climbed over Mason and sat next to me. He kissed the tip of my nose right in the place where it freckled. "If the kids aren't exhausted, I am. I'm going to round them up." He called after them and then yelled when they scattered down both sides of the beach.

"It's going to be a noisy house," said Mason.

"I kind of like it," I said.

"Did that lady buy the *Sentinel?* Gloria said she's liquid, whatever that means."

"She was married to a senator once. Geraldine Montague. I met her on a flight to Charlotte and she wrote down my name, gave me her card. I just picked up the phone one day and asked her if she'd like to hear a business proposal. She likes this area. It's close to her grandchildren. She thinks of the *Sentinel* as a hobby. Gloria said she brought by paint samples yesterday. That's always a good sign."

"Grandpa says he doesn't think he's going to like Rocky Mount." Mason sounded just like Dad.

"Let him complain. The house we're looking at has plenty of places for him to read, and it's not near the water and that should satisfy him. Besides, he's keeping the cottage and that is what reminds him most of my mother."

"I looked at the atlas, and Rocky Mount is right in between where we live and where they live," Mason said.

I began rolling up the blanket and gathering the collection of plastic beach toys strewn around our little spot on the sand.

"I've been thinking about Grandma Joan, and she doesn't make sense."

"Toss me that sand pail, please, will you?" I asked.

"If she wanted Dad's land so badly, then why did she give it right back to me?"

"So I tried a little kindness. Don't look at me like that."

"You're turning into a wimp, Mom. I kind of like it." Mason clumped together an armload of sand toys and headed toward the parking lot with four squealing Arnetts on his heels. Colin opened the doors to let them clamber inside, a tangle of bare feet powdered with sand in every nook and cranny of every bend in every limb.

"Hold it! I want to take a picture," I said.

Colin groaned. Every Arnett child along with Mason clambered out of the vehicle and gathered around the tailgate posing like contortionists and body builders.

I considered the lovely sight of each one and how God used the small things to hold back life's tides.

Author's Note

IN THE MIDDLE OF WRITING *SANDPEBBLES*, OUR life took a tragic turn when three Huntersville policemen showed up at our door to tell us "Your daughter, Jessica, was in a terrible car accident. She didn't make it."

I say this to you, the reader, because some who hear of our tragedy may think that this sudden twist in our road fomented this story when, instead, our sudden loss caused the work already in progress to shift as I descended into a valley I did not want to travel. A valley that soon became a canyon.

In this canyon, I discovered many new things about pain and about the Lord: a deeper understanding of the Suffering Savior; how to offer real comfort to those in pain; and thirdly, a higher appreciation for the healing qualities of laughter. Within weeks after committing our angel girl eternally into the arms of Christ, the wonderful people from W Publishing and Women of Faith invited me along with the other fiction authors of this line to join them for a weekend of refreshing at the Nashville 2001 conference. I suddenly found myself surrounded by a unique sisterhood of authors and speakers who lifted my spirits, took me closer to the cross, and made me laugh until the pain was nothing but a soft pillow. I had taken a sabbatical from writing *Sandpebbles,* or anything for that matter, and did not know if I possessed the creative energy to return to my writing desk. But I realized that weekend that when I am an emotional wreck, Christ can handle all of my engine work. I returned home renewed and determined to write this story with a deeper understanding of pain and a hopeful measure of laughter. I had discovered a new elixir and wanted to share it with as many women as possible. And although laughter is addictive, you won't have to check into the Betty Ford Clinic when you overdo.

It was only a few months later that our nation was shaken by its own tragedy. Suddenly the world was reeling in the aftermath of a modern-day holocaust that affected every American somehow, some way. Through these dark days, God helped me realize that when pain takes up residence in my heart, hopelessness tries to wiggle through the door right behind her. And that is when I have to post an eviction notice—no hopelessness allowed.

Several weeks after our April tragedy, I noticed that my Bible promise desk calendar yet remained on the date of Jessica's death. April 27, 2001 was coincidentally decorated with her favorite flowers—daisies—and inscribed with this scripture: *"I waited patiently for the* LORD *to help me, and he turned to me and heard my cry. He lifted me out of the pit of despair, out of the mud and the mire. He set my feet on solid ground and steadied me as I walked along"* Psalm 40:1–2 NLT.

If you're up to your knees in life's mud and your pits have become canyons, this is my prayer for you—that Jesus Christ, who hears your cry, will lift you up onto His solid ground and keep you moving ahead, steady as you go, walking on Sonshine.

—Patricia Hickman

Acknowledgments

I WANT TO EXPRESS HOW GRATEFUL I AM TO THE following people for their advice and expert knowledge that lends accuracy to my story. Very warm thanks to Pastor Wade Malloy of Southlake Presbyterian Church for sharing facts about Presbyterian traditions and doctrines of faith. Additional thanks go to attorney Jeff Rothwell for providing me with legal facts and trial information. And thanks so much to John Bordsen, travel editor of the *Charlotte Observer*, who helped immensely in the early stages of *Sandpebbles* as I developed March Longfellow's eclectic newspaper career. Thanks to my wonderful friend, Shannon Anzivino, for lending the medical facts to this story as well as being a prayer warrior for this project. And to Deb Raney, massive thanks to you for assisting me in developing the quirky office staff and setting for the Candle Cove *Sentinel*. Your knowledge of small-town newspapers is as vital to this story as your own stories are to the CBA market.

I also want to thank the W Publishing Group family and the Women of Faith family for being a family to me during our trying year. Thank you for your patience in waiting for this story to finally come to its completion. Thank you, Debbie Wickwire, for being such a wonderful sister in the faith. Thank you, Stephen Arterburn, for your vision for this line of fiction. Thank you, Mary, Patsy, Barbara, Thelma, Marilyn, Sheila, and Luci (who is always last) for propping us up with your prayers and sharing your profound jewels of wisdom. Thank you to Mark Sweeney, Ami McConnell, Diane Eble, and the W editing staff and marketing team for your expert attention to detail and commitment to excellence in fiction. Thank you to Greg Johnson and Rick Christian of the best literary agency in the country and for being our friends. Lastly (but not leastly), thanks to my WOF Fictionette sisters, Angie, Terri, and Karen, and the ChiLibris family of writers for surrounding the Hickmans with your love and prayers. You have no idea . . . words just cannot express how deeply you touched our lives and helped us down the healing path.

stranded in
paradise

By Lori Copeland

WestBow™
PRESS
A Division of Thomas Nelson Publishers
Since 1798
visit us at www.westbowpress.com

Published by W Publishing Group, Nashville, Tennessee, in association
with the literary agency of Alive Communications, Inc., 7680 Goddard
Street, Suite 200, Colorado Springs, Colorado, 80920. All rights reserved.

Library of Congress Cataloging-in-Publication Data

Copeland, Lori.
    Stranded in paradise / by Lori Copeland.
      p. cm.
    ISBN 0-8499-4378-7 (softcover)
    1. Colorado—Fiction. I. Title.
PS3553.06336 S77 2002
813'.54—dc21   2002008987

This book is a singular gift from God, and I praise His name that He would allow this author to extol His glory through Women of Faith.

And to Thelma Jean Keithly Bilyeu: mother of nine children, grandmother of twenty-two, great-grandmother of twenty-one, and great-great-grandmother of one. Thelma was called home to be with the Lord as I was finishing this book. A devoted follower of Christ, Thelma enjoyed many hours of Christian fiction. Thelma, you will be sorely missed by family, friends, and loved ones. Until we meet again . . .

Let the LORD's people show him reverence, for those who honor him will have all they need. Even strong young lions sometimes go hungry, but those who trust in the LORD will never lack any good thing.

—PSALM 34:9–10
NEW LIVING TRANSLATION

1

Jan. 10, 8:55 A.M.
Denver, Colorado

"Boy, Kim. This weather is freaky! A tropical depression forming in the Pacific—in January?"

"Weird. I thought hurricane season was over two months ago," the female disk jockey said. But this is Denver and I want snow!"

Tess Nelson signaled, then switched lanes on the busy interstate. The Acura surged ahead, passing a slower-moving vehicle before shooting back to the right lane. The digital clock turned to 8:56 A.M.

The disk jockeys kept up their banter, "Imagine a summer thunderstorm, a dark, hulking brute towering over ten turbulent miles into the heavens—black, rolling clouds spewing blinding rain, hailstones, and lightning. Then picture a line of these monsters seventy-five miles long, standing shoulder to shoulder," Rocky said of a developing storm in the South Pacific. "Take that line and wrap it around into a circle 230 miles across and spin it counterclockwise at 140 miles an hour and you're in the eye of a hurricane. . . . Must be something to experience . . ." She frowned at the radio, as she wondered how long it took for those storms to fizzle out. She had a business trip planned for the following week in Hawaii and the last thing she needed was some tropical depression to foul up her plans.

The Acura wheeled into the underground parking garage. Tires and power steering screeched as she ascended from the first floor to the second level. She turned into spot seven, shut off the engine, and looked at the clock. 8:57—oops. 8:58. On time.

Her newest twenty-something temp was waiting when the elevator doors opened to the fourteenth floor.

"Suit wants to see you." Judy chewed gum and pointed an acrylic-nailed, three-ringed finger toward the executive suite one floor up.

"I need to drop these things off in my office and get a cup of coffee—"

"No time, Kiddo. The Man says now. Mucho pronto." The temp blew a bubble and popped it back into her mouth in one swift move.

Tess shifted the armload of folders, sunglasses, briefcase, and purse, then pilfered a notepad and pen from her secretary's desk. "Please spit out your gum." She pointed to the wastebasket.

"Yes ma'am."

Ma'am? Tess flinched. She had to speak to Nick in personnel about the help he was sending her lately. The last one had taken breaks every hour to do her yoga stretches right there on the office floor. She didn't know how long she could deal with the endless array of teenyboppers behind the desk.

Stepping into the elevator, she punched floor thirty-seven and tapped the pen against the notepad as she watched the numbers change above the elevator's doors. To hear Len refer to the executive office as "his office" sounded strange. He'd taken over as chief executive officer of Connor.com upon the sudden death of his father, Dave Connor, the man who had started the company five years earlier. While dot com companies had been rising fast in the late nineties, Dave Connor had moved with caution, investing back into the business instead of buying new equipment and hiring employees he wouldn't be able to keep for the long haul. He was a man of vision. But Dave hadn't planned on dying at the age of sixty-one of a heart attack.

Dot com companies sell service, not a product, and Dave had built a strong, self-sustaining business because he cared about his customers. Connor.com allowed clients to let bids on large-ticket or small-ticket items online. If they wished, they could even do a closed bid.

Under Dave's management, changes were constantly made to meet a client's needs. Most of the schools in this area used Connor.com to order supplies like hand soap, detergent, grease-breaker soap, and soap for mopping kitchen floors, tile floors, and hardwood floors. One catalog they maintained listed over twenty thousand different soap items.

A company of this size needed a lot of people: a chief executive officer, chief financial officer, chief operations officer, chief technical officer, plus middle management people and a ton of technical geeks. Not everyone could manage a company this size the way Dave had done. She hoped Len was up to it.

Tess had met Dave at a Chamber of Commerce mixer five and a half years ago. He was a kind old man who had treated her like a daughter almost from the time they met. When he had asked her to join his company a few months later, she'd jumped at the opportunity.

The job was a human resource manager's dream, with a lot of potential for advancement. She was ready for the challenges. For the past two years Dave had been grooming her to take the position of vice president of human resources, second in command of Connor.com.

Apparently, this morning Len was ready to announce that he was moving her into the job. She knew she was ready to steer the company through the turbulent waters of mergers and acquisitions, setting up profit sharing and a 401(k) program that would attract experienced and loyal employees. This was the crowning achievement of all her hard work.

As she reached Len's office, his secretary, Nancy, was coming out. "Hello," Tess chirped.

"Go on in," Nancy murmured, refusing to meet her eye. Odd. Nancy Silva was one of the friendliest people Tess knew. From the look on Nancy's face she wondered if something awful had happened to her.

"Thanks," Tess said as Nancy turned her back.

She opened the door. Len had made few changes to Dave's office. When she entered the world of mahogany and Prussian blue she found Len leaning back in Dave's chair, phone to his ear, staring out the big window behind the large desk that had been his father's for over twenty years. Len had that familiar pose, forefinger tapping the back of the phone as he spoke as if prompting whoever was on the other end to hurry it up. His sandy hair fell against his forehead in that boyish way he had. Tess felt her back stiffen as the old feelings tried to wedge their way back in. Yes, Len had his charms, she told herself, but there was a selfish side to the man.

"See you the first of the week," Len said into the receiver, then hung up the phone and swung around. "Ah, Tess."

She smiled, reminding herself of what this meeting was no doubt about. "Ah, Len." She'd waited a long time for this moment, put in many a long day and given up countless weekends to make deadlines.

She sobered when he didn't return her smile, and uneasiness grew in the pit of her stomach. His life had changed tremendously when Dave died, she reasoned, he was just having a hard day.

She could be of invaluable help now that Dave was gone, of course, and she would. She knew the ins and outs of the company better than anyone, Len included. "Have a seat," Len invited.

She sank into one of the familiar leather chairs where she'd spent many an evening after five sitting, talking business, and laughing over Dave's corny jokes. She wondered briefly if she and Len would have the same kind of relaxed, creative relationship after working hours. Maybe the man could change. She looked up into his eyes.

"You know the dot com business is a little bizarre right now, with so many companies folding," Len said quickly as he raked a hand through his blond hair.

"Yes . . ." Tess replied uncertainly, wondering where he was headed. Was Len thinking of merging with another company? Connor.com was financially stable but right now wasn't the best time—

"The good news is a lot of qualified people are suddenly available."

She shrugged. "True."

"I was talking to a friend I went to college with. We were fraternity brothers, in fact."

"Oh?" She crossed her legs and focused on him, wishing he'd get to the point. "What's his background?"

"Chuck Vinton has been V.P. of human resources at a West Coast firm, but they were bought out . . ."

A prickle of apprehension snaked down her spine.

"—and he's free, so I've hired him as our new vice president."

For a split second, she felt nothing, as if she were in a tunnel without sound or reason. Vice president, he had said—vice president of human resources.

"I don't understand," she said through her fog.

Len met her eyes. He enunciated the words this time, speaking slowly as if she were unable to comprehend. "Chuck's going to take over. He's exactly what Connor.com needs."

Tess shifted forward in her chair. "You hired a *fraternity* brother for my job?"

"I knew you would have a hard time with this, Tess. Chuck isn't exactly taking your position. Your situation here with Connor.com has been unusual—Dad gave you a lot of responsibility. He may have made promises but that was when he was . . ."

"Promises be hanged! Len, you know me. I've worked seventy-hour weeks, skipped vacations, erased my personal life—"

"And I appreciate your hard work but I think the company's better served by hiring someone with more experience. Chuck has ten years under his belt."

He toyed with an eraser, sitting up in his chair to slam dunk the rubber into a glass ashtray.

She seethed. Her life was falling apart and the dunce was shooting hoops.

So there it was: all her hard work, setting up the department from the company's foundation, was being tossed aside because Len Connor ran into an old college buddy. She should have known he'd pull something like this.

"I see." She struggled to hold on to some shred of professionalism. "Then you're saying that I will be working for Mr. Vinton."

Len swirled a gold pen between his fingers. "Well, you *could,* I guess, but the thing is . . ." he paused and she could see his jaw tense. "Chuck is bringing his own people; you'll have to apply for any openings that are left."

"He's bringing—" She tried to absorb the shock. Her mind whirled. "So either I start from square one or I'm fired?"

Len shrugged. "Sorry."

"You're *firing* me?" She stood up, pen and pad fluttering to the floor. The Uniball rolled under the desk.

"There is another open position in which you would fit well—"

"Where?" Her voice was almost a screech.

"Payroll." He smiled, but there was a hint of condescension in that twinkle in his eyes.

Her lashes narrowed. "You're offering me a job in *payroll?*"

He lifted his shoulders. "It's a good position. Decent pay. Punch out at five o'clock."

She stopped him cold. "I am a manager, Len, not a

payroll clerk. I have five years of experience hiring and managing *departments* full of payroll clerks and a dozen other employees. Len, this is a huge professional insult!"

His tone firmed. "I'm only doing what's best for Connor.com. You know that we've tightened our belts, that we've frozen new hires—"

Anger welled inside her.

"But you can bring in your fraternity brother and *his* people? Do I look that stupid, Len?"

He shifted closer to the desk. Beneath the polished wood, his foot tapped erratically. "Your years of service have been duly noted, Tess. It's a tough break, but you're resilient. In a few years, who knows, maybe you'll prove me wrong."

She swallowed back an acid retort. "I'm thinking you're right. I can do better than Conner.com. Chuck does sound like the man to head the helm."

Len shrugged. "Of course the choice is yours. Perhaps you need a few days to think about it . . . "

"I don't need a *vacation*." Right now she needed a two-by-four. A good solid plank to wipe the smirk off his silver-spoon-fed Harvard face.

He calmly met her wintry stare. "I'll hold the payroll position until I hear from you." The phone rang and he picked it up, dismissing her with a nod.

She pivoted on her heels and walked out.

Fired.

Sacked.

She had just been squeezed out—regardless of the "options" Len thought he was giving her. Payroll indeed!

Vaguely aware that Len's secretary was bent conspicuously over a file cabinet, she mustered a pleasant smile and made her way out.

Ducking into the executive washroom, Tess locked herself in a stall, refusing to cry—crying would leave her eyes red and puffy—but she breathed deeply for several minutes as she tried to harness her emotions. She would keep her dignity if it killed her.

Minutes later, she wet a paper towel and pressed it to her eyes, checked to ensure that her makeup was still flawless, then she returned to her office. There, laying on the top of her desk, sat the airline ticket for her business trip. A lot of good that was. The airline wouldn't allow her to transfer it into another name.

She stood staring at it. It would serve Len right to lose the cost of the ticket. She wondered why he hadn't mentioned her upcoming trip. Maybe he'd forgotten. She lifted the envelope and turned it over in her hands. Then in one swift move she tucked it into her briefcase. She wasn't sure why.

She had to get out of the office before she started blubbering, or worse yet before she went back and gave Len Connor a piece of her mind. She reached for her purse and briefcase, then, lifting her chin, walked quickly to the elevator. Len Connor would soon discover that Tess Nelson couldn't be replaced by a fraternity brother or anyone else.

The perky temp went on point. "Are you leaving for the day, Miss Nelson?"

"I'll be out of the office a couple of weeks," she said weakly. Maybe by then Len will have called begging her to come back. She pushed the lighted button, aware of the curious eyes following her. She straightened, her chin lifting a notch. She knew that news of her firing would spread faster than small-town gossip once she left the building. Would anyone care that she'd been dumped? She doubted it; she'd made few friends among her coworkers but who had time for a social life with her workload? Anyway, she wasn't there to socialize. She was there to work. As they should be. That was how she'd gotten where she was, after all . . .

Mona.

The dread word surfaced in her consciousness as she rode to the ground floor. She could hear her mother's voice now: *Well, the news doesn't surprise me. You always mess up somehow.* She slid into her Acura, and flipped on the car defrosters. As she drove out of the garage, she realized that the rain was falling in sheets. She pulled into traffic, erratically swerving to miss an oncoming public transportation bus.

Len Connor could not humiliate her this way. She had

helped his father build Connor.com. She couldn't be replaced by a ruthless whim, and that was all this ploy was. Len had always been jealous of the trust his father had put in her. Now that he was in charge he was rubbing her nose in it.

But he'd see Connor.com couldn't run without her—and it wouldn't take Len long to recognize it. Not once things started falling apart.

Tess unlocked the door to her condo and flicked on the light. More than anything else, her home was a deliberate reminder of how far up the ladder she had climbed. Colonial blue walls with white trim, white sofa, blue-and-white striped Queen Anne chairs, a tall lemon-yellow vase holding a silk arrangement of willows and forsythia had all been chosen to create an impression of pristine cleanliness. She remembered the dirty, dismal house she had grown up in and shuddered. How had she survived?

Shucking off her shoes, she made her way to the kitchen, where she scooped up a bowl of ice cream and topped it with a drizzle of Hershey's syrup. She dug her spoon in and lifted it to her mouth when she noticed a long hair trailing out of it. "Eww!" She groaned and gazed down at the counter where three more strands innocently lay. "Not again," she said. She set the ice cream down and made her way to the bathroom where she studied herself in the mirror. It didn't *look* like she was losing her hair, but lately it seemed as if she'd found strands everywhere: in her checkbook, on reports for work, in her food . . .

She lifted a brush from the counter and gave her taffy-color hair a few strokes when the phone began jangling.

"Tess?" a voice said when she picked up.

"Beeg?" Tess said. Bee Gee had been her college roommate. She'd since made a name for herself as an artist working primarily in watercolor.

"Say, I was calling about your trip next week. There's this show in New York—"

"Oh, Beeg!" She moaned, the tears she'd so carefully held in now flowing freely. "That, that oaf Len Connor had the gall to fire me this morning! Can you believe this?"

"Oh, honey," Beeg consoled. "I'm so sorry."

Tess sobbed in big gulps. "He actually thought I'd take a job in *payroll* when he knows I've been practically running the company these past few months."

"So, what are you going to do about it? How high up is his office? Maybe you could throw rocks at his window."

That brought a smile to Tess's waterlogged cheeks.

"You always could cheer me up."

"Maybe you should come next week anyway. It could

be a vacation instead of a business trip. I'm sure you have money squirreled away."

"I do still have the ticket . . ." She glanced at her briefcase by the door. "But it wouldn't be right. I didn't pay for it."

"Was it right for Len Connor to fire you?" Beeg defended.

"No . . ."

"So you need time to regroup, think through what you want to do next. What better place than in Hawaii with your best friend?"

"You know I'd love to spend some time with you," Tess began, "but I just don't know if I'm ready now. There's just too much . . ."

"And your perfect little schedule can't adjust?" Beeg said with kindness in her voice. "I know all about it. But if you change your mind . . ."

"I know where to find you," she finished and Beeg chuckled.

"In the meantime," Beeg said, "why don't you go find some nice big rocks to throw at that window? Boulders, maybe."

After she hung up the phone, Tess returned to her ice cream and sat at the kitchen table as she ate. It had been at least six years since she'd seen Bee Gee Harris. No one had ever been a better friend to her.

She held her spoon up, gazing at her reflection in the concave surface that made her nose look disproportionately large. She laughed aloud, then realized how hollow it sounded in the silence of her home.

Maybe it would be good to go see Beeg, she thought. At least she'd have someone to have a good cry with. Who knew, maybe some time on a Hawaiian beach would give her the direction she needed.

Jan. 14, 2:30 P.M.
O'Hare International Control Tower

Carter McConnell sat at his terminal and watched snow blowing in driving sheets against the tower windows. Perched in the glassed-in birdcage, weary air traffic controllers gazed at their radar monitors.

It had been one of the worst nights anyone could remember. During the past few hours they had efficiently handled close to four hundred incoming and outgoing flights. Planes were sitting at gates, others systematically landing and taking off, but the rush was nothing compared to what it had been earlier.

From his vantage point high atop the airport terminal, Carter focused on the red beacon lights moving about the runway. He wished he was home. His head ached and his throat felt scratchy and tight. He wanted to kick back, relax, give his dog, Max, a tummy rub, and eat a nice bowl of mint chocolate chip ice cream. But he still had an hour before his shift was over.

He glanced at the ground-surveillance radar and suddenly sat up straighter. A quick reading on the bright display indicated that a United Boeing 727, still ten miles out, was coming in fast. Carter quickly flipped a switch on the panel in front of him.

"Approach, this is Ground. Clipper 242 looks to be coming in hard. Does he have a problem?"

"Ground, this is Approach. Yeah, he's picking up heavy ice. He's been cleared to land on Runway 36."

Carter glanced at the ground radar again and frowned. If Tim Matthews, the approach controller, had accurate information, they were in trouble. Carter's ground-surveillance screen indicated an unidentified airplane taxiing toward the approach end of Runway 36.

Carter grabbed the binoculars and scanned the snow-covered tarmac. His jaw clenched when he saw the lighted tail section of a Global Airways DC-9 disappearing toward the runway.

"Global, this is Ground—" The sharp crackling at the other end took Carter by surprise. "Global, this is Ground. Do you read me?" The question was met with an ominous silence. Flipping a second switch, Carter shouted, "Local, we've got a problem. I've got a Global Airways DC-9 taxiing on Runway 36 and a Boeing 727 about to land on him. He's not responding!" His voice rose another decibel.

"What's he doing out there?" a voice screeched over the airwaves.

"That's what I'm trying to find out. Advise the Clipper."

"Roger." Max Lakin flipped a switch on his panel. "Clipper 242 be advised we have a no-radio Global DC-9 taxiing southbound on Runway 36. Be prepared for a go-around."

The Clipper's pilot came back. "Local, what's the Global doing out there?"

"Beats me. We're trying to reach the aircraft."

"I'm low on fuel. You're gonna have to get him out of there!" The United pilot shot back.

Carter listened as he kept a close eye on the runway visual-radar indicator. Visibility was down to 2,400 feet. For the past four and a half hours the pilots had been relying solely on instruments.

The nerves between his shoulder blades tightened as he hit the radio switch again.

"Global DC-9, this is Ground," Carter's urgency seeped through his voice. "Exit runway immediately! Do you hear me?"

Wiping a shaky hand across the back of his neck, he eased forward in his chair as the tower supervisor threw down the papers he had been reading and came to stand behind him.

"What's going on?"

"I've got an unauthorized DC-9 taxiing on a reserved runway and he's not talking to me."

Carl Anderson frowned. He was fiftyish, with a large waist and graying hair.

"He obviously thinks he's been cleared," Carter muttered. He tried to reach the DC-9 again. "Global DC-9, exit to taxiway immediately! Repeat. Exit to taxiway immediately!"

Carl leaned over Carter's shoulder and watched the screen as the two planes continued on their courses on Runway 36.

"Tell Local to advise Clipper to go around," Carl said as Carter started pressing the necessary switches.

"I'll try it again—Local, this is Ground. Advise Clipper 242. Unauthorized DC-9 still on runway. Go around immediately! Repeat. Go around immediately!"

"Roger!" Local quickly punched another switch. "Clipper 242, this is Local. Aircraft on runway. Go around. Repeat. Go around."

Carter heard Local talking to the Clipper. Then he heard the pilot's voice, "I'd love to oblige, Local, but this ain't no crop duster I'm flyin'."

"Well, you'd better find a way, Clipper, unless you want to be headline news tomorrow morning," Carter warned. He watched the screen as the two dots drew closer.

All Carter could hope for was that the timing of the two aircraft would be a split second apart and a collision would be avoided. He breathed a silent prayer: *Lord, I've done all I can do on this end. It's up to You.*

Carl hurriedly reached for the crash phone to alert the fire station and emergency crew of an impending crisis. Carter tried to raise the Global DC-9 again, "Global, exit to taxiway *immediately!* Repeat. Exit to taxiway *immediately!*"

Riveted to the screen, the men watched in tense silence as the two blips on the radar screen rushed closer and closer together. The room had become unnaturally quiet as the other flight controllers performed their duties in hushed tones.

"Well, start praying," Carl advised.

"Already have."

The wide-bodied Boeing 747 touched down on the landing strip and came streaking along the runway as the DC-9 inched its way forward.

"Move it, move it, move it," Carter breathed, then he held his breath as the plane rolled laboriously across the path of the incoming 747.

The strained voice of the Clipper pilot cracked over the wire, "Get out of the way, buddy!" Carter cringed as the pilot's voice willed the DC-9 out of his path.

The dots closed in on each other on Carter's screen as the Clipper roared down the landing strip at more than two hundred miles per hour. The blips grew closer and closer.

Suddenly they split apart and the DC-9 eased off the runway as the 747 shot by him in a screech of flying mud and snow.

Carter threw down his pencil and leaned back in his chair weakly as Carl let out a loud war whoop.

"Thank you, God!" Carter said.

"What was that?" yelled the pilot of the DC-9 over the wire, the man obviously shaken.

"Global, you're on an unauthorized taxiway!" Carter snapped. "Where have you been? I've been trying to contact you for three minutes."

"I'm sorry. We've had a radio malfunction—I just heard the contact . . ."

"Well, take some advice, when you have a radio problem don't just go strolling down a runway!" Carter flipped off the radio switch and rubbed his face with his hands. He was trembling and flushed.

Carl laid his hands on his shoulders and gave them a supportive squeeze. "You okay?"

Emotionally and physically drained, Carter could not will himself to respond. He leaned back in his chair and stared at the ceiling. There was no longer any doubt about it. The pressure of the job was getting to him. True, he'd experienced closer calls, but his palms had never felt so sweaty or his stomach been in such a tight knot.

When Carl had hired him nine years earlier Carter had been self-confident; he'd have brushed off this sort of incident without another thought, considering it a part of the business. Perhaps be energized by it, even. But tonight was different. It shouldn't be. He was a seasoned professional, but tonight was—enough. It was enough. He couldn't do this any more.

His supervisor clapped a friendly hand on his shoulder. "Come to my office when you get a minute."

Carter's pulse jumped. "Sure."

His supervisor was on the phone when he arrived. He glanced up and motioned Carter to help himself to the coffee. Carter shook his head. The last thing he needed was more caffeine in his system. He settled his large frame into the upholstered chair opposite Carl's desk.

Carl finished his conversation in a few moments. "Sorry." He nodded toward the phone. "The higher-ups drive me crazy."

"No problem."

The older man stepped to the hotplate and picked up a carafe. "One more cup of this stuff is gonna kill me. Wanda would have a fit if she knew how many I've had today." He shrugged, then poured the strong black brew into his cup and added a couple packets of sugar. "I'm going to die of something, so I figure I might as well go alert."

Carter acknowledged Carl's attempt at wit with a slim

smile and waited patiently until he sat down again. Carl was always worrying about what his wife thought about his bad habits, but never enough to change them.

Carl sipped the strong coffee cautiously, and then sipped again. He seemed to be doing a lot of fidgeting. Carter wished he'd get to the point of the powwow. "You're doing a great job, Son," Carl finally said, meeting Carter's eyes. He set his foam cup aside and leaned forward on his forearms.

Carter glanced up, surprised by the unexpected praise. "Thanks."

"I'm sending you on a vacation."

The statement was firm and straight to the point.

"Vacation? I can't. Not right now."

"Sure you can. You leave tomorrow morning."

"Come on, Carl—"

He was about to argue the point when he saw determination creep into his supervisor's face. He could sit here and argue all day but in the end Carl would have the last word. He always did.

"No buts, Buddy." His superior's tone may have softened, but Carter knew his resolution hadn't. "In the past nine years how many vacations have you taken?" He looked Carter in the eye.

"Well . . . I . . . ." Carter stammered.

"You're too valuable a controller for me to lose. I've sat by and watched you for weeks now, and I think it's time we did something. We all reach the end of our limit at some point—most boys take a lot less than nine years to get there. You deserve some time away."

Carter knew better than to disagree. He hadn't been himself lately.

"Sorry, Carl, I know I haven't been giving you my best."

Carl leaned back in his chair and studied his coffee cup. "You're one of the most conscientious, moral men I have. I'm only trying to see that I don't lose you. You're tired, Carter. I hate to call it burnout, but something's affecting you both physically and mentally. You need a little R and R. Relax. Have some fun. Forget about the job and its pressures."

"You're worried about my competency."

"You're top-notch, Carter, but this is a high-stress job. We all need a little down time." Carl leaned forward, and his eyes held Carter's gaze. "Look, it's nothing to be ashamed of. We all have our limits. You're conscientious, focused. That's good. But this sort of concentration takes a lot out of a man. A couple weeks of lying in the sun and you'll be back complaining that you've used up all your vacation hours. As far back as I can remember you've used your vacation time for church mission trips to Uganda to help build houses for orphan children. That's good, and God bless you, Son, but you need to take time for yourself. Even Christ took time to renew Himself with His Father. You should do the same. Besides, you can fly anywhere in the world for next to nothing. You should take advantage of that."

"My absence will leave you short-handed," Carter reminded. "If I could get over this cold—"

"You will. Bake it out in the sun." Carl grinned.

Carter stood up. While he didn't like being forced to go on vacation, something inside him said he needed it. Two weeks without coping, without thinking, without breaking into a cold sweat, without sitting on the edge of his chair. . . . Maybe rest was all he needed.

"I don't suppose it will do any good to argue with you?"

"None at all. Soon as Randy gets here, consider yourself out of work for the next two weeks, or longer, if you need it. You let me worry about your replacement. That's what I'm paid the big bucks for." He grinned.

Carter reached to shake his supervisor's hand, gratified by the other man's concern. "I appreciate this—"

"Don't worry about it." Carl glanced at his watch. "Uh oh, look at the time. I've got to call Wanda and tell her I'm going to be a few minutes late." He flashed Carter an apologetic grin. "The woman thinks I've dropped dead if I'm not home by six on the dot."

Carter left the tower, groaning when he saw the inch of ice accumulated on his windshield. Starting the motor, he flipped on the defroster and pulled on his gloves as he sat waiting for the windshield to clear.

He knew Carl was right. He'd been working so hard for so long he wasn't even sure he knew *how* to unwind. But the truth was, rest was exactly what he needed. He'd been on "automatic" for too long. And it wasn't an emotional recharging he'd been lacking. He'd transferred his work habits to his spiritual life. He'd been going full-tilt doing "the right things" but not taking time to just be with God—this was the wakeup call he needed and he knew it. Now he only had to think of where he would go to find the sun and privacy he wanted. Hawaii—the thought came to him. He'd never seen the island and now was the perfect time. What he needed was a good book, a couple packages of Oreo cookies—chocolate crème peanut butter—and complete solitude for the next two weeks. He could pack everything he needed into a couple of bags. Sun, sand, a hotel with room service, and he was set to go—to regenerate.

2

A yellow cab slowly inched its way along snow-packed Pena Boulevard Tuesday morning. Rain had turned to snow and the worsening weather was brutal. Traffic to Denver International snarled onto the exit road.

"Will I be able to make my seven o'clock flight?" Tess asked anxiously as she stared out the back window, her warm breath frosty in the cab's arctic air.

"I'll have you there in twenty minutes." The driver peered over his shoulder. "Sorry, the heater's on the fritz. It was working fine an hour ago. Can't imagine what could've happened to it."

She sighed. She'd been in the backseat for the last forty-five minutes of that hour. Why shouldn't the heater fall apart?

The taxi driver peered at her through the rearview mirror.

"Um . . . Miss? Are you all right back th—"

KAABOOMMM!

Tess's heart shot to her throat as she instinctively ducked at the sound of the sudden explosion. Briefcase and purse toppled to the floor.

"Ho, boy!" The driver fought the steering wheel and finally managed to ease the cab over to the side of the exit road. "I think we've got ourselves a flat tire."

After bringing the crippled taxi to a halt, he turned halfway around in the driver's seat. "Now, don't worry. I'll get you to your flight on time."

She wanted to *scream*.

As soon as she'd gotten home last night the white stuff had started to fall. Every snowplow in Denver had been working nonstop for the past ten hours. Travel had slowed to a crawl. Six-foot-high drifts made finding a clear spot to pull off the road impossible, but the cab driver managed to get the vehicle off the main thoroughfare. Now an endless string of frustrated motorists inched past the disabled cab, often leaning on their horns as if that would somehow even the score.

"I'll have the tire changed in a jiffy," the driver promised as he got out.

She inched lower in the backseat. What difference did it make? She was going to miss the plane anyway. She would be stuck at the terminal for hours. Why did Len have to do this to her? She ran her hands through her hair, and a clump of strands clung to her hands. *Great,* she thought, *what else could happen?*

No, she wasn't going there; she was going to Hawaii for a nice vacation with her best friend. She would not give Len Connor the satisfaction of ruining her good time.

She was going to relax, consider her options, her career. And she was going to think about it in a lounge chair with a cool fruit drink in her hand in the land of pineapples and grass skirts.

While the driver changed the tire, Tess sat in the frosty silence of the cab, watching snow drift past the car window. The swirling flakes were hypnotic, and she let her mind float back to Len's office and that awful afternoon six days ago. What had happened? She had been so certain that she finally had life under control—

She rested her forehead against the cold windowpane and she laughed humorlessly. *Well, Bee Gee, you don't know what you've gotten yourself into, inviting this nutcase to your house.*

She'd tried to call Beeg a couple of times again last night to confirm their plans but she'd gotten a busy signal. She'd try again the moment she landed. She should have tried to reach her this morning, but because of the three-hour time difference she'd decided to wait. Besides, Beeg had told her to come.

Her thoughts were interrupted when the cab driver climbed back into the cab. Snow crusted thick on his heavy coat and eyelashes.

"All fixed," he said.

Tess nodded. She had a little over forty minutes to check in and make the gate.

With her luck she would set off the metal detectors, be searched and questioned. She'd miss the flight and have an eight-hour wait before the next one.

"Can you step on it?" She asked. "I'm never going to make my flight."

"Even if I have to make this taxi sprout wings, I'll get you there!" The cabby promised. "I've never caused a passenger to miss a flight yet."

Yes, but you've never had me in your cab. True to his word, the cab driver delivered her in front of United Airlines with thirty minutes to spare. She tore through the crowded terminal, dodging the throng of travelers. The check-in line moved swiftly; she got her boarding pass and made it past security. She had ten minutes left before takeoff time.

As she breathlessly neared the gate, a slow-moving elderly gentleman ahead of her dropped his boarding pass and stooped to retrieve it.

Bags flying, Tess skidded to a stop, gasping in pain when she felt her right ankle give—the same ankle she'd broken in a skiing accident three years before. Fighting the hot sting of wrenched muscles, she bent and collected her briefcase and purse.

The elderly man turned around, apparently oblivious that he had been the cause of her injury. "You okay, little lady? Looks like you had a little tangle."

"Fine." She gritted her teeth against the white-hot pain. "Just dandy."

She straightened. Her ankle throbbed.

"Shouldn't be in such a big hurry. Folks got to learn to slow down. Everyone's in such an all-fired hurry," the man complained as he proceeded slowly on down the corridor, his words of wisdom trailing behind him.

"And 'have a good day' to you, too," she muttered.

She deftly tested her weight on the injured ankle. The ache was awful. She would have to swallow the anguish and hobble on if she was going to make the flight.

She managed to board seconds before the Jetway detached from the plane. Sinking gratefully into her assigned seat, she reached for the seatbelt and fought against the unfamiliar urge to cry. Tess Nelson did not cry. If Mona had taught her one thing it was that a Nelson was in charge of her own life—she and she alone was responsible for herself and her actions. Only whiners and losers cried.

As the 767 roared down the tarmac, she reached to rub her swollen ankle. The pain had turned to a constant ache. She wondered if she would be able to get her boot back on if she took it off during the flight. Deciding some relief from the pressure was worth the risk, she warily pulled off the footwear and examined her ankle. It was puffy but maybe with luck it wouldn't get any worse. Suddenly aware of the guy setting next to her, she lifted her gaze and met a pair of amused artic blue eyes. A grin hovered at the corners of his tanned features as his gaze dropped to her Nerf-ball-size foot—certainly not her best feature.

Snapping around in her seat, she clicked the belt in place and pretended interest in the in-flight phone. If he said *one* word she would strangle him.

Dropping her head against the headrest, she closed her eyes and felt the familiar tug in her stomach as the plane lifted off and soared into the void of swirling snow. Right now all she wanted to see was a hole open up and swallow the passengers.

"Predicted to add up to fourteen inches before it's over," the radio announcer said. "But we're the lucky ones. Over in the Pacific, trouble is brewing. Some off season tropical depression has developed. . . . Sustained winds from twenty to thirty-four knots, that's twenty-three to thirty-nine miles per hour, for us lay people. It could turn into a doozy before all's said and done. Stay tuned for further updates."

She tuned out the radio and the teenage boy who wore it. His head bobbed in time with some sort of rap music that she wished was anything else. Even country would've been better. As she returned her tray to the upright position, the "fasten seat belt" sign came on and she settled back to await final descent into Kahului Airport.

At precisely 3:37 P.M., Maui time, the Boeing 767 landed. Heavy trade winds gusted through the open walkways as Tess followed the throng of wary fliers to the baggage claim terminal. By now her ankle had swollen to nearly twice its normal size. She had pulled and strained to force her boot back on, groaning aloud in agony. The hunk beside her had looked more than a little awkward at her state, and yet what could he have done? Pushed her bulging ankle from the other side?

Her ankle ached as if a bull had kicked it. She couldn't zip the boot, so the top flapped open, snagging her hose. Her eyes searched the concourse for signs that she was actually in Hawaii. No one met her with a flowered lei, and she didn't spot a single hula girl. Swallowing an odd sense of disappointment, she limped on. Maybe Don Ho was waiting for her in the baggage claim.

I'm in paradise, she thought. *I'm going to relax, bake on the beach, and forget about Len Connor.* She wondered if he'd figured out the new 401(k) deductions they'd worked on with the new investment broker. No doubt *Chuck* would have it all buttoned down in no time.

As she approached baggage claim an energetic pre-schooler throwing a full-blown temper tantrum caught her attention. He was screaming and kicking his feet on the floor as his nervous-looking mother pled in a mousy voice, "Now, Tommy, you won't get any gum that way. Please be a good boy for Mommy." Tommy bounced back up and bolted away from his mother . . . straight at Tess.

Suddenly paralyzed in the face of the oncoming disaster, she tried to sidestep the human missile but Tommy must've had a homing device because he changed course with her.

The sudden impact knocked her breathless as she threw her weight solidly on her sprained ankle. She bellowed at the sheer agony that shot up her leg as her purse and briefcase went flying. Again.

At precisely the same moment, her right eye blurred. She slapped a hand over her eye to save the dislodged contact but it was too late.

"Thomas Lee! You stop this moment!" The child's

mother marched over to take the little imp by the scruff of the neck from where he lay sprawled at her feet. Tommy's mother turned the child toward her. "What have I told you about running?! Say you're sorry to this nice lady for bumping into her!"

The harried mother turned to Tess who by now had dropped to her hands and knees and was crawling frantically around on the floor of the terminal, desperately groping for the missing contact lens.

"It's all right," Tess muttered. "I'm sure Thomas didn't mean any harm—" Where was the thing? It couldn't have gone far!

She was as blind as Mr. Magoo without her contacts. She smiled gratefully when other blurs she assumed were people paused to offer help with the search. Soon four other travelers were on their hands and knees scanning the multicolored tile.

The contrite mother had a firm grip on her young son now. The boy stood rooted to the spot as Tess crawled around on the polished floor.

"I'm so sorry about your contact," the mother repeated.

"Don't worry," Tess assured her. "I have my glasses with me."

The boy crossed his arms and looked up at his mother. "Sowwy," he finally managed.

She smiled at the blurred image. "It's quite all right— but don't run anymore. You'll hurt yourself."

The mother ushered her son through the crowd as she gathered her personal belongings and thanked her co-searchers before limping steadfastly toward the luggage carousel.

🌴

The luggage hadn't arrived, so she stepped to a nearby pay phone. Her cell phone was buried in her luggage, a mistake she realized in the cab. She searched her purse and coat pockets for change, but all she managed to come up with were six pennies, a nasty-looking nickel that had part of a breath mint stuck to it, and a Canadian coin she had picked up somewhere.

By the time she'd limped to the nearest newsstand for change and limped back, all the phones were in use. She patiently waited while a frazzled-looking housewife gave instructions to her husband and children. "I left some TV dinners in the freezer for tonight. And there's some lettuce and tomatoes for a salad—oh, I forgot to buy Ranch dressing . . ." the woman kept going. When the lady finally ran out of time and dashed off to catch her shuttle ride, Tess moved up to the phone. She dropped her coins into the slot and tapped out Beeg's work number. She breathed a sigh of relief when she heard the phone start to ring—several times with no answer. Replacing the receiver, she frowned. Maybe this was some sort of Hawaiian holiday. She dropped more coins into the phone and dialed Beeg's home number.

Beeg's familiar voice came over the line on the second ring. "Hello! This is Me!"

Relief flooded Tess. Thank goodness. "Hi, Beeg! This is—"

"I'm sorry I can't come to the phone right now," her friend's sunny voice interrupted. "At the sound of the tone, please leave your name and number, and I'll return your call as soon as possible."

When she heard the beep, she squeezed her eyes shut in disgust and pressed the receiver against her forehead. One more delay, Tess. You should be used to that by now.

Since the luggage was late in arriving, Carter decided to mosey back to the shop. He bought a pineapple-guava-orange smoothie and a copy of *Newsweek,* then walked back to the luggage area. People occupied the benches, so he took a stand near the phones. When he heard the young woman beside him suddenly slam down the receiver, he turned to look.

She fumbled in her coat pocket and extracted a number

of tissue wads, which she discarded into the trash receptacle. Finally she took one wad and held it to her nose as she leaned against the wall and took deep, hiccupping breaths.

He fished a fresh package of tissues from his carry-on and handed it to her, tapping it against her arm to get her attention.

"Thanks," she mumbled, her eyes momentarily meeting his. She wiped her eyes and blew her nose. She looked as if someone had just shot her dog.

"Looks like you're having a rough day," Carter said.

"I've had better," the woman replied, sniffling.

"It could get worse . . ." Carter said. "They could always lose our luggage." He offered her a smile which she returned shyly.

The woman handed the pack of tissues back.

"Keep it," he said. "I've got more."

"I'm going to sit." She motioned toward her foot. "I . . . hurt my ankle."

He watched as she hobbled over to the waiting area and sat down.

Her shoulders lifted in a sigh as she unwrapped a piece of gum and stuck the stick in her mouth, then blindly fished about with her right hand in her purse, finally withdrawing an emery board. Crossing then uncrossing her legs, she filed her nails and jiggled her left foot erratically.

Busy, busy, busy, Carter thought. He looked around the waiting area. Fifty out of a hundred passengers either had a cell phone pressed to their ear, answered a pager, typed on a laptop, or consulted a hand-held Palm Pal. Looking at them, he realized that he was no different. Until two days ago he'd been in the same boat, but not anymore. He strengthened his resolve to learn how to be a calm, relaxed person. He didn't want to end up so worn out he was sobbing in front of strangers at the airport.

Ten minutes later, a siren blasted and bags started to drop and roll along the conveyor belt. Easing her way through the throng, Tess eventually found herself standing beside the man who had given her the tissues.

He smiled. "Hello again."

"Hi." They stood, watching. Waiting for their bags. Two hundred and fifty suitcases passed in front of them before she discovered she and the tissue man were the only ones left standing.

He glanced over with a questioning expression in his eyes.

She looked back, shrugging.

She glanced at the baggage opening and prayed that she wouldn't hear the conveyer shut off. The motor continued to hum.

They silently focused on the rotating carousel. Suddenly a single bag belched out of the rubber flaps and lumbered down the belt.

"Finally," she said. "I thought I'd have to go naked *and* blind."

The man ventured a polite, "Huh?"

"I lost my contact earlier."

He grimaced. "I *thought* you looked familiar—you were the woman crawling on the floor."

"Yes, why?" She turned to look at him. "I lost my contact . . ."

He drew a deep breath. "Well, I think I may have stepped on it."

Nostrils flared. Suddenly the air left Kahului terminal. "You did what?"

"I was coming down the corridor and . . . I stepped on what I thought was a piece of hard candy. I'm sorry—"

She shook her head. The information didn't surprise her. "It isn't your fault," she said. "I told you this hasn't been my day. It isn't your fault," she repeated, more to convince herself than him. "I tried to find it, but—"

"Too many big feet." He had a kind smile and eyes that crinkled in the corners.

"You couldn't have known," she said as she latched onto the bag, but his hand grabbed it at the same time

"Excuse me," he said.

She closed her eyes. "*What* now?"

"I think you're mistaken. This is my bag—see. Big scar on the right side." He laid his hand across the deep dent in the side of the leather bag.

She evaluated the bag with thinned lips. "No. You're mistaken. This is my bag. Mine has a nick on the left side—received last summer, in New York."

He focused on the piece of black Samsonite. "No, it's mine." He picked up the bag and turned to walk away. Tess felt her temper rising.

She whirled and limped after him. "Wait just one minute! Set my luggage down this very minute!"

He turned around slowly, a look of condescension growing in his eyes.

Dropping the bag on the floor, he then knelt on one knee. "This matter is easily settled. All we have to do is read the nametag. I'm sure you're mistaken."

She stood, heat rising to her cheeks. Their dispute was being closely observed by incoming travelers from other flights, impatient to retrieve their luggage.

"No," she said. "You're mistaken."

Carter pulled the tag free and squinted to read. "Let's see what we have here." Glancing up a moment later he said solemnly, "I was wrong. The bag isn't mine."

"I know." She smiled. "That's what I've been trying to tell you."

He picked up the suitcase and held it out to her. "Here you go, Harry."

Her hand was already wrapping around the handle when the name suddenly penetrated. "Harry?"

He lifted an eyebrow. "You aren't Harry Finnerman?"

"Of course I'm not Harry Finnerman."

"Oh. That's too bad," he said, "because this bag belongs to Harry Finnerman." A grin grew on his face.

"Are you sure?" She squatted to peer at the tag, squinting one eye closed. When she indeed discovered that he was right, she lifted her gaze.

"Don't gloat," she grumbled. "People are watching us." Straightening, she muttered, "Well, I guess my bags are still somewhere."

"As are mine," he agreed.

Just not where any of them are supposed to be.

"I thought you said it couldn't get any worse," she said. He shrugged.

They stepped back to the revolving carousel to wait. A moment later another bag shot out and thundered down the conveyor. Score one more for Harry Finnerman.

A moment later the carousel stopped.

Then a siren blasted, and the conveyor on the right began spitting bags out from a later flight.

"There must have been a mix-up somewhere," the man said quietly.

"Both of my bags are missing," Tess said, feeling her forehead to see if she was getting a fever. No, she was cool. Three hairs stuck to her hand and she quickly flicked them away.

The man turned and walked to the Claims Department while she limped behind.

A half hour later, she and the tissue man were still standing in line, filling out forms. They finally completed the paperwork regarding the lost luggage, and with the airline's promise to deliver the bags as soon as they were located, they left the terminal.

Giving a pleasant nod, the man left. She turned to hail a cab and glanced up at the sky.

Maui weather was definitely better than Denver. Crystal blue skies, fluffy cumulus clouds drifting overhead. Taking a deep breath, she sniffed. Plumeria. The flower scented the tropical breeze with a heady perfume.

"Hello again," a voice sounded over Tess's shoulder.

She turned, as he tucked a brochure of some sort into the pocket of the coat he now carried draped over his arm.

He was back.

"Everything settled?" he said.

She nodded, glancing down at her snow boot that looked about as useless in the eighty-degree heat as a life preserver on a duck.

"Looks like that ankle's in bad shape—better have a doctor check it out as soon as you can." A taxi braked to the curb and the man opened the door. "This one's yours."

"No," she shook her head. "You take it."

"I insist." He held the door open wider.

"No, *I* insist."

"Look," he said. "You need to get ice on that ankle." He smiled. "Besides, if we don't decide soon, the cab will leave without either of us." A couple who stood ahead of them on the curb shot them dirty looks.

She said quietly, "I suppose we could share."

"Get in. I'll get your purse and briefcase," he offered.

"Thanks."

He positioned the items between them in the backseat, got in, and slammed the cab door.

"Where to?" the gum-chewing driver asked.

"Pioneer Inn for me," the man said.

She slid the man a peripheral glance, and gave the driver Beeg's address.

Twenty minutes later, the driver braked at the front entrance of the historical Pioneer Inn, overlooking beautiful Lahaina Harbor. The tissue man stepped out of the cab and paid his fare.

Now this was more like it, she thought as she gazed around. Boats bobbed in the harbor, steel guitar music floated from the music stand on the corner. With a final wave, he said good-by. Now she could get on with her vacation.

Forty minutes later, the cab wheeled back onto Wharf Street and deposited Tess at the Pioneer Inn. She had knocked and rung Beeg's doorbell for over ten minutes before a neighbor informed her that Ms. Harris was away.

Away.

What did he mean by "away"? Had she gone for a picnic at the other side of the island? The neighbor wasn't much help. "Just asked me to look after the place for a few days," the smallish man said.

Biting her lower lip, she had asked the neighbor to call another cab. Reasoning that she could call Beeg's cell phone once her luggage arrived with her address book, she decided to try the Pioneer Inn. It looked like a nice place, and she kind of liked the carved wooden captain she'd seen through the lobby windows.

She paid the fare and hauled her purse and briefcase out of the backseat, glad to be minutes away from a long soak in a hot tub. Ibuprofen and relaxation—the thought left her feeling giddy.

Tess emerged from the Pioneer Inn minutes later and lifted her hand for a cab. So much for lighted harbors in a beautiful historic setting. Unfortunately the driver was the one she'd left five minutes earlier. He smiled. "Back so soon?"

She heaved her purse and briefcase into the backseat and said simply, "No rooms."

The clerk called ahead to a place called the Mynah Nest. It was only six blocks away, and from the looks of it, it was rated down near the one-star range. Shutters hung askew from the windows, whose paint had peeled long before. The sign had a faded mynah bird painted on its top—the creature looked so worn it could've dropped from exhaustion alone. "Only one problem," the driver said over his shoulder.

She shut her eyes. "What?"

"The staff went out on strike two weeks ago."

She got out and paid her fare, mumbling an "I might call you back—we'll see," before shutting the door.

The place had a definite odor—and it wasn't Plumeria. It had more of a rotten-egg quality. The carpet was a good decade past its last shampooing. The orange, rust, and brown design was dizzying, especially blurred by her inability to see it clearly. She walked up to the front desk, where she was met by a squeaky-voiced boy with hair that stood up at spiked angles. She wasn't sure if it was an intended 'do or not.

"Can I help you?" he asked.

"I heard your staff was on strike," she said.

"Yes, Ma'am. I'm the manager here."

She raised a curious brow. "I guess I'd like a room . . ."

"I can assure you that, despite the inconvenience of no staff, we will extend every effort to make your stay as comfortable as possible."

She nodded, squinting her eyes. He spoke like a professional. "Is there an optometrist close by?"

"Oh, yes, Ma'am." She wished he'd stop calling her that. "There's all kinds of optical places in Maui." He wrote down an address for her.

"I'll need ice right away." She pointed toward her ankle. "And can you please phone the airport and inform them that I'm staying here? I have a couple of missing bags. I'd like them brought directly to my room the moment they arrive."

"Certainly, Ms. Nelson. Your room is 465. We hope you'll enjoy your stay."

The young manager handed her the key with a flourish, managing only to drop it at her feet. She bent painfully to retrieve it. At this point she didn't care if they put her on a sofa in the lobby, just so her foot was elevated and she had an ice pack and some aspirin.

"Where are the elevators?"

"Oh, sorry, Ma'am." The freckle-faced boy flashed an embarrassed grin. "That's another tiny difficulty we're experiencing. The elevators are out of order right now—but we've called a repairman. He's due any minute. I'm sure he'll have those puppies up and running in a jif." His youthful features turned serious. "If you want to hang out in the lobby it's okay. There are house mints—they're free. You can have all you want."

She lifted a finger to her pounding temple. *Hang out in the lobby and eat house mints?* "No, thanks." Straightening, she reached for her purse and briefcase. "I'll take the stairs."

At least she didn't have two heavy pieces of luggage to tote.

She limped up four rickety flights, briefcase under one arm and her purse under the other. By the time she reached the fourth floor, she was wishing she'd joined a gym years earlier. Sagging against the plaster with sections of lathe peeking out from the peeled walls, she gasped to catch her breath. Her heartbeat had to be at least two hundred sixty-five.

Working her way down the dimly lit hall, she followed the line of closed doors, squinting at the numbers. 465 was the room farthest from the stairway.

She unlocked the door, flicked on the lamp, and fell across the bed in exhaustion. Her ankle throbbed with every beat of her heart.

She lay on her back and studied the room. It sure wasn't fancy. The same rust, brown, and orange carpet lined the floors, and the bed had a padded vinyl "pillow" across its middle. She looked over toward the TV and noticed a pair of cowboy boots on the floor to the side. She wondered if the room had been cleaned. She shivered at the thought. Right now she didn't have the energy to deal with another crisis. By tomorrow she would connect with Beeg and this nightmare would be over.

She wondered how Len was managing without her. Would he realize how much she'd contributed to Connor.com and want her back? She recalled Len's smug expression as he told her she was being replaced like an outdated pair of jeans. And what had she done? She'd limped away to lick her wounds like an injured pup.

Her mother would say she had gotten what she deserved. She had placed her trust in someone other than herself and that was never wise.

She'd been dismissed as if she hadn't sacrificed both private and work life to Connor.com these past five years.

The sun was sinking behind the strand of palms outside her window before she was able to convince herself to get up to check on what had happened to the ice bag the clerk had promised to deliver. "I've been washing sheets and I forgot," he said, then he apologized profusely and said he'd be up in a little while. She rolled off the side of the bed and limped into the bathroom. Minutes later, balanced on her good foot, steam floating around her, she anticipated the heavenly tub of hot water.

Suddenly there was a sharp rap at the door.

She groaned. "Just a minute."

The knock sounded again. "Keep your shirt on!" she called as she turned off the water and hobbled toward the door.

"Yes?" She stood and listened.

Silence.

She waited a few moments then slid the security chain free and cautiously eased the door open. Sitting there were four pieces of scuffed black Samsonite with a bag of ice draped across the top.

"I can't believe this."

She had only two pieces of luggage missing. Not four. She stepped into the hall, hoping to catch the manager, but he was long gone.

She consulted the tag on the first and second bags and confirmed that the luggage was hers. The other two belonged to a Carter McConnell, whoever that was. Probably the guy from the airport, she surmised.

She sighed and dragged all four pieces into the room, then dropped the bag of ice into the sink and hobbled back to the bathroom. After her soak and a few minutes with ice on her ankle, she'd call the front desk and inform the clerk about the mix-up.

As far as she was concerned, if Mr. McConnell had been without his luggage this long, another hour wouldn't make any difference.

3

Tess slowly turned off the hot water with her big toe and lay back in a tub of hot salts as she let the steamy fragrance assuage her weary senses.

She hadn't thought that last week could be topped, but today had been worse. Beeg was missing; surely they were crisscrossing each other's path. Early tomorrow morning she would call Beeg's house, and if that effort failed to reach her, she would go to The Lopsided Easel, the small Front Street gallery where Beeg worked. They would share a cup of Kona coffee and have a good laugh about the whole thing—if she could remember how to laugh. She wiggled deeper into the hot suds.

As far as Connor.com—she'd let Len stew in his own juices for a few days. It wouldn't take a genius to discover that Tess Nelson contributed more to the company than Len ever dreamed. He would be calling her, begging her to come back; she'd bet the farm on that. She just needed to decide what her answer would be. Did she want to work for a man who could dismiss her with a wave of the hand? Didn't she have more self-respect than that?

Settling deeper into gardenia-scented water, she decided to wait a day or two before she checked her home messages. Then she would return to Connor.com on her own terms.

The delicious thought warmed her and made the last twenty-four hours tolerable.

Her fingers and toes had pruned and the water had cooled to chilly before she summoned enough energy to dry off and rub some fragrant cream on her skin. It felt so good to have her personal articles back. She'd recovered her glasses, cell phone, and address book, so she felt a measure of comfort.

Tightening her robe sash, she sat on the bed with her leg elevated on a pillow and the cool of the now-melting ice on her ankle. She stared at the two extra pieces of luggage beside the bed. Carter what's-his-name would probably appreciate having his items as much as she did. She needed to report the mistake.

The teenybopper manning the front desk answered her call in a piping little voice that harbored an adolescent crack.

"Yeah, what is it!"

"This is Tess Nelson in room 465. Two pieces of luggage have been delivered to my room by mistake."

"No joke?"

She rolled her eyes. "No joke. Would you please send up someone to get them?"

"Sure thing, Lady. Do the bags have a name on 'em?"

"The tags say Carter McConnell."

"McConnell, McConnell—" The young man repeated the name under his breath. Tess could hear him frantically rummaging through some papers.

"Yeah, here ya go—Carter McConnell. He just checked in—he's in room 464. Just down the hall from you. Uh, sorry 'bout the mix-up there, Lady. Tell ya what I'm gonna do. Soon as I can get a few minutes I'll hop on up there to get 'em."

Good grief. She looked at her melted bag of ice and thought of the hour she'd already wasted and knew Mr. McConnell would want to have his personal effects as soon as possible.

"If it isn't against hotel policy, perhaps I could just set Mr. McConnell's luggage outside his door?"

"If you don't think it's too much hassle . . . hop to it."

"Okay, I'll take care of it."

"Thanks a wad, Lady," he said, then hung up.

She gingerly placed her weight on her injured ankle. She was pleased to note it didn't hurt as much as before although it had taken on numbness. Adding a fraction more bulk, she flinched and nearly fell.

She scooted the pieces of luggage to the door. Talk

about weight! The man must have packed bricks in one of the bags.

Shoving the bags into the hall, she wondered if knocking and leaving them in front of the door of room 464 would be sufficient. That was the way the bags had been delivered to her. But, she reasoned, if the man weren't there the bags might be stolen before he returned to his room.

She tapped lightly on the door, then allowed ample time for the man to respond. When there was no response, she knocked, louder this time.

🌴

What idiot was knocking on the door?

Carter rolled over onto his back and opened his eyes, trying to remember where he was. The antihistamines he'd taken had his thinking process on the blink. The mix-up at Pioneer Inn, thinking he had a room only to discover that his reservation had been eaten by the computer and he couldn't get a room until tomorrow night, then the frantic search for another room, and being reduced to a stay in the Mynah Nest, was enough to throw him off balance. He'd wanted to get settled, start the relaxing process. It would be another day before he could get in to the Pioneer Inn.

The persistent knock rattled him.

He couldn't remember the last time he'd felt so dragged out. Now some nincompoop was trying to beat down the door.

Annoyed, he rolled out of bed as whoever it was pounded on the door again. He stumbled, bumping his knee on the desk, and finally reached the door, but not before his big toe found a straight pin some former guest had dropped on the carpeted floor.

Pain shot up his calf and he sucked in a breath as he dropped to his knees to extract the blasted harpoon. The slight trickle of blood when he pulled the pin free made him sick to his stomach. He was a lily-livered coward when it came to the sight of blood, especially his own.

Another brisk knock on the door brought him back to his feet.

"Okay! Okay! I'm coming!" Hopping on one foot, he slid the security chain free and cracked the door a fraction.

Oh, great. The wren. What was *she* doing here? And in a bathrobe? He averted his gaze to the floor.

"Mr. McConnell? I'm sorry to bother you but—"

Carter opened the door wider and Tess stepped back, clearly startled. They stared at each other. Finally Carter prompted. "How did you find me here? Are you following me?"

She stood speechless. Her lips moved but no sound

came out. "You're Carter McConnell?" He nodded his head.

"How dare you!" she sputtered. "I am not the kind of person who follows total strangers! Besides, you were staying at the Pioneer Inn."

He leaned on the doorsill, still fighting sleep. "I *thought* I was staying at the Pioneer Inn. Some mix-up with the reservations—computer glitch. I move to the Pioneer tomorrow night." He yawned, running his hand through his tousled hair. "So, what do you want if you're not stalking me?"

"The airline delivered your bags to my room by mistake—I thought you'd want to have them right away. Of course, I wouldn't have disturbed you had I known . . ."

He glanced from the towel on her head down to her bare feet. Her left ankle and foot looked like an over-inflated water balloon. "That's looking worse." He pointed at her foot. "What was your name?"

"Tess Nelson," she spurted. "And I'll thank you to mind your own business." She turned and marched toward her room. Carter tugged his luggage into his room and then dropped across the bed and fell asleep before he could think another thought.

4

"Looks like that nutty depression is intensifying, Erin," the radio announcer began. Tess lifted her head to see what time it was—7:12. "The meteorologists are picking out names as this baby grows, with sustained winds up to fifty miles per hour. Hurricane season is over but who knows what Mother Nature has up her sleeve?"

She turned off the alarm. So much for sleeping in today. If she were home she'd already be on her snack break. She stuffed the thought aside. She was on vacation. She was going to enjoy Hawaii—storm or no storm. How bad could it be this late in the year?

As she stepped out of bed the pain in her foot surged. She needed to find a doctor and see about getting a contact lens, but not before she got ahold of Beeg.

Picking up her cell phone and address book she called Beeg's home number again. The answering machine picked up. When it beeped, Tess said, "Hey, Beeg, I'm here in Maui

but I seem to keep missing you. Call me on my cell phone
. . ." She hung up and stared at her phone. Where could
Beeg be? It wasn't as if she didn't expect her to come.

Padding to the bathroom, she brushed her teeth and
then took out a brush and started in on her hair. A big
clump of hair dropped into the sink. She looked at it in
disgust. She'd have to wear a hat today, definitely.

"This is not my idea of the perfect vacation." Tess exited
the hotel in search of an eye and foot doctor. She'd
decided to stop back at the airport to rent a car too, since
she hadn't gotten ahold of Beeg and taking taxis everywhere was getting quite costly.

Once that was taken care of it was time to attend to
her injuries. Her ankle now looked like a bloated corpse,
and the sprain needed a doctor's attention.

Thirty minutes later she was sitting in a clinic, fanning herself with a coverless issue of *People* magazine—
recently and thoroughly mangled by the four-year-old
sitting next to her.

A nurse appeared through an outer door. "Ms. Nelson?"

"Me." Tess laid the magazine aside and stood up and
hobbled to follow the white uniform. Upon entering

examining room 4, she was sat on a narrow table with a long strip of white paper where the nurse efficiently recorded her blood pressure and temperature. Stripping the sphygmomanometer off, she then scribbled notes before positioning a clipboard on her trim stomach. "What can we do for you today?"

"I sprained my ankle running to catch a plane. It's very painful."

She nodded. "Visiting Hawaii?"

"Yes."

She clipped the pencil on the board. "Doctor will be in shortly." The door closed behind her, and Tess drew a deep breath, holding her foot out in front of her to reassess the damage. The ankle was blue and distorted—could she have chipped the bone? The prospect added another unwelcome angst to her growing list.

Thirty minutes later the doctor appeared. Tess sat up quickly: she'd finally given in to the uncomfortable table and laid back. Absently smoothing her hair, she smiled at the gray-haired physician with a noticeable paunch.

He peered at the chart in his hand. "Having ankle problems?"

"I sprained it while I was running to catch a plane. It's been throbbing for hours."

"Hummm." Setting the chart aside, he took her bare foot and examined it.

"Yes . . . hummm. There's considerable swelling and bruising."

"I've taken Advil and used ice packs but nothing helps." She waited, heart pumping erratically. What if it was broken and she had to endure a hot cast—which would undoubtedly mean crutches. . . . Her heart banged against her rib cage.

"Humm. . . ." He bent closer and carefully manipulated the smarting appendage. Tess gritted her teeth and closed her eyes.

"Hurt?"

Pain! Searing agony, you masochist!

She grinned. "A little."

"Hummm." Straightening, his eyes focused on a mole on her left arm. Narrowing in on the site, he examined the barely distinguishable discoloration. "How long have you had this?"

The heart again. Thumping wildly, crowding the back of her throat. "All my life—I think." She tried to remember—she'd had the mole all her life, hadn't she? The blemish looked vaguely familiar—but maybe it had come up lately. She felt faint.

"Does it look strange? *Dangerous?*" She turned to peer at the now definitely suspicious looking *thing* on her left forearm.

"Hummm." He pulled a light over to the table, switched it on, then reached for a magnifying glass.

Wide-eyed, she studied his grave demeanor, ankle forgotten. Drawing the light nearer, he scoured the object for what seemed an inordinately long time.

"What?" she asked faintly.

"Hummm. . . ." The magnifying glass moved back and forth—an inch here, half inch there. . . .

Sweat broke out on her forehead.

Straightening, he snapped off the light and pushed the stand back. "I'm going to write you a prescription for pain and something to relax those muscles. Before you leave I'd like to take an x-ray of that foot, but I believe we're dealing with a simple sprain."

Nodding mutely, she tried to fathom how pain and muscle relaxants could relate to a suspicious looking mole? Dear God—she'd *never* noticed. Len had thrown her into such a tailspin, and she'd been so busy with work. . . . Had she overlooked something? Melanoma. She'd read article after article about the dreaded skin condition. She lifted her forearm and stared.

The doctor wrote on the pad. Her mind faintly registered the scrape of ball point against paper. She'd have to fly home immediately—consult her doctor, who would then refer her to a specialist. How good were Denver oncologists? Her hands trembled. She would fly to the Mayo Clinic in Rochester, Minnesota—she'd have the best of care there—maybe even extend her life a few more years. . . . Her heart sank. There was so much yet to do—so many things she'd wanted to experience. Motherhood. She wanted to spend a summer in Ireland, take an Alaskan cruise.

"I'll wrap the ankle—should give you some relief," the doctor was saying. He tore the prescription off the pad. "You call the office tomorrow and my nurse will give you the results of the x-ray. Meanwhile," he smiled, "enjoy our beautiful island."

She nodded, numb now. "The . . . mole. Should I see . . .?"

"The mole?" He flapped the air. "Perfectly normal. You've probably had it all your life." He turned and walked out, closing the door behind him.

Weakly lowering herself flat on her back, she stared at the ceiling, trying to still her racing heart.

An hour later and two blocks away, Tess walked through the door of an optical service whose flashing red sign promised, "ready in one hour." *Now to get rid of these glasses.*

For the next hour and a half, she read magazines and filed her nails. One whole morning in paradise shot on medical emergencies plus the visits cost twice what she'd have paid on the Mainland.

"Ms. Nelson?"

Tess tossed the magazine aside and for the second

time that morning hobbled into a small cubicle—this one filled with strange looking apparatus for a preliminary exam. She read numbers, pointed right and left, and pushed a button each time a flash occurred.

She jumped when a blast of air hit her right eye: glaucoma test. Moments later she was ushered into the optician's chair. When the man entered, she did a double take at his bottle-thick lenses, which he repeatedly shoved to the bridge of his nose with his forefinger.

"Lost a contact?"

"In the airport."

"Shame." Up went the glasses. After a series of tests— ptosis, exophthalmos, lesions, deformities or asymmetry problems—he got down to the business at hand.

She heard a flipping sound. "Is A better, or B?" the doctor asked.

"B."

She heard a click. "B or A?" Up went the glasses.

"A."

Click. "A or B?"

"Uh . . . A—no wait. Let me see B again."

Click.

"What was the question?"

"A or B." Up went the glasses.

"B. No, A."

"A or B?"

"A."

She was getting dizzy.

Click. "B or A?"

"B—A—I don't know. They both look the same."

Twenty minutes later she walked out, after paying for the examination and ordering one contact, which she now had to kill an hour before she could get. She settled on lunch and a brief excursion through a trendy dress shop where she purchased a silk blouse for an outlandish price. All in all, she considered the morning had cost her close to three hundred dollars, and it was barely noon.

Breezing out of the optometrist shop, she smiled, relieved to be free of the annoying glasses. Her foot hit something sticky on the sidewalk and she paused and lifted her heel, groaning when she saw a wad of pink bubble gum stuck to the leather sole. Lowering the good foot, she scraped back and forth, keeping an eye out for curious bystanders. Her sandaled foot moved back and forth, back and forth, each rub producing nothing more than a long, stringy, sticky piece of gum-based latex.

Sun glared down on her and she felt perspiration running down her neck. Her wrapped ankle throbbed. Gum was stuck tight as an eight-day clock. She could remove the shoe, but walking barefoot on the warm pavement didn't interest her—not when she had to shuffle anyway. She'd have to make it back to the car and get rid of the sandal.

With a goal fixed in mind, she limped down the concrete, trailing a long gooey slick of pink bubble gum on the hot pavement.

This vacation was going nowhere but to the dogs.

With her health care needs dealt with, Tess decided to walk to Beeg's gallery near the historical Baldwin Missionary Home. She crossed the street and stopped to gawk at the Banyon tree in the middle of a small park where craft vendors peddled their wares. The tree branches spread for blocks.

"Something, isn't it?" a voice said.

She turned to see a nicely dressed woman sitting on a bench, smiling at her. She wore her iron gray hair braided and looped in a coronet. Even sitting on a rustic bench, her posture and the way she held her head appeared almost queenly. Her eyes, blue as Hawaiian skies, were warm and alert, expressing a friendly interest. A native woven basket containing cut Plumeria and Birds of Paradise sat next to a shopping bag. Tess glanced at a loaf of fresh baked bread and a carton of milk in the shopping bag.

"The tree was planted by the sheriff of Maui in 1873 and is now the largest in the state," the woman offered.

"It is amazing." She turned back to study the tourist attraction. Where the tree's roots thickened, they formed a series of columns like tendons in the tree's neck to support the ever-lengthening branches.

"Ficus benghalensis," the lady said in explanation. "The tree now stands nearly sixty feet tall and covers more than two-thirds of an acre." Her timeless features softened as she stared up at the sun filtering lacey fingers through the branches. "One of God's many marvels."

Tess smiled and moved on. *God's marvels.*

She'd never thought of it that way.

Trekking by ocean-front stores, she spotted the Lopsided Easel half a block away. The small upstairs gallery looked inviting with its colorful array of watercolors decorating the window. She paused to read the list of artists represented there; of course Beeg as well as other talents like Don Jusko, Michael Krahan, and Jim Kingwell, who was noted for his watercolors of local scenes.

She entered the store, alive with color, space, and movement, and smiled at the pretty young Polynesian girl behind the counter. "Hi," she said. "Tell Bee Gee her past has come back to haunt her."

New York City.

Bee Gee had gone to the Mainland for an art showing and she'd be gone two weeks! She vaguely remembered Beeg saying something about New York. She wanted to pull her hair in sheer frustration. But she knew with the state her hair was in that it wouldn't be wise. The clerk at the gallery had given her the Marriott number where Beeg was staying, but what good would it do to call? Beeg was in New York and she was in Maui.

After she'd left the Lopsided Easel, she had aimlessly wandered the streets of Lahaina, trying to gain control of her emotions. A cacophony of tropical bird calls and Don Ho's voice blared from street corner vendors' stereos.

Now what? Should she book the next flight back to Denver or stay in Hawaii and force herself to enjoy her time off?

She needed aspirin.

Depressed, she drove back to the Mynah Nest. The foul odor of rotten eggs met her again. Well, Tess decided, the least she could do was find a nicer place to stay. She drove to the Pioneer Inn where the clerk assured her there were now open rooms.

When the clerk gave her the key to her room she smiled and made her way up. This room was markedly cleaner and smelled fresh. Still, Beeg was gone. She had no one to share her time with. She hung the "Do Not Disturb" sign on the door and then did exactly what she promised herself she wouldn't: she called home to check her messages. She had a three o'clock dental appointment on Monday that she'd forgotten to cancel. The jewelry store had the broken locket fixed. She could pick it up anytime.

She downed two aspirins and went to bed.

5

In spite of the impending storm which, according to the weather bureau, had just kicked up another notch, she was determined to relax. The storm would veer away and dissipate soon. The travel brochure she had picked up in the Pioneer Inn lobby claimed that there was nowhere on earth more beautiful to witness at sunrise than the summit of Mount Haleakala. Her ankle was stronger this morning so she rented a car, purchased a latte, and made the two-hour drive to the crater and the short hobble to the summit. As she watched, the blazing ball eased up over the dormant volcano crater radiant light gradually spreading until it infused the sky with brilliant golds and yellows. It was the most glorious thing she had ever seen. On her drive home, she was still affected by it, almost as if it were a religious experience, as if she'd somehow seen a bit of God in that sunrise.

She knew she was far from spiritual. She thought

about the times her grandmother had taken her to Mass when she was a child. It held the same sense of reverence and hushed awe. Mom, of course, didn't like priests, or the church.

"Religion gives outgoing folks something to do on Sunday mornings. But really—God? You're smarter than that, Tess."

"But Mom," Tess had said. "The nice woman in the black robe and funny-looking thing on her head—that 'Sister'— she says there is a God, and that He loves little children."

"And there's a pot of gold at the end of the rainbow!"

Tess hadn't known what to think. She'd wanted to believe in a God who cared about her, but as she'd grown older she'd seen too little of such kindness, especially with people like Len Connor. She felt more and more certain that her mother was right.

🌴

As Tess drove into Maui she felt as though she was marooned on the moon.

Restless now, she decided to ignore her smarting ankle and do *something*. Food. She needed a decent meal to put events in perspective, to put her life into perspective. When she asked where she could find a good meal, the concierge suggested a luau—the Old Lahaina Luau located within easy walking distance of Pioneer Inn. She had been thinking more along the lines of swordfish and salad at the grill below the hotel, but maybe a little entertainment would jumpstart the vacation mode.

Returning upstairs, she dressed in a pair of white walking shorts and a butter-yellow T-shirt and pulled her hair atop her head and stuffed it into her hat. Slipping on a pair of sandals, which looked awful with the injured ankle wrapped, she went back downstairs and exited the hotel.

The air outside was scented with tuberose and jasmine—or so she tried to imagine—after all this was "paradise." Actually the scent of hamburger from that cheeseburger joint a couple blocks away accompanied her as she took her time walking to the luau. Gusty winds had slackened to a nice breeze though the evening was slightly overcast.

The luau grounds were typical native Hawaiian. Palm trees, grass huts, and steel guitars blended to create an authentic setting. A handsome Polynesian young man wearing a brightly flowered *tupenu* smiled as he looped an orchid lei over her head. Her mood lightened as she accepted a glass of fruit punch with a fresh orchid floating in it. Demonstrations of lei making, coconut cutting, and Ti leaf shirt weaving lined the walkways. She wandered the grounds, sipping her drink.

After posing for the required souvenir picture with said Polynesian hunk, Tess was directed to her seat. As she approached her chair, she did a quick double take. Sitting at the same table, binoculars lifted as he studied the bobbing boats in the harbor, sat none other than Carter McConnell. When he lifted his eyes and saw her, disbelief crossed his face. She set her drink on the table and sat down. "Now who's stalking whom?"

"Nice to see you again, too."

She glanced at the binoculars as he held them aloft. "Thirty-nine fifty. Hilo Hattie's," he said in explanation. "Want to look?" He held them up for her.

"No," she said as a gust of wind lifted her hat. She quickly pulled it back down, shoving it tightly onto her head.

A pair of lovely Polynesian girls came by, grass skirts rustling. "Would you two like a hula lesson?"

She looked over at Carter's face, which had turned a dark shade of pink. "Uh," he stammered. "No thanks." One of the girls wiggled her hips and made a waving motion in front of herself with her arms. "It's not hard," she encouraged. "I bet your wife would love to get a picture of you doing it."

Now it was her turn to blush. She felt the heat rise up her cheeks.

The second girl pulled Carter to his feet and positioned his hands in front of him, showing him the foot movement.

"This is the Ami'ami," she explained. "Now move your hips back and forth." Carter jerked around like a marionette on a string. "No, it's a smaller movement, a little jiggle like this." She demonstrated. Tess swallowed back her amusement as he let the girls make a fool of out him.

When Carter spotted Tess's growing jollity, he leaned over and said something to one of the women. Smiling, they hula-ed over, hips gyrating wildly as they drew a protesting Tess into the act.

"My ankle," she objected.

Carter grinned. "If you can walk on it, you can dance. Come on, give it a try."

The women positioned her next to Carter, draped a grass shirt around her trim hips, and showed her the proper movements. At first she felt conspicuous, but soon she was gyrating along with the others. The four *Akalewa* swayed their hips from side to side, in a graceful interpretation of the native art, *Ha'a*. Tess figured the hand movements were beyond her, but she could swing a grass skirt with the best of them.

"A new talent to wow the homefolks," Carter said.

"I can just imagine doing this at a board meeting." She laughed and tried to mimic the hand movements, which looked easy and graceful, but somehow didn't translate well when she tried them.

"Just what a flight controller needs: hula proficiency." He exaggerated a gyration. "I'll add it to my resume."

The crowd watched, laughing at the playful antics. Before Tess realized it she was actually having fun.

By the time they made their way back to the table she was glad for the reprieve. "I haven't moved like that since my last junior high dance," Carter said.

"What about senior high?" she teased.

"I gave up dancing." There was a twinkle in his eyes that she hadn't noticed before. "What about you?" he said.

"I did the ballet thing for a while. At least until my ballet teacher told me to take up football. I never caught on." They shared a chuckle.

"It looks like they're pulling the pig out of the pit," Carter said. "Want to go watch?"

They stood side by side as the animal with the apple in its mouth was lifted onto the main serving table.

"Where I come from, you don't bury a pig then dig him back up and eat him," she told him. He grinned.

After they had filled their plates, she noticed that he briefly bowed his head before he ate. Praying, she supposed. He didn't seem like one of those religious fanatics who said "Bless this and bless that." She made a note to ask him about it later.

The food, pork included, was surprisingly delicious: Lomi Lomi Salmon, Pulehue Steak, Guava Chicken, Haupia, otherwise known as coconut pudding, banana bread, Taro Rolls, Poi, and Kalua Pua's.

"That's free-range pork," Carter supplied after consulting the menu.

They looked at each other and repeated in unison: "The pig."

"How can a pig be free-range anyhow?" Carter leaned over and whispered. "Was it raised in its natural environment? And where would *that* be?" Tess laughed and looked at him. He sure seemed different than the grumpy guy whose luggage she'd delivered the day before. But then she'd been pretty exhausted too, so she guessed she could understand the change. He was an easy person to be around.

By the time the entertainment began she felt relaxed and happy. They applauded the performance of the beautiful ancient hula Kahiko and 'Auana. For the first time since she'd arrived in Hawaii she felt as though everything was going to be all right. She couldn't say why, exactly. Nothing had changed. She was still without a job. Maybe it was making a new friend.

The wind tossed the dancer's hair, and Tess pulled her hat down tighter.

Cramming a piece of roll into his mouth, Carter applauded. Then leaning over he asked, "Is it supposed to rain?" He tilted his head toward the sky that had taken on a starless appearance. The wind kicked up again.

She shrugged. She'd heard Beeg mention that rain showers were frequent on this side of the island so she wouldn't be surprised—though the cool feel in the air hinted at something stronger than a tropical mist. She studied Carter's relaxed manner. Like her, he was wearing a flower lei some Polynesian lovely had draped over his head. He was smiling, having a great time in spite of their rocky beginning.

"Nice, huh?" he said, laugh crinkles forming around friendly blue eyes.

She nodded. The luau was therapeutic, a sorely needed diversion from a hectic past few days.

She looked up. The wind was whipping across the lawn so strongly that the dancers were having trouble keeping their balance; costumes were wrapping around their bodies, and the girls' long back hair flailed around their faces, making it hard for them to see. A gale whistled through the musicians' microphones, sending an ear-piercing shriek of feedback.

Servers darted about to set desserts—Haupia pudding, Haupia cake, pineapple upside-down cake, guava cake, and coffee—in front of the guests before the full gale hit. Tess leaned to cut a slice of pineapple upside-down cake when the wind whipped a glob of brown sugar into the hair of the woman two chairs down. The woman gave her a dirty look and then left in a huff.

Thunder grumbled. Guests dressed in flimsy island wear clasped their forearms in an attempt to keep warm, teeth chattering as the skies opened up. Waiters and waitresses rushed to rescue the food, pulling out carts they quickly loaded with platters and took inside. Waiters handed out flimsy yellow plastic rain ponchos and guests tried to wrestle the gear over their heads in the whipping wind.

"Are we having fun yet?" Cater shouted into the wind.

"A blast!" Tess replied, "Help me put this on." Carter reached over but the wind persisted, making it impossible to find the narrow slits in the sides.

Chairs overturned. The entertainers courageously plowed ahead on the semi-circular stage below as Poi-logged spectators made for higher ground. Rain sluiced down but the musicians bravely played on.

". . . the missionaries brought many changes to our island," the announcer intoned. *Shreeeek, shrilllll,* the reverb sounded.

". . . King Kalakaua . . . Drat!" The announcer flung the mike to the ground as lightning forked the arena.

"Let's get out of here!" Carter took her hand and the two ran-hobbled toward the lobby's thatched roof. "Are you okay?" Carter released her hand and looked at her drenched face.

"I'm fine," Tess said. "Wet. But fine." She looked down at her feet; the foot without injury had a broken sandal strap.

"Rats!" She said. "Now I need to go sandal shopping, since this is the only pair I brought."

"You need an excuse to shop?" It was a question.

"That's a stereotype, I'll have you know. Not all women love spending money."

"I didn't mean it as an affront," Carter held up both hands and smiled. "Truce?"

She blushed. "Truce."

"Let me hail a cab," Carter offered.

"Are you all right?" he asked again as he helped her into the backseat when a taxi finally pulled up. Water streamed off her chin in rivulets. *How can he be so calm?* She thought.

"Fine. I just want to get into dry clothes."

6

She wasn't about to let bad luck get her down, Tess decided the next morning when she woke up.

Dazzling sunlight filtered through the window as she lifted a slat to look out. Paradise shimmered like a priceless jewel in the rain-drenched harbor. *Papahanaumoku*—Earth Mother—as the emcee had called it last night, looked to be in a better mood this morning. And so was she. Smiling, she dropped the louver back into place.

Her thoughts drifted to Denver. She was tired of wondering what was happening at Connor.com. Len Connor could take a flying leap; Chuck Somebody could wrestle with hiring, resource allocation, compensation, benefits, and compliance with OSHA laws. After an eighteen-hour day manning the phones and handling Connor.com's problems, the "good ol' boys" could kick back, have a beer, and try to figure out the mess.

Tess wasn't going to lift a finger to help. The thought was liberating.

She stared at her reflection in the mirror. A tan—she needed one of those billboard browns that would be the envy of every woman in Denver. She wanted to look her loveliest when she spooned crow onto Len Connor's plate.

After eating pineapple and cinnamon toast in the grill, Tess then headed to Makena Big Beach with a new umbrella and a bottle of Maui Baby, Maui Island's Secret Browning Formula. She'd bought a beach chair, too.

She braked in the public asphalt parking lot and hauled the newly purchased items out of the trunk. By the time she got to the beach, the shoreline was already swarming with scantily clad men and women as they staggered beneath the weight of overloaded backpacks, boogie boards, and snorkel paraphernalia.

After turning the beach umbrella just so, she reached for the tanning lotion and peeled out of her turquoise-and-hot-pink-Hawaiian-print sarong. What she'd do with the superfluous piece of clothing in Denver she didn't know. Pretzeling herself into the chair, she began applying the lotion then leaned back and relaxed behind oversized sunglasses, prepared to spend a leisurely morning. Lazy wavelets of aquamarine water lapped against the shoreline. Feathered fans of palm leaves wove a dark tracery against a sky so blue it made her heart ache. A gentle breeze brought the tang of sea salt mixed with the intoxicating aroma of flowers. An exotic blended fragrance not found in a bottle.

She wondered what Connor.com peons were doing. Slaving away over copy machines, no doubt, staring numb-minded at blinking cursors and answering ringing phones.

She sighed. She missed it. Missed the hassle, the adrenaline rush—really missed it. But she wondered, was that the meaning of life? To slave away at a job she got no recognition for? Or worse, for just a paycheck. Wasn't there supposed to be a deeper meaning in all of this?

Sun beat down. The sound of laughing children's voices drifted toward her. The kids were building a sandcastle on the beach. Children. Precious little miracles. Would she ever have any of her own? She'd been so busy building a career that she had never really paused to consider the question. Thirty-two wasn't ancient, but she could hear her biological clock ticking—or was that the idiot's rap music, farther down the beach, blaring in her ear?

Lazily warm, she dozed, opening her eyes occasionally when she heard the excited cries of a beachcomber who'd spotted a whale frolicking near one of the islands jutting out of the water. *Big whoop,* she thought irritably.

Suddenly the wind shifted. Sand kicked up—instantly coating the Maui Baby tanning lotion in a grainy sheet.

She sat up, shielding her eyes as sunbathers started to race past her. Big Beach had suddenly turned into the

Sahara Desert with a sandstorm approaching. The wind machine-gunned gritty pellets at unsuspecting sun-worshipers.

Spitting sand, she sprang up and grabbed the umbrella. Wind caught the frame and stripped the fabric inside out. Another hefty gust sent her nearly airborne as she stumbled around, trying to wedge her toes into a pair of rubber flip-flops. "Stupid thongs!" she muttered. Sun-blistered snorkelers boiled out of the churning water to make a dash for the shoreline.

Grabbing her belongings, she set off for the car. Her hat blew off and she went to retrieve it. The injured ankle gave way then, and she stumbled, then pulled herself upright before she hobbled on.

Ramming what was left of the shredded umbrella into the nearest trash receptacle, she lunged for the car. Once inside, she dug sand out of her eyes and ears and places where sand didn't belong.

Grasping hold of the steering wheel, she batted her forehead against the backs of her hands. *Why-why-why?* Why *couldn't* she have a nice relaxing vacation?

After a moment, her nerves calmed. A shower. She needed a shower to get rid of this sand. She turned the key in the ignition . . . and heard nothing.

Nothing.

She whacked the steering wheel. "Don't do this!"

She turned the key again.

Nothing.

"No. *No.*" Gritting her teeth, she tried again. Grinding. Grinding.

Again.

Nothing. Grind.

Clamping her eyes shut, she heaved an exacerbated *oooomph*. Faced with the inevitable, she fumbled in her purse for her cell phone.

Grimacing against the feel of gritty sand in uncomfortable places, she listened for the dial tone and found she had none. Of course. *Tess, you're losing it, girl. Okay.* She looked around, deciding she had to take charge of the situation. Sand still pitted the car's windows. Who knew how long this would keep up? She'd just have to borrow a cell phone from a fellow sun-worshiper. So, pulling her hat down on her head and retying the sarong around her waist, she opened the car door and began to make her way in the wind and sand to the phone. The back of her sand-logged swimsuit hung a good two inches too low as she walked backward through the gale, trying to avoid getting more grit in her eyes. "Hey!" a voice said as she felt a thump against her back. "Watch where you're going, Lady!" a tall, tanned Adonis said in a gruff voice.

Her face flamed. "Sorry. Can I use your cell phone?" And for once, the man had one. Her luck was picking up.

"I don't *know* what's wrong with the car," she told the

rental agent. "It won't start. I turn the key and nothing happens."

"We'll send someone right away—Big Beach, right?"

"Right." Big *sandy* beach. The clerk didn't mention that help was still two hours away.

And so as the sun set on Lahaina Harbor on Tess Nelson's third night in paradise, she was in her room, soaking a sprained ankle and trying to get the taste of sand out of her mouth. Too weary to eat, she skipped dinner and fell asleep before eleven, only to be awakened by the wind around three A.M. Peering out the window blinds, she watched palms bending to the onslaught, loose fronds whipping across the parking lot.

"Gilligan's Island," she conceded. "I'm trapped on Gilligan's Island."

What would Mona think of her now?

"She's so pretty." Tess stared at the beautiful creature lying in a pink velvet box. Its blue eyes opened and closed, and when she pressed its tummy, the baby cried real tears. She never cried. Mona spanked her when she cried.

"Please, Mommy. Can't I have this doll?"

"Oh, all right, you ungrateful twit. You can have the stupid doll. I hope you're happy."

Mona glared at her daughter as she paid for the purchase. They left the store and got into the car to go home.

But before Mona turned on the ignition, she looked at the doll and said snidely, "It looks like it's lying in a coffin."

Tess felt her heart drop. Why did her mother have to spoil everything?

She lowered the window blind. What had made her think about Mona and that silly doll? Unpleasant events of the past few days? It wasn't as if she didn't have dolls—but that one was special—a child's delight.

Other girls at school—girls with pretty clothes and Beaver Cleaver mothers—sailed through life on a magic carpet. Their mothers had pretty polished nails; Mona's hands were rough from factory work and they perpetually smelled of cigarette smoke. Other girls' moms came to PTA and were room mothers who visited school on holidays and birthdays bearing pretty plates of cupcakes and cookies.

Mona never came to anything. She didn't have time to bake cupcakes and cookies or be a room mother. Once she promised she would, but she hadn't. Only recently had it occurred to her that Mona had had to work—the family needed two incomes to survive. Maybe if Mona had talked to Tess about it, she might have understood, maybe even accepted the fact that not everyone lived the ideal family lifestyle.

Still, her mother and father were forever making

promises to go to the movies or get ice cream, but when the time came they were too tired. She had vowed to herself that when she grew up, she would take care of herself. She'd eat all the ice cream and go to all the movies she wanted. She might even make enough money to buy a movie theatre and be the envy of every girl in class. She'd have a home with good furniture, not some old pieces of junk from the thrift store, and she'd buy it all with her own money that she'd work hard for, and no one would ever take it away from her because she was tough—even though sometimes it hurt to be tough.

Sunday mornings, she'd watch her friends, all dressed up in their nice clothes as they drove away to church with their PTA mothers and Ward Cleaver fathers. She imagined the happy families coming back to eat pot roast and mashed potatoes and gravy, sitting at a table with pretty plates and saucers and even fresh flowers, and she'd wonder why, if there were a *God*, did he love some people more than he did others? Because it was obvious that he did.

"Your problem is that you're too trusting, Tess," Mona said. A cigarette dangled from the corner of her mouth and the stench of smoke filled the room. "You need to grow up," she said. "Now come away from that window. Those folks are putting on airs. Jack Pierson may look like the perfect hus-

band and father, but I know for a fact Jack likes his brandy. Don't be fooled by people. Do you really think anything in this life is that perfect?—that trusting in some mystical God to run your life is going to keep you from having troubles? Now set the table for breakfast and maybe we'll all go for a ride later."

"Promise?"

"Promise."

Mona was right. She had let down her guard and placed her trust in Len Connor. And Len had shafted her big time.

I'm hiring a fraternity brother. But there's that position in payroll . . .

Mona would give her an earful when she heard that she had been demoted—fired, whatever. She should call her, but they rarely talked. Guilt nagged her when she thought of how little time she allotted family—but then the Nelson family gave a whole new definition to "family."

She picked up a travel brochure and leafed through the pages. A drive to Hana promised spectacular waterfalls and freshwater pools. Hawaiian "cattle country." African tulip trees, towering Baldwin pines, colorful exotic plants and flowers, the variegated greens of the endless tropical scenery—none of which really interested her. At least not right now.

Wadding the paper, she threw it aside and started to pace. She hated this feeling, this panicky feeling of not knowing what was going to happen next. Fear of the unknown set her teeth on edge. Maybe she'd been wrong to leave. Maybe she should go back and fight for her job. If she stayed and waited for Len, would he ever recognize his mistake? Suddenly she felt overwhelmed, as though she were drowning. A headache bloomed at the base of her skull.

7

Sitting at the small table in her room, Tess casually leafed through "Driving Maui" while she finished breakfast. Her eye caught the "Whale Watch" excursion. Humpbacks migrated from the North Pacific to Maui's southern and western shores during late November through March to mate, calve, and nurse their young in warm Hawaiian waters.

Whales. Well, why not. She wished she didn't have to go alone. Her thoughts turned to that man she'd spent time with at the luau and she wondered what he was doing today. Then just as quickly, she tossed the idea aside.

Donning a pair of shorts, a T-shirt, and flip-flops, she reached for her sunglasses, binoculars (thanks to Hilo Hattie's), and sunscreen, and looked at her reflection in the mirror. Was that a bald spot near her left temple? She moved closer to see, running her hand through the strands, a few of which came loose and clung to her fingers. "Great!" she murmured. Nerves had her going bald. Great. She grabbed a bandanna and tied it securely around her head, then left for the wharf to purchase a ticket.

Captain Commando Humpback Whale Picture Patrol— a certified thirteen-passenger inflatable boat—bobbed at its mooring.

Water, wind, and surf. She climbed aboard, and leaned back as the captain set out to sea. The boat skimmed foamy waves. She gazed at the immensity of it all. Hadn't she heard somewhere that God showed Himself in nature? She wondered if even God was surprised by His handiwork the day He formed the oceans.

No, she supposed. Nothing surprised Him, not even the beauty she saw this morning.

So, ol' girl, why can't you let go and let God handle the rough spots in your life? If He's smart enough to create all you see, maybe He's big enough to oversee your piddling crisis. Name me one man or woman who doesn't have problems, but the wise soul doesn't fool himself into thinking he controls it. But she'd been in charge of her life for so long she didn't know how to even begin.

A couple of miles offshore, the captain stopped the boat. "We got to be quiet and watch," the overweight man with the standard captain's hat said, finger to lips. The other ten tourists gazed with hushed awe, turning in circles to see who would be first to spot their prey.

After a few minutes a teenage boy with bright red hair pointed as he squeaked, "Thar she blows!" The excited tourists heaved to portside, causing the raft to shift. Men, children, and women jostled for position, binoculars to their eyes, shouting, "portside!" then, "starboard!" pointing out each sighting.

It wasn't long before she tired of trying to catch a glimpse. She moved to the back bench. She'd stuffed a novel in her backpack; she'd read and leave the whales their privacy.

Sitting back, she opened the book and yawned. Sun reflected off the water and made her drowsy. Tess closed her eyes and soaked up the rays.

A second later they snapped open in time to see a humpback surface starboard, so close that a shower of seawater from its blowhole drenched her. Flinging water off her book, she grabbed the sides of the raft for support as the rubber tipped and shifted. Whale lovers screamed and trampled in her direction, tripping over each other to get the photo op. There wouldn't have been more chaos if the humpback had tried to mate with the boat.

She tried to scramble out of the way but her bad ankle got caught on a rope and she tripped before a portly man slammed into her. "Get . . . off . . . of me!" she managed. The man offered a vague apology before climbing to his feet and rushing to the latest sighting. Cameras whirred.

"Portside!"

Gripping the sides of the rubber raft, she gritted her teeth until the whale submerged and the crowd scrimmaged back to the front. She dropped back to the seat to examine her foot.

"Oh, yeah, that's gonna swell. Again!" she murmured, clamping her eyes shut.

Soaked pages in her novel curled in the sun.

Tess braked the rented car behind the hotel, exhausted. A trip to a local supermarket after whale watching for soda and chips to keep in the room proved interesting. Asparagus: nine dollars a pound. She didn't think she'd be cooking much asparagus if she lived here. She had purchased tape and an Ace bandage as well, since the first one smelled of seawater.

After dropping her goods in her room and rebandaging her ankle, she made her way back outside. The harbor gently beckoned to her. Lahaina was beautifully lit tonight. Festive strings of tiny multicolored lights reflected from boats tied to the moorings.

She walked slowly along the water's edge, drinking in the scenery. The air smelled tangy yet fresh. Palm trees rustled in the breeze. The ocean surf beat steadily along the shore.

Her eyes strayed to couples walking hand and hand, and emptiness welled inside her. Something was missing in her life—was it a man? Was it family? No, she didn't need a man to make her life complete, and her family had proven less than satisfying years ago. She didn't need anyone—maybe that was the problem.

Lanai Island lay dark against a background of sailboats awash in their tiny lights. A couple stood, arms wrapped around each another, and gazed at the splendid sight. She felt the weight of her aloneness. She *was* alone. Most of the time it didn't bother her, but seeing couples walking with their arms looped around each other, honeymooners kissing in secluded corners, made her realize what an empty life she lived.

Why couldn't she be like those people, tourists enjoying their vacation, laughing, enjoying life in general, even having their pictures taken with those ridiculous parrots in front of the hotel? She thought of the smiling tourists she'd seen crowded into shops, buying colorful Polynesian shirts and sarongs as if there would be a souvenir famine in the very near future. They'd never wear the things. They'd take them home, show them to their friends and families, and then they'd stash them in a bottom drawer and at some future time the treasures would go into a garage sale or become someone's Halloween costume.

Wasting money like it grew on trees—

She cringed when she realized how much like Mona she sounded. Mona.

The pit of her stomach felt like a stone. What difference did it make to her how those people spent their money? It made absolutely no difference to her. They were having a good time and that was what mattered, wasn't it?

Mona was the perennial wet blanket at every party, the one who couldn't have fun if her life depended on it: "Why would you buy me something like that?" she'd ask when Tess gave her a thoughtfully chosen birthday or Christmas gift. "What am I going to do with that? Such a waste of money."

Not much different than you wondering why tourists buy sarongs and brightly flowered shirts, is it, Tess?

Was she turning into her mother?

Sleep didn't come easily that night. Noises drifted from the harbor—the sounds of happy voices, of someone strumming a ukulele and singing "Shiny Bubbles" and laughing.

People having fun. People unlike Tess Nelson, who'd die before she slaughtered the song, "Tiny Bubbles."

"Relax," she whispered. "Relax and enjoy Hawaii."

Connor.com *couldn't* run smoothly without her. Why, she'd established all of the H.R. systems, factors that kept the employees happy—everyone knew that happy employees equaled productive employees and that meant money in Connor.com's pocket. She was the backbone of the systems, which were the backbone of the company. Logic said Len needed her, that Connor.com needed her.

Logic.

Carter shoved his room keys into his pocket as he let himself into his room. He slid the window open to welcome a breeze and automatically turned on the TV. The cheeseburger he'd eaten fought with the double-dip Häagen-Dazs coconut pineapple cone he'd bought on the walk back to the hotel.

Sitting down in a chair, he propped his feet on the bed and adjusted the sound on the TV as his eyes scanned the stack of coupon books he'd acquired.

". . . tropical storm . . . better watch this one, folks, could be upgraded to hurricane status before the night's over . . ."

Spotting a coupon for "Mexican Madness Night" at Moose McGillicuddy's restaurant, he leaned over and carefully creased the paper then tore it out. $16.95 for two. He shrugged. Not bad—he was a "one" but he'd eat what he could and leave the rest.

Adjacent to the Madness coupon was one for a free coffee mug at Hilo Hattie's, with a twenty-five-dollar purchase. The binoculars and puka beads had already cost him fifty, but he might find something else he liked—maybe take Carl back one of those hula skirts. He snickered when he tried to imagine what the macho supervisor would do with two half coconut shells and a grass skirt. The coupon joined the others on the nightstand.

He stretched out to relax and let the cheeseburger settle. Carl had been smart to make him take a vacation. He'd needed the time away to refocus and relax.

Thanks for calling my limitations to my attention, he thought. *Help me to lean more fully on You.*

Clicking off the TV, Carter lay in the darkness, doing what he'd come to do in Hawaii: spend time with his Best Friend.

Lord, You know my heart. Let me do more thanking and less complaining. Grant me patience to wait on You. I recognize my need for Your assurances, for Your strength for Your hand on my life. I stand guilty: guilty of weak faith and the if-I-can't-fix-it-by-Friday-I'll-turn-it-over-to-God thinking. Thank You for reminding me that it is You I need, not You who need me.

8

Startled from a sound sleep, Tess sat bolt upright in bed. Shouts—someone pounding on her door.

Fighting off the dregs of deep sleep, she shook her head and tried to focus on the lighted numbers on the travel alarm on the nightstand. Six A.M.? What was going on now? Deciding the racket wasn't going to stop, she grabbed her robe and stuffed her arms into it, then rammed her left foot in a loafer. Failing to find the other, she dropped to her knees to search under the chair.

Someone pounded on the door again, then a man's voice yelled out, "Open up!"

She found the missing shoe as the hammering persisted. Springing to her feet, she banged her lip on the edge of the bed frame.

"Ouch!" The tip of her tongue worried the swelling knot as she grabbed the shoe and stuffed it onto her right foot. "Ouch!" She'd forgotten the sore ankle. Fire alarms were shrilling in the hallway.

Her tongue was still exploring her bleeding lip as she reached the door and jerked it open to find a fireman in full gear standing in front of her, ax in hand, his face blackened with soot. Two air tanks were strapped to the man's back

"What's going on?"

"We're evacuating the building."

She caught the scent of smoke. This wasn't a drill; it was the real thing. Panic swelled in her throat.

"We need you to leave the hotel immediately."

"Ah . . . yeah. I just need to—"

"Leave everything. Get out of the building." The fireman moved on.

"Take the stairs at the end of the hall. Don't use the elevator," the man turned to warn over his shoulder before he continued down the hall, pounding on doors and calling out evacuation orders. The firefighter's heavy black leather coat with Maui County Department of Fire Control disappeared into the blue haze hanging in the air.

Hotel guests in various stages of undress rushed past her. Coughing, she reached inside for her purse and then went to the bathroom to retrieve her glasses. As she passed room 215, the door flew open and Carter stumbled out.

"Are you still here?" Carter frowned.

"I had to go back for a minute."

"For what?"

"My glasses." Her mouth firmed. "I can't see without them and I didn't have time to put my contacts in."

Carter glanced at her door number. "What are the chances of us being on the same floor in the Mynah Nest and Pioneer Inn?" The siren kept up its blare as pajama-clad guests raced for the stairwell.

"Hey, you two! Keep moving. Get out of the building. *Now!*"

Carter grabbed her arm and propelled her toward the exit stairway. As he opened the heavy door a cloud of thick smoke belched out and he quickly shielded her with his body. Tess's mind raced as other people turned and searched for an alternate escape.

"Down here!" someone shouted.

She edged closer to Carter. "Do you have this uncanny feeling that we're caught in some ludicrous crisis time warp?" she said, trying to sound unconcerned even as tears stung her eyes.

"I'm beginning to get that feeling."

Her body trembled beneath her thin robe.

By now the firemen were swarming; one beefy man stood by a fire exit and motioned guests through an open window. Tess and Carter managed to keep ahead of the smoke. Fire sprinklers were going off; water ran along the carpeted hall in streams.

"Ouch!" she cried.

Carter stopped. "What?" He looked at her.

She pointed down. "My ankle." He scooped her up in his arms and raced toward the window, waiting until a man and his wife climbed out onto the metal stairway. Her fingers wrapped in his shirtfront, "I can't do this—"

"Sure you can—we're not talking options here."

She looked down at the thirty-foot drop, then back to him. "I can't do this. What if I fall?"

"You can do it." He gently pried her fingers loose from his T-shirt.

She shook her head, clamping her eyes shut tightly.

"Just hold on. I'll carry you down—"

"No! You can't!" Her grip tightened. "I can't—really. I can't."

"We're only two floors up. We'll be safe. I have eagle footing. Keep your eyes closed and pray."

"I don't pray . . ." she said weakly.

He glanced down, his face puckered in a frown. "Okay, I'll pray for both of us." He helped her through the window and climbed out. "Lord, we're coming through!" he shouted. Sirens wailed. Thick black smoke roiled from a downstairs vent. Firemen unraveled long water hoses from pumper trucks. Ladder trucks arrived.

She clung to his shirt, refusing to open her eyes.

"Just hold on." His voice was low, gentle. He started to ease his way down the fire escape. "We're going to make it just fine. Don't worry. Keep your eyes closed, and don't look down."

He cautiously felt for each step.

"Are you all right?" he asked.

"Are we down?"

"Not quite. Still one floor to go."

"Still one!"

"We're doing fine. Keep your eyes closed."

"Don't worry." It wasn't until he set her down on solid ground that she slowly loosened her grip. Fawn-colored eyes opened. She fumbled in her robe pocket and slipped on a pair of eyeglasses.

"You couldn't see anyway?" he exclaimed with a laugh.

"I wasn't taking any chances—all my clothes are up there. What about my clothes? I'm not dressed."

Carter ran his hand through his hair. "I don't know. We'll have to see how bad the fire is."

Someone handed the displaced guests cups of hot, fragrant coffee, and a blanket, which Carter protectively wrapped around Tess. Threading their way through the crowd, they wandered across the street, sat on the curb, and stared at the ground floor, where black smoke rolled from broken windows.

A moment later Carter looked over to find a woman

sitting on the curb beside him. Startled, he stared at the yellow cat draped around her neck in collarlike fashion.

The woman sent him a peripheral glance and smiled. "There's nothing like a bit of excitement to stir the blood, is there?"

"No, Ma'am." His eyes focused on the animal. How did she get the cat to do that? Wasn't that thing hot around her neck? Where had she come from? He hadn't seen her at the hotel.

She gave him a smile peppered with experience. "Don't worry. God has everything under control."

"Indeed He does," Carter replied.

Nodding, he turned back to Tess, who leaned close and whispered, "I've seen her. She was sitting on the bench at the Banyon tree a couple mornings ago."

The lady turned with Tess's hushed observation. Their eyes met, and she smiled benignly. After a moment she turned back to stare at the historic old building engulfed in smoke.

"Everything we brought with us is up there," Tess said.

The woman nodded. "Clothing and luggage can be replaced. But a soul—now that's another thing. I must go, but I'll see you again." She stood and walked over to one of the waiting ambulances.

"She's an odd duck," Carter said more to himself than to Tess.

They watched as fire belched from the kitchen area

and flames spread. He sat with his wrists hanging over his knees, staring at the ground. "This is turning into some vacation."

She laughed humorlessly. "And I came to Hawaii to get away from it all."

He smiled. "Me, too—I'm supposed to be relaxing. Too much stress in my life."

"Well—" leaning back on his elbows, he stared at the burning hotel, "things could be worse. Like the lady said, material possessions can be replaced. At least no lives were lost."

She nodded. "Wonder how the fire started?"

He shrugged, and then sat up straighter. "I don't know about you, but I could use some breakfast. Are you hungry?"

"Well," she looked down at the robe and blanket. "I'm not exactly dressed—"

"Nobody's going to care. Let's find some scrambled eggs. We're down to nothing except what's on our backs. Do you plan to starve, too?"

The corner of her mouth quirked "No."

"Me either. Let's go."

He ushered her into the warmth of a nearby small café. The eating establishment was deserted—everyone, it seemed, was out watching the fire. Carter chose a table near the back of the room. She pulled the blanket closer around her robe as if it were a queen's cape, and sat with her back to the wall. Small tables with rush-bottomed chairs waited for customers. Vases of flowers placed on each table added a festive air, and a mural of palm trees and ocean waves covered one wall. The pretty waitress carrying menus and glasses of water looked as if she would feel right at home in a grass skirt.

"What can I get you?" the woman asked.

"Black coffee for me," Carter said without consulting a menu. "Two scrambled eggs, toast, and some of that tropical guava jelly."

Tess nodded. "Same."

The waitress smiled, a deep dimple creasing her twenty-something face. "You two from the hotel?"

"Yes."

"Too bad. Lose everything?"

Tess studied the table, the knuckles of her hand white from clutching the blanket that wanted to slip off her shoulders.

"It would seem so," Carter answered. "I don't know when we'll know for certain."

"Lose your money, too?"

Carter had to smile. "I have my billfold."

"Well, if you need to run a tab—I'm Joanie, and I own the place."

"Thanks."

When Joanie left to retrieve their order, Tess planted her elbows on the table and thrust her fingers into her hair. "I simply cannot believe this!"

Carter shrugged. "Life sometimes throws sliders. The way I see it, we're still alive, we're in paradise, and this vacation has no where to go but up."

She leveled her gaze on him. "What planet did you say you were from?"

"Earth." He grinned, and then leaned closer. "Temporary journey until the real thing."

She groaned. "You're one of those Christians, aren't you? I knew when I saw you bow your head at the luau."

"You mean the fun luau? Yes," he said quietly. "I believe in God. He's seen me through a lot."

"I thought so. You're too . . . comfortable with disaster."

"I've never heard that one before."

"I'm sure you have your perfect little life; it's a free ride with God, right?"

"No." He leveled a gaze at her. "Why are you so uptight?"

That stopped her cold. She sat back and let her hands drop to the table. She looked down and noticed some stray strands of hair. Her face flushed.

"I'm not trying to offend you," Carter went on. "You just seem . . . stressed." She lifted her eyes to his.

"I'm not a Christian and I'm sorry I got defensive. Maybe I am stressed. With the fire and all . . ." Her gaze dropped to the bag in her lap. She laughed. "I just realized how stupid I am. I didn't grab my purse; I grabbed a makeup bag."

"Well, you may be broke but you'll look good," he said.

"I wasn't thinking," she said. "That's not like me. I'm usually a logical, organized, in-control person."

"Losing your britches to a fire will shake up anybody."

"It's *not* the fire—or Beeg being gone or the weather or losing my contact. It's *everything*—everything about this whole rotten episode called life."

The waitress set two cups of coffee on the table. Carter stared at the steaming liquid as silence took over. Finally he reached for sugar packets, eyeing her. "What do you mean by 'everything'?"

She sat silent for a moment, wondering if she'd said too much. Yet there was something about a man in a T-shirt and pajama bottoms and a woman wearing a robe and blanket that transformed strangers into confidants.

"I lost my job."

"Lost your job," he repeated. "That's all? I thought you were going to say you'd been given three weeks to live."

"I might as well."

"Come on, now. Losing a job isn't the end of the world. You're alive; you're in good health—I presume. You're in paradise." He smiled, as if hoping to coax the black look off her face. "What's so bad?"

"I was replaced by the boss's old fraternity brother. Fired."

Carter dumped sugar into his coffee. "That's bad."

She lifted an indifferent shoulder and grabbed for the blanket when it started to slide. "I know it probably sounds trivial to you."

"Well, no. Not trivial. But you have to admit it's not one for the books. It happens more than you'd think."

She absently shredded a napkin. "Dave—that was my boss's dad, who founded the company—had groomed me to be his right hand. I was in line to be the next vice president of human resources. I'd worked hard for the job— my private life the past five years has been practically nonexistent. But then Dave died suddenly . . ."

"And sonny came in and the dream disappeared."

"Pretty much. He did offer me another position . . ."

"And the choice was?"

"Payroll, two levels below my current position, or leave the company."

"Ouch."

She piled up the napkin pieces. "I think Len brought in his friend to get back at me. He seemed jealous of the working relationship I had with his father—he felt intimidated by me."

Carter sat back in the booth and studied her.

"That's pretty cold. Could be the best thing that's ever happened to you."

"Yeah, well, Len has quite an ego. I went back and realized I still had a plane ticket to Hawaii—it was supposed to be a business trip . . ."

"He paid for this trip?"

"Well . . . technically . . . yes." She shifted in her chair. "It was a nonrefundable ticket . . ." her voice trailed off. She really hadn't given it much thought but when put that way she felt a guilt she hadn't felt before. "I guess I should pay Connor.com for it when I get back . . ."

Carter smiled reassuringly at her. "So what are you going to do for work when you return? A bright, intelligent woman like you shouldn't let one jerk get you down."

"Bright and intelligent, huh? I wonder what kind of impression you'd have of me when I'm not doing a Three-Stooge fest." She pointed to her ankle and puffy lips.

"It's in the eyes," Carter said half-joking.

"Oh, the eyes," she repeated. "Seriously, I don't know what I'm going to do. Yet." She balanced her coffee cup in one hand, studying the thick mug as if she'd never seen a cup before.

"So, now what?"

"Now I wait until Len realizes his mistake—and he will. He'll beg me to come back and I'll probably go—under my terms. I've spent too many years with the company to walk away now." She leaned back in the booth. "In another five years I'll move on, manage an even larger Human Resources department, and maybe even move into labor relations." She looked up sharply. "With my experience I can work anywhere I want."

He lifted his hands with mock surrender. "I'm on your side."

"Well, don't think for a minute that Len's decision is anything but a minor roadblock—because it isn't. I've spent the last five years building my career—Len Connor isn't going to diminish it or *me* with one brief conversation."

"Got it all under control, do you?"

Joanie arrived with two plates and slid breakfast in front of Carter and Tess before pouring fresh coffee.

"Can I get you anything else?" Joanie asked.

"Nothing," Carter said. "Thanks."

The waitress walked off. Tess sat staring at the plate.

"Do you want something else?" Carter looked at her.

"I'm not hungry."

"You've got to eat something." Carter spread jelly on a piece of toast and held it out to her. "Try this. One bite at a time."

"I can't—"

"Tess Nelson's in control, isn't she? Eat."

She snatched the toast and bit into it.

"That's it—I love a woman with an appetite."

Picking up her fork, she sobered. She looked up, her eyes intent. "You talk to God, don't you?"

"Sure. My faith is important to me."

"I suppose He talks back to you?"

"Every day—in a loud, thunderous voice often accompanied by wind, thunder, and lightning." He took a sip of coffee, and then dipped his head when he saw the heat in her eyes.

"He doesn't *talk* to me—not in the way you imply. But we have ongoing communication."

She shrugged. "My grandmother took me to church once in a while, but I didn't then nor do I now understand all the hoopla. Lately I've been trying to comprehend . . ." She glanced out the front window of the café. "Right now I have more pressing concerns to consider; do I have any identification left, any clothes, and any money—"

"Don't worry about it. I'm sure the hotel will help."

She felt herself choke up—she wasn't sure why exactly, but she sure wasn't going to let Carter McConnell see her turn into a blubbering mass. "I thought about sending the tickets back to Len, but then I thought, why not? Why not get out of Denver, leave the snow and cold behind? That's easy enough, I thought. Consider my options.

"But then the taxi had no heater and I nearly froze. The driver drove like a maniac. I sprained my ankle at the airport and had to limp down the Jetway. When I got to Maui, a little boy ran into me, knocking my contact out. My best friend, whom I was really coming to see, is on the Mainland showing her watercolor originals." She sighed. "The luau was a disaster, the beach a worse failure, and now there's been a fire in the hotel kitchen, which happened to be directly below my room." She looked up. "Does this God of yours have a warped sense of humor?"

"Yes, God has a sense of humor, but it's not warped." He leaned closer and whispered lightly, "Nothing about God is warped. He loves us—without reservations."

Tess felt herself swallow hard. The kindness in his voice threatened her resolve to not cry. Carter straightened. "What about family? Mom? Dad? Brothers or sisters? Why not go home for a long overdue vacation?"

"Never. Mona wouldn't welcome the intrusion. She's the last person I want to know about losing my job. I haven't seen my brother in twenty years. He's off photographing another war somewhere—I can't remember the last time we talked."

"Mona?"

"My *mother.*"

The way she bit the word out translated to al-Qaida terrorist. Mona bin Laden.

His tone softened. "What a pair we make. I'm here in paradise because my boss thinks I'm stressed out; you're here because you *are* stressed out . . ."

"I didn't say I was stressed out," she defended.

Carter smiled knowingly. "Okay. Never mind," she conceded.

She glanced down at her soot-blackened robe, the blanket, and shrugged dismally. "I'm going home—the moment the stores open and I can buy something other than this robe and blanket to wear."

Carter salted his eggs. "I suppose—" His words halted

in midsentence as a man suddenly burst through the restaurant's front door and barreled toward the table. The Popeye—a spinach-eating looking brute twice Carter's size and clearly of Polynesian descent—grabbed him by the shirt collar and pulled him out of the booth.

"What th—?" Carter's eyes bulged as the oaf dangled him in midair by the nape of his cotton/polyester blend T-shirt. The hulk glared at Carter as if he were about to take him apart piece by piece.

"The question is, what you think *you're* doing, Chump!" The man's voice sounded like gravel on metal.

"Let–go–of–me!" Carter wrapped his hands around the man's tree-branch-like wrist and tried to wrestle free. His air supply diminished.

Tess slid out of the booth, throwing down her napkin. "You let him go this instant!" she demanded. "Who do you think you are?"

Carter felt like a fool, dangling by his shirt collar from the hand of this . . . this *leviathan,* while Tess confronted the guy like a teacup poodle facing down a pit bull.

She snapped her finger and pointed at the man with authority. "I'm warning you! *Let* go of him!"

Standing in bare feet, she was five foot nothing of blazing wrath in a nightgown and smoky bathrobe.

The bully let go of Carter's collar and shoved him against the booth. Carter felt his hip hit with a sickening thud. He straightened against the pain, about to pull himself up between Tess and the giant when Tess spoke again, her voice low but filled with grit, "Just what do you think you're doing?"

The man's cold eyes fixed on her. "This is between him and me, Short-Stuff."

She got in his face. "Not when you come in here and disrupt my breakfast, Buster!"

He started to ease off, shooting Carter a murderous glare. "I don't know who you are, Lady, but this chump has been seein' my girl. Nobody cuts into my time."

"Wait a minute!" Carter protested but Tess held up one hand to stop him.

"And who is your *girl?*" she asked coldly.

"Irihapeti Tehuia—ask him." He pointed at Carter.

"I not only don't *know* an Irihapeti Tehuia, I can't even spell it." Carter sat back down, raising a hand to his crushed windpipe.

"Never heard of her," the ape scoffed. "I got word that you two was seen havin' a cozy dinner last Friday—"

"I wasn't in Hawaii last Friday." Carter met his furious gaze. "Your information is wrong."

"You—"

"He wasn't," she interrupted. "Neither one of us got here until Monday night."

"You'd lie for him—"

"Maybe. But I'm telling the truth right now." She crossed her arms, her eyes daring him to repeat his claim.

The brute's features coiled like a snake. "You're not Frank Lotus?"

"I'm not Frank Anybody. Look, fella, I don't know who you're looking for," Carter said, "but it isn't me. Why don't you just leave, talk to this woman you're having trouble with, and try to get the mistake straightened out." Carter massaged his swollen throat. The dufus had bruised his windpipe!

Pivoting on his heel, the stranger lumbered out of the café. Tess sank back into the booth and released a sigh of relief.

"Well, that was interesting," Carter said.

They sat for a moment, and then burst out laughing. Carter was glad to see that she was feeling better, even if it took his broken neck to wipe the gloom off her face.

"If this situation can get any worse, I'd like to know how," he admitted.

"Oh, I'm sure it can." She wiped her eyes with the corner of a napkin and eyed the mound of congealed eggs on her plate. "Actually, it's starting to get interesting."

9

"*Alana* has now been upgraded from a tropical storm to a hurricane. She could make landfall in the Hawaiian Islands within thirty-six hours. But she's switched course before. Stay tuned for updates as they become available . . ."

The bartender reached up and switched off the news. Murmurs about the rare approaching storm spread among the guests, but Tess was oblivious to the building concern.

Sitting in the Pioneer Courtyard, surrounded by palms and lush vegetation, she and Carter waited for the hotel management's instructions on how to weather the storm.

With all the mishaps she'd had, the thought that she'd be smack dab in the center of a hurricane had never entered her mind.

She finished off a glass of iced tea and sat back. "You have been very nice about all this."

Carter had been more than nice; he'd been courteous and kind and ever optimistic. That was more than she could claim for herself.

Pioneer Inn management had rounded up the fire-displaced guests and asked them to wait in the courtyard for further instructions. A female employee found a pair of jeans and a shirt for Tess, and she had changed in the ladies' room. Carter and several other men still wore pajamas. The smell of thick smoke hung onerous in the air, and the guests buzzed with stories of the harrowing escape.

"You've been a good sport, too," he acknowledged. "What did the doctor say about that ankle?"

Medical staff was on site to help, so she took the opportunity to have the injury looked at again. By now, a sprained ankle was the least of her worries.

"He said it's healing nicely."

"You're still limping."

"My ankle is the least of my problems. Where do you think they'll put us now that the hotel is devastated?" The first floor was a black pit, especially where the kitchen had been. While the upper floors had been saved from the fire's ravage they had not been spared from the sprinkler system that had left everything a soggy, dripping mess.

The hectic hours surrounding the kitchen fire had shown people's true nature. Everyone was helping the victims. The management provided free trays of food and fruit and hot coffee they brought from the nearby grocery. Strangers brought blankets, clothes, personal items. It was truly a heartwarming thing to see. The manager appeared. Tired lines around his eyes testified to the past tense hours. Clearing his throat, the short, pudgy man got the crowd's attention. "Best Western wants to assure each guest that they will be taken care of with the utmost expediency, and hotel management deeply appreciates each person's willingness to cooperate. We are trying to locate rooms for every guest, but it's proving to be a difficult goal. Hotels on the island are at their maximum because of conventions and the Skins games this coming weekend. At the moment, kind Lahaina residents are offering to take guests into their homes until other arrangements can be made."

Tess's gaze switched to Carter. "I don't want to stay with a stranger," she whispered. It was barely eight o'clock in the morning yet she felt exhausted. She wanted to leave, to be back in her quiet, safe home. But, with the storm approaching, the odds of getting a flight back to the Mainland tonight were slim to impossible, though she certainly intended to try. If she couldn't get out, she was stuck. Stranded in paradise. The absurdity struck her as funny and she supposed lack of sleep was the culprit more than true humor, because the situation was about as humorous as a bubble gum machine in a lockjaw ward.

Carter shook his head. "I don't like the thought either, but it sounds like we have little choice."

"We will have employees standing by to introduce you to your hosts," the manager went on. "In the meantime, coffee, tea, and breakfast rolls are being served."

Tess and Carter got up, milling with the crowd. Young men and women worked their way though the pack, taking names and addresses.

The manager waved to her and Carter as they stood to the side of the fountain. He approached, his ruddy features dark with concern. "Mr. McConnell and Miss Nelson—I am so sorry for this inconvenience. I have a lovely woman who is willing to open her home to you—"

Tess met Carter's gaze and shook her head.

"Miss Nelson doesn't feel comfortable staying with strangers," Carter said. "Is there someplace else we could stay?"

"Only the beach," the manager concluded, then shook his head. "And I wouldn't advise sleeping on the beach."

"No—of course not." Carter ran his hand over his whiskered jaw. "You mentioned a woman?"

"Stella DeMuer." He leaned in close. "Ms. DeMuer is a bit eccentric, but I can assure you she's perfectly harmless. She has a lovely beach home in Kihei with a guesthouse in back for your comfort, Mr. McConnell."

"Kihei—"

"Only twenty-five minutes from Lahaina—lovely town," the manager assured. "You have a car?"

"I have one," Tess said. "But I really don't like the idea of staying in someone's private home."

Carter spotted a woman walking his way and he frowned when he saw the large yellow cat draped around her neck.

Tess paled and edged closer. "That's the woman we talked to after the fire, the one I met by the Banyon tree."

Stella DeMuer emerged, larger than life despite her petite size, her weather-beaten face wreathed in smiles. "Hello again. Please," she extended a blue-veined hand. "I have a very large house that I am too willing to share." She turned to look at the homeless throng and her features saddened. "Since meeting you this morning I am certain that you two are the ones I'm meant to help. Come." She extended a gnarled hand with rings on every finger to Tess. "A nice hot bath and a cup of Earl Grey will do you a world of good."

Tess backed up, eyeing the hand skeptically. She wouldn't rest a moment wondering what she'd gotten herself into. "If you'll excuse me, I need to make a phone call."

She slipped away, leaving Carter to deal with the woman. He shot her a questioning look, but Tess kept walking. If he wanted to take a chance that this DeMuer character might be an ax murderer, that was his prerogative. She was going to try the airport first.

The airline clerk only laughed when she requested a seat on the next flight out. "I have 198 seats and I've booked 207."

She bet the nine that showed up expecting to go home wouldn't see the humor.

"Monday night is the earliest I could manage—then you'll be on standby—unless you know someone with a private plane. And with this storm coming, I'm not even sure about that . . . Unless you have the cash to charter your own flight. . . ."

Biting her lower lip, she switched to Plan X—the last option short of death, and punched the cell phone's automatic dial. The phone rang twice before her mother's familiar growling voice answered. "Yeah."

"Mona?"

"Tess?" She heard the expected sigh. "Now what's wrong?"

"I'm in a bit of a fix, Mother." She decided not to sugar-coat the situation—it wouldn't matter to Mona anyway. She could be standing on the top of a high-rise with her hair on fire and Mona would only ask how much the call was costing. "I've lost my job. I'm in Hawaii, and the hotel where I was staying had a fire. I have no money, credit card, or identification." She swallowed, pushing back the bitter taste of gall obstructing her throat. "I need your help."

"Lost your job? What did you do now?"

"Nothing, Mona. Downsizing. It happens all the

time." Lies, all lies, but the truth would matter less to Mona. Mother wouldn't care that she'd worked sixty- and seventy-hour weeks to please Conner.com, that she'd skipped lunches to stay on the phone with their health care provider while they ironed out their benefits package, that she'd searched the ends of the earth to find the best 401(k) for company employees. She'd endured crude jokes from VPs and fought off married men's advances—all without endangering the company/client relationship and all in the name of advancement. Yet Mona would see what she wanted to see.

Steel tinged her mother's tone. "A Nelson has never lost his job. Surely if you were attending to business the company would have found a way to keep you. How many times have I told you, Tess, you control what hap- pens to you—don't be blaming your problems on down- sizing. That's a tidy, predictable euphemism for being fired. Was it your stubborn pride? And what do you mean you're in Hawaii? Hawaii? How can you be in Hawaii if you've just lost your job? You bring about your own problems, exactly like Roy . . ."

Tess interrupted Mona's tirade. "Could you just *please* wire me five hundred dollars until I get back to Denver? I'll pay you back. Three days at most, Mona. I'm at your mercy."

There it was again. The sigh. The tedious, almost-silent I-wish-I'd-never-had-you sigh. Well, she wished the same thing, but neither she nor Mona could have do-overs.

"Do you think I'm made of money? I barely have enough to scrape by, thanks to Roy Nelson, your esteemed, drunken father. Do you think my mother thought about me when she kicked me out of the house at fifteen? I had nowhere to go, Tess. I had to depend on myself, and if I've taught you nothing else it's to depend on yourself. I'd do you no favor by pandering to your weakness. You were irresponsible enough to go to Hawaii without a job to come back to, now you figure a way to get back."

The line went dead. Tess closed her eyes, blinking back tears.

Fine. There went your Mother's Day card.

After setting the phone in its cradle, she rested her head against the back of her chair. Why had she called Mona when she knew what the response would be? Mona was as cold as penguin droppings. Especially since Dad had left her once the kids were grown. He died of liver cancer at the age of forty-seven.

Tess sucked in bitterly sharp air and huddled deeper into the lining of her thin coat as she followed Mona and Troy down the railroad tracks. Troy was only two years old. Tess felt that funny sickness in the pit of her stomach again, the one she felt every weekend. I hate weekends. I wish there was no such thing as Friday and Saturday. That was when Roy would stay late at the bars and come home with that awful smell on his breath. Then Mona would start yelling. If she'd only learn to shut her mouth when Dad told her to, things would be better. He wouldn't get so mad. He wouldn't hit her with a trowel of plaster.

Flecks of white dotted the back of Mona's print dress. Tess stared at the design as she walked. Today was Saturday. Saturday meant that he was drunk by noon; Saturday meant there would be no peace in the house until Sunday afternoon when he slept it off. Saturday meant they wouldn't go home until late. It was cold, so cold. Tess hated that. She hated the walking and sitting on the railroad tracks wishing she was anybody else on earth but herself. She thought about all the kids in school who were sitting in warm homes with kind, smiling moms and dads.

They sat down on the cold tracks. She wondered if a train would come by. Maybe it will hit us and kill us, she thought. Then Mona and Troy and Dad will be sorry.

She wanted to go home, even if Mona and Dad did argue. She hated this feeling.

"I'm going to leave him when you kids get bigger," Mona promised, glancing over at her.

She had heard that so many times that the promise didn't touch her anymore—it didn't make her happy or sad. It was just another promise from Mona, a promise not to be trusted.

"I *hate* this idea," Tess confessed as she drove the rental car down Highway 31. In the passenger seat, Carter frowned as he tried to decipher Stella DeMuer's directions.

"Ms. DeMuer is trustworthy or the manager wouldn't have set this up—and if I, for one moment, think otherwise we'll get out of there." The map rattled as he shook it out. "You have to admit that God's provided for us; we don't have to sleep on the beach tonight."

"Yeah, well, He could have done better—He could have gotten me on that flight home tonight."

"That would've been unfair to me. We're just getting to know each other." Carter grinned. "Relax. Before we know it—"

"What are we looking for?" Her voice interrupted. "The directions say that once we pass Harlow's restaurant we keep going a few blocks. Apparently the DeMuer house faces the ocean, and the back of the house faces the highway."

She motored through the tropical streets of Kihei, past shops and restaurants, condominiums with vivid beds of Draceana, Heliconia, and Anthrurium, coffee huts with signs touting lattes and piña colada smoothies. To Carter's left, senior tourists wearing khaki shorts, knee-high socks, and sandals took leisurely strolls, passed by an occasional jogger. Sun worshipers lay on the beach, determined to get as much benefit from the rays as possible, although the gentle breakers had been replaced by rolling whitecaps. Tess prayed the island would be spared and this crazy storm would dissipate.

"Why do you think Stella wanted *us* as her houseguests?"

Carter refolded the map. "Maybe she's lonely and wants company."

"That's it over there." She pointed toward a house. "Number 204, right?" To the right, the beige stucco structure was surrounded by overgrown tropical vegetation. Baldwin pines jutted up beside the red-tile roof that reflected hot sun. The dwelling had been at one time a magnificent showcase of opulence and grandeur. But time and neglect had taken its toll. Today the house looked slightly run-down and sad.

Flipping on the turn signal, she turned into the driveway. Stella DeMuer was sitting on the back step, waiting to greet them. Her face lit with expectation as Carter got their smoky-smelling, damp bags out of the trunk and transported them to the back door.

"Welcome," Stella enthused, clasping her hands together theatrically. "I've been expecting you. Come." She got up, lifted her cat around her neck, and walked down the stairs, where she led Carter and Tess to a small guesthouse. She was wearing a funny-looking red hat and short veil, with a feather poking up.

"You should be comfortable here, Mr. McConnell. I had Fredrick lay out clean towels and soap for you." Tess lifted her brow and Carter knew she was thinking the same thing: Fredrick? The old woman had servants—or was she living in the past?

"Please. Call me Carter."

"Of course, Carter. Such a handsome name."

The guesthouse was old but meticulously clean. A tropical-scented breeze filtered through partially opened vertical glass panes. Bookshelves lined two walls, and four matching watercolors, not prints, of surf and sand hung above the faded blue sofa. Oriental-style throw rugs were scattered over the tile floors. "Thank you. This is nice." Carter dropped his bags on the floor and looked around. "Very nice." He reached for a banana in the bowl of fruit "Fredrick" had left on the coffee table. "Tess and I appreciate your opening your home to us."

"Very kind of you," Tess murmured.

"Nonsense, you're doing an old woman a favor. I get very lonely here, and the days are very long. Now you, my dear Tess, will come with me." Stella turned and motioned to Carter. "You can come too. I know you must be hungry."

She led the way back across the cobblestone drive and into a side porch. Glass stretched across the front of the house where sofas, settees, and overstuffed chairs, old but in their heyday pricey, were lined up in conversation nooks. Beyond the glass wall, the Pacific glistened as waves rolled in. Tess's bedroom sat off the kitchen at the back of the house. She laid down her bag, and Stella and Carter drifted off to make small talk and chicken salad sandwiches for lunch. She was grateful for some time alone and glad to get off her ankle.

She lay back on the sunshine-smelling pillowcase and closed her eyes. Maybe this wasn't such a horrible idea after all. She considered Carter's earlier remark about God being good to them. Indeed, they wouldn't have to sleep on the beach tonight, and Mrs. DeMuer seemed like a kind old lady, although she did find the cat thing more than odd.

She felt herself starting to drift as she listened to Carter's clear baritone drifting from the kitchen. Maybe, if she were a praying woman, she ought to thank God for pairing her up with this gentle man. He had helped her in so many ways with his kind yet no-nonsense approach to life.

She could have done a lot worse.

Later she sat in the kitchen and ate sandwiches and cheese curls with Carter and Stella. The cat occupied himself by taking a bath in the sunny alcove window. Perhaps things finally were turning around for her. She could only hope.

The earth softened around the edges; the sun slid lower, spreading an amber blanket across the water. Tess meandered down the beach alone. The wind was blowing hard now, tangling her long hair. Her gaze moved across the ocean. Heavy waves lapped the shore, and distant snapping sails sounded like mini-shotgun blasts.

What was she doing here on this beach? What was she doing in Hawaii when everything important to her was in Denver? This was insane. She should go home and get her life back on track. Mona was right; no one was going to wave a magic wand and make her troubles disappear. Certainly not Mona and certainly not Len Conner. She'd been foolish to ask for Mona's help. The woman had always been as cuddly as a porcupine.

Her greatest fear was that she would become Mona, that she would become a critical, joyless woman. Was that what she wanted? She despised the thought. She wasn't a child any longer. Mona was right about one thing—she needed to take charge, and the first area she was going to work on was not allowing Mona's nagging to keep sending her to that fearful place she'd gone to as a child. That cowering child with no self-esteem needed to be laid to rest. But that was easier said than done.

"Tess?"

She turned around to see Stella waving, the breeze battering her floral caftan. She waved.

"Mind if I join you?" Stella said as she came closer.

"Come!" Tess said.

Stella walked with an amazing vitality for a woman

her age. Tess guessed her host to be somewhere in her early eighties, but then she'd never been good at guessing ages.

She bit back a grin. At least this afternoon Stella had left the cat at home. The woman was warm, interesting, and definitely eccentric, yet Tess had never met anyone who intrigued her more.

"How is that ankle, Dear? You haven't been walking too much, have you?" Stella's gaze was kind and very focused. She patted Tess's hand. "You look tired. Vacations are supposed to be restful."

The two women walked on. Stella lifted her face to the fading sun. "Trade winds are heavy; storm's getting closer."

"Thank you again for your hospitality," Tess said. "I won't be in your hair for long—I'm flying home Monday. Hopefully."

The woman smiled. "The island is really lovely this time of the year. I'd be happy to show you the sights. You're welcome to stay with me as long as you want."

Her heart wasn't in it anymore. She'd been too beaten down.

"Thanks, but I couldn't intrude—"

"Intrude," Stella scoffed, waving a dismissive hand. "I'm rattling around in that big house. All those rooms— for an old woman and a cat. Fredrick goes home at night. I love the company, and you're meant to be here. I know that with a certainty. You have things to learn, and I can help with that." Her eyes softened. They reached a sharp, rocky outcropping and turned back toward the house.

"Tell me about yourself," Tess nudged. "Have you always lived here?"

"Edgar had the house built in 1950. I waited until construction was complete before I moved here from Los Angeles." She smiled and her eyes crinkled as if her memories were sweet. Tess felt a tug of envy. Quite obviously Stella had loved this man deeply.

"Edgar? That's your husband?"

"Edgar's dead now." Mist shimmered in Stella's eyes. "My, how I miss that old fella." She glanced over. "You and Carter are in love?"

"Me and Carter?" Tess choked out. "No—I barely know him. We met through a series of events, starting at the airport." As far as love . . . she wasn't sure she knew the meaning of the word. She'd been "in like" with men a few times. Respected one once, but love? She didn't know if she knew how to love.

"Stella, what made you decide to take us in? There are all kinds of sickos walking around. You don't know us—"

"I know you well enough." Stella smiled and nodded. "Yes, I know you well enough. It was meant that we meet."

Tess brushed a piece of hair out of her eyes and thought about Stella's declaration: *It was meant that we meet.*

What was that supposed to mean?

Friday morning, the aroma of hot coffee filled the air when Tess emerged from the bedroom. The previous night she'd managed to launder her smoke-laden clothes and air out her luggage. She'd gone to bed around 11:00 but rising wind had kept her awake most of the night. She smiled at Carter, who was stretched out across a lounge chair, reading a newspaper.

"Good morning," he said.

"Morning." Yawning, she scratched her hair and thought maybe she should have combed it into some semblance of order. She wondered if her bald patch was noticeable. She hadn't found any more hairs lately. Perhaps that malady was abating. She hoped. But then she wasn't trying to impress anyone. Her eyes moved surreptitiously to Carter, who didn't seem to notice the train wreck—or if he did, he was kind enough not to comment. Len would have said something.

Carter glanced up, his smile sending an odd shiver down her back.

Stella's lilting voice drifted from the kitchen. "Waffles and eggs benedict coming up! Are you hungry?"

Not if you're cooking with a cat around your neck, Tess thought with a smile.

"Starved!" Carter said.

Tess wandered into the sunny kitchen where a large, open window carried the scent of fresh ocean air.

"Help yourself to the coffee, or there's fruit juice on the counter," Stella said in her sweet way. "Make yourself at home." She turned from the stove, clasping her hands. "I'm so glad to have someone to eat with this morning. This is wonderful."

"You're a godsend to us," Carter said as he walked into the kitchen. "Thank you, Stella." He stretched, then pressed his hand to the small of his back. "And my bad back thanks you. Just thinking about a night on the sand hurts."

Tess smiled. "Coward."

"When it comes to pain? You're looking at the worst." He winked.

Well, at least he was honest, she thought. Clean cut, nails neatly trimmed, hair cut in classic style, freshly shaven and smelling faintly of Old Spice, and *honest,* to boot—she'd begun to think the breed had disappeared with the T Rex.

"Oh, we'll have such fun," Stella crowed. "Now, you sit," she directed to Carter. "I'll take up the eggs." The waffle iron beeped that it was done. "Tess, would you work on waffles, please?"

Tess reached for a plate and the butter dish. "Sure."

"Here we go," Stella sang out softly a few minutes later, setting plates of steaming eggs and waffles in front of Tess and Carter, and then setting a third on the floor for the cat. "There now," she crooned, calling the cat from his spot by the window. "Eat up, Henry."

Henry. Tess glanced at Carter. The neck muff's name was *Henry*. She picked up her fork and was about to take a bite when she froze as Carter asked if he could say grace.

"Oh, would you?" Stella beamed.

Stella closed her eyes, hands clasped with reverence.

Carter bent his head and offered thanks: brief, but with such sincerity and sweetness of thought that Tess was afraid to look up. She'd never heard anyone speak to God like that before. It was as if God was his friend and not some distant deity who struck terror at will. When the amen sounded, she glanced up to see Carter unfolding his napkin, his eyes discreetly appreciating the mound of fluffy yellow.

He picked up his fork. "Food looks great, Stella."

Stella got up to pour herself a cup of coffee before rejoining them at the table.

"Aren't you going to eat something?" Tess asked Stella as she spread strawberry jam on a piece of toast.

"Oh, no," Stella waved a hand in the air in what was now a familiar gesture. "I'll eat later."

She felt uncomfortable with Stella watching but she managed to devour the meal in nothing flat.

"So, you're going home Monday?" Stella asked.

Tess smiled. "I hope. I'm on standby. What about you, Carter?" She peered over the rim of her juice glass. "Are you going to try to get a flight out Monday?"

Carter resalted his food. "I'm here so I'll stick it out for a couple of weeks."

"Stick it out? That doesn't sound very vacationerish."

"The reason I'm here in the first place is to get rid of stress. I guess the Lord is testing me."

"The Lord does indeed hold us to our word." Stella propped her chin on her hands. "By the way, did you two know that pesky hurricane's turned directly toward the island?"

10

"You're going to get an ulcer from all of this." Carter sat on Stella's worn sofa, thumbing through a worn copy of *New York Times* as Tess frantically dialed another number.

"I have to get out of *here*—did you hear what Stella said?"

Carter nodded. "They've upgraded the freaky storm to hurricane—but only an F-1 hurricane, Tess. It's just a gale. With the proper precautions we'll be fine."

"How do you know this?" She hadn't allowed a forecast to register since leaving Denver.

"I'm an air traffic controller at O'Hare. I know my storms."

The man was the Rock of Gibraltar. Didn't he know that he and his "flight controller's" attitude was about to be blown off the face of the map?

She dialed the third charter flight number and met

with the same results: no flights were leaving the island until the storm passed. Slamming the receiver back into the cradle, she dropped into a chair and crossed her arms.

"Need a Tagamet?" Carter said, his gaze never leaving the magazine.

"Very funny." She turned to him. "Aren't you the least concerned that we're *trapped?*"

"I'm concerned, but I'm smart enough to know that I'm not in charge of the situation." He got up to look out of the windows. Wind lashed the tops of palms; a garbage can lid whipped by the window. "I called to find out where the nearest shelter is—if we need to go there we can."

"We'll be safe," Stella said. She sat on the sofa with the cat around her neck again, a pleasant demeanor on her face. The cat appeared to be sleeping placidly. "Henry and I have ridden out many a tropical storm and lived to tell about them. Remember '92, Henry? Hurricane Iniki. It was September; the storm wasn't predicted to have any effect on the island, but we woke to the sound of air-raid sirens. Iniki had decided to do a switchback overnight and was headed straight for us. I filled every pot and pan in the house with water—even filled the bathtubs. The radio said to put plywood on all the windows. I watched television until the announcer said the power would be turned off when the wind speed reached 45 knots, and that we should expect sustained winds to 165 miles per hour. Iniki had become a category five hurricane—the largest they get." Stella reached up and ran a spider-veined hand along Henry's side. "We did our share of visiting with the Lord that night, didn't we, boy?"

Tess got up and began pacing.

"Relax," Carter advised. "We'll take whatever precautions are needed." He glanced at Stella. "Do I need to do anything? Nail plywood, close the storm shutters?"

Stella smiled. "Not yet. Let's see what Ms. *Alana* does next. Often storms veer off and we just get the rain and wind, but this one's packing an attitude. We'll not wait much longer."

Tess closed her eyes and rubbed her temples. She felt a pressure in her head that she was certain would balloon into an aneurysm any moment. Why weren't they doing *something?* Surely there was some precaution they could be taking other than this maddening sitting and waiting around for whatever came their way. This just wasn't right!

Seconds later, she felt the gentle pressure of Carter's hand on her right shoulder. She opened her eyes. "The NHC has issued a 'Hurricane Watch'; this means the storm will make landfall normally within twenty-four hours—but the watch usually includes a fairly wide area. Like Stella says, could be we'll only get gale-force winds, high water, and flash flood situations."

"And this doesn't alarm you?" Where *was* the Tylenol?

"All flights will be canceled until the storm abates," Carter said, a sympathetic look on his face.

"Come sit, dear." Stella patted the seat next to her. "We'll likely have a rough time of it, but nothing our Lord isn't in charge of. We'll be fine."

"The point is," Carter added quietly, "we need to heed the warning and take precautions. But we're here, Tess, under God's grace and His protection."

Grace. God had never shown her any grace. Had He shown grace by letting Len fire her? Had He shown grace through Mona? Had He shown grace by putting her in a situation in which she had no control?

"How long does it take for a hurricane to pass?" she asked weakly.

"The storm will be here in a few hours, most likely, and then runs its course in a few days," Stella said.

Ten days.

And Tess couldn't do a thing to stop it.

Grace.

She might as well wish for a million dollars.

11

Midafternoon, rain began as a faint pitter-patter, nothing to hint at the hulking monster it was destined to become. But soon heavy wind gusts battered the beach house's windowpanes. Tess sat listening to the storm's growing fury.

After a while she got up to pace. Peering outside, she turned around to face Carter, who was listening to radio reports on the storm. "Shouldn't we close the shutters?"

Carter looked to Stella.

She nodded. "You may close the shutters—but we'll wait another hour or two before the plywood goes up. I keep enough in the garage for just such an event."

"What about moving to higher ground?" Tess thought about Kula—the town was high atop Maui.

"Absolutely not!" Stella's chin shot up. "I will not leave my home. We'll wait—see if it's upgraded. I've been through many a warning—some legitimate, some a waste of time and money. We'll wait." She absently stroked the purring cat's neck.

Tess could not understand Stella's ability to just sit there. Neither Stella nor Carter seemed worried, although she had detected a faint light of concern in Carter's eyes now that the wind had picked up. She wondered if Stella was truly of sound mind or if she and Carter should overrule her wishes and proceed with defensive measures. She looked over at Carter who said, "I'm going to check out that garage—see how well stocked we are. Just in case." His gaze shifted to Stella. Tess breathed a quiet sigh of relief—at least someone was moving forward.

"Do you need some help?" she whispered.

"No," he said. "You keep an eye on our hostess. I'll see to things." He quickly left, and she returned to her stool by the counter.

"So, Stella," she said. "What did you and Edgar do before you moved to Hawaii?"

"Oh, we lived in Beverly Hills. That's where all the movie people lived. Guess perhaps they still do—" Her voice drifted off.

"Were you and your husband in the film business?"

Stella laughed. "Oh, yes, I was but you wouldn't remember. You're far too young. And they don't show my movies on the late, late, or even very late show anymore." She chuckled.

Tess turned. "You were a movie star?"

"Oh, my yes. Starred with some of the biggest. Why I—have you seen *Orphans of the Storm?* No," she mused, "I supposed you wouldn't have—that was 1922."

1922? That made her what—over 100 years old? Tess was amazed at the woman's memory.

"What about *Three on a Match*—? No, I made that film in 1924."

"You were a silent film star?" Stella DeMuer suddenly fell into place in Tess's mind. She could picture eccentric Stella in the old melodramatic films with heart-tugging plots.

Stella's bottom lip quivered. "Surely you've seen *Casablanca?*"

Tess grinned. "You were in *Casablanca?* With Bogart and Bergman?"

"Oh yes—and that lovely Paul Henreid. Paul was such a gentleman, you know. Of course, that was later, when speaking parts were in—and truthfully, I had a support-ing role in that particular film. Edgar, my husband, was unhappy about the casting, but I seized the opportunity to work with Humphrey and Ingrid," she confessed.

Humphrey and Ingrid.

"Then of course there was *Anna Christie,* with Greta—"

"Garbo?"

Stella blinked. "Why, yes—is there another Greta?"

"No—there isn't another Greta Garbo." Tess chuckled.

"*The Girl from New York* was my favorite, but then there was *Moonbeam, Jacob and Esau*—I played their conniving mother. I loved the part. Oh, there were a dozen others, names only those interested in movie history would recognize today."

"Why, you were a movie queen!" Tess said, amazed. She moved to the couch next to Stella and pulled a pillow onto her lap as she drew her feet underneath her. The wind beat against the panes. "I've seen *The Girl from New York*. It's timeless. Was your husband an actor as well?"

Stella blushed at the question. "He was a director in the mid- to late forties. We met on the set of *Moonbeam*. I was just twenty and he was twenty-five. I remember . . . I was losing my yourthful 'bloom' but he was smitten with me at first." She paused and looked over at Tess with a faraway gaze in her eyes. "He was talking to the cameraman and, well, there was just something in his eyes. I can't really explain it. He was such a good man. It wasn't long before we were very much in love."

Tess felt a second twinge of envy. The love shimmering in Stella's eyes when she spoke of her husband, even after so many years, was real. Magic.

"We weren't married nearly long enough." Her features closed momentarily. "I still miss him so much sometimes it's a physical ache." She dipped her head and blushed and the smile returned.

"I don't know if I'll ever find a love like that," Tess confessed.

"You have to start with trust—if you don't have that you don't have anything."

"I haven't been too successful in that arena—"

Carter came back. Water dripped off his rain slicker. "It's wet out there."

Stella pushed out of her seat. "Well, now, it's getting to be our nap time. You two just make yourselves at home. We'll keep a close eye on the storm." She picked up Henry. "Come, my love. It's nappies for us."

When the former movie queen reached the doorway, she suddenly turned. Her eyes softened. "Don't be afraid of life, Tess. Put your trust in Someone who deserves it. God is good; He keeps His promises when no other will." She turned and disappeared down the long hallway.

Tess gazed at the spot where she had stood. *Put your trust in Someone who deserves it?* For some unknown reason, she wanted to do just that—she wanted to trust, to find someone worthy of trust.

For a moment neither she nor Carter spoke. Then she said cautiously, "Do I look like someone who can't trust? What's with that remark?"

Carter lifted an innocent brow. "A nap doesn't sound like a bad idea."

12

"The NHC has now upgraded *Alana* to a category two storm." The TV meteorologist waved his hand over the mass of white on the map behind him as he spoke. Carter sat watching, a warm cup of coffee in hand. "The eye of this dangerous storm is expected to make landfall in the early hours of Saturday morning, the 24th on the island of Oahu. Island residents should be making plans to move to nearby evacuation centers. Remember to take your Disaster Supply Kit. Do not forget to make plans for pets if you must evacuate. *Alana* is a treacherous category two hurricane with winds capable of 96–110 miles per hour." Carter switched off the TV and clasped his hands together across his knees. Sheets of heavy rain pelted the windows. He needed to find a way to protect Tess and Stella, even if Stella refused to move to the storm shelter. He reached to pick up his Bible, looking for the true Source of wisdom he'd learned to rely on. Tess thought he wasn't scared. Right. With a hurricane forming outside their window.

Lord, if only I were spiritually mature enough to trust You totally in the face of danger. I ask Your shield for Tess and Stella. Grant me the wisdom to do all that I can to protect these two women.

Could he help Tess? She needed more than shelter in a hurricane; she needed protection from a danger far greater, one all men were powerless against without God's help. Yet she seemed unwilling to relinquish that control to anyone but herself. Was he "man" enough to step out of his comfort zone and offer a solution—with God's Word to back it up? Face-to-face witnessing never came easy for him. He'd learned long ago that he couldn't whip a person into submission; the need and desire had to be there to begin with.

Instead, his witness was to build houses for orphaned children and tell them stories about God's love, but the innocent eyes that had looked back at him then were childlike, trusting. Experience had hardened Tess's eyes. Someone somewhere had instilled doubt in her, and he would bet the problem went back to an early age. It troubled him to see a young woman wrestling with life when relief was near and so obtainable. She had such potential, far beyond what she could accomplish at a job.

Carter thought back on his own journey toward God. He had accepted the Lord as Savior after a chain of rebellious years. He'd hit bottom, and he'd hit hard—social drugs, drinking, and wild women. He'd thought life couldn't get any better until he looked in the mirror one day and saw an empty shell of a man. He'd been missing work, losing friends. His life had become a cesspool so dank that he didn't know how to climb his way out. That was when a next-door neighbor had invited him to attend a men's retreat.

At first Carter had laughed. Men's retreat. At the time the event held the same attraction as a Barbie Doll convention.

But for some reason he'd gone. Life had gotten so unbearable, he knew his next step would've been suicide. That weekend he'd ended his restless search. He'd found what every man, woman, and child wanted: significance, security, and acceptance.

Could he share his faith with Tess? How would she react? Would she think he was a religious fanatic—a kook?

He suspected she already did by the looks she gave him when he prayed or picked up his Bible.

Am I not still God? a voice whispered.

Resting his head on the chair back, he closed his eyes and communed with the still, small voice, ever present.

When he opened his eyes, wind still battered the shutters and tore at the canvas awnings as though they were made of paper. Even with the storm upgrade, Stella had made it clear that she would not leave her home. The beach was the worst place they could sit it out, but Carter didn't intend to leave the old woman alone. He consoled himself that if the house had withstood a category five hurricane then surely it would hold tight in this storm.

The door suddenly flew open and a frenetic Tess appeared in the front hallway. Carter bolted, feet flying upward. Muddy water pooled on her tennis shoes. Her hair was plastered in wet, noodlelike strings to her head. Slamming his hand to his heart, he asked above the thrashing jackhammer of the wind. "What happened to you?"

"I was out on the lanai—this thing is getting worse." She pointed to the sheets of water running down the window glass. "We've got to do something."

Closing his Bible, Carter laid it on the table. "Stella isn't going to leave, and I'm not leaving her here alone."

"Six-foot breakers are battering the shoreline. It won't be long until the roads are impassible." She brushed past him to approach the window. "I'm scared, Carter. Honestly scared. We could be killed in this thing."

"We could get killed crossing the street." Taking her by the arm, he gently drew her away from the frightening sight. "Is Stella awake?"

"I don't know—I don't think so."

Stella walked into the room, blinking sleep from her eyes. "My, it's nasty out there, isn't it?" she said with her gaze toward the window.

The former movie star was wearing Henry. The cat snoozed, perfectly at ease with Nature's show of fury.

Carter frowned. "Stella, the storm has been upgraded to an F-2 hurricane. We need to do what we can to save the house, and then get to a public shelter."

"No," Stella contended. "I told you I won't leave my house." She smiled. "It's like an old friend; I need to be here to protect it."

Carter wheeled Stella's old '72 Chevy pickup around the barricade and headed back on 36. "Stella has plenty of plywood and nails for the windows—if it isn't too windy to put them up now. Thank heavens her house is only one story," he said. "There's an old generator too, but I don't know if it works—it looked awfully old. We'll pick up fresh flashlights and radio batteries and buy an emergency kit—canned goods, that kind of thing. Then we need to find out where we need to go when this thing *really* hits."

Tess looked out the windshield at the slanting rain. "*If* we can go anywhere."

He grimaced. "You're right. There's nowhere to run but into the ocean."

She swallowed back her rising panic as the truck plowed through sheets of standing water.

Wal-Mart was teeming with frantic islanders preparing for destruction. They ran toward the entrance with their hoods and purses held over their heads as if that would keep the pummeling rain from reaching them. Carter parked the Chevy on the last row adjacent to the blue-and-white building and they made a run for the front door.

Once inside, Tess headed for batteries while Carter wandered off in the direction of the snack bar. Tess hurriedly gathered a handful of C, AA, and D batteries then proceeded to a long line where she waited for over half an hour to make the purchase. Her feet hurt, and her hair looked like a wet dog's fur. She'd give a king's ransom for dry underwear.

She heard snatches of anxious inquiries.

"Is the storm still moving in our direction?"

"Has it picked up speed or strength?"

She gazed along the rows of shoppers and saw Carter rolling a cart loaded with a small portable generator and black, heavy plastic sheets. Among the storm paraphernalia, he'd set a tuberose lei. He held two cups of steaming coffee in his hands. Handing one to Tess, he then draped the floral offering around her neck with a smile. "I thought you could use a pick-me-up."

Touched by his simple act of kindness, she nodded

her head and gratefully accepted the hot coffee—how he'd managed to roll a cart and carry two steaming cups without losing the contents confounded her.

Men.

Carter was pounding on the defroster when she climbed back in the truck cab. He'd thoughtfully pulled to the front entrance so she wouldn't get wetter. "It's not blowing right," he explained before starting off again. Wheeling back onto the highway, Carter eased to the edge of the seat and mopped up moisture coating the inside of the windshield. The old heater clanked and chugged, and worn wipers tried in vain to keep up with the steady downpour.

"I read an Oprah book once about a woman whose boyfriend dumped her off at Wal-Mart and never came back." She held the dashboard with a white-fingered grip as the rain slanted in its heavy beat. Sweat beaded on her forehead.

"Really?" Carter reached over her to mop the passenger side of the windshield.

"The woman lived there for a few days without anyone noticing."

"Lived in Wal-Mart?" Carter said as if it were a sunny day and they weren't driving through foot-deep flooded streets.

"Yes—and she was expecting the moron's baby. Had the child on the pots and pan aisle—or somewhere like that, if I'm remembering correctly. The employees found her the next morning. That must have been pretty shocking." She lifted one hand to wipe her forehead and ran her fingers through her hair. Five or six hairs came loose in her hand. She looked out the window.

"You can see the road okay?" She asked, wondering if she would be able to find the pavement in these blasts of wind and rain.

"We're fine." He put a hand consolingly on her arm. "You can calm down."

Sheathed in the cab's rain-tinged air, she started to relax. She edged closer to him, hanging on to his sleeve. He turned to look at her and grinned. Shame washed over her. He had to deal not only with a hurricane, but with a hysterical woman. She'd bet his challenges at O'Hare paled in comparison to this. Yet she'd never heard him complain.

She eased closer to his warmth and ignored the curious look he gave her. Their closeness allotted a sense of security—as if he had a direct pipeline to . . . well, somewhere . . . or someone that she didn't. She supposed some men would consider the move a come-on but Tess wasn't thinking about propriety. She just wanted to feel safe. Sitting near like this, breathing in his cologne mingled with the tuberose of her lei . . .

Well, a woman had to admit that his thoughtful gifts were special—nothing like the obligatory red roses or Godiva chocolates that made a woman shun the scales for weeks afterward.

Carter McConnell was a nice guy—and the only thing solid she had to hold onto right now.

"I admire your composure," she admitted as Carter drove the pickup through the streets.

He chuckled—a nice, manly baritone timbre that gave her tingles. *Tingles. Whoa, Tess.*

"On the inside, I'm just as scared as you are. Maybe even more," he admitted. "I have yours and Stella's safety to consider."

A man willing to admit weaknesses.

"But you don't show it—you seem so . . . calm."

"If I am, the credit belongs to the Lord, not to me."

She averted her gaze to stare out the window.

They fell silent as he wiped the windshield clear again.

"You think I'm terrible, don't you?"

He crammed the rag in his side pocket. "No. Why would I think you're terrible?"

"Because I don't *believe.*"

"Faith is an act of the will; you have to desire to know the truth, and you haven't desired it yet."

"And what is that supposed to mean?" Even as the words left her lips, she realized she sounded defensive.

"If I tell, you will think I'm a religious fanatic," he said.

"Too late; I already do." She grinned, then sobered. She'd seen him pray before every meal, read his Bible, saw him live as if his faith were something alive and real. Hardly the stuffy religion she'd heard about from Mona.

"Okay," Carter said. "You asked."

"I asked."

His eyes softened and he spoke calmly without censure. What she heard in his voice was concern for her, love. "No one can believe without the Spirit's help."

"Then you're saying God picks and chooses who will know Him? That hardly seems fair."

"God opens the doors, invites us to come to Him—He loves everyone, Tess, including you. But He's like us; He doesn't stay where He isn't wanted." Carter glanced over to meet her eyes.

Why, he *was* a religious nut, trying to frighten her into believing! She looked away. "Sorry. I can't understand the concept of a loving God. Sometimes I think He's downright mean."

"He is a God of justice and a God of mercy."

"Mercy. Now there's a crock. Where was God on September 11, 2001? Where was God when my friend Jennifer's husband died of brain cancer and left her with two young daughters to raise?" she asked.

Where was God the day Mona Nelson gave birth to her? She glanced at Carter as tears glistened in her eyes.

Carter reached over and rested his hand on top of hers. "I can't explain the bad things that happen in the world; I don't even try. But I do know that without the Holy Spirit a person is incapable of grasping God's words, and without God, life is meaningless. Acceptance is an option. But for me God's love was so compelling I couldn't resist it. It's the only thing that gives me hope in this world."

She turned her head to gaze at the pouring rain as his words had resonated strongly within her. Right now, hope was what she desperately needed.

13

"Hurricane. From the Taino word meaning 'evil spirit.' In the Caribbean the storms are called the 'God of All Evil,'" Stella said as she sipped hot cocoa.

Carter had gone out to the garage to get the plywood to begin boarding the windows.

Tess divided her attention between the kindly old woman and another television weather bulletin. She turned her head to scrutinize the strengthening storm out Stella's front windows. The monster was getting down to business. Palm trees bent their heads to the bully, deferring to its greatness.

"Beautiful, isn't it?" The featherlike touch of Stella's hand on her shoulder drew Tess from her reverie. Breakers lashed against the fawn-colored sand, churning it to dark chocolate, kicking up heavy spray. An *a lae keokeo*—Hawaiian coot—drifted with drafts, his shrill cries echoing through the stormy late afternoon.

"Even in her fury, Nature is an awesome sight." Stella spoke in a soothing, confident tone—one Tess knew should have calmed her. Her thoughts kept returning to Carter's words on the way home from Wal-Mart: *It's the only thing that gives me hope.* The thought had begun to take root in her heart and now it seemed to echo over and over, answering her heart's plea.

"I never cease to be amazed at His power," Stella's voice interrupted her reverie.

"God's power?" Tess tasted the name on her tongue, foreign—neither sweet nor sour.

"God's power. If you'll excuse me." Stella tuned and left her alone in the living room. Rain lashed the window.

Tess closed her eyes and drank in the scent of the rain. Her thoughts drifted. What kind of man was Carter McConnell? Certainly the first man she'd ever met who openly spoke of his faith, of commitment to God. She wasn't sure what to think about that. Her grandmother's faith was born of the need to avoid hellfire rather than the alive kind of faith that Carter claimed.

She had always felt that Christians made awkward, bumbling attempts to express *why* they were so happy, why they existed in a perpetual state of spiritual euphoria. Carter had experienced no such hesitancy. He truly believed what he practiced.

She turned from the window as Stella breezed back through the doorway, carrying a large tray filled with a teapot and two cups. A plate of lemon cookies sat beside the cream and sugar.

"Thought you might enjoy something warm. I wonder how Carter is managing that plywood."

Tess turned on the threadbare sofa, and leaned forward to accept her tea. "I should go help him. . . ." Her thoughts returned to their current dilemma. The storm's intensity grew minute by minute. Outside, torrential rain hammered the storm-tossed sea, scattering sea foam like dried orchid petals. She felt a sudden urgency to go help Carter even though he'd told her he wanted her to stay with Stella.

"It should have been done earlier," Stella confessed. "Fredrick's talked about it for days, but you never know about these storms. Often they blow themselves out before they hit land. Who would have thought that with the normal threats behind us a rebel cyclone would decide to rear its ugly head in January?" She lifted the cookie plate to offer one to Tess before placing it back on the coffee table. "Would you do the honors, dear?"

Shutters banged against the stucco exterior.

Stella frowned. "I do worry about Carter out there. I wonder if he'd like some tea. It's chamomile."

Stella glanced over and her tone softened, "He'll be fine, Dear. If he needs your help he'll tell you."

Startled that her thoughts had been so easily read, Tess changed the subject. "You said your husband was a movie director?" She noticed with a frown that the spoon was tarnished yellow. She wondered if Stella would mind her polishing the silver; she was still itchy to help in some way—*any* way.

"Yes—but I doubt you'd know any of his films." Stella proceeded to name half a dozen films that Tess had indeed seen on the Nostalgia Channel. After telling her so, Tess grinned and spooned sugar into her cup. "I'm honored to be in the company of a *famous* Hollywood celebrity."

"Well, you shouldn't be." Stella laughed ruefully. "Scandalous would be a better word choice."

"Oh?" Her smile faded.

"My husband was called to appear before the Army-McCarthy hearings."

Tess slowly lowered the cup back to the saucer. McCarthy hearings. Didn't that have something to do with a Hollywood blacklist back in the fifties? "I've heard of the hearings; I'm not sure what they were about."

"They were nothing but a witch hunt," Stella snapped. The old woman visibly bristled, her eyes turning as chilly as the howling wind. "The hearings were convened to investigate a series of charges leveled by Senator Joseph McCarthy."

"By the Army? How did your husband get involved?"

The old woman's eyes hardened. "It's a complicated story, one much too involved to tell."

"No." Tess scooted to the edge of the sofa. "Please. I'm interested."

For a moment it looked as through Stella wouldn't comply—that the memory was still an open wound. Then, slowly, she set her cup back on the tray. The thin china rattled. "It was Edgar's destruction."

Stella studied her cup for a moment, and then continued, "McCarthy had a consultant on his staff named David Schine who was drafted into the army in 1953. Roy Cohn, McCarthy's chief counsel, began a personal campaign to pressure military officials into releasing Schine from service, though he'd been drafted, so he could return to Washington. Early in 1954—March, I think—the army retaliated by documenting what they called Cohn's 'improper intrusions' into Schine's military career. McCarthy responded by claiming the army was holding Schine 'hostage' to keep his committee from exposing communists within the military.

"Well, it rolled on from there. The Senate Permanent Subcommittee on Investigation, of which McCarthy was chairman, voted to investigate. They also decided to allow live TV coverage of the inquiry." Stella glanced up.

"You weren't born yet, of course. For four years, beginning in 1947, McCarthy had been accusing people of being communists, destroying the lives and careers of ordinary people, and a number of people in the motion picture industry, but no concrete evidence had ever been shown that linked any of the accused to the Communist Party. But that didn't stop him.

"Several hundred performers whose only 'crime' was belonging to or supporting organizations or causes that McCarthy named as 'subversive' were blacklisted. No one would hire them."

"Couldn't someone do something?" Tess asked. "I mean—"

"The Screen Actors Guild, the Screen Writer's Guild, the Screen Directors Guild made no effort to stop this . . . this evil. On the contrary, they cooperated. If they tried to protect their members, they knew that the American public would think the guilds themselves were subversive, which would mean the public would stop going to movies, which would lead to a massive loss of jobs.

"One accusation was that the communists were placing subversive messages into Hollywood films and were in a position to put negative images of the United States in films that would have an international distribution."

Tess leaned back to digest the information. "And your husband was involved?"

"Yes, Edgar was involved. In 1946 the Screen Actors Guild was listed as a union with communist influences. So, some so-called friendly witnesses were called before the Un-American Activities Committee to be interviewed. Robert Taylor, Richard Arlen, Adolphe Menjou. Jack Warner, head of Warner Brothers Studio, named people on the studio's payroll that he suspected of harboring left-wing sympathies, including my husband."

"*Was* he involved?" she asked.

Stella drew a deep shuddering breath, and Tess could see that simply talking about that time in her life disturbed her. "I'm sorry. This is too sad for you."

The old woman stroked Henry, her eyes misting with unshed tears. "It's still painful, yet when I look back on my life I see this as one of those defining moments on which life-altering decisions were made. Edgar was called before the committee in Washington, D.C. He didn't want me to come, and I was busy on a film so I didn't go. Now I wish that I had. I'd have known what was happening. He never talked about it later, but I knew Marsha Hunt and she told me what happened.

"Marsha, too, had been blacklisted. She went to Washington with Humphrey Bogart, Lauren Bacall, and Danny Kaye. They hoped to generate positive publicity for those trying to defend themselves against those horrible charges, but their good intentions backfired. They had prepared statements that they planned to read when called to witness. But only one was allowed to read his statement. The rest were dismissed from the witness table, almost before they started.

"Anyway, others had better luck. Lucille Ball's testimony was so garbled and meaningless that she was allowed to be excused without stigma. That wasn't like Lucy at all—Lucille was a brilliant woman. If only Desi could have stayed away from the women . . .

"Writers like Clifford Odets never wrote again. Others managed to work behind the scenes, using other names, or worked in Mexico and in Europe. The rumor mill said John Garfield's death was linked to his appearance before the committee. It was an awful time." Stella shook her head as if to clear away the memory.

"Many directors kept working but changed their names. Edgar wouldn't do that. He said he couldn't pretend to be someone or something other than what he was. He was called before the committee after being named by Jack Warner; we don't know how that happened. Jack was probably trying to protect his studio. We could never find any real reason for his actions."

"It must have been a terrible time for both you and your husband." Tess stared at the cold cup of tea.

"Edgar never worked again." Stella's trembling fingers wrapped around her coffee cup. "He told the committee that he'd never been to any kind of meeting that could be called communist. I wasn't sure. I wasn't sure what was right or wrong, truth or lie. People you trusted turned on friends. You didn't know if you were next. It was a horrible time.

"Edgar went into a depression. Nothing I could do or say would draw him out of it."

"You . . . had reservations about your husband's innocence?"

Stella's head snapped up. "I'm sorry to say that I did—

at first. There were days, sometimes weeks, when I was confused. Edgar refused to deny or confess anything. He was a man of principle," she said proudly, "and he expected his actions to speak louder than any statement. We left Hollywood and moved here, to Maui."

"Was your husband's name ever cleared?"

"Eventually, but it was too late. By then he was dead."

Tess cleared her throat to break the rickety silence. "I'm so sorry. It's so unfair."

Stella looked up, her hands resting on Henry's glossy coat. "Life isn't about fairness."

Tess kept silent.

"I should have trusted Edgar more; I wouldn't have missed out on one of the most important things in my life: the ability to help Edgar in his darkest hour." Her eyes met Tess's.

"If God's so powerful, why doesn't He just make the bad things go away?" The words materialized from Tess's mind and she bit down hard on her lower lip.

"I can't answer that question. But I do know that time did teach me about faith. Adversity tends to do that; it forces us to sink our roots deep into God's faithfulness or we'll surely topple over."

"Then God let Edgar be destroyed in order for what? To make your faith stronger?"

"I don't know what His purpose was; I will never know until I speak with Him personally. But the experience did make me stronger."

"But your husband's name was cleared too late."

"Perhaps. But if it had been cleared earlier, we wouldn't have moved here, wouldn't have had those *wonderful* years together. We'd have kept working day and night, wasting more time on the pursuit of fame and earthly possessions than on being together." She smiled. "Everything that we work so hard for will either be used up, discarded, or belong to someone else someday. It's a sobering realization, isn't it? I think the reason I had occasional doubts was because Edgar and I had taken too little time to get to know each other. Here, in this beautiful paradise, we were given that time. What a precious gift!"

Tess picked up a throw pillow and held it tightly to her chest. Inside, her emotions churned. What would it be like to trust so implicitly that the outcome didn't matter? To rest so completely in another person's—or deity's—love that the outcome simply wouldn't matter? Something deep inside her twisted—and ached for such a belief.

"You find trust very difficult, don't you, my dear?" Stella gently stoked Henry's fur. "Once I felt the same, but I wish I could help you know the peace that comes from trust—trusting with all your heart."

"Faith and trust weren't Nelson family values," Tess admitted.

"I'm sorry to hear that." Stella's features softened. "We

can't pick our parents; we can only become wiser as adults."

Tess straightened, pitching the pillow aside.

"I think I'll see if Carter needs my help."

Stella smiled, reaching for the teapot. "You do that, Dear. Perhaps God has provided this time for the two of you to become better acquainted."

14

"We'll be dry in here." Carter opened the door as she ducked into the garage, where stacks of plywood littered the floor. He had managed to get all the boards put up along the back and sides of the house, but the wind made the work difficult, pushing against the plywood as he carried it out. Turning around, his eyes registered her comical attire. Stella had lent her Edgar's old coveralls. They dragged on the floor by a good four inches, and the seat drooped practically to her knees.

"They're not a fashion statement, but they'll help keep you dry," the old woman had promised.

Carter smirked and turned back to his work. He gave a pull on the generator's cord. It roared to life. After a few minutes he turned it off. "That's ready, should we need it." He glanced up at her, then motioned to a paint can on the concrete floor. "Best seat in the house."

She took a discarded rag and dusted off the top before

she sat down. Dried pink spatters lined the rim of the bucket. Rain hammered the tile roof, but the shelter's interior felt almost cozy compared to the chaos outside.

"How's Stella?"

"She's holding up okay. She seems pretty calm about all this."

She stared at dark stains dotting the concrete floor. "I don't understand why she's treating the storm so lightly. She doesn't seem concerned about the house, and she knows how destructive hurricanes can be."

"Maybe she's lived through enough storms that she has a sixth sense about the danger—though it's risky reasoning. Older people feel a need to protect their homes . . ." his words trailed off.

Carter sat down on the cold cement beside her. The dampness made dark curls in his hair.

She found herself staring at him. "Naturally curly hair?"

Carter's face turned bright crimson. He leaned to wipe a streak of wet hair off her cheek. The simple, innocent gesture warmed her.

They listened to the roar of the waves. Then Tess's halting voice emerged from the fading daylight, "Did you know that Stella's husband was blacklisted by the McCarthy hearings?" She told him about Edgar, and the injustice that had befallen him and Stella in the late fifties.

"Edgar was a strong man," she concluded. "Or maybe he wasn't. He died too soon still thinking that his name was besmirched."

"I imagine that he knows," Carter said quietly as gusts of wind and rain battered the small garage.

When she remained quiet, he reached over and tugged her pant leg. "You don't agree?"

"If you're implying that he was a Christian so therefore today he is in heaven . . . I think I'd be a little bitter, if I were Edgar."

"And how would bitterness enrich your life?"

She shrugged.

"You're a tough nut to crack, Nelson. Bitterness destroys *you*—not the thing or person you're bitter against."

She reached over and yanked his earlobe playfully. "More Christian philosophy?"

He grinned and lay back, cradling his head in crossed arms. She and Carter fell silent—the nice kind of shared silence that didn't produce a need to talk. After awhile he said, "I guess I should be out there hammering plywood again. Only four windows to go. Care to help me haul these boards?"

"I guess not." She couldn't see how he was going to get the wood up in gale winds. Carter hummed as he gathered up his supplies for another round of hammering.

Lulled by the sound of rain striking the roof and the soft timbre of Carter's voice, she closed her eyes. The camaraderie between them was nice, more than nice. Trusting. She had enjoyed few such relationships.

Wind snapped a branch and the limb shattered a windowpane. She jumped and scooted closer.

"What's wrong—the glass didn't get you, did it?" Carter shouted above the roar of the storm.

"No—don't you have a flashlight?" Darkness was quickly approaching. They had gotten all but this last piece of plywood in place. At least the board would keep out the rain until the glass could be replaced.

"Yes—somewhere."

He scooted around, trying to locate the object. Eventually his hand closed around the aluminum and he crawled back to her. Switching on the beam, he pointed the beam in her eyes. She pulled it out of his hand and directed it at the hole in the glass. "Let's get this up fast," she said, grabbing the corner of the piece of plywood and wrestling it into place. Carter quickly pounded nails into the four corners first before adding a few more along the sides. When he was done he looked over at her rain-soaked face. "What's wrong?" he said, pulling her inside the house.

"Okay. I'm scared. Happy?"

"Delirious." He shifted back to show her a cheesy grin. "What's not to be happy about? We're in a hurricane. We've had nine days of nothing but whale watching, luau's, and—hey—did you get your picture taken with the parrot? The one that digs his claws into your shoulder and draws blood?"

"I missed that."

His playfully drew her closer and in a mock conspiratorial whisper and said, "Now tell Carter what Tess is afraid of. Wind?"

"I hate storms, and no, I . . . I don't like wind. I was in a tornado once. I—I can't stand the sound of wind—"

"Yeah, well. I don't like wind, either. But together we'll ride this thing out."

She rested her head on his shoulder and closed her eyes for just a moment. Oddly enough she felt better. Tomorrow she would regret this spurt of idiocy, but right now she was going with it.

"Have you seen the movie *The Perfect Storm?*" she ventured.

He gave her a wry look. "Chatting about *The Perfect Storm* right now makes about as much sense as United Airlines featuring an airline disaster movie on their transatlantic flights." He squeezed her shoulders. "We're taking proper precautions, and now we turn it over to—"

"God." Her defensive tone was gone. For the first time in her life she started to believe it. Carter smiled that broad, beaming smile of his.

"How many children are there in your family?" she asked, suddenly wanting to know more about him.

"I have an older sister. No other siblings."

"I have a younger brother. What's your favorite dessert?"

"Cheesecake—with red stuff swirled through it."

"Lemon pie."

"*Lemon* pie?"

"That's my favorite. School?" she asked.

"Humm?"

"Where did you go to school?"

"High school—Chicago. Graduated from Baylor University in Waco, Texas. Business major."

"DePauw; Indiana. Master's degrees in finance and psychology."

He let out a low whistle. "Two? As suspected, you're an overachiever."

"What about your grades?"

"They were okay. Dean's list every semester."

"Dean's list is better than 'okay.' What kind of car do you drive?"

"What's this interrogation all about?"

"Nothing." She was suddenly defensive, "I thought since we've become part of each other's lives in the last nine days we should know something about each other."

Carter gently released her gaze and pushed to his feet. "We better see what Stella's up to." He looked through the small opening he had left in the window. The fury intensified.

She lifted her voice. "Is it the hurricane?"

"I'd say." Carter said. "By the looks of things, the eye isn't going to miss us by much."

"It's really kicking up out there," Carter said when he and Tess came into the living room, after going to their separate quarters to dry off. With the storm's approach, Stella had insisted he take one of the other guest rooms inside the main house so he wouldn't get doused every time he had to pop into his room. They found Stella sitting peacefully in a chair, feeding Henry pieces of dry Eukanuba.

Tess shook her head in amazement. Neighbors and business owners had battened down hatches and headed for Up Country days ago. Yet Stella calmly fed her cat tiny pieces of food, indifferent to Nature's mugging.

She followed Carter into the kitchen, where he switched on the radio and scanned the range of the dial, looking for up-to-the-minute weather advisories. She bent to listen over his shoulder.

He frowned. "Will you stop that—you're putting gray hairs on my head."

Stella smiled gently when Tess paced back into the

living room. "Rest, Child. Have faith that God is in His kingdom and all is right with the world. "

She came to sit down on the sofa. The wind had become a shrieking woman bent on murderous revenge. "Did you have faith?" she asked, trying to take her mind off the storm. "When your husband was accused of being a communist and couldn't work?"

Stella smiled. "Not at first. I remembered nights that he was gone to meetings. I assumed they were about scripts. They could have been something else. I never asked. I was selfishly involved in my own career." She gently lowered Henry to the floor. "You see, I never really completely believed Edgar. Some bit of gossip, a thought-less word, speculative innuendo always made me think that perhaps he'd fallen in with someone, attended some sort of meeting, maybe had done something innocently that had somehow connected him to the Communist Party. I felt there had to be a 'reason' for Jack Warner fin-gering him as a communist sympathizer.

"So, I waffled between my husband's guilt and inno-cence. But then, I realized there was nothing I could do about any of it, if Edgar were guilty. What was happen-ing was out of my hands. When my husband lost his job, we began to lose possessions—things that had meant much to us. We lost our home in Los Angeles. Friends. I began to lose opportunities. Scripts stopped coming. Worse, the rejection was a cancer on Edgar's soul."

Tess reached for a throw pillow and held it on her lap. "Go on."

A smile lit the old woman's eyes. "God knew what we needed. This house—" Stella's gaze swept the room, "was his gift to me. The only thing that remained of his empire."

"You'd lost everything?"

"We lost possessions. But possessions are only things. We lost nothing of value. We still had each another and we managed to keep the house. We retained our faith in God; they couldn't take that from us."

"Was faith enough when Edgar died?"

"Nothing is enough when you lose the one you love most in the world—not at first," Stella said gently. "But without my strong conviction that ours was only a temporary parting, I would have died with Edgar." Stella's gaze drifted away and she quietly excused herself to go to her room.

Tess heard Carter switch off the kitchen radio. She got up to rejoin him.

"This thing is going to get a whole lot worse before it gets better," he said grimly.

15

". . . moving offshore now. Dangerous storm . . . tuned for updates . . ."

Wind shrieked as Stella serenely adjusted Henry more comfortably around her neck. "I've never left this house in a storm, and I don't plan to start now. But if you kids would feel more secure, go. Drive to Kula. I have a friend there who would be willing to let you sit out the storm with her."

"I think we *all* need to move to a public shelter," Carter said.

Tess could hear a television commentator's sober voice repeating evacuation instructions. Stella couldn't stay here—not alone.

The old woman shook her head. Tess brushed by her and entered the living room. "What's that pounding sound?"

Carter inclined his head, and then proceeded to the front door, calling back to her, "Someone's here." Air pressure pushed the door in the moment Carter turned the knob. Rain came in gusting blasts. Stella appeared in the hallway, eyes curious. "Fredrick?" Her smile widened when she spotted the rain-drenched couple huddled together on the porch. Both man and woman were stoop-shouldered with wet gray hair peeking out from beneath yellow rain slickers. "Ben! Esther!" she called out. "Come in! Come in! It's a wonder you didn't blow away out there!"

The elderly couple stepped inside the foyer, greeting Stella warmly. The man extended an arthritic hand as rain made muddy puddles on the marble entryway. Stella made the introductions. "Ben and Esther Grantham, this is Tess Nelson and Carter McConnell, my houseguests."

Carter shook the white-haired gentleman's hand. "Tess was just asking Stella if we shouldn't move to higher ground."

The man's wizened features creased. "It could be more dangerous getting to shelter now than staying put. Esther and I have been through some pretty rough ones. We'd stay at our own place except we're so close to the shore. The wind took out a big tree in our yard. It crashed into our dining room. We didn't figure it was a good idea to just let it pummel us." His gaze roamed the darkened living room. "Looks like you got this place buttoned up tight. Do you mind if we keep you company until the storm blows over?"

"Of course, you're welcome to stay, Ben." Stella led the

couple into the kitchen, motioning for them to sit at the table. "Carter got all the windows covered, so we're nice and cozy in our little cocoon. When the fury worsens we'll have to move to an inside wall of the bathroom."

Tess's stomach hit the floor. *Worsens?* Crashing noises—like a garbage truck dumping a load of glass—thudded outside the windows. Then the noise switched to one of a freight train running through the beach house.

"Thank you, Stella." The old gentleman reached out and ruffled Henry's belly, then seated his wife in a chair adjacent to Stella's. Worry hovered on Esther's matronly face.

"Goodness—it is getting bad." Esther's eyes darted to the window when the sound of a limb snapping and hitting the side of the house crashed.

Tess watched with something like envy as Ben patted his wife's shoulder.

The small group sat in the candlelit room, waiting. Inside Tess, an emotional storm built—a hurricane of circumstances. Nine days ago her biggest worry had been Len Connor; now she was afraid for her life. When asked a week ago what she valued most she would have answered justice. Right now, what she wanted most was another few years—another sunrise. An opportunity to make something of her life, something lasting and worthwhile. She could find another job; she could blot Len and Connor.com out of her mind and put them where they belonged in her priorities. What mattered were the people in her life, her family. And as much as she had tried to deny it, had let the bitterness of her childhood blot it out, the truth was she loved her family. She had chosen to remember only the bad times, but there had been good times too. Sunday afternoons reading the paper together, laughing at the funnies. She had been so preoccupied with finding someone to blame for the downward spiral in her life, she'd forgotten to look for the good. Sure, the bad times had been just as real, but it hadn't all been bad. As she sat here with the wind threatening to blow their house in, it became crystal clear to her. It was Mona she had to contend with— Mona she had to tackle head-on before she could ever resolve the real tempest in her life.

16

Around midnight Ben and Esther started to nod off. Stella and Henry dozed in a nearby chair.

Carter nudged Tess's leg with his foot. "Hanging in there?"

The wind shrieked loudly in the eaves. She looked nervously toward the roof and placed a hand on her stomach.

Carter rested his head against the rim of the sofa and listened as flying objects struck the shuttered windows. Something hard thumped the side of the house, and in the distance storm sirens wailed. He envisioned himself in a war zone, his face white as he ducked reflexively every time a foreign object slammed into the house. Trash receptacles weren't SCUD missiles, but at the moment Carter couldn't distinguish the difference.

He smiled, studying Tess's worried features. She was a pretty woman, who had a lot to offer a man if she would only release the bitterness in her heart. Carter wasn't usually impulsive; it took him six months to get to know the average woman and even then he moved with caution, but there was something different about this woman.

A nonbeliever.

Was God testing his resolve to follow Him all the way?

Tess shifted and moved closer to the sofa. She seemed almost like a fragile kitten who would look up at him with those doleful eyes, something he could drape around his neck for the rest of his life. Carter shook his head at the thought.

He'd known this woman nine days . . . nine mind-boggling, problematic days, and something was happening inside of him, something bothersome. She was intelligent and goal oriented; and she couldn't trust anyone if her life depended on it. God, man—the recipient didn't seem to matter. She was incapable of placing her trust in anyone.

Therein lay a major problem; Carter believed that eternal life, and his personal security, hinged on nothing less than the ability to trust.

Trust wasn't concrete—an object that he could hold in his hand and claim ownership of. He had to work at trust as hard as manning his command station, but willingness—the desire to believe—made faith possible.

Oh, Lord Almighty, blessed is the man who trusts in You.

He absently stroked his hand across the top of Tess's hair. The fragrant mass felt soft and smelled of wind and rain.

Her sleepy voice drifted up. "When this is over . . . will you call me?"

Carter smiled, burying his face into the floral silk. "Sure. What shall I call you?"

He could feel her laughing. "Beautiful would be nice." She twisted to look up at him. "No commitment, you understand. But I'd like it if you could call to say hello once in a while, let me know how you are—if those new runways point toward Denver."

"I'd like that. And if you think about it, you can give me a ring every now and then."

She didn't miss a beat. "What sort of ring do you want?"

A smile caught the corners of his mouth. Flirting. They were flirting, and it felt good. "Is this where I'm supposed to say 'a wedding ring'?"

She twisted her body to meet his eyes. "Of course not—"

His tone sobered. "I won't forget this vacation."

Her gaze softened. "Nor will I."

The moment stretched. Finally, she eased free of his embrace, as if she knew that the moment and the relationship was fleeting. "I'm hungry."

Was he glad she'd broken the mood? Maybe. Relieved?

Yes.

The only thing he knew for certain was that the relationship wasn't going anywhere—she wasn't a Christian—and the thought stung.

"Nelson? When this is over I'll buy you a sixteen-ounce steak at Moose McGillicuddy's."

"Deal." They shook hands on it.

According to Carter, she didn't have faith because she'd never asked for it.

Just ask for it. Desire it.

Right.

She buttered a piece of bread. Two A.M. approached; the eye of the storm was near.

She was a businesswoman. If a customer didn't place an order, then according to Carter's theory, the customer didn't know they wanted something.

Salvation couldn't be compared to ordering floor wax, but she knew the difference.

Did faith work that way? It sounded too pat—too easy—and in her world, when something sounded "too good to be true" it generally was.

She was savvy enough to know that those professing

faith did not live trouble-free lives. If that were the case, then Carter would have had a perfect vacation. He wouldn't be sitting in a stranger's kitchen, eating cold bread and jelly while Maui was getting blown away—or sounded like it.

"Suppose," she mused, setting the bread sack in front of Carter. "Suppose I buy into your theory. My grandmother had faith, but Mona turned out awful. Why would God allow my mother to not inherit her mother's faith?"

"God isn't Santa Claus. Mona had her own choices to make." He offered the spoon, and she licked the remains of the sticky sweetness.

She took a bite of her meal. "Is that what you really think?"

"I think someone you loved very deeply disappointed you," Carter said, taking a bite of his bread also. "I think they broke a trust, and now you find it hard to believe in anyone or anything."

Her jaw dropped. Then she clamped it shut. Tightness formed around her eyes. "You can't know that."

"No, I can't. But you asked me what I thought. I think that's why you work so hard—you figure since you can't trust anyone to help you, you have to do it all on your own—the perfect career, the perfect life. . . ." He lowered his gaze to the counter. "I'm sorry. I have no right," he said.

Tess had always been cognizant of her need for security. She'd accumulated quite a bit for her age. Stella's earlier words flashed through her mind. *Everything you own will be discarded, used up, or belong to someone else.*

Sure she had a nice apartment, nice furnishings, made some good, solid investments, a healthy 401(k). She'd worked hard for what she had. She had never thought she could take it with her. She wasn't that naïve. Maybe she'd thought that her children would be the benefactors of her hard work, but then, she had no marriage prospects, no plans for children. So, what if the worst happened? What if *Alana* claimed her life? What would the long hours, pressure, incessant travel have done for her? Wasted her life?

🌴

Fierce winds pounded the sheets of plywood nailed across windows, and rain poured rivers through gutters. The restless hurricane seemed intent on showing its true force of power. The sea responded with a show of uncompromising strength as it hurled brutal waves against the battered shoreline.

Tess awoke around five A.M. from a brief nap and lay listening to the wind. Her stomach churned when she thought of being devoured by the angry sea. But a short distance away, Carter lay sleeping on the floor, strong and solid, a symbol of comfort. How had he managed to penetrate her heart in so short a time? His words of faith echoed like a voice in a canyon, resounding until her soul couldn't help but feel compelled to reply. It wasn't a strong answer. No. It was more a faint whisper, but it came nonetheless and reverberated through her soul. She wanted the desire Carter spoke of, the desire to believe. Now the only question was, how did she get this peace?

With the morning, the storm began to blow itself out. The ruthless winds calmed as the day lifted its head from behind gray clouds.

"Looks like it's about over," Ben said from the front door. His perceptive eyes scanned the aftermath of destruction. "The old houses stood the test yet another time."

Carter walked to the doorway and stood for a moment, listening. "Silence," he said.

Outside, distant voices sounded up and down the beach. Residents had started to come out of houses.

Tess stretched lazily then touched the small of her back. The floor was hard as a brick. "Is it really over?" She combed her fingers through her tangled hair.

"It's stopped raining and the winds have let up."

When they stepped out onto the patio a moment later, they were greeted with the sight of downed trees. Palm fronds carpeted the saturated ground. In the driveway, a power line hung, snakelike, over her rental car.

"Oh no, look at that," she said. "Do you suppose it hurt the car mechanically?"

Carter squinted cautiously at the line. "I don't know, but we'd better stay clear until we know for sure the power's off."

Turning their backs on the car, she and Carter headed out to inspect the beach. Stella was already out walking, Ben and Esther leading the way.

Debris covered a large area. A mattress floated lazily in the water. Sheets of plywood and dead sea life littered the shore. Tess spotted a New York Yankees hat, the lid to a blender, and a shower cap. One beach house's upper triangular walls had blown in. Carter picked his way among felled birds and fish tossed onto the shore while she followed close behind. Numerous buildings were blown down. A pair of men's pants hung in a palm tree. Briefly she closed her eyes to block out the vision of ruin. Where hours ago shopkeepers and tourists had bought and sold souvenirs and macadamia nuts, now the seaside town of Kihei looked like a war zone.

"And what, fair lady, shall we do on this tenth day of our lovely vacation?" Carter paused to stare at a beach chair bobbing in the ocean, his tone light but his eyes serious. "Want to try for ten pipers piping?"

"Naw, the nine drummers drove me nuts." She regrouped

and matched his tone. "But there's still so much we haven't done, Carter! Earthquakes, locust plagues, aviation disasters—"

Mentally, she began to rehearse the catalog of folly that had been her "vacation." "Let's see what we *did* manage to accomplish—my cab had a blowout on the way to Stapleton. I had to run to make the flight and I turned my ankle in the process."

"So? I had a miserable cold and my ears killed me on the flight over." Carter stood poised for the battle of who-had-the-worst-vacation.

"Oh, how sad!" She grinned as the tension of the past hours gradually released. *Alana* had left behind destruction, but the storm had spared the island residents—she'd heard no report of death or serious injury. "You didn't have cold pills in your luggage?"

"I didn't *have* luggage by that time."

"But you could have bought some Sudafed when you arrived at your hotel."

"Oh, by then I had my luggage back."

"You did?"

"Oh yeah. Only the hotel burned down, and I lost it again."

"Oh, that hotel!" She was enjoying their game. "I was staying there. Pioneer Inn? Lovely historical place. When I had to vacate the room, I grabbed my makeup bag instead of my purse."

"Go figure."

"Then I spent half the day running around dressed in a blanket."

He viewed her with mock surprise. "You're *that* woman?"

She sobered as her eyes skimmed the storm damage. It would take Kihei months to recover, but the little seaside town had heart. She remembered Beeg—safely in New York. What would Beeg do if she came home to find her gallery destroyed and her watercolors ruined?

Every earthly possession will be used up, given away, or belong to someone else.

She sighed. Carter reached out for her hand and she for his. "Heck of a vacation, Ms. Nelson. Who's your travel agent?"

She paused, then admitted, "Actually I was thinking your travel agent looks a little more . . . trustworthy."

The damage to Stella's house was appreciable. Tiles had blown off the roof, shutters were damaged beyond repair. Downed tree limbs scattered the lawn. Snakes, insects, and rodents driven to higher ground were everywhere—causing more than a little anxiety for cleanup crews.

Carter and Tess skirted puddles as they returned to the beach house. Carter coughed hollowly.

He smiled at her concerned look. "I need hot coffee. Lots of coffee."

Ben, Esther, and Stella were still down the beach inspecting damage. They had the house to themselves. Pouring two cups of coffee, Carter sat down at the table.

Tess remained at the window, arms crossed, staring out.

"Coffee's getting cold."

"I don't want coffee."

He poured cream into his cup and stirred. "What do you want, Tess? Do you know?"

"How does anyone really know what they want?" she asked, her gaze still outside the one window Carter had freed from its plywood imprisonment.

"I suppose they don't," Carter said quietly. "Not without serious thought about what's important to them."

"I want to trust in God like you do," she admitted. "But how do I do that?"

"A child stands on the edge of a swimming pool and says, 'Daddy! Catch me!' and jumps almost before the words are out of his mouth. How does he know his daddy will catch him?"

"Because he always had caught him?"

"Childlike faith. The unwavering trust in his father,

knowing that he's never dropped him, never failed to catch him. That's what faith in God is all about."

Her top teeth worried her bottom lip. "I'm going home, Carter."

He glanced up. His eyes darkened at the announcement. "There won't be any flights out for a few hours."

"I know—but when there are I'm going back to Denver. I need to know that I'm not just feeling this way because of the strain of the storm. . . . I don't want to be a Christian in hard times. If this is real and true, it needs to be for always. I need to go home and think . . ."

Shoving back from the table, Carter said quietly, "Then as soon as the airport opens we'll get you a flight."

Around eight o'clock, an employee from Pioneer Inn arrived. Rapping on the door, he stood on the back porch and waited. Tess spotted him through the kitchen window. Lifting the sill, she called, "May I help you?"

"Tess Nelson?"

She frowned. "I'm Tess."

The boy waved an envelope. "This came for you day before yesterday. Sorry, because of the storm this was the soonest I could get here."

Drying her hand on a towel, she went to open the door. When she looked inside the envelope, she found a voucher for five hundred dollars and a note from Mona.

Life hasn't been easy without Roy; money is always tight. I will need the cash back as soon as you can repay it. Mona.

Tess felt hot tears sting her eyes. She'd sent the money. Mona had not let her down. For the first time in her life, Mom had come through.

Her throat ached from the lump of emotion suddenly blocking her windpipe.

17

A power company crew working the area late Sunday night removed the line from Tess's rental car. Unfortunately, the jolt of power from the line had zapped the car's electronic ignition system, leaving the vehicle undriveable. Stella immediately offered her the use of her battered truck.

After stowing her soot-covered bags in the back of the Chevy pickup Monday morning, Carter climbed into the driver's seat. Air traffic out of Kahului Airport had resumed operation. Main throughways had been cleared of power lines and debris.

Stella carried Henry in her arms as she walked Tess out to the truck. "I know you want to go home. You have choices to make about your job, and I trust you will make those decisions wisely. But I have so much enjoyed knowing you, having you here." She smiled fondly at Carter. "Both of you. You are welcome in my home any time. And I pray the Lord will return you someday to Maui—preferably under more pleasant conditions. The island really is paradise, you know."

Tess smiled though tears stung her eyes. The former movie queen turned to address Carter, "Now, young man, you are to spend the remainder of the afternoon with me. I'll have Fredrick prepare us a nice fruit tray— the pineapple is extra sweet this year—"

The old woman turned as a white-haired gentleman rounded the corner of the house. She broke into a beam. "Fredrick!"

Tess gaped at Carter.

"Stella, my dear." The distinguished gent dressed in a white suit and spats—yes, spats—bent to place a succinct kiss on each of Stella's red-rouged cheeks. "I have been so worried about you. I trust you made it through the storm without any real harm?" His eyes lifted to curiously size up the two strangers.

Stella introduced Tess and Carter and explained how they had come to stay with her.

"The Lord was with us, Fredrick. And my new friends have been with me all the time—and Ben and Esther."

"I am so relieved to know that Stella had someone to keep her company," Fredrick confessed as he shook Carter's hand. "I wanted to call, but heavy trade winds took my phone lines down two days ago."

"Good to meet you, Fredrick." Carter grinned. "Tess

and I were beginning to wonder if you really existed."

"Oh, indeed I do, kind sir. Indeed I do." With a snap of his heels, Fredrick bowed. "If you will excuse me, I must see to the house, and Stella's lunch."

Draping an arm around Stella's waist, Tess steered her new friend to the passenger side of the cab. "You've been wonderful to both Carter and me. I wish I knew how to thank you."

"Oh, my dear, it is I who should be thanking you. You and Carter have brought sunshine into my life—even in the midst of a storm." For a split second, Stella embraced her. "You will stay in touch? Perhaps give an old lady a call occasionally?"

Tess enfolded her fragile frame and hugged her tightly. "I promise."

As Carter backed the truck out of the drive, Stella suddenly quickened her steps. Her eyes deepened with concern. Reaching out, she grasped onto her fingers through the open window. Tess held on tightly.

"Remember the things we talked about," Stella called. "About trust, and faith and love."

"I will." She knew that she would never forget the time she'd spent in Stella's house, or the long talks, and the woman's wisdom. She swiped at tears stinging her eyes.

The Chevy was old, and rattled as if it would fall apart. Carter seemed unusually quiet, Tess assumed because he was concentrating on driving. Or was he avoiding conversation? The air between them was charged, as if they both had something weighing on their minds and neither could push past politeness to speak. His stern features indicated that he was troubled. Maybe he thought that rushing back to Denver would only cast her back into the same mold she'd always been in. And perhaps that could happen, but she didn't think so. Ever since she'd gotten the telegram and money from her mother a new thought had been forming within her. Now, as they made their way along the cluttered, storm-strewn streets of Kihei she saw with clarity why she'd always held back, had been so terrified of trusting. Mona. The one person she'd tried so hard to trust, who had invariably failed her, finally came through, and with that one act, Tess felt her foundations shake. If Mona, who was far from perfect, could be trusted, perhaps God, the God Carter loved so dearly, deserved her trust too. But first she had to go to Indiana, to see her mother for herself. Indiana held the key to her problems.

She looked over at Carter. The thought of never seeing him again left her hurting. Somehow it seemed wrong to walk away from this man; why, her practical side couldn't fathom. But like the air she breathed, it just was.

Carter peered at the vacillating dash gauges, seemingly unaware of the turmoil going on inside her. "The gas gauge is sticking. Stella and Fredrick must not believe in maintenance." His voice fell to silence.

She studied the pineapple fields as the old truck rattled along Highway 30. She was heading home; Carter was going back to Chicago and his job at O'Hare—his church work. She recalled the dedication in his voice when he spoke of his mission trips to faraway places like Bosnia, El Salvador, and his newest project, an orphanage in Uganda. How she wished she could do something so noble, so *meaningful* with her life.

Her eyes switched to the Bible lying on the seat between them. She picked it up and glanced over questioningly. Carter turned the wheel and they headed down 380. His jaw locked, and she wondered if she'd aggravated him by handling the book. Even he would have to admit that not everybody carried a Bible in their front seat. Maybe Jehovah's Witnesses . . . pastors.

Carter answered her silent inquiry. "I've fallen behind on my reading lately."

She lightly skimmed the worn pages. Passages were highlighted in yellow; notations made to the side.

She closed the Bible. "If the Bible is the best-selling book in the world, what's the second?"

He shook his head. "I have no idea."

"Would you think I'm full of myself if I told you that I knew?"

He glanced at her.

"Well, I don't—I haven't a clue either," she admitted lightly, "but I do know the Bible sells over a million copies a year—read that in a Crimson and Brown report. Why that particular fact was mentioned in a human resource periodical, I can't imagine." She lifted the heavy black book again and stared at it. "Have you read this through?"

"Several times."

She lifted her eyebrows. "Several times? Why? Does it update itself?"

"No, it doesn't change—only my comprehension changes. Every time I read it, I discover something I didn't know before."

She could see she was getting to him. He gripped the steering wheel, staring straight ahead. Not the relaxed Carter of days past. He seemed on edge, tense. Distant. Well, maybe that was what she wanted: distance. The relationship had all the signs of . . . what? Turning serious? Hardly. After today she would most likely never see him again.

She laid the book back on the seat between them.

He turned to focus on her. "Are you sure you aren't leaving for different reasons?"

"Like what?"

"Maybe you're afraid."

"Afraid!" She scoffed. "Of what?"

"I don't know." Carter turned onto the exit. "Afraid

of discovering that God loves you more than you can imagine."

"Why would that frighten me?"

"Love is a terrifying thing—it gives, yes. But it asks a lot more in return. You'd have to give up everything for Him—for Jesus. A lot of people turn back because of that. You'd have to let go of your unholy twins."

"Unholy twins?"

"Hurry and Worry."

"Hurry and worry," she repeated. "Whatever."

"You hurry too much, and you're going to worry yourself into an early grave."

"Now just one minute—"

"*Face* it, Tess. That's why you're in such an all-fired hurry to leave Maui. You can't stand the thought of rejection, that Len Connor fired you. You can't wait to get back and have the last say."

His observation stung; and he couldn't be more off base. Well, maybe there was a grain of truth in the accusation but who was he to butt into her personal life?

"Quite obviously you don't live in the same world I do, Mr.-Perfect-Carter-McConnell. Worry is a natural extension of any high-pressure job."

"You can't say my job isn't high pressure," he reminded her.

"And you couldn't take the stress—you said so earlier. The only reason you came to Maui was because you were forced to slow down. So don't talk to me about hurry and worry. Those *twins* are on your back too!" She could feel her blood pressure boiling. Then she added insult to injury. "Plus, you have it EASY, Carter. You aren't upwardly mobile like I am. You've reached your goals."

"Have I, now?"

"Haven't you? You sit in a tower, directing planes to safe landings and takeoffs."

When he refused to capitulate, she baited, "Isn't that true? You've already reached your potential?"

"My potential won't be reached until I see Jesus face to face."

She crossed her legs and her arms. One foot twitched erratically.

She sobered as the years fell away and she once again squirmed beside her grandmother in a pew as the priest's words filled the large sanctuary.

"Are you far more valuable to Him than the birds of the air? Can all your worries add a single moment to your life?"

"The Jewish have a saying," Carter's voice broke into her suddenly melancholy reverie. "'Worms eat you when you're dead. Worry eats you when you're alive.' Worry erodes the machinery of our lives. Faith and trust are the grease that keeps it running smoothly."

She felt helpless to argue. Memories had stripped her of self-assurance; confidence momentarily deserted her. Passages long forgotten drifted back to her.

"Look at the lilies and how they grow. They don't work or make their clothing, yet Solomon in all his glory was not dressed as beautifully as they are. And if God cares so wonderfully for flowers that are here today and gone tomorrow, won't He more surely care for you?"

"I don't understand God," she admitted. "I just don't. But, you're going to have to trust *me*—I want to. I really do."

Carter reached for her hand and held tightly.

A few minutes later his "Uh, oh," broke the silence.

"What's the matter?"

The engine sputtered, and then coughed. She glanced at the gas gauge as the old wheezer started to buck. "Don't tell me we're out of gas!"

The Chevy rumbled and spat a couple more times. Carter swerved the vehicle to the edge of the road. "Okay," Carter agreed. "But somebody needs to inform you."

Panic crowded the back of her throat. *Out of gas?* The truck was out of *gas* and she had a flight out in one hour? Her eyes darted, trying to locate a nearby gas station.

Carter switched off the ignition. "I'll bet nobody's put gas in the tank in months." He opened the door and unfolded his long legs out of the cab. "We passed a convenience store half a mile back."

She went on point. "You have to walk? How long will that take?"

"I don't know. I'm not an Olympic sprinter, but I'll be back as soon as I can."

She scooted across the seat and shouted after his retreating back. "My plane leaves in *one* hour, Carter! It will take me that long to get through security!"

"I'm aware of when your plane leaves, Tess."

Carter trekked back to where they'd come from while she kept track of his progress through the back window. It didn't take long for the truck's cab to heat up. She wished she'd dressed a little more casually. Her nylons were already sticking to her legs.

She thought about getting out of the truck and standing somewhere cooler. She opened the truck door, hoping to catch a breeze. Twenty minutes passed. Finally she slid out of the truck and paced the side of the road.

About the time she decided something awful had happened to Carter and he was never coming back, a rattle-trap truck sped down the road and skidded to a halt beside her. Carter clambered out and lifted a gas can from the truck's bed.

"Thanks!" he called.

"Aloha!" a voice returned before the truck sped off.

Carter lugged the heavy can to the back of the truck and uncapped the tank. Tipping the can, he poured gas into the empty tank. Sweat rolled down the sides of his flushed face. "Relax. You'll make the plane."

Relax. She resumed pacing.

By the time Carter returned the gas can, filled the tank, and parked the truck in "short term" parking, the plane was due to take off in twenty-five minutes. Tess's nerves were raw and stretched to the limit as Carter lugged her bags to the curbside check-in line. Minutes later, after retrieving her boarding pass, she made a break for the gate. Halfway there, she turned around and stopped. Harried passengers swerved around her to avoid a collision.

Carter stood in the opening of the breezeway, watching her. She hadn't said good-by. She realized this was the moment she had been avoiding all day.

Turning around, she walked back. They stood for a moment, breathing deeply of tuberose-scented tropical air. Paradise.

Silence stretched. Then he leisurely held out his arms and she walked into them. Holding on tightly, she closed her eyes and savored the last few hints of his cologne. She searched but couldn't find the words to say what she wanted to say. For the past ten days he had been a source of strength and hope that she never knew she needed.

"Thank you," she whispered.

His hold tightened. "You weren't kidding about staying in touch?"

"Do you want me to?"

"I want you to."

She wasn't sure how he kept his voice so calm, so level, when all she wanted to do was cry.

Gently releasing her, he stood back and smiled. "Take care of yourself, Tess Nelson."

"You, too, Carter McConnell." She grinned. Tears stung her eyes as she turned away and walked toward the gate. She heard his voice calling above the noisy room.

"I'm holding you to your promise to call. Don't forget me."

Forget him? Impossible.

Moments later, she raced down the Jetway and onto the wide-bodied plane. Breathless, and fighting back tears now, she located her seat. Buckled in, she fumbled for a tissue. She wished she'd never met Carter McConnell—knowing him only added another confusing equation to her messed-up life.

The plane remained unmoving in its place at the gate. Tess thumbed through a copy of United Airline Promo Magazine and listened for the door to seal. She checked the time. Back to her magazine.

Thirty minutes had passed when the pilot announced there would be a slight delay.

What *now?* If she could only get *out* of paradise— away from Carter—away from this feeling that because of this Chicago flight controller and his beliefs, her life would never be the same.

Another thirty minutes crept by. Passengers fanned themselves with newspapers; babies cried.

"Ladies and gentleman." The pilot's grave voice came

over the intercom. "Sorry about the delay. Seems there's been a security breach. Passengers will have to deplane."

She slammed her head solidly back against the seat. Why not? What *ever* made her think she was going to get off the island this easily?

With a sigh of resignation, she picked up her purse and stepped into the aisle.

"How long?" she asked as she passed the flight attendant.

The lady shrugged. "Stay close. The airline will keep you informed."

18

The message light on the answering machine was blinking when Tess turned the key and let herself into the apartment. She glanced at it. Twelve calls. Her thoughts drifted: Len.

He'd taken his good ol' sweet time to call.

After dumping her bags the bedroom, she returned to the hallway and jacked up the heat. Though the apartment was exactly as she'd left it, the place didn't feel like home anymore. What had changed? Her?

The two-hour delay at Kahului had given her time to reflect on her life and the direction she'd been going. She hadn't cared for the insight. Always the smug career machine, the Tess of the past had attributed success to self-achievement, but vacation . . . and Carter McConnell . . . had made her realize that no man—or woman, for that matter—was an island. Tess Nelson needed help.

She unpacked and then addressed the imminent problem: her phone messages. The first message came on. "Tess . . . ?" It was Len. He sounded contrite—no, penitent. "Tess—sweetie. I tried the hotel in Maui, and the clerk said there'd been some sort of accident—fire— something. Anyway, call me the minute you get home. We need to talk."

Beep.

The lack of genuine concern in Len's message irritated Tess. How about an, *"Are you okay? Were you hurt in the fire?"*

Then message two started in. "Okay," it was Len again. "So, Chuck isn't working out as I'd hoped. . . . Are you calling in to hear your messages? . . . Um, call me."

"Hey, Tess," Len again, for the third message, "Look, Babe—we're hurting here—I've been following *Alana* on the Weather Channel. Looks like she got pretty ugly. Air traffic's resumed—I know you didn't stick around to help with the cleanup so I know you're back. Where are you? Come on, I'm waiting to hear from you. Things are a mess here. Connor.com needs you. . . ."

All in all there were eleven calls from Len, all essentially the same. The twelfth call was from Carter, checking to see that she'd arrived safely; sweet, unselfish Carter.

Her finger hit delete. She'd waited, had been sure Len

would make just such a call, but somehow it didn't satisfy as she'd hoped. There was still a hollowness in the pit of her stomach.

A second later, the doorbell rang. Groaning, she thought about ignoring the intrusion. She was tired, had severe jetlag—the last thing she wanted right now was to relive the events of her vacation in paradise.

Whoever it was leaned on the bell with persistence. Len? He wouldn't dare show up—not without warning her first. When she opened the door, she found her next-door neighbor, Herb Franklin, steadying a large vase of red roses. He smiled when he saw her. "Thank goodness—I thought we had a prowler." His features sobered. "I thought you planned to be away a few more days. I heard someone come in and I came to investigate."

"Lucky criminal," she said as she eyed the voluminous bouquet. And such lovely extravagance—at least three-dozen crimson American Beauty's were arranged with sprigs of baby's breath. "Are those mine?"

Herb handed her the crystal vase. "They came today—and one yesterday just like it, and a similar one the day before." He flashed an apologetic grin. "It will take me a few minutes to get the vases all over here." He turned and trekked back to his residence. For a fleeting moment she hoped they were from Carter but just as quickly she realized that would've been impossible since he couldn't very well have sent them when she was still in Hawaii. She opened the card and read the inscription:

We need you, Tess. *Call* **me. Len.**

At 12:50 A.M. Tess sat up and pitched the heavy comforter aside. Denver streetlight filtered through the bedroom curtain. Tylenol; she needed a pain reliever. The smell of roses was overpowering. A jackhammer pounded in her right temple, and her ankle ached. Even an earlier soak in the whirlpool tub had failed to loosen the tight muscles coiled in her shoulders. Having grown accustomed to the sound of surf breaking along the shoreline, now Tess found herself disturbed by Denver's sirens, the crunch of steel-belted tires on packed snow, and wind howling up the apartment eaves.

Getting out of bed, she crammed her feet into slippers and pulled on her robe. As she walked through the front room, she switched on lamps. The darkness bothered her, the gloom, the uncertainty of what lay in the shadows.

I'm being maudlin, she warned herself as she entered

the kitchen and picked up the teakettle and filled it with water. *You're weirding out, Tess.*

Waiting for the water to heat, she sat at the table and peeled an apple, watching the peel grow longer and longer. She was so fascinated by the progression that when the teakettle blasted a shrill whistle she jumped as though someone had fired a cannon through the window.

Moments later she dropped a bag of Lipton in the cup, thinking about Len's earlier messages. *Call me.*

Well, Len, I have called you—everything in my arsenal of bad names.

Propping her chin on her hand, she dunked the bag up and down in hot water and wondered why she didn't feel justified. Cleansed. She had gotten want she'd wanted, hadn't she? Len Conner on all fours. He had called. Her position with Connor.com was waiting to be reclaimed.

With a fat raise and a sizable bonus at year's end, no doubt.

So where was the elation? The thrill of victory?

Life wasn't fair. Wasn't that what Stella had said? And the old movie queen's wisdom was profound.

Her mind flew back to her talks with Stella and Carter. Hadn't she told Carter that she wanted to finally trust God? Yet she knew that if that was ever going to happen she had to let go of the one thing that held her back—no, the two things, she decided. First, she needed to get over what Len Connor had done, and second, she needed to forgive her mother. She absently stirred the cup of tea as the apple lay forgotten beside the cup.

Starting tomorrow morning, she was going to find the real woman. The real Tess Nelson.

The dilapidated row house stood like a war-weary soldier backlit by the early morning Indiana skyline. Tess had never come to see her mother without calling first, but then this January had been anything but typical for her.

She proceeded up the snow-packed walk. Her breath puffed a frosty vapor in the bitterly cold air. A man wrapped in a shabby-looking overcoat and wearing a fedora exited the building carrying a long-handled shovel. If the tenants wanted snow off their walk it was up to them to remove it. There was no hired help to do it here as there was in her condo.

The man nodded as she passed. Years of bleak existence looked back at her.

"Morning."

"Good morning." She opened the glass door marred by hundreds of handprints and stepped into the foyer. Mailboxes lined the chipped, painted wall; a potted plant that might once have contributed oxygen no longer even tried. Dead leaves gathered in a shallow pool at the base of the cracked terra cotta-colored plastic.

She pressed the elevator button. The cables clicked as the car slowly started its descent to her. Her eyes scanned the squalid conditions and she was assuaged by guilt when she thought about her warm apartment, filled with trendy furniture and Beeg's watercolor prints. How could Mona live here? Steel doors labored open and Tess waited for the bouncing elevator car to stabilize.

Hesitantly entering the cave, she removed her winter gloves and pressed the sixth-floor button. The tiny room smelled of perspiration and wet dog. She watched the light buttons and thought about how hard it would be for a woman Mona's age to transport heavy sacks of groceries to the sixth floor. She leaned and pressed the button again. Then twice more before the door shut.

Getting off on six, she walked down the long hallway that reeked of fried meat and burnt toast. She paused in front of Mona's apartment: 607.

Drawing a deep breath, she rapped on the door that held a pink faded plastic floral bouquet on its surface. She could hear Katie Couric and Matt Lauer chatting with Al Roker in the background, something about the unexpected snowfall in the Big Apple that morning.

She listened to the sounds of footsteps and bumps emanateding from inside the apartment, as if someone was searching for something to throw on. Shortly the door creaked open a crack and for the first time in sixteen years she met her mother's eyes.

"Mama?"

The door shut as the security chain rattled, and then the door opened fully. Mona stood in front of her with a faded turquoise chenille housecoat half off her shoulder, hair poking out of red Velcro curlers. A Winston sagged from the corner of her mouth. Clearly she was surprised to see Tess, though she made some effort to remain unreadable. "Who died?"

Tess managed a wavering smile. "Nobody. I know I should have called, but I . . . thought maybe it's been too long. I should pay a visit in person."

Mona's gaze raked her and Tess was suddenly self-conscious of her blatant show of affluence compared to her surroundings. Why hadn't she worn jeans and running shoes? Her mother stepped back, motioning her inside. "You don't need more money, do you?" she said.

"No, Mother."

She entered the cubicle of an apartment, her eyes skimming the interior. A closet ran the length of the entryway. Small living room, tiny kitchenette. One bedroom off to the left. At least the bed was made. A stack of books was piled on the end table with prescription medicine vials—six of them. A pair of glasses lay open beside them.

A twenty-one-inch television, with what looked to be

an ancient Nintendo attached, blared from its perch: a scarred, inexpensive pressed-sawdust table that could be purchased at Kmart and hand assembled. Her eyes skimmed the picture taken shortly after Mona and Roy's marriage. She'd seen it throughout her childhood. The photo had been taken in front of a Woolworth's in Texas. A nineteen-year-old Roy was wearing a sailor cap, and sixteen-year-old Mona wore her hair upswept. The smiling couple looked happy.

Once Tess took a seat, Mona closed the door and slid the security chain back into place. "Thought you were in Hawaii."

"I got back day before yesterday."

"Is it nice?" Mona took her coat and draped it over the back of a kitchen chair. Dishes with dried food cluttered the sink. A skillet of bacon grease congealed on the two-burner stove.

She shrugged. "It's tropical."

"Expensive, I hear."

Tess smiled. At nine dollars a pound for fresh asparagus, she guessed it was safe to say prices were high. "Very."

Shuffling past her, Mona made her way to the frayed sofa. As she passed the table bearing the Nintendo, she switched the television off. A deck of cards in Solitaire order splayed across an aluminum television tray facing the couch. An ashtray, overflowing with butts, lent its evidence to the smoky smell that permeated the tiny quarters.

Grinding out one cigarette, Mona flicked a Bic lighter and lit another one as she studied Tess beneath shaded lids. The years had been cruel to Mona Nelson. Lines etched her leathery skin like erratic road maps, paving the way to eyes shrunken deeply back in her skull.

Tess fished in her purse for the envelope. "I've brought your money back."

"Good." Mona peered at the offering through a veil of blue smoke.

She laid the money on the end table. Silence surpassed the sounds coming from the low-rent housing hallway—someone running a vacuum, an infant crying in the distance.

A child was the product of his environment, that she would agree. Sadly, for the last thirty-two years she had practiced Mona and Roy's belief, lived under the assumption that Christianity was a lie. Yet in the past week she'd come to see that they had been wrong, she had been wrong. She had witnessed not only God's existence but His love for her. She'd seen it in Stella and Carter, in their willingness to reach out to her. Now it was her turn to reach out in forgiveness.

Her eyes scanned the squalor. There had to be a stronger reason for life than this. Tess saw before her a woman who did not need to be feared, but a woman to be pitied. Her heart swelled with a long forgotten love. Mona had lived her whole life in an aura of distrust and desperation. Perhaps her lack of spiritual awakening was a by-product of her own painful childhood. Instinct told Tess that Mona held the key to her emotional restoration, and she knew the key could not turn in the lock without forgiveness and compassion. Mona was sixty-two years old. She lived in an empty world of cigarettes, computer games, and soap operas.

"Is there anything I can do for you—anything you want?"

"No, I do okay. A neighbor lady takes me to the grocery store and to pick up my medicine on Saturdays. I do all right."

"I want to pay your bills each month." She drew a long breath. "Send me the amount you need and I'll send you a check."

"I don't need your charity."

"I know you don't. This is something I want to do."

"Well." She shrugged. "If you have money to burn go ahead."

Tess suddenly bent to give her mother a stiff hug. She felt Mona's hand touch the back of her hair.

"Well," Tess straightened, pasting on a smile, afraid she would cry. "I need to be going."

Mona got up and opened the door. "I suppose there is one thing you could do for me."

"What's that?"

"I'd like to have a PlayStation."

"PlayStation? One of those computer toys?"

She nodded. "Roy's old Nintendo is just about to give out on me. I'd sure enjoy a PlayStation, maybe a few extra games—if that wouldn't be asking too much."

"No— I'll send you a PlayStation when I get back to Denver."

For an instant Tess looked deeply into her mother's eyes, and she wanted to believe—oh how she wanted to trust that what she saw in the faded brown gaze was more than regret for lost years, maybe even a hint of love for her.

"Bundle up tight. It's cold out there," Mona said.

She obediently fastened the bottom button on her coat, and pulled on warm gloves. "Take care of yourself, Mom."

Mona nodded. "You too."

19

Airport gift shops were about as personal as a blender for Christmas, but Tess found a stuffed cat that looked a whole lot like Henry. She purchased the cat, and included the toy with a large box of chocolates and had the gifts mailed to Stella along with a note thanking her for her hospitality. Stella had offered more than hospitality; she had offered new insight. Tess had sadly been lacking in that commodity. Stella also offered friendship. Friendships took time to cultivate and nurture. Over the years Tess had worked too many long hours and weekends to develop close relationships. She needed to change that.

As she was paying for the chocolates, her eyes centered on a box of nuts and she thought of Len, whose frantic calls she had yet to return. They would serve as a succinct answer to his pleas for help. *Nuts to you.*

"I'll take a box of nuts, too."

"Certainly." The clerk reached behind her and snagged a five-pound assortment of almond Macadamias. "Will there be anything else?"

"Yes. I want to enclose this note with the gift." She scribbled a brief message that read, "Thanks, but not interested. Tess." She handed the card back to the woman. "Will those go out today?"

"Sometime late this afternoon."

"Thanks."

Tess left the shop, pausing outside long enough to blow air out of her cheeks. She still had to send the check for the airline ticket, but it was over.

Man. She gave the air a jubilant right hook. That felt good. *Really good.*

Groundhog Day arrived on the heels of a Denver blizzard. Punxsutawney Phil emerged from his burrow and saw his shadow, so weather forecasters predicted winter would hang around for another six weeks.

Trudging through nine inches of snow with more falling in the mall parking lot, Tess huddled deeper into the lining of her wool coat. By the looks of the empty lot, not many Denverites were out shopping today.

Inside the sprawling Denver Mall complex, Tess stomped snow off her boots and made her way to B. Dalton's bookstore. On the flight home from Indiana two days ago she'd come up with a plan—an "enlighten Tess" strategy. There was no way on earth that she was going to read and understand the King James Bible, but logic said there were other ways to learn about the gospel.

Thirty minutes later she carried her purchases to the counter. She didn't blink when the clerk perused the two titles: *The Complete Idiot's Guide to the Bible* and *No Brainer's Guide to the Bible*.

Back in her own habitat, she shrugged out of her coat and boots and emptied the sack of reading material on the sofa. Wielding a yellow highlighter, she started to read. Noon passed, and she didn't break for lunch.

Late afternoon, she ate a handful of Ritz crackers and some bologna. When she came to a thought or paragraph that she questioned, she highlighted it. Rereading her scribbles she realized that every other line in the first two chapters was highlighted. And this was the easy version.

By nightfall, instead of Dan Rather's voice filtering from her apartment, Tess's mystified exclamations of "Huh?" and "Oh, now how can that be?" or the occasional "Give me a break" shattered the silence.

But after reading most of the day, she slept better that night than she had in a long time. When she awoke in the night she tried praying. Her novice attempts were halting at first. She prayed about the weather—and Herb Franklin's continuing good health. Stella's name came up once or twice. Carter's more than twice. She felt a sense of peace overtake her, a sense that she was no longer alone. God could be trusted because He loved her—He loved Tess Nelson.

The following morning, she found herself talking out loud as she dumped coffee grinds to make a fresh pot.

That night Carter was still on her mind—she sincerely hoped that he wouldn't look back on his time in Maui and remember Tess Nelson as a nut case who'd spoiled his vacation.

Reaching for the phone, she called Beeg. When her college roommate's voice came on the line, she grinned. "Well it's about time."

"Tess! Is that you?" Beeg squealed. "I'm so sorry I missed you—When are you coming to Maui again?"

She sank down to the sofa, speechless. "Do I have a story for you."

For over an hour, she told of her exploits and how she'd weathered *Alana* in paradise. Bee Gee told her about the damage to her shop—most everything had been lost; insurance covered the building but couldn't come near to the value of her lost artwork.

"Stella DeMuer—the old movie queen? You stayed in Stella DeMuer's beach house?" Beeg exclaimed when Tess told her about her accommodations after the fire.

"She's wonderful, Beeg. Could you go visit Stella sometime? She's so lonely, and you would love her."

"Sure, I've always wanted to see the inside of her home. Does she really wear a cat around her neck?"

"Henry." Tess grinned.

Beeg's tone had softened. "You sound different, Tess. Happier. Have you met someone?"

Had she met someone? Carter's face flashed through her mind. Besides the Lord? "Could be—and I am happier, Beeg. I've been reading the Bible lately."

"Yeah? Me too! I've been going to church with a guy. You know, there could be something to this religion thing."

"Yeah," Tess agreed. "I think there really could be, Beeg."

That night she dug Carter's home phone number out of her purse and dialed Chicago. She knew the games women were supposed to play—don't be pushy. Wait for him to call. Don't appear too needy.

Well, Carter's and her relationship wasn't Romeo and Juliet's. But she wasn't going to play any games. If he mistook a simple phone call between two acquaintances to be anything other than innocuous, that was his problem. She drummed her fingernails on the end table as she listened to the first ring.

Then two.

Three. Her heart took a nosedive. He wasn't home.

She wondered if he'd stayed in Maui. She absently flipped the remote to the Weather Channel.

On the fifth ring, Carter's voice came on the line. "Hello."

Relief flooded her. "Hey. I was about to hang up."

"Hey—is this Tess?"

She sat back on the sofa, closing her eyes. It felt so good to hear his voice. Suddenly it seemed the weight of the world had lifted from her shoulders. "Ms. Unlucky Charm in person."

His tone modulated. "Hi, Girl."

"I see you made it back to Chicago."

"Smooth as silk this time. What about you?"

"We had to deplane for a couple of hours because of a security breach—the airlines never said what kind of a breach. After that the flight was uneventful. So, how are things? Back to work yet?"

"Not yet. I'm scheduled for next week, though."

They chatted about nothing. Then about everything. She had forgotten how easy he was to confide in.

"Hey," he said.

"What?"

"When's your birthday?"

"July fourth. Why?"

"No kidding. July fourth? I woke up in the middle of the night last night and remembered you hadn't included that with your address."

She smiled, recalling the night of the hurricane and

the candid sharing of their lives as they sat on Stella's cold garage floor.

"When's yours?"

"July fifth."

"No way."

"Why would I lie about my birthday?"

"Well." She debated the next line. The "rules" would strongly advise against it. "Maybe we'll share a birthday cake this year."

"Sounds good to me. I hope you like German chocolate."

"I love chocolate of any nationality."

They laughed.

"I like you, Nelson." This from Carter.

"I like you too, McConnell."

"Exactly when do you think that happened? When I handed you the package of tissues at the airport? Or maybe it was over the luggage carousel when you had such charitable thoughts about my stealing your suitcase."

She felt color dot her cheeks. "I think it was . . . about the time you looked at me as if I'd lost my mind on the hotel fire escape and you had to haul me down two flights of stairs." They laughed and then a comfortable silence lengthened.

"Are you back at Connor.com?"

"No. I'm not going back. I figure I can trust my future to God."

"That's great, Tess. Really great to hear."

She stalled, aware they'd been talking for over an hour, but she needed to tell him that she valued his integrity, his kindness . . .

She bit her lip. "Hey, call me sometime."

"You too. I'm home most days. If I'm not leave a message and—"

"You'll get back to me." She laughed.

When he spoke this time there was unevenness in his tone. "I think about you a lot."

"I think about you, too."

"What's the weather like in Chicago?" She needed him to keep talking so she could hear his voice.

"It sleeted today."

"Here, too." Dead air. "Well . . . talk to you soon."

She replaced the receiver and sat alone in the apartment.

The phone shrilled. She sat while the instrument cycled and the answering machine picked up. Len's agitated voice came over the line.

"What's with the box of nuts, Tess? And this note: 'Not interested.' Are these nuts supposed to represent your answer—some kind of a joke—is this your way of getting even? Have you lost your *mind?*"

Smiling, she rested her head on the back of the sofa. Maybe she had, Len. Right now it sure looked like it.

20

Tess came home from the post office Thursday afternoon to find a large manila envelope jammed in the mail receptacle. She had been waiting almost a month now for the right job opportunity to open up. She hoped this would be the answer to her prayers. Maneuvering the wrapper free, she caught her breath and held it when she saw that the letter was from Caltron—one of Denver's largest pharmaceutical companies.

Inside was the prize she sought. Was she available for a ten o'clock appointment on the eighteenth?

Was she ever.

The morning of the interview, she dressed carefully in a red wool suit and white silk blouse. She studied her image in the mirror, trying to decide if she should wear her hair up or down, changing earrings twice before she was satisfied that she looked appropriately professional.

Glancing at her watch, she picked up her purse and

started out the door. Then she stopped. Her nerves were side straddling her backbone.

Tossing her purse onto the couch, she dropped to her knees. She'd taken to praying more and more in the past month, until now; she couldn't imagine *not* taking her concerns to the Lord. She took a moment to collect her thoughts, desperately wanting to get this right.

"Dear Father in Heaven." She paused. "Dear God. You have been so faithful to me, even when I wasn't aware of it. Help me to trust You, to know that no matter how this turns out, You're in control. I only need You—to know You more."

She relaxed once the words were said. A peace came over her.

"I desire to know and receive Your Spirit."

And she did—oh, how she did.

"I give You all my doubts and insecurities. I willingly place every facet of my life in your hands, Father—I surrender all." Tears dripped from the corners of her eyes; she'd have to redo her makeup. "I respectfully remind You that there will be more times when I'll want to take it all back than times I will walk solely in faith, but I pray Your grace will not allow me to remain in the darkness for long.

"I need to know that You are walking beside me—every day. I ask for the faith that Carter and Stella have—I want the peace and assurance as I leave this room today that my life is no longer temporal, but eternal, in Your service. . . ."

"Hey McConnell."

"What's happenin', Nelson?" Carter fingered the cupid tie around his neck and grinned. Sure, the men at work razzed him for wearing the gift Tess had sent for Valentine's Day, but so what? It had her written all over it.

"I had a promising job interview today," she said.

Carter unwrapped a stick of spearmint gum and stuck it in his mouth. In the background, flight controllers went about their business. His eyes habitually focused on the blinking blips on radar.

"And?"

"I won't know for a few days."

"Well, I'll ask God to make a special dispensation in your case." His grin widened. "How's the ol' stress level?"

"What stress?" He could sense her subsequent smile. "I've decided to look at my job differently—I'm happy all those fly jockeys are fighting over me. I'm popular."

"Carter." She took a deep breath.

"Yo."

"I've accepted Jesus as my Savior. I did it awhile ago, but it's been sort of growing in me this past month. This morning though, it seemed very *real.*"

His tone instantly sobered. "You did?"

"I'm taking baby steps," she confessed. "I'll need help from you."

"You don't become an adult overnight—you don't grow in Christ overnight. If you've placed the order, Tess, God will deliver. I'm so proud of you."

Shoot. Was that emotion suddenly crowding the back of his throat? Shoot. It was. He took a swipe at his eyes and chewed hard on his gum to control the surge of tears.

"I know you only have a few minutes for your break—I just wanted to tell you."

"Thanks." He spit the gum out in a tissue and leaned closer to the mouthpiece. "Hey. Nice work, Nelson."

"Thanks"—and here she drew not upon her *Dummies* guides, but upon her heart—"but the credit belongs to the Lord."

21

March arrived on the heels of strong winds, and kites began flapping in East Denver Park District. Tess's long-distance bills to Chicago were astronomical, but her new position with Caltron paid more than she had hoped.

When she'd gotten on that plane to Hawaii her life had been in shambles, and look what God had done.

Wonder flooded her anew. What a change a few weeks had brought. She wanted to tell Carter personally, to see him face to face. The idea brought her up short as she doodled on a scratch pad in her new office overlooking the Denver skyline.

Well, why not?

For less than one month's phone bill she could fly to Chicago and spend an entire weekend. She and Carter could talk without wondering about how the other person looked, without *wishing* that they could kiss each other good night.

Reaching for the phone, she gently eased the door shut with the tip of her leather shoe.

She drove to Denver International Airport on her lunch hour and sat in the car and studied the control tower, trying to envision Carter's world. Doubts assuaged her. Should she really fly to Chicago? Show up unannounced and uninvited? On the pretext of delivering a greeting card?

Feminists would have a cow.

Well. So what. She couldn't get through another week without seeing him. She sat with her window cracked so she could hear the roar of jets taking off and landing. Carter needed her. She *knew* he did. He needed someone to come home to. Someone to share his life, someone who would love him, care for him, nurture him—

He needed her and she needed him.

Together, with the Lord's blessing, they could conquer the world!

22

Tess Nelson handed the cabby a twenty and slid out of the backseat. She had an hour and a half to make the Chicago flight.

Sprinting toward the busy terminal, she disregarded lingering ice patches still clinging to the walkways. Suddenly she was slip-sliding across the frozen glaze, groping wildly for anything to latch onto for leverage.

Dropping her suitcase, she lunged for a handrail moments before she would have sprawled face first. But not quickly enough to prevent her left ankle from twisting.

Deja vu.

She grasped the injured appendage and groaned out loud. No! There was something about Denver International and ankles that didn't mix.

She took small comfort in the knowledge that her right ankle had finally healed and this time it was her left that was rapidly ballooning. Picking up her suitcase, she limped on.

In a rush to board her flight, she limped right past the handsome man who had dashed out the exit door.

🌴

Carter skidded to a halt and whipped around when he saw Tess hobbling in the opposite direction, carrying luggage.

She was *leaving* town as he was arriving.

Panic seized him and he yelled, "Hey! What's wrong with your ankle now?"

Dropping his overnight bag, he sprinted after her, threading his way through a throng of oncoming passengers. "Nelson!"

The sound of Carter's voice brought Tess to a halt. "Carter?" She whirled, dropping her case when she spotted him, and raced toward him, oblivious to the pain.

Carter twirled her around as she latched onto his neck and held on tightly. Oh, he smelled *so* good! So Carter.

Catching her up in his arms, he kissed her, oblivious to the fact that they were blocking traffic flow.

"What are you doing here?" she exclaimed when they finally relinquished their hold.

"The oddest thing—I was trying to find a stamp to mail your St. Patrick's Day card, and I thought, 'Hey, McConnell, why don't you just take her the card in person?'"

She interrupted. "Carter! That was my line! And a lame one at that."

"No way."

"Way!" she argued.

He drew her back into his arms. "What are *you* doing here?"

"I'm going to see *you*."

"I'm *coming* to see you."

"Hey." His tone softened. "Aren't we blessed. We've both found what we're looking for." He leaned slightly to kiss the tip of her nose. The gesture promised a lifetime of commitment. "I love you, Tess Nelson."

Only through His grace could her life have taken such a wonderful turn, Tess realized. Only through God's grace.

"What made you change your mind—convince yourself that you can trust me and God?"

She smiled, tightening her hold around his neck. "If I can trust God, I can trust you."

He chuckled. "Lady, I hate to tell you, but you can trust God a lot more that you can trust me."

"Hey, McConnell, speaking of God." she grinned, then sobered, "thanks for the introduction."

He winked. "My pleasure."

Draping his arm around her waist, they walked back to the line of waiting taxis.

"Hey, Tess."

"Yes, Carter?"

"What would you think about me flying to Denver, say—for the next year, every weekend?"

He leaned to give her another kiss. Pausing, they stopped to hold each other as the crowd dodged around them. Finally, he stepped back and said softly, "Maybe you and I could go out to dinner those weekends—give ourselves a chance to get to know each other better?"

She nodded. "I'd say that is a definite go."

"Good." Carter suspected he already knew all he needed to know about Tess Nelson—but he wanted to enjoy their courtship. He picked up his flight bag and they continued toward the cabs, arm in arm. He glanced up at the lowering sky.

"Have you heard what the weather's going to do?"

"No," she said. "And I *don't* want to."

THE END

Dear Reader,

I wonder if you found *Stranded in Paradise* to be lighter reading than most Christian fiction? If you did, I'm glad! I truly
believe laughter is sound medicine and a gift from God. In a
world where we often experience sarcasm and bitterness, I'm
so thankful God blessed us with the escape valve that enables
us to smile in the midst of chaos and uncertainty!

So when I was asked to write a novel for the Women of
Faith Fiction series, I happily resolved to make laughter a key
ingredient in the novel. Since my husband and I visited
Hawaii for the first time early this year, I knew that tropical
location was another key ingredient for my novel. After all,
the island is pure tropical paradise—the pineapple sweet and
the vibrant rainbows a touch of heaven! But like everything
else on earth, storms occasionally disturb the island's tran-
quility. And that understanding is the books final and perhaps
most profound ingredient.

My family has been richly blessed, but we still have personal
storms that make us pause and examine our foundation. In
such times of trouble, it helps me to realize that I'm not in
charge of my day…God is. In his book *Day by Day*, Chuck
Swindol uses an illustration from the life of an oyster to aptly
describe God's role in life's troubles. "An irritation occurs when
the shell of the oyster is invaded by an alien substance—like a
grain of sand. When that happens, all the resources within the
tiny, sensitive oyster rush to the irritated spot and begin to
release healing fluids that other wise would have remained dormant. By and by the irritant is covered—by a pearl. Had there
been no interruption, there could have been no pearl."

What a comforting thought to carry us through the God appointed storms of life! Through periods when we're forced to stop and ask, Is my spiritual foundation truly sound? Will the occasional upheavals sweep away my house, or hold firm to the solid rock? I like to think that my foundation is unwavering, but when the storms come, I all too often focus on the irritant. As the storm passes and bright sunshine suddenly breaks through a wall of clouds, God is there, where he's always been, guarding my foundation. Protecting his child, creating, if not a pearl, a stronger oyster.

Swindol reminds the reader of J.B. Phillips' paraphrased James 1:2-4: "When all kinds of troubles and temptations crowd into your lives, my brothers, don't resent them as intruders, but welcome them as friends! Realize that they come to test your faith and to produce in you the quality of endurance…let the process go on until that endurance is fully developed, and you will find you have become men {and women} of mature character."

As you turn your thoughts to the discussion questions that follow, I hope you'll prayerfully reflect on the simple truths in *Stranded in Paradise*. How firm is your foundation? Is your spiritual house built on sand or solid rock?

And have you focused on the irritant or on the pearl?

I praise God for the opportunity to share my beliefs and my hope for eternity. May God richly bless each and every one of you.

Lori Copeland
Summer 2002

discussion questions/ study guide

1. In the opening chapter of *Stranded in Paradise*, Tess Nelson loses her job—the job that she had given the bulk of her time and efforts to, to which she had devoted her very *life*. Discuss how this seemingly catastrophic incident initiates a bizarre series of events—a twisted ankle, lost luggage, a hotel fire, and a hurricane, to name a few—that remarkably lead to healing and restoration for Tess.

2. Carter McConnell's early encounters with Tess are less-than-perfect. As one of the first Christian characters Tess meets, how does Carter's "bad" behavior affect Tess's concept of Christians? Could his actions be considered beneficial—lending authenticity to his character?

3. Through flashbacks to Tess's childhood memories, we see that her early life was riddled with painful experiences. Discuss how this past pain shaped Tess's personality. Was her reaction to Carter's compassion and kindness emblematic of someone with her history?

4. At what point did it become obvious that Carter and Tess were drawn to each other by more than friendship? Did Carter, knowing that she was not a believer, handle himself with the appropriate amount of restraint? Did he, at any point, allow his emotions to control his actions? Discuss.

5. Stella DeMuer is an eccentric former movie star whose husband, Edgar, was wrongfully linked to the Communist Party

in the McCarthy hearings. What influence did this elder woman's hospitality and personal story have on Tess's faith?

6. In the midst of Hurricane *Alana*, Tess does a great deal of soul-searching, considering the reality of God's love for her. What role did panic play in her eventual conversion? Do you believe panic is a common element used in evangelism? Is this good or bad?

7. Characteristic of her deliberate, thoughtful nature, Tess decides she must return home to ponder all that has happened on her ill-fated vacation before submitting herself totally to God. Was this a wise decision? Why or why not?

8. Tess Nelson's tropical vacation in Maui was supposed to be *paradise*. Yet mishap after mishap seemed to indicate that this beautiful island was anything *but* celestial. Discuss the symbolism of Paradise—what it means in superficial, earthly terms and what it means in eternal, heavenly terms.

9. Upon her return to the states, Tess visits Mona, her mother. Removing her filter of anger, Tess sees Mona's life through new eyes. How does Tess's impression of her mother change? How do you think the relationship between these two women will evolve?

10. The character of Tess Nelson truly comes full-circle— quitting a job she previously devoted herself to, reaching out to a mother she once loathed, and embracing a God she never understood. Discuss the ramifications of Tess's past decisions and how God used even her disobedience to direct the path of her life.

acknowledgments

Thanks to E. W. Woolly, who showed the Copelands Maui for the first time, and then took time to read the manuscript and give me a "second opinion." Thanks, E. W. and Linda, for rainy luaus, sandy beaches, and extra sweet pineapple.

The following Internet web sites provided important background information for this book:

Untied States Air Force Reserve

Fema for Kids: Hurricanes

Fema: Fact sheet: Hurricanes

Access Noaa: In The Eye of a Hurricane, Cmdr. Ron Philippborn, NOAA CORPS (retired)

USA Today; Weather Basics

Ask a Hurricane Hunter

Flight into a Hurricane

Astronomy and Earth Science:
The Greatest Storm on Earth

ABC News: Birth of a Hurricane

Stages of Development: The Growth of a Hurricane

the PEARL

By Angela Hunt

WestBow
PRESS

A Division of Thomas Nelson Publishers
Since 1798

visit us at www.westbowpress.com

Library of Congress Cataloging-in-Publication Data

Hunt, Angela Elwell, 1957-
        The pearl / by Angela Hunt.
            p. cm.
        ISBN 0-8499-4366-3
        1. Women in radio broadcasting--Fiction. 2. Radio broadcasters--Fiction. I. Title.
PS3558.U46747 P43 2003
813'.54--dc21   2002153181

Printed in the United States of America

So he took me in spirit to a great, high mountain, and he showed me the holy city, Jerusalem, descending out of heaven from God . . . The twelve gates were made of pearls—each gate from a single pearl! And the main street was pure gold, as clear as glass.

—JOHN THE APOSTLE, FROM REVELATION 21

One

As my prerecorded voice began extolling the virtues of a Posture Perfect Mattress, Gary Ripley, my producer, came through the doorway and shoved a stack of freshly printed hate mail beneath my nose.

"New batch." He dropped the pages onto the desk. "Thought you might want to stir something up in the next hour. The what-to-do-with-Grandma topic is getting old."

I cocked an eyebrow at him, but he only grinned and leaned against the wall, lifting his hands in a *don't-shoot-the-messenger* pose.

I picked up the first letter, which opened with a string of expletives, then pronounced me the worst excuse for a counselor the world had ever seen. *"The advice you gave that woman in Atlanta came straight from the pits of hell,"* someone, probably a man, had written. *"Leave her husband? Marriage is for better or worse, but you want to overturn God's laws and institute your own."*

I felt my cheeks burn as I leaned back in my chair. Though I had grown accustomed to vitriolic mail of all types, criticism never failed to sting. Beneath the bluster and bravado I'd adopted as part of my radio persona, I constantly worried that I would hurt someone in a reckless moment of glib patter.

"Gary"—I glanced over my shoulder—"do you remember a woman calling from Atlanta?"

"Yeah." He snapped his gum. "Yesterday. You told her to pack up and run like mad."

"That was the abuse case, right? The woman with the broken jaw?"

Gary nodded. "The husband had put her in ICU the month before. How could you forget that one?"

"I didn't forget." I fingered the edge of the paper as I studied the e-mail. "I just wanted to be sure I remembered it correctly."

No, no cause for guilt on this one. God did want us to weather good and bad in our marriages, but I have never believed he intended women to be used as punching bags. The nameless coward who had sent this note could bluster all he wanted; my counsel in that situation had been sound.

I slid the paper to the desk and glanced at the clock. Nine fifty-eight, so I still had two minutes until the top of the hour, followed by eight minutes of news and commercials. Plenty of time for a break.

I flipped through the remaining e-mails. "Anything interesting in here?"

Gary shrugged. "The usual. People calling you intolerant and a hardhearted witch. Oh, and one calling you a child-abuser."

I snorted a laugh. "Because I told that one woman to swat her kid on the rear?"

"That's the one. The lady says she's going to report you to Social Services."

"She'll have to catch me swatting my kids first." I stood and stretched, then pressed my hands to the small of my back and grinned at my producer. "My kids never need swatting. They're angels."

Gary made a face at that, but he didn't argue. Truth was, my kids *were* good kids, and he knew it. At eighteen, Brittany Jane's only major flaw was her stubborn refusal to keep food out of the cluttered cave she called a bedroom, and Scott Daniel, age five, was a bundle of pure delight.

Taking advantage of the break, I left the studio as Gary followed. We visited the coffeemaker in the snack area, filled our mugs with liquid caffeine, then stood and drank, enjoying the quiet break while keeping a careful eye on the clock.

Our building, owned by Open Air Communications, housed several radio stations—among them WUBN, the Gulf Coast's hard-rock headquarters; WSHE, soft rock from the sixties and seventies; WNAR, home of the county's best jazz; and WCTY, the voice of new country. At any given hour you could walk down the halls and peer into studio windows of a half-dozen broadcasters, all saying something different on the invisible airways that carried our words, healthy and perverse, across the nation.

Sometimes the thought left me feeling a little dizzy.

Gary took a final sip from his mug, then pointed to the clock. "Time."

I nodded, then followed him down the hall. A door swung open as we passed WCTY, allowing a stream of country music to flow through the hall. I shook my head as the lyrics followed us: *I'm so miserable without you, it's like having you here.*

As Chad Potter, our sound engineer, punched up the theme music for my show, I slipped back into the air studio and took my place behind the desk.

On the phone, a half-dozen blinking buttons flashed at me; each of them representing someone who had called and remained on hold through the commercials, the news, and the theme music. I would never cease to marvel at the patience of some callers. Most of them would hang on even through the monologue I delivered at the beginning of every segment.

As the theme music faded, I settled the headphones on my head— the better to hear my producer and sound engineer from the control room—and leaned forward on the desk.

"Welcome back, friends and neighbors, to another hour of the *Dr. Sheldon Show.* You know, some people look for flowers and robins as a herald of spring; I look for the Nordstrom catalog. I know I'll be on the cutting edge of fashion just by perusing its contents, and this year I was not disappointed. Now I know some of you may think it's not possible to be fashionable by osmosis, but I beg to differ. I mean, what is fashion, but clothing that's *in* one year and *out* the next? Right now my closet is stuffed with things from when I first got married, so something tells me I'm about to ride the crest of high fashion once again."

I paused to pick up my notepad, then ruffled the pages in front of the mike. "As I flipped through the catalog this year, though, one group of products confused me. I don't know if you've seen these things in the stores yet, but what is the deal with toe toppers and foot tubes? I mean, have you *seen* those things? I suppose they're for wearing with slides and sandals, but they kind of defeat the purpose. The toe toppers—I know, it's hard to imagine anything with that silly a name being practical—are half a sock. They start at the toe like an ordinary sock, and end at the arch of your foot. Now I ask you, what is that about? Do you wear them with high-heeled, elegant sandals? And have this terrycloth *thing* hanging out?"

Silently I counted out a beat, then laughed. "And foot tubes—have you seen *those*? They're like the calf warmers we all bought when that Jennifer Beals movie came out . . . you know, the woman welder who wanted to—*Flashdance*, that was it. Anyway, these foot tubes are like calf warmers, but they cover only the middle part of your foot. Your tootsies and your heels are still left out in the cold to freeze or sweat, depending on whether you're wearing them in Montana or Florida."

Looking through the rectangular window that opened into the control room, I saw Gary holding a hand over his face. Because he knew women comprised the majority of my audience, he tolerated my female-oriented monologues, but just barely.

"Toe toppers and foot tubes." I breathed a heavy sigh into the mike. "Somebody please tell me this fad will pass."

I glanced up at the list of names on the computer monitor, then pressed the first button on the beige plastic phone. "Carla! Welcome to the show."

"Dr. Diana! Goodness, I can't believe I'm really talking to you."

I cast Gary a *didn't-you-tell-her-to-get-to-the-point?* look, then shoe-horned a smile into my voice. "Have you seen those toe toppers in the stores yet?"

"No—and I agree, they sound silly."

"I think so. But how can I help you today?"

"It's my mother—I mean mother-in-law. She's mousy—I mean *mouthy*—good grief, I'm nervous!"

"Calm down, Carla. We haven't lost a caller yet." I glanced up at the computer screen, where next to Carla's name Gary had typed *MIL insults her constantly. Advice?*

Though the woman might be nervous simply because she was on the radio, I knew her anxiety might also have arisen from the fact that her mother-in-law could be listening . . . so I'd have bet my bottom dollar that *Carla* wasn't her real name.

My caller exhaled into the phone, eliciting an agonized expression from Chad at the soundboard.

"Okay. It's like this—I love my husband, I really do, but his mother is driving me crazy. Everything I do, she has to criticize—my clothes, my cooking, the way I keep house. I have a job, you see, so what does it matter if the shelves get a little dusty? Her son doesn't read books anyway, so what does she care? And lately Joe and I have been talking about having a baby—"

"Joe is your husband?"

"Yes. Sorry, I should have said that."

"And how long have you been married?"

"Six months." She exhaled another deep breath, obviously grateful that I had taken control of the conversation.

Flashing a grin at Chad, I silently tapped the windscreen on my microphone with two fingers, reminding him that I knew better than to huff and puff into his expensive equipment.

"I'm glad you called, Carla, and I'm glad you didn't wait to address this issue. Because if you allow this situation to continue, you will be dealing with the problem for as long as your marriage lasts—which, in my opinion, won't be long past your fifth anniversary. Men who allow their mothers to criticize their wives tend to lose their wives' respect, and respect is one of the most important ingredients in marriage."

I paused a moment to let my words take hold. "Let me ask you this, Carla—do you know much about your mother-in-law's history?"

"Um . . . not really. Should I?"

"It might be helpful. We'll talk about your husband in a moment, but first let me remind you of one of my favorite profound sayings. Are you ready?"

"Yeah, sure."

"Here it is: Hurt people . . . hurt people."

In the control room, Chad played the blast of a trumpet, the usual sound effect for one of what he called *Dr. Diana's pronouncements*.

Grinning at him, I pulled the mike closer. "If your mother-in-law is honestly vindictive toward you, she may be acting out of pain. Somewhere, someone has hurt her badly, and she has not yet learned how to deal with that hurt. You may be the source of her pain, through some direct or indirect action, or her issues may spring from something completely unrelated to you."

"So what do I *do* about it?"

"You do this—first, you ask your mother-in-law if you've done something to offend her. Say you've noticed that she seems out of sorts around you, and ask if you can do something to make things right. If she names something—say, for example, you inadvertently ran over her petunias—then apologize and offer to replant her flowers. If, on the other hand, she denies her attitude or says you've done nothing to hurt her feelings, then your conscience should be clear.

"Second, you talk to your husband and tell him you love him dearly, you admire him to death, but you married him, not his mother. So the next time his mother criticizes you, if he doesn't politely excuse himself and lead you out of Mama's presence, he'll be disappointing you tremendously. Leave and cleave, Carla—that's what marriage is about. Leaving the parental nest and cleaving to your spouse. If your husband doesn't want to be firm in the face of his mother's wailing—and believe me, she will wail the first few times he stands up to her—then you'll just have to resign yourself to the fact that you married a spineless mama's boy."

In the control room, Chad clicked a key and sent the wail of a frustrated baby over the airwaves.

I grinned at him while Carla sputtered protestations. "But I thought men who took care of their mothers were, like, *programmed* to take care of their wives! My mother always said I should notice how a boy treats his mom, and he was always so deferential to her—"

"There's a vast difference between treating a woman with respect and kowtowing to her every demand." I lowered my voice and leaned closer to the microphone. "I know it's not easy, Carla, but your husband might need a *lot* of encouragement before he'll be able to stand up to his mom. I wish you'd noticed his disposition toward docility while you were dating."

"I did notice his—whatever you said. But I was sure he'd change once we were married."

"Men don't change, sweetie, apart from acts of God. They fossilize."

I cocked my index finger toward Chad, who clicked the next button and took us into commercial. After pulling the headphones from my ears, I picked up the telephone. The promo for Nutriment Weight Loss Solutions dropped to a muted mumble when Chad saw I held the receiver.

"Carla," I spoke into the phone, "we're off the air now. Listen, dear, I'm not saying you should give up on your husband. I'm saying you and Joe need to open the lines of communication. Tell him you love him, make him feel like your protector. That's probably all he needs to rise to the task. If you make him feel like he can take on the world, taking on his mama will be a lot easier."

"I'll try." Carla sniffled into the phone, a sound I'd heard a thousand times, but still it got to me. "Thanks, Dr. Diana."

"You're welcome, sweetie. God bless."

I disconnected the call, then glanced at the computer monitor where a queue of bright green rectangles listed all holding callers. Gary moved interesting people straight to the top of the list; he relegated weirdos or off-topic calls to the bottom.

Rarely did we resort to bottom-feeding.

Four callers were now waiting—according to Gary's notes, the woman at the top of the queue was dealing with a blended family, the man after her was calling about a troubled sixteen-year-old, and the name beneath his belonged to ten-year-old Tiffany, who wanted to ask a question for her school report. The last caller, Lela, was wondering about the wisdom of leaving her money to a spoiled grandchild.

Lifting a brow, I peered through the rectangular window before Gary's desk. Lela was bound to strike a nerve with my local audience, so she must have sounded like a real dud to earn last place in the lineup. Though my show was syndicated and broadcast on sixty-two stations nationwide—with new stations signing on every week—the folks in Tampa cared deeply about elder issues. Probably 75 percent of the people in my local listening audience were retired snowbirds, particularly in this month of March.

Through the wide windows separating me from the technical brains of my program I could see Chad, my engineer, hunched over his board, his magic fingers adjusting knobs and sliders whose functions remained a mystery to me even after five years in radio. Gary, my producer and call screener, hunched over the phone, his brow crinkled in concentration as he greeted another caller. His hands moved to the keyboard, and in a moment he'd click *enter* and send the information to me.

As the commercial played out, I settled the headset back on my head and glanced at the computer screen. I didn't often buck Gary's suggested order, but I wasn't in the mood to discuss blended families. The ten-year-old might be more fun.

I clicked the button for line three as the intro music faded away. "Tiffany, honey, are you there? This is Dr. Diana."

A heavy breath whooshed into the phone, then, "Hello?"

"Hello, Tiffany. Did you have a question to ask me?"

More heavy breathing, followed by a decidedly childish giggle. "Is it really you?"

"It really is. And I hear you have some kind of school report to write?"

Another loud exhalation. "Yes."

"What's your topic?"

Yet another heavy sigh. "Dr. Diana."

I laughed. "You're doing a report on me? Well, sweetie, I hope you're kinder than my critics. Is there something special you wanted to know about me?"

"Yes."

I smiled. "And that is?"

"Ask the question, dummy. She's waiting."

Despite Tiffany's obvious proximity to the phone, I had no trouble hearing a woman's sharp voice. A second later, Tiffany exhaled again, then asked, "Do you have any pets?"

I clenched my fist, wishing for a moment that I could climb through the phone line and speak a few strong words to whoever would burden this tender ten-year-old with a label like *dummy*.

"Yes, sweetheart, I have a pet." I spoke in the warmest tone I could manage. "I have a Chinese pug, a little guy we call Terwilliger. He spends most of his time in my son's room, 'cause they're the same age. They're best friends."

Tiffany laughed, a lovely two-noted giggle. "He sounds cute."

"He is, honey, and he's smart, too. Sometimes people look at him and think he's not so smart, 'cause he has this little mashed-in face, but they're wrong about him. Terwilliger—we call him Twiggy for short— is a great little dog. And he doesn't care what people think, 'cause he knows he's okay in my book." I hesitated. "You understand, sweetie?"

"Uh-huh."

"Is that all you need from me?"

"Uh-huh."

The woman's voice shrilled again in the background: "Say thank you, idiot, and get off the phone."

Rage burned my cheeks. "Who is that, Tiffany? Your mom?"

"Uh-huh."

"May I speak to her, please?"

No answer but the clunking sounds of a telephone in transit. A second later the woman's voice came over the phone, the sharp edges smoothed away. "Hello?"

"Are you Tiffany's mother?"

"Why, yes, I am."

"She's a charming little girl."

"Why, thank you."

"What's your first name, dear?"

"Anna."

"Well, Anna, I don't know your situation, and I suppose I could be way off base, but I do know this—your daughter deserves better than you're giving her now. Maybe you're having a bad day or something, but no child responds well to words like *dummy* and *idiot*. What I've heard from you in the space of two minutes amounts to verbal abuse—"

A definite click snapped in my ear. I glanced up at Gary, who shrugged as if to say *she's gone.*

"Well, folks," I said, aware that Tiffany and her mom might still be listening. "Let's remember one thing, shall we? Sticks and stones may not break bones, but they certainly can wound a spirit. If you have to give your child a nickname, let it be something endearing. My husband has always called our daughter *sweetness*, and"—I forced a laugh—"he calls me *gorgeous*, whether I measure up to the name or not. But he makes me *feel* gorgeous, and that's what we need to do for our loved ones . . . give them room to soar."

Pressing the next button, which took us into a twenty-second pre-recorded bit of patter, I glanced at the call screen, where a new name had appeared at the top of the queue. Gary's thin voice filled my right ear: "A live one coming through. Be careful—he may be a crank."

"Got it."

I read the detail line, where Gary had typed: *Tom—thinks his wife is planning to leave him. Sounds desperate.*

Nodding, I picked up a pencil and tapped it to the syncopated rhythm of my ten-second lead-in, a hyped-up, whispered version of my name recorded over a funky Latin beat.

I felt good. The morning had offered a string of interesting calls, all practical problems without a single tedious question about capital punishment, politics, or abortion. I had strong opinions on those issues, but so did my callers, so the resulting merry-go-round resulted in frustrating radio for host and audience alike. On the few occasions callers did manage to bring up one of the irresolvable topics, I usually ended up having to cut them off, particularly if they became abusive. I didn't mind disconnecting rude callers, but afterward I always had to spend another hour defending my actions to well-meaning folks who thought "free speech" meant "free access to the airwaves."

As the intro died down, I punched the button for line one. "Hi, Tom! Thanks for calling the show."

"Dr. Diana?" The voice came out garbled, as if the man were strangling on repressed emotions. His tone, coupled with Gary's warning, raised my adrenaline level a couple of percentage points.

I straightened in my chair. "I'm here, Tom. Did you want to tell me about your wife?"

"She's leaving me."

I waited only a second for him to continue, then hurried to fill the dead air. "How do you know she's leaving?"

"She's outside putting suitcases in the car. And she's taking my little girl with her."

I looked up at Gary, who crossed his arms and nodded.

"Tom"—I rested my elbows on the desk—"I'm not sure there's anything I can do for you at this moment. Have you talked to your wife about why she wants to leave?"

"Yeah. She's found another man—she's moving in with him. I told her it would just about kill me if she left, but she doesn't care."

"I'm sure she cares, Tom, but perhaps she's confused at the moment."

"She doesn't give a flip."

I stiffened at something I heard in his voice, something jagged and sharp.

"She doesn't even care that I got the gun out of the dresser drawer. She saw me pull it out, but she just kept moving toward the car, dragging my daughter with her."

I pressed my hands to the headphones as the muscles in my chest constricted. "You have a gun?"

"Right here in my hand. It's loaded, too."

I looked at Gary, whose concerned expression had intensified to panic. Chad, on the other hand, looked almost gleeful at the prospect of unexpected drama.

"Tom, you need to put the gun away. You must have frightened your wife; perhaps that's why she's leaving with your daughter."

"I'd never hurt them." He paused, his words hanging in the silence as if he'd paused to question his own statement, then he pressed on. "But I'm going to kill myself. And when she comes back into the room to see if she's forgotten anything, she'll find me lying here. And maybe she'll pick up the phone, and you can tell her why I did it."

I braced my hands against the edge of the desk. "Whoa, Tom. I don't think I can cooperate with your plan. And we shouldn't rush into anything."

Oh sweet Jesus, I need you now.

My mind raced backward at warp speed, summoning up the standard protocols in crisis counseling. When a patient threatens suicide, the counselor has to stay calm. Remove the weapon if possible. Take charge. Insist you're not going to leave, you will get help, and anything is better than suicide. Be loving, but above all, be firm.

Silently praying for wisdom, I leaned into the microphone. "I'm glad you called, Tom, because I want to help you through this. You've gone through a lot today, but this is not going to be the end of your world, you understand? Your wife is leaving. But even if she drives away with your daughter, she can never take away the special relationship between you and your child. You'll always be her father, right?"

As Tom mumbled incoherently, I picked up my notepad. Grabbing a Sharpie someone had left on the desk, I wrote *CALLER ID?* in block letters, then ripped out the page and flashed it toward the window. Gary read the note, then nodded.

"Yeah, I'll always be her father." Tom was weeping now, his ragged voice scraping like sandpaper against my ears. "But I don't want her to remember me like this."

The adage I had so glibly recited only a few moments before flittered through my brain: *Hurt people . . . hurt people.* Would Tom hurt someone before the day ended?

I scrawled *CALL 911* on another page, then yanked it from the notebook and held it up. Gary made the OK sign, then hunched over the phone.

I had to keep Tom talking. "You don't want her to remember you like *what?*" I gentled my voice. "Tom, I know you're confused, but you have to see the illogic in your statement. You don't want your daughter to remember you as sad and upset, but would you rather she remember you as a bloody corpse on the living room floor?"

"I'm in the kitchen." I could barely understand the words through his sobbing.

"Think, friend. Let your daughter remember you as a man who recovered from a temporary loss and grew strong enough to be the father she needed as she grew up. How old is your daughter, Tom?"

More weeping, then, "Four."

"Four? Oh, Tom!" I released a dramatic sigh, a breathy stream of air that defeated the purpose of Chad's prized windscreen. "You haven't had time to see her lose her first tooth, walk to her first day of kindergarten, or smile at her first boyfriend. Don't you want to be around when she goes on her first date? Even if you're not with your wife, don't you want to be nearby when your daughter wants to talk to someone about her relationship with her boyfriend? Don't you want to be the man who walks her down the aisle on her wedding day?"

He did not answer, but I wouldn't give up—not as long as I could hear him sniffling.

I had to distract him. "I have two children, Tom. A son and a daughter. I don't talk about them much on the program because my daughter's at the age where she doesn't want to admit she even has parents."

Dead silence on the other end of the line. A flicker of apprehension coursed through my bloodstream, then I heard another sniff.

He was still with me. Frantic, I pointed at Gary, giving him the sign to open his mike. I needed feedback from someone, and I didn't want to pull words from Tom if he didn't feel like making small talk.

"My kids," I said, giving Gary purposeful direction. "They're something, aren't they?"

Gary shot me a deer-in-the-headlights look through the window, then leaned into his mike. "Your daughter's a wonderful girl."

I sent him a grateful smile. "Yes, she is. And that, ladies and gentlemen, is the seldom-heard voice of Gary Ripley, my producer. Gary's listening, too, Tom, and we're going to get you some help."

"I don't want help." Tom's whisper was faint and flat, the voice of defeat. "Thanks for trying, Dr. Diana, but if you'll just tell my wife why I did it—"

"My son, however, loves having his mother around—then again, he's only five." I pressed on, not wanting to give Tom an opportunity to sign off. If I could keep him listening, even arouse a little indignation, the emergency rescue personnel Gary had called—*please, God, let no snafus arise on that end*—would have time to reach my distraught caller.

I rattled on as if I hadn't heard Tom's last words. "Most five-year-olds are wise enough to realize they didn't spring from the primordial ooze and parents had something to do with their appearance on earth. My daughter, on the other hand, has decided that eighteen equals complete maturity and she should be allowed to do as she pleases."

Gary's wide eyes warned me away from the topic—talk of the tumultuous teen years would not comfort a suicidal caller.

I backed away and tried another approach. "What's your daughter's name, Tom?"

He hesitated, cleared his throat, then said, "Casey."

"That's a lovely name. Is she your only child?"

"Yeah."

"Children are wonderful, aren't they? I didn't think I would ever be a mother. My husband and I were married five years before we became parents, and our first child arrived through adoption. For three years we tried to create a biological child, then the doctors told us the odds of pregnancy were pretty much one in a million. So because we wanted a baby more than a pregnancy, we adopted our beautiful daughter. I thought our family was complete, but apparently God had other ideas. Twelve years later, surprise! The rabbit died—or, in this technologically advanced age, I suppose I should say the home pregnancy test proved positive. My husband and I found ourselves on the receiving end of an unexpected pregnancy, and now when I look at my son I see undeniable proof that God still works miracles. My boy is a little angel, as delightful as any kid you'd ever want to meet . . . and I'll bet he's a lot like your Casey."

I glanced toward the control room, hoping Gary would have some sort of update for me, but he had turned away, concentrating on whatever he was telling someone on the phone. His voice was a dull murmur in my headphones, not clear enough for me to catch his words.

Without missing a beat, I returned to the tale of my family's creation, a story I'd told a number of times at pro-life rallies and mother-
daughter banquets. For security reasons I rarely talked about my
family on the air, but this was an exceptional occasion.

"I love my children, Tom, and I'm sure you love your Casey, too.
I'd lay down my life for my kids, no doubt about it, but I know it's
also important that I be there for them. Because I want to be around
for my daughter's wedding, I try to eat right and exercise a couple of
times a week. Because I want to be able to play ball with my son, I
don't smoke. In a way, I guess you could say I'm living for them—and
I know you are, too. When parents love their children, living for them
just comes naturally. Wouldn't you agree?"

More sniffling sounds, followed by a muffled, "Yeah."

"That's great, Tom. I'm glad you feel that way, too." I forced what
I hoped was a relaxed laugh. "Just this morning my little boy bounced
into my room and woke me by covering my face with kisses. At first
I thought I was dreaming, but when I opened my eyes, he was standing beside me in his little pajamas, dragging his monkey by one arm.
I asked what he was doing, and he said, 'I'm kissing you good morning, Mommy. You kiss me good night, don't you?'"

My next laugh wasn't at all forced. "Isn't that sweet, Tom? I'll bet
your Casey sometimes does things like that." I narrowed my eyes, listening intently, then smiled when I heard his reply.

"Yeah, sometimes she does. She likes to stand on my feet when we
dance. 'Course it's not really dancing—it's me rocking back and forth
while she stands on my boots and hangs on to keep from falling off."

Frantic hand-waving from Gary's window caught my eye. He
pointed toward Chad, who was holding up a sign: *SWAT TEAM
OUTSIDE THE HOUSE.*

I closed my eyes as my uneasiness shifted into a deeper and more
immediate fear.

"Tom, I need you to do something for me. You called today to
talk, and I've enjoyed our conversation very much. But I'm in the

business of providing help, so we have done our best to help you. I've just learned some people have arrived outside your house."

"What kind of people?" An edge in his voice verged on the threatening. Apparently Tom couldn't see out a window from where he stood.

"Well, your wife and daughter are out there, right? You said they were outside. Have they come back into the house?"

"Nobody's come in."

"Did you hear the car leave?"

"I didn't hear anything. The windows are closed, 'cause it's cold outside."

He definitely wasn't calling from Florida.

"I'm glad it's quiet. Listen, Tom, I want you to put the phone down and go outside to see if your daughter and wife are still in the driveway. But before you go, promise me you'll leave your gun on the kitchen table—we wouldn't want to frighten Casey with it, would we?"

The edge melted away, leaving only soft concern. "I wouldn't want to do that."

"Fine. Leave the gun on the table, Tom, and step out the front door. Make sure Casey is okay and give her a hug for me."

I winced as the phone rattled against something hard—probably the kitchen counter—and the studio went silent as we held our breaths and listened. Perhaps this was the one occasion where dead air would not be a curse.

I slid my hand toward the next button, wondering if we should go to commercial in case something went drastically wrong. I glanced at Gary, who was staring up at the clock, counting the seconds. Ten . . . fifteen . . . twenty.

Hurt people . . . hurt people.

How long would it take to subdue a man? Surely longer than it would take to *shoot* one . . .

I glanced at the computer screen. Chad had cued a station promo to run next. In five more seconds I would hit the next button and go with the promo, but—

Gary's voice buzzed in my ear. "Diana? Why are you waiting?"

"I don't know why I'm waiting." I spoke into the mike, filling some of the dead air. "I just think I should."

We heard sounds—muffled voices, a shout, and odd clunking noises. I flinched as a new male voice rumbled over the phone line. "Is this Dr. Diana?"

"It is. Who are you?"

"Sergeant Michelson, of the Memphis police. We're in the house."

"And Tom? The man I was speaking to?"

"One of our officers subdued him, and he's safe. We're taking him to a hospital for a psych exam."

From the control booth, Chad triumphantly punched the next button, and a glance at the clock told me why he'd been quick to cut off the conversation. Local news aired at the top and bottom of every hour, and a suicidal man in Memphis, Tennessee, didn't qualify as local news.

I picked up the receiver to continue my conversation with the police officer. "We're off the air now, Sergeant. Were the wife and daughter outside?"

"They were gone by the time we arrived. But after the 911 call came in, we kept listening to your show so we'd know what was happening inside the house. When he went out the front door, two of our people went in the back to secure the weapon."

"Thank goodness." I leaned back in my chair as relief flooded my bones. "And you'll make sure he gets help? Unless he does, he may try something again, Sergeant. And suicidal people don't always use a gun."

The cop's short bark of laughter had a bitter edge. "Tell me something I don't know, Doc. But thanks for your help."

I hung up the phone, then paused to bow my head. As the newscaster in the next studio read the news, I exhaled a deep breath and let the Spirit pray for me. The best I could manage was a heartfelt, "Thank you, Lord, for averting a tragedy."

When I finally looked up, I leaned into the mike to ask Chad to run the long promo and a two-minute sound bite after the news. I needed a quick trip to the ladies' room and a splash of cold water on my wrists.

I slipped off the tall, padded chair and moved toward the doorway, waving to Gary as I left. If the SWAT team had fired upon Tom or he'd gone outside with his gun, that call would have resulted in an unmitigated disaster . . .

Heaven had smiled on me this morning.

Two

DR. STEVE SHELDON EXITED THE SMALL STOREROOM his staff jokingly referred to as his *prayer closet*. The appellation was not off the mark, because he often retreated to the confined room when he needed a quiet place to pray. His tiny office held too many files and charts to be closed off when he needed real sanctuary, yet sanctuary—and silence—was what he'd wanted when he realized his wife had a seriously disturbed caller on the line.

He'd been listening, as he always did, on a pocket-sized transistor radio left over from his college days. The small and unobtrusive earpiece allowed him to work while he listened to Diana's show, a far better option than flooding his office with topics that were often not suitable for the ears of young children. Most of the time he was able to concentrate on his patients and listen to Diana in the background; this morning, however, he'd been in the middle of filling a cavity when he realized his wife was facing serious trouble.

He had immediately finished with his patient, handed the chart to Melanie Brown, his dental hygienist, and retreated to the storeroom. Melanie must have realized the source of his distraction, for she didn't once rap on the door to disturb his concentration. His patients could wait, and they did—children rarely clamored to greet their dentist.

Now he sidled past Melanie and grinned at six-year-old Joseph Walker, who sat in the reclining chair like a stiff-armed plastic doll. "Hey, Joseph." Steve perched on a padded rolling stool. "Miss Melanie tells me you have a beautiful smile. Mind if I take a look?"

The clearly petrified kid nodded, then slowly lowered his jaw until a quarter-inch gap appeared between his lips.

"Sorry, partner." Steve grinned at the boy, then pulled the surgical mask over his face. "But you're going to have to give me a crocodile-sized smile so I can see all your choppers."

With an agonized expression, Joseph Walker complied, his gaze rolling up to the ceiling.

"My son's only a little younger than you." Steve pressed a gloved fingertip to the edge of the boy's upper teeth. "And he's already lost a tooth, can you believe it? I thought he'd wait until six to lose his first tooth, but he's growing up real fast. He already likes the Tampa Bay Bucs and can name every player in the starting lineup—with a little prompting."

Steve's gaze drifted toward the boy's eyes in case a spark of interest flickered there. But as the metal tip of his probe encountered the enamel of a bicuspid, Joseph's eyelids lowered and clamped tight. But the brave lad spoke.

"I loss a toof when I was five." The blue eyes opened and sought Steve's.

"Then you're a big boy just like my Scotty." Steve smiled, hoping to offer reassurance, but he knew the sight of smiling eyes above a surgical mask would likely do little to ease Joseph's tension.

Better to hurry and put the kid out of his misery. Keeping up a steady stream of comforting chitchat, Steve checked the molars, asked Joseph to bite down, and noticed that the boy already had a sizable overbite. With his small jaw, he would definitely need braces in a few years.

No need to mention orthodontia to Joseph. Mrs. Walker would need to know, though.

Steve dropped his probe onto the tray, then clapped his hands.

"You're all done, kiddo." Snapping off his rubber gloves, he rolled them into a ball and tossed them toward the trash can, which Melanie opened at the appropriate instant.

"What teamwork—you, me, and Miss Melanie." Steve unhooked the paper shield from the boy's neck. "Together we'll keep those cavities away, okay? So when you're as old as I am, you'll have all your own teeth."

Joseph nodded wordlessly.

"Good boy. Now, Miss Melanie's going to give you a toothbrush, a tube of toothpaste, and let you pick a toy from the treasure chest. I'm going to go to the desk and talk to your mom. You're doing a good job on the brushing, Joseph, so keep up the fine work."

Joseph slid out of the chair and followed Melanie to the playroom while Steve met Mrs. Walker at the reception desk. As she frowned and wrote out the check, he explained the boy's future need for orthodontia. "He has a small jaw and a sizable overbite. He's still growing, but I think within the next couple of years you should take him to an orthodontist for an evaluation."

Mrs. Walker's brow lowered like a thundercloud. "How can you know that when he doesn't even have his permanent teeth?"

Steve forced a polite smile. "Baby teeth are smaller than permanent teeth, and his teeth are already crowded. He'll be fine for a while, but since orthodontia is expensive, I want you to be prepared."

Mrs. Walker sighed loudly, then handed her check to the receptionist. "If it's not one thing, it's another. I don't know why I ever wanted to have kids. They're costing me a fortune."

"They *are* expensive," Steve agreed, backing away. "But they're worth it, don't you think?"

Mrs. Walker heaved a weary sigh as she turned on her heel. "Ask me later, Doc, after I've had my dinner and a cup of coffee."

He watched in bemused dismay as Mrs. Walker called her son from the playroom, then pulled him toward the front door. Melanie witnessed the scene, then approached the reception desk.

"Makes you wonder about American motherhood, doesn't it?"

Steve shook his head. "Don't judge Mrs. Walker too harshly. She has six others like Joseph at home, and each one of them either has or will need orthodontia."

He grinned at his hygienist, knowing she had a twelve-year-old son. Over the six months she'd worked for him, he had learned that her husband had walked out on them years ago, but she seemed to manage single motherhood as well as any woman he'd ever met. "Tell me, Melanie, do you ever wonder why you had kids?"

Her blue eyes sparkled. "Oh, I know why. 'Cause I got swept off my feet by a fast-talking, two-timing, no-good glob of bucket slime."

Steve tilted his head, not quite sure how to respond, but she patted his arm. "Don't you worry about me, Dr. Steve. My boy B.J. and I are doin' just fine. As long as he doesn't drive me crazy wanting the latest Nintendo game, we'll make it."

She crinkled her nose and looked toward the receptionist. "You got more kids for us to torture, Gerta?"

Gerta Poppovitch, the woman who'd been administrating the office for the last fifteen years, ignored the hygienist and fixed Steve in a steely glare. "For you, Dr. Steve, Tommy Oliphant has been waiting ten minutes in room two." She slid a bright yellow chart across the blue Formica counter. "And for you, Melanie, here's the chart on Audrey Williams, a real charmer. On her last visit she bit our hygienist."

Melanie pretended to shudder. "I suppose it's a good thing my tetanus shots are up to date."

As she stepped forward to get the chart, Steve checked his watch. Diana was beginning the third hour of her show. At noon he'd have to call and congratulate her on a problem handled well.

Whistling, he moved down the hall to where Tommy Oliphant waited.

Three

GARY RIPLEY LEANED BACK IN HIS CHAIR AND GRINNED at the string of lights. All ten phone lines were blinking; they hadn't stopped since the SWAT team intercepted Tennessee Tom in the last hour. Diana had come back on the air and continued, cool as a cucumber, but Gary had been sweating bullets the entire time she talked to the suicidal man. It was a good thing she pulled it off, a *great* thing, or the press would be calling her "Dr. Death" or "Dr. Die" from this day forward.

A phone line at the far right of the bank of buttons began to blink. For an instant he stared at it, wondering how a caller had managed to access one of their private lines, then he hurried to press the key.

"Morning Show."

"Is this Ripley? Diana Sheldon's producer?"

"Yeah—can I help you?"

"Conrad Wexler, vice president in charge of network talk shows. Just wanted you to tell Diana we've heard about what happened on your show this morning—"

Gary's stomach clenched.

"—and we're amazingly proud of her. My assistant is trying to get the story to the TV networks for some prime-time airplay. Shoot, if

Barbara Walters can do a special on that ten-year-old kid who foiled a bank robbery in Houston, she can certainly do one on the talk-radio shrink who stopped a family massacre in Tennessee."

Gary looked at Chad, who was oblivious to everything but Diana's chatter.

"It, um, wasn't exactly a massacre, sir. The guy was threatening to kill himself."

"But his wife and family were outside, right? And he had a loaded gun?"

"Um, yeah. Apparently."

"And in the good doctor's professional opinion, could the situation have escalated?"

Gary glanced through the window at Diana, who was trying to convince a woman that wearing a formal white gown to her fifth wedding wasn't such a good idea.

"I'll have to ask her. I do know she was nervous."

"Then it was certainly a *potential* massacre, and our Dr. Diana averted it. That guy could have gone outside and killed the wife and kid, then turned the gun on himself. He could have taken out one of the SWAT guys. It happens all the time—I read about something similar in the paper just last week."

Gary bit his lip, not wanting to argue with a head honcho. Wexler had to be calling from L.A., headquarters of the Prime Radio Network and home to all the big-name national radio talk shows. Diana was only a small star in the Prime Radio crown, but today might bring her an opportunity to shine a little brighter . . . which would reflect nicely on her producer.

"Prime-time TV would be great, sir." Gary swiveled his chair to keep his star in view. "Diana would be a natural."

"I know she would. You tell her I called, and keep us in the loop if you hear anything else from Tennessee. Maybe we should think about changing the focus of her show—what would happen if we made it more suicide-centered?"

Gary made a face. "I, um, don't think she'd buy that, sir. She wants to keep the show focused on family problems."

"So where do you think suicides come from? Messed-up families."

Gary studied the dusty ceiling tiles before answering. "I think Diana would say she wants to help families *before* they get majorly messed up. Besides, if we did nothing but suicides, we'd be bound to lose a few. And people get sued for things like that."

Wexler fell silent for an instant. "You're right, the liability would kill us. But the drama, man, the drama!" He blew into the phone. "Well, you tell her I called and to keep up the good work. You, too, kid. You'll hear from us."

Gary opened his mouth to say good-bye, but the phone had already gone dead. He dropped the receiver to the desk and glanced up at the caller screen—Diana was now talking to a fifteen-year-old girl whose mother wouldn't let her get a tattoo.

"It's *my* body," the girl was saying. "And if I want a tattoo, I don't see why I can't get one."

"At fifteen," Diana said, "you're only a shadow of the person you will one day be. Your tastes will change as you grow older, and the tattoo you love today may be the mistake you hate in twenty years. Listen to your mother, sweetheart, and keep the peace at home. When you're older and on your own, if you still feel you *must* have a tattoo, then you'll be able to get one. But until that time comes, remember one thing—Mama knows best."

Gary grinned. Part Erma Bombeck, part Dr. Laura, and part Emily Post, Diana had an answer for everything and everybody. Despite her show's growing popularity, until this morning she had been one of the best-kept secrets in America.

Now he had a feeling everything was about to change.

four

BRITTANY SHELDON PULLED HER BOOKS TO HER CHEST and leaned forward, one sneakered foot flat on the floor, the other flexed to propel her out the door.

As the bell chimed, she rose with thirty classmates. "Hold it," Mrs. Parker called. "Read the last three pages of *Hamlet* for homework. Find out what happens to the prince—and count on a quiz tomorrow."

Brittany moved toward the door, then rolled her eyes as her best friend, Charisse Logan, fell into step beside her. "Gonna read that play?"

"No."

Charisse grinned. "Gonna fail the quiz?"

"Probably."

"And you don't care?"

"Got that right."

They followed the crowd into the hallway, where sunlight streamed over the sidewalk and spilled onto the dented lockers clinging like barnacles to the walls of Seminole High School. After finding her own locker, Brittany twirled the dial as Charisse leaned against a concrete pillar and snapped her gum.

"I hate Mrs. Parker. Did you see that skirt she had on? I'll bet she's had it since the eighties. I swear, I think the fabric was plastic."

"Mrs. Parker is retarded." Brittany slammed her heavy English book into the locker and wondered why she'd even bothered to carry it to class. She was practically cross-eyed from reading Shakespeare and all those stuffy British writers Mrs. Parker adored. Why couldn't they read something *interesting* for a change?

A squeal cut through the roar and crash of students and slamming lockers. "Brittany Sheldon!"

"Oh, brother."

She turned in time to see Sierra Smith threading her way through a group of sophomore geeks. Sierra, an eleventh-grade varsity cheerleader who seemed to bounce through the halls even when she wasn't wearing sneakers, was so perpetually bubbly she wouldn't recognize a snub if you got in her face and told her to take a flying leap.

Charisse lifted a brow. "What do you think *she* wants?"

Brittany snorted. "Probably wants us to sell flowers or something for the prom."

Apparently oblivious even to the goofy looks from the geeks, Sierra kept coming. Finally she stood beside them, a positively putrid package of perkiness. "I'm so glad I caught you girls! Did you hear the news?"

Brittany modeled a look of exaggerated curiosity. "Golly gee, what news?"

The cheerleader beamed. "Your mother! She saved some guy's life on the radio this morning. He had a gun and everything, but she managed to talk him out of killing himself while somebody called the police."

Brittany glanced at Charisse. "And how would you know about it?"

"Mrs. Hamilton plays the radio in the library every morning, and she let us listen when things got interesting. It was so awesome! Now they're giving updates on the news every hour—"

Cutting Sierra off with an uplifted hand, Brittany gave her a plastic smile. "Thanks, Sierra. You're so right. I have the coolest mom!"

She waited until the bubbly girl bounced away, then suddenly unsmiled. "Let's get out of here."

Charisse slowed her gum-chewing. "You wanna ditch?"

"You bet." Brittany glanced over her shoulder, then set out toward the parking lot with long strides. Her pickup truck waited there, her chariot of escape.

Charisse double-timed to keep up. "But—"

"There'll never be a better day," Brittany said, thinking aloud. "I heard about my mom's little adventure, you see? And I was so upset I forgot to check out or call to get permission to go home. All I have to do is tell Mom I was worried about her, and she'll write me an excuse." She shook her head. "I feel like such a stupid baby. I can't go to the bathroom without a note from my mother."

"Join the crowd," Charisse said, then added: "So it'll be okay if your friend goes with you?"

Brittany shrugged. "You're upset, too, and you want to keep me company. If your mom doesn't buy that, I'll have my mom call her. No problem."

"But where do we go? Your mom'll be home in a couple of hours, and my mom is probably still in bed—"

"We go to the beach." Brittany tilted her face toward the sun, already hot and bright. "And we start working on our summer tans."

Charisse's narrow face beamed. "I like the way you think, girl."

"Thinking's easy"—Brittany narrowed her eyes as they moved from the mob on the sidewalk into the unpopulated parking lot—"when your mother is a flippin' genius."

five

"YOU WERE JUST TOO COOL, DR. SHELDON."

"Thank you, Charity, but I was only doing my job." Charity from Buffalo was a regular caller with a penchant for sharing quotable quips, and I knew she had called with more on her mind than praise for my performance earlier that morning. Gary was doing his best to screen all the gushing calls.

I glanced at the clock. We were winding down, and I hoped Charity had something worthwhile to share as we moved into the close. "What's on your mind today?"

"As I listened to your program, I couldn't help but think about oysters. Do you know much about oysters, Dr. Sheldon?"

Oysters? The woman was determined to send us out on an irrelevant note. "Can't say I do, Charity. I don't even like to eat them."

The woman's gentle laugh rippled over the airwaves. I didn't know much about this woman, but I pictured her as about sixty with clipped gray hair, glasses, rouged cheeks, and a librarian's love of reference books.

"Oysters are one of nature's most wonderful creations. When a grain of sand enters their shell, they don't even try to eject the irritation. Instead they embrace it, pull it close, and surround it with their very essence. In time, their ability to wrap beauty around trouble results in a pearl. That's what you did today—you wrapped beauty around the trouble in that man's life and saved a lost soul."

With a lot of help from above.

I tilted my head toward the mike as the clock advanced to 11:58. "Thanks for sharing that, Charity. I must admit, I never cared much for slimy oysters, but I *do* like pearls. Thank you for your kind comments, and thanks for calling."

I cocked a finger toward the control room and Chad hit the next button. I signed off over "the bed," two minutes of funky rhythms designed to send listeners on their way with an upbeat attitude, careful to keep a light note in my voice as I wished my audience a good day and a good attitude.

No sense in letting the world know I felt as wrung-out as my grandmother's dishrag.

"Talk to you tomorrow," I finished, keeping an eye on the clock counting down the seconds. "And remember—the next time you have a problem, don't do anything you'll regret. Call me, and let's talk it out."

The music faded, Gary slumped in relief, and I slipped the headphones from my ears. Inside the control room, the noon news would have begun to blare from the speakers, but in my soundproof chamber the only noise was the quiet thump of my own heart.

I took a deep breath and lowered my head, not wanting Gary or Chad to see the play of emotions on my face.

Man, oh man.

I propped my elbows on the desk, then dropped my head into my hands. I'd had a live one today, and by the grace of God alone we had managed to pull success out of what could have been sheer disaster. If Tom from Tennessee had blown himself away on the air, or hurt his wife and kid—

Chad would have used the ten-second delay to keep the sound of a gunshot from reaching the airwaves, but the delay button wouldn't have been able to disguise the fact that something had gone terribly, drastically wrong. No matter how we tried to spin it, the world would have been witness to Dr. Diana Sheldon, pop psychologist and queen of morning radio, spectacularly failing a desperate caller. Within minutes the national media would have smelled blood in the water, and the tabloids would have engaged in a feeding frenzy. People who never listened to talk radio would have heard every gritty detail . . .

"Diana?" Gary's voice came through the intercom speaker at my left hand. "Can you come in here? I have news."

"In a minute."

I swiveled my chair to face the thick gray wall behind me. My coworkers had decorated every spare inch of space in the control room next door with girlie pictures, but nothing hung here except a promotional banner for the station.

WFLZ, the Voice of the Gulf Coast.

My voice could have blown it big time today.

I reached back and picked up my coffee cup, then brought the brew to my lips. Cold coffee wasn't the most appetizing thing in the world, but it was wet and my throat was dry. I needed to be on my way after gathering a quick report from Gary, because Scott Daniel would be standing in a line of kindergartners at the Gulf Coast Christian School, waiting for chauffeur moms to arrive.

I needed a minute, though, to gather my thoughts. The media might still pick up the story of my suicidal caller, but now it would play as a feel-good feature, not a news brief. We might even get some good publicity—and good publicity was priceless. My program was doing well, airing in several major markets, but something like this could propel us to the level of Paul Harvey or Rush Limbaugh . . .

I slipped from my chair and grabbed my purse from under the desk, then passed through the doorway and into the hall. A half-dozen interns stood outside, their eyes wide.

I hesitated. Young guys were always hanging around the Open Air Building; radio attracted them like a fistfight draws a crowd. But never before had they congregated outside my studio.

I passed through them, then turned. "Hey, guys, what's up?"

They nodded in wordless greeting, then a multiple-earringed kid who didn't look a day over sixteen hurried to open the door for me.

"Thanks." I gave him a puzzled smile, then stepped into the control room, pulling the door closed behind me. No sense in letting the interns eavesdrop if Gary had bad news to report. Anything could have happened in the last hour, including Tennessee Tom's suicide while in police custody.

I dropped my purse on the worn couch behind Gary's chair. "Well?"

Gary spun around to face me, a grin overtaking his usual preoccupied look. "Dr. D, what can I say? You were unbelievable this morning. The phones haven't stopped ringing."

Long ago I learned not to pay much attention to gushing praise, but kind comments from a coworker always filled me with a rush of warmth. Still, I couldn't have handled that call alone.

I shrugged. "I wasn't that unbelievable, and I nearly blew it at least once. I did what any crisis counselor would do."

A glint of wonder filled Gary's eyes. "Still, it was pretty impressive."

"Your husband called a minute ago," Chad added, glancing up as his big hands roved over the soundboard. He was monitoring the news being read two studios away.

"Steve called? Was something wrong?"

"He heard the show," Chad answered, using the computer mouse to drag and drop a commercial into the lineup on the monitor. "He told me to tell you he had been praying for you."

For Chad, a rough-edged agnostic, to even pronounce the word *praying* was something of a miracle.

"Really?"

"And what Charity said there at the end was good." Chad shrugged as he stared at the flickering meters on his board. "She seemed to tie it all together."

"That oyster analogy is as old as the hills, but yeah, it did fit well." I sank onto the couch against the wall and shifted my attention to Gary. "Anything else important?"

Leaning against the console, my producer delivered the next bit of news with an air of solemnity. "Conrad Wexler called."

"Wexler?" I tapped my fingers on my knee, trying to place the name.

"He's the vice president of talk shows for the network. Our boss."

"Oh." Wide-eyed, I met Gary's gaze. "So—are we fired?"

His grin widened. "Apparently we nearly gave him a coronary, but he loved what he heard. Told me to congratulate you on a job well done and mentioned that he was planning to alert the media. I wouldn't be surprised if the people from ABC News or *People* magazine show up on your doorstep this week."

"As long as they don't come today." I glanced at the clock mounted above Chad's board—twelve minutes after noon already, which meant I'd be so late that Scott Daniel might get anxious.

I pulled the straps of my purse to my shoulder. "I've got to run, guys. I'll come in early tomorrow, though, to tape those promos we discussed earlier—"

"Let me sleep on this latest development," Gary interrupted, "and maybe I can think of something to highlight what happened here today. Nothing that will come across as exploitative, but maybe something punchy like 'Dr. Diana can handle your 911 call'—"

I couldn't stop a shudder. "I don't think we want to encourage suicidal callers. If we give desperate people an audience, they're likely to call and kill themselves on the air just because they know they can."

Gary sank back, his body language suggesting he'd been hurt. "It was just a thought."

"I'm glad you're thinking. But let's think some more."

I gave him a grin, then stood and reached out to touch Chad's shoulder. The burly sound engineer could be as explosive as a chunk of C-4, but he knew how to solve all kinds of technical problems. I didn't know what we'd do without him. "Good work today, Chad. Thanks for your help."

He tossed a quick smile in my direction. "No problem, Dr. D."

Six

AFTER GIVING HER RESTLESS YOUNG CHARGES A STERN glance, Kathy Marshall bent to peer out from beneath the portico where a line of cars was creeping along at slug speed. The sun had disappeared, and the now-gray sky, heavy with drizzly rain, sagged toward the parking lot where moms and minivans waited with headlights on and windshield wipers beating in rhythm.

Rain always seemed to activate the wiggle gene in her kindergartners, and the visiting balloon artist hadn't done anything to calm them down. Taking advantage of the extra time afforded by their rain-canceled recess, he had taken pains to fashion a different balloon animal for each child—long, thin creations that were now clasped tightly in twenty-two pairs of small hands.

Mrs. Hawthorne, a vegan earth mother who drove an old VW bus that probably burned more fossil fuels than any vehicle in the line, leaned sideways to open the door for her squirmy daughter.

"Here you go, Placentia." Kathy caught the door and opened it wide, then helped the little girl into the front seat. Mrs. Hawthorne, apparently assuming that Kathy had things under control, leaned back against her seat and tapped the steering wheel in time to the Beach Boys tune playing on the radio.

Kathy forced a smile as she dragged her hand through the pile of McDonald's wrappers wedged into the space between the seat and the door. "Placentia, where's the seat belt?"

"It's there." Placentia pointed toward her mother's belt, hanging loose from the opposite door.

"Not your mother's belt, honey. *Your* belt. I can't let you ride away until you are safely tucked into your seat belt."

Mrs. Hawthorne, obviously oblivious to Kathy's rapidly ebbing patience, begin to sing: "And we'll have fun, fun, fun, now that Daddy took her T-Bird away."

"Mrs. Hawthorne." Leaning over the child, who began to bat Kathy's cheek with the tail of a balloon brontosaurus, she assumed her best let's-be-serious expression. "Can you help me belt your daughter into this seat?"

"Of course." Mrs. Hawthorne gave Kathy a wide-eyed smile, then jerked her thumb over her shoulder. "Get in the back, Placentia, where the belts work."

"I doan wanna!"

"You need to."

"But I wanna ride in front!"

Lifting both hands, Mrs. Hawthorne gave Kathy a helpless shrug.

Dimly aware that she was exhibiting a less-than-flattering pose to the other children in line, Kathy dived into the backseat of the car, then pinned Placentia to the seat with her forearm. The girl sang along with the Beach Boys, keeping time by bopping Kathy's cheek with the balloon—

If she ever invited another balloon artist, she ought to have her head examined.

Finally she felt the seat belt click. With difficulty she extracted herself from between the VW's bucket seats, then slammed the door with a bit more force than necessary.

Closing her eyes, she slowly inhaled as the next car approached.

"Miss Marshall?"

She looked down to see Scott Sheldon holding his balloon centipede with both hands.

"Yes, Scott?"

"My balloon doesn't have any legs."

Careful to keep an eye on the approaching car, she smiled at the boy. "Yes he does, Scott, we drew them on with black marker."

"But those aren't legs, they're just marks. Everybody else's animals have legs that bend."

She opened her mouth to answer, but at that moment Mrs. Lipps opened the door for her daughter. Reaching for Jacqueline Lipps with one hand, Kathy nodded to Scott. "We couldn't very well put a hundred bent legs on that balloon, could we?"

She bent to help Jacqueline into the car, belted the child in, then gave Mrs. Lipps a weary smile.

When she returned to the line, Scott Sheldon was waiting with another question. "Miss Marshall?"

Kathy lifted her hand, waving the next car forward. She ought to send Scott to the end of the line because his mother was nearly always one of the last to arrive. But he'd think she meant to punish him if she did, and somehow she couldn't stand the sight of pain in those big blue eyes.

As the next driver inched forward, Kathy turned her attention to Scott. "Yes, honey?"

"If I bring him back tomorrow"—his gaze shifted to the long, unbent balloon in his hands—"can we maybe give him a couple of legs?"

Kathy laughed softly as she motioned for Kimmie Jones. The quiet little girl was carrying one of the cuter balloon creations, a poodle that almost looked like a poodle.

"I tell you what, Scott." She winked at the boy as she placed her hand on Kimmie's shoulder. "Bring him in tomorrow and we'll see what we can do."

Turning to smile at Mrs. Cragle, Kimmie's mother, Kathy bent to buckle the girl's seat belt.

She was digging for yet another belt clasp when she sensed commotion behind her. The rising wind was spitting rain onto the children and making the girls squeal. She turned in time to see Natalie Wright throw up a hand to keep rain out of her eyes, then a gust of wind snatched the balloon kitten from her grasp.

Leaning on the open car door, Kathy called out a warning as Scott Sheldon ran after the balloon. The kitten flitted across the sidewalk, then landed in a puddle in front of Mrs. Cragle's front fender. Kathy took a step to haul Scott back into line, but the car door blocked her way. She sidestepped, intending to move around it, but the car lurched and she heard sounds that froze her scalp to her skull—the clasp of a safety belt, a soft thump, and a faint splash.

"Stop!" Terror lodged in her throat, making it impossible to say anything else. Something in her voice must have struck fear into Mrs. Cragle, for the woman's wandering foot slammed on the brake. Kathy pushed her way past the car door and covered the distance to Scott Sheldon in three frantic strides.

He lay chest down on the wet pavement with his head turned so she could see that his mouth was slightly open below eyes as wide and blank as windowpanes.

Seven

"DON'T YOU HAVE TO GO?"

Gary's comment broke my concentration. I had moved toward the door several minutes ago, but I paused to check the plastic correspondence tray mounted to the wall. Gary usually printed out new e-mails after the show, but some of our eager-beaver interns often pulled mail from the Web site while the show aired and dropped copies into the tray. Technology never ceased to amaze me, but I was usually grateful that I could hear so much from so many people in so short a time.

Though I was running late, I hadn't been able to resist skimming through the stack, hoping for a virulent piece of hate mail that might serve as a springboard for tomorrow's program. After today's drama, anything less than dazzlingly controversial would seem like a snooze. I might even tackle an abortion letter tomorrow, if I could find someone who'd debate intelligently instead of screaming at me.

Deep within the recesses of my purse, my cell phone played its melodic ring.

"Rats." I tucked the stack of printed pages under my arm, then began the laborious process of digging past wallet, checkbook, and sunglasses case in search of my Nokia. I had to be quick if I wanted to catch it before the automatic voice mail picked up.

I found the phone after the second ring, glanced at the digital readout, and saw "Steve's Car" in the caller ID box. Why would my husband be calling from his car? He usually ate lunch in his office, but maybe he'd known I'd be swamped after such a stressful show and was offering to pick Scott up himself, sparing me from a mad rush to the school. Or maybe he'd decided to take me and Scott Daniel to lunch. An impromptu celebration certainly fit the occasion.

The phone had sent him to voice mail, so I dialed his cell number and waited for him to pick up. "Steve?"

"Honey, it's me."

I frowned as I caught Gary's eye. My husband wasn't the type to state the obvious. I turned slightly and lowered my head. "Everything okay? You don't sound like yourself."

"There's been an accident at the school."

Something cold slid down my spine, leaving a trail of dread in its wake. "What kind of accident?"

"They say Scott's dead." My husband's voice, usually so calm and soothing even in the most trying circumstances, broke into shards. "They've got to be wrong, but I'm on my way to the school to see what the trouble is."

As my knees turned to water, I sank onto the couch. "Scott Daniel? *Our* Scott?"

"They said he was hit by a car." His words grated and cracked as they tumbled over one another. "It's raining, you see, and apparently the driver didn't see him step into the road . . ."

His strangled voice died away, and some part of my brain wondered how he could simultaneously drive and relay this terrible message. But a cloud, formless and heavy, swallowed up that insignificant thought as it began to fill my brain.

Jesus, Lord, this news couldn't be true. Don't let it be true. Take my life, my body, my *world*, but don't take my son. You couldn't do that, you wouldn't do that. Let him be hurt, let it be a mistake, let this be a dream . . .

"Of course it's not true." I said the words automatically, gripping the phone so tightly my fingers hurt. "You go there, and you'll see. I'm leaving the station now. You call me when you know what hospital they've taken him to, and I'll meet you there."

"Okay."

The line clicked and Steve was gone. Somehow I stood and turned toward the door.

"Everything okay?" The look on Gary's face told me he knew nothing was as it should be.

"Scott's hurt." I stared at him as a series of words and stuttering images filled my brain. "I'm to meet Steve . . . someplace. He'll let me know."

Gary slipped from his tall chair. "Your hands are shaking, Diana. Let me drive you."

I would have protested, but a quick glance at my hands confirmed his observation. Besides, having Gary to negotiate Tampa traffic would leave my mind free for more important things . . . like taking Steve's next call and straightening out this horrible mistake.

Nodding, I turned toward the door. "Okay."

I paused, frustrated by the moment Gary took to murmur something to Chad, then together we pressed through the crowd of starry-eyed interns still loitering in the hall.

"You might want to take an umbrella, Dr. Sheldon," one of them called. "It's raining outside."

Ignoring him, I concentrated on placing one foot in front of the other. After the news I'd just received, how could a little rain possibly hurt?

Eight

DRIVING MORE CAREFULLY THAN USUAL BECAUSE OF the rain, Gary turned the car onto the six-lane Gandy Boulevard and drove west toward the bridge and Pinellas County. Diana and Steve lived in Hunter's Green, an exclusive gated community between Largo and Seminole, but on the west side of Tampa Bay. Brittany, their daughter, attended Seminole High School, while Scott went to a private kindergarten at a church near the family home. Diana was usually careful to leave the station as soon as the show had finished, but even on the best of days she was one of the last mothers to arrive at the kindergarten pickup, depending upon the pace of traffic from Tampa.

He risked a glance at his stunned passenger. Though almost twenty years his senior, he'd always thought his boss an attractive woman. At this moment, however, the color had fled from her cheeks, the liveliness from her eyes. She sat very still, her eyes narrow, one hand clutching the seat belt across her chest.

He summoned the courage to speak. "Did, um, Steve give you any details?"

Keeping her eyes on the road ahead, she shook her head. "Not really." She spoke slowly, as if carefully considering each word before pronouncing it. "He said something about the rain . . . and about a car. I suppose somebody bumped Scott Daniel as he waited in the pickup line. But it can't be serious. Those people are very careful, and cars *crawl* through that portico where the children wait on rain days."

Gary sighed. Thank goodness. The show was going well, and today had been a red-letter day. He couldn't afford to have his star sidetracked by a family emergency.

"I'm sure Scott is fine," he said, handling the car with more confidence than he'd felt when they left the station. "Now, where are we going?"

Diana didn't answer, but the hand on the seat belt tightened until he could see the white bone of her knuckles.

"How am I going to get my car?" Abruptly, she gave him a pointed look. "How am I supposed to get to work tomorrow?"

"Don't worry, just give me your keys." He forced a smile. "I'll go back and get Chad, and when he gets off we'll take your car to your house. That way you can hook up with Steve and you won't have to worry about the car."

He pulled left to pass a slow-moving truck. "Diana, we're near the bridge. Where are we going? Did I hear you mention a hospital?"

"I don't know." Her face had drawn inward, a pale knot of apprehension. "Steve's supposed to call when he learns where they took Scott." She tossed her head slightly, as if shaking off the shock that had attacked her in the studio. "I think"—she gestured left—"you should head south toward St. Pete. They'll probably take him to All Children's."

Nodding, Gary increased the pressure on the accelerator. The Gandy Bridge would deposit them in St. Petersburg, and with a little luck they'd reach the leading children's hospital before Steve, who'd be coming from his office in Clearwater.

They were fortunate to have a specialized children's hospital in the area. Gary didn't know much about kids, but they were resilient, weren't they? His mother had always said kids practically had rubber bones. And doctors worked miracles these days.

Threading his way through the traffic, he gave his passenger a confident smile. "Everything's going to be fine."

Nine

GARY HAD NEARLY CONVINCED ME THAT STEVE'S CALL was nothing but a terrible mistake when my cell phone chimed again. I dived for it, catching it before the second ring.

"Steve? Gary's driving me, but which hospital?"

My husband spoke in an odd, flat voice. "No hospital, Di. They've taken him to the medical examiner's office. I'm here now, waiting for you."

I stared at the windshield, where the wipers thumped out an encouraging beat. *Not . . . dead . . . not . . . dead.*

"But—why? Surely they need to get him to the hospital."

The cellular silence between us filled with dread, then Steve's voice broke. "He's gone, sweetheart. His neck was broken. He wasn't breathing when the teacher reached his side, and the EMS personnel never found a pulse."

I looked at Gary, who was doing his best to act as though he wasn't listening. Seeing him—my employee—reminded me that I was a person with some authority.

"Listen, Steve, he can't be dead. Remember when that little girl down the street fell in her pool? She had no pulse. She didn't breathe for nearly ten minutes, but they revived her in the ambulance."

"But her mother had been doing CPR . . . and her neck wasn't broken."

I closed my eyes as horrific images pushed and jostled and competed with each other for space in my brain. My boy could not be dead. This was a mistake; it had happened to some other child or it hadn't happened at all.

"How can they be sure that's what happened to Scott? I want him taken to the hospital; I want the doctors to do CPR or whatever they have to do. Little boys don't go from being perfectly healthy one minute to dead in the next—"

"Diana." He whispered my name in a tattered voice. "We're waiting for you here at the ME's office. Come as soon as you can . . . because I don't think I can do this without you."

Do what? Give up on my son? I wouldn't do that, I *couldn't* do that, but if I had to go there to demand that they act in a reasonable manner, I certainly would. And if Scott Daniel was dead, if there was nothing else they could do—

A wave of pain threatened to engulf me, but I pushed it back and backpedaled away from that thought.

"Where *is* the ME's office? I haven't a clue."

"Ulmerton Road, about a mile west of the sheriff's department. I'll meet you outside."

He disconnected the call, but I sat for another three seconds with the phone pressed to my ear before I realized he had gone. Without warning, without so much as a good-bye.

My beloved Scott Daniel would never leave like that.

I turned to Gary, dropping my phone into my purse. "We have to go to the medical examiner's office. It's on Ulmerton Road—I think I know the building."

Gary nodded wordlessly, and I felt an instant's relief in knowing I wouldn't have to repeat anything Steve had said. After all, Gary had heard half the conversation, and surely he knew they didn't take still-living little boys to places that had more in common with a morgue than a hospital.

A morgue. Upon waking this morning, I could not have named a place less likely to house a meeting between myself, my husband, and my son.

I lowered the phone and dropped it back into my bag, then stared at the tops of my knees, bony lumps beneath the hem of my plaid skirt—a skirt I had liked until ten minutes ago. Now I knew I'd never wear it again.

I shifted my gaze to the window, then propped my elbow on the car door and stared at the traffic trailing by. Something had gone terribly wrong at that school. Some teacher had messed up, some driver had been reckless, and some principal had been out of his mind to even *think* of letting the children line up on a rainy afternoon like this one. Some EMS worker had been careless or lazy—why else hadn't they done something to stop the spark of life from leaving a perfectly healthy little boy?

Someone—perhaps many someones—had committed a grievous wrong today, and I would not rest until they had been confronted and made to realize the vastness of their mistake.

Scott Daniel Sheldon was not supposed to die today.

My baby lay on a steel table, his narrow chest covered by a sheet. His eyes were closed, his lashes pale fringes upon cheeks that had been rosy and warm when I kissed them this morning.

I cupped the smooth cap of shining blond hair against my palm. His name leaped to my tongue and stuttered against the back of my teeth, but I could not speak the name of a living boy in the presence of this empty shell.

So I stared at the child on the table, cold and pearl blue in the fluorescent lights. The hollow mockery before me did not seem capable of containing a life as robust as Scott Daniel's, but on the cheek I saw the scrape from his fall last week as we skated on the driveway. I had warned Scott that he wasn't ready to go down the steep slope, but in the minute I turned to pull mail from the mailbox, he tromped up the grass. I looked up in time to see him launch himself and sail down, his eyes wide with terror and his mouth open in a gleeful squeal. And, as I had feared, his skates hit the crack at the intersection of driveway and side-walk and he went flying; fortunately, a patch of Floratam sod cushioned his face-first fall. His cheek, however, had encountered a stray rock.

Now I brushed my fingertip across the shallow scar. Scott Daniel, bone of my bones, blood of my blood, had inherited more than my blonde hair and blue eyes. My stubborn will had also passed through the placenta that fed him, yet it was somehow tolerable in this pack-age . . . perhaps because he had also inherited his father's easygoing smile. The first time I held him in the delivery room, I knew he was a special gift, a boy God would use for some glorious purpose—

But not this. This—this death, this day, was not God's plan. This was completely wrong.

To my left, Steve was sobbing softly, one hand pressed to his face, the other across his chest in a primitive defense posture. *It won't help,* I wanted to say. *Something evil attacked us today, God stood back and allowed it, and for a moment, at least, the world turned upside down.*

I would not have been surprised to learn that in the last hour ter-rorists had destroyed the United Nations or an earthquake had ejected California into the sea. Surely God had been sleeping . . . and surely he would make things right.

But how?

I turned to my husband, the hideous and alluring question on my lips, but he had closed his eyes to the sight of our dead boy. The med-ical examiner, a quiet man in a white lab coat, stood near the door, respecting our time with our son. He had met us in the lobby and explained the accident, but the words had fallen upon my ears like an overturned can of Tinkertoys, jumbled and disorganized.

He gave me details, not answers.

None of this made any sense.

I don't know how long we stood there, but after a while I found myself in a small lobby decorated like the lounge at the car dealership where I routinely waste three hours every six months: leatherette couch against the wall, oak-laminate coffee table with chrome legs, dozens of tattered year-old magazines stacked on a matching table at the side of the couch.

I heard the crackle of cheap vinyl as I sank onto the sofa. Why did a morgue need a lounge? This wasn't a place where one came to wait for an outcome.

A moment later, I understood. As if he'd been summoned by some wireless pastoral-emergency network, our pastor, John Thompson, arrived. Breathless and red-faced, he pulled me to my feet, gave me a quick embrace, then greeted Steve in the same way.

"I'm sorry it took me so long to get here." Pastor John pulled a handkerchief from his pocket and offered it to Steve, who was still weeping freely. "Please, Diana, Steve, let's sit down. I'm sure you want to talk about this, and I'd like to pray with you."

Dry-eyed and shivering, I sat, but all I could see when I looked up at the man in charge of shepherding my eternal soul was an employee on autopilot, a man who routinely offered prayers for the sick and consolation for the grieving. I was a professional counselor; I knew how easily words of comfort became rote.

I stared at him, indignation mingling with rising disbelief. How could he comfort us? Though we had often talked to him at church, he had not known Scott Daniel. To my knowledge, he had never taught my son a Bible verse or prayed with him—Sunday school teachers and the kindergarten staff had done those things. Scott Daniel had not yet made a profession of faith, so Pastor John had not even baptized him.

I doubted he had ever heard my beautiful son laugh.

The pastor tugged at his pocket, probably looking for another handkerchief, then halted when he looked into my dry eyes. I would not weep before the man responsible for the kindergarten where my son died.

A flush colored his face as awareness thickened between us.

"I'm sure you want to know details of the accident." Looking away, he clasped his soft hands and lowered himself into a charmless chrome-and-vinyl chair. "I've talked to the teacher, the parent driving the car, and the police officer who wrote out the report."

"Tell us." My voice sounded chilly in my own ears. Beside me, Steve was noisily blowing his nose, but I had never felt less inclined to weep. "Tell me why my son is dead."

The pastor blanched, then spread his hands and looked to Steve. "The kindergarten teachers had all the children in line for rainy-day pickup. Only one car can fit beneath the portico at a time, you know, so the children were growing restless. By 12:15, however, most of the students had been picked up."

I took the blow without flinching. If he intended those words to carry a payload of guilt, he succeeded. By 12:15 I was usually crossing the Gandy Bridge, nearly at the school, but today . . .

Today I had been celebrating in the control room.

Still avoiding my gaze, Pastor John brought a hand to the back of his neck. "The kindergartners had animal balloons, you see—a balloon artist had visited the classroom and entertained them by making those twisty animals. When the little girl beside Scott lost her balloon in a gust of wind, he ran after it. Unfortunately, he darted in front of a driver who was distracted with buckling her child into the front seat. The car struck Scott from behind."

I brought my hand to my temple as a sudden dart of pain scorched the back of my brow. My angel was lying in the next room for the sake of a five-cent balloon?

"Given his height and the point of contact," Pastor John continued, "the police officer figured the impact broke Scott's neck instantly. The teacher could not get a pulse. When the EMS technicians reached us at 12:23"—finally, his gaze crossed mine—"Scott was gone."

Twelve twenty-three . . .

I had been sitting in the studio, grinning while Chad and Gary praised my silver tongue and quick-thinking wisdom. They had been crowing because I saved a life . . . but what if my delay had caused my son's death? If I'd been on time, would things have been different?

No, a rational voice assured me. Even in the best of circumstances, I hardly ever made it to the church before 12:25. If this had been an ordinary day, I still wouldn't have arrived in time to keep Scott from being hit.

So why didn't someone else prevent this accident?

"Where was the teacher"—my fist bunched at my side—"while my son was running into the road?"

"Kathy Marshall was standing right beside the children." A faint thread of rebuke lined the pastor's voice. "She was close enough to reach out and tap Scott on the shoulder, but he surprised her, darting out like that."

He lowered his gaze to the mottled commercial carpeting. "Kathy feels terrible about this, as do we all. But the police officer and the other teachers have assured her she did nothing wrong. No one can predict the impulsive actions of a child."

My temper flared. "Perhaps you should."

A strangled sound came from my husband's throat, but I pressed on. "Aren't you supposed to make allowances for the impulsive actions of children? No one can predict car accidents, either, so we make people wear seat belts even to drive around the block."

Pastor John gave me a look of patient exasperation. "We've painted a yellow line on the sidewalk. The children know they are not supposed to step over it unless they are escorted by a teacher. We drum that rule into their heads from the first day of class. Unfortunately, in his hurry to save his classmate's balloon, Scott forgot."

So now it was Scott's fault. The man was blaming my five-year-old child for his own death.

I rubbed my temple as the pastor kept apologizing. His words said "I'm sorry," but all I could hear was "Please don't sue us."

As if my husband would ever sue the church where he was an elder and a Sunday school teacher.

The door opened again. The white-coated medical examiner stepped in and handed Steve a clipboard. "I'm sorry to intrude, but this is necessary," the doctor said, his eyes filled with sadness and his voice rough. "The state of Florida requires an autopsy for all traumatic deaths. After the autopsy, we will release the body to whatever funeral home you select."

Steve looked at the clipboard as if he had forgotten how to read. "And this is?"

"We need permission to autopsy the body, so you'll need to sign at the bottom. The second sheet is a list of local funeral homes. You may select one now or make inquiries and call to tell us which one you'd like to use."

Did he really expect us to shop for a funeral home as if we were buying a new car? As the keeper-of-the-family-checkbook, I was usually the one who researched things like appliances and furniture, but I could not imagine how one went about choosing a mortician to care for one's child after an autopsy.

I watched in abject horror as Steve signed the first form, then flipped to the second page and put an *X* next to the box for Whitlow's funeral home.

I gave him a quizzical look. "Why them?"

His hands trembling, he offered the clipboard to the doctor. "I don't know. The name sounded familiar, I guess."

The doctor took the clipboard, then nodded. "They're good people. I'll have the director at Whitlow's give you a call."

I lowered my head into my hands as the words echoed in the silence.

Our pastor cleared his throat. "Will you want to have a service at the church?"

Steve didn't hesitate. "Of course, Pastor—and we'd like you to do it."

A surge of bile rose in my throat. I wasn't sure I wanted this man anywhere near my baby, but what other options did I have?

"I'd be honored." Pastor John nodded, then stood, undoubtedly anxious to get back to doing whatever he did all day. Tonight when his work was finished, he'd go home to his wife and three sons, none of whom had ever been struck by a car on church property. None of whom had ever even been in the hospital, much less the morgue.

Steve lifted his head. "We need to call Brittany—get her out of school, I guess."

I winced. How did one go about asking the school to release a child in this situation? "Excuse me, Mr. Principal, but Brittany Sheldon's brother has died. Yes, died. D-I-E-D. If you'll send her home, we'll be sure she has a proper note tomorrow."

"Why?" My voice broke. "It's not like she has to rush to the hospital to tell her brother good-bye." I glanced at my watch. "She'll be home in a couple of hours. Let's tell her then."

The words rolled off my tongue even as my brain resisted the idea of sitting down and sharing this disastrous news with our daughter. If I could put off telling Brittany, I could give her a few more hours of life in a world where horrible, unthinkable things did not happen on rainy Monday afternoons.

Pastor John lifted his hands, reminding me of how he stood to address the congregation after the call to worship on Sunday mornings. "Shall we pray together before I go?"

Steve bowed his head; I blinked in incredulity.

"Father God," the pastor prayed, stepping forward to drop a hand on each of our shoulders, "we know you are the healer of broken hearts. You know the pain of losing a son, and you have walked through the valley of the shadow of death. Be with Steve and Diana now, be the rod and staff that comfort as they walk through this time of grief and sorrow. We ask these things in the name of Jesus, our Lord."

Steve was weeping again, and something in the prayer brought tears to my own eyes. But they were not tears of grief—they were flecks of irritation.

I didn't want a rod and staff—I wanted my son. And God couldn't understand my pain; how could he? He was God, he knew how the play would end. Yes, he lost his beloved son, but only in a finite dimension, and he knew he'd have his son restored after three days.

I stared at the floor, my watery eyes blurring the floor covering into a homogeneous smear. I'd always heard that God understood our pain, but at that moment I couldn't believe it. Comparing his loss to mine was like a millionaire losing a hundred bucks on a bad day in the stock market.

"We'll be praying for you, Steve and Diana." The pastor's deep voice rumbled into my thoughts. "I'll be praying that God would show himself near and dear in this time of trouble."

How could God be *near* when he had obviously been napping this afternoon? And *dear*? Somehow the word didn't fit this situation.

I had been a Christian since childhood, and I'd never felt inclined to hide my faith. At the station, I'd borne more than my fair share of cutting remarks because I professed Christ. I'd learned that you could be a Buddhist, a Muslim, a Wiccan, or a multi-pierced moon-worshiping pagan without eliciting too much comment, but you couldn't be a born-again Christian without attracting various versions of the uplifted brow and snide smile. Yet I had always remained faithful to my testimony, speaking clearly and often even a little eloquently about the reality of faith and God's enduring love.

So was *this* how God repaid me for years of faithful service? Where had his love been today? And why would God, who had so miraculously given Scott Daniel to us only five years ago, abruptly call him home on a rainy day in March?

Another thought—one I'd ignored earlier—jabbed like a splinter in my heart, radiating waves of agony every time my mind brushed against it. At 12:23, I had been thinking about work and radio—*why hadn't I known?* I should have felt something; my mother's heart should have intuited that my son was in trouble. The Spirit of God should have alerted me to the danger, but I heard no inner voice, felt no warning premonition . . .

Something had gone horribly, drastically awry.

Pastor John opened the door and left, leaving Steve and me alone in the silence. For a long moment we sat like statues under the hum of the fluorescent lights.

Finally Steve reached out and took my hand. "Let's go, darling." I stood with him, but as we passed through the doorway he turned right toward the parking lot while I turned left toward the room where my baby lay.

"Diana . . . where are you going?"

"To see Scott Daniel."

"But you've seen him."

I pulled my hand from his grasp and took another step toward the large, cold room. Odd, how that lifeless room called to me. "I need to see him again."

Something in Steve seemed to soften. He took my arm and led me back into the place where our baby lay on a steel table. Someone had wheeled in another sheet-draped body during our absence, and the form beneath it was definitely adult. No mourners stood near to remark upon it.

How could I leave my son with a stranger?

After pulling back the sheet, I ran my fingertips through Scott's hair, noticing how, even in death, gold sparked among the fair threads. He had been born with a wealth of white-blond hair, and when the other boys cut theirs short and wore moussed spikes, Scott had allowed me to keep his in a longer style. His hair was as soft as a kitten's ear, as sweet as baby's breath . . . and after today it would be out of my reach.

My mind flashed back to the crazy days of my teenage years, when after football games we drove along River Road in Rockledge, carefully managing the curves of that oak-shrouded road while searching for the fabled mausoleum. According to local legend, a man had buried his wife on his property in a glass-covered casket, and if you peered into the coffin you could see her hair and nails still growing.

It wasn't true, of course. Nails and hair were dead once they left living follicles and nail beds, but you couldn't have convinced me of that at sixteen. We never did gather the courage to visit the mausoleum . . . never did actually find the place. Now, standing with my son, I would have wagered there was no glass-covered coffin on River Road. Who would want to witness a loved one's decay?

I wanted to remember Scott Daniel as he was this morning—a joyful, curious little scamp. The boy who held my face to give me smacky kisses that never failed to smear my lipstick. The boy who rode on his dad's back while they stomped around the house waiting for dinner to materialize from my disorganized kitchen.

I'm not sure how long we stood there, but after a while I felt the gentle pressure of Steve's hands on my shoulders. "Honey, we have to go."

I bit my lip and nodded, then allowed Steve to lead me toward the door. Like a bandage long stuck to a wound, I felt myself being pulled from the son I had succored and birthed and nurtured. And as Steve guided me through the parking lot, his arm around my shoulders, I hunched forward as the agonizing pain of separation tore me in two.

How long would it hurt? The counselor part of my brain knew the pain would ease in time, but my heart didn't buy it.

My heart felt they should bury us together.

Ten

I THINK EVERY WOMAN, IF SHE IS HONEST, WILL ADMIT to having a contingency plan in case disaster befalls her family. In more thoughtful moments over the years, I had mentally mapped out the funerals of both my husband and my parents.

My parents proved unexpectedly helpful in this regard, having prepaid and preplanned their funerals years before they passed away within months of each other. They had both sensibly opted for cremation instead of burial, thus avoiding all the hassle with a casket, viewing, and graveside service, yet I always thought I would bury Steve if he were to die unexpectedly. My reasons had nothing to do with superstitions about the body, nor did I think myself morbid enough to spend long hours sitting in a cemetery revisiting his memory. I wouldn't need any kind of special setting for that—the Lord had used him to mold and shape my life over the past twenty-two years, so I would take him with me no matter where I went.

No, I had thought to have Steve buried for my children's sakes. At some point Brittany and Scott Daniel might appreciate a permanent memorial to their father. As a popular and beloved dentist, Steve's practice was practically a community institution, and I thought it might be nice for my children to visit a quiet place and commemorate the life they had known all too briefly.

I had made tentative plans for my parents, my husband, and myself (no frills, no media, no open casket, thanks). What I had never considered was planning a funeral for one of my children.

The day after Scott Daniel's accident, I lay in bed with a migraine, nauseous and disinclined to speak to anyone. In the preceding hours I had retold the story of Scott's accident several times, enduring fresh agony with each retelling. I couldn't speak anymore, couldn't tell another visitor or caller how my son had died.

Fortunately, Steve rose to the occasion, handling the details of death as deftly as he'd handled things in the ME's office. He arranged everything with the funeral home, choosing a small white casket lined with silver-gray satin, and a burial plot beneath a live oak at Serenity Memorial Gardens. We would have a funeral service at the church without the casket, in deference to any of Scott Daniel's classmates who might attend, then we'd have a simple service at the graveside for family members.

Tuesday afternoon, Steve came into the bedroom and described all this for me, inviting my comments of approval or disapproval, but I could only stare at him. Only once did I gather enough strength to break through my paralysis—Steve had gone into Scott Daniel's closet and brought out a white shirt and the navy blue blazer I'd bought for Scott to wear last Easter. My boy had looked like a blond cherub in that coat, but he'd worn it only about ten minutes before shucking it onto the Sunday school table and joining his little friends on the playground.

I rose out of bed when I spied the blazer in Steve's hand. "Not that. That's not Scott Daniel."

Steve gave me a look of sheer exasperation. "What, then?"

"Wait." Steeling myself to the necessity of action, I went into Scott's bedroom and rummaged through the closet until I found his favorite shirt—a child-sized Tampa Bay Buccaneers football jersey. I stood there, the jersey in one hand, and wondered what else he should wear. Steve had been carrying only the shirt and jacket—weren't the dead allowed to wear pants?

I shook my head. I didn't care how the funeral home people usually did it; my son would be fully dressed when we said good-bye for the last time. I pulled a clean pair of underwear from his drawer, found two sports socks with no holes in the heels and a pair of black knit basketball shorts. The funeral director might think the shorts undignified, but I didn't care. Scotty had loved them.

Taking the clothes to our bedroom, I dropped them into a shopping bag and handed it to Steve. "Tell them to dress him in these."

Steve peeked into the bag. "They told me he'd only be visible from the waist up."

"Take all of it." I bit my lip. "What about shoes?"

Steve closed the bag. "He didn't wear shoes to bed, did he?"

"Get his tennis shoes. I don't want him going—I don't want him to have bare feet."

I watched Steve walk away, noticing for the first time how weariness showed in the drooping slope of his shoulders. He needed rest. I needed rest. Both of us needed to close our eyes in healing sleep, but neither of us could. Not yet.

Strange, isn't it, how we assign metaphors of sleep to death. We speak of putting the body to *rest,* of people falling *asleep,* and meeting again when they *wake.* We even dress a casket to look like a bed, with pillows and ruffles and satin linings. But I knew Scott Daniel wasn't asleep—according to all I believed in the Bible, to be absent from the body meant to be present with the Lord, so my son wasn't sleeping in any sense of the word. He had vacated his fragile body, and we would treat it tenderly, but he would have no more use for that bit of mortal flesh until the day Jesus returned and refashioned it for use in his kingdom.

I knew all the relevant theology. Before getting my masters in psychology and my doctorate in counseling, I'd graduated from a Christian college with a degree in biblical studies. As a counselor and a radio talk-show host, I'd been dispensing the proper answers for years—God doesn't send trouble, but he allows it. Death is not a final good-bye, but a temporary parting. Tears endure for a night, but joy comes in the morning.

Funny how the answers didn't feel at all proper when the time came to deliver them to myself.

As the hours until the funeral ticked by, the pat responses felt less and less comforting. We had entered a surreal world where time and ordinary life seemed somehow suspended. Brittany, who had received the news in shock followed by noisy tears, floated through the kitchen only when we left it, then retreated to her bedroom. The counselor in me knew she needed someone to talk to; the mother in me was too paralyzed to volunteer for the role.

Our house filled with food as strangers rang the doorbell and handed over warm casseroles, speaking in hushed voices as if we, not Scott, were asleep. Kathy Marshall, Scott's teacher, and Winnie Cragle, the woman who had hit him, dropped by to blubber apologies that buzzed against my eardrums like static from a foreign radio station. People I didn't even know sent letters, notes, and e-mails. Cards sprinkled the foyer tiles, dropped through the mail slot in the front door. The phone rang so insistently that we turned the ringer off and let the answering machine relate the pertinent details: Funeral Wednesday morning, 10:00 A.M., Gulf Coast Community Church. In lieu of flowers, please send contributions to the Scott Sheldon Memorial Fund in care of the church, and together we can help children in need . . .

The memorial fund had been Steve's idea, of course—on Tuesday I had not been able to string two coherent thoughts together, let alone come up with a plan as meaningful as this one. Yet Steve knew our situation would attract media attention, so why not arrange to have good come out of tragedy? With the money from the memorial fund, we could do something practical the next time we heard about a family left homeless by fire or a child who lacked decent clothes for school.

At the time, I thought the memorial fund was Steve's way of making sure "all things work together for good" proved true. As for me, I didn't feel at all inclined to help God out.

On Wednesday morning I dressed with numb fingers, fumbling with the buttons on my white blouse. Was a navy-and-white suit proper attire for a child's memorial service? As a rule, the people of our church didn't wear black to funerals, for how could we mourn when our loved ones were in heaven? I understood the sentiment, but wearing red or green or pink to my son's service seemed about as appropriate as wearing a negligee to church.

Moving in a fog, I went downstairs and joined my family in the black limo provided by the funeral home. When the car pulled through the neighborhood security gate, the unexpected click and whir of cameras snapped me out of my stupor. A phalanx of press people stood beside the landscaped entrance while a local news van, satellite extended, idled at the side of the road.

"That's got to be her car!" I heard someone call. "Dr. Diana!"

Some still-functioning part of my brain realized that the national media had picked up the story. I hadn't read a newspaper in two days, nor had I spoken to anyone from the network. Gary had called Monday night to say they could run prerecorded "best of" programs for at least a week, and his reassurance had been enough to mute the tiny lobe of my brain eternally preoccupied with career.

Ignoring the reporters' shouted questions, the driver sped away, taking us to the church where we alighted in a private area, then walked to the front pew of a crowded sanctuary.

I didn't turn around. In the place ordinarily filled by a casket stood an easel bearing a twenty-by-twenty-four-inch photograph of my heaven-sent miracle, my smiling boy. Two extravagant bouquets stood beside the picture, spangling the front of the church with red roses, baby's breath, and silver streamers.

Some idiot had tied a balloon to one of the flower stands.

I lowered my head as tears stung my eyes. I might never be able to look at a balloon again without thinking of the senselessness of Scott Daniel's death . . . which meant that for the rest of my life I'd be sending regrets to birthday party invitations.

Drawing a deep breath, I opened the printed program. The brief publication listed Scott's full name, his birth date, and the date of his homegoing. It listed his survivors—*a child has survivors?*—as his mother, his father, his sister. All four of his grandparents were in heaven . . . and that thought, at least, brought a twisted smile to my face. He'd be well looked after until we joined him there.

My smile vanished a moment later. Beneath the order of service, some well-meaning imbecile from the funeral home had written, "Heaven needed another angel, so they sent for the brightest and best."

My empty stomach churned as I glanced at Steve. Aside from bad theology, the sentiment was cloyingly maudlin. Had he approved it? Probably. In his current state of mind, he would not have wanted to raise a fuss about anything.

The minister spoke, a woman sang, the children from Scott's kindergarten class walked up in wide-eyed silence and dropped crayoned pictures onto a table near his photograph. Later—in ten years, maybe—Steve and I would look through these tributes.

On Steve's left side, Brittany sat as quiet as a stone, her arms crossed at her waist. I looked at her during the kindergartners' promenade, expecting to see tears in her eyes, but she was staring at the carpet, one sandaled foot swinging in a restless rhythm.

Were we keeping her from the *mall*?

I averted my eyes as shame scorched my cheeks. The counselor in me rose up to waggle a finger and point out that as a teenager, Brittany was not well-acquainted with death. Her grandparents had lived miles away; they had not been part of the daily fabric of our lives. I could not expect her to mourn as we did; I really shouldn't expect anything from her at all. Right now she was mourning Scott Daniel with shock and silence. In time she would miss her brother, then she would learn how to deal with the loss. Children were amazingly resilient, weren't they?

At the conclusion of the service, everyone stood while Steve, Brittany, and I walked alone out of the church. After sliding into the waiting limo, I saw a crowd emerge from the church, their curious eyes following us as we pulled away for the drive to Scott Daniel's final resting place.

The fog-filled dream through which I had been sleepwalking ended at my baby's graveside. Seeing him in the open box, seeing the box next to fresh-turned earth, my anguish burst the last shreds of my control. I wept like a woman who has never known the release of tears. Alone with the pastor and my family, I bent and ran my fingers through Scotty's silky hair one final time.

I wailed when Steve pulled me away so they could close the casket. He tried to lead me toward the car as they removed the spray of flowers, but I resisted until Pastor John took my other elbow and gently helped Steve escort me forward.

As we stepped out from beneath the funeral canopy, again I heard the clicks of camera shutters. Security had kept the press at bay during the graveside service, but now that we were in public, the press considered us fair game. Steve slipped his arm around me, sheltering me from the intrusive cameras.

We drove home, where a posse of church friends was guarding the house. I gave them a glassy-eyed nod of thanks, then slipped out of my jacket, dropped it on the antique pew in the foyer, and climbed the carpeted stairs.

My baby, my miracle child, had moved to heaven, and I wanted to join him. I walked toward my bedroom, then whirled in an abrupt about-face and entered the little room I had wallpapered with red-uniformed tin soldiers on one wall and the Tampa Bay Bucs logo on the other.

With the quiet of the house wrapping around me, I kicked off my pumps and curled up in the middle of Scott Daniel's twin bed. His favorite toy—a rubber-faced black-and-yellow monkey beloved since infancy—sat propped against the pillow.

I pulled the monkey close to my heart and breathed in the scents of my son, then whispered the prayer I had recited at his bedside since his infancy: "Now I lay me down to sleep . . ." If God was merciful, perhaps he would fulfill that prayer and take my soul to join Scott Daniel's.

After a while my eyelids drifted shut, and I surrendered my senses to blessed numbness.

Eleven

SITTING IN THE FOYER OF HIS SILENT HOME, STEVE stared at Scotty's just-delivered portrait and felt a lone tear trickle down his cheek. His only begotten son, the child of his heart—

Now, God, I can empathize with you.

He missed Scotty dreadfully, and knew he would continue to miss him as the years lumbered forward. During every ball game, soccer tournament, and fishing trip, he would yearn for his son's companionship. Time might lessen this gnawing grief, but nothing would prevent Steve from missing the lighthearted boy who had suddenly disappeared not only from their lives, but from their futures.

Steve would attend no high school basketball games to watch Scotty play. There'd be no first car, no driving lessons. No teaching him how to shave and reminding him to use deodorant. No heart-to-heart conversations about girls, sex, and how to know when love is real.

He'd have no grandchildren through Scotty's branch of the family tree—and since Brittany was a grafted branch, no biological grandchildren at all. Not that it mattered . . . but he'd be lying if he said he hadn't thought about it. Most men want to father a son to carry on the family name, and he'd been no exception.

Leaning against the staircase banister, he closed his eyes and opened the door on a host of memories too precious to revisit amid the bustle of a houseful of guests. Scotty as an infant, mewling and helpless in Steve's hands. Scotty as a toddler, teetering forward in that ridiculous padded snowsuit Diana had made him wear to guard against bruises. Three-year-old Scotty excitedly blowing out the candles on Brittany's sixteenth birthday cake, then clapping in delight while she fumed.

Steve released a choked, desperate laugh, then opened his eyes. Such memories could be dangerous . . . if he wanted to make it through this time with his faith intact.

He picked up the picture, considered hanging it at the foot of the stairs, then decided to wait. Yesterday he had given their minister a copy of Scotty's most recent studio portrait, and Pastor John had been kind enough to have it enlarged. One day Diana would appreciate that kindness, but Steve didn't think she was ready to have a twenty-by-twenty-four-inch photo of their lost son staring her in the face first thing every morning.

In a few months she was certain to remember the portrait and ask about it. Then he'd bring it out so they could hang it in the den, a bright spot where they could enjoy it every day. And in years to come, as Brittany and her husband and kids came over to gather around the television to eat popcorn and watch animated videos, they could look up and see Scotty's picture, and think of him waiting for them.

In heaven. Steve had always thought of the place as being similar to life insurance—it was something you desperately needed, yet didn't need to contemplate—but now he found himself hungering for eternity. With Scotty there, heaven would feel more like home than this house did without him.

Twelve

BRITTANY SHUT AND LOCKED THE DOOR TO HER room, then kicked her shoes in the general direction of the closet. Terwilliger the pug lay curled in a pile of clean clothes she'd pulled from the laundry basket. Looking up as she approached, he opened his mouth in a panting smile and waggled his stump of a tail.

"Dumb dog." She stared at her clothes, now covered in white pug hairs. She'd have to throw the whole pile back down the laundry chute.

The dog would probably pester her to no end, now that the Scottster was gone. Ignoring him, Brittany perched on the edge of the bed and picked up the phone, then punched in Charisse's number.

"Hey."

"You back?"

"Yeah."

"How was it?"

"How do ya think? It was a funeral."

"Man." The phone line hummed for a second, then Charisse added, "You okay?"

Brittany leaned against the headboard. "I guess."

"What's it like at your house?"

"Quiet. There's a bunch of people in the kitchen putting food away. Mom's in Scotty's room, and Dad's in his bedroom. Nobody's talking much."

"Bummer."

Brittany shrugged. "Nobody but the Scottster ever talked much anyway. He ran his mouth all the time—so much I always wanted to slug him."

Charisse laughed, then clamped off the sound, apparently remembering that funerals and laughter didn't exactly go together.

"So—you wanna do something later?"

"Maybe. This place is creepy."

"Wanna go to a movie?"

Looking up, Brittany studied the dust tails hanging from her ceiling and stirring slightly in the breath of the slow-moving fan. "I guess."

"I can pick you up. About ten?"

Brittany considered. Ordinarily she had to tell her parents where she was going—a rule she found restrictive and stupid, considering that she'd be a high school graduate in two months—but neither Mom nor Dad seemed in any mood to care right now. And with all the coming and going at the house, she could probably slip out and not even be missed.

"Yeah, pick me up at ten. Let's hit the late showing."

"Anything special you want to see?"

"Something to make me laugh."

After hanging up, Brittany leaned back on her pillows and crossed her arms. The house was an absolute disaster, with assorted church people stumbling all over themselves downstairs. People she didn't even know were answering the door and tending some strange mourners' buffet in the kitchen while her parents had gone into seclusion. Mom had managed to hold herself together until the cemetery, then she absolutely lost it. And Dad, who'd been openly weeping since Monday, had pretended to be strong when Mom crumbled like a sandcastle hit by the incoming tide.

She tugged on the sleeve of her sweater. What if *she* had been the one hit by a car? Would her parents be carrying on over her like this? No sense in asking, really, because hypothetical questions were generally stupid. Still, the thought rankled—would they weep for her in the same way?

She knew her parents loved her. Mom had a baby book stuffed with photographs, and she had loaded her vanity in the master bath with fancy-framed pictures of Brittany in Christmas dresses, dress-up costumes, and tutus from ballet lessons. When she was little, her parents entertained her for hours with the story of how they had prayed for a baby to love, so God sent them a chosen child through the miracle of adoption. They talked about how they went to the hospital to pick her up, how they thanked her "tummy mommy," how they kissed Brittany and hugged her and dressed her in special clothes they'd picked out just for her—

But she'd been a kid then, and easily entertained.

When she was small, Mom and Dad had done everything parents could do for a daughter . . . until the Scottster arrived from out of the blue. Then everything changed.

At first she, too, had been caught up in the miracle of Scotty's conception. The idea of having a little brother was cool, especially after having been an only child for so long. But by the time Scott was born, she was thirteen, and ready to make her own life with her friends.

She had loved the Scottster—after she recovered from the initial embarrassment of walking around with a big-bellied, forty-three-year-old mother. But if movie stars like Jane Seymour could have babies in their forties, why not her mom? Mom had always kept herself in good health, and she didn't let herself get *too* repulsive while she was pregnant. Brittany even used to exercise with her after the baby came; the two of them would lie on the carpet in the den and do sit-ups while Scotty rocked in the baby swing, fascinated by the flailings of the women in his little life.

Yeah, the Scottster had been cute as a baby, and in the early days she had begged to baby-sit. "Maybe when you're older," Mom had answered, and Brittany sulked because her mother didn't trust her enough to handle an infant. Her first baby-sitting opportunity came when Scotty was two, and by the time he had passed his third birthday, Brittany was sick and tired of being asked to "stick around" to watch the kid while her parents ran to the store or went out on the weekends. Didn't they know teenagers had a constitutional right to a social life? Couldn't they understand that no high school student wanted to be caught dead with a toddler in tow?

"You're killing my reputation, Mom!" Brittany yelled one night. "People think he's *my* kid!"

That was an obvious lie, since Scott was as blond as moonlight and Brittany's hair more the color of a bonfire. Truth was, she didn't look like either of her parents, though well-meaning friends were quick to assure her she acted just like them.

Sheesh. As if that were a compliment.

Last year she and her parents had agreed on a compromise. Brittany would be asked to baby-sit no more than two nights a month, and in return she'd be allowed to stay out until midnight two weekend nights a month. Her parents still clung to the antiquated notion of an 11:00 P.M. curfew, but she and Charisse had found a way around it. After all, when two adults tumbled into bed at eleven after a long day of work coupled with dealing with a little kid, they weren't exactly vigilant about guarding the driveway. And a nice climbing oak grew right outside Britt's window . . .

The dog, tired of being ignored, jumped onto the bed and sat next to her, then dropped his chin to her knee. He blinked his round eyes, then looked at her with a woebegone expression.

As Britt dropped her hand onto Terwilliger's round head, her gaze fell upon an odd shape jutting from the dust ruffle at the bottom of her bed. Reaching down, she felt the hard bumper of the Ford F150, the red truck Scotty loved to "drive" all over the house. He must have had it in here Sunday night when she'd gone out with Charisse. He was probably chasing the dog with it.

Unexpected tears clouded her vision, and she blinked as she brushed them away. Death really rotted. The abruptness was the worst thing about it. The Scottster had been here one morning and gone the next. She'd had no warning, no chance to tell him good-bye or say she was sorry for all the times she acted like a snot when he didn't deserve it.

Wonder Boy could be a pain sometimes, like when he wanted to come into her room while she was trying to talk on the phone. A couple of times he'd managed to overhear choice information and blab it at the dinner table, and more than once she'd wanted to wring his scrawny little neck.

But she had never wanted him dead. God above knew that. And she had loved her brother—it was hard not to love his cute little face and those chubby cheeks. But though she would miss him, she'd leave the weeping and wailing to her parents.

If God counted the number of tears people shed for others (and why wouldn't he, if he counted hairs on heads?), then her parents had wept enough today to fill her quota, too.

In the last three days, they'd probably done enough for a lifetime.

Thirteen

MARCH TIPTOED UP TO APRIL WHILE I WASN'T LOOK-ing. The seasonal change is subtle in Florida. Our March winds are alley cats, and our April showers light. No tulips raise their heads to herald a new season here, no daffodils or hyacinths sprinkle our flowerbeds. If I had been more observant, I would have noticed the flocks of thong-clad spring breakers descending to cover the beaches, and the migrating, hoary-headed snowbirds who fly northward right around Easter . . .

I realized April had nearly arrived when I returned to work the Monday following Scott Daniel's accident. The eager girl at the reception desk had turned the page on her huge calendar a day early, and the vast amount of white space caught my eye before I noticed the watchful look she gave me—a sympathetic smile anchoring wary eyes, as if I were a bomb that might explode with the slightest shift in emotional pressure.

I saw the same look mirrored on dozens of other faces as I negotiated the maze leading to our studio. I walked down the hallways with measured steps, returning the fragile greetings with a nod and a stiff smile, determined not to let anyone crack the thin veneer of composure holding me together.

Gary had said I could take another week off if I wanted to, but I knew returning to work would bring normalcy back to my life. I'd been a working woman for so long I didn't know how to relax at home. Because I began my radio show while I was pregnant with Scott Daniel, I used to joke that you could measure the length of my career by the number of my son's birthdays.

I wouldn't make that comment anymore.

The friends and church members had all gone back to their own lives; Steve and I had washed the casserole dishes and Tupperware containers and returned them to their owners. Now the house felt empty, though it was still fragrant with flowers sent in a vain attempt to brighten our gloom.

As though that could possibly help.

Nothing could dispel the gloom haunting our home. You could shine a searchlight into the vaulted halls of my heart and the resident shadows would viciously snuff that beam like a puny candle flame.

Yes, we knew our son was in heaven. Yes, we knew Jesus had promised to bear our burdens. But those promises were like engravings on a tall marble wall, far beyond my reach and cold as death itself.

With relief I entered our control room and closed the door behind me. Chad and Gary sat in their places, while a pot of fresh brew bubbled beneath the coffeemaker on the counter.

"Morning, guys." Though I'd had two cups of coffee before leaving the house, I crossed the room in search of my mug.

Gary responded first. "Good morning, Diana."

I caught the guarded look Chad sent him, but charitably pretended not to notice.

"Um, Dr. D?"

"Yes, Chad?"

"I was real sorry to hear about your little boy."

This from a man who had attended the memorial service and would probably have run the other way if I had tried to thank him for

637

coming. But I understood. People like Chad weren't comfortable with overt emotion of any kind . . . and this situation was loaded.

"Thanks." I found my mug, held it on my palm for a moment, then turned to face my coworkers.

"Guys, it's been a tough week at my house, but I'm a professional in the studio. I'm not sure what's going to happen today—actually, I'm not sure of anything anymore—but I'm going to do my best to carry on as usual. I just wanted to say that up front."

Turning back to the coffee machine, I picked up the pot. "Anything good in the mail this week, Gary? I feel like starting off with something divisive—maybe a juicy piece of hate mail."

When I glanced back, Gary had squinched his face into a *how-do-I-tell-her* look.

"Spit it out, guy."

"Um—90 percent of the mail last week was condolence letters. The other 10 percent was just stupid stuff."

I winced. "Nothing really interesting?"

He fidgeted on his stool, his knees shifting back and forth like the legs of an overanxious adolescent. "Gee, Diana, you're like a national hero. I haven't seen anything like this since the nation rallied around that pregnant woman whose husband died when the plane went down on 9/11."

My mind whirled. "But I didn't do anything."

"Doesn't matter. You were a hero to lots of people before this happened, and then Tennessee Tom called on the same day you lost your son—" His features tensed, as though he was suddenly aware he'd broached a difficult subject. He swallowed hard. "Now nearly everyone admires you."

I exhaled softly. I had not read the stories, but well-meaning friends had dropped off multiple copies at the house. Nearly every newspaper in America had picked up the story about how my son died minutes after I talked Tom Winchell of Memphis, Tennessee, into going out to meet a SWAT team. I couldn't blame them. No news editor worth his salt would pass up a story that rich in irony.

"What on earth do they admire me for?" I asked. "Not cracking under the pressure?"

Gary flushed as he looked away. "For getting through, I guess. For bearing up under the cameras and all."

I poured a packet of sugar in my coffee and stirred. I didn't want to be any sort of hero; I didn't want my private grief to overlap my work at all. On the other hand, I'd been in the radio business long enough to know the price of celebrity—if you create an appetite for your material in an audience, you shouldn't be surprised when the audience hungers for more. The key to survival is in knowing how much you can give without being eaten alive.

I took the spoon from my coffee mug and dropped it on a tray stained with the leavings of a week's worth of sloppy coffee drinkers, then turned to face my staff. "This is what we'll do. We'll take the first five minutes of the monologue to talk about the accident, and I'll thank our listeners for their support. I'll tell them we are working through our loss, but I'm still committed to the show and helping them with their problems. Then we'll cut to the most ridiculous caller you can find."

The dimple appeared in Gary's cheek. "You want Matilda?"

A caller springing completely from Gary's imagination and penchant for mimicry, Matilda was our ace in the hole whenever things got slow or we needed to voice an outrageous opinion that proper Dr. Diana simply couldn't verbalize. Most of our listeners were perceptive enough to realize Matilda was a fictional figment, but occasionally we did get letters from listeners who were convinced sixty-nine-year-old Matilda McGuillicutty really did live in a freezer box outside the Lake Bongo Vista Horseshoe Stadium.

"You bet. Have Matilda call and ask about sending her goldfish to therapy or something, and before you know it we'll be back on track."

"Perfect!" Gary spun around to scribble on his legal pad, and I knew he'd be thinking hard about what Matilda could say.

"Anything on the newswire?" I glanced out the window, where one of the ubiquitous interns was gazing wistfully at the soundboard, no doubt dreaming of the day he'd be allowed to push buttons and slide thingamajigs.

"One of our state senators is proposing a bill that would allow transsexuals to adopt children," Gary muttered in a distracted voice. "But you don't want to tackle that today, do you?"

"Why not? I'm an adoptive parent."

Before last week, I had been an adoptive *and* a biological parent . . . but I wouldn't think about that now.

I sipped from my coffee, pulled a thicker-than-usual stack of correspondence from the tray on the wall, then headed toward the door. "I'm going to the air studio to read through these. Yell if you need me."

Gary didn't even look up from his notes. "Sure thing."

In truth, I wanted some time alone, and the padded and soundproof walls of the air studio seemed infinitely more soothing than the girls-in-bikinis-wallpapered control room. Gary and Chad were sharp young men, but neither of them could truly appreciate what had happened in my life. Last week, in an instant, I had lost a child. The most precious thing those two had ever lost was probably their virginity.

Nodding at another starry-eyed intern, this one a young woman, I slipped into the air studio and perched on my chair. The headphones dangled from the boom, but I left them hanging, knowing Gary would understand I wanted quiet. When I wore those, I could hear every murmur and roar made in the often-busy control room. Gary would hail me on the intercom if he needed me.

Steeling myself for horrific spelling and a fresh assault of emotion, I pulled on my reading glasses and began to skim the letters and printed e-mails. From all over America my listeners had written, some bemoaning my loss, others urging me not to give up.

Did they think I was suicidal? I had been wounded, but I still had a husband, a daughter, and a career. In the last week I'd been too numb to act like much of a wife, mother, or career woman, but I would find my footing soon.

Maybe.

One woman from Idaho reminded me that the pain would lessen in time, for she had loved and lost, too, and loving and losing was better than not loving at all.

"Original," I murmured, turning another page on my desk.

The next two letters assured me that my son was now an angel in heaven. Wrong.

I flipped the page. The next note came from a medium who offered me a chance to speak to Scott one final time—for a reasonable fee. "If you like, we can barter a deal," the so-called psychic wrote. "Free radio advertising for one year will get you three thirty-minute sessions with your son's spirit. Call me today, Dr. Diana—I know that little guy wants to talk to his mommy!"

I wadded that page with one hand, then flung it toward the trash can where it—and its author—belonged.

The next letter came from a lawyer offering her services in case I wanted to sue the school, the driver, or the state of Florida for any reason whatsoever. Another handwritten note came from a barely literate woman who had no legal experience whatsoever, but was convinced I could persuade a jury to give me five million dollars, a million for each year of my son's life.

"Think of all the things you could do with the money," she had scrawled across the bottom of a sheet of notebook paper. *"You could end hungry around the world, starting right here in air town. Sence I know your to busy to feed all those kids, I'd be happy to take care of the money for you."*

"Sure you would," I muttered. "But it'd take a lot more than five million to satisfy your greedy soul, wouldn't it?"

I glanced toward Gary in the window, but he was busy with something at the computer and not looking my way. I satisfied my urge to vent by tossing the last letter into the garbage, too, and found myself wishing that I could meet some of these idiots face-to-face. As a radio personality, I'd grown used to receiving letters from all sorts of zanies, but never had they struck so close to my heart.

They weren't all bad. Sprinkled among the outrageous letters were cards and notes from kind people who knew how to string words together in a reasonably coherent pattern. Most were from women, though several came from men. I blinked back tears as I read these, and wondered if I should take some of them to Steve. He had been handling his grief reasonably well. He had gone back to work the day after the funeral and seemed to find comfort in staying busy.

Nighttime was the most difficult part of the day, and the family dinners we had enjoyed were rapidly becoming family history. Scott Daniel had been the glue holding us together, for Brittany certainly had no desire to eat dinner with her parents. Every night this past week, after coming home from school, she had gone straight upstairs to take a nap, sleeping through supper. With no desire to disturb what was certainly an adolescent coping mechanism, Steve and I ate take-out on TV trays in the den, pretending to watch the evening news so we wouldn't have to speak. Later, as I slipped into bed, I would hear the beep of the microwave downstairs as Brittany warmed up whatever leftovers she could find in the fridge.

My daughter had proved remarkably unflappable, and once again I marveled at the emotional elasticity of children. She had wept when we told her about the accident; she had stood with crossed arms at the graveside, an obvious defensive posture revealing volumes about her frame of mind. But logic assured me she could not blame herself—a common danger with children—nor could she blame us, for Scott's death could not have been more accidental.

She would miss him, we all would, but she would go on. She had her circle of friends, and she had a new life for which to prepare. In less than six months she would be leaving the nest and heading off to college. I would not want her wings to be laden with grief or guilt.

Without warning, tears stung my eyes. I dropped the letter in my hand and pulled off my glasses, swiveling my chair to block anyone watching from the windows as I swiped wetness from my lower lashes.

I had wanted to come back to work and return to the routine of ordinary life. I had even hoped that listening to the problems of others would take my mind off my own situation, but if my emotions kept ricocheting like this, how would I ever get through the day?

I reached into my pocket and pulled out a tissue, then furiously dabbed at my eyes. I had to get a grip. This control room, with its microphone and buttons and flashing phone lines, was blessedly removed from my home. At home, time had stopped, appetites had ceased, and the flesh-and-blood people had become ghosts while Scott Daniel laughed and giggled behind every corner . . .

I still listened for his tread on the stairs, paused at the threshold of his room at night, waited for his kiss to rouse me in the morning. His shoes, which still fit in the palm of my hand, littered the floor beneath his bed, and his favorite juice boxes lined the bottom shelf in the refrigerator.

My home had become an alien place, but here at the station . . .

Here I was safe. Scott Daniel had never even visited the Open Air complex. This place held no memories of him, so here I could find relief.

Glancing at the clock, I saw we had five minutes to air. Framed by the window linking me to the control room, Gary perched on his stool, his eyes intent upon me.

Giving him a thumbs-up, I reached for my headphones, then settled the band over my head.

"You okay?" His voice sounded thin in my ear.

I set my hands to the task of positioning a pad of paper and a pencil within easy reach. "I'm fine. You might want to pull up a couple of extra comedy bits, though. If you see me start to lose it, just let them roll, okay? I think I'll be fine, but sometimes I surprise myself."

"Don't worry, Dr. D," Chad breathed into the mike. "We've got your back."

Nodding, I took another sip of the fragrant coffee, then rubbed my hands together and took a deep breath.

Another week, another Monday morning, another show. But the first without Scott Daniel.

Fourteen

I WAITED UNTIL STEVE'S OLD BMW SHUDDERED TO a halt, then wrapped my hand around the seat belt across my chest. "I really don't want to do this. It's not too late for us to go home."

Steve halted, his hand on the door. "This will be good for us, Diana. Give it a try, just this once. If you absolutely hate it, I'll go alone from now on."

I blew out my cheeks, ruffling the bangs over my eyes. "I don't know why you need this. You're a mature man, you can find peace in your faith. And you're married to a counselor, for Pete's sake—"

"I need to do this for *me*. And I think you need it, too, though that stubborn will of yours has blinded you to your own need at the moment."

Unable to face him, I turned my eyes toward the window. If I looked over and saw a smile on his face, so help me, my palm would itch to slap it off.

"Have it your way, then."

As I unfastened the seat belt, I marveled again that Steve had even been interested in attending a support group for bereaved parents. The week after the accident he'd dropped a few hints about visiting the grief recovery group at our church, but I vetoed that idea before the words could finish leaving his mouth. Open our hearts before people who *knew* us? Having a pap smear in the middle of I-275 at rush hour would be far more appealing.

When he came home with a brochure about this parents' support group, I'd been adamantly against it, too. We didn't need help, we didn't need the exposure, and we sure didn't need to share one blessed word about our private grief with the world. Ever since taking my first radio job, I'd been careful to guard my family's privacy. Life was hard enough for my children because their dad had cleaned the teeth of practically every other kid in the county. My radio exposure had increased the pressure, especially on Brittany, who'd been a tender thirteen when I took to the airwaves.

"It's hard enough having two doctors for parents," she once whined to me. "But having Dr. Diana for a *mom*? People think I should never have any problems!"

With her plea in mind, I tried to distance my private self from the job. I refrained from using my radio voice in neighborhood conversations, I described my occupation on parent questionnaires as "communications," and I never offered to bring my kids along when the station booked me for promo appearances. My radio listeners knew I had a son and a daughter; thanks to the national media, they now knew my son was dead. That was all I wanted the world to know. My memories of Scott Daniel were too precious; I would not dilute them by sharing them with the world.

Not being a celebrity, however, Steve had never had to divide his life between public and private worlds so his sense of potential publicity land mines was undeveloped, at best. A good man with nothing to hide, he had no fear of the media and believed most reporters were friendly and sympathetic.

Ha!

I shuddered to think of a reporter lying in wait, then plying Steve with a smile and an innocent question about our family. Steve would erupt like Mount Vesuvius, spewing stories, snapshots, and quotes that would not always be understood by people outside our family circle.

Even before the accident, Steve *loved* to talk about our kids to anyone who would listen. Now the sympathy of strangers seemed to assure him of Scott's uniqueness, but I didn't need assurance. Scott Daniel was a special blessing from God, and I didn't need anyone to remind me of that.

The single reason I agreed to come tonight, the *only* way Steve could ever get me to appear at such a public venue, was my belief that Christian wives should submit when their husbands won't back down.

Of course, that belief hadn't stopped me from resisting during the drive from our home to this little frame building in Largo. On most occasions when we disagreed, I convinced Steve to swing around to my point of view. But he hadn't been in a swinging mood tonight, so here I was . . . because I respected my husband and wanted to please God.

And because Steve had promised I would have to come only once.

I glanced up toward the small building that had obviously been a home in a former lifetime, probably sold to the city as the population moved out of the urban center. A sign hanging from the porch eaves announced that we had come to the "Pinellas County Community Services Center."

Sighing, I picked up my purse and opened the door. Steve had no idea what I was risking in this act of submission—exposure, for instance. What would the press say if word got out that Dr. Diana Sheldon, professional radio psychologist, was attending a support group for desperate, pathetic parents? The idea was ludicrous.

Besides, I could already predict exactly what variety of psychobabble we'd be served tonight. I knew about letting go and moving on; I knew about venting and releasing and identifying the stages of grieving. My rational brain understood why I could burst into tears at any moment for no reason at all, and my scientific brain had begun to count squares on the calendar, for such outbursts usually tapered off after a period of forty days. The ancients had been wise when they allotted that length of time for mourning—physiologically, we humans seemed to require forty days to regain our equilibrium after a significant personal loss.

Steve and I were on day sixteen, still in the heart of the unsteady stage . . . yet another reason why we shouldn't be appearing in public.

Yet Steve apparently needed outside help, and it was only after he threatened to attend this meeting alone that I decided to rethink my position. Yes, I wanted to honor my husband's wishes, but I was also terrified of what he might say if I weren't along to stem the tide of words. Unaccompanied, he might freely talk about me, my job, or the pressure of raising a child in the spotlight of celebrity. My dear, naive husband might air our personal problems and feelings to anyone who would listen, even if one of them happened to be a reporter, a freelance writer, or a neighbor with a glib tongue.

I agreed to join him with two stipulations. I would speak as little as possible, lest anyone recognize my voice, and while we were in the meeting Steve would refer to me by my middle name, Juliet. According to the brochure, the group maintained a no-last-names policy, but I knew how friendships could spring up outside the confessional circle. No way was I going to let someone drag our family onto the pages of the *National Gossip*. That rag had already printed a grainy photograph of us at the cemetery.

The sound of Steve's footsteps on the gravel grated against my nerves. "Coming, *Juliet*?"

I gritted my teeth at the sound of sarcasm in his voice. He thought I was overreacting. He thought my security concerns resulted from paranoia, and he probably believed my desire to disguise my identity sprang from pure egotism. But in this age of reality television and overnight celebrity, I would take no chances.

I slid out of the seat, brushed the wrinkles from my skirt, and joined Steve on a narrow sidewalk that led into the community center. The place looked like most city-owned buildings—a little dingy and too garishly painted—but it was brightly lit and uncluttered. Through the screen door I could see wooden floors glowing with a patina of long use, and folding chairs stacked against the wall. A dozen chairs had been arranged in a circle in the center of the room, and most of these were filled by men and women of all ages. None of them were smiling.

Steve dropped his hand onto my shoulder as we paused to open the door, and I felt a sense of relief when I walked through and stepped out of his reach. Our disagreement vibrated like a force field between us, and I knew it wouldn't dissipate until we had successfully navigated the evening.

I spied two empty seats and strode toward them, leaving Steve to follow, his heavy shoes clunking against the wooden floor.

He flashed a smile around the circle of faces. "I'm sorry we're late."

"It's all right. You must be Steve and Juliet. I'm Mary Fisher." This reply came from a heavyset woman with a throaty voice. I sank into a chair, dropped my purse onto my lap, and rested my forearms on it, well aware that I was transmitting a forceful message in body language: *Don't come too close.*

Steve, on the other hand, sat down and leaned forward, then opened his hands in an apologetic shrug. "We didn't mean to interrupt. Thank you for allowing us to come."

As if they would turn us away! The sight before my eyes proved one of my mother's old adages—misery *did* love company, because these had to be the most miserable-looking people ever assembled in one room.

"You are welcome." Mary's voice was an echoing purr in the room. "You are among friends."

I resisted the urge to jam my finger down my throat. As a counselor, I had sat in the lead chair and murmured those same words many times, so I knew how automatic they were. Any vague hope I'd harbored of finding *real* help was shattered by Mary Fisher's appearance—she had adopted the uniform of a garden-variety social worker, a type I knew well from graduate school. Though she was probably on the far side of forty, she wore her gray-streaked hair long and straight. Her eyes, round with concern, peered out at us through untrimmed bangs, and her full patterned skirt flowed over her thighs and puddled on the floor like curtains in a formal dining room. Her skin was pale, for she was surely an indoor girl who only went outside to hug trees in the moonlight, and her lips were lined from the habit of pressing them together in thought. She wore no wedding ring, so odds were good she was liberated, divorced, or lesbian, and I knew without looking that if I were to peer into her purse I'd find a cell phone, a voter registration card establishing her affiliation with the Democratic Party, and a bottle of echinacea. Once she hit fifty, she'd be carrying ginkgo biloba, too.

"We are gathered here tonight," Mary said, her wide eyes sweeping the group as a heavy charm bracelet jangled at her wrist, "to support one another through one of the worst tragedies that can befall a loving parent. We are here because we have been united by loss. We are here because we care, and we long to care for others. We may have lost our children, but we have not lost the ability to care."

I closed my eyes. The sentiment in here was so thick you could haul it up by the bucket and sell it by the pound.

"Steve and Juliet—"

The sound of our names snapped me back to attention.

"—I'm sure you'd like to get a feel for things before you speak, so why don't we let the others start us off with introductions?"

She looked around the circle, her eyes wide with appeal, and finally one gray-haired man shuffled his feet and met my gaze. "My name's Ted." He shifted his blue eyes to Steve, then reached out and clasped the hand of the frail woman beside him. "We lost our son ten years ago. He was murdered on his way home from his after-school job, and his killer has never been found."

As a murmur of sympathy ran through the circle, I wondered how many times they had heard his introduction. Had Ted been coming to this group for ten years? The psychologist in me protested, but the parent in me understood. If someone took Brittany from me, I wouldn't be able to let the matter rest until the police found the killer and helped me answer a single question: *Why?*

A red-haired woman next to Ted lifted her hand like a child in school seeking permission to speak.

Mary nodded. "Go ahead, dear."

The redhead looked straight at me. "I'm Tilly. My daughter died from a drug overdose six months ago. She was only fourteen. I know who killed her—those nasty punks who make pills available to inno-cent kids. What I can't understand is why nobody's doing anything about it."

I looked away, lest Tilly read the thoughts in my eyes: lose the anger, lady, or it'll eat you alive. And don't forget who swallowed those pills—your daughter made the choice, right?

"I'm Meg—and I lost a baby at birth." The sweet girl who uttered this clutched at her young husband's hand and sent an apologetic smile winging toward Mary. "I feel a little like I don't belong here, because I didn't have much of a life with my baby. You all had a chance to really *know* your children—"

"The loss is the same," Mary interrupted. "You belong here, never doubt it. Loss comes to us through different situations, but we feel the same emotions. Sometimes we feel anger, sometimes despair, and sometimes we try to bargain with ourselves or with our conception of a higher power—"

"I don't blame God."

I stiffened as my husband spoke.

"God gave us our son five years ago—I'm sorry, I should introduce myself. I'm Steve, this is my wife, and we lost our five-year-old son in an accident only two weeks ago."

Another murmur of sympathy rippled through the circle, but this time it felt about as genuine as canned laughter. What did these people know about us?

"And I don't blame God—we weren't supposed to be able to have kids, you see, so when Di—when my wife got pregnant, we were thrilled. We saw Scotty as a gift from God, a miracle, and we just *knew* God was going to do something special with his life. That's why we're having a hard time with his death. Why would God take something he'd given us so miraculously?"

"That's an interesting thought, Steve." Mary's smooth voice flowed over us like honey on a raw burn. "But not everyone here believes in God, you know. If you do, that's fine, and I'm sure it helps if you can visualize life in a larger picture. Life brought you an unexpected gift, and now circumstances have taken it away. So what was the reason for that life? Was it not to love and be loved? Isn't that why we are all here? If you look at it that way, even a simple flower has a purpose—to bloom, even for a day, and bring pleasure to others."

I resisted a sudden urge to laugh, for my dear husband was staring at Mary as if she'd suddenly sprouted dandelions on her scalp. "I don't understand what flowers have to do with my son, and of course we loved Scotty. But there's more to life than love."

"Really?" Mary tilted her head, then spread her hands. "Group?"

"Love is all there is." This from a big-haired woman in tight jeans. "My son had Down syndrome and he was the embodiment of love. Some people are amazed I could miss him like I do, but I can't help it. I feel like I've lost an angel who flew into my life for a few years, then flew away."

"Love doesn't go very far when you're dealing with teenagers— you've got to have a lot of steel in your spine, too." Tilly's eyes flashed. "I loved my daughter and I miss her, but there are times I'm actually glad I don't have the hassle anymore. Then I feel guilty, but the truth is, raising a teenager is hard. All those nights I waited up because I didn't know where she was, or what she was doing, or who she was with—well, it was hard on a single mom. Now all I have to cope with is her absence—and, well, sometimes that's easier than coping with her presence, if you know what I mean."

As Tilly's voice faded away, Ted reached over and patted her hand. I felt a rueful smile cross my face. These people weren't likely to find answers here, but at least they had found companionship.

"I know how frustrating the teen years can be," Steve said, his voice softening. "But we hadn't reached that point with Scotty. Even so, somehow I doubt life with him would ever be hard. You may think I'm biased, but he really was a great kid. Everybody loved him and he loved everybody. That's why we were so sure God had a glorious future mapped out for him . . ."

As his voice trailed away, Steve looked at me. I knew he was hoping I'd pick up the conversational ball and run, but I couldn't. Even if I had wanted to participate, at that moment a lump the size of a football was lodged in my throat. I knew I'd be bawling like a newborn if anyone so much as looked my way.

I shook my head in a barely discernible gesture, then looked down to study the dusty toes of my shoes. Steve had brought us into this emotional huddle, he could get us out.

Fifteen

REACHING ACROSS THE CONSOLE, STEVE POWERED OFF the car's AC. Though the night was heavy and warm for April, the chilly breeze emanating from his wife threatened to frost the windshield.

He turned the BMW through the twisting side streets of downtown Largo, then headed south on Starkey Road. A light rain had begun to fall during the meeting and the highway shimmered beneath the streetlights. April showers were supposed to bring May flowers, but this rain held only the promise of more tears.

He had been the only one to cry during the meeting. All of the people in the circle had lost children, and, after hearing the others' stories, he knew none of them had yet arrived at a place of acceptance, whatever that meant. Yet he was the only one who wept.

Had the others learned to master their emotions? Or had their grief evolved to some feeling too deep for tears?

He glanced toward his wife, who sat with one arm propped on the door, her face turned toward the window. Diana had been too angry to cry. She had not spoken during the meeting, and her chilly attitude had silently warned everyone away. Even Mary, who could probably warm the cockles of Scrooge's heart, had deferred to Diana's frostiness and left her alone.

A few months ago Diana's aloof behavior would have embarrassed him, but embarrassment now seemed like such a trivial emotion. Once you have broken down in hiccuping sobs before police officers, church friends, your hygienist, and a medical examiner, what else on earth could possibly prove embarrassing?

At work, he'd been careful to maintain his composure before his young patients—children didn't understand loss, and in a perfect world, they shouldn't have to encounter death and disaster. But today's kids lived in a fallen world where Bad Things happened all too often.

He brought his hand to his jaw as a sudden dart of guilt pricked him. Diana was angry, but she was also in pain. He recognized it in the set of her jaw, the watery glint of her eyes. Stoicism was part of her nature, so she wasn't easily given to tears. He had always admired her strength, but now it seemed unnatural that the man of the house should weep and wail while the woman watched with glassy eyes.

He supposed part of his wife's self-control resulted from her work. The act of absorbing other people's heartbreaking situations had to toughen the heart somehow . . . or had her heart been tough all along? The most common comment he heard when people realized he was married to the famous Dr. Diana was "I don't know how she can sit around and listen to people's problems all day."

Maybe Diana was good at what she did because she had a heart strong enough to weather the emotional storms that knocked most people off their feet.

She wasn't unbreakable, though. Two nights ago he had come home to find her standing in the den, the contents of a half-dozen photograph albums scattered over the couch and coffee table. The desperate look in her eyes had alarmed him, and the fury with which she wailed, "I can't find one!" made him wonder if something inside her had snapped.

"You can't find what?"

"A picture of Scott Daniel snaggle-toothed. You know, a picture with his front tooth missing." She raked her hand through her hair, then stood there, one hand clawing her scalp as if she could dredge information from her brain. "How could we forget to take a picture of him like that? We knew he wouldn't stay that way forever!"

He had joined her in the middle of the mess, trying his best to remember the last time he'd taken the camera from the desk drawer. "Didn't we take pictures at his birthday party?"

"He had both his teeth then. He didn't lose his front tooth until January."

Steve pressed his hand to his chin. He had hauled out the video camera at Christmas, so they'd have those memories, but he couldn't remember shooting any pictures of Scotty's gap-toothed smile.

"We didn't do it, did we?" Tears were streaming down her face, but she wasn't really crying, it was more like an overflow of emotion. "How could *you,* a dentist, not think to take a picture of him like that?"

He opened his mouth, not sure if he should defend himself or soothe her, and suddenly she was in his arms, beating his chest with slow, heavy thumps while she wept in earnest.

No, Diana wasn't unbreakable.

Reaching through the empty space between them now, he squeezed her arm. "Is Britty home tonight, or did she go out?"

Diana lifted one shoulder in a shrug. "I'm not sure. She may have left a note on the kitchen table, but you didn't give me time to check."

He removed his hand, hearing the accusation in her words. After rushing home from the office, he had time to do little more than wash his hands and grab a slice of pizza from the box on the counter. She, on the other hand, had been home for at least three hours, but she'd say she had been busy reading letters or preparing for her show.

Still . . . he would keep trying to offer an olive branch.

Determined not to be drawn into a fight, he drew a deep breath. "Britty spends an awful lot of time at Charisse's house. Have you met the girl's parents?"

"Brittany is eighteen, Steve, she's not a toddler anymore. We don't have to request detailed biographical sketches of her friends' parents."

"But shouldn't we at least know what they're like? She's over there four nights a week."

"I've spoken to the woman."

"When? When you called their house looking for Britty?"

She turned, a swift shadow of anger sweeping across her face. "Why the sudden interrogation? Brittany and Charisse have been friends for three years. I hardly think they're about to run off and become drug dealers."

He took pains to keep his voice level. "I'm just saying we need to keep tabs on our daughter."

"Why? So God won't snatch her, too?"

Steve blinked, stunned by the force of his wife's reaction. He did not answer, but drove through the security gate, greeted the guard in the gatehouse, then turned down the street that would lead him home.

Silence reigned until they pulled into the driveway. As the automatic opener lifted the creaking paneled garage door, he gripped his wife's hand. "Diana, I know you're hurting. I know you didn't want to come tonight, and I appreciate the fact that you did. But just now I wasn't talking about Scotty. I only wanted to know about our daughter."

"Brittany's fine."

"Is she? I haven't seen much of her in the last two weeks."

Diana reached for the door handle. "She's doing better than either of us. Think about it, Steve—she lost less than we did, so she'll recover quicker. She lost a brother, but her world never revolved around Scott Daniel the way ours did. Plus, she has her friends to take her mind off things."

"Maybe she needs more than friends. Maybe she needs someone to talk to."

Diana arched a brow. "Like who?"

"Well . . . like a counselor."

Her nostrils flared. "Are you *nuts*? *I'm* a counselor, and she doesn't need anyone else. If I were to send her to someone, she'd think she was damaged goods or something. I'm sure she's only experiencing ordinary emotions in an ordinary way. We're a normal family, Steve, probably a lot better than normal."

Steve slammed the steering wheel with the meaty part of his palm. "What's *normal*? I must be nuts, Diana, because I can't find normal anymore. I get up, I get dressed, I go to work, but nothing feels right. You might be Superwoman, but I felt the need for this support group tonight, and somehow it helped to know other people have felt what I'm feeling. I can't help thinking that Britty might benefit from someone who can listen to what she's thinking and help her sort through all this."

"Brittany has us to talk to. Have we ever turned her away? If she needs to talk, she'll come to us."

"Will she?"

The question hung between them, unanswered, and for an instant Steve saw uncertainty flicker in his wife's eyes. Then her face froze in a mask of resoluteness.

"She would come to us." Her voice rang with finality. "I believe that with all my heart."

Sixteen

THAT NIGHT I TOSSED AND TURNED FOR THE BETTER part of an hour. When Steve's deep breathing assured me that he had nodded off, I slipped out of bed and padded down the hall. A thin strip of light and a faint stream of music had poured from beneath Brittany's door at eleven when I went upstairs to bed. Now her room lay as silent and dark as my own.

I walked past her closed door and hesitated at the threshold to Scott Daniel's room, breathing deep.

Everything I'd heard at the support group tonight told me I should go back to bed, close my eyes, and concentrate on tomorrow's tasks. If I couldn't move past this loss, I'd become as pitiful as Ted, who still sought comfort and counsel after ten years of bereavement.

But the heart and the mind speak with two separate voices, and the cry of my heart could not be ignored. Trailing one hand along the papered wall, I stepped into Scott Daniel's room and felt my flesh pebble in a shiver of delight.

Amazing, that after sixteen days a room could still retain the essence of a living, breathing boy. In the dim glow of the automatic nightlight I crossed to his dresser, then fondled the ears of a stuffed bunny, a beribboned gift I had meant to slip into his Easter basket.

Quietly opening the top drawer, I trailed my fingertips over the neat piles of underwear and socks. A shuffle of baseball cards had been shoved into the corner—I pulled them out, tapped them into a neat stack, and placed them in between the pairs of rolled tube socks.

Opening the second drawer, I instinctively recognized the things I sought—a swirl of unlaundered T-shirts and sweaters, still smelling of Scott Daniel Sheldon.

I pulled his Buccaneers sweatshirt from the melee and pressed it to my face, breathing in the scents of cookies and grass, boy and school paste. Then, still clutching the shirt, I crawled into his bed and climbed beneath the covers. His monkey, wide-eyed and rubber-faced, lay beside me as it had lain beside my son since infancy.

Retreating here had become a secret ritual for me, the only way I could relax enough to sleep. Lying in Scott Daniel's bed was like wrapping myself up in him. As I drifted in the haze between wakefulness and sleep, his favorite monkey in my arms, I could almost convince myself that he might burst through the door at any moment.

Memories of the day crowded my thoughts as I closed my eyes and drifted. The broken, agonized voices of the parents in the support group echoed in my consciousness while their sympathetic faces hovered before me, their eyes grazing mine. A few of those faces had held traces of skepticism when Steve explained how Scott had been our special gift from God, but not even Mary the agnostic social worker would ever be able to convince me otherwise. We had wanted so desperately to be parents; we had worked so hard to adopt Brittany. Once she came home, we settled back to concentrate on parenting, a job we loved.

Years later, with unbridled joy, disbelief, and a great deal of giddiness we announced Scott Daniel's pending arrival. The barren womb had become fruitful, and like Elizabeth, Hannah, and Rachel of the Bible, I wanted to sing and praise God in unbounded ecstasy.

Even in a shallow doze, I smiled at the memory. My doctor had warned me about late-life pregnancies; he had quoted statistics about complications, Down syndrome, and health risks to the mother. But

God proved faithful, and in the October of my forty-third year, I gave birth to a healthy son. Pastor John came to the hospital to pray with us, and I still remember how Steve, John, and I held hands over my hospital bed with the baby propped against my bent knees, taking in his first prayer.

God had been so generous—so how could he now withdraw his gift? We hadn't asked for a miracle baby, but we had fallen in love with him once he arrived. Why would God give us the unspoken desire of our hearts and then snatch it away?

Fully awake again, I rolled onto my back and opened my eyes. Streaming moonlight through the window made a rectangle on the floor, brightening the room enough for me to see the pictures on the ceiling. Scott Daniel had asked Steve to pin posters of his favorite basketball players above his bed, so in the gloom I could see the muscled profiles of Michael Jordan and Scotty Pippen, my son's personal favorite.

Unbidden, tears spilled from my eyes and trailed into my hair. Steve and Scott had often talked about getting tickets to go see Pippen play in Orlando, but life got in the way. Now that day would never come.

Turning onto my side, I felt the soft pressure of Scott Daniel's pillow against my cheek. How many nights had I peered through the door to see him sleeping here, his lips full and slightly parted, one arm wrapped around his monkey, one bare foot sticking out from under the covers. He loved wearing socks to bed but he kicked them off, so I was forever fishing them out of the sheets—

My thoughts came to an abrupt halt as the stairs creaked. I lay as if paralyzed while fear blew down the back of my neck. I would have heard a click if one of the bedroom doors had opened, so the person climbing the stairs was not Steve, not Brittany, and certainly not Scott Daniel.

Every muscle in my body tightened as I threw back the covers and placed my bare feet on the floor. Reaching for Scott Daniel's tee ball bat against the wall, I crept toward the hallway, where a dark shadow was moving toward Brittany's room.

My trembling fingers found the light switch. When the overhead lamp blazed, I found myself staring into the wide eyes of my daughter.

Fear faded to relief, then veered toward astonished anger. "What are you *doing?*"

Brittany blinked in the brightness.

My brain struggled to make sense of the situation. It was nearly one o'clock and a school night—and Britt had been in her room when I went to bed . . . hadn't she?

Mouth agape, I studied her. She wore a light jacket and shoes, and her purse hung from her shoulder. She hadn't been downstairs raiding the refrigerator.

I nailed her with an *I-mean-business* look. "Young lady, I asked you a question."

Lifting her chin, she met my gaze head-on. "I was with Charisse."

"At this hour? It's a school night, and your curfew is 10:30."

Disdain filled her eyes. "Nobody else has to be in that early."

"You do. So what were you doing just now?"

"Nothing."

"Nothing?" Anger, so successfully restrained earlier this evening, stretched its limbs inside my chest and pounded on my heart. Thrumming with rage, I marched to her room, threw open the door, and flipped the light switch. The bed was empty, though a decidedly lifelike lump lay beneath the quilt—a maneuver straight out of *Ferris Bueller's Day Off.*

Stalking toward her nightstand, I saw how she had managed to turn the lamp off—a timer, one of those square plastic gizmos you can buy at any grocery store, had controlled both the light and the radio with the aid of an extension cord.

For a moment I hovered between fury at her deception and wonder at her ingenuity. Fury quickly won out.

"This"—my finger trembled as I pointed to the timer in the outlet—"is pure deception, young lady. Why have you been lying to us?"

Brittany plopped on the bed, crossing her arms. "Well . . . I'm sorry. But my curfew is too early. Every other senior I know can stay out at least until midnight."

"You'll never convince me your friends' parents allow them to stay out until midnight on a school night. But that's beside the point—it's *1:00* A.M.!"

"Well . . ." She twirled a strand of flaming hair around her finger. "I guess we forgot to look at the clock."

I sputtered in stupefaction. "And where were you while you were forgetting to look at the clock?"

"Nowhere bad—just the Waffle House."

I stared at her in speechless incredulity. *The Waffle House?* Since when had my daughter acquired a love of pancakes and coffee?

I placed a hand on my hip. "You don't understand. Anything could happen to you late at night, anything at all. It only takes one drunken driver, one tired man on his way home from work—"

She rolled her eyes. "I'm not going to die, Mom."

I clenched my hand, resisting the urge to slap her impertinent face.

God would have to help me through this. He had given me this teenager, and in another minute or two I'd be more than happy to give her back.

I closed my eyes and clenched my jaw. What now, Lord? How much more do you expect me to handle?

Seventeen

THE SOUND OF VOICES WOKE STEVE FROM A RESTLESS sleep. He blinked at the green numerals of the digital clock, orienting himself to the time and place, then slid out of bed and threw on his robe. Brittany and Diana were going at each other about something, but what in the world could have set them off at 1:15 in the morning?

Diana's face was tight with fury when he entered the fray. Britty sat on her bed, her arms wrapped around herself, her chin jutting forward. Neither of his girls looked happy.

He brought his hand to his brow, shielding his eyes from the blinding light. "What's going on here?"

Diana whirled to face him. "I heard a noise and stepped out into the hall. I found our daughter climbing the stairs. While we thought she was asleep in bed, she's been out with Charisse. They think they're immortal."

"We weren't doing anything bad," Brittany mumbled.

"Wait." Steve held up his hand, fishing around for a misplaced thought, then found it. He gave his wife a triumphant smile. "She couldn't have been out. Her truck's been in the driveway all night."

Diana's brows lifted, graceful wings of scorn. "She had Charisse pick her up." She pointed to the nightstand. "Look behind that lamp—she purposely put her light on a timer to deceive us! And I want to know how long this has been going on!"

Steve looked at Brittany, who seemed to be weighing the consequences of the truth against those of a plausible lie.

Leaning against the doorframe, he folded his arms. "Where were you, Britty?"

She gave him a look of wide-eyed remorse. "The Waffle House. We go there because it's open twenty-four hours. But we don't do anything bad. We just drink Cokes and talk."

"Who was with you?"

Britt's cheeks went a deeper pink. "Um . . . Charisse."

"Anyone else?"

"No, Daddy."

Red flags flew at the word *Daddy*. She hadn't called him by that little-girl endearment since the last time he'd caught her engaged in intentional mischief.

He fixed a grim look to his face, one guaranteed to ensure compliance. "Your mother and I will not tolerate this kind of behavior. We don't want you out this late."

"But we weren't doing anything wrong!"

He lifted a hand to silence the outburst. "What you were doing doesn't matter. I worry about the drunks on the road, the oddballs who hang out in open-all-night places, the trouble you might encounter on the road after midnight. When your mother and I go to bed, we want to know you are safe and sound. We want you home."

He glanced at the timer in the outlet, disturbed by the evidence that his daughter had not only broken the rules, but had done so with premeditation. "You're going to be grounded for this—for a while, I think, probably as long as a month. We'll talk in a couple of weeks and see what lessons you've learned."

"Daddy!"

"That's it." He tightened the belt of his robe. "I'm not going to discuss this any further tonight."

Britty turned and buried her face in her pillow. She wasn't happy, but he could handle her anger.

Diana swept past him, leading the way out of the room. He followed, eager to hear her thoughts, but she had few to offer.

"Well done, Counselor," she murmured, each word a splinter of ice.

"You would have done something different?"

She didn't answer, but strode back into the darkness of their bedroom and got into bed, turning her back to him.

Steve slipped out of his robe, tossed it over the footboard, and pulled up the comforter.

Women. He had lived with two of them for over eighteen years, and he was no closer to understanding them than on the day he had married Diana. Scotty, on the other hand, had been as easy to read as large print.

Pain squeezed his heart in a sudden spasm. He missed his son. Never more than now.

Eighteen

"Hello, Sharon, and welcome to the program."

"Dr. Diana?"

I forced a laugh. "Speaking."

"I can't believe it's really you."

I looked at Gary in patient amusement. "Last time I checked, Sharon, I was still me. What's on your mind?"

"Well . . ."

She paused, and that's never good. One of my brows shot up to my hairline while I silently asked Gary, *What gives with this one?*

I was about to disconnect the call when Sharon found her tongue: "Actually, Dr. Diana, I don't have a question for you. I called because I wanted to tell you something."

I checked the screen. "You told my producer you wanted to talk about a problem with your adult son."

"Actually, I wanted to talk to you about *your* son. I think it's terrible the way you've been carrying on as if nothing has happened when I know you have to be dying inside—"

I clicked the disconnect button. "Sorry, Sharon, but people who fib to Gary get cut off." I glanced at the monitor—Todd occupied the next space in the queue, and he was calling about a problem between his fiancée and his poodle.

"Good day to you, Todd; you're on the air. How can I help you?"

"Dr. Diana?"

"Who else?"

"Oh. Sorry."

Another case of broadcast blank-brain? "Todd, you have a problem with your fiancée?"

"I did, but—man, I heard what you did to that last caller. You were cold, Dr. Diana."

If he knew the details of the night I'd just endured, he wouldn't be so quick to pass judgment. "You think I ought to encourage people who lie in order to get on the air?"

"No, but—"

"Neither do I. Now state your problem or get off my show."

Beyond the window, Gary dropped his jaw.

"I, um—" The caller cleared his throat. "It's my fiancée."

"What about her?"

"My dog doesn't like her. My mother doesn't like her, either. She's a great little gal, but my mom keeps cutting her down—"

"Excuse me, but do you hear yourself, Todd? I'm having a little trouble understanding how you can recognize belittlement when you seem intent upon doing it yourself."

"Huh?"

"You just said you were engaged to a great little gal."

"Yeah. So?"

"So don't you see how condescending your attitude is? If your fiancée has grown up with people who criticize her, it's only natural she'd gravitate toward a man who treats her the same way. If you want your mother to stop belittling your girlfriend, I suggest you take a look at your own attitudes first."

Todd sputtered in confusion. "I don't belittle her—"

"Didn't you just call her a *little* gal?"

"Yeah, but I've always called her that."

"You don't think that's condescending?"

"Not when she's five-foot-one."

I stared at the screen, momentarily forgetting that dead air and radio don't mix. Behind the glass, I could see Chad laughing so hard he was in imminent danger of falling off his stool.

I pressed my hand to my forehead. "Your fiancée is short."

"Yeah. Comes up to my shoulder if she's wearing high heels."

"Well, then"—I shook my head, pretending not to notice Chad's histrionics—"I beg your pardon, Todd. I misread the situation."

Todd didn't miss a beat. "I think you misread that other caller, too. She was only trying to help you—"

"I don't need help with my personal life, Todd, and that's not what this show is about. So—tell your girl no one can make a doormat of her unless she lies down, and tell your mother to mind her manners and welcome this young woman to the family. As far as the dog goes—well, either come up with a way to keep them separated, or get yourself a new dog. Because the woman deserves first place in your heart."

I pressed the next button, then disconnected Todd. As a commercial for Neutrogena hand soap filled the speakers, I leaned back in my chair and exhaled a deep breath. "Good grief, when did our callers grow fangs?"

"You're okay," Gary reassured me. "You just have to remember they're trying to help. They listen to you every day, they've read about you in the newspaper, and they care about you."

"Thanks, but I don't want the show to turn into my own private pity party. Tell 'em when they call, okay? No talking about my problems. I'm here to talk about theirs."

"Help's on the way," Gary said. "Look at the list—Charity's on the line."

"Good. I could use a quotable quip this afternoon."

As soon as the intro faded into oblivion, I punched Charity through. "Charity? Welcome to the *Dr. Sheldon Show.*"

"Good morning, Dr. Diana." Her voice had that quivery, unsupported tone I always associated with older people. "This morning I ran across a particularly poignant quote I wanted to share with you."

I grinned at Gary. This woman was as predictable as the sunrise. "I'm all ears, Charity."

"It's from the Talmud, and it goes like this: 'The deeper the sorrow, the less tongue it hath.'"

My lungs contracted so I could barely draw breath to speak, but I forced out a reply: "True enough."

"I would imagine," her voice was soft with compassion, "that's why you don't want to talk about your son."

For a full five seconds I struggled to force words past the constriction of my throat. "And that, ladies and gentlemen"—I pushed the words into the mike—"is why I must ask you to refrain from broaching a difficult subject. Talk radio depends upon *talk,* and I can't talk about some things right now. Maybe not ever. So thank you, Charity, for expressing my reality so eloquently, and I'll thank you, listeners, not to mention my personal situation again."

I pressed the next button, then slumped in my chair as the *Dr. Sheldon Show* theme music led us into the top of the hour. According to the clock, we had sixty seconds before the newsbreak, so I pushed my chair back and stood. During the news I'd have time to walk down the hall and stretch my legs, maybe read a few of the e-mails that had come in during the last hour. I wouldn't be surprised if we had already received a handful either supporting or chastising me for reacting so strongly in this last segment.

The studio door opened. One of our interns, a red-haired youth named Craig Somebody-or-Other, stepped into the room, a sheaf of papers in his hand. He gave me a cautious smile. "Gary said you might like to see these."

"Don't worry, I won't bite." I took the letters and skimmed the first page. A rather bland greeting, thanks-for-changing-my-life, the usual stuff. I flipped through the others. "Anything good in here?"

Craig slipped his hands into his jeans pockets. "Nothing really controversial. Someone sent you a note about the latest healthcare bill before Congress—"

"Boring. People don't care about political issues unless there's a personal story attached."

"Well . . ." As Craig tilted his head, strands of hair that had come loose from his ponytail fell across his cheek. "There's a letter from a guy who says he wants to talk to you about something a little weird." His face flushed. "He, um, says he can clone your son."

Not sure I had heard correctly, I looked up from the page I'd been reading. "Say again?"

Craig took a half-step back. "He's with some group called Project One, and they're into human cloning."

"That's illegal in this country."

"The guy says he's from France."

I handed the stack of e-mail back to the intern. "He's a kook. Put these in my box, will you? I'll pick them up on my way out."

I pointed to the clock as I moved toward the door. "If you'll excuse me, I plan to make wise use of this break and take a walk down the hall."

At least he didn't follow me into the ladies' room.

Nineteen

ALONE IN HER BEDROOM, BRITTANY LEANED AGAINST the mountain of pillows on her bed and ran her fingers through her hair.

"So then what'd he say?" She kept her voice low. Though her mother hadn't specifically forbidden the use of the telephone, that was probably an oversight. The witch had certainly been mad enough to take away everything that made life endurable.

"He just grinned," Charisse answered. "Then he asked when you'd be free, 'cause he really wants to ask you out."

Brittany felt her cheeks grow hot. Being grounded was bad enough, but to have Zack Johnson *know* she was grounded was beyond terrible. "I am *so* bummed."

"Bummed because you're grounded, or bummed that he wants to ask you out?"

"Both." Brittany exhaled in a loud sigh. "Zack's timing stinks. Nothing in my life is going right now, and my parents are totally messed up. The witch is still furious, and my idiot dad keeps knocking on my door and coming in here to annoy me. He's been in twice since he got home."

"What does he want?"

"Nothing—he just comes in, messes with my hair or leans against the wall and tells me some stupid joke he heard from one of the kids in his office. Then he goes into his room and sits in his chair to cry. He thinks nobody knows what he's doing, but I hear him in there. He does that every day."

Charisse fell silent for a moment. "He's still sad about your brother?"

"They both are. I guess they just express it in different ways. Dad gets sad and Mom gets mad."

"What about you?"

"I'm okay. I mean, what can I do to change anything? They liked him better, anyway. He was their little angel. I'm their problem child."

A hollow clanging sound filled the phone, then Charisse snapped her gum. "Got a song for you. I wrote it this afternoon."

Brittany rolled her eyes, but she didn't dare complain. Charisse was a fairly decent singer, but her songs and guitar playing could use a little polish. Some of her lyrics made no sense at all, others had no real tune. But Charisse loved to compose, and Brittany felt she had to listen. After all, Charisse was the only person on earth who would sit and listen to her complaints.

"Girl with her dreams," Charisse sang, her voice cutting through the strum of the guitar. "Poor seventeen. Told what to think, how to dress, how to hide your deep distress . . ."

Brittany listened for three or four minutes, checked her watch, then picked up the remote and powered on the little television in her room. She hit the mute button as soon as images filled the screen— no sense in having the witch storm in here and declare the TV off-limits, too.

And Charisse wouldn't appreciate knowing she didn't have Brittany's full attention.

"That's where I'm stuck," Charisse said, abruptly stopping the song. "I can't think of a way to end it, and in performance you can't fade out the way they do on a CD."

"You'll think of something."

"I'd better. 'Cause this is going to be my signature song when we open the coffeehouse."

The coffeehouse was their brainchild, the Great Adventure they were going to embark upon as soon as they could manage to tear away from the Parents. They'd probably have to put in at least a couple of semesters at college to keep their folks off their backs, but then Brittany and Charisse were going to open The Spot, which would soon become the coolest hangout on the Gulf beaches. Charisse would sing every night while Brittany handled the business and made sure all the male hotties got good seats up front.

"Hey, I saw a For Sale sign on that biker bar just down the street from Luigi's," Charisse said. "It's closed now. We could go after school tomorrow and check it out."

"How are we going to check it out? We have no money."

"You don't have to pay just to look through a window, moron. We can drive over and look around. I know that place probably won't be available by the time we're ready to open The Spot, but the layout might give us some ideas."

Brittany wasn't sure how a biker bar would help them plan their coffeehouse, but anything was better than coming straight home. "Okay—wait, I forgot. I'm not supposed to go anywhere after school."

"Not even for ten minutes?"

"Not even. If the witch finds out, she'll add another month to my sentence."

"How will she find out?"

"She gets off work early, remember? She doesn't have to pick up the Scottster anymore—"

An unexpected lump rose in her throat, and she coughed to get rid of it. Trouble was, the more she coughed, the tighter her throat became so she had to cough again just to clear her airway.

Two minutes later, teary-eyed and wheezing, she thumped herself on the chest and managed a strangled question: "You still there?"

"Good grief, Britt. You okay?"

"Fine. Just breathed in the wrong way or something. What were we talking about?"

Charisse strummed the guitar a moment, then clicked her tongue. "Going to look at the biker bar. You said you can't go."

"Right. The witch is always here when I get home now, and if I'm late, she'll know it. She might be too busy to notice, but if she does, I'm busted."

"Bummer."

"Got that right."

They sat for a moment in companionable silence, then Charisse sighed. "Well . . . guess I better go at least *look* at my English book. I'll be grounded, too, if I don't pass Mrs. Parker's class."

"You'll pass."

"I wish."

"You will, you always do, you brain."

"Don't call me names."

"You brain."

"You moron."

"Get outta here."

"I would, if you'd let me get off the phone!"

They laughed, then hung up.

And as she lay back on her pillow, Brittany closed her eyes and knew that conversation would be the most fun she'd have all day.

Twenty

SLIDING TO THE EDGE OF MY CHAIR, I LEANED CLOSER to the dangling microphone. "Let me get this straight—you made an adoption plan for your baby eighteen years ago, and now you want to be involved in the boy's life?"

"Yes, that's right."

"Are you out of your *mind*?" I paused to let the words echo in the silence. "Bear with me, will you, while I spin a little analogy. Let's say life is a play, and the parents are the directors who train a child—he'll be the actor in this little drama. They place him on the stage, they clap madly when he takes his first step and says his first line. They are coaching from the wings, supporting our young thespian throughout every dramatic trial and tempest." I paused. "Janice, are you with me?"

"Still here."

"Good. Now—let's suppose our hardworking theater company is suddenly approached by another director, a woman who says she not only deserves a place in the wings, but on the stage as well. Our parent directors are trying to teach the child to be independent, they're allowing him to move away from them, but the new director wants him to move *closer* to her. How do you think that makes our hardworking parent team feel? And what about the child? With two sets of directors coaching him, how can he *help* but be confused?"

The caller, a woman from Alabama, sputtered in indignation. "But that's not fair—if it weren't for me, the boy wouldn't even be alive."

"Perhaps, but if not for those other people, he wouldn't be on the stage. If not for those people, you wouldn't have had the freedom to pursue whatever sort of life you've pursued for the last eighteen years. You may have made a selfless decision to make an adoption plan for your baby, and with everything in my heart, I applaud you for that. It takes a brave woman to realize that children deserve to grow up with a mother and a father who are absolutely nuts about the kid. For what you did eighteen years ago, I salute you, Janice. For what you want to do now, I say shame on you!"

Silence rolled over the phone line. I glanced at the control room window, where Gary and Chad were watching with wide eyes.

Maybe I had come on a little strong. Dr. Diana was supposed to be outspoken and occasionally outrageous, but a genteel lady from Alabama might not appreciate such brusqueness.

"Janice? You still there?"

"Yes." Her voice was lower now, subdued.

"Please." I gentled my tone. "Think again before you go knocking on that family's door. See if there's an adoption registry in your state. If by chance your son has registered and expressed an interest in a reunion, then and only then would you have my blessing to proceed. If he has not, please reconsider. Your son is at the age where he needs to make a life of his own. If he wants to meet you, he'll find a way to let you know. If he wants to move ahead with his life, let him. Eighteen years ago you made your choice. Now let the reunion be his choice."

Without wasting a moment, I clicked to the next caller, then grinned. "Good day to you, Charity, you're on the *Dr. Sheldon Show.*"

"Good morning, Dr. Sheldon! And how are you this lovely day?"

"We're all fine as frog hair, Charity. What's on your mind?"

"I ran across a profound thought the other day. I thought you would appreciate it."

I winked at Gary through the window, then propped my head on my hand. "All right, Charity. Can't wait to hear it."

"It's a quote by Samuel Johnson. He said, 'When grief is fresh, every attempt to divert it only irritates.'"

I drummed my nails on the desktop, knowing the sound would carry over the airwaves. "That's . . . interesting, Charity. What made you think of Sam Johnson today?"

"Why you, Dr. Diana. For weeks I've been listening to you try to divert people from your grief, and I know the effort has to be irritating your soul."

I answered in my breeziest voice. "Thank you for your concern, Charity, but my family and I are coping as well as anyone can expect."

I clicked on the next caller. "Stewart? Hi, this is Dr. Diana. Welcome to the show."

"I'm so glad I reached you. I've been trying to get through for days, but the lines are always busy."

I laughed. "What can I say? The problems of society just keep piling up outside my door. So what's your question?"

"No question, really. I just wanted to call and talk about the change I've noticed in you."

I glanced at the call screen. According to Gary's notes, Stewart from Chicago wanted to talk about his wife's meddlesome sister.

"I thought you had a sister-in-law problem, Stewart."

"I do, actually. But first I just want to say that lately I've been extremely disappointed in you."

"Oh?" I grimaced at Gary. "Sorry to disappoint you, Stu. But I gave up trying to please everyone a long time ago."

"It's just that I heard you were a Christian. And some of your recent responses haven't been very Christlike."

"Ohhhhh, I see." I pressed my fingertips to my temple, where another tension headache had begun to pound. "Tell me, Stu—do you read the Bible?"

"Sure."

"And in your Bible, did Jesus ever get upset?"

Stewart hesitated. "He was never mean or cruel. He couldn't have been, because he never sinned."

"I beg to differ, Stu, not about the Lord's sinlessness, but about the cruelty, because that quality is usually subjective. Do you recall the afternoon Jesus cleansed the temple?"

Three seconds of silence, followed by, "Uh-huh."

"I daresay some of those moneychangers thought Jesus was being a little heavy-handed, perhaps even cruel. And what about the Pharisees? Jesus did not mince words when he confronted them with their hypocrisy. But the Lord understood that sometimes one must be cruel in order to be kind."

"Um . . ."

"Get off your high horse, Stu, and don't toss my religion in my face. I could say a few things about people who read the Bible without understanding the larger context, but, unlike you, I'm going to practice a little self-control and keep my opinions to myself. For now, at least, I'm going to think of that Elvis song—know the one I mean?"

The ever-amazing Chad had successfully followed my train of thought. As I launched pious Stu into never-never land, Chad hit the next button and Elvis began crooning "Don't Be Cruel."

When we'd heard a good thirty seconds of the King, I gave Chad the cut signal and leaned into the mike. "Friends, let me tell you a story I heard the other day. Seems an old-time Quaker preacher had the original church in the wildwood, so to speak. His people came to Sunday meeting from all over the mountains, but, unfortunately, most of them had to pass by a big bear's cave on the way. The bear didn't take kindly to having his Sundays disturbed by so many churchgoing folk, so whenever he heard the sound of their singing on the path, he'd run out and bite a few, just for sport. Of course this upset the mountain folk, and pretty soon most of them stopped going to church."

Following my drift, Chad punched in a twanging banjo song for background music.

"Well, the preacher couldn't have that, no sir. So he went down the mountain to have a talk with the bear. He told him that God had meant for the animals and mankind to live in peace, and that the bear would be truly blessed if he could find it in his heart to turn the other cheek and not bite folks when they disturbed his rest. This sounded logical to the bear, who was a naturally God-fearing creature, so he promised to stop biting.

"Well, the church people began to come back to meeting and after a while they got brave enough to stick their heads in the bear's cave and speak to him. Some of the boys, though, became downright foolish. One afternoon they coaxed the bear out with promises of honey, then they pelted him with stones and clubbed him with branches. They beat that poor bear to a frazzle!

"The minister happened by the next day and heard the bear's moaning. As he knelt by the wounded creature's side, he heard about how those boys had not only lost their fear of the bear, but their respect as well. 'You told me I'd be blessed if I didn't bite,' the bear said. 'And I've kept my end of the bargain. But look what God has allowed!'

"The preacher shook his head. 'Friend bear,' he said, 'I told you not to bite. I didn't say you couldn't *growl*.'"

I clicked the next button, which played one of my exit riffs, then leaned in for a parting shot: "Think about it, friends. And forgive me when I growl."

I yanked the headphones from my ears, then leaned my elbows on the desk and massaged my temples. Half an hour to go before I could go home and forget about everyone else's problems . . .

The intercom at my elbow buzzed. "Dr. D? You've got a personal call on line six."

I glanced at the blinking row of telephone lights. Who could be calling on one of the private lines? Steve was at work and Brittany at school, but either one of them could be dealing with an emergency . . .

Rattled by an uncomfortable sense of déjà vu, I lifted the phone and clicked the blinking button at the far right. "Hello?"

"Dr. Diana Sheldon, please." The voice was cultured, masculine, and flavored by an upper-crust accent. European, probably. Maybe British?

"Speaking."

"My name is Andrew Norcross. I won't take up much of your time—"

"I'm in the middle of a show, Mr. Norcross, so if you're selling something—"

"I'm not selling anything, Dr. Sheldon. I wanted first of all to offer my sincere condolences on the death of your son."

I would have tossed him as easily as I bounced other callers who spoke of Scott, but the man's calm voice acted like a balm on my raw nerves.

"Thank you. But I haven't time—"

"Would you, Dr. Sheldon, like to hear about a miracle of modern medicine? Through our work in the field of reproductive technology, I believe odds are good we can reproduce and restore your son."

My hand froze on the phone. Was this some sort of sick joke? This man had to be a shyster, a con man, the worst kind of slime-ball ambulance chaser.

Fury flooded my voice. "Why, you—"

"I don't expect you to believe me or to make a decision now," he interrupted, his voice a soothing stream in my ear. "But you can discover the truth about our organization on the Web. I know you're grieving. And when your heart leads you to a place where you can move past the pain, visit us at www.projectone.org. You'll find the details of our program there."

The name snagged a memory in my subconscious. "You're with . . . that group involved in human cloning. And that's impossible."

"Why should it be? With samples of your son's tissue we can determine his complete genetic makeup and replicate it in the lab. The resulting boy won't *be* the son you lost, but he will be exactly *like* your son, genetically programmed in exactly the same way. Our motto is 'reproduction, not resurrection.' We can't bring your son back from the dead, but we can give you a baby with your son's exact genetic makeup. He would live in your son's environment, which has been changed only through the passage of time and circumstance." He hesitated a beat, then asked, "Why shouldn't you have another son identical to the one you so tragically lost?"

I could not speak. This was no bumbling unemployed worker with nothing better to do than listen to talk radio and moan about his personal problems—the man on the other end of this line was an articulate, thoughtful, and persuasive individual. Still, the idea of cloning was ludicrous—

He gave me no time to object again.

"Thank you for your time, Dr. Sheldon. I understand your reticence, even your doubt, but I believe you'll be pleasantly surprised when you read about our program. When you're ready, you can find my number on the Web page. Until then, I wish you well."

The line clicked, and suddenly the phone in my hand felt as heavy as a dead thing. I dropped it back into its cradle, my mind spinning with horror, bewilderment, and more than a niggling of curiosity.

I'm not quite sure how I got through the final half-hour of the program. The callers were unimaginative, their problems routine, my answers quick and to the point. Wedding protocol, a child's right to privacy, how to address the remarried father's new wife—I handled the questions easily, then pointed to Chad, who took us out with the bed while I made breezy small talk and promised an interesting discussion the next time we met.

The guys didn't even seem to notice my switch to autopilot. Thrilled with their technical prowess, they were high-fivin' each other when I looked through the window. "Not a single operator error," Chad crowed in my earphones as the bed faded into the noon news. "I love it when a show comes off without a hitch."

While Chad grinned and lined up the commercial breaks for the news, I took advantage of the quiet to turn to the laptop at my right hand. A high-speed modem connected it to the Internet, and within seconds I had arrived at a Web page featuring a picture of a perfect baby boy, umbilical cord still attached. "Clone Humans?" the caption read. "Why not?"

I scrolled down the page and began to read the text.

Our first goal at Project One is to develop a safe and reliable method for the cloning of human beings. Since the birth of Dolly, the first cloned mammal, several other experiments performed on mice, cows, and cats have demonstrated that cloning leads to healthy offspring. As of this writing, several human pregnancies involving clones have been established. Once the first cloned baby is born, we plan to offer our unique service to individuals throughout the world.

If you would like to be among the first to participate in our cloning program, please contact one of our project coordinators . . .

The Web site listed Andrew Norcross as the American coordinator, and added, "We anticipate the fees for our service will be approximately $300,000 U.S."

The article went on to describe how cloning would enable sterile, homosexual, or genetically impaired couples to have children. An affiliated program, ClonaPet, would offer the duplication of domestic animals, so "you will never have to say good-bye to a beloved pet again!"

A final blanket statement covered all the bases: "If you are interested in cloning for any reason, Project One has a program for you."

"Diana?" Gary's disembodied voice blared from the intercom. "We've got some ratings reports you might want to see."

"Coming." I clicked the Web page away, but not before making a mental note of the URL. Andrew Norcross, whoever he was, was probably just a slick salesman and these Project One people mere dreamers, but still . . .

I shoved the thought aside and stood. Zanies and nut cases were a given in the world of talk radio. If I were smart, I'd consign Andrew Norcross and his call to my mental trash bin and forget I'd ever heard of human cloning.

If I were smart . . .

My own admonition rang in my ears as I began the long drive home.

Like anyone else, I have flaws, and one of them is that I'm not as smart as I sometimes think I am. Growing up, my mother took great pains to avoid mentioning my intelligence—which was never exemplary, but occasionally noticeable enough to get me in trouble at home, especially when combined with my lack of humility. Seems I had a healthy ego without any sort of reinforcement—the self-esteem lessons they now teach in public schools would have turned me into a self-indulgent monster. I don't remember this, but to her dying day my mother swore that one afternoon in eighth grade, I calmly informed my parents they would soon need a dictionary just to converse with me.

(If I said that—and I'm still not sure I was that cheeky—I probably deserve the sassy daughter heaven sent me. In full humility I can say, however, that I have never deserved my son. Nothing I ever did could merit such a blessing.)

Though I had always thought of myself as reasonably bright, on the drive home from the station I was ready to cop to pure stupidity . . . because I could not get Andrew Norcross and his fantastic proposal out of my mind.

Clone Scott Daniel? At first glance the idea seemed ridiculous, even sacrilegious. Didn't the Bible teach that each individual possessed a single soul, and that soul went to heaven when the body ceased to function? I knew where my son was—Scott Daniel was in heaven with the Lord, waiting for us to join him.

Still . . .

In the past few months, medical science had pulled some pretty amazing rabbits out of its assorted hats. Technology hadn't been able to do anything to save Scott, though, and part of my brain still couldn't accept that a single glancing blow—a simple thump—could sever a child's spine and leave the emergency technicians with nothing to do but shrug their shoulders.

Was cloning a way to rectify that medical shortfall? Strange as it was, the idea made sense to me. I still could not accept that it had been God's will for Scott Daniel to die on March 24. I could believe Scott died because a driver was distracted, but I could not believe God had anything to do with the accident. Surely not everything that happened on earth was God's will. His perfect will could not include murder, rape, or terrorist attacks, could it? He did not want people to sin or behave foolishly. And hadn't Scott been acting a wee bit foolish when he darted into the driveway to chase that balloon?

I chewed on my lip, then shifted to the right lane where I could drive slower and think deeper.

If it had not been God's will for Scott Daniel to die . . . perhaps God was now giving me an opportunity to right a wrong.

Pressing my lips together, I lifted my thoughts toward heaven. *God, could it be? Five years ago you gave us an unexpected miracle; are you willing to grant us another one?*

Cloning was not so commonplace that we would be automatically assured of success. Despite Andrew Norcross's confident manner, I knew the process was still far from foolproof: doctors made mistakes, experiments went awry, embryo transfers failed. But if God put his creative hand on the process, perhaps I could have my baby restored.

I know it sounds crazy, Lord, but it's no crazier than me having a baby after so many years of infertility. It's no crazier than you telling Joshua to blow trumpets around Jericho or allowing Hezekiah to live another fifteen years after he begged for his life on what should have been his deathbed.

Reproduction, not resurrection, Norcross had warned. Still . . . wasn't reproduction the nexus of life? In my biology classes I had sat through countless films depicting the ageless struggle of sperm to enter the egg, salmon who leaped rapids to reach their spawning grounds, animals who sacrificed their lives in the drive to reproduce. Every living thing on the planet focused on reproduction; even Christ commanded us to go and bear fruit by sharing the gospel.

The thought brought a twisted smile to my face. God created Scott Daniel five years ago. Couldn't he help a few doctors re-create him?

The idea carried me all the way home.

Twenty-one

AFTER CLOSING THE CAR DOOR, STEVE TURNED THE key in the ignition, pointed the air conditioner's vent toward his face, and closed his eyes in the stream of cool air. Tears pressed against his eyelids, salty springs that had threatened to overflow several times during the day.

"God," he whispered, resting his hands on the steering wheel, "how am I supposed to do my job when every tenth or twelfth kid is a blond-haired, blue-eyed reminder of Scotty?"

Heaven didn't answer, but the simple act of asking the question eased some of the pressure upon his heart. All his life he'd heard that Christians were supposed to be overcomers; lately he'd felt fortunate to think of himself as an endurer.

Given his present circumstance, he couldn't think of a more stressful occupation than his own. He had gone into dentistry because the discipline appealed to him; he had specialized in the pediatric branch because he liked kids. But now his hands trembled when he held x-rays toward the light cabinet, and his voice often broke when he spoke to the youngsters in his chair.

Few of his young patients knew of the loss he'd suffered, and he worried that his emotional instability might frighten them. Kids were nervous enough around dentists—the sight of a weepy, red-eyed man behind a mask could only unnerve them further.

His staff knew everything, and they'd been surprisingly unembarrassed the first time he burst into tears without warning. Melanie had simply pulled him out of the exam room and walked him to his office with her steadying hand in the center of his back. Once inside, she'd handed him a box of tissues, then closed the door with a promise to handle things until he wanted to resume.

Now he breathed deeply, wiped his eyes with a handkerchief from his pocket, then put the car into gear. A few moments later he pulled into China Gate, his favorite Chinese restaurant, and went inside. At the counter, he ordered three dishes to go.

The young man behind the register raised an eyebrow.

"No Kung Pow tonight?"

Kung Pow had been Scotty's favorite. He loved the peanuts.

Steve shook his head. "Not tonight, thanks."

A few moments later he was heading home with the scents of fried rice and sweet-'n'-sour pork filling the interior of the old BMW. The sweet-'n'-sour was Brittany's favorite dish, and Steve had been thinking of her when he decided to pick up Chinese. She had scarcely spoken ten words to him since the night they had to ground her, so maybe this would help bring her out of her pout.

She'd always been a reserved, private child—more like Diana, really, because he'd always been willing to spill his deepest thoughts to almost anyone who cared enough to listen. Diana never shared her secrets unless the act of sharing was expedient and sensible, and the recipient of her thoughts could be trusted.

Brittany, on the other hand, never seemed to share her feelings with anyone—anyone over thirty, that is. She and Charisse Logan were as tight as ticks, but Steve couldn't remember the last time she had sat down and told him about her day. In all the length of his memory, he *knew* she'd never asked about his.

Maybe she was going through a phase. After all, weren't all ado-lescents self-centered?

He slowed for a red light, then stopped and tapped the steering wheel with his fingertips. He was no psychologist, but he was fairly certain eighteen-year-olds were supposed to be difficult. Kids at that age naturally pulled away, testing their independence while they tried to find their way in life. The parents, on the other hand, functioned like guardrails on a highway, getting bumped and battered as they struggled to keep the kid on the right road.

He had certainly given his parents fits at that age. At eighteen, he'd been running with a group of guys who stole beer from minimarkets for kicks, then spent the night drinking and playing pool in various family rec rooms. Only the grace of God had prevented him from being arrested or killed in an accident.

His blood chilled as his wandering thoughts tripped over a sensi-tive nerve. Accidents happened all the time, even to innocent kids like Scotty.

As the light turned green, Steve eased down on the accelerator and slipped back into thoughts of Brittany. She had been especially surly since Scotty's accident, and he suspected the roots of her discontent went far deeper than their recent discipline. Even before Diana caught Britty sneaking in late, the girl hadn't exactly been treating them with respect, much less love. Diana complained that Britt treated their home like a hotel, checking in only to use the phone, grab something to eat, and crash when her body ran out of energy. Sometimes Steve felt more like an answering service than a parent, and whenever he popped into his daughter's room to try to have some fun with her, he usually got a rude "Go away!" for his trouble.

Parenting a teenager was difficult . . . especially when compared to parenting a five-year-old. Scotty hadn't been perfect, but teaching him had been a simple pleasure compared to playing guardrail for a teenage girl determined to have her own way. Teenagers had access to such dangerous things—cars, drugs, guns, even sexual diseases. Every time the phone rang when Brittany was out late, Steve would snap to alertness while images of a thousand terrible tragedies flashed through his mind.

Bad things happened even to kids from good families. And if those kids *chose* to do stupid things . . . Steve shook his head. God must have legions of angels working overtime to save today's kids from their own risky behaviors.

The worst part of raising teenagers was knowing unleashed anger could drive them to do almost anything because kids tended to act first and reflect later. Practically every other week Steve opened the paper to read about another teen who had picked up a gun to do harm to others or committed suicide just to prove a point. He would never be able to forget the local boy who stole a plane and crashed it into a Tampa skyscraper. No one ever knew why.

He swallowed the lump that had risen in his throat and flipped on his turn signal. The most fiendish thing Scotty ever did in a tantrum was run into the dining room and yell "Greasy slimy gopher guts!" during one of Diana's dinner parties.

Steve bit his lip as another tide of tears threatened his eyes. "Please, Lord," he whispered, easing his car through the security gate at the entrance to his neighborhood. "Keep your hand on Brittany when I can't reach her. Don't let us lose our daughter, too."

Twenty-two

My heart leaped as I heard the creak of the rising garage door. Steve was on his way in.

I scooped up the Web pages I'd printed and thrust them into a folder, then walked to the entrance of the small study I used as a home office. Steve stood in the front hallway, a bag from China Gate in his arms.

"Hi, guy." I felt a little breathless, even giddy, but half hoped he wouldn't notice my eagerness until I was ready to talk.

I was in luck. He scarcely looked at me, but continued through the foyer toward the kitchen. "Hi. Britty home?"

"I'm not sure." I glanced at the computer screen to be sure I had clicked away Project One's Web page, then followed my husband. "She may have come in, but I was doing some work on the computer. I've been pretty much preoccupied the last few hours."

Steve grunted in a noncommittal reply, then set the bag on the kitchen island and began to unpack it. "I got that sweet-and-sour stuff she likes. I got you chicken and broccoli, if that's okay."

"That's great." I glanced back toward the stairs, then lifted my voice. "Brittany Jane!"

Steve winced. "She won't hear you even if she's up there. She's probably either on the phone or wearing her headphones."

I really didn't want to traipse up the stairs in search of my daughter; I wanted a few moments alone with my husband. "If she's hungry, she'll come down."

Perching on a barstool, I rested my chin in my palm and studied my husband. Grief had etched deep lines into his forehead, creases that hadn't been apparent only a few months ago. My face probably bore the same lines, but what if they could be erased with news of a miracle?

"I had an interesting call today," I began, easing into the subject that had staged a coup d'état of my thought processes.

"Someone on the show?"

"Someone who called during a break."

Steve opened a container, releasing the warm scent of soy sauce and rice into the kitchen. "So—who was it?"

I lowered my hand and adjusted the salt and pepper shakers someone had knocked out of position. "At first I thought he was a kook, but then I checked out his organization's Web page. The more I read about this group, the more interested I became. And now—okay, I'll admit it. I'm really curious."

Steve made a face as he pulled two pairs of wrapped chopsticks from the bottom of the bag. "We don't have a lot of cash to throw around right now, not with Britty going off to college in a few months. So if this guy was selling stock options or something—"

"Not stock options. He's into medical research." I paused as I heard the creak of the stairs. "But we can talk about it after dinner."

Steve nodded without comment. After twenty-two years of marriage and eighteen of parenting, our marital shorthand had advanced to the point that we could easily halt a conversation in midstream if one of the children popped into the room.

Brittany breezed into the kitchen, lifted her nose in what might pass for a nod of appreciation, then slid onto her favorite barstool.

Steve pushed a foil container toward her. "I got your favorite."

"Thanks." She pried off the plastic lid, then looked at the paper-wrapped utensils. "You expect me to eat with chopsticks?"

Steve grinned at her. "Give it a try. Might be fun."

Brittany rolled her eyes and slid off the stool. I watched in silence as she went to the drawer and grabbed a fork, then stalked to the cabinet for a glass.

I shifted my gaze back to my husband. "Good day at your office?"

He shrugged. "Fine."

"Mine, too. The usual kinds of callers, I guess. And Gary showed me a ratings report—we've picked up five new stations. We're finally making headway in the Northwest. Of course, some of these new stations don't have the morning slot free, so now I have to remember not to say 'good morning' on shows that will be rebroadcast in the middle of the afternoon."

"That's great, Di."

Taking his foil container, Steve perched on another barstool. Once he had moved away from the counter, I stood to glean whatever was left in the bag—a container of chicken and broccoli, an egg roll, another pair of chopsticks, and a handful of fortune cookies.

Turning, I pulled a plate from the cabinet and scooped some rice from the open container, then spooned a healthy portion of the chicken and broccoli over it. At the pantry, Brittany popped the top on a can of Coke and slurped at the rim.

"Brittany!" I made a face. "I hope you don't do that in public."

She poured a stream of caramel-colored liquid into her glass. "None of my friends would care."

"Well, I care. And anything you do unconsciously becomes a habit soon enough."

She rolled her eyes in reply. Not wanting to wage war over something so trivial, I backed off, then opened the fridge long enough to pull out a jar of dill pickles. Long ago I'd learned that a dill pickle after a meal killed my craving for something sweet. I figured pickles had kept me from gaining thirty pounds over the years.

I wrapped my palm over the jar, then twisted. Nothing.

"Here, Steve." I slid the jar over the counter. "I need some brawn."

He gave me a quick grin, then untwisted the lid with one quick motion. I speared a pickle with a fork, then set it on a dessert plate to sit until after my meal. Dill pickles, on my sensitive teeth at least, are best served at room temperature.

Taking my plate, I took the barstool next to Steve at the counter, willing my eyes not to glance at the empty table to our left.

The square pub table had been perfect for the corner of our kitchen—informal and antique, in happier days it brought all four of us together over meals when our schedules allowed us to eat together. In the days following the funeral, however, we grazed through the kitchen like roaming horses, nibbling from the dozens of casseroles that had materialized in our refrigerator.

Now we were eating as a family again, but none of us had made a move toward the antique table. I don't think any of us had the heart to sit across from Scott Daniel's empty seat.

Steve positioned his chopsticks between the fingers of his right hand, then glanced at our daughter. "How was your day, sweetness?"

She shrugged and leaned back in her chair—a maneuver I'd forbidden a hundred times. Not only was she weakening the joints of my chairs, but if those back two legs slipped on this tile, she would almost certainly fracture her skull. The last thing I needed was another visit to the hospital.

I was about to rebuke her again when her face split into a sudden smile. "Mrs. Parker threw up in English class."

I grimaced. "Must we hear about this now? We're eating."

Steve furrowed a brow in concern. "Your teacher? Is she all right?"

"Yeah, we think she ate something that disagreed with her."

Steve's chopsticks froze in midair. "That could be serious. If there's food poisoning in the school cafeteria—"

"There's not. Mrs. Parker is too cheap to eat at school; she always brings her lunch. But at least we got a substitute and got to goof off the rest of the hour."

Brittany's smile was wide and real, the first sign of genuine pleasure

I'd seen on her face in weeks. And what had brought it on? Goofing off and the sickness of a teacher.

I drew a deep breath and regarded my broccoli chicken. I could launch into another lecture, but Brittany had heard my entire repertoire. Besides, she was smiling, and we were eating dinner like a family.

I shouldn't spoil it.

We sat in silence for a few moments, Steve managing fairly well with his chopsticks, me fumbling to keep up with him, and Brittany unabashedly eating her dinner with a fork.

"It's not fair," I finally said, trying to inject a note of humor into the heavy silence. "I think you're so good with those things because you work with thin little instruments all day."

Giving me a wicked grin, Steve waggled his chopsticks at me. "Practice makes perfect, Diana darling."

"I don't have the patience for it." Dropping my chopsticks to the counter, I picked up a fork and winked at Britt. "Maybe our daughter has the right idea."

For my efforts at camaraderie, I got another roll of the eyes. She gobbled a last bite of pork, then slipped from her chair and grabbed her glass. "I've got homework."

"No Coke upstairs, young lady," I called before she could make a break for it. "Your carpet already looks like a minefield."

She huffed again, then set the glass on the counter. I knew she'd be back for it once I vacated the kitchen.

But for now I was glad to see her go. I waited a moment, then allowed my thoughts to swing back to the subject I'd been about to broach when Britt came downstairs.

No time like the present, they say, and the hour certainly seemed appropriate. Steve was as relaxed as I'd seen him in days.

Steeling myself to my course, I plunged ahead. "Remember the call I mentioned earlier? The guy who called on my break?"

Steve regarded me quizzically for a moment, then nodded. "Yes—the one with the Web page?"

"That's right. He works for a company called Project One. Medical technology."

Steve took a big bite of chicken, then lifted a brow and swallowed. "So you said."

"They are researchers involved with cloning . . . people."

My husband's face twisted into the human equivalent of a question mark. "Don't tell me you're taking this guy seriously."

"It's not as bizarre as it sounds, Steve. According to what I read on their Web page, we should not think of clones as drones or science fiction monsters. A clone is merely the identical twin of someone else, separated through time."

His brows rose as he leaned back in his chair and twisted to look at me. "Okay—so why did this guy call you? Is he trying to get you to do a segment on cloning?"

My heart thumped against my rib cage. Might as well tell the truth, the whole truth, and nothing but the truth.

"Not exactly—he didn't mention the show at all. He called because he'd read about Scott Daniel."

The line of Steve's mouth clamped tight for a moment, then his throat bobbed as he swallowed. He lowered his chopsticks, braced his hands against the table, and met my gaze head-on. "I'm not sure where you're going with this, Di, but I don't think I like it."

I waved his concerns away. "Don't make snap decisions. The idea turned me off, too, until I did some reading. Cloning isn't what you think."

"I don't know what I think. It's too new, too far out, and, if memory serves, it's illegal in this country."

"Legality is not an issue—they can perform the procedure in a country where cloning *is* legal." I let the silence stretch a moment, then reached out to gently touch his arm. "The people at Project One have a saying, Steve—cloning is reproduction, not resurrection. I know we can't have Scott Daniel back, but we can have a boy just like him. We can give that boy another chance at life."

"Have you lost your *mind*?" Steve gave me a look that said his brain was working hard at a new set of problems. "I don't know why you would ever think"—his voice broke—"we could replace Scotty."

"I'm not trying to replace him! I'm just trying to make things right!" I shifted to face him. "Give me a few minutes, Steve, will you just *listen*? Let me explain everything, then you can make an informed judgment."

He crossed his arms, his face locking in neutral. "I'm listening."

I hesitated, wishing for a moment that I'd brought my notes from the study. "Okay. Well, first it's important to realize that a clone is not an exact replica of the original person. We won't have another Scott Daniel, but we'll have a boy genetically identical to him. He will have all of Scott's inbred abilities and the same tendencies that are built into a kid, but he won't be the same. And we won't expect him to be."

A muscle worked at Steve's jaw, but he didn't interrupt.

I forced a laugh. "It would actually be a great experiment in nature versus nurture—noticing the differences, I mean. But what they would do is take a cell from Scott's tissue samples—and the medical examiner has all the genetic material we'd need—and insert the DNA from one of Scott's cells into a female egg—one of mine or somebody else's, it doesn't matter. The egg will have been emptied so it's nothing but living cytoplasm. When Scott Daniel's DNA is inserted, the egg will begin to divide. When it reaches the embryo stage, it will be implanted into a woman . . . and that woman could be me."

A little overcome by the sheer wonder of the process, I paused to draw a deep breath. "Just think, Steve—I could have the baby. Our miracle boy would be born all over again, but this time we'd know exactly what to expect. The baby would look just like Scott Daniel and he'd be hard-wired like Scott Daniel, but he'd be different, too. And we'd have another chance to parent him."

Steve frowned in a way that made me wonder if he was trying to remember Scotty's birth or trying to forget every word he'd just heard.

His next words settled that question: "I think the very idea is repugnant. That sort of manipulation is against nature. It's not right."

I knew I had married a man who thought with his heart instead of his brain, but never had that tendency annoyed me more. Couldn't he grasp the logic of my argument?

"Everything we do these days is against nature! Do you think it's *natural* to have plastic surgery, or take pills, or get false teeth? We've learned how to use technology to our advantage, so why not use this?"

His brows drew together. *"God* creates people, not man. He makes each of us unique—"

"We are unique individuals, yes, but at this moment the planet is populated by over one hundred fifty million people whose genetic codes are *not* uniquely individual. Identical twins, for instance, and triplets. Do you find twins unnatural? Of course not. Do you find triplets repugnant? I don't think so. In fact, I seem to recall you describing the Brown triplets in your practice as *adorable*."

Steve spread his hands. "I don't know, Di. Don't you see why this guy called you? He wants to use you. You're a celebrity, and since Scott's accident you're even more in the public eye. If he gets you to sign on to his cause, you'll be setting a dangerous precedent. Human life has been cheapened enough with stem cell research and embryos being created to be used as living collections of spare parts. Do you want to endorse the way they are tinkering with stem cells and modifying human DNA? What if they make mistakes we cannot rectify?"

"Project One is concerned with cloning, Steve, not genetic engineering. They are two completely different things. Genetic engineering involves the modification of human DNA; cloning is simply the copying of it."

"But those people aren't going to stop at one threshold. If you give them permission to proceed with this kind of research, human genetic engineering is the next step."

I forced my lips to part in a calm, curved smile. "Read your medical journals more thoroughly, hon. Gene therapy has been going on for years. And it's changing lives for the better."

"But what about the cheapening of human life? Cloning will not always be successful, so what about the babies who die when something goes wrong?"

"People die all the time, Steve." My voice filled with a harshness I could not suppress. "You and I know that better than anyone. Yes, the cloned child might die through miscarriage or even stillbirth, but every pregnant woman faces that risk. And do you know how many patients sign up for experimental cancer treatments every year? Thousands. Should they be restricted from trying new protocols just because something might go wrong and they might die?"

His eyes rested on me, alive with speculation. "You're comparing apples to oranges. It's not the same."

"I disagree. And death is part of life. Over forty thousand people die in auto accidents every year in the United States, and yet nobody has ever suggested we do away with automobiles. Yes, some cloned embryos might die . . . but maybe they weren't really embryos, only collections of cells. Who can say?" I paused to push a stray hank of hair behind my ear. "I think that's a risk I'd be willing to take."

Steve looked at me in bewildered horror, but didn't speak.

"I'm not asking for a decision right now." I lowered my voice. "I just want you to think about it. I'm not completely sure if this is right for us, but I think I'd like to talk to this man from Project One and investigate some of the details."

A range of emotions played across my husband's face—uncertainty, fear, and a trace of anger—then he reached out and gently took my hand. "I know you miss Scotty, Di. But we can't bring him back."

I lifted my chin. "You don't have to tell me what I already know. I just want to do a little research. To see if maybe—"

"It isn't right, Diana. I'm not as good with argument as you are, but I know when something is wrong. And this has wrong written all over it. But if you want to have another baby—"

"It took us twenty years to conceive the first one. The odds of me getting pregnant again are about a million to one." I pulled my hand from his, knowing I wouldn't win the argument tonight. But the seed had been planted, and Steve would be considering the idea for the next few days. And while I knew his doubts were strong, his love for Scott Daniel was stronger.

While he pondered, I was going to launch a full-scale investigation . . . and contact Andrew Norcross.

I gave Steve a quick smile, then carried my dishes to the sink.

Two hours later I sat before my computer in the study, fretting at the keyboard as I typed in yet another search phrase. I didn't really want to know all the scientific details involved in the cloning procedure, but it would help if I could assure Steve that the process was safe and effective. I thought I had a good understanding of the medical procedure, but in my research I stumbled across some interesting considerations.

I had forgotten that an American company, Advanced Cell Technology, first announced the successful cloning of a human embryo in October 2001. Horrified by the implications, the U.S. House of Representatives promptly voted to ban human cloning. The Bush administration went on record in favor of the ban.

Public reaction dumbfounded the researchers at ACT. The CEO of that company, Dr. Michael West, told the press he never intended to clone a human being, but had instead taken the first steps toward therapeutic cloning. "We took a human egg cell and removed its DNA," he told a reporter from CNN. "So now we have the beginnings of life with no blueprint. And we put a human cell from a different person into that egg cell. The egg cell then does somewhat . . . wonderful things. It takes the patient's cell back in time, so that it's embryonic again. And it's sort of, you know, back to the trunk of the tree of cellular life. So that we could then make anything identical to the patient."

West went on to say that his work centered on treating illness, not creating human lives. "We're talking about human *cellular* life, not a human life," he told the reporter. "A human life, we know scientifically, begins upwards, even into two weeks of human development, where this little ball of cells decides, 'I'm going to become one person or I am going to be two persons.' It hasn't yet decided. No cells of the body of any kind exist in this little ball of cells, and that's as far as we believe it's appropriate to go in applying cloning to medicine."

I clicked the print key so I could show Steve a copy of the article. I knew he'd be concerned about the possible destruction of human life, but if those cells were only the *potential* for human life . . . therein arose another problem. Could we differentiate between life and *probable* life? In God's eyes, when did a person become a person? A lump of skin was cellular life, but it certainly wasn't a person. An embryo, on the other hand, *was* a person, even if tiny and dependent. If the scientists pursuing therapeutic cloning could train a little ball of stem cells to grow into a kidney, they were creating human organs, but not human life.

Could science determine when personhood begins?

My head ached from all the technical terms I'd digested in the last hour. Technically, a fertilized egg, or *zygote,* contained the forty-six chromosomes that inhabited every human cell, but as it grew it moved through other stages, becoming a morula, blastocyst, embryo, and fetus. I read that many dedicated pro-lifers—a term I'd always used to describe myself—claimed that any being with forty-six chromosomes was a person, but I had to admit that definition seemed too simplistic and even inaccurate. After all, people with Down syndrome had forty-seven chromosomes; were they not people? And apes had forty-eight, so you could not say that a being with "at least forty-six" qualified as human.

The *morula,* I learned, was the proper name for the shapeless mass of sixteen cells existing four days after fertilization. The term *blastocyst* described the cells' development from the morula stage to the *bilaminar,* or two-layered stage, which began during the cells' second week. At fourteen days, the *primitive streak* appeared—a visible marking that would eventually develop into the spinal column. Until the appearance of the primitive streak, the morula, blastocyst, or embryo could divide to become twins or even triplets.

So how could we say a blastocyst was a person?

I shook my head, weary of my internal debate. None of this really mattered to me; I wanted to *have* a baby, not destroy one.

"Many religious people," I read on a seminary-affiliated Web page, "oppose cloning on the grounds that it is impossible to know if the soul can be cloned. Since the soul is invisible and immeasurable, who but God can say whether or not it exists inside a clone?"

I clicked my tongue against my teeth. My personal theory, unprovable but logical, held that the soul emanated from the invisible and immeasurable breath of life God exhaled into man in the Garden. That spark of life—which man had yet to replicate from nonliving matter—passed from parents to child. I couldn't say with perfect certainty at which stage of cell development the soul formed, but neither could any theologian.

Two weeks earlier I'd spent ten minutes with a caller who insisted that life began at conception. Recognizing the beginning of an abortion discussion—which usually provoked great passion, but turned at least half my audience off faster than slime on a dinner plate—I sought to direct the old debate down a different trail.

"You're wrong, my friend," I'd told him. "Life doesn't begin at conception. It began in the Garden of Eden, when God breathed life into Adam. Life was passed from Adam to Eve when God formed a woman from man's living rib, and it's been passed from parents to children ever since."

"Yeah, but scientists can make babies in a test tube now."

"Can they? They can't do squat without a living egg. The spark of life, or whatever you want to call it, has to exist first. Think about it— your hand is alive as long as it's attached to your body—cut it off, and those cells die within minutes. Likewise, a sperm and egg are alive, so when they join to form the beginning of an embryo, life is not created, it's merely transformed."

"Well . . . okay. But I don't believe in a literal Garden of Eden. That's just a myth."

"So are you, caller. Ciao."

I had disconnected him and moved on, but now my own words whirled in my brain as I read a paper on religious arguments against cloning. A flush of pleasure flooded my cheeks when I discovered an actual term for what I had expressed to the caller: *traducianism,* the belief that a child inherits a soul as well as a body from its parents.

Somehow I'd missed that one in my college Bible classes.

The idea made sense, even in a cloning situation. A baby created from Scott Daniel's DNA would still be the genetic offspring of my chromosomes and Steve's. The DNA, a nonliving blueprint, would be placed into a living egg to direct the cell's division and growth. The embryo would be sheltered and nourished by my own body. If there was a chance, however small, that the soul was somehow transmitted through the living egg, then I'd stipulate that we harvest one from my ovaries. The doctors would undoubtedly protest on account of my age, but I would insist.

And life would beget life. The resulting child would possess a soul every bit as vibrant and alive as Adam had been in the Garden of Eden.

I rested my chin in my hand, feeling a smile stretch against my palm. Steve would accept this argument. Once he felt the baby's first kick, he'd know God had blessed us with a new life and a new soul. Still—

My smile shriveled. Steve had other concerns, more practical arguments that couldn't be dismissed by polysyllabic words and foggy theology.

Was it right for us to pursue a risky procedure? I remembered reading about the first successfully cloned kitten back in the spring of 2002—scientists tried one hundred eighty-eight times and created eighty-two embryos before achieving one successful pregnancy. Andrew Norcross had assured me that the technology had improved, but what if it had not?

What if I got four months into the pregnancy and discovered the developing fetus was abnormal? As a Christian, I considered all life a sacred trust because it sprang from the hand of God. If the cloned baby developed some sort of severe problem, would I have the heart to carry it to term and deal with the consequences? Some people might be quick to point out that the clone had sprung from *my* hand, not God's, therefore I would be bringing one more suffering child into a world filled with suffering children . . .

Could we afford to care for a severely disabled child? We had a daughter preparing for college; our retirement years loomed on the horizon. We were no longer young. I was forty-eight, Steve fifty, and the care of a severely deformed or dependent child would drain our energy and financial resources. We were financially stable, but three hundred thousand dollars for medical fees to Project One, none of which would be covered by insurance, would take a healthy bite out of our retirement savings. I would still have my career and Steve could always count on a profit when he eventually sold his practice, but the nest egg we had spent years building would be gone—

"You're still down here?"

I flinched as Steve's voice broke into my thoughts. He stood in the doorway, his arms crossed as he frowned at my computer screen.

Instinctively, I swiveled my chair to block his view. "I was doing some research."

The corners of his mouth were tight, but determination shone in his eyes. "I've been thinking about it, Di, and cloning is just a little too 'brave new world' for me. I don't think we should do it."

I looked away. In the interest of domestic peace, I didn't want to contradict him at this late hour, but I didn't see how he could have given the idea enough thought. After all, I'd spent the entire night doing research while he'd been sitting in his favorite chair. How could he make up his mind so quickly?

"Don't make a hasty decision." I propped my head on my hand. "I'm going to call this man from Project One and I'll ask him about all the issues troubling us. I'm not completely sold on the idea, either. It's a lot to think about."

My words seemed to reassure him, for the line of his shoulders relaxed. He nodded toward the stairs. "Coming up?"

"In a little while. I just need to clean up a few things down here."

He nodded. "Okay."

He turned to leave; I swiveled back to my computer. But before reaching for the lamp a few moments later, I copied Andrew Norcross's number from the Web site onto a sticky note, then slapped it onto a page in my calendar.

Twenty-three

ANDREW NORCROSS AND I PLAYED PHONE TAG FOR three days. After the conclusion of my Tuesday show, I finally managed to reach him. He apologized for my difficulty in pinning him down, but explained that due to the controversial nature of Project One's work, he maintained an office at an undisclosed location in New York. "This is my cell phone number, but I'm not always available to answer it."

I laughed at the thought of this cultured man holding clandestine meetings in darkened alleys. "How on earth do you conduct business?"

"We have a post office box where you can send whatever documents we need, but for meetings, I'll come to you rather than have you come here."

Sitting in the studio, I turned away from the windows and faced the blank wall. "Sounds secretive—and, to be honest, such secrecy hardly inspires confidence, Mr. Norcross."

He chuckled. "There is no need for concern, Dr. Sheldon. When you are ready to make a commitment, we'll fly you to France, and you may inspect any of our facilities. My superiors are very open about our operation, but necessity forces them to be a bit publicity-shy, particularly in the States."

"I would like to meet with you," I told him. "My husband and I have some concerns and questions about the entire process."

"I would love to come down. Do you have room in your schedule on Friday?"

I blinked. "You'd come so soon?"

"Certainly. We know how important it is to act while interest is keen, and experience has taught us the value of face-to-face meetings. Let me know when you have time available, and I'll arrange to meet you."

I checked my calendar, suggested a lunchtime meeting, and Andrew readily agreed. I gave him our home address for his files, then suggested that we meet at an Applebee's restaurant near the station. I also offered to pick him up at the airport, but he insisted he could find his way with no trouble.

"I'll look forward to meeting you," I said, "but I have to be honest—my husband has expressed serious reservations about the entire idea, so this trip may be a waste of your time."

"I would be surprised if you both didn't have reservations. In fact, I consider thoughtful hesitation a good sign—you're asking hard questions, and we want our clients to know everything before beginning a procedure. Don't worry, Dr. Sheldon, I'm sure we'll be able to dispel any worries you might have."

I ran my hand through my hair, steeling myself to ask the question uppermost in my mind. "Before you go, there's one thing I really must know."

"Yes?"

"Why did you call me?"

The bluntness of my inquiry didn't seem to rattle him. He laughed, then answered with a smile in his voice. "Your celebrity was a major factor, of course. We would not have heard of you if not for the press coverage of your son's death. But if we can turn your tragedy into something good, if we can demonstrate how cloning has the power to mend broken hearts and a broken home, we'll be taking giant strides forward. In a few years, perhaps, you may be part of the reason we won't have to be so secretive about our office locations."

"But what if my husband and I don't want to go public with the story? We have always tried to shield our children's privacy."

"And we will respect your wishes once the baby is born. The news of your pregnancy and the child's birth will make headlines, but after the delivery you will be free to live your normal life. I would imagine we would want to hold a press conference in the hospital where you give birth, but we would never send reporters to your doorstep."

I frowned, remembering the media's intrusion on the day of Scott's funeral. "Sometimes they come without prompting."

"If they do, you will deal with them as you always have. Frankly, we enjoy working with celebrities because they are accustomed to dealing with the press. You would not have a press-free life even without your interest in cloning, and you have already established boundaries between your professional and personal lives."

I glanced toward the window, where a pair of interns were casting covetous glances toward Chad's soundboard. Norcross was right; I had lived in a goldfish bowl for years. Surely this would be nothing new.

"You're right, Mr. Norcross. After what we went through at the funeral, I think we can handle a birth announcement."

"I look forward to meeting you, Dr. Sheldon."

I thanked him, then hung up. And as I lowered the phone, I realized Steve had been right about one thing—Andrew Norcross had been up front about Project One's blatant plan to use my celebrity to advance their cause.

But would it really matter? They would use my name, but with God's help, I would bring a beautiful new life into the world. Surely the end result would be worth whatever price I had to pay.

Twenty-four

STEVE POINTED TOWARD HIS REGULAR BOOTH AND nodded at the hostess as he passed. "Good afternoon, Shirley. Mind if I seat myself?"

"No problem, Doc." She grinned as he walked by. "Want your iced tea now?"

"Bring it on."

After sliding into the booth, Steve plucked the laminated menu from its holder, even though predictability was one of the nice things about eating in the same restaurant every afternoon. The waitresses at this Denny's knew what he liked: unsweetened iced tea, a small garden salad with French dressing on the side, and either a club sandwich, French dip, or veggie burger, depending on his mood.

Today he didn't know what sort of lunch his mood dictated. Last Thursday he'd been emotionally hung over from the parents' support group meeting; his stomach had been too queasy for anything more than a plain club sandwich. Last night he had made a point of skipping the meeting—not that Diana noticed—but the quiet night at home had done little to improve his outlook. The thick cloud of grief that had surrounded him since Scotty's death had not abated, but a new current stirred the air—Diana's notion of cloning. She had set up a Friday lunch meeting with that fellow from Project One, and Steve had promised he'd be hospitable and open-minded.

He still didn't feel right about pursuing the cloning idea, but Diana had a knack for making the far-fetched sound perfectly plausible. Daunting on the radio, she was nearly irresistible in person. When she took it upon herself to present a case, people were usually nodding in agreement before she had moved from point one to point two. Last year she'd gone before the Hunter's Green community association to promote the idea of salary increases for the two guards who staffed the security station. Before she'd finished, the association had voted to grant Christmas bonuses, too. If Diana had spoken five more minutes, Steve wouldn't have been surprised to discover that the association had voted to raise monthly maintenance fees to establish a Hunter's Green Security Guards' Retirement Fund.

He had just decided that the glossy picture of a French-dip sandwich amounted to culinary pornography when a deep voice broke into his concentration. "Afternoon, Dr. Sheldon. They let you out of that office for lunch?"

He looked up. Wilson McGruder, one of nearly a dozen pastors on the staff of his church, stood with one hand tucked into his belt, the other pressing against the edge of the table as if for support. The elderly McGruder ministered to the "senior saints," a large and active group of older adults who, when they weren't in church, spent most of their time traveling from one tourist attraction to another.

Steve was surprised McGruder even knew his name.

"Pastor." He extended his hand. "Sorry for not standing, but this booth has me pinned."

"No problem, young man." McGruder shook his hand with a firm grip, then inclined his head toward the empty bench. "Do you mind if I join you a moment?"

Steve smiled. "Not at all. Join me for lunch if you like."

"Ah, no, I don't want to be a bother." The older man slipped into the booth, then folded his hands on the table. With the sure instincts of a homing pigeon, Shirley came toward them, order pad in hand.

"Just an iced tea for me," McGruder said, "and whatever the doctor's having can go on my tab."

Steve protested, but the pastor waved his objection away. When Shirley had taken Steve's order and retreated to the kitchen, McGruder leaned forward.

"I'm glad the Lord set you in my path today, Dr. Sheldon. I've been meaning to tell you I was very sorry to hear about your son."

With an effort, Steve pushed words past the boulder in his throat. "Thank you, Pastor."

The minister's dark eyes, startling beneath a shock of white hair, drifted toward the window. "I go to a lot of funerals in my work, and there's something beautiful in the death of an elder who knows the Lord. The death of a child is no less beautiful, for I know the little ones go straight into the arms of Jesus, but it's harder for those of us who are left behind with our questions."

Steve could do nothing but nod.

Shirley returned a moment later, two iced teas in hand. Correctly divining the prevailing mood, she set the glasses on the table and left without a word.

"Is there anything we can do for you, son?" McGruder's eyes glinted with kindness. "We're here to serve you."

"Everyone has been very kind." Steve pulled a pink packet from the sugar rack, ripped it open, and dumped the stuff into his tea. "We had enough food at the house to feed a battalion."

"Ah, but the weeks following a funeral are the hardest. After the food and the guests disappear, that's when loneliness smacks you upside the head."

Steve closed his eyes until he could rein in his emotions. This man wasn't just spouting words; obviously, he had lived through the emotions he was describing. Of course, a man of his age had undoubtedly experienced many things.

"Pastor"—Steve opened his eyes—"what do you know about human cloning?"

The man's heavy brow furrowed. "Cloning?"

"Yes. My wife has been doing some research on it, but I'd appreciate hearing a minister's opinion."

McGruder snorted with the half-choked mirth of a man who wasn't sure he should be laughing. "Son, what I know about cloning could fill the head of a pin three times. I'm afraid I don't keep up with those kinds of things."

Steve shrugged to hide his disappointment. "That's okay."

The pastor scratched his head. "There was one thing, though—let me recall. I think—no, that was something else—yes, that was cloning. I was preparing a lesson on cults for the saints' Monday morning Bible study, and I ran across a new group. Seems to me they were into cloning, though I never understood why."

Steve frowned. "A cult?"

"Yes. Wait a minute—there, I remember. They're called the Raelians, and they're nuttier than fruitcakes, in my opinion. Founded back in '97 by a man named Rael. He claims that the name of God in the Old Testament, Elohim, isn't a reference to Jehovah at all." He squinted at Steve. "Because Elohim is plural, don't you see. Apparently the idea of the Trinity hasn't occurred to them."

Steve didn't see, but he nodded.

"Anyway, these Raelians say that since Elohim is plural, God must have been a race of superior beings—aliens—who began life on earth through a sort of cloning process. They think Jesus was resurrected through cloning, too. According to them, he really did die on the cross, but the aliens levitated his body and sent a clone back to earth."

Steve sat back, stunned. "That's crazy."

"Not to them." McGruder shrugged. "There's a cult born every month, seems like, and they get nuttier and nuttier. But the Bible says people will believe a lie in the last days. Since folks have been believing lies for years, I take that verse to mean people of the last days are going to believe the most illogical things you could ever imagine."

Steve glanced out the window. "These Raelians—are they American?"

"Praise God, no. We have more than our share of cultists, but these guys are European. I forget which country they hail from."

Steve shifted his gaze back to the pastor's face. "Could it be France?"

McGruder looked thoughtful, then nodded. "I think that's it. I'd have to check my notes to be sure, but I'm sure it was someplace in the European Union. They started a company, you see, to do human cloning because it's illegal here. I didn't pay much attention to that part of what I was reading, though. Didn't seem relevant to the senior saints. And I couldn't imagine anybody buying into that heresy."

If only you knew.

Steve drew a deep breath. "Pastor, apart from the cult business, how do you feel about cloning?"

The man sighed as he ran his hand over the crepe at his throat. "I really don't know enough about it to comment, Steve. Wish I did."

"What if I told you it was almost like artificial insemination or in vitro fertilization. Those procedures are performed all the time these days. In a church as large as ours, I'd be willing to bet some of our own members owe their children to IVF or AI."

A smile gathered up the wrinkles at McGruder's lined mouth. "You know, sometimes I miss the good old days. Having babies was a lot less complicated then. Most children could tell who their parents were without having to consult a medical record."

"I know." Steve sipped his tea, then lowered the sweating glass to the table. "So you don't have any strong feelings about the cloning procedure itself?"

McGruder shook his head. "I don't know what to say, son. I can only tell you I'd be highly suspicious of anyone affiliated with people who find it more sensible to trust aliens than God. I find it much simpler to believe in a loving God who created me, chose to bless the earth through Israel, and will take custody of my immortal soul at death than to spend my time and money trying to clone myself over and over just so I'll last until the aliens come back."

"Me, too." Steve leaned back as Shirley approached with his lunch. After thanking her, he looked at the plate and lifted the top of the bun.

McGruder leaned forward and sniffed the veggie patty suspiciously. "That thing really fit to eat?"

"It's healthy."

"But is it good?"

Steve grinned and reached for the catsup. "Anything's good if you put enough catsup on it."

"I'll leave you to your lunch, then." Grinning, the pastor slid his hand over the check Shirley had left on the table. "Sorry I couldn't be of more help, son. But if I come up with something useful, I'll let you know—if that would be all right."

"That"—Steve extended his hand toward the older man—"would be much appreciated."

Twenty-five

I WAS NOT HAPPY TO HEAR THAT STEVE WANTED ME to cancel my appointment with Andrew Norcross because old Pastor McGruder believed in aliens.

"The appointment's for tomorrow afternoon," I pointed out, settling into the easy chair by our bedroom window. "He may already be at a Tampa hotel. I can't cancel now; it'd be bad manners."

"I don't think manners matter much in this situation." Steve sat on the edge of the bed and pulled off his shoes. He'd been called to the emergency room after dinner—one of his young patients had been in an auto accident and needed several permanent teeth replaced—and we hadn't had a chance to talk. Now he was tired, obviously irritable, and in no mood for compromise.

"I can't believe you're still pursuing this." He threw me a sideways glance, his face flushed in the light from the overhead lamp. "I thought you were about to give up on the idea."

"Well, I haven't. I'm not going to give up until I've given Andrew a chance to answer my questions. For Scott Daniel's sake, I'm going to persevere."

"This afternoon I did a little research of my own—did you know Project One is affiliated with the Raelians?"

I frowned. I'd seen the name on one of the Web sites I'd visited, but I'd been so interested in the process I really hadn't paid much attention to the fine print at the bottom of the page. "And who are they?"

"The cult Pastor McGruder told me about. Apparently they believe aliens created all human life, and through cloning we're supposed to stay alive long enough to see them come again. I don't understand it all, and neither does Pastor McGruder. I'm not sure the Raelians understand what they're supposed to believe, but they're really into the idea of cloning."

I snorted. "I doubt Andrew is affiliated with little green men from outer space."

"But he might be affiliated with the Raelians."

"So what if he is? I don't necessarily agree with my Muslim dry cleaner, but I still need to get my clothes cleaned."

"Your dry cleaner isn't involved in your family life . . . and he won't be using your name to promote his business."

Steve had me there. Andrew had freely admitted that the people at Project One intended to use my name to promote their work. If their work included preaching the doctrine of aliens . . . I blew out my cheeks. That would mean trouble.

I picked up the novel I'd been trying to read ever since Scott Daniel's accident. "We'll just have to ask Andrew about it tomorrow. If he is a Raelian or whatever, we'll tell him to keep the medical aspects of our case separate from the religious aspects of whatever it is they believe."

"Some things are too closely linked to be separated."

"Anything can be separated, Steve. Even an atom."

My husband didn't answer, but the piercing look in his eyes stirred something in my soul—whether it was guilt, anger, or grief, I didn't care to analyze.

I dropped my unopened book onto the floor, then shifted to face my husband. "Honey, forget about the aliens. I want you to come to this meeting tomorrow with an open mind. I told Andrew we'd meet him at the Applebee's near the station—"

"I'm not going to the meeting."

"But you promised!"

"I promised I'd be hospitable. I didn't promise to go." Steve spoke in a firm and final voice, and I knew he would not change his mind. My rock of Gibraltar could be as stubborn as stone, too.

Girding myself with resolve, I lifted my chin. "I'll go alone, then. But I am going. It's too late to back out."

In that moment I knew we had come to a crossroads—never in the twenty-two years of our marriage had I opposed him so completely. Usually we talked through problems when we disagreed, and nine times out of ten Steve saw the wisdom in my arguments. But by the set of his chin and the look in his eye, I knew he wouldn't be changing his mind, at least not within the next twenty-four hours.

I glanced at the clock—11:15. I should be going to bed, but the thought of crawling beneath the sheets with such a stubborn man made my stomach clench. Besides, years ago we had promised never to go to bed angry with one another. That promise hovered above us now, inviting me to apologize and attempt to bridge the gap that yawned between us . . .

I knew what I *should* do. I should apologize, I should soothe his ruffled feelings, I should put off all talk of cloning for another day . . . but I couldn't do any of those things. Not anymore.

So I wouldn't go to bed.

As my heart pumped outrage and indignation through my veins, I stood and picked up my book. "You're tired, and I want to read, so I'm going down to the study. Don't wait up."

"I won't."

I left him, my heart pounding as I jogged down the stairs. Why couldn't he see how important this meeting was? Cloning might be the only way to make our family complete again. We had lost Scott Daniel, but we could fill that empty space.

We had to. I have tasted desperate desire only a few times in my life—first, when I met Steve and knew I would never be happy without him at my side; second, when it became apparent we were not likely to have biological children and I yearned for a child of my own; and third, when I learned that I was pregnant with Scott and begged God to give me a healthy baby.

On each of those three occasions I had prayed like Hannah, weeping and groaning with emotions too deep for words. And each time God had answered, so I was confident he would answer my prayers again.

As I turned the corner and entered my study, Charity's quip of the day washed through me, shivering my skin like the touch of a wandering spirit. This morning she had called in the first hour to share the words of some nameless mystic: "Life contains two tragedies," she told me, her voice wavering over the airwaves. "One is not to get your heart's desire . . . the other is to get it."

The only tragedy here, I resolutely told myself, would be for Steve to ignore my pleas and my research. We would have another son, and God would smooth our path and keep this baby from harm.

I had never wanted anything so badly in my entire life.

Twenty-six

IN THE UPSTAIRS BATHROOM, BRITTANY STEPPED closer to the locked door and pressed her ear to the surface. Her parents must have assumed she was asleep in her room, for they had made no effort to lower their voices.

Her parents never argued—at least, not like the people she saw on television. Her father was so easygoing he wouldn't even honk at drivers who weren't paying attention at traffic lights, and Ms. Counselor always said yelling accomplished nothing.

Her parents conducted their arguments in supercharged voices, and the discussion Brittany had just heard was intense enough to cut through the space between their bedroom and the hallway. She had been caught by the mention of Scott Daniel—a name rarely spoken these days—then the conversation veered off to cults and space aliens. She had no idea what her parents were arguing about, but one thing was clear: her mother desperately wanted to talk to someone named Andrew, and her father just as desperately wanted to avoid talking to this person.

Who was this Andrew guy? And why did he have the power to make her usually reasonable parents bark at each other?

She turned out the light, then cautiously opened the bathroom door and peered into the hallway. A light still burned through the half-open door of her parents' room, but she had heard her mother go downstairs. Mom was probably in her study, which meant she was either working late or too ticked to stay in the same room with Dad.

Slipping like a shadow through the darkened hall, Brittany entered her own room and closed the door. After diving for the comfort of her bed, she huddled beneath the comforter and curled into a ball.

Around her, the house waited like a living thing, silent and anxious. Last week her parents had been yelling at her. Tonight they were fighting with each other. Next week—who knew?

What had happened to them? Their family wasn't perfect, but it had never been as messed up as some of her friends'. Both her parents were as straight as sticks and as predictable as June weather. Sometimes she wished one of them had a secret life, something really juicy, but they had no skeletons in the closet, no tattoos in private places, no gay siblings or cousins who rode with the Hell's Angels. Her parents were the most conventional, boring people on the planet . . . which was why she couldn't understand why they were arguing about aliens.

What did aliens have to do with the Scottster?

She lay perfectly still, the only sound the rhythm of her pulse in her ear. Why did things have to change? If Scotty were still alive and sleeping in the room next door, Mom would have come by to tuck him in. On her way through the hallway, she'd have thrust her head into Britt's room, made a face at the mess, then pointed an accusing finger at the pair of half-empty Coke cans on the window sill.

A few minutes later Dad would have come through the hallway, stomping over the floor like a giant as he did his ridiculous "Fee Fie Foe Fum" routine, bellowing about smelling the blood of "his Scotty son." In time, he would have come to Britt's door, too, but he would have rapped lightly with his knuckles and offered some stupid knock-knock joke he'd picked up from one of his patients.

The sweetness of the image drew tears from some deep place far behind her eyes. She dashed the wetness away, then pressed her face into her pillow.

Why was she feeling so weepy? Her childhood was long gone, and she didn't want it back.

Scott was gone, too . . . and, at the moment, her parents were way beyond her reach.

But life had to go on, didn't it?

Twenty-seven

WORN OUT BY MY ARGUMENT WITH STEVE, WHEN I did go to bed I fell asleep almost immediately. For a while I tossed and turned in a fretful doze, then my hold on reality relaxed and at last fell free. Through the magic of sleep and the subconscious, my brain transported me to a dream landscape almost as vivid and real as the world around me.

I found myself again sliding out of Gary's car in a numb sense of panic. This time, however, he had not dropped me at the morgue, but at the children's hospital.

I stood on the concrete sidewalk wearing the same plaid skirt I'd worn the day Scott died. I carried the same purse on my arm, and if I had checked the screen of my cell phone, I knew I'd see Steve's number displayed there. He had called me to meet him . . .

"Diana!" Steve's voice, electric with tension, cut through the shushing sounds of passing cars. Still wearing his lab coat, he stood near the hospital entrance. "This way."

I hurried to join him. "Where's Scott Daniel?"

"Somewhere in here." He paused before moving through the automatic glass doors, and as I looked into his eyes I saw no trace of grief or sorrow, only the fear of a parent who had received news of an accident. "Come on, let's get to him."

He didn't have to ask twice. I followed my husband, easily keeping pace with his long-legged stride. We passed the receptionist's desk, where a pair of elderly men with trembling hands were pulling Medicaid cards from their wallets; we hurried by a long line of pregnant women in wheelchairs, all of them staring into space with expressionless faces.

My heart was pounding in a joyous rhythm by the time we reached the elevator. I caught Steve's eye. "I knew it was all a mistake. He's alive."

Concern and confusion warred in Steve's eyes. "Of course he is. They would tell us if he weren't."

"I know." I smiled, then looked away, barely able to repress the fount of hysterical laughter bubbling up within me. Steve didn't know what I knew, how absolutely awful this day could have been . . .

My heart lifted when the elevator chimed. I stepped forward, eager to charge ahead, but when the doors opened a mob of faceless men, women, and children flooded into the hall. Shoved and turned by the crowd, I cried out in frustration, then finally reached the elevator. I had lost Steve, but I jabbed the nearest button and sighed in relief when the double doors finally slid together.

The elevator deposited me on a floor unlike any hospital ward I'd ever seen. The walls gleamed like alabaster, and milky fog streamed around the ankles of the nurses monitoring the hallways. Part of my brain registered this as odd; the larger part of my brain drove me forward. An orderly in white stood behind the desk, and when I asked for Scott Daniel Sheldon, he pointed to a room directly behind me.

A sudden chill climbed the ladder of my spine as I approached the door. I knew I was dreaming, but I didn't want to wake. If I could be with Scotty, I could adjust to the faceless people and mist-carpeted hallways. Better to have Scott living in a dream than dead in the real world.

I pushed on the swinging door, then stared at the multitude in the room. Steve and Brittany sat by the bed, while Pastor John, Gary, and several of our friends from church lined the walls. Bouquets of flowers stood on tables and shelves, spreading their sweet fragrance throughout the room.

I hurried to my son's side. He looked small and pitiful in that big bed, but his skin was rosy, his lips full and pink. The small scratch still marred his cheek, but his hand, when I held it, was warm. Leaning over the bed railing, I turned his hand and pressed my fingers to his wrist—a pulse, strong and regular, flowed through those blue veins.

"He's alive." I whispered the words over the whoosh and click of the machines in the room.

Steve dropped his hand upon my shoulder. "Yes, sweetheart, he is. But we're waiting to hear what the doctor will say."

Ignoring my husband, I trailed the back of my hand along my son's sweet face. "Scott Daniel, wake up, honey." I spoke in the lilting rhyme with which I used to wake him as a baby. "The sun's come up and so should we, snugglebugs though we may be."

No answer. I began again, a little louder this time. "Wake up, sweetie. The sun's come up and so should we, snugglebugs though we may be—"

The phone rang, interrupting, and I turned to glare at it. But there was nothing on the bedside table but a plastic pitcher and a paper cup.

Reality jolted me back to wakefulness. The phone on my nightstand was ringing . . . at 1:20 A.M.

Shock yielded quickly to fury. I fumbled for the phone, then snapped, "Hello?"

The phone clicked as the caller hung up. Fuming, I dropped it back into its cradle, then lay back down and raked my hand through my hair. The caller had to be one of Brittany's friends, someone who could tell by my voice that this was not a good hour to call.

Good thing he or she hung up. If I knew who had interrupted my time with Scott Daniel, I'd probably go for his or her adolescent throat next time we met.

I turned onto my side and closed my eyes, my mind grasping for the dream, reaching for it with terrible longing. But the thin sleep I had enjoyed proved to be all my body would accept.

A cruel joke, courtesy of my subconscious mind.

After an hour I got up and went downstairs to read and weep . . . alone.

Twenty-eight

OVER THE THUMP OF THE MUSIC THAT CARRIED US into the noon news, Gary's voice buzzed in my ear. "Good show, Dr. D."

I looked up at him through the window, gave him a thumbs-up, and slipped the headphones from my head.

I didn't have time to hang around and chat. In exactly fifteen minutes, I was to meet Andrew Norcross at the restaurant down the street.

I grabbed my purse, hurried through the hall, then stuck my head through the doorway of the sound studio. "Anything urgent, guys?" I glanced at the correspondence folder. "Anything that can't wait until tomorrow?"

Gary glanced around his desk, then shrugged. "Don't see anything. But the paychecks haven't arrived yet."

"Don't care about the paycheck; I'm outta here. Call me later if anything comes up, but I'm going to be incommunicado for a couple of hours."

To emphasize my statement, I pulled my cell phone from my purse, dramatically pressed the power button, then winked. I left them to wonder if I had a secret life, then smiled my way through the usual cluster of interns gathered in the hallway. Today they were holding court outside the country music studio, and as I peeked in the window, I realized why—Marcia Lane, a beautiful and buxom rising star from Nashville, was sitting at the mike for a live interview while her latest hit, "'How Can I Miss You if You Won't Go Away?" warbled through the speakers over the door.

The sun was warm on my face as I moved through the parking lot and unlocked my car. Summer would be upon us before we knew it, then my walks through the parking lot would become mad dashes to hurry from one air-conditioned sanctuary to another.

Scott Daniel had always enjoyed summertime. I had taken him to a water babies class as an infant, and after that he could never seem to get enough of the pool. I had to be careful, though. The chlorine would turn his beautiful hair a strange shade of green if we didn't slather on the conditioner after every swim.

I found myself smiling. Was a love of the water a result of nature or nurture? Would the new baby like the water as much as Scotty did?

Applebee's was buzzing by the time I arrived. I stood in the entry-way with my arms folded and tried not to be conspicuous as I scanned arriving customers. I knew Andrew was traveling alone, so I could safely ignore groups of women and couples. I found myself examining young-to-middle-aged men with the concentration of a surgeon.

When a taxi pulled up at the curb, I knew I'd found him. A tall, thin fellow with a leather briefcase stepped out and rubbed the back of his neck with one hand while studying the front of the building. He wore a dark, tailored suit unlike anything modeled by the locals.

With a confidence born of certainty, I moved toward the door and motioned him in. "Andrew Norcross?"

His narrow face split into a smile. "Dr. Sheldon?"

"Welcome to Tampa. I've got the hostess holding a booth for us."

I immediately felt at ease with my guest. Having been a student of psychology and a professional counselor, I can usually form an accurate impression of people within a few moments of meeting them. Andrew was handsome in a European model sort of way—gaunt cheeks, wavy hair, dark eyes. His hands were clean, his nails manicured, and the corners of his eyes crinkled into nets when he smiled—and he smiled a lot.

I felt a frisson of guilty pleasure because Steve hadn't come.

After exchanging introductions and pleasantries, we studied the menus and placed our orders. Nerves had tightened my stomach into a ball, but I didn't want Andrew to feel uncomfortable eating alone. I ordered a mandarin orange salad.

Once the young waitress had taken our menus, I folded my arms on the table and looked across at my guest.

"Good flight?"

"Uneventful, thank goodness. I'm hoping for another quiet flight this afternoon."

Working around the heavy table, he pulled his briefcase onto the bench and proceeded to extract a folder and a glossy brochure. My mouth almost watered at the sight of the papers—I hungered more for information than food. "I really appreciate your coming all this way, Mr. Norcross."

"Please call me Andrew."

"All right. I'm afraid I must begin by apologizing for my husband."

He lifted a brow. "Has he been detained?"

I smiled, trying to put a pleasant face on the situation. "I'm sorry, but my husband is a dentist, you know, and sometimes things . . . come up. He won't be joining us today."

A look of concern crossed Andrew's face, then he shrugged and smiled. "The organization prefers that I meet with both prospective clients, but since we also work with single parents, I'm sure we'll be fine. I know you'll relate all the information." He leaned forward and handed me a brochure featuring a beautiful blond boy on the cover. My heart twisted. The boy could have been Scott Daniel's brother.

Andrew wasted no time coming to the purpose of our meeting. "As you know, Dr. Sheldon, we are a not-for-profit organization, but we do have operating costs—quite extensive expenses, as I'm sure you can appreciate. The controversial aspect of our work has forced us to be slightly clandestine about the operation of our labs, but I can assure you everything is regulated. The French government monitors our medical and research facilities, and an independent panel of accountants audits our books each year."

I nodded, eager to move into the more difficult aspects of the discussion. "I understand all that, Andrew, and I have no problems with your organization. My husband, however, heard some troubling news—something about Project One's affiliation with a group called the Raelians."

Andrew's smile deepened. "I'm not surprised you are concerned."

"Are you tied to them?"

"Project One's founder is affiliated with the Raelians, yes. And many Raelians have registered with our company for one project or another— cloning has religious significance for them, you understand."

"Actually, I don't understand at all."

"It's not relevant to your situation. The important thing for you to know is that Project One is an independent entity with no official ties to the Raelian Movement. We accept no monies from them, nor do we distribute any funds to them."

I leaned back against the seat, wondering if a separation of funds was enough to counter Steve's objection. The Raelians' bizarre beliefs had so turned him against the concept of cloning—

"Correct me if I'm wrong," Andrew pressed into my thoughts, "but don't several American religious groups dabble in commercial enterprises? The other day I was watching a religious show on television, and they offered a credit card to supporters. Apparently every time someone uses the card, a small percentage of the transaction amount goes to support the Holy Water Spring Retirement Community for Sensible Saints."

His comment brought a smile to my face. "I'm not sure you've got the name quite right, but yes, you're correct. Religious groups use all sorts of means to raise money."

"Does your husband find that offensive?"

I shifted my gaze toward the window as I considered the question. Steve had strong opinions about religion and money. While he wasn't opposed to students selling candy to support the Christian school, he didn't think it right for the church youth group to do the same thing. I could scarcely see the difference, but according to Steve, the Lord's church should be supported by tithes from the Lord's people. The Lord's school, I supposed, would have to survive on tuition and candy bar sales.

Sighing, I turned back to Andrew. "That question has too many variables for me to answer."

A smile found its way through his mask of uncertainty. "Perhaps he will be content to know the Raelians do not use Project One for fundraising or proselytizing. We are a business operation, pure and simple."

"Yet one tied to a religious group."

"Don't other organizations sponsor programs as a service to their members? Look around—in this country alone you can find Catholic hospitals, Christian retreat centers, Baptist universities. The other day I saw an ad for a Christian mortgage company. Those people offer a service because they believe it will benefit people of like mind. But they do not forbid others from enjoying the same service, nor do they always proselytize."

"Point taken, but we are accustomed to those groups and affiliations. I'm afraid my husband finds the Raelians a little strange. Incomprehensible, actually."

Andrew quirked a brow. "Try explaining the doctrine of transubstantiation to someone who's never heard of Jesus Christ."

I laughed. "Where are you from?"

"Britain. But I lived all over Europe as a child; my parents fell victim to a case of wanderlust, I'm afraid. I've only been in the States two years."

"Long enough to get a good feel for our society, though."

He grimaced in good humor. "It took several months to readjust my perceptions of America. From watching American exports on

European television, I formulated a notion that all Americans were like the people on *Jerry Springer* and *Baywatch*."

He glanced at the brochure on the table. "I suppose we should get back to our discussion. Is there anything you'd like to know before I launch into the standard spiel?"

"I think you can skip the spiel and cut to the heart of the matter. I've already done a bit of research, so I think I know all I want to know about the actual cloning process."

"So you've covered the basics."

"I'm familiar with the process—in nontechnical language, at least. But I'd like to know more about certain ethical issues." I tented my hands. "My husband has strong reservations, and I imagine my radio audience will, too—if we decide to go through with this."

Andrew nodded. "The most important thing to remember is that a clone is not a carbon copy. It would be more accurate to describe a clone as a time-delayed identical twin of the original. The clone and the donor would have different fingerprints. Remember Cece, the first cloned cat? He and his donor were different colors. Because a clone will grow up in different circumstances than the donor, environment will play different roles in shaping certain characteristics. A clone will not inherit the donor's memories, personality, or likes and dislikes. A strong likelihood that he or she will develop in the same way exists, but so does a chance the clone will not."

As the waitress approached, I leaned back into the booth and smiled. The new child would encounter different things than Scott Daniel, but he'd probably look the same and have a similar personality. And, when a few years had passed, I'd have another opportunity to capture Scott Daniel's goofy gap-toothed grin on film.

Andrew, who had ordered tea, set his cup off to the side and seemed more eager to talk than fuss with his drink.

Fine with me.

When the waitress had walked away, I pushed my soft drink to the side, too. "One thing does concern me, Andrew—no matter how safe the procedure becomes, I fear many Americans will be resistant to the idea of cloning. We are a nation of freethinkers, and people believe clones will be like zombies, mindless Frankensteins who will wander through life as a mere shadow of the donor. My husband and I would face this prejudice—as would my son."

"Nothing could be farther from the truth. Clones are real people, and in the United States all people have rights and responsibilities. I've heard the same arguments in Europe. People think we are creating clones to create a race of slaves, but that's ridiculous. Once a cloned child is born, he or she will be protected by the same laws protecting other individuals. Clones are fully human, and they must share in human civil liberties."

"Once the child is *born*." I underlined the latter word. "Therein lies another potential problem. Fetuses do not always have rights under American law, and my husband and I both strongly disagree with the devaluation of preborn human life. We would not want you to create a dozen embryos and use only one. We would not be comfortable with the implantation of, say, four embryos, and the selective abortion of the weaker fetuses—"

"Then you do not have to deal with those things—we will not implement those strategies in your situation." Dismissing my concerns with a shrug, Andrew unwrapped the flatware in his napkin, then withdrew the spoon. "After studying the matter for some time, I feel the only objection to cloning that holds any merit at all is the claim that the technology is not yet foolproof. But we have come amazingly far in the last few months, and I can almost guarantee you will not be confronted with a problem in the embryo stage." He plucked a lemon wedge from a plate on the table, squeezed the juice into his tea, then dropped the rind back onto the plate. "Again, let me remind you—cloning is not genetic engineering. We are not modifying human DNA, we are simply planting it to grow in new soil."

I parked my chin in my palm. "My husband, if I may be frank, is more than a little dubious about the entire idea. He spoke with a pastor at our church, an older fellow who knows nothing about modern technology, and Steve got a little rattled. I've a feeling our pastor simply dismissed the idea as playing God."

Andrew shook his head in weary resignation. "We hear from religious protesters every week. In contrast to abortion, which results in the *destruction* of human life, we are about the *creation* of life. Moreover, we hear that 'playing God' argument every time medicine takes a major step forward. At one time the arguments against birth-control pills and heart transplants consisted of the same two words. When people see what good can come out of advanced technology, the protests usually die away."

I accepted a glass of water from the waitress, then set it on a napkin. "All right, Andrew, I'm now thinking more like a radio host than a mother. When—if—word of this gets out, I know I'm going to be hounded on my show and in the press. People will be calling me everything from Mary Shelley to Hitler. What am I to say when they accuse me of personally ushering in the end of the world?"

"Don't let the critics shake your confidence. Tell them cloning is perfectly ethical, legal, and well on its way to being accepted worldwide." Andrew opened the brochure and flipped several pages. "Cloned children are perfectly protected under existing American law, but regulations concerning the actual cloning process still need to be instituted around the world. On these pages you'll find operational guidelines that were proposed by our people, approved by the International Association of Physicians, and subsequently adopted by the European Union. They do not yet exist in this country, of course, because cloning is still illegal here."

I leaned forward to peer at the page.

"First," Andrew said, "human clones should have the same legal rights and responsibilities as any other human being. Second, no living person should be cloned without his or her consent. An individual should be entitled to automatic copyright for his or her own genetic code. Just as you cannot take my published words and use them for your own benefit, one person should not be able to benefit from the DNA of another without consent."

I stared at the page, my mind opening to a new realm of possibilities. "I hadn't thought of that."

"It's important. Imagine what might happen if someone got ahold of Michael Jordan's hairbrush. They could take the DNA from a single strand of his hair and impregnate scores of women with Michael Jordan clones. Those children may grow up to hate basketball, but they'd all have Michael Jordan's body, his genetic code, and whatever elements are hard-wired into his personality. That sort of identity-theft should be illegal."

I closed my eyes, imagining an entire room of Osama bin Laden or Hitler clones. That idea alone could generate hours of discussion on my show.

"Third"—he glanced down at the page—"human clones should only be gestated and delivered voluntarily by adult women. Though the Japanese are currently working on an artificial womb and some researchers have theorized that clones might successfully gestate in the wombs of cattle, we know human embryos are profoundly imprinted during the prenatal period. Infants who miss out on the sounds of human conversation, touch, and even music during gestation would be severely deprived at birth."

I could only stare at him. The implications of what he was describing were enormous. The people at Project One might be kooky in their theology, but someone had demonstrated a great deal of wisdom by preparing these regulations.

"Finally"—Andrew tapped the last paragraph on the page—"the cloning of convicted murderers and other violent criminals should be banned. Since evidence suggests that a propensity for violence can be inherited, the use of criminals' DNA for cloning should be prohibited under any circumstances. The world does not need another Stalin, Lenin, or Hitler."

I smiled as the opposite thought occurred to me. "But what about the world's truly wonderful people? We could create another Anne Frank . . . another da Vinci and Ben Franklin."

His mouth curved in a smile. "Can you imagine the inventions da Vinci and Franklin might come up with if they were allowed to work together? With today's technology at their fingertips, there's no limit to what they could achieve."

"Amazing." My thoughts drifted toward the future, where my own beloved son might attend medical conventions with clones of Thomas Edison and George Washington . . .

"Many people have talked about the possibility of correcting the mistakes of the past," Andrew said. "Now we have a chance to do just that."

His comment snapped me out of my reverie. "Correcting a mistake?"

"Like the Holocaust. Those who complain that cloning will somehow cheat the world of genetic diversity fail to realize how we could actually restore the genes of millions of people who died under Hitler's regime. Consider the hundreds of thousands of doctors, scientists, and scholars murdered in Stalin's purge—wouldn't it be wonderful if we could restore those people?"

"You're not worried about overpopulating the planet?"

He laughed. "I doubt we'll engage in the mass production of human beings until food supplies are likewise being mass-produced. With the help of genetic engineers, other groups are cloning food products—super-productive fruits and vegetables, disease-resistant livestock, and the like." He lifted his glass, but paused before bringing it to his lips. "I've learned never to say never, Dr. Sheldon. While we wouldn't be able to restore every Holocaust victim, enough locks of hair and bits of bones remain for us to make tremendous headway in righting the wrongs committed by a previous generation."

While the idea of restoration intrigued me, I was far more fascinated by the possibility of righting a *recent* wrong—Scott Daniel's death. So far Andrew had talked philosophy; I needed practical details.

I cleared my throat. "Andrew, if I were in your position, I would want to be sure any prospective parents were mentally healthy before proceeding."

He nodded. "Naturally, family stability is a major concern. In that sense, we're a bit like an adoption agency. We want to be sure our babies are going to live with stable parents."

I held up my index finger. "My family, on the other hand, is recovering from a death in the family. I'm not sure *stable* is a word that describes us at the moment."

He reached out and lightly touched the back of my hand. "I think I know what you're going to say, Dr. Sheldon, and I understand. We know you will need time to grieve, but the process of cloning takes time, too. We'll have to get tissue samples from you, then we'll have to do the actual DNA implantation. If you're to be the egg donor, you'll have to take hormones in order to produce several eggs at the proper time, then you'll have to travel to Europe for the implantation. You'll go through the nine months of pregnancy, then you will welcome and raise your child."

His smile held a tinge of sadness. "I'd say that was the easy part, but I think you're experienced enough to know that grief and motherhood often go hand in hand, right?"

I looked away as tears stung my eyes. The man was perceptive. From the first moment we hold our little ones, mothers know the grief of letting go is inevitable.

"We may be a little more flexible than most American adoption agencies," Andrew went on, rambling, I thought, to cover for my sudden weepiness. "For instance, we would have no problem approving a single woman who wished to become a mother through cloning, or a homosexual couple. We don't hold our clients to an outmoded definition of family, but we do expect prospective parents to be of sound mind and body."

Steve would have seen red upon hearing Andrew talk about new definitions of family, but what did Project One's unconventional views have to do with us? Besides, Steve didn't spend his days listening to callers try to explain their convoluted interpersonal relation-ships. I did, and I knew the stereotypical family had become a thing of the past. As of the year 2000, the "two parents with their own chil-dren" designation applied to only 24 percent of American households. The situation of the American family wasn't ideal, but few civiliza-tions throughout history had been as stable.

I dashed tears from my eyes, then watched silently as the waitress advanced and set two salad bowls before us. I picked up my fork and speared a bite of chicken, giving Andrew implicit permission to eat while we talked. "You mentioned tissue samples—where am I to get those?"

Andrew picked up his knife and fork. "I'm assuming an autopsy was performed after your son's death? The medical examiner should have tissue samples on file. They may even still be fresh—unfrozen, that is. If there were no other choice we could use something as simple as a strand of hair, but an assortment of cells would be far better."

"Will the ME give them to me?"

His dark brows drew downward. "Not usually. Often you'll have to engage a lawyer to see results. Sometimes an intimidating letter in the right tone will persuade an ME to hand over tissue samples. But you might have to get a court order to see results."

I bit my lower lip. "And then?"

"You have a medical examination. If you're not yet menopausal—"

"I'm not."

"—then you take hormones designed to encourage hyperovula-tion. When the time is right, you will fly to France, where in our lab the doctor will remove several eggs from your ovary. They will be emptied of all genetic material, then one will be injected with your son's DNA. The others will be placed in storage."

"If my eggs . . . aren't suitable?"

"Then we will use another woman's. The origin of the eggs is not really important, because none of the egg donor's DNA is passed onto the clone. Once the egg is denucleated, nothing remains inside but cytoplasm."

And perhaps the spark of life . . . the seeds of a soul.

Automatically, my hand dropped to my lap and touched the soft place where I had carried Scott for so many months.

"I would really like to use my egg, Andrew. I don't want a donor."

He hesitated over his salad, one brow lifting, then he shrugged. "I don't foresee a problem."

"Once the egg divides, what then?"

He held up a warning finger, stalling me until he had swallowed his last bite. "Once the embryo has reached the six-cell stage, it will be implanted inside your womb. You will remain under our doctor's care for a few days so we can monitor your hormones to be sure your body doesn't reject the pregnancy. When all is as it should be, you will fly home and return to your normal activities. Go to your regular obstetrician, have whatever tests he or she recommends. Within forty weeks, you will give birth to a normal child who will be the genetic offspring of you and your husband . . . and the identical twin to the boy you lost."

I had read the material, I had pondered and weighed it until I could have provided many of the details myself, but hearing Andrew explain the procedure in a matter-of-fact voice reassured me, for his was the voice of authority. I, on the other hand, was a new convert desperately seeking a smidgen of faith.

"And you say several women are now pregnant with clones?"

He stared at me, his eyes sparkling, then gave me a tentative smile. "I shouldn't say anything." He lowered his voice to a conspiratorial whisper. "But the first two clones were born two weeks ago. A set of twins, delivered in London. Mother and boys are absolutely healthy. To be safe, however, they're going to keep the news quiet until the boys are three months old."

I felt a tide of gooseflesh ripple up each arm and crash at the back of my neck. "You're not kidding?"

His grin widened as he shook his head. "My supervisors would have a fit if they knew I told you. But I thought you should know.

You won't be the first in the world, if that pressure worries you. You might not even be the first American woman. You'd definitely be *among* the first, though. A pioneer in the field of fertility technology."

I sat back, letting my gaze rove over the diners beyond our booth. Cloning was no longer a dream, nor was it mere scientific prattle. It had happened, it would happen again, and it could happen for me . . . if I were willing.

"Who?" I turned back to Andrew. "Who did the London woman clone?"

One corner of his mouth quirked upward. "I'm not at liberty to divulge that information. I can tell you, however, it was someone remarkable."

I pressed my hand to my forehead as images swirled in my brain like bits of glass in a kaleidoscope. Who had been cloned in London? Winston Churchill? Prince Charles? No—they wouldn't clone a living person without his permission. But what if they'd *had* his permission?

I smiled as an absurd idea lifted its head. Given the long life spans of women in the royal family, rumor held that Queen Elizabeth might reign for another twenty or thirty years, leaving Charles with little time to do the job for which he'd been born. What if *another* Prince of Wales had been created? A pair of identical princes—another heir and a spare. The younger versions of Charles would have every hereditary right to rule and every opportunity to reign if he died soon after the queen reached the end of her natural life span. William and Harry might object, of course, but so far those young men had not shown any burning desire to assume the throne . . .

I shook my head, clearing away the fantastic ideas. Five years in talk radio had expanded my thought processes far beyond the rational realm.

"Okay." I took a deep breath. "So cloning is possible. It's probable. Now tell me about the expense."

Andrew lowered his fork, then slowly clasped his hands. "The process is quite costly. But I've been in touch with my superiors back in France. Because of the favor you'd be doing us—because, as we dis-cussed, we fully intend to use your name and position to advance cloning in the United States—we are prepared to offer you a 50 percent reduction in fees. We will cover everything—the implanta-tion, research, hormone treatments, even hospitalization, should you require it—for one hundred fifty thousand dollars."

I caught my breath. Since I'd been expecting to hear a figure twice that amount, I felt like I'd won the lottery.

"One hundred fifty thousand? That's all?"

"Absolutely. And payment can be spread out over the time of your treatment, but we'll need a deposit. The typical amount is 10 percent."

Fifteen thousand dollars . . . about what I'd intended to pay for Brittany's college tuition next year. But fifteen thousand, even one hundred fifty thousand, was a paltry amount when compared to the value of my son's life.

My thoughts shifted to more practical matters. "What about the publicity? When, exactly, would it begin?"

"From our side, not until after the pregnancy is established. You, of course, are free to tell anyone you like of your plans—we would only ask that you not reveal our office locations on national radio." He grinned. "We have attracted enough controversy; we would natu-rally be reluctant to invite more."

"Thank you, Andrew." I picked up my fork and punched at a piece of chicken hiding among the lettuce folds. Slipping through the restraints of my self-control, a smile spread over my face. "I'll go home and discuss these things with my husband. I'm quite sure we'll be sending you a check next week."

Dollar signs and baby booties danced in my imagination as I drove back to the station. Coming up with one hundred fifty thousand dol-lars wouldn't be easy, but we could manage it. Throughout our mar-ried life, we had taken financial chances—stepping out in faith to buy our first house and the dental office, taking our first scary steps into the stock market—but God had always provided what we needed. I was convinced he would provide this time, as well.

Well, Lord, you've opened a door . . . now provide the means we'll need to go through it.

Sitting at a red light, I took a mental inventory of our financial affairs. The bill-paying checking account was always in a state of flux. The savings account was only slightly more substantial, for even though we made regular deposits, unexpected expenses regularly drained it. That left our retirement accounts, the equity in the house, and the money-market fund we had opened as a savings account for Brittany's college tuition.

I didn't want to sell the house—I wanted our new son to grow up in the same room that had sheltered Scott Daniel. But we'd been living in the house ten years, so a home equity loan or a second mortgage wouldn't be out of the question.

And both Steve and I were well employed. My husband made a good living from his practice and I was one of the highest-paid radio personalities in Florida, if not in the nation. I hadn't checked Dr. Laura's paycheck stub lately, but at contract negotiation time my agent had assured me I was on my way to playing in her league.

Once I told Steve how easily we could restore our son, his reservations would ebb away. The expense might give him pause, but he'd soon agree it would be money well spent. After all, he had never been tight-fisted; we both believed money was something God gave us so we could minister to the needs of others. What better cause for our investments could we find? Perhaps our example would encourage a doctor in Italy or France to clone St. Francis of Assisi or even St. Paul.

I laughed softly as a sudden thought occurred to me—a clone of Paul raised in a messianic Jewish household! In a century with satellite television and the World Wide Web, what a preacher that firebrand would make! Modern medicine might even find a way to heal the troublesome illness he had referred to as his "thorn in the flesh."

I pulled into the parking lot, shut off the engine, then leaned against the door as an indefinable feeling of *rightness* swept over me. Jesus spoke of the "pearl of great price," the thing a man would sell his soul to gain. I knew the analogy pertained to salvation, but couldn't the pearl also stand for other precious things?

For me, the pearl of great price would be the restoration of my precious son. For him, I would empty my bank account, mortgage the house, sell my own blood.

One hundred fifty thousand dollars was nothing.

Twenty-nine

WITH SOME DIFFICULTY, I MANAGED TO TEMPER MY excitement while I returned to the air studio, taped a series of promos, then ran to the grocery store to pick up a short list of family necessities. As the grandfather clock in the foyer chimed six o'clock, I swept into the kitchen on a tide of rising euphoria. Steve and Brittany were eating sub sandwiches at the bar while my dinner, still wrapped in waxed paper, waited on the counter.

I heaved the grocery bags onto the stove, then cast my family a faintly reproving look. "What? No waiting for the mother?" The note of cheer in my voice contradicted my rebuke, and at the sound of it both Steve and Britt looked up, clearly suspicious.

Not willing to broach the subject of cloning with Brittany in the room, I grabbed my sandwich and sat next to Steve, forcing myself to relax. I would explain the cloning project to him first, get his approval, then tactfully approach Brittany. Thoughts of a new brother or a pregnant mother would not thrill her, but by the time the baby came she'd be away at college. She could begin her new life while we started over again with our new son.

I took a bite of the low-fat club sandwich. Amazing what they could do with meats and peppers and a little lettuce. "Delicious." I smiled at my husband. "Thanks for getting dinner."

"What are you so cheery about?" Steve gave me a dubious glance. "Pick up a couple of new stations today?"

I shrugged and swallowed. "Maybe. Things are going well with the show."

Brittany must have sensed something in the air, for she gulped the remainder of her sandwich, took a perfunctory swallow of her Coke, then left the table, beverage in hand. I watched her carry the forbidden glass up the stairs and decided to let the infraction slide. I needed to speak to Steve, and I didn't want to wait.

"I had lunch with Andrew Norcross today." I kept my tone light and bright. "He was very interesting and well-prepared. I think you would like him."

Steve kept eating, but his eyes said, *Oh, really?*

I pressed on. "Because we'll be helping Project One by allowing them to go public with our story, they're willing to give us a break on the fees. They'll take care of everything—all treatments, services, and follow-up, for one hundred fifty thousand."

Steve found his voice. "Dollars?"

"That's right."

"American dollars?"

"Of course, American dollars! And I was careful to mention all your concerns. Yes, you were right, the founder of Project One is a Raelian, but the cloning group in no way disseminates his religious beliefs. And Andrew assured me they will respect our pro-life convictions. They will withdraw several eggs from my ovary, but they will use only one at a time for the DNA transfers. If the first embryo doesn't implant, for instance, they'll process another, but they will not create several embryos and then freeze them. I told him we couldn't allow that."

He lifted one brow, suggesting in marital shorthand that I had taken leave of my senses. "And you *trust* him?"

"Of course I trust him. They are ethical people; a board of directors oversees every step of the process. Furthermore, they have considered details I wouldn't have thought about in years. Here." I spread the brochure on the counter. "I read most of this after lunch and now I'm even more impressed with their organization."

Annoyance struggled with disbelief on his face as he stared at me. "You're still serious about this?"

"More than ever."

"And nothing I said means anything to you."

"Of course it means something, Steve—but Andrew had an answer for each of our concerns. He explained everything to me, and if you read this brochure, you'll see that cloning is safe, practical, and quite possibly the answer to several medical problems." My voice broke with huskiness. "It *is* possible, Steve. The first cloned twins were born last month in London, with no complications. We could be the first Americans—"

"Is that what's driving you?" His eyes sniped at me. "Are you doing this for the *publicity*?"

I took a wincing breath. "Is that what you think? I'm not pursuing this for publicity, I'm doing this for us. I want to restore our family."

He looked away, his eyes brimming with threatening tears. I shifted my gaze back to my sandwich.

I'd sprung a lot on him tonight and I shouldn't push. He needed a few minutes to collect his thoughts, to lick his wounded feelings, to find the humility to admit he'd been wrong to object to my plan.

Steve glanced at the pages of the brochure, then cleared his throat and met my gaze. "Where do you think we're going to come up with one hundred fifty thousand dollars that aren't in our budget?"

I swiveled to face him. "I've been thinking about it all day. We have fifty thousand in Brittany's college fund, so I could take the deposit—fifteen thousand—from that. And we have at least two hundred thousand invested in the house, so we could get a second mortgage or a home equity loan."

"It wouldn't be fair to dip into Britty's college fund for this. I also don't think it's right to risk our house for a procedure that may not work. We're already making huge mortgage payments. How are we supposed to afford a second?"

He met my gaze without flinching, and for an instant I felt like a spoiled ingénue telling her father that she really, *really* needed a new dress for the debutante season.

The feeling didn't last. I wasn't a spoiled girl; I was a mature woman with a successful career. "We can afford it, Steve. We'll just cut back for a while. And Britt won't need all that money this year. If for some reason we're not able to completely reimburse her account, we could always take out an educational loan."

"So you want us to pay for a student loan, a second mortgage, the original house payment, and two car payments? The only thing free and clear around here will be Britt's truck."

I snorted. Brittany's old red pickup—the vehicle of her dreams and her sixteenth birthday present—hardly deserved to be called a truck, but at least it was paid for. The insurance premium, however, made me see double every six months.

Leaning forward, I propped my elbow on the counter and pinched the bridge of my nose. Closing my eyes, I murmured, "Don't give me grief about money, Steve. You don't pay the bills, so you don't have the headaches. I think I know what we can handle."

"If it's causing you so much stress, maybe I should take the checkbook."

"It's not stressful." Lifting my head, I met his gaze. "I know we'll be fine, we always are. Hasn't God always provided what we needed?"

"I'm glad you finally got around to thinking about God."

The remark stung. Did he think I hadn't prayed about this decision?

Leaning back in his chair, Steve fixed me in a stern-eyed gaze. "Diana, you could bring home an entire encyclopedia of information saying cloning is okay, and I'm afraid I wouldn't change my mind. I've been praying about this, and I have a clear sense that cloning is not for us." Dampness shone in his eyes as he rubbed his hand over his jaw. "Maybe it is okay for some people, I don't know. But I don't think it's God's will for us. It won't bring Scotty back and it won't ease our pain."

His voice fell to a whisper. "Our son is with God, Diana, he's not waiting in some test tube or petri dish. I don't think cloning will honor the Lord."

For the first time in my life, I could not find words to fit my emotions. My usually reserved husband had exerted his authority without apology . . . but I didn't like his decision. He was wrong, I *knew* he was wrong, but I didn't know how to convince him he was making the biggest mistake of his life.

"Steve." I reached out and brushed his hand with my fingertips. "I know what you're feeling. You're still grieving for Scott Daniel—so am I. You think you need more time. Well, you'll have the time you need because the cloning process won't happen overnight. It'll take months, probably more than a year. And while we're waiting you'll move past the pain and soon you'll be ready to move forward and embrace the idea of a new child. But you can't give me an emphatic denial now. We'll need to put some things in motion as soon as possible, and these things can't wait. Besides"—I forced a laugh—"we're not getting any younger. So if we're going to be parents again—"

"You talk as if we're not parents at all." Raw hurt gleamed in his eyes. "Diana, we still have two children—Scotty in heaven, and Brittany right here."

Beneath the table, I clenched my fist, desperate for him to understand. "I haven't forgotten anything, and I've been praying, too. And I really believe this is God's will for us—"

"God's will?" His voice cracked. "How can you know cloning is God's will?"

"Easy. We know God sent Scott Daniel to us, right? And we know God wants us to raise our children in the nurture and admonition of the Lord. But we didn't get to raise Scott Daniel; the accident took that opportunity from us. Cloning will turn back the clock, and out of all the people in this country, God sent *us* the opportunity to restore our son—"

"Have you lost your mind? No one can turn back the clock."

"Now we can."

"No! God wills that we live this life as it comes, that we remember our time on earth is only temporary—"

"It's not that temporary!" I was shouting now, but I didn't care if Britt overheard. "You can't tell me it was God's will for a five-year-old miracle to be snatched from our hands before we even had a chance to walk him to first grade! The loving God who gave Scott to me wouldn't take him like that! You can never, ever convince me otherwise!"

"You think you know God's mind?" Steve laughed, the sound hoarse and bitter in my cozy kitchen. "You spend all day on the radio talking to people as if you *are* God, and you only point them to him when you can't think of anything else to say. You're what people call a 'worldly Christian,' someone who gives godly advice only when your own self-reliance, common sense, and intuition have failed."

Helpless to halt my rising anger, I scraped my hand through my hair. "What are you talking about? I do more good for people on the radio than you do in that stuffy dentist's office!"

He flushed, his features contorting with shock and anger. "I do what God called me to do." His words were sharp, as pointed as an ice pick. "And I thought you were doing what you felt called to do. But if you think you're being called to pursue this cloning thing, you're not hearing God. I don't know who you're hearing, but it's not God."

"Who are you to say what I'm hearing?" I gripped the edge of the counter, my temper rising beyond my limits of control. "Where is it written that God speaks to only the man?"

"A husband is supposed to be the spiritual leader in his home."

"Then stop wallowing in your grief and start leading! You're not doing anything, Steve—you sit in your easy chair every night and cry for half an hour, as if that would help anything. At least I'm trying to do something constructive."

"You call cloning constructive? You will destroy our privacy and expose all of us, even Brittany, to the glare of international publicity. With this cockeyed scheme you will attract more wackos and vigilantes than that stupid show of yours could draw in a hundred years—"

"While you're doing nothing! *Do* something, Steve. Help me put this family back together!"

My words hung in the silence, vibrating in the space between us. For a moment Steve gaped at me, his eyes blazing with amber fire, then he slowly placed his hands on the table, palms down.

We had both said more than we should have. We had both ventured beyond the boundaries of safe discussion into the territory of personal insult. And we both knew it.

But neither of us felt like apologizing.

"I am grieving for my only son." Steve stared at the tips of his fingers as if he'd never seen them before. "I loved him. And Scotty deserves to be missed."

"I loved him, too. And I know he deserves another chance at life." The words slipped out before I could stop them, and while I knew they weren't technically accurate, they expressed the yearning of my heart.

Steve looked at me, accusation mingling with anger in his eyes.

Slowly I stood and placed my trembling hand on my husband's shoulder. "Steve, please try to understand. I haven't forgotten God in all this. I believe he sent Scott Daniel to us as a miracle, and I believe he had nothing whatsoever to do with that terrible accident. God didn't kill our son. And now he's given us a chance to—"

"God may not have killed our son"—Steve lifted his head—"but he certainly allowed the accident. And with all my heart I believe he took Scotty's soul to heaven."

I lifted my hand, unable to remain in physical contact with a man who would offer such a simplistic defense. "Then tell me *why*." I sank back to my stool, facing my husband. "Why did God take our son when it would have been no big deal to have Scott avoid that car? Or suffer a broken arm instead of a broken neck?"

Steve shook his head. "I don't know."

"But I want answers!"

"Sometimes we can't find the answers this side of heaven."

Frustrated beyond words, I slid off the seat and backed away. "I want answers, I *need* them! If God isn't going to provide any, I'm going to find them on my own!"

When an audible gasp broke the heavy silence, I looked up to see Brittany standing in the kitchen doorway, her hand wrapped around the doorframe as if for support. White-faced and teary-eyed, she stared at us a moment, then pivoted on the ball of her foot and strode toward the stairs.

"Now look what you've done." Rebuke saturated Steve's voice. "As if she didn't have enough on her mind."

"Britt? What terrible things are on her mind? School and zits are not the most pressing problems in the world, you know."

"You, *Counselor*"—he spat the word—"should know how traumatic it is for children to hear their parents arguing. As far as I know, this is the first time she's found us like this."

I drew a long, quivering breath, mastering the fury boiling within me. "Most kids deal with more than this every day. Brittany has been sheltered her entire life; maybe it's time she caught a glimpse of the real world. Kids need to know their parents sometimes argue."

"But she's hurting! She lost a brother."

"We lost a *son*. And we'll lose another one if you don't support me in this."

Steve's eyes went hot with resentment, and I knew I'd lost the battle. Despite my assurances, proofs, and pleas, he would not help me bring another child into this family.

I looked at him, biting my lip until it throbbed like my pulse, then slowly shook my head. I'd explained the situation as best I could, but my words were powerless against Steve's stubborn will. If God was going to restore our son, he was going to have to either change Steve or show me some way around him.

Abandoning my husband in the silence of the kitchen, I turned and retreated to my study.

Thirty

"You okay, Britt? You sound funny."

Brittany sniffed, then dabbed at the end of her nose with a tissue. "I'm fine. Just having an allergy attack."

"Oh." Charisse fell silent. "So . . . you want to do something tonight, or are you still grounded?"

Brittany hiccuped, a lingering result of her sobbing. "I'm still grounded."

Charisse sighed. "Bummer. But hey—I heard that. Are you drunk?"

"I wish." Brittany threw the wadded tissue in her palm to the floor. "I'd give anything to get wasted and forget about this place."

"So—wanna sneak out later?"

Biting her lip, Brittany considered the idea, then decided against it. With her parents squalling and squabbling, either one of them might be roaming the house in the wee hours of the morning. She'd get caught for sure.

"Can't. I'm not feeling good, either."

"Too bad." Charisse strummed the guitar. "Well . . . since there's nothing else to do, you wanna hear my new song?"

"Sure." Brittany lowered her head to the pillow, then positioned the phone on her ear. "Play away. I'm listening."

As Charisse strummed and sang a new song that made no sense at all, Brittany closed her eyes against the hot geyser that pushed at the backs of her eyelids. She brought her fist to her mouth in an effort to stop any sound that might rise from her throat, because if Charisse heard her crying, she'd ask what was wrong.

And Brittany couldn't say.

All she knew was that nothing in her life was right. Everything in her world—her house, her schoolwork, her car, her makeup, her clothes, her shoes, her weight, her hair, even the dozens of nail polish bottles lined up on her dresser—absolutely nothing about any of it was good. Zack Johnson had been avoiding her in the halls, and who wouldn't? Nobody wanted to be around anyone who oozed *loser* from every pore.

She'd been a loser from the beginning. Her birth mother hadn't wanted her, so she'd dumped Brittany at Social Services. Mom and Dad had been good for taking her in when nobody else wanted her, but then Scotty came along, and their hearts filled with love for their *own* kid . . .

While Charisse sang, Brittany bit her fist and struggled against the tears she refused to let fall.

The shadows beneath the palms and hibiscus were already deep and dark when Steve stepped out onto the front porch. Thrusting his hands in his pockets, he walked down the steps toward the sidewalk, taking comfort in the soft scuffing sounds of his shoes on the concrete. Such an ordinary sound on an ordinary night, coming from an ordinary American home.

Except nothing in his house was ordinary anymore.

A tear trickled down his cheek. He swiped it away, angry at his own weakness. How could one loss disrupt a family so? He knew some marriages splintered over the deaths of children, but he had always assumed his marriage could survive anything. After all, he and Diana were Christians, reasonable people, and financially stable. They had a lovely daughter who was successfully growing into young womanhood, and they'd had a darling son who charmed a smile out of everyone he met. They maintained successful careers, as many friends as time would allow, and a comfortable home in a tidy, gated neighborhood.

How could their lives fall apart in a single instant?

He strolled down the sidewalk, passing his neighbor's house where a TV blared through a cracked downstairs window and music drifted from their thirteen-year-old girl's upstairs bedroom. The Hudsons were nice people—Janice was a dedicated schoolteacher, and Robert a pharmacist down at the local Albertson's. With their three teenage girls, they attended Mass once a week and seemed to weather every storm life sent their way. But as far as Steve knew, life hadn't sent them many storms. Their daughters were good students, athletic, and pretty. Probably the most serious problem the Hudsons had to face all year was the damage they'd discovered at the corner of their front porch.

Subterranean termites, Bob had confided to Steve, his eyes somber. Trouble with a capital *T*.

Steve quickened his pace, moving into the circle of light provided by the streetlight in front of the next house. He didn't know the Emersons, but according to the grapevine the quiet, elderly couple wanted nothing more than to enjoy their retirement years and occasionally entertain their grandchildren. A single light burned in an uncurtained window downstairs, and through the panes Steve could see a sedate living room with traditional furniture and groupings of smiling family portraits on the walls.

He averted his eyes, not wanting to invade his neighbors' privacy. They hadn't invaded his, even immediately after the accident. This modern neighborhood was tidy and circumspect; each resident minded his own affairs and pretended not to notice when the sounds of raw, real life seeped past the boundaries of the carefully clipped lawns. Once a year, on the first Saturday in July, they met in the street for a neighborhood block party—skateboarding kids at one end, moms in the middle, dads with barbecue grills and beers at the business end. They talked, they laughed, they engaged in polite games of one-upmanship.

You got a raise? How nice. I made partner.

You bought a Lexus? Nice car. I went with the BMW.

Steve grimaced as he considered this year's convocation. This summer he could top them all: *You had a baby? Good for you. We're carrying America's first clone.*

Staring down at the sidewalk, he snorted softly. His neighbors had no idea what had been happening in his house. Through the last few difficult weeks, he and Diana had continued to smile and go to work, toiling in the traces of their daily lives as if nothing had happened . . . when in fact their world had turned upside down.

From an open window he heard the sudden sounds of barking. From within the shadows of anonymity, a man yelled, "Sadie! Shut up!"

Steve increased his pace, not wanting to upset the animal further. In another month, maybe two, none of these windows would be open, for Florida's muggy heat would lie upon them like a blanket even at this first hour of dark.

How could Diana presume to know what God had in mind for their family? He was supposed to be the head of the house, and thus far he'd had nothing but unsettling feelings when she mentioned cloning and the idea of another baby. In his youth it was hip to call these feelings *bad vibes,* and the expression still fit. A creeping unease slithered at the base of his gut whenever he thought about the Raelians, and the entire Project One setup felt a little too sci-fi for his comfort. Diana might well be right about the promises they'd made to her, but how would she know if those scientists decided to tinker with the DNA they transferred? And how could she guarantee they wouldn't create a half-dozen embryos and freeze several for future experimentation? Their labs were located in France because the United States wouldn't allow this sort of organization to operate within its borders. Though Steve didn't always trust the government, he had to respect the men and women who had studied the situation and declared cloning a bad thing. If they'd seen enough danger to prohibit the practice, their conviction was good enough for him.

Still . . .

He loved his wife, and struggled to understand her point of view. She had lost the only baby she had carried within her womb, and he grieved with her for that loss. But she needed to understand his feelings, too. He had lost the boy into which he had deposited all his father-son dreams. Diana and Brittany shared that unique mother-daughter thing where one day they were best friends and the next they were hissing at each other, but he and Scott had experienced a father-son bond the girls would never understand. Though Scotty was still young, already the two of them had ventured deep into male bonding. He had taught Scott how to bait a hook. They had begun to play ball together, and Scotty had even begun to ask questions about the day when he would become a daddy . . .

The memory brought a twisted smile to Steve's face.

"Will I ever have a little boy?" Scotty had asked one day as they fished on the bank of Walsingham Lake.

"Sure you will, son."

"But where will he sleep?"

"I'm sure he'll have his own room, just like you do."

Scott's little face squinched into a knot. "But where will Brittany and Mommy sleep?"

Steve had patiently tried to explain that they would not always live together because one day Scotty would leave home to go live somewhere else—

As he had . . . sooner than anyone expected.

Another squadron of tears ran down Steve's face, silent, steady sentinels of the grief that still overflowed his heart. He had learned not to resist them. They sprang up whenever summoned by memory or thought, they flowed until the reservoir had emptied. In time, perhaps, the bitter springs would not flow as freely, but Steve doubted they would ever disappear completely.

Amazing, that a mature Christian could feel such pain. He had been taught by godly parents, he knew the Scripture, he knew Scotty was with Jesus. With all his heart he believed the Lord would comfort, heal, and carry every daily burden. With all that knowledge he had hoped to alleviate the agony of death, but the pain would not be denied. When Paul wrote, "O death, where is thy sting?" he must have been writing with an eternal perspective in mind. Here, on earth, death still stung like an adder.

Scotty had been a tender tree planted in the fertile ground of Steve's affection, and death had ripped the young tree out by its roots. Despite his certain faith, Steve would never think of heaven without feeling the ache of the empty hole in his heart.

Sighing, he wiped his cheeks with his shirt cuffs and pressed into the darkness, circling the block. Diana knew the Scriptures, too. As a professional counselor, she knew about grief and its effects on those who mourn. But that knowledge had not helped her after the accident. She insisted on handling the situation like a clinician, pressing toward cloning while denying the clawing pain ripping her soul apart.

"Doctor," he murmured, slipping his hands into his pockets as he looked up at the star-spangled night, "heal thyself."

What had happened to his wife? In the beginning she had mourned as he had, but while he continued to weep, she had girded herself in determination. The only tears she had shed lately were tears of frustration brought on by another of their arguments.

She no longer slept in Scotty's room, no longer clung to the boy's stuffed monkey. For a few days Steve had actually felt jealous of her quick recovery, but now he wondered if she was healing at all.

Then again, what did he know? He knew how to treat teeth, not hearts.

Diana had always been quicker to respond than he. In basic temperament, they were opposites—Diana was an introvert, but when she turned on the charm she could be bright, persuasive, and delight-fully domineering. In household matters he usually deferred to her because she always researched their options and made sound recom-mendations.

This time, however, grief had wrecked her reasoning and skewed her thoughts. She might have law and logic in her corner, but he had an unswerving conviction that cloning was wrong. Scotty could not be replaced, and God had brought them to this dark place for a pur-pose. Whether or not they discovered that purpose . . . well, it didn't matter. Some answers could only be found behind heaven's door.

So . . . his family had come to a rough place, and his job was to steer them safely through it. But to please Diana, he would either have to capitulate and approve her plan to bear a clone or suffer the con-sequences of denying her. Those consequences would not be pleasant. He had never seen such determination in her eyes.

He hesitated beneath the sheltering arms of a huge live oak on the corner, a thick old tree that had barely escaped a neighborhood asso-ciation vote to cut it down. Yes, it did obscure the streetlight, and yes, it did shed several pounds of leaves in the spring. But the regal tree had probably outlasted more hurricanes, tropical storms, and winter freezes than any soul in the neighborhood.

If only he had half the strength of that tree.

He lifted his eyes to the spangled sky serving as a backdrop to the gently swaying branches. "Do I give in to her, Lord? Or do I hold my ground?"

He heard no answer in the darkness, no divine message through the whispering branches. But an inexplicable peace settled about his heart, and, clinging to it, he turned and began to walk back home.

Thirty-one

ON MONDAY MORNING, I DRESSED AND HEADED OUT early for the office, grateful beyond words for a job that offered distraction and distance from my recalcitrant husband. At eight minutes past nine, the intro to my show began. Perched on my swiveling chair, I adjusted the headphones to a more comfortable position, then checked my notes for the monologue. I usually began each hour with a brief intro about family life or life in general—something to warm up the audience and give callers time to get to the phone. As my producer, Gary, willingly played Ed McMahon to my Johnny Carson.

As the intro died out, I leaned into the mike. "Good day to you, guy friends and gal pals across the fruited plain! Dr. Diana Sheldon here, bringing you words of wisdom from the home front, the house front, and the business front, wherever you happen to be."

I tapped my pencil on the desk. "I was thinking about something on the drive to the studio today—sort of mentally planning my day, you know, and thinking about what I'd have to do when I left work this afternoon. Then my mind flipped back to the days when my children were small. I don't know about you, but when my kids were babies I prided myself on motherly conscientiousness. No ready-made baby food for my offspring, no sir! Instead I bought fresh vegetables, cooked them, puréed them in the food processor, then I froze those smashed foods in ice cube trays."

Behind the window, Gary grinned and leaned into his mike. "What's an ice cube tray?"

I groaned. "Heaven help us, I keep forgetting my producer is on the young side of thirty. An ice cube tray, my naive ignoramus, is one of those plastic things with dividers. You fill them with water and place them in the freezer, and in an hour or two you have frozen ice cubes."

"Some of them were metal," Chad added helpfully. "My parents had metal ones in their icebox."

"Spoken like a true antique aficionado." I placed one hand on the mike to whisper into it. "Help me, friends. I am surrounded by American youths. The studio next door is filled with youngsters, and you should see the hallway . . . but I digress."

Grinning, I leaned back and resumed my normal banter. "As I was saying, I was so proud of feeding my children home-prepared foods with no additives, no preservatives, nothing but foods as natural as God made them." I thumped the desk for emphasis.

Gary recognized his cue. "And then?"

"Then my kids grew up. And they began to eat fast-food French fries, hamburgers, and fried chicken fingers. My son thought pizza was one of the major food groups. When my daughter decides it's time to get married, she'll probably choose Styrofoam as her china pattern.

"But the worst of it is what this relaxed attitude about food has done to me. Saturday I was in the kitchen, thinking I would do something dramatic like actually boil a couple of eggs for egg salad. I thought it was about time I made an honest-to-goodness home-cooked meal for my family, so I decided to whip up some egg salad. I was pretty sure I could find some bread smashed up behind something in the freezer."

Chad pressed the sound effect button. In unison, a chorus of awed voices whispered, "Wow."

I laughed. "You *should* be impressed. Anyway, I found a couple of eggs in the fridge, dug out and dusted off a saucepan from the cabinet, and put the eggs on to boil." I paused dramatically. "Then I approached the most daunting step of the adventure."

From the control room Gary quipped, "Was one of the eggs, um, occupied?"

I groaned. "Ugh. Nothing so gross. No, I opened the fridge and launched a search-and-rescue mission among the many bottles stuffed inside those plastic compartments built into the door. Finally, success! I discovered a jar of mayonnaise with about half an inch of mayo at the bottom."

"So?" Gary asked. "What was the problem?"

"Well, this is April, right? So I thought I should check the expiration date, because everyone knows mayo can go bad and breed salmonella. So I turned the jar sideways and upside down until I found the date in tiny little letters: July 13."

"So you were good to go, right?"

"Not hardly. The date was July 13, 1998!"

I pointed at Chad, who punched the next button and sent a funky riff out over the airwaves while a prerecorded announcer reminded listeners of our toll-free number: 1-888-555-HELP.

I didn't even have to resume my patter before the phone lines lit up. Relieved, I glanced up at the computer screen, then punched the line for the first caller. "Hello, and welcome to the *Dr. Sheldon Show*!"

"Dr. Diana?"

"Good day, Charity."

"How'd you know it was me?"

I laughed. "I see all, my friend. I'm assuming you have a snippet of wisdom to share with us today?"

"Oh, yes. Friday I heard that one woman moaning about her husband's weight."

"And you can shed some light on the subject?"

"Yes, indeed. Are you ready?"

"Lay it on me."

Charity cleared her throat, and, on cue, Chad pressed a button launching the sound effect of a drum roll.

"Overweight," Charity said, "doesn't happen overnight. It snacks up on you."

Ch-ching went the sound machine.

I groaned. "Very punny, Charity."

"I know. Wasn't it cute?"

"Uh-huh. Got anything else for us?"

"Not today. But maybe I'll call again tomorrow."

"I'll look forward to it." I clicked to the next caller, a man named Bill from New York. "Good morning, you're on the *Dr. Sheldon Show.*"

"Dr. Sheldon! Let me first say that I love your program and agree with you 98 percent of the time."

Uh-oh. That remaining 2 percent was going to give me trouble. I worked a smile into my voice. "Thank you, Bill. Did you have a question?"

"Why, yes—at least, I think it's a question, maybe I just want to pick a bone with you."

Automatically, my hand went toward the phone. If Bill from New York felt compelled to talk about Scott Daniel—

"The other day I heard you say you were a Christian."

My hand relaxed. "Yes, I am."

"Well, don't you find your beliefs to be discriminatory? To my knowledge, Christianity is the only organized religion that says only its adherents are going to make it to the next life. Most other religions see God as the person at the hub of a wheel, and just as there are many spokes in a wheel, there are many ways to reach God."

I glanced at Gary, then exhaled noisily. "Boy, Bill, you like to start off the week with a bang, don't you?"

He chuckled. "Well, that's why they pay you the big bucks, Dr. Diana."

"Yeah, right." I laughed along with him. "First, let me take exception to your claim that Christianity is the only religion that limits entrance to heaven. I think you'll find that most cults are quite specific in their beliefs that *they* are the chosen ones. They keep people in their group through fear and intimidation."

"Well, I wasn't sure about that. But you've got to admit, Christianity is pretty specific. I grew up in a hellfire and brimstone kind of church, and I've heard all those speeches about 'narrow is the path and few there be that find it.'"

"I'm glad you were listening. Yes, the path is narrow, but heaven is not some sparsely populated country club. It's going to be filled with people. Sociologists tell us that as many as 70 percent of all humans ever born never live to celebrate their eighth birthday"—I felt the old knot rise in my chest, but kept going—"and Scripture indicates that children go to heaven when they die. If you add to that figure the millions of babies murdered by abortion every year, and then add those who profess Christ—let's say that's 10 percent of the forty billion or so people who have ever lived on earth—the grand population of heaven is going to be more than thirty billion. That's nearly three-fourths of all human beings ever created."

"Yeah, but—"

"No buts about it, Bill. Doesn't it make sense? I mean, why would God, who knows the future, create the human race if he planned to send the vast majority of us to hell? I don't believe he would."

"Yeah, but you're set in your ways. And you can't say that other religions are worthless. Anyone who teaches peace and love and tolerance is doing good for humankind—"

"Forget your hub-and-the-wheel analogy, Bill, and let me tell you a more appropriate story. There was once a king who had three sons. He also had one ring of pure gold. Concerned about rivalry among his sons after his death, he had two rings fashioned from false gold and upon his deathbed he ordered his wise men to give the three rings to his sons. Calling his sons near, he told them the truth: one ring was real, two were false, but the person with the pure ring would always be kind, good, and blessed of God. So, Bill, what do you think happened next?"

"For the love of heaven, how am I supposed to know? You're spinning some silly story while I'm trying to—"

"Of course, Bill, thanks for playing. All three sons strove to be kind and good because each of them wanted the people to believe he had been blessed with the real ring."

"See? See?" Bill was practically beside himself, shrieking into the phone. "I'm *right*. All religions have value if they teach people to live peacefully with one another."

"Anyone who practices good will be regarded as good by those who can't see the secrets of the human heart," I answered. "But all the good in the world won't change the truth—only one son had the real ring. The other two were living a lie. Think about it."

I pressed the next button, sending us into commercial, then leaned back and stretched. Though it was only Monday, the morning felt more like Friday.

A glance in the mirror this morning revealed that fatigue had settled in pockets under my eyes. Steve and I had endured the weekend in an awkward state of truce, pretending politeness and burying our noses in newspapers or books whenever circumstances forced us to sit in the same room. Pleading a headache, I slipped out of church after the early worship service, leaving Steve to teach his Sunday school class alone.

I spent most of Sunday afternoon in my bed, surrounded by copies of the *St. Petersburg Times*, the *New York Times*, and the *Tampa Tribune*. Talk radio demanded a working knowledge of current events, and Steve left me alone to read most of the day, coming in at 11:00 P.M. to change, shower, and crawl under the covers on his side of the bed.

At least Brittany seemed immune. She'd asked for and received permission to spend most of the weekend at Charisse's house.

Chad's voice buzzed in my headphones. "How's the level in there?"

"Good, Chad. Everything's great."

"Got a couple of local calls on the line," Gary said, making small talk while my prerecorded voice extolled the virtues of all-natural bee pollen supplements. "Their topics will play in Peoria, though."

"That's fine."

I rocked in my chair, waiting for the commercial to run out, then idly tapped my fingers on the desk during the ten-second lead-in. I was anxious to finish the show and get out of the studio, for this afternoon I planned to visit the bank. I needed to mail a cashier's check for fifteen thousand dollars to Project One in New York.

As the intro died away, I clicked on the phone and greeted my next caller. "Cynthia? Welcome to the show."

"Dr. Diana?"

"That's me."

"I'm having a terrible problem with my husband. I know you believe in marriage at all costs—"

I cut her off before she could put more words in my mouth. "Wait a minute, dear. Marriage at all costs? I don't think I've ever said that. Doesn't even sound like my lingo."

"Well . . . I mean, you believe in marriage."

"Yes, I do. But first tell me about the problem with your husband."

"Well—we just aren't getting along these days. We fight all the time, and I've been asking myself whether it's better for my kids to live in a quiet house with one parent or a stressful house with two."

"Let me ask you this—did you come from a divorced family?"

The caller hesitated. "Yeah."

"And do you have a career?"

"I'm a nurse."

"Okay. How many children, and how old?"

"Two boys—they're five and three."

I let out a low whistle. "So tell me why you'd be willing to contribute to the divorce rate in order to stop squabbling with your spouse?"

"Well . . . isn't it true that children are happier when their parents are happy? And divorce happens half the time, I hear. I don't think my kids would be hurt if we split up."

"That 50 percent divorce rate statistic is a lie, Cynthia. Think about it. They tell us in any given year two million marriages and one million divorces are recorded, so people assume half the people who get married also get divorced. But that's not comparing the *total* number of existing marriages to the *total* number of divorces. When you look at it in the proper perspective, the divorce rate is about 13 percent."

"So? It still seems like everyone I know has been divorced at least once."

"You need to widen your circle of friends, dear. And have you considered what divorce is doing to our nation's kids? We are sowing troubles we'll reap in later years and future generations. Psychologists tell us three out of five children of divorce feel rejected by at least one parent. Five years after their parents' divorce, more than one-third of divorced children perform markedly worse in school than before the divorce. And half still suffer from the slings and arrows of parents who fight as much *after* the split as before! So don't tell me you want to divorce your husband for the sake of your children. I don't buy it."

When I heard nothing but silence from the other end of the phone, I wondered if I had misread the situation.

"I would never"—I lowered my voice—"tell a woman to remain in a marriage if she is being abused or threatened, or if her children are in danger. If that is your situation, my advice would be to take your kids and get out. But if you and your husband just can't get along, for the love of Pete, solve your petty problems and learn how to cooperate! Marriage is a partnership. Every day one of you is going to have to surrender to the other, and in successful marriages, partners take turns being flexible."

"I guess," Cynthia said, "but it seems like I'm always the one giving in."

"Then you tell your husband it's time for a change. If he loves you—if he's committed to your marriage—he'll listen. Love isn't lording your will over someone, it's learning how to bend when the winds blow. Choose your battles carefully, Cynthia; don't force your hand on unimportant issues. But when something really matters, stand your ground and state your reasons for feeling as you do. And perhaps your confidence can sway your husband to see things from your viewpoint."

I paused, giving her a chance to respond, but apparently Cynthia had nothing to add.

"So, listeners—get with the program so many of our grandparents followed. Think of marriage as a lifelong journey, not a short-term fling. For the sake of our children, let's show a little character and make things work."

I pointed to Chad, who let the next commercial roll, then propped my chin on my hand and studied the list of callers in the queue. A woman named Doris wanted to talk about her husband's annoying postretirement habits, a homeschooled child had a question about her mother's discipline, a man named Stephen was having a problem with his wife. Americans had nothing but problems, and over the course of my career, I'd heard about everything. Each day in the studio was different, but few days held any surprises.

Thinking it might be interesting to hear the male side of a marital disagreement after Cynthia's call, I waited until the commercial played out, then leaned into the mike.

"Hello, Stephen, welcome to the *Dr. Sheldon Show*."

"Good day, Dr. Diana."

I froze as my husband's voice reverberated through the studio.

For an agonizing moment my mind went blank. Score one for Steve—he'd managed to surprise me. I stared at the computer screen, not daring to look at Gary lest he see the panic on my face, then forced out my usual reply. "Go ahead."

"I'm calling about something that's happened in my family. Nearly a month ago, we lost our young son in a tragic accident."

"I'm sorry." The words felt stiff and heavy on my tongue.

"Thank you. My wife and I grieved together for a while, but now she seems intent on chasing a ghost. She will not let our son go."

Closing my eyes, I wavered between reason and emotion. The professional, rational side of me knew the proper response, but my emotional side recognized the trap my husband had set. He wanted me to say something like "She needs to move on" or "No one can live in the past," but those instructions didn't apply in our situation. We didn't *have* to move on; we had another choice—but I knew he wouldn't mention the word *clone* on national radio.

"I'm very sorry for your loss," I said, shifting into semiautomatic mode, "but your wife will handle things in her own way. Give her time—she might surprise you."

Before Steve could say anything else, I hit the next button. Chad's head jerked up as one of our prerecorded comedy bits began to play, and Gary shot a puzzled look through the glass.

"Listen," I whispered into the phone, knowing we were off the air. "I don't know what you think you're doing—"

Steve interrupted in a calm voice. "I'm trying to help you see reason. Maybe if you look at yourself from another perspective—"

"Get off the phone and don't ever call here again."

I punched the disconnect button, then dropped the receiver into the cradle. While my prerecorded voice laughed and whooped it up on the airwaves, I held my head in both hands and tried to gain control of my seething emotions.

Gary and Chad probably thought I was sick and needed a break—and they wouldn't be far off the mark. The encounter with my husband had left me feeling queasy.

The guys didn't know the truth. And I wasn't about to tell them.

I was still boiling from Steve's little telephone stunt when he came home at six o'clock. I sat in the study, my nerves stretched tighter than a bowstring, and waited for him to pause in the doorway and say something.

I wasn't prepared for the sound of a second male voice.

"Come on in, Pastor," Steve said, his tone unusually bright for this hour of the day. "Have a seat in the living room, and I'll get us something to drink. Diet Coke okay with you?"

"That's fine, Steve, thanks."

I cringed as I recognized the voice of John Thompson, our pastor. For a moment I searched my memory, wondering if I'd forgotten about a dinner appointment, but found nothing. Which meant Steve had invited the pastor to our home for some sort of ambush.

That realization fanned the anger that had been boiling beneath my skin. Spontaneous human combustion suddenly seemed possible.

I heard them move from the foyer into the hallway, then their voices echoed in the kitchen amid the chink of ice cubes and glasses. Steve would probably settle the pastor into a comfortable chair, place a soft drink in his hand, then come to fetch me.

I glanced toward the door. My purse lay on the table, so I could grab my keys and run out the door, later claiming I had to make an emergency run to the grocery . . .

"Diana." Steve leaned against the doorframe and peered in at me. "Do you have a few minutes? I've invited Pastor John—"

"I heard." The laserlike glare I shot at him could have sliced through steel. "What is this, a sneak attack?"

Steve took a half step back, his face a mask of pleasant blandness. "It's nothing of the kind. I wanted to talk to John, so I invited him to the house. You're welcome to join us, but only if you want to. I understand if you have work to do."

I narrowed my eyes. Steve was not usually the conniving sort, but this charade wouldn't have fooled even an innocent like Scott Daniel.

"I have a lot of work." I gestured toward the printed wire reports scattered over my desk. "But if I get caught up with my reading, maybe I'll come in."

"That'd be nice." Without another word Steve left me, and a moment later I heard him rummaging around in the kitchen, probably searching for some snack that would hold the men until dinner.

I stared at the computer screen, then gave my reflection a lopsided smile. My husband was not a subtle man; obviously he'd called in reinforcements. Apparently he thought the Reverend John Thompson could attack my stance on cloning, but I doubted our minister was up to the challenge. Trouble was, neither of them would realize the futility of their position if I retreated from the battlefield.

With quiet assurance I stepped out of the study and joined the men in the kitchen. Steve had done his best to provide refreshments for his guest, setting a plate of battered Oreos in the center of the kitchen island.

Pretty pitiful battle rations for a mercenary.

"Give me a minute, guys." Breezing past Steve, I opened the cupboards and found fresh chips and a jar of salsa, then arranged my offering on our best snack tray. After setting it on the counter and making certain each man had a full glass of soda, I took a seat at the bar across from the pastor.

I gave him my brightest smile. "John, I know you didn't stop by just to chat about Steve's Sunday school class. So why don't you tell me why you're here?"

Fire the first shot, if you dare.

The pastor looked at me, a betraying flush brightening his face. "Well, yes, Diana, Steve asked me to stop by to talk to you about this matter of cloning. He thought I might be able to shed some light on the subject."

I cocked a brow in his direction. "Have you light to shed?"

A cheap shot, maybe, but if he was unprepared, he deserved it.

"Well"—he glanced around; I had the feeling he was looking for notes—"I believe it's intrinsically wrong, and that's the most important thing. People who say these little cloned embryos are not human are mistaken. If allowed to grow, those cells will develop into a human baby just like those cloned sheep cells grew into a lamb—"

"But the cells are not always allowed to grow, John. Some of them are halted before the egg divides past the six-cell stage. It's not an embryo yet, no organs, nothing but elementary stem cells."

"It's human, isn't it?"

"Yes, if you mean that it has forty-six chromosomes like every other human cell. But the cells of your thumb have forty-six chromosomes, too, and while they're human, they're not a person."

He frowned. "We shouldn't be playing God with this kind of thing."

"An old argument, John, and not effective. Are we playing God when we shock someone's heart back to life? When we do a heart transplant? God does hold the power of life and death, but sometimes he allows men to wield that power, too. Would you outlaw defibrillators because they can literally bring people back from the dead?"

John glanced at Steve, then spread his hands. "I can't argue science with you, Diana. You know more than I do about the technology. So let me ask you—why do you feel you have to clone your son? You know the process won't bring Scotty back."

I stiffened, a little surprised by the feint and counterattack from another direction. "I know cloning won't bring Scott Daniel back, but it will right a wrong. I honestly believe God never meant for our son to die that day. So maybe he is allowing us to explore the miracle of cloning so we can have another chance with a genetic twin."

Lines of concentration deepened under John's eyes. "God is sovereign, Diana. He doesn't make mistakes. Scott Daniel died, so you have to accept that God took him home."

Swallowing hard, I lifted my chin. "God didn't take Scott Daniel from us. He wouldn't do that."

"God ordains everything that happens in the lives of his children." John spoke in a soft and careful voice. "If you are a Christian, everything that happens to you is filtered through his perfect will."

I shook my head. "He may not have stopped Scott's death, but I'll never believe he actually *permitted* it. Why would he? It makes no sense."

Drawing a deep breath, John pressed his hands to his knees. "Your daughter Brittany drives a red pickup, right?"

Steve nodded. "That's her."

John smiled and looked at me. "Okay. Suppose, Diana, Brittany came to you and asked permission to take Scotty to the candy store. She knows she can't take him without your approval. You grant that permission, so even though she's driving, the trip is happening according to your will. If you hadn't agreed, Brittany would not have the authority to take your son. The ultimate decision was yours."

I nailed him with my sharpest glare. "Are you saying Satan took my son with God's permission?"

The pastor's eyes clouded with hazy sadness as he lifted his hands. "I don't know, I don't know if we *can* know these things. But this I do know—Scripture tells us that the Lord does not abandon anyone forever. Though he brings grief, he also shows compassion according to the greatness of his unfailing love. For he does not enjoy hurting people or causing them sorrow."

"He hurts people?" I had steeled my heart in defense, but those words slipped away from me like the mewling of a kitten caught in a crossfire. Hastily, I reinforced my defenses. "I serve a God of *love*. He doesn't do evil things."

"God is not the author of evil, but neither is he its victim. He takes the evil that happens to us, even the evil we bring on ourselves, and uses it for his highest good."

I lifted a finger. "That's why I think good can come from cloning. If Scott Daniel had not died, we would never have considered it. God will bring good out of it, but I can't believe he did this to us on purpose."

The pastor closed his eyes and opened his mouth—a clear signal that my volley had utterly missed the mark.

"If you believe God merely allowed this tragedy to happen," he said, speaking as slowly as he would to a child, "then you must also believe he was either unable or unwilling to intervene. If he was unable, then he is not greater than evil, and therefore not an all-powerful God. If he was unwilling, then he behaved far more callously than any father I can imagine."

Lost in confusion, I stared at him. He was painting pictures of a God I didn't recognize, and I'd been a Christian most of my life.

"If, as you say, God took my son"—the words tasted sour in my mouth—"then *why* did he do it?"

The pastor smiled, but with a distracted, inward look, as though he had transferred his attention to a field of vision beyond my reach.

"I don't know why," he said simply, "but God does. And if you seek him, he may give you the wisdom you need to understand."

Aghast at the answer, I looked at Steve. My husband was staring at the floor, twin tracks of tears on his face.

"I do believe one thing," Pastor John said, standing. "When tragedies like this happen in our lives, God is far more interested in our reactions than our actions. So I would caution you to be careful, Diana and Steve. Don't run out and do things you might regret. Turn your thoughts inward and see if God might be trying to do something in your spiritual life. Spiritual things, after all, are eternal things. Nothing else really matters, does it?"

Stunned by an assault I hadn't counted on, I sat at the counter in silence as the pastor bent to pick up a cracked Oreo, nodded a farewell, then accompanied my husband out into the night.

That night I visited the hospital again. The dream came back with startling clarity, rushing into my consciousness the moment I began to drift in sleep.

I stepped out of Gary's car, felt the familiar scratch of my plaid skirt, saw Steve standing near the door.

"Diana," he called, looking as if he'd been waiting for me. "This way."

Overcome by an eerie sense of déjà vu, I didn't speak, but followed him through the doors, past the reception desk, and down the hall where the pregnant women in wheelchairs were still staring into space. I drew a deep breath as we paused at the elevator and took a moment to look around—the corridor to my right ended in a brick wall; to my left I saw the bustling waiting area and dozens of people who waited restlessly to see a physician.

The elevator chimed. This time I braced myself for the onslaught, stepping aside as the faceless, animated mannequins poured out of the elevator and scattered into the waiting room. Steve vanished again, but I didn't hesitate. I stepped into the elevator, pressed the only button, and soon found myself on the alabaster floor with the white-garbed nurses.

I didn't pause to ask for Scott Daniel's room, but turned immediately for the place I'd last seen him. Though I knew what to expect, a thrill shivered through my senses as I crossed the threshold and saw my son lying in the hospital bed. Steve and Brittany were there, still keeping a vigil, while Gary leaned against the back wall. Pastor John had left the room, as had the friends who'd been present on our previous visit, but they didn't matter.

Only Scott Daniel. I moved immediately to the bed and leaned over the metal railing, pressing my lips to his warm forehead.

He lived. My son still lived.

"He's alive." This time I spoke the words in a firm voice, to be heard above the mechanical clicks of the machinery around the bed.

As before, Steve dropped his hand upon my shoulder. "Yes, sweetheart, he is. But we're waiting to hear what the doctor will say."

I ran the back of my hand along Scott's round face. "Wake up, honey." Again I whispered our good morning refrain. "The sun's come up and so should we, snugglebugs though we may be."

He did not wake, but I thought I saw a slight flutter behind his eyelids.

I leaned closer to whisper directly in his ear. "Wake up, Scott Daniel. The sun's come up and so should we, snugglebugs though we may be."

No answer, but was that a flush on his cheek?

"I think his color's improving." I tossed the words over my shoulder to anyone who would listen, then paused. Brittany and Gary had left the room, leaving me alone with Steve.

Steve's voice, firm and final, fell upon my ear. "We have to wait for the doctor."

"Scotty?" I leaned far forward, gently drawing my son into my arms. Perhaps that was the problem. At home I used to crawl into bed with him, holding him close as I recited our little rhyme. "The sun's come up and so should we, snugglebugs though we may be—"

"Diana?" The resonant voice behind me was familiar, but I couldn't place it. A quick downward glance revealed dark shoes and pants topped by a white lab coat. The doctor, surely.

I returned my gaze to my son. "Don't you think he looks better, Doctor? I thought I saw a little movement a moment ago."

"He's gone, Diana." He spoke the words without malice, but they fell with the weight of stones in still water, spreading endless ripples of pain and betrayal.

"Nooooooooo." Biting back a sob, I traced a thread of gold in Scott Daniel's hair. "He's alive."

"His body is being kept alive through the science of machines, but his soul departed long ago. He is safe and happy, but he is not here."

Unable to speak, I shook my head. How could this idiot doctor say such things, when I held a living, breathing boy in my arms? Scott Daniel was here with me, the scar on his cheek was *healing,* for Pete's sake, and I would not let him slip away.

"Diana." The doctor's voice was closer this time, and gentler, almost as if he stood behind me whispering in my ear. "You have to let him go."

"I can't."

"You must. You can't live in this place."

"I can." The words felt like daggers ripping up my throat. "I will. I will stay here for as long as it takes my son to wake up; I'll sleep for the next two weeks if I have to—"

A hand squeezed my shoulder and I turned, ready to rail against the doctor who refused to see the life still burning in my son. But the room melted into blackness, and when I focused my eyes, I found myself lying in bed. A shadow-shrouded Steve leaned over me.

"You okay?" His voice sounded uneasy. "You were whimpering in your sleep."

Wearily, I lifted my head. By the dim glow of the bathroom night-light I saw the outline of our bed, the nightstand, the fringe on the window blind. Drab, dark reality.

"Sorry." I dropped my head back to the pillow. "Dreaming, I guess."

He grunted and turned away from me; a few moments later I heard him softly snoring.

When I was sure he slept, I buried my face in my pillow and released the hot tears of loss and fury that had begun to rise the moment he woke me.

Thirty-two

STEVE'S PASTORAL AMBUSH WAS NOT ENOUGH TO upset my campaign. Though that skirmish had momentarily bewildered me, one truth remained: the Bible had nothing to say about cloning. Since I still believed the Project One opportunity could be part of God's plan for us, I pressed on.

I had hand-delivered the letter with my fifteen-thousand-dollar cashier's check to the post office on April 21. Within a week I received a "to-do" list from Andrew at the New York Office of Project One.

First on the list: obtain Scott Daniel's tissue samples. On my most formal stationery I immediately fired off a letter to the Pinellas County medical examiner; a week later I shot off a second note.

Finally, on May 13, I received a response. Dr. Joseph Spago, the ME I had met on the day of Scott Daniel's death, replied with a form letter regretfully stating that he could not release the tissue samples for my use. To do so would violate policy.

Ten minutes after opening the envelope, I was on the phone. After navigating a bewildering voice-mail maze, I punched in Dr. Spago's extension, answered several annoying prerecorded queries, then finally found myself talking to the man I sought.

I reminded the doctor that we had met in March.

"Dr. Sheldon." Immediately his tone became solicitous. "Of course I remember meeting you. What can I do for you?"

"I'm holding a letter from you, Doctor, refusing to release a selection of my son's tissue samples."

From the way he awkwardly cleared his throat, I realized he hadn't recognized my name when he signed the letter.

"I'm sorry, Dr. Sheldon, but it's against our policy to release specimens. We have to keep specimens from all unnatural death cases in the event some sort of litigation arises. This is particularly important in accident cases like your son's."

"But you have several samples from my son's body. I'm only asking for one."

A second of silence followed, then, "May I ask why you want this?"

Rolling my eyes, I turned my chair to face the window. "I don't think that information is pertinent to my request. I am a parent, I want a tissue sample from my son's body—preferably one that has not been frozen."

"I'm truly sorry, Dr. Sheldon, but the answer has to be no. I would love to oblige you as a professional courtesy, but I answer to higher authorities."

I sighed. "All right, then. What would it take for me to obtain one of those samples?"

He exhaled into the phone. "I'm not positive, but since we are responsible to the courts, I suspect nothing less than a court order will suffice."

"Thank you, Doctor."

I disconnected the call, scribbled a few notes on a legal pad, then reached for the phone book. Steve and I had not met with our lawyer since revising our wills shortly after Scott Daniel's birth. This call would be a surprise.

Parker Oliphant, our family lawyer, seemed genuinely pleased to hear from me. "Diana Sheldon! Don't tell me someone has decided to sue you for radio malpractice."

"Nothing so tedious, I'm afraid." I leaned back in the chair and stared at the ceiling, mentally marshaling my facts. "I'm in the midst of an unusual situation and I could use your help. I'm thinking a strongly worded letter might do the trick."

I heard the creak of his chair. "What's the story?"

"It concerns my son, Scott Daniel." Against my will, a lump rose in my throat and threatened to strangle my words. "You may have heard about the accident a few weeks ago."

"I did and I'm very sorry. I sent a card; did you get it?"

"Yes, and thank you very much." In truth, I had no idea if I saw Parker's card—the kitchen table had been littered with stacks of cards and letters I hadn't had the courage or the heart to open. Steve's receptionist, Gerta Poppovitch, had acknowledged them for us.

"Parker, what I'm about to explain is controversial, so I'd appreciate it if you kept this quiet. I'm not sure of all the legal terms or procedures, but I need you to write a letter to convince a judge to release tissue samples held by the Pinellas County medical examiner's office."

The chair squeaked again. "There's no need to do that, Diana. If you're planning to sue the driver who struck Scott, the ME will automatically provide the data we need—"

"I'm not suing, Parker. The accident was . . . an accident."

A deep silence echoed over the phone, broken only by the scratching of a branch against my windowpane.

"I'm sorry, Diana, if I'm sounding a little dense—but why did you want this tissue sample?"

"It's for medical research, Parker—for the baby I plan to have next year. I don't want to go into details, but I desperately need one of those tissue samples. I'm asking you to do whatever you must to get it for me."

Silence rolled over the line, then he said, "You're talking about cloning."

"Yes."

Parker did not respond for a long moment, but I could hear the ghostly chatter of a keyboard as he made notes about the conversation. "Well," he finally said, "as the parent, you have more right than anyone to your own child's tissue. After all, after the autopsy the ME's office signed the body over to you, didn't they?"

"Yes. They said they needed to keep samples in case of possible litigation, but that's a moot point in our situation. Besides, I'm not asking for every tissue they have, just a representative sample."

The keyboard chattered again. "Steve's on board with this?"

I drew a deep breath, torn between truth and a careful dodging of the question. "Well . . . not exactly. Will it matter if he disagrees with me?"

"Only if he openly resists you."

"So if Steve says nothing, the judge will grant my request?"

"The odds are pretty good."

"But if Steve wants to fight me?"

"Then you're in trouble. The judge might even dismiss your request as frivolous."

I hesitated, counting the costs. I was about to suggest something that went against everything I'd believed for years and every precept I'd ever proclaimed on the air. Families were the basis of America, and nothing mattered more to a happy family than a happy marriage, but could I be happy if Steve refused to allow me to restore our son?

If he did not change his mind—and from everything I'd seen, I didn't think he would—could I be happy remaining in this marriage? *With* Steve, I'd continue to be an example of a faithful wife, but inwardly, I'd be dying. *Without* Steve, I could be a happy single mother, devoted to my son.

I'd been married for twenty-two years . . . but I'd only been allowed five years as Scott's mother. I'd been cheated, but by having another son I could bring balance to my life.

Gathering my courage, I asked the question that would change everything: "What if I petition the court as a single woman?"

I heard Parker's quick intake of breath. "But you're not single."

"I could be."

He laughed, but I heard no humor in the sound. "I don't know what you're thinking, Diana, but I think you'd better work things out with Steve before you petition the court. A judge is not likely to think highly of your mental stability if you can't decide whether or not you want to be married."

I thanked him for his time, promised to call later, and hung up.

Dinner that night was strained, but for once I wasn't the primary cause of the disruption. Steve had come home at five and gone straight to the kitchen, where he deposited takeout boxes from Durango's. Eager to see a smiling face, he'd tiptoed up the stairs to greet his daughter, then caught Brittany smoking in her bedroom.

Ten minutes later we all sat at the kitchen counter, silent and tense. Steve kept shooting pained glances in Britt's direction while she fastened her gaze to her plate and stabbed at a slice of roast beef until the meat had more holes in it than a sieve.

When I could bear the tension no longer, I looked at her. "Are you done?"

Her jaw tensed. "Yes."

"Then you may be excused."

Bolting like a deer before the hounds, she pushed back from the table and stomped toward the stairs, but not before grabbing a box of cheese crackers from the pantry.

I noted the food and sighed, wearily making a mental note to vacuum her carpet tomorrow. No one could mess up a bedroom faster than my daughter.

Once she had gone, I pulled the ME's letter from my pocket and slid it across the counter.

"What's this?" Steve asked, his expression blank.

"Read it."

He pulled his glasses from his shirt pocket and read with a stony expression. As he folded the page again, however, a look of triumph flashed in his eyes.

"So the medical examiner won't cooperate. Surely that's a sign."

"What are you talking about?"

"A sign from God. If he had wanted us to pursue cloning, he would have smoothed the road before us."

Crossing my arms, I stared at him. "Maybe you're wrong. Maybe he's making our way difficult to stretch and test our faith. After all, he certainly didn't make things easy for Paul or the disciples."

"They were working to advance the kingdom of God. You're trying to advance a personal cause."

"For the love of Pete, will you make sense? Why can't you agree with me?"

"Because you're wrong. You're in denial, Counselor, and you can't see how you're lying to yourself."

Something rose within me, a bitter and acrid emotion I had never felt toward any living person . . . yet it was directed toward my *husband*. How could this be happening to us? I was a Christian, I loved Steve, and until now I had always wanted to be a submissive wife. Hadn't I gone with him to that stupid support group when everything in me railed against it? Yet this time he had gone too far. He was forcing me to live a life I was never meant to live.

"I'm going to ask you one last time." Rancor sharpened my voice. "Will you support me when I ask for a court order to get those tissue samples? Will you help me parent our new son?"

He dropped his fork, touched his lips with his napkin, then lowered it and met my gaze head-on. In a voice as steady as my own, he answered. "I will not."

A trembling rose from deep within me, but I would not weep. "Then I'll move forward without you. And you know what that means."

The set of his jaw did not change, but his brow wrinkled and something moved in his eyes. "I suppose I do."

"I want a divorce."

I thought my statement would shock him. Perhaps it did. But in that moment he did not flinch, nor did he protest. We both sat as immovable as rocks, two partners caught in a standoff because neither would capitulate.

"You have no grounds for divorce," he finally said.

"How about mental cruelty? You have denied me the one thing I desire most in life—my child."

He looked at me and blinked hard. "I have never been cruel. I have been firm."

"That's what most abusers tell their wives."

His brows shot up. "Oh, come on, Diana. You can't say I have abused you."

"I prefer to cite 'irreconcilable differences,' if anyone asks. But your refusal to support me feels like cruelty."

"I can't help your perceptions! Besides, I meant you have no *biblical* grounds to divorce me."

"Abuse isn't a biblical reason for divorce, either, but I would never tell an abused woman to stay with her husband." I straightened in my chair, readjusting my shattered dignity. "Besides, I think the Bible makes that point about adultery being the only allowable reason because people were putting their spouses away so they could marry someone else. I'm not planning to remarry. I want to have my baby. I'd love to reunite our family, but if you can't join us . . ."

I shrugged and lowered my gaze, hoping he'd understand. I hadn't fallen out of love with him—after twenty-two years of marriage we weren't exactly passionate in our relationship, but our marriage was comfortable and I had always considered Steve my best friend. I knew I shouldn't toss that aside, but neither should he ignore my desperate desire to restore our son.

I cast him a sidelong glance. "I'd love to be married to you forever, Steve, but I'm going to have this baby. If you change your mind, and if you don't hate me after all this, well, maybe there's hope for our future together. But if you can't support me, I want a divorce."

I watched a host of varying emotions twist his expression as he looked out the window. First, emotion softened his eyes, then a random thought tightened the corners of his mouth. "You know what this makes you," he said, his eyes averted. "The biggest hypocrite to ever hold court on radio."

"I am *not* a hypocrite." I threw the words like stones. "I have always been true to my beliefs in public and in private."

"I've heard you tell callers how divorce hurts children. You say parents should bend, practice give-and-take—"

"I've been bending for twenty-two years. And as far as our children are concerned, Scott Daniel is dead, Brittany is finished with childhood, and the new baby won't even draw breath if we stay married."

His squint tightened. "You talk as if we already have a third child. We don't. We shouldn't. Not like this."

"I should, I can, and I will, whether or not I have your help. If you won't join me, I'll have him without you. If I have to leave you to do it, I'll leave."

Picking up his fork, Steve stared down at his plate. "Suit yourself." The words were a hoarse whisper. "But you won't take our daughter. I won't lose two children."

That statement felt like a slug hitting the center of my chest. "You can't be serious. Daughters belong with their *mothers.*"

"Daughters belong in a stable and loving environment." Calmly he picked up his knife and proceeded to slice his roast beef. "At this moment, I'm the one who can best provide what Britty needs. I'm sure any judge would agree after my lawyer describes your plan to put this family on the front page of every newspaper in the nation."

Shock whipped my breath away. The room seemed to spin, the bright yellows and reds of my kitchen mixing in a mad whirl. Instinctively, I reached out to grasp the edge of the counter, then closed my eyes and held my head to stop the nauseating sensation of vertigo.

I don't know how long I sat there—four minutes, maybe five—

but when I lifted my head again, Steve had risen and walked away. Three plates remained on the counter, all of them filled with food no one had eaten or enjoyed.

I stood and carried my dishes to the sink, then used a fork to scrape my untouched beef into the disposal. The act reminded me of the surfeit of food we'd known after Scott's accident. No one wanted to eat when death came calling.

Even when death struck a marriage.

Thirty-three

AT ONE POINT IN MY CHILDHOOD—I'M NOT SURE, but I think I was six or seven—I decided to run away. I even picked out the place I would run to, a pretty little home by the lake. My parents and I often drove past that house on our way to church, so I had mentally mapped out the route I'd take to reach it. Any people who lived in such a nice house, I reasoned, had to be nice, too.

I had no real reason to leave home, but kids on TV and in books ran away all the time. My parents were loving and firm, not monsters. Still, I planned my escape.

One afternoon I went so far as to pull all the things I'd need from my bureau drawer. Item by item I pulled out shirts and shorts, socks and underwear, and I remember being shocked when I turned to discover that I had emptied my entire dresser. I either had inflated ideas about my needs or a pitiful lack of clothing.

One night after my mother tucked me in, I thought about how much I would miss her when I ran away. Despite my best efforts to hide it, a tear slipped down my cheek and caught my mother's attention.

She knelt by my bed. "Diana, honey, what's wrong?"

I shook my head. "Nothing."

"Are you sure?"

I was sure of one thing—I couldn't tell her about my plan to run away. So I lied and told her I was fine, I wasn't upset, everything was a-okay. Which it was.

I think all my life I've been planning to run away. I've just been waiting for a reason.

I didn't want to divorce Steve. I didn't believe divorce honors God. I knew it would damage my testimony before an unbelieving world. And, as I was constantly telling my radio audience, I believe in marriage and partnership and staying together for the sake of the children. I hated what a separation or divorce might do to Brittany, even at her age.

Still . . . Steve and I had reached an impasse, a place where I could not bend and he would not yield.

Wednesday morning found me searching the classified ads in the station's break room. Apartments were plentiful in Tampa, and several were located within a ten-minute drive of the station. I'd need a two-bedroom, of course, because Brittany would have to come with me . . .

If Steve would let her. I dropped the paper, abruptly aware that I was moving too quickly. Steve could be stubborn when he wanted to be, and last night he'd indicated he'd fight me for custody of our daughter.

I'd need a good lawyer.

I glanced at my watch. With only ten minutes till air, I didn't have time to start a search through the yellow pages. But I'd work on it in the afternoon, because with each day of waiting my eggs and Scott Daniel's tissue samples grew older.

I could not afford to waste time.

Thirty-four

STEVE STEPPED THROUGH THE PRIVATE EXIT OF HIS office and stood for a moment in the parking lot, wincing in the glaring sun. Lately life itself seemed intent upon causing him pain.

"You okay, Dr. Sheldon?"

Prying one eye open, he saw Melanie Brown standing beside him, her eyes sheltered by a pair of wire-rimmed sunglasses. Her shoulder-length blonde hair ruffled slightly in the breeze while her lips curved in a soft smile.

"I'm fine." He brought two fingers to the brim of an imaginary cap, then pointed to the sun overhead. "Just a little blinded, that's all."

"You should get some Ray-Bans." She moved toward her car, a lima-bean-colored VW bug she'd named Lily. Pausing by the door, she eyed him with concern. "You want me to pick you up a pair of sunglasses while I'm out for lunch? I'd be happy to do it since . . . well, I know things are rough for you right now. You probably don't feel like going to the mall."

He resisted the urge to snort in derision. A crowded public shopping center was the last place on earth he wanted to visit on his lunch hour, but she didn't need to know the reason for his melancholy.

"Thanks, Melanie, but I'll be fine. You drive carefully, now."

She flashed him a smile and got in the car, then waved before pulling out and driving away. He watched her leave, realizing that she was going to have lunch amid a happy bustle of people while he ate a sandwich by his son's grave.

Grief tiptoed close to press a cold palm to his shoulder. Angrily he shrugged off the chill, then slipped his hand into his pocket, searching for his keys.

What had happened to his carefully ordered world? In the last few weeks his wife, formerly a fount of wisdom and stability, had morphed into a woman he scarcely knew, let alone understood. He had tried talking, waiting, and empathizing, but though two months had passed since Scotty's accident, she showed no signs of returning to her old self. Somehow she had turned a corner he thought she'd never reach, and last night she had been dead serious when she asked for a divorce.

He found his keys, unlocked the car, and slid into the seat, leaving the door open so the heat could escape. Slipping the key into the ignition, he started the engine, then positioned the vent to blow cool air onto his face.

A divorce. When he was a kid, his mother had nearly worn out Tammy Wynette's recording of that tune. As Tammy warbled on about her pending D-I-V-O-R-C-E, he had sounded out the word and wondered what in the world could be so bad people had to spell it in a song.

Now he knew. Divorce was awful enough when it happened to other people; when it happened to you, it was like a death. Worse than death, actually. Scotty's accident had been a shock, but death had come swiftly and almost painlessly for Scott. Divorce tore the limbs from a family torso and left the raw nerve endings exposed.

If this divorce went through, Brittany would be ripped in two. At a time when she desperately needed both parents and wanted neither, what would she do?

He'd been praying ever since Diana first mentioned the horrible word. He'd asked God to change her heart, but somehow he knew God didn't force his will on his creations. Free will was both a tremendous gift and a tremendous burden . . . especially to those whose loved ones used their freedom to make destructive choices.

He closed the car door, then sat for a moment with his hands braced against the steering wheel. He didn't know what to do next. An inner voice urged him to take action, but as he saw it, he had only three choices: capitulate to Diana and proceed with the cloning; resist her efforts in the cloning and the divorce; or allow her to proceed in her plans with no resistance whatsoever.

The first option was untenable for several reasons. First, he did not want to be associated with the Raelians, no matter how loose their affiliation with Project One. Second, producing a replacement twin for Scotty seemed disrespectful to his son's memory. Though Steve felt certain he could love another child should Diana want to again consider adoption, he did not think it fair to expect another baby to fill Scotty's shoes. Third, the idea of cloning disturbed something in Steve's spirit, and throughout his life he'd come to rely upon the peace of God as a sure indicator that he'd chosen the right thing.

If he resisted Diana and contested the divorce, the media would be drawn to their family like fleas to a hound. Diana's career would suffer, Brittany would be tormented, and his practice, built on years of trust, might collapse. No parent would want to take their child to a dentist whose name appeared regularly in the tabloids.

He shuddered to think how reporters might turn innocent moments of their family history into lurid escapades for the gossip trade. Snoops from the *Tattler* or the *National Gossip* would take one look at their children—one adopted, then, thirteen years later, a miracle birth—and portray Scotty's arrival as some sort of alien encounter or, even more believable, the result of an adulterous fling. Brittany, whose exotic flaming-haired loveliness stood out in any crowd, would be fodder for photographers and reporters who might say or do anything to pry a provocative quote from her lips.

But those things would be only background for the real story once Diana's plans to bear a clone became public knowledge. Even divorced, they'd forever be known as the "Warring Clone Couple." The resulting child, if he survived, would inherit a legacy of speculation, rumor, and gossip . . .

Steve couldn't allow that. He loved his family too much.

Which left only one option—to allow Diana to make her choices freely, to step back and make it easy for her. Didn't the Bible say something about letting an unbelieving husband or wife go free? God wanted his children to live in peace.

Trouble was, Diana wasn't an unbelieving spouse. She was as strong a Christian as he was, but in the last few weeks grief had strapped blinders over her eyes. He could think of about ten spiritual principles her recent decisions had violated, including that verse about wives submitting themselves to their husbands . . .

Diana was a twenty-first-century woman. She didn't submit to many people. On the night he'd brought Pastor John to the house to try to speak sense to Diana, she'd faced him with the steely resolve of a gunslinger with nothing to lose.

He chuckled bitterly as the words of an old-time preacher came back to him on a tide of memory. "My wife and I have been married fifty years without a single argument," the preacher had said, thumping the pulpit for emphasis. "In the beginning, we made an agreement—she'd let me decide the major issues, and she'd take care of all the minor matters. And in fifty years of marriage, we've never had a major issue come up."

Steve exhaled a deep breath. His marriage had been much like the preacher's until God tossed a decidedly major issue into his lap. Trouble was, his wife was not willing to let him lead.

Sighing, he put the car into reverse, then turned to look behind him. The parking lot was clear, which was more than he could say for his future.

Brittany crossed the threshold, then winced as the security system beeped softly. She'd learned how to get around her mother's little tattletale setup at night by going out a window, but just once she'd like to come home from school without the house announcing her presence.

The soft glow of a lamp came from her mother's study, accompanied by the plastic clatter of the keyboard. Maybe her mom was concentrating and wouldn't notice as she slipped through the foyer.

Lowering her head, she moved past the doorway to the study, then felt her heart sink when the computer clatter ceased.

"Britt?"

She paused in mid-stride. "Yeah?"

"Good day?"

Brittany took a step back, enough to bring her within view of her mother at the computer desk.

"Okay day."

Her mother nodded, then turned back to face the computer monitor. That was it, then.

She hesitated. "Dad home?"

"Not yet." Her mother's voice was flat, abstracted.

"He picking up dinner?"

Her mother shook her head. "Don't know. Haven't spoken to him."

All right. Brittany rolled her eyes and moved away from the door, digesting her mother's diffident reply. Her parents usually kept close tabs on each other, especially at dinnertime. They had an arrangement—Dad picked dinner up on Mondays, Wednesdays, and Fridays, Mom cooked on Tuesdays, Thursdays, and Saturdays, reserving Sundays for leftovers. But even when Mom didn't cook, Dad usually called ahead to ask her what she wanted for dinner . . .

Brittany paused with her hand on the banister. Something was rotten in Denmark, as Mrs. Parker would say, something foul. Something not even Diana Do-Right and the World's Most Perfect Kiddie Dentist could handle.

She snorted softly as she climbed the stairs. Life as the child of two nearly perfect adults (or so everyone thought) had been hard enough before the Scottster died, now things were really spinning out of control. Diana Do-Right was looking a little frayed around the edges, and Dumbo Dad hadn't been himself in days.

Going into her room, Brittany swung her backpack onto the bed, then closed the door and turned the lock. She moved to her CD player, slid in her favorite disc, then slipped on her headphones and turned up the volume.

Closing her eyes, she let the drums and rants of the lead singer take her mind off home. Better to think about life on the streets of New York and in the L.A. hood than to dwell on the miseries of life at 3957 Hunter's Lane in Pinellas County, Florida.

Funny, though . . . until her parents started fighting, she would have sworn her mother was getting better. Dad was still moping around the house; she often found him sitting in his easy chair with damp cheeks. But in the last few weeks, Mom had almost seemed like her old self. She spent a lot of time at her computer, she walked with the old spring in her step, she had resumed her complaining about clutter in the house. Last Saturday afternoon Britt had heard sounds coming from the Scottster's room. She had peeked in to find her mother sealing all of Scott's stuffed animals in plastic bags and storing them in the closet. The rubber-faced monkey had disappeared from the bed, the plastic robots had been swept from the shelves, Scott's raincoat had vanished from the hook by the closet door. Everything, Brittany guessed, from looking at the neat piles in the closet, had gone into storage.

She wasn't sure what that meant, but she'd seen enough Lifetime television movies to know that people who did such things had usually accepted a tragic event and were ready to move on with their lives. Apparently Mom was ready and Dad wasn't, so maybe that accounted for the trouble between them.

Stretching out on the bed, she rested one hand on the book she was supposed to read for homework and clutched her pillow with the other. The friction between her parents was something new . . . and a little unnerving. She'd seen them get a little snappish with each other when they were tired, in a rush, or if one of them had just come home from a really bad day at work. But when one was down, the other managed to be up, and by talking things out they somehow managed to level out.

She rolled onto her back and stared at the ceiling. Maybe that was the problem with her folks now—Dad was down, Mom was up, and the talking wasn't working.

From the depths of her book bag, her cell phone rang. Brittany sat up and dived for it, then checked the caller ID. She felt a little flutter in her stomach. She knew this caller.

Snatching off her headphones, she pressed the talk button. "Hello?"

"Britt? It's Zack."

Holding the phone against her ear, Brittany settled back onto her pillow and grinned. "Whatcha doing?"

"Nothing. What's up with you?"

"Nada. Just lying here."

"Cool. Hey, I was thinking—you wanna go over to Tampa tonight? There's a new band playing in Ybor City. They're supposed to be really good."

Brittany bit her lip. Technically, she was well past her month of being grounded, though neither Mom nor Dad had officially come out and said she was off the hook. But even if she was free to go out, these concerts went late—the no-name bands usually started playing at nine or ten, and the featured groups didn't take the stage until eleven or twelve. But she hadn't gone anywhere all week and she was bored.

"I'd love to go—but I can't leave here until ten. Can you pick me up then?"

"Yeah. For you, I'll wait."

She glanced in the mirror, glad he couldn't see the blush that had risen to her cheeks.

"And Zack?"

"Yeah?"

"Don't come to the front of the house. Just pull to the end of the street and park in the cul-de-sac. I'll walk down and meet you there."

"Whatever you say."

As she clicked the call away, Brittany considered her plan. She'd come up to bed early, turn out the light, let her parents think she'd gone to sleep. Their house lay a good sixty yards from the end of the street, so she could go out the window, shimmy down the oak tree, and walk down the sidewalk in darkness. Once the concert was over, she'd reverse the process to beat the security system.

Sighing, she closed her eyes and pulled the headset back over her ears. Her parents wouldn't even know she was gone.

Thirty-five

THE REMAINING DAYS OF MAY STRETCHED THEM-
selves thin while Steve worked to preserve his home and family. After
Diana's startling request he had gone to his pastor, who listened sym-
pathetically and with genuine tears in his eyes. When Steve finished
explaining their situation, Pastor John promised to pray for the family, then gently reminded Steve that if the divorce went through, he
would have to give up his Sunday school class and resign his position
on the elder board. Church policy was based upon literal Scripture: a
man could lead in the church only if he were blameless and "the husband of but one wife." No divorced persons need apply.

Steve had left the pastor's office with a new emotion stirring in his
breast: shame. Not only had he failed to keep his wife and daughter
safe from an attack on their family, he had also proved himself an
unfit example for other believers. When he went home to sleep in the
guest room that night, he lay down in misery so acute it manifested
itself in real stomach pains.

After two weeks of pointless arguing with Diana and persistent
pleading with God, Steve climbed the stairs to talk to his daughter.
Diana thought they should talk to Brittany together, but something
in Steve wouldn't—couldn't—give Diana that satisfaction. Display a

united front now? How could they, with the fabric of their family torn in two? Refusing to participate in that charade, Steve waited until Diana left the house to speak at a Tuesday night meeting of professional women, then he climbed the stairs.

They had come to an arrangement. Brittany would graduate from high school on Friday, May 30, and Diana wanted to file for divorce as soon as possible after the milestone event. "To hurry the medical examiner," she'd said, crossing her arms. "My lawyer sent a letter, but it had no effect. The only way to get the tissue samples is by a court order, so we'll have to file a petition."

Without being told, Steve knew she wanted to petition the court as a single woman. No judge would grant her petition if her husband protested, and some might not even grant it if the *ex*-husband protested. But after pondering and praying about the matter through many sleepless nights, Steve had come to a decision: he would not fight her. Not in the divorce, not in the court petition, not in the cloning. If he resisted, Diana would blame him for any subsequent troubles or failures. If he stepped back, she would have no one to blame but herself.

At the head of the stairs he turned and looked at Brittany's closed door. Diana would be furious that he had spoken to Britty without her. But her actions had caused this standoff, and their daughter deserved to know the truth from someone who wanted to hold the family together.

He knocked on Britty's door, received no answer, then tried the knob. Locked, as usual.

He knocked harder. "Brittany!"

Pressing his ear to the knob, he heard rustlings from within. Finally his daughter opened the door and stared at him in puffy-eyed bewilderment.

"What time is it?" she asked, her voice heavy with sleep.

"It's 7:30." He stared into her messy room. The golden glow from a lamp on the table revealed schoolbooks scattered on the floor next to an assortment of magazines. The comforter on her bed was rumpled, and the noise she called music buzzed from the headphones on her pillow.

He looked at her in concern. "You feeling okay? You don't usually go to bed at seven o'clock."

She closed her eyes. "I'm tired, Dad. I need a nap."

"You can sleep in a few minutes, then. I want to talk to you."

Huffing in resignation, she moved to the bed and sat on the edge of the mattress, hugging her pillow to her chest while she lowered her head. Steve pushed a pile of jeans from the chair at her desk, then sat down, his gaze roving over rows of nail polish and cans of hair goop.

Had she ever used this desk to *study*?

She lifted her head. "Am I in trouble?"

"No, nothing like that." He swiped at an imaginary piece of dust, then smoothed the desktop with a fingertip. "Brittany, your mother and I have been talking about some pretty serious matters for the last couple of weeks."

Her eyes narrowed.

He drew a deep breath. This was not going to be easy.

"This is hard to explain, honey, but your mom and I have come to a place in our marriage where we cannot go forward together. Neither of us has been unfaithful to the other, you don't need to speculate about anything like that. But because we can't stay married, I'm going to leave the house this weekend, after graduation. Your mother says she's going to file for divorce. If she does, I'm not going to contest it."

Both her eyes were wide now, her mouth a small *O*.

"I know this will be hard for you," he continued, lowering his gaze to her stained and strewn carpet. "So as much as I'd like to have you with me, I'm going to let you stay here this summer so you'll be in a familiar place as you get ready for college. But if you want to stay with me at any time, all you have to do is let me know. I love you, Britty, and I want to be near you. The thought of leaving—I can't—I'm sorry."

Sorrow ripped at his voice, leaving him with tatters of useless phrases, and when he looked up again, his daughter's eyes had gone glassy with wetness.

"I'm so sorry, honey." He stared at her, his heart breaking under the weight of a million regrets. "I wish it didn't have to be this way."

"You're getting a *divorce*?"

"It's what your mother wants."

"My parents will be divorced." She spoke in a tentative, flat voice, as if taking the words for a test drive.

He pressed his lips together as an unexpected surge of anger caught him by surprise. If someone had told him he'd ever hear those words from the lips of his child, he never would have believed it. Even during the most difficult times, *divorce* had never been in his vocabulary, but he hadn't counted on Diana finding the audacity to speak the word.

Brittany clutched the pillow and stared at the crumpled comforter on her bed. "Most of my friends have divorced parents." She released a hollow laugh. "I'll finally fit in."

"Britty—"

"Is it—" She looked up, a question on her face. "Is it because of what happened to Scott?"

He sighed, wishing he could explain, but it wouldn't be fair to burden her with the full story now. If Diana persisted in her plan, Brittany would understand soon enough.

"Scotty's death put a strain on our relationship, but we could have made it through."

Her eyes filled with anguish. "Is it because of me? Because of something I did?"

Compassion flooded his heart. "No, honey. You should never think that." He rose and crossed to the bed, then pulled her into an embrace. "You didn't have anything to do with this. Trust me on this one. In time you'll understand, but for now . . . well, just trust me. In a few weeks I may not be married to your mother, but I'll always be your father and I'll love you forever. Never forget that."

He released her and stepped back. She stared at him with a slightly bewildered expression, as if a question lurked in her mind, but not the courage to ask it.

"You had nothing to do with this," he repeated, in case the unspoken query had been spurred by guilt. "This is something between your mother and me."

He turned then, leaving her in the numbness of discovery, but he knew the tears would begin to flow soon enough. He was well-acquainted with grief, and he knew she would pass this night in soul-searing tears. As much as he wanted to spare her, he couldn't.

As for him, a new emotion took up residence in his heart. For making him hurt his daughter and for bringing agony upon them all, rage toward Diana boiled at the core of his soul.

Brittany sat in stunned silence as the door closed. For a moment her mind went blank—she could not seem to formulate words, even clear thoughts—then a sharp surge of sadness pricked the heavy balloon of guilt she had been carrying for months. Remorse poured out in a flood, streaming down her cheeks.

She had often hoped her parents would split up. When she was feeling defiant, she used to fantasize about divorce bringing an end to that "united front" her mother always babbled about. Sometimes she secretly envied friends who spent weekends with their dads in apartments on the beach or summers with their moms someplace a world away.

Still, wishing was one thing and reality something else altogether. She could scarcely imagine her parents separated. How could Diana Do-Right do something as crazy as this? Was this one of those nutty midlife crises they were always poking fun at on TV? Or was her mother having an affair? Her father had said she wasn't, but maybe he was lying. Maybe her mother was lying to them both.

Her eyes lifted to the mirror above her cluttered dresser. She saw herself there—young girl, big eyes, pale skin, flaming-red hair. Abandoned at birth and now abandoned again.

Her face twisted, her eyes clamped tight to trap the sudden deluge of tears, but there were too many. Bending from the waist, she buried her face in her pillow and gave vent to the agony of confusion and hurt.

How could her parents do this, and right when she needed them to be there for her? Graduation, which should have been the best night of her life, would be a sham. She would stand between them in photographs, everyone would smile at the camera, but the whole thing would be a lie. Everything in her life was a lie, and everybody a liar.

She hated them—her mom and dad both.

Her dad drove her crazy with his teasing and nosing into her business, but she couldn't imagine him not being around when she needed twenty bucks or her truck was making weird noises. And as annoying as his continual questions were, she couldn't imagine walking out the front door without hearing him ask where she was going and when she'd be coming back.

And as much as she resented her mother for bringing them all to the brink of divorce, she couldn't imagine living without her, either. While it might be fun to visit Dad in an apartment somewhere, living without Mom would be like living in a house without electricity. On good days, in the old days, she seemed to keep the house warm. Without a doubt, she kept the house running. She was the one who reminded Dad of school events, who made the dentist appointments, who paid the bills, who did little things like keeping fresh flowers on the kitchen table and in the foyer . . .

"Oh, man." Brittany sat up and reached for a tissue, then blew her nose. She couldn't think when her head was stopped up, and her head felt like a ball of water, wet and slippery and gross. Last night, out with Zack, she had felt pretty and flirtatious and mature.

Good thing he couldn't see her now.

After blowing her nose again, she rolled onto her side, punched her pillow, and wiped her cheeks with her shirtsleeve. Maybe the divorce wouldn't matter. After all, she was eighteen, legally an adult, and she'd be off to college in less than three months. She wouldn't even be living here, so the problems of home shouldn't really matter. Dad would help pay her college bills and Mom would handle all the paperwork just as she handled everything else. When Christmas came around, she'd spend a few days with Mom and a few days with Dad . . . but where would she spend Christmas Eve?

She balled her hands into fists, fighting back the hot tears swelling behind her eyes. Why was this so terrible? She'd probably be like 97 percent of the other kids in her freshman class, just another girl whose parents had two different addresses.

Cold, common sense rose up to shine the hard light of truth on her words. No—it would not be life as usual if her parents split up. The word *divorce* tasted terrible on her tongue, and she still couldn't accept the possibility. And though her dad had said the breakup had nothing to do with her, an inner voice whispered that she'd been flirting with disaster for over a year. Every time she slipped out the window, every curfew she broke, every lie she told added to the stress in her parents' lives. Though they didn't know the half of what she'd done—and maybe never would—she was not blameless. She had been rebelling against her family for months, and the stress had finally cracked the foundation.

Maybe this was God's way of paying her back. He knew what she'd done. He saw everything and kept records, didn't he? In Sunday school she'd learned to think of him as a shining and holy old man who sat in a big white chair surrounded by angels and hundreds of black books on stands. Every time you did something to break one of the rules he put a black mark next to your name, a mark that could be erased only when you repented and confessed and prayed in Jesus' name.

But even when you did those things to make it right, you still had to suffer the consequences. And this time she'd committed one sin too many, piled on the straw that broke the proverbial camel's back.

Her family was broken, and she could do nothing to fix it.

Thirty-six

ON MAY 30, STEVE AND I JOINED THE HUNDREDS OF other parents jamming the War Hawk stadium to witness the high school graduation. We sat together in chilly silence, our shoulders not touching even once, and applauded like zanies as Brittany crossed the stage to accept her diploma and have her tassel moved from one side to the other.

As I watched, I couldn't help but think that the timing of our divorce, while not perfect, was probably the best it could have been. Our daughter was preparing to leave home for college; she was already cutting ties to high school friends. Loosening the apron strings that bound her to us was a logical next step. The divorce could not touch any fond memories she retained of her childhood, and I was reasonably sure Steve and I would remain civil in the years ahead. I had even dared to dream of reconciliation after the baby's birth—if Steve could find it in his heart to forgive me for this struggle, I knew his love for Scott Daniel would lead him to love the new baby. Love for our family would bring him back.

After the graduation ceremony we drove back to the house, then Brittany ran upstairs to change into jeans and a sweater. We waited until she came down; we hugged her and kissed her and sent her out to celebrate with her friends. Then Steve calmly told me good-bye and went to his car, which he had discreetly loaded with suitcases before the graduation ceremony. As I watched from the doorway, he slid into the BMW and drove away to his new apartment, his new furniture, and his new life.

As we had agreed, I went into the study and turned on the computer. In March 2002, Florida had become one the first states in the country to offer uncontested on-line divorces. For two hundred forty-nine dollars, conveniently payable by credit card, applicants could spend thirty minutes answering a series of questions and have their divorce petition filed in court. Petitioners would have to appear at the final divorce hearing, but the on-line application appealed to me. It was fast, private, and inexpensive.

Because Steve had decided not to contest the divorce, I made no demands on him. With lucrative careers, we agreed neither of us needed money for alimony or child support since Brittany's college fund would cover her expenses until she was ready to step out on her own. We agreed that I would keep the house until Brittany left for college, then we'd put it on the market and I'd move to a smaller place. When it sold, we'd evenly split the proceeds.

My dreams of keeping the house so the baby would grow up in Scott Daniel's room had fled with Steve's refusal to support the idea. Without Steve's income, I was now counting on selling the house to reimburse the money I'd borrowed from Brittany's college fund and to finance the cloning. If all went well, the house should sell just as I needed the balance of Project One's fee. I'd still be short about thirty-five thousand, but if I cut down on expenses and asked my agent to book me for a few profitable speaking engagements, I'd eventually be able to cover the balance.

Time passed. Moving in the relaxed haze of a steamy Florida summer, I went to work, spouted advice, then came home to sit by the pool with Terwilliger. Whenever a pang of loneliness struck, or I found myself listening for Steve's key in the door, I would remind myself that I had done a desperate thing for a valid reason. Within a year, God willing, I would have my son again. Then, if God willed, perhaps Steve would come home.

I kept a watchful eye on the calendar, counting off the days, and stored my emotions on a shelf. Next year, when I was snuggling with my son, I would call Steve, apologize, and beg him to consider rekindling our marriage. Until then . . . I'd steel myself to the sight of his empty chair, his unrumpled pillow, and the spotlessly clean second sink in our master bath.

On June 30, four weeks after filing our divorce petition, Steve and I stood in a judge's chambers, assured him we were parting amicably, and walked out of the Pinellas County courthouse as unmarried individuals. We crossed the courtyard and stepped onto the asphalt parking lot together without speaking, then walked side by side to our cars. We reached his BMW first.

I hesitated. With my wealth of experience in counseling I should have known what to say, but nothing had prepared me for this good-bye.

Steve stood still, staring at his keys as he spread them over his palm. Only the tightening of the muscles in his throat betrayed his emotion. "Will you answer one question for me?"

Squinting at him through the hot glare of the June sun, I felt perspiration trickle down my spine as a suffocating sensation tightened my throat. "What question is that?"

He looked at me with something very fragile in his eyes. "Do you still love me at all?"

I could not bear the touch of his gaze, and the look of hurt behind the question. I crossed my arms and looked away to safer territory. "I'll always love you, Steve. But now it's time for me to love our son."

I held my breath, hoping the enormity of what we had just done would bring him to his senses, but he only lowered his keys and unlocked the door. "Good-bye, Diana."

That was it, then. No second thoughts, no last-minute promises. Only a weight of sadness on his lined face, and a brief good-bye.

"Bye." Feeling guilty and selfish, somehow I forced the word over the despair in my throat, then lowered my head and hurried through the parking lot.

The next morning I sat at the studio microphone rubbing the naked joint of my ring finger as I listened to yet another "I-can't-get-along-with-my-mother-in-law" call. This man, at least, had experienced a unique situation. The last time he had forgotten to call and say he'd be coming home late from work, his mother-in-law had rushed to comfort her distraught daughter (who was certain her hapless husband was having an affair), then locked the hardworking man out of his own home. "It's all because my wife's first husband was a no-account jerk," Jim told me. "They seem to think I'm the same way, but I'm not."

I pushed a heavy sigh over the airwaves. "Jim, are you up for a story?"

"Uh—sure, Dr. Diana."

"Okay. Picture an old-timer sitting on his front porch in his rocker, watching new folks drive into town. A family comes by, and they stop to ask for directions. 'We're thinking about moving to the country,' the husband says, 'and we're wondering what this town is like.'

"The old-timer narrows his eyes a minute, then says, 'Well, tell me about your old neighborhood.'

"The wife rolls her eyes and says, 'Oh, things are terrible where we're living now. The neighborhood is going downhill, the people are a bunch of snobs, and the schools are just awful.'

"The old-timer shakes his head. 'Hate to tell you folks this, but things are pretty much the same here. If I were you, I'd just keep going.'

"So they did. A few minutes later another family pulls up for directions, and the husband comes out to ask about the town up ahead. The old-timer gives them the once-over and says, 'Suppose you tell me about the place you're living now?'

"The wife steps out and says, 'Oh, it's a perfectly lovely town; we hate to move. The schools are wonderful, the location is lovely, and the people are as nice as can be. We wouldn't move at all, except—'

"'That's okay,' the old timer interrupts. 'I don't need to hear anymore. You just mosey on into town, and I think you'll like what you see. You're going to feel right at home.'"

I hesitated a moment. "Jim, you still with me?"

"Yeah, Dr. Diana."

"Do you understand? What did my story say to you?"

"Umm . . . that I should move out of town?"

I glanced at Gary, who was rocking with laughter behind the window. "Not quite, Jim. The point of that story is that the town didn't change; the attitudes of the people made all the difference. People with a negative outlook tend to carry that perspective into everything they do. Not always, of course, but I'm amazed at how certain people manage to find the negative in everything. I have a feeling your mother-in-law may be one of those people."

Jim managed a choking laugh. "So I'm stuck with her?"

"Yes—and no. What your mother-in-law did was wrong. You have a right to enter your own home whenever you choose. But instead of fixating on your mother-in-law's overreaction, why don't you concentrate on pleasing your wife? Call her when you're going to be late. Bring her flowers, tell her there's no woman in the world that can match her smile. Make her feel loved and special, and she'll stop doubting you. Treat her with the same consideration you'd like to receive, and I guarantee your mother-in-law will run out of reasons to lock you out of the house. Her attitude will change, but it might take time."

Jim stuttered for a moment, then grew quiet. "I guess that'd work. But the woman's still a witch."

"She's a crazy-maker," I said, laughing. "Know what crazy-makers are? They're people who drive us nuts, but they also make us stronger. Learn to live with a crazy-maker, and you'll learn to tolerate the other trials in your life."

I looked up when I heard a tapping on the studio window. Gary was standing at his desk with a printout in his hand. He pointed to the paper, then drew his index finger across his throat in an abrupt gesture.

Glancing at the clock, I saw that we had five minutes until the newsbreak, but Chad could fill the time with commercials and one of our prerecorded bits if some emergency had come up.

"We'll be back with more of your calls after the news," I said, keeping my tone light. When Chad hit the first commercial, I slipped off the headphones. I was about to stand and go into the control room, but Gary burst through the studio doorway, the mysterious paper in his hand.

Leaning back in my chair, I gaped at him. "Have we declared war on somebody?"

He smiled a grim little grin as he handed me the ragged page. "The news of your divorce just hit the wire. I think you'd better read this, then we have to decide how we're going to handle the matter."

Keeping one hand over my fluttering stomach, I skimmed the wire report. Beneath a headline of "Pro-Family Radio Psychologist Knocks Blocks from Beneath Crumbling Marriage," I read that my divorce had become part of the public record. An astute journalist had obviously seen the court report this morning and called Steve at his office. "When asked the reason for the divorce," the reporter wrote, "Dr. Steve Sheldon would only say, 'Ask my wife.'"

I groaned. "Wouldn't you know they'd go after Steve?"

"He's easier to reach than you." Gary took the paper from me. "So, how do you want to handle this?"

I took a deep breath. "How broad is the coverage?"

"I think it's a safe bet that it's national by now. This came out on the wire half an hour ago, which means CNN will probably put it in their noon news loop. By tomorrow it'll be old news and you'll be playing defense."

I nodded, understanding his point. "So if I address it today—"

"Your audience will see you as being straightforward and honest. It's hard to paint something as a scandal if no one's trying to hide it."

Running my hand through my hair, I weighed my options and settled on a decision. For the last four weeks I'd been considering different ways of announcing my divorce. I knew the news would become public; I just hadn't expected it to hit in the middle of my show.

I picked up a pencil and reached for my notepad. "After the news break, I'll address it in the monologue. Find me some moving background music—something soothing without too many violins. Maybe the soundtrack of *Pearl Harbor.*"

Gary nodded and went out while I twirled the pencil between my fingers and stared at the blank page. How could I tell thousands of devoted listeners that one of the stoutest defenders of marriage in the modern world had felt it necessary to divorce a loving husband? It would have been easy to say Steve was abusive or controlling, but I could not sully his reputation to save my own skin. Besides, we'd be seeing blood in the water on this one no matter what I said.

I'd have to account for the divorce . . . and soon I'd have to explain the cloning. My lawyer had already filed my petition for the court order to obtain the tissue samples; we were only waiting for a judge to review the case and give us a ruling. If all went well, I could be pregnant within a matter of months.

So I owed my audience two revelations, and reaction to the second might well overshadow disappointment for the first. It'd be a coup for the network if I broke the cloning story on my show. Project One wanted to share my story with the world, well, why not share it with my audience first?

My gaze drifted toward the windows where Gary and Chad worked. Unfortunately, I hadn't told my staff about my plans for the baby. It hardly seemed fair to drop that bombshell on them without warning because a subject this huge would change the nature of the show for weeks to come. Cloning would become the hot topic of the *year,* and Gary would find himself fielding callers who used words like *traducianism* and *denucleated.* Some of our conservative listeners would find my plans so shocking they'd leave in droves, while we'd undoubtedly attract new listeners from the fringes where UFO and conspiracy buffs dwelled . . .

If I dropped both bombs today, I'd be facing major damage containment and an eventual audience readjustment. But why not press ahead? Our nation's recent history was replete with examples of people who'd been caught in far worse things than divorce and survived by moving ahead with their lives.

During the news break I jotted down a few thoughts, then sat silently as the intro music played. As the last refrain of the "Dr. Diana theme" faded away, I lifted my notepad and saw that my fingers were trembling.

"Welcome back, friends, to the *Dr. Sheldon Show.* This monologue will be a little different, but I need to take a few moments to share my heart with you. For five years now, I've been listening to your problems and offering honest, truthful answers, and now I'd like you to hear about a problem I've experienced. The media has painted me as some sort of sanctimonious holier-than-thou counselor, and that's not an accurate picture. I believe God ordained specific principles to create a healthy, functioning human society. I also believe certain bedrock philosophies, when followed, result in strong homes and happy families.

"Which is why it breaks my heart to sit with you and reveal that yesterday my twenty-two-year marriage ended in divorce. My ex-husband is a good man, a fine man, but we can no longer remain married. You've often heard me speak of the importance of maintaining a united front when raising children—well, my husband and I have turned in two different directions. I do not wish to reveal private details in a public forum, but you should know that we are both committed to loving our children to the best of our ability and we are fully aware of the stress divorce can bring. But unhappiness in the home can bring stress, too—as can a marriage in which two people can no longer agree on the basic requirements for a life together."

I paused, searching for words beyond those on my notepad. "I know some of you will have strong feelings about this—some may even think I have betrayed you by seeking a divorce when I have always stressed the importance of marriage. All I can do is remind you that I have never said you must remain married no matter what. Neither my husband nor I have been unfaithful in this marriage; no third parties were involved. We are aching, publicly and privately, so don't feel you must throw stones to make sure we're feeling an adequate amount of pain."

I glanced up at Gary, who had no idea of what was coming next. "Now I want to tell you something else—something I have never revealed in public. Modern science has given me a unique opportunity to experience a miracle."

Lowering the phone in his hand, Gary looked at me with a troubled and questioning expression.

"As most of you know"—I paused to clear a frog from my throat— "I lost my beloved five-year-old son a few months ago. Scott Daniel was the joy of my life. Now, through the miracle of technology, medical researchers have given me a chance to bear my son's identical twin. He won't be the same child, but a genetic duplicate. I will carry him in a normal pregnancy, I will love and cherish him just as I loved and cherished Scott Daniel before the accident claimed his life. And once again I will experience the inexpressible joy of motherhood."

I shivered, overcome again with the wonder of the future, then pointed at Chad, who rolled the soft version of the riff that signaled a return to the telephone queue. "Before I take your calls"—I dropped my voice to a whisper—"be forewarned. Today I will not discuss my divorce or my future plans. Tomorrow, perhaps. I know this news will ignite controversy, and I'm prepared to deal with the repercussions. But I must ask you to respect the privacy of my daughter and ex-husband. They are not public figures, and they have a right to privacy."

I glanced up at the screen, and saw that Cheryl from Waco wanted to ask if I had the recipe for the Cabbage Soup Diet. Ordinarily I'd have consigned her call to the bottom of the heap, but today such triviality seemed a blessing.

Thirty-seven

STEVE GLANCED TOWARD GERTA POPPOVITCH, WHO had just slammed the phone down in an unusual display of temper. "Sorry, Dr. Steve," she said, catching his eye. "But those reporters are about to drive me buggy."

"Ignore them." He picked up a patient chart on the counter, then flipped it open and tried to make his brain focus on his handwritten notes. His ability to concentrate seemed to have vanished along with his marriage, and he found himself taking twice as long with patients as usual. Melanie, bless her heart, covered for him whenever she could, but by four o'clock he usually had a waiting room filled with impatient parents who pointedly glanced at their watches and grumbled about homework to finish and dinners to prepare.

He was falling apart. Losing Scotty had been hard enough; losing his marriage in the face of intense publicity was a nightmare beyond anything he had ever encountered.

Yesterday Diana had gone public with the news of their divorce and her plans to clone their son, and last night a phalanx of reporters had been waiting outside Steve's building, cameras at the ready. He charged through them and their stinging questions, and in between each panting breath he heard himself muttering "No comment, no comment" as though he had developed an acute case of Tourette's syndrome.

Hurrying into the apartment, he leaned against the door, a new kind of fear quaking his body from toe to hair. His phone was ringing; the answering machine blinked with thirty-seven messages from representatives of the media and one call from Diana, who had phoned from the station to tell him she had broken the news.

How considerate.

The situation hadn't improved with the dawn of a new day. Another corps of reporters had been waiting outside his apartment when he left for work, and through the tiny window in his office he could see another group waiting on the sidewalk outside his office building. Gerta said at least half a dozen parents had canceled their children's appointments, and the children he did see were more nervous than usual, spooked, no doubt, by the reporters and the harried look in their dentist's eye.

Through all the confusion, Melanie had been a godsend. She double-checked his charts before giving them to Gerta to file; she flagged suspicious teeth on several x-rays before he entered the exam room. And when he paused in the break room and debated running the media gauntlet to fetch a cheeseburger for lunch, she had offered to go pick something up and run it right back. He gratefully accepted her offer, and within minutes she had gone out and returned with two taco salads.

"Don't worry, Steve," she said as they ate together in the tiny break room. "This won't last forever. They'll probably keep after Diana, but as long as you refuse to have anything to do with her, you'll fade out of the picture." She lightly laid her hand on his wrist. "And if and when you need to talk to someone, know this—I'll be there for you. Anytime."

He did not answer, but winced slightly, as if her touch had nipped his flesh. A month ago the eager look in her eye would have set off his inner alarms and sent him into a hasty retreat, but he was no longer a married man.

He was single. And, according to his church, no longer an example of virtue.

Not knowing what else to do, he took a bite of his salad and gave her an appreciative smile.

Thirty-eight

FOUR DAYS AFTER BREAKING THE BIG NEWS TO MY radio audience, I sat alone in my kitchen, absorbing the sounds and silences of a nearly empty house. Terwilliger slept under the table and atop my foot, his legs twitching as he whimpered in sleep, probably chasing a cat in his dreams.

Poor little guy. Until the accident he had belonged to Scott Daniel. In the past four months he had drifted from person to person, trying to find another constant companion. "Looks like you're stuck with me," I murmured, glancing down at his chunky little body. "Everyone else is leaving."

I sipped my coffee and counted the chimes from the grandfather clock in the foyer. One. Two. Three. Three o'clock, and no husband coming home later either for dinner or with dinner. I didn't expect to see Brittany until at least midnight, if then. Since graduation, she had taken to spending most of her time with her friends, and I wanted to give her the freedom a high school graduate deserved. Steve was worried because she didn't want to be with either of her parents, but I assured him her avoidance of us almost certainly had less to do with the divorce than with the fact that she'd be leaving for college in less than two months. She wanted to be with her friends, period.

Over the last few days, the oddest sense of disconnectedness had crept over me. I was the same person I had always been, with the same coworkers, friends, and job, yet there were moments when I felt like that man in the *Outer Limits* episode who wakes up to find that he's somehow managed to sleep through the world's nuclear destruction. Whether walking through the house or driving in the car, I kept wondering who would care if I decided to stop off at the grocery instead of going home. If I obeyed a wild notion and drove to Fort Lauderdale one afternoon, would anyone notice that I hadn't been home at dinnertime? If I collapsed in the bathroom, how many hours would I lie on the tile floor before someone realized I needed help?

The term *single* fit me about as well as a size 3-X jacket; the word felt uncomfortably loose and revealing.

"You'll get used to it," I told myself, lifting my mug. "You can get used to almost anything."

I took another sip of my coffee, an afternoon pick-me-up I sorely needed. This morning's show had been a near-disaster. Three-quarters of the callers seemed more intent on blasting my decisions than listening to reason, and when I spoke logically or recited facts, they resorted to yelling, as if an argument could be won by sheer volume.

The other callers, the 25 percent who supported me in the divorce, the cloning, or both, were more enthralled than interesting. I was so brave, so courageous, such a model for others, yada, yada, yada. While it was nice to hear from people who didn't think I'd evolved into the wicked witch of the west, those callers tended to put me—and my other listeners—to sleep.

The most comforting words had come from Charity, who had not failed to call with her quote of the day. "A ship in the harbor is safe," she had said, "but that is not what ships are for. Maybe you should launch out into the unknown, Dr. Diana."

Taking her words to heart, I now sat with my trusty legal pad and struggled to come up with ideas for a slightly adjusted format—something to take my focus away from traditional conservative family issues but not deny the foundational principles I still espoused.

I scratched on the notepad, then held it up to consider what I'd written: *Technology with a Twist.*

I grimaced. That tag sounded more like some kind of cocktail than a radio program. One of my colleagues at the station used "the fusion of entertainment and enlightenment" as his promo line, so maybe I could go with something like "modern thought meets universal truth."

Then again, why not describe the show as the WWF of modern ideas? The World Wrestling Federation wouldn't mind . . . but their lawyers might.

Sighing, I dropped the notepad, then rested my elbow on the table and propped my chin in my hand.

I hated to admit it, but Steve's absence had been a shock to my system. He'd taken an apartment in Clearwater Beach, only a fifteen-minute drive away, but the thought of him living in another zip code unnerved me. I'd known I could not walk away from twenty-two years of marriage without feeling some major side effects, but the little things were affecting me most.

Like no snoring to break the deep silence of the night.

No one to take out the garbage without being asked.

No one to keep me company when I waited up for Brittany to come home.

I nearly jumped out of my skin when the phone shattered the stillness. "For the love of Pete," I grumbled, pulling my foot free of Terwilliger's warm little body. "Get a grip, Diana."

The phone had rung almost constantly during the last week, but old news was not news, so I hadn't fielded any press calls today. As I predicted, the news of my plan to bear a clone overshadowed the announcement of my divorce. I stalled most of the reporters with a comment about how it was premature to discuss the future, and every night I thanked God for the security guard outside my gated community. Though the press hounded Steve and me persistently for a couple of days, no one had bothered Brittany. I doubted if anyone had been able to find her.

I scanned the caller ID, not willing for my solitude to be interrupted by a telephone solicitor or a reporter, then hastily picked up the receiver. Someone was calling from the station.

"Diana?"

Gary's breathless voice alarmed me. "Is something wrong?"

"Did you hear?"

"Did I hear what?" Automatically, my gaze shifted toward the television in the family room. If there'd been some sort of disaster, Gary would want me to know as soon as possible so we could discuss how to handle it on tomorrow's program.

"The network dumped us. The word came down a few minutes ago—this morning was the last show we'll do from WFLZ."

Unable to speak, I stood as if fastened to the floor.

"Diana? You there?"

I gulped, forcing down the sudden lurch of my stomach. For a moment the color ran out of my kitchen and the hum of the phone faded into oblivion.

"That's—that's impossible," I managed to stammer. "They wouldn't dare dump us. We make them too much money. Even with the controversy—"

"They dared and they did. I spoke to Conrad Wexler myself, who said they hired you to speak for family values and parenthood, not science freaks and cultists."

"*Cultists?* Who's he been talking to?"

"What's this about, Diana?" A note of panic vibrated in Gary's voice. "You didn't say anything to me about cults. And you didn't warn me that we were stepping into a weird area. One minute I'm thinking you're brave for coming clean about your divorce, and the next minute you're telling the world you're taking us into the honest-to-goodness Twilight Zone."

I pressed a hand to my face. "Hush, Gary. I need to think."

"Why didn't you do that sooner?"

"I did. But I didn't foresee this." I turned and leaned against the kitchen counter, my thoughts racing. Score one for Conrad Wexler—he had managed to surprise me. Landed a knockout blow when I wasn't looking. But though my stomach felt empty and my lungs breathless, I wouldn't be down for the full ten-count. No way.

"Let's see—did you call the station's lawyer to ask for clarification? Maybe there's a clause or something to prevent this. They can't dump us for no reason."

"They have a reason. You can't change the format of your show without approval."

"We didn't change the format."

"Not officially, but you changed the content, and they say that's the same thing. And Conrad Wexler didn't sound exactly reluctant to let us go. I think he was personally offended by what he's heard about your plans."

"Wexler? I thought he was a progressive liberal."

"He's a conservative Catholic. Before last week he was one of your biggest fans."

"But he employs all those raunchy talk-show hosts—"

"He's a businessman; he goes with what makes money, as long as it doesn't cross a certain line. I didn't know where his line is, but obviously you've crossed it. So we're out. Out of the station, out of the network. We get six weeks of severance pay, and that's it."

I pressed my hand to my forehead and rubbed the tender spot at my temple. My eyelashes began to twitch, a sure sign of stress. I used to drop everything and call Steve when things like this happened . . . now I could only call on God. But he was enough.

Father, help. Please. You brought me to this place, so please see me through.

Drawing in a deep breath, I forced myself to calm down. "Don't worry, Gary, and don't pack your suitcase. I'll have my agent get on top of this."

"You do that. But he'd better be prepared for both barrels. Wexler didn't mince any words with me."

I hung up, then moved to the kitchen sink and bent to brace my arms against the counter. Gary had to be exaggerating, but he wouldn't joke about us being fired from the network. Being dropped by one station was troubling enough, but if we lost the network, we didn't lose one station, we lost more than sixty that wouldn't turn around and pick us back up—not if they wanted to stay in good graces with the higher-ups, that is. Worst of all, we lost our facility, our access to equipment, our support system.

I was no longer a successful radio star; I was an unemployed has-been.

I had to call my agent. But in a minute, when I wasn't feeling so nauseous.

I turned on the water, ran my fingers through the cool stream, then rubbed the pulse points at my throat. What would I do without my job? I'd been depending on that income to make a living; I'd been counting on the network for health insurance and maternity leave benefits.

Unbidden, Steve's name floated to the front of my brain, but I shoved it aside. He was a good man, the sort who would help if I asked, but I couldn't ask him for anything now.

Not even for the baby's sake. From the moment I had realized Steve could not approve of the cloning, I knew I would not ask him to support the baby in any way. If he would not acknowledge our son, I didn't want him to have any claim to the boy. The baby would be mine alone, an amalgamation of my body and Scott Daniel's DNA.

But without a job, how could I support myself and come up with the money I needed for the procedure? If I dipped into Brittany's account, I'd bankrupt her future . . . and her trust.

I lowered my head, feeling like one of those weepy people who called my show to complain about suffering the consequences of their own foolish actions.

Overcome by despair, I leaned over the sink and wept.

Thirty-nine

RECALLING CHARITY'S QUIP ABOUT SHIPS LEAVING the safety of the harbor, I licked my wounds, called my agent (who was as distressed as I about the bad news, and no help at all), then set about reordering my future. I spent the July 4 holiday at my desk, outlining a plan that would take me out of radio and into the adventure of my life.

Because the Prime Radio Network was the biggest in the business, I knew my career in radio was over. No other network could match my salary or Prime's market base, so unless I wanted to do a Sunday morning show for some little independent station in Kalamazoo, I would have to surrender the idea of a radio talk show.

But TV loomed as a distinct possibility. At my age I wasn't exactly Miss America material, but neither would I send viewers screeching in horror. I could come up with a format and tape a couple of shows at the local public broadcasting studio. I'd have to rent the facility and pay the crew, but I would consider it an investment in my future. While the tape made its rounds at the networks, I would concentrate on getting Brittany off to college, selling the house, and winning permission to use Scott Daniel's tissue samples.

My lawyer had petitioned the court the day after the issue of our divorce decree, and he warned me that the process of judicial review could take four or five weeks, maybe longer. I saw the delay as God's perfect timing. By the time I had legal access to Scott Daniel's tissue samples, everything else should have fallen into place. Britt would be on her way to school, the house would be listed with a real-estate agent, and I could leave the area, maybe head out to New York, Los Angeles, or one of the other major markets.

Brittany wouldn't care where I went. She would have said farewell to her high school friends and she'd be excited about meeting new people at college. Steve would probably be thrilled not to have me living across town, and maybe he'd find it easier to start a new life if I weren't in the picture.

Then again . . . perhaps he'd come out to visit after the baby was born. And maybe, if love and nostalgia softened his heart, Steve would see that my idea was actually a blessing and he'd change his mind about accepting our son. If he did, I'd willingly come back to Tampa. We could remarry and start over in a cozy condo on the beach, one with a guest room where Brittany could stay when she came home on breaks from school. I could get a local studio to host my TV show. If Oprah could make Chicago her signature town, I could do the same for Tampa.

My celebrity as the mother of the first American clone would help my career if I used it carefully. Instead of focusing so much on traditional values, my TV show could explore the world of contemporary medicine and shifting ethical boundaries. I'd still maintain my pro-life positions, condemning fetal experimentation and partial-birth abortion, but I wouldn't be such a hard-liner that I couldn't be open and receptive to new ideas. Good things could come out of modern medicine and reproductive technology. I would stress that years ago people were repulsed by the thought of test-tube babies, but now such procedures were common. Perhaps my first show could be about heart transplants, which had once seemed a perversion of the natural order.

As the mother of the first American clone, I'd be the perfect person to embody all that was good about medical technology. Together my son and I would help bring a fearful nation into a new century of possibilities.

The Project One folks would be thrilled if I moved to TV, and my son would be a living advertisement for their work. Perhaps they'd even sign a contract promising to sponsor my show—a promise that would be appreciated by the networks. My agent would *love* to sell a program with a tested format, a well-known host, and a wealthy sponsor ready and waiting.

As the day wore on, I felt my flagging self-confidence begin to rise. At dinnertime I interrupted Gary at his family picnic to tell him we were moving the show to television. He sounded a bit distracted as I explained my plans, but he thanked me for calling and wished me a happy Fourth of July.

Eleven P.M. found me doodling dollar signs and possible salary figures on my notepad when the phone rang. I glanced at the caller ID. The number was Charisse's, so Britt was probably calling to tell me she'd be stopping by to pick up twenty bucks for the late movie . . .

Sighing, I reached for the receiver.

"Yeah?"

"Hey." Charisse giggled, and at the sound of her laughter I knew trouble was afoot. Brittany was supposed to be with Charisse, but the girl's casual greeting told me otherwise.

"So"—the smack of her gum cracked over the line—"did your mom see the hickey on your neck?"

Like a witness to an unexpected accident, I sat absolutely still. During the ensuing silence, Charisse stopped cracking her gum.

I would have given anything to see the look on her face.

"No." I switched into Motivated Mother Mode. "I didn't see anything on my daughter's neck. Should I look again, Charisse?"

Dead silence filled the other end of the line, then I heard a click. Charisse obviously had few defense mechanisms, but at least she hadn't tried to lie.

I lowered the phone back into the stand, then dropped my head onto my hand and groaned. I didn't even know Brittany had a boyfriend—or did she? Maybe the girls had gone to a party where they played those adolescent kissing games. That didn't sound like something Britt would do, but who knew what kids these days were up to? Or maybe Charisse was kidding, and the mark on Britt's neck was only a bruise. Or maybe there was no mark on my daughter's neck at all.

Yet one thing was clear—Charisse thought she had been speaking to Brittany. Despite the lack of a biological link between us, Britt had picked up my vocal inflections. She was always telling me it drove her crazy when people said she sounded like Dr. Diana.

I reached for the phone to call Steve, then dropped my hand as an acute sense of loss sideswiped my heart. Old habits were hard to break. I was the custodial parent; I would have to deal with this. Rationally.

My daughter apparently had a love bite on her neck, and Charisse knew all about it while I knew nothing. And—a new realization dawned—my daughter, who was supposed to be spending the night with her best friend, was in fact AWOL and I had no idea where she could be.

I felt an instinctive stab of fear, then took a deep breath and pushed the pain away. This was the twenty-first century, and Brittany had been carrying a cell phone since her fifteenth birthday. Apart from those toddler leashes parents needed in airports and amusement parks, the cell phone was the best parental tool ever invented.

I reached for the phone again, punched in Britt's number, and waited.

The phone rang.

And rang.

And rang.

Still holding the phone to my ear, I stood and pushed the lace curtain away from the window. Her red pickup was nowhere in sight.

I closed my eyes, trying to recall the events of the day. Britt had slept late, not coming downstairs until nearly lunchtime. I'd been working hard on my proposal when she went out the door, and I had barely managed to flap my fingers in an absent-minded wave when she said good-bye.

Biting my lip, I disconnected the call, then flipped through my address book for Steve's new number. Maybe she had gone to the beach to see her father. If they had been watching a movie or doing something, she might have decided to stay at his place instead of going on to Charisse's house . . .

Someone picked up after the third ring. I nearly melted in relief when a female greeted me, then I tensed.

This was *not* my daughter's voice.

"May I speak to Steve, please? It's his—it's Diana."

"Just a minute."

Was it my imagination, or did that voice cool when she realized who I was?

I cleared my throat when Steve came on the line. "Sorry to interrupt—"

"You're not interrupting. It's just a little Fourth of July party for the office staff."

"At 11:00 P.M.?" I squinched my eyes together, unable to believe that a serpent of jealousy wriggled in my breast. What business was it of mine?

"Melanie's son is watching a video." Steve spoke in a soft, almost weary voice. "She wouldn't let him borrow it, so he's staying till the end."

"Oh." I felt a flush burn my cheeks. How could I sit here and act like some sort of green-eyed monster when our daughter was missing? "Listen, Steve—is Britt with you?"

"I haven't seen her." The softness fled his voice, replaced by sharp concern. "Where is she supposed to be?"

"She's supposed to be at Charisse's house, but Charisse just called here to inquire about a hickey on Britt's neck."

"What?"

"You heard me." I glanced at the clock. Nearly 11:15, and still no sign of my daughter. Her curfew was midnight on weekends, so she wasn't officially overdue yet, but it wasn't like her to go out without telling us where she was going . . . or was it? She'd been spending the night with Charisse for years, and we had never had any cause to doubt her word.

"Steve, I'm worried."

"Don't panic. Did you call her?"

"Of course. She didn't answer her phone."

"Maybe the battery's dead."

"Not likely. She keeps it charged—heaven forbid that she miss a call from one of her friends."

"Is it possible she went to some other girl's house?"

"Anything's possible—but who else?" I raked my hand through my hair, frantically trying to come up with other names. Brittany had been a member of a large peer group in middle school, but as she grew older, the girls drifted apart. She and Charisse had been best friends for the last three years.

I couldn't come up with a single name. "I don't know. I can't think of anyone."

"Good grief, Diana, she and Charisse have to hang out with some-body. You know kids of that age, they travel in packs."

"I know, but I don't know any of her other friends. They don't go to our church, and I don't think they even go to her school."

My thoughts whirled away, then zoomed back to focus on one sharp and disturbing realization. As a teenager, I was always bringing my friends home because Mom and Dad kept a supply of frozen piz-zas in the freezer and cases of soda in the pantry. Britt had *never* wanted to bring her friends to our house, and deep inside, I knew why. She didn't want everyone to know she lived with Dr. Diana the radio shrink and Dr. Steve, the kiddie dentist with the big treasure chest.

I brought my hand to my forehead. "Think, Steve. What do we do?"

"What time did you tell her to be home?"

I swallowed hard, trying not to reveal my growing irritation with his questions. "I didn't tell her anything; she's supposed to be at Charisse's."

"Does Charisse know where she is?"

"Obviously not, since she called here expecting to find Britt."

That fact alarmed me more than anything. Even Charisse didn't know where Brittany was, and I was sure those two knew almost everything about each other. So if Britt had a secret she hadn't shared with her best friend—

"Steve, I'm scared."

"Wait till midnight, then call the police. She has to be somewhere."

"But where?"

Disturbing images blurred in my brain—Brittany strapped in her seat belt while the pickup sank in a culvert, lying battered and unconscious in a hospital bed, or drugged and being raped at some out-of-control Fourth of July party—

"Lord, help us," I whispered. "Bring our baby home."

Forty

HEARING THE RISING PANIC IN DIANA'S VOICE, STEVE took a deep breath to calm the racing of his own heart. "Why don't you call her?"

"She didn't answer the first time!"

Steve gripped the phone, resisting the alarm that had sent a surge of adrenaline through his bloodstream. Diana needed calm counsel, not words to fuel her fear. "Try again. Maybe she was in the bathroom or something."

"All right. I'll call her. And so help me, when I reach her I'm going to let her have it for scaring us like this—"

The phone clicked. Steve pressed the talk button and punched in his daughter's number, determined to reach Britty before Diana did. His wife—*ex*-wife—was angry, and she didn't always think straight when in the grip of fury.

Fortunately, he had Britty's cell phone programmed into memory, and he heard it begin to ring a moment later. "Come on, Lord, let her pick up," he whispered, breathing a prayer into the phone. "Just let her be okay."

From the backseat of Zack Johnson's car, Brittany heard the phone ringing inside her purse.

Again.

"Ignore it," Zack whispered, his breath coming in short gasps.

"I ignored it last time. What if something's wrong?" Grateful for an opportunity to pull away, she sat up and reached for her purse, digging the phone out after only four rings.

"Hello?"

"Britty, where are you?"

Her father's voice slammed into her conscience with the force of a speeding locomotive. A shiver ran up her spine, a shudder that had nothing to do with the rush of cool air on her bare skin.

"Daddy?"

"You're supposed to be at Charisse's—but obviously, you're not. So would you mind telling me where you are? Your mother's frantic."

Brittany glanced behind her, where Zack leaned against the seat, one hand reaching out possessively to stroke her arm. Instinctively, she pulled away.

"I'm with a friend."

"Well, you'd better get home. Your mother's not happy that you lied about where you were going."

Brittany pressed her lips together as a wellspring of shame rose within her. She wanted to confess, to cry out that she was sorry for something far worse than her father would ever imagine her doing, but she couldn't say those things in front of Zack. And she still needed him to take her back to the beach where they had left her pickup.

"I'm going," she whispered. "I'll be home soon."

She rested her forehead on the back of the front seat. Why did everyone make such a big deal about sex? There had been no wonder here tonight, no oneness, no passion. Only discomfort, awkwardness, sweat . . .

And fear.

"I'm going home, Dad," she repeated, half hoping he'd hear her unspoken need. "I'm sorry."

"Okay." His voice was calmer now, the worry replaced by relief. "I'll call you tomorrow, okay? Even though you're not living with me, I still care about what's happening to you."

She wanted to cry, to hang her head and weep until she shuddered with hiccuping sobs, but she couldn't do that here.

"Okay, Dad."

She hung up the phone, then lowered her head and cast Zack a sidelong look. "I'm busted. You need to take me back."

He gave her a smile, and she could see he hadn't noticed the change in the quality of her attention. "Aw, baby, the night is young. Let the old coots wait awhile."

"You don't know my parents—and you especially don't know my mom. If I'm not home in half an hour, she'll call the cops. And she won't just go to bed—she'll sit up waiting for me. The longer she waits, the madder she'll get."

Zack heaved a heavy sigh, then pulled his T-shirt from the back of the front seat. "Okay, babe, good enough."

She stared at him. "Zack, do you love me?"

He laughed. "'Course, Britt."

Spurred by an innate modesty, she turned to look out the window as she fumbled with the buttons of her blouse. He loved her. So maybe the pain was worth it.

Her phone rang again, and without looking Brittany knew who was calling. She debated whether or not to answer, then decided she'd better.

"Hi, Mom," she said, just after hitting the talk key. "I'm on my way home."

"Where are you?" Her mother's voice was an angry buzz.

"In Madeira Beach."

"Where in Madeira Beach?"

"Um . . . in the park. I'm with a friend, Mom, and we're on our way home."

"Have you lost your mind, girl? You're supposed to be at Charisse's—"

"I'll be home in a few minutes."

She clicked the phone off and dropped it into her bag, wishing she could cut herself off from the last few months of her life as easily.

Forty-one

AFTER HANGING UP THE PHONE, I COULDN'T RELAX; I couldn't even sit still. The public park in Madeira Beach was a good half-hour away, and if Brittany was with someone, she might have to drop the friend off someplace . . .

Restless, I went up to my daughter's room, turned on the light, and looked at the usual assortment of teenage girl clutter. Nothing in the scattered clothes or magazines explained why my daughter had become a liar.

What had happened to my Britt? When had she changed, and how had I missed the signs?

I looked over the top of her dresser, then opened her underwear drawer and lifted out stacks of panties, bras, and socks. Nothing to explain how the good Christian girl I had raised could tell me bold-faced lies.

Had she *planned* to stay out all night? She regularly spent the night with Charisse; sometimes Friday and Saturday nights on a weekend. How many times had she actually been out running around the county, sleeping who knows where . . . and with whom?

My heart shook off the disloyal thought. Brittany wasn't a bad girl; she had never given us anything more than ordinary teenage trouble, and I had always considered myself an expert in differentiating between normal growing pains and outright rebellion. Our adult friends thought of Britt as sweet, polite, and relatively dependable. Sure, she rolled her eyes a lot and avoided us like the plague, but I attributed those things to adolescence, not character flaws. Besides, she had accepted Christ at an early age and she went to church with us every Sunday morning.

So how could she be the kind of girl who would lie and sneak around behind our backs?

I opened another drawer; nothing but shorts.

Another; bathing suits and tops.

I moved to the nightstand, where a stack of slick magazines toppled onto the floor as I opened the door. I scanned them for signs of incriminating evidence, but they were just magazines—not the sort I would have chosen, but how could I stop her from spending her allowance on junk when I wasn't around?

Sinking to the floor, I made a face at one particular cover—the magazine was called *Skank,* and one headline read, "Does he love your bod or your brain? Five ways to tell." The headline beneath it proclaimed, "Sticky fingers? Ten ways not to get caught."

Caught—what, *shoplifting?*

I pitched the magazine into the trash, then bent to look under the bed. Amid the childhood detritus of trolls and beheaded Barbies, I found a collection of CD cases. After pulling them out, I skimmed the names of the groups and realized I'd never heard of any of them. But I was not a fan of punk rock or whatever the kids were listening to these days, and Britt often went to concerts for local bands who burned CDs as easily as we used to make cassette tapes.

On a whim, I flipped open one of the plastic covers and read the words of a song. I don't know how they sounded set to music, but the lyrics were bad poetry and contained profanity that would have made my mother faint and attitudes that made my heart shrivel. Rebellion, despair, talk of suicide and hopelessness . . .

I dropped the CD cover as anguish seared my soul. Did my daughter *enjoy* listening to this junk? If she did, she had been feeding her heart and mind with soulless drivel while I sat before a microphone and admonished the parents of America to be vigilant about what went into their children's ears.

"Garbage in, garbage out," I whispered, gazing at the trash my daughter had chosen for entertainment. I knew each younger generation tried to be a little more outrageous than the previous one, and my generation had been pretty wild. I'd come of age in the seventies, when pot was cool and rebellion expected. But I had been a Christian, and my religious convictions had kept me from making really serious mistakes.

"What happened to my daughter, God?" The words came out as a wail. "Why haven't the things that worked for me worked for my daughter? Why haven't the things we've drummed into her since childhood kept her on the right path? Is she ignoring everything her father and I ever told her about truth and goodness and purity, or did we fail her somehow? Did we teach her about truth often enough and loud enough, or did we only assume she would pick up what she needed to know from Sunday school?"

I sank to the edge of the bed as my heart bulged with a question I didn't have the courage to speak aloud: *Were we to blame for this?*

The anxieties that had been lapping at my brain crested and crashed in a terrifying, painful roar—what had happened to my daughter's soul? I would have sworn her commitment to Christ was genuine. As a young girl she regularly read her Bible, she went on missions trips with the youth group, she seemed to honestly enjoy her relationship with God. But if she were a sincere believer, how could she live like this? Why wasn't the Spirit of God knocking her flat with conviction?

I lowered my head as tears welled in my eyes. Perhaps wishful thinking had skewed my perception of Brittany. Maybe it was all a lie—her salvation experience, her participation at church, her testimony. Peer pressure was a powerful force even in the early teen years; maybe she had only said and done the things she thought we expected her to say and do. Now that she had achieved a degree of independence, maybe she was showing her true colors away from our home and our supervision. Psychologists had a saying: the person your child is away from home is the person they'll become at maturity. I'd always taken comfort in that truism because no matter how often Britt rolled her eyes at us at home, in public she had always been well-mannered and polite.

What if I'd never seen the real Brittany?

Feeling as though some large, lumpy object pressed against my breastbone, I swallowed hard and braced myself to face the truth. I was losing my daughter. I *would* lose her, unless somehow I could identify the problem and correct it.

That's when I saw the leather corner of a blue book jutting out from beneath the mattress. I pulled it out and ran my hand over the leather cover.

A diary. An expensive one that did not lock, but closed by means of a leather strip that looped around the spine and fastened at the edge.

Should I read it? Ordinarily I would not pry into Britt's thoughts, but this was no ordinary night. I was fighting for my daughter's life, for her *soul,* and at the moment I was woefully unprepared for battle.

With trembling fingers, I untied the leather strap. Propping my back against the side of the bed, I flipped open the pages and began to read. The back of the book was blank, but at one point Britt had been faithful to write every night.

Thursday, September 5:

I swear, Mom never comes in my room anymore except to gripe about how messy it is! She's been a real witch lately, and I think she's all freaked out about the Scottster at kindergarten—as if that were the end of the world. Now it's like the only time she thinks of me is just to yell about something—my room, or the fact that I came in ten minutes late. Ten minutes! Like the fate of the universe hangs on ten minutes.

I wish she'd just go to bed and leave me alone—I mean, none of my other friends have a warden for a mother, just me. And Dad's just as bad. He's so dumb sometimes. Everybody loves him, but not everybody has to live with him.

Sometimes I'm so angry I just want to leave. Sometimes I think about getting married and not inviting them to the wedding—that'd serve them right. Sometimes I think about my mother being in a car wreck and in the hospital, and find myself wishing it would happen. At least she'd be out of my hair a few days. I think I could watch her drive into a lake and just sit there, not even getting up to call 911.

My Dumbo Dad could be in the car with her, I don't care. I'm sick and tired of living here. I'm sick of their rules and everybody telling me what I'm supposed to be. Everybody thinks I'm some kind of angel girl because of who my parents are, and that's not fair. It's like I've never had a chance to be who I am—whoever that is. I'm told what to think and what to wear and what kind of music to listen to. People think I'm one way, but they don't know the real me at all. I guess only Charisse does, but she's always in such a fog. She doesn't have a clue about anything really important.

Most of the time I hate them. I hate Scott. I hate everybody at church and at school. I hate my entire messed-up life.

Britt hated *Scott?* Trying to comprehend what I was reading, I checked the date again, then realized she'd written this well before the accident. I'd been telling myself this was mere backlash to the emotional trauma of losing Scott, a reaction to grief and loss, but Brittany had been feeling this anger for nearly a year.

I sat perfectly still and felt my heart break. It was a sharp, searing pain, probably much like the warning pang of a heart attack—the sort that makes old men clutch their chests and fall to the ground in agony.

How could she? Sadness pooled in my wounded heart, a gray despondency unlike anything I'd ever felt before. How could my beloved daughter have felt such rage toward us? We had never done anything but try our best to love and protect her.

I flipped to the back of the diary, then ruffled the pages until I found a more recent entry.

Saturday, June 14

Z has been asking me to sleep with him. I haven't yet—probably because I'm a little afraid of the whole idea, but I might change my mind. I've been so crazy lately, and Z seems to be the only person in my world who actually has his act together. He got a summer job at the record shop in the mall, and C and I like hanging out there. Sometimes Z and I slip into the stock room and make out for a while. It feels a little scary and weird, but maybe that's what love is.

I used to think I would never have sex before marriage because my parents would kill me if they found out, but I don't think that's so major anymore. I mean, what's the big deal? It's not like they're going to find out, with Dumbo Dad living in Clearwater and the witch with her nose stuck to the computer screen. The best thing about graduating is that they don't bug me as much as they used to about coming in on time . . . or maybe the witch just doesn't care anymore.

I do know this—all that stuff about marriage being holy and pure and for life is a crock. I always thought my parents loved each other, but you should hear them now. I don't know what's going on in their heads, but I know it's not good. It sure isn't holy and pure.

All I know is that Z says he loves me and I believe him. And if he asks, you know, the question again, I'll probably say yes.

Why not?

I froze as the front door slammed. My head felt numb and my heart still throbbed from the knowledge I'd just gleaned, but the sound of the door roused me to action. I stood, about to shove the diary back under the bed, then stopped.

No. There should be no more secrets between us.

Wrapping my courage around the strands of my raveled, bleeding heart, I tucked the diary under my arm and went to greet the daughter I no longer knew.

Forty-two

THE SHADOW MOVING ACROSS THE FOYER'S TILED FLOOR was too large for Brittany, and for a moment my breath caught in my throat. Then the unidentified visitor moved into the circle of lamp light.

Steve.

I had never been so relieved to see another adult in my life. "Steve," I called, clinging to the banister as I crept down the stairs. With its heavy secrets, the diary beneath my arm felt like a fifty-pound weight.

I paused at the bottom of the steps, not certain how to begin. If ever a situation called for a united front, this one did.

Stepping closer, he looked up at me. "Forgive me for letting myself in. Old habits, you know." His shoulders rose in a faint, helpless shrug. "I decided to come help you. Not that you need help, but . . . I thought I should be here."

The wave of indignation I'd felt earlier came flooding back. "What about your party?"

"Everybody went home when I told them I had a family emergency."

I closed my eyes to trap a sudden rush of tears. *Thank you, God, that I still have an ally in Steve.*

"I'm glad you're here." I stepped off the stairs and showed him the diary. His questioning gaze traveled from the book to my eyes, so I hurried to explain. "I found this in her room. I don't usually snoop, you know, but I had to see if I could find something to explain why she would lie to us." I took a deep, unsteady breath. "I discovered I don't know our daughter at all."

He slipped his hands into his pockets, then inclined his head toward the living room. "Want to sit and talk?"

"I'd like that. She's not home yet, but I expect her any time now."

We moved into the living room, where Steve sat on the couch while I sank into the wing chair. I turned on the lamp, then opened to the page I'd been reading when he pulled up.

"She hates us," I said simply. "She thinks of me as a witch, and you're Dumbo Dad—and those, I think, are her more affectionate terms for us. But what frightens me is the anger she expresses here. I can't believe any child raised in a loving home can feel this way. I certainly never hated my parents like this."

"You're not Brittany." He spoke softly, though his eyes glowed with the same pain I felt. "I don't think we can judge her through the lens of our experience."

I propped my elbow on the arm of the chair and pushed at the hair on my forehead. "I don't know what to do. We should send her to a counselor, I suppose."

His sharp laughter caught me off guard. "Do you honestly think Brittany would agree to see a counselor? For heaven's sake, Diana, she's lived with a counselor for eighteen years! Counseling is the last thing she wants!"

"But she needs it! I've only read a few pages of this, and I'm scared to death. The girl who wrote this is filled with hate, and anger, and fear. She's also thinking about sleeping with some guy. I'm frightened for her."

He brought his hand to his stubbled jaw, then gave me a brief, distracted glance and tried to smile. "What would you tell a caller who called your show with this problem?"

I blinked at him. "What would I—I can't answer that. It's different when it's your own child."

"It shouldn't be. You're the professional counselor, the family expert. You've been telling people what to do for years."

Whether or not he intended it, the words stung. I sat back, a frown puckering my mouth as I realized how right he was. I was a phony. My show was a sham. The so-called advice I'd been dispensing over the airwaves held about as much value as empty air.

Disappointment struck like a blow to my stomach. I lowered my eyes, looked at my empty palms, then shook my head. "I don't know. If she doesn't repent and turn around, I might say the parents have to kick her out. After all, if they allow her to continue to lie to them, aren't they enabling her to continue doing wrong?"

I hauled my gaze from my helpless hands and returned my attention to the man on the sofa. "It's not like this is the first time Brittany has lied. Remember the timer and the lamp? Only the Lord knows how many nights she fooled us with that setup. Now I'm wondering how many nights she's been out running around when we thought she was with Charisse. Sometimes tough love is the only option. Sometimes you have to be tough if you want to preserve your own sanity . . ."

I let my words trail off, not willing to verbalize all the pictures that had crystallized in my mind over the past half-hour. Though I had never imagined my daughter in such scenarios before, I now pictured her sporting hookerwear and sipping from a bottle of Scotch in a den of drug dealers. What if she had contracted a venereal disease? What if she had had an abortion? Would I even know about it?

Looking at the man who had once been my best friend, I longed for the protectiveness of his arms, then shoved the longing away. "If you were the professional counselor, what would you advise?"

He brought up his hand to cover his mouth, closed his eyes for a moment, then let his arm fall to his side. "I don't have a clue, but I know who does. What other parents do and say doesn't matter in this situation. What my folks did with me or what yours did with you doesn't count for anything. We've just come through a terrible ordeal, and this situation is unique."

"Other families have gone through terrible ordeals—"

"Their experiences don't have anything to do with us. There's only one person I trust to prescribe behavior for us now, and that's who I'm going to ask for advice."

I gave him a look of sheer disbelief. Steve had never read a psychology book in his life, as far as I knew, unless he'd taken to reading them in the five weeks since he'd moved out.

"And that expert would be?"

"The heavenly Father."

Silence stretched between us. I lowered my gaze as a fresh wave of guilt washed through my soul, followed by a tide of indignation. I thought about God all the time. I had been praying for Brittany in the last hour. What else was I supposed to do?

I smiled to cover my annoyance. "And how are we supposed to arrange an appointment with God?"

"Think about it—how does he react when we are filled with anger and hate? And we do resent him sometimes, even though we're his children." Steve trembled slightly, as if a chilly wind had blown over him. "I resented him plenty after the accident. I couldn't understand why he'd take Scotty . . . and once I asked why he'd take our son, who adored us, and leave us with a teenager who didn't give a flip about our family. But even in the face of my ugliest honesty, he didn't turn away. Even when I angrily pounded the arms of that easy chair, he never left my side. His Spirit kept telling me to trust him . . . one day at a time."

A trace of unguarded tenderness shone in Steve's eyes as he met my gaze. "She may choose to walk away from us. But no matter how angry you are for Britty's betrayal, no matter how hurt you are by what you've read, you can't give up on her, Diana."

"Part of me wants to." I thought of the vitriol running like a flaming thread through her diary. "Honestly, right now I'm ready to get her out of the house. She's been running around for God knows how long, lying to us, hating us—how can she hate us when we're the ones who work to put clothes on her back and a roof over her head? We've done nothing but support her and love her; we've tried to teach her the right things. We've brought her up in the best home we knew how to make, yet look how she has chosen to repay us!"

Steve rested his cheek in his hand. "I know, honey. I'm feeling the same things. But we can't make a mistake now, because our reaction to this could affect the rest of her life. We have to think and pray and proceed carefully."

"The parent of the prodigal," I murmured, my thoughts wandering.

"What's that?"

"Something our 'quip of the day' lady said a few weeks ago. She said that at some time, every parent is the parent of the wandering prodigal, with nothing to do but keep the house open to hope."

"She's right." The warmth of Steve's smile echoed in his voice. "She's exactly right, Diana. We have to hope and pray that Brittany comes around."

I listened, I heard, but I wasn't sure I was ready to take his advice. God might be long-suffering and forgiving . . . but I wasn't God.

Forty-three

IN A SUDDEN FLASH OF REVELATION, BRITTANY REAL-ized that nothing felt as awful—or as wonderful—as walking into the foyer and seeing her mom and dad in the living room beyond.

Awful, because she'd been caught in a lie . . . and the lie was the least of what she'd done tonight.

Wonderful because her parents were together.

Terrible because neither of them looked inclined toward sympathy. Somehow the infamous united front had pulled together over the divide of divorce.

Better face the music.

Drawing a deep breath, she took a step forward. "I'm sorry."

Ignoring the apology, Mom straightened in her chair. "Where were you?"

"And who were you with?" Dad's brows lowered in a frown.

Crossing one arm over her chest, Brittany knew it'd be best to tell the truth . . . or as much of the truth as they could handle.

"I was with Zack Johnson." She glanced from her mom to her dad. "You don't know him."

Her mother fixed her in a hot glare. "You told me you were spending the night with Charisse."

"I didn't."

"Is this the first time you've lied to us?"

Looking at the floor, Brittany weighed her options. If she confessed to a few things, maybe the other things would remain hidden. "No. I've been out a couple of times with Zack."

When she looked up again, her father wore a look of astounded horror. "What do you *do* all night?"

"Nothing, Dad." She shrugged. "We go to Dunkin Donuts or Steak 'n Shake . . . or sometimes we just go to the beach and talk. A couple of times he's taken me back to Charisse's house."

Mom's hand went to her throat. "Charisse's mother lets you come in at all hours of the morning?"

"Charisse's mother goes to bed." Brittany dared to meet her mother's burning gaze. "I just tap on Charisse's window, and she gets up to let me in."

"Brittany—" Her father leaned forward, resting his elbows on his knees. "I don't understand why you felt it necessary to lie to us. If you want to date this boy, why didn't you bring him home to meet us? We're not opposed to you dating. We're not monsters."

Lowering her gaze, Brittany shrugged.

"Your father asked a good question." Her mother's voice came out hoarse, as if forced through a sore throat. "Despite what you think, we are not your jailers. I am not the wicked witch, and your father is a far cry from a Dumbo Dad."

A shiver struck Brittany's spine. Shifting her gaze, she saw a blue book on the coffee table. *The* blue book.

Her mother had read her diary. No wonder she was hacked.

She dared to risk indignation. "You *snooped*?"

"You gave me reason to," her mother answered in a level voice.

"I've always respected your privacy, but you lied to me. And when you break trust, Britt, you lose privileges. Even the privilege of privacy."

Brittany crossed one arm over her chest. "Can I go upstairs now?"

"I'm not sure we're done here." Mom looked at Dad. "Anything you want to say to your daughter while we're together?"

Dad nodded. "You bet there is."

Forty-four

I SANK BACK IN MY CHAIR, ALL TOO RELIEVED THAT Steve had come and was now talking to our daughter. He had been right about one thing: I was too hurt, too angry, and too wounded to handle the situation rationally. I couldn't forget what Brittany had written about me driving into a lake and how she wouldn't call 911 if I were drowning.

What had I done to evoke that kind of hostility? I had done nothing but love the kid, sacrifice for her, and pray for her. I hadn't been a perfect parent, but I'd done the best I could . . . hadn't I?

When Steve and I first married, I had wanted a baby more than anything. After nearly three years of riding the infertility roller coaster, we decided to adopt—and signing the agency agreement had been a huge leap of faith. Steve was just beginning his practice, still paying off school bills, and I was struggling to finish my master's degree. Money was tight in those days, but somehow we obtained a second mortgage on our small home and forked over a check to the adoption agency. We passed another anxious eighteen months before the agency placed Brittany Jane with us.

As sure as I lived, I knew God wanted us to be parents. Steve loved children, and motherhood was the desire of my heart. How could a loving God fail to grant the position he had designed us to fill?

He didn't. At six weeks of age Brittany came home, a tiny, beautiful pink bundle of smiles. We adored her, and I finally felt truly fulfilled. I took her everywhere, even to school when I studied in the library. When I walked up to get my diploma, I carried Britt in a Snugli on my chest.

I had been made for motherhood, or so I thought. When Brittany went to school, I took pains to be available whenever needed. I served as a room mother, I baked dozens of cookies for her class and served as a minivan chauffeur on field trips. I attended every science fair, speech meet, concert, and fund-raising event. Steve, who by that time had built a thriving practice, reserved Saturdays and Sundays for family outings and church.

I thought life couldn't get any better. And when Britt entered middle school and wanted to be let out of the car at the corner so her friends wouldn't see her with me, I reminded myself that this behavior was typical for the age. Pulling away was natural and normal; she had to learn to stand on her own within her peer group. She was becoming an exotically beautiful young lady, and my heart sang every time I looked at her.

Then Scott Daniel came. My thoughts turned again to diapers and sleepers, but this time the miracle had happened within my own body. I breast-fed him—a wonder!—and sometimes I think we bonded in a way Brittany and I never had. Because my radio career began while I was pregnant with Scott, I worked extra hard to do all the things I had done for Britt. I didn't have time for much else, but by then Brittany had dropped out of her extracurricular activities, and seemed intent on pretending she didn't even have parents—

I felt the truth all at once, like an electric jolt through my spine.

I had nearly lost my daughter.

"We love you, Britty," Steve was saying, "and you will always have a home with us. But if you lie to us, if you demonstrate that you cannot be trusted, you will face the consequences. If you cannot function as a part of this household with a compliant spirit and a willing heart, you are free to leave. We will help you pack your things, and we will set you free."

His voice softened as his eyes filled. "We don't want you to leave. We want to support you in college; we want to stand by you through life. But if you cannot live with us, Brittany Jane, you can live without us. The choice is yours to make."

Britt's chin wobbled as she looked up. "I'm sorry." Her gaze fell on the diary, and I knew she had to be thinking of all she had written— things I hadn't even read.

"Take some time," Steve said, "and think about your decision, because this isn't something you can dismiss with a simple apology. I'm sorry we haven't caught this pattern of disobedient behavior sooner, and I apologize for not being as vigilant as I should have been. Now you need to decide whether you want to be part of this family or step out on your own."

Her face twisted. "How can you say that? This isn't a *family* anymore."

Oh, no. I would not allow her to shift the blame for her misdeeds to our shoulders. And if she wanted to match pain for pain, the events of this night had left me armed and bristling for battle.

"You said you wouldn't even call for help if I drove into the lake—" Anguish choked off my voice. I stared at her. "You wouldn't care if I *died*?"

Her eyes filled with tears, but I couldn't tell if they sprang from shame, fear, or guilt. I waited, but she did not apologize, nor did she deny a word she'd written.

And in that moment I experienced what psychologists describe as the fine line between love and hate. My passionate yearning for my daughter, wounded by her words, flamed into an equally passionate revulsion.

"Finish up with her," I told Steve, weeping as I rose from my chair. "I can't stay here."

Leaving them together in the living room, I crossed the foyer in swift steps and let myself out into the darkness.

forty-five

STEVE LOOKED AT HIS WEEPING DAUGHTER AND KNEW she'd not soon forget this night. This was not a simple matter of being caught in a lie. Tonight they had pulled back the curtain and seen their daughter as she really was.

Charisse's phone call had been a blessing in disguise. If she hadn't called, and if Diana hadn't found the diary, they might still believe their daughter was no more than a moderately troublesome teenager.

"We love you very much, Britty." He stood in order to look directly into her eyes. "But you've hurt us deeply—not only by your actions, but by your words."

Her chin trembled when he gestured toward the diary. He thought she wanted to deny the things she'd written, but couldn't.

He slipped his hands into his pockets. "I know it hasn't been easy being our kid. That's why we're offering you a way out. But home is the place where you'll always be welcome, and we're the parents who will always love you."

Weeping in earnest now, she sank to the love seat in front of him. "I could live with you." She paused to swipe at her cheeks. "Mom's mad at me, so if I lived with you—"

"Your mom's anger will pass, but it's going to take her a while to get over the hurt. I'm hurt, too. You can't treat us with hate and disdain and expect us not to feel anything in response."

"I'm sorry, okay?" She shifted, clearly unwilling to meet his gaze. "Can I go upstairs now?"

He nodded. "If you have nothing to add, I suppose we're done here."

Rising, she whirled away and took the stairs two at a time.

Exhaling slowly, Steve sank back to the sofa and watched her go. He would have liked to see something more from her, some sign of genuine brokenness as opposed to regret that she'd gotten caught. But for better or worse, this situation was finished. She would decide how they'd play the next act.

He lowered his head to his hand. Never in a hundred years would he have believed he'd reach the point where he'd have to ask his beloved daughter to leave home, but he couldn't stand by and do nothing while she lived in rebellion.

Abashed at his choice of words, he shook his head. It felt ridiculous telling a kid to leave home when there was no more unified home to leave. Most kids would do what she had suggested—if they had a falling out with Mom, they'd move in with Dad until things got tough there, then they'd hightail it back to Mom's house. Back and forth, like some kind of human ping-pong ball, forced out only when both parents had endured all the trials they could handle . . . or they just couldn't care anymore.

Thank God, he still cared. And, though she had been cut to the quick, Diana still cared. The bond between her and Britty had been forged years ago, and it would grow strong again when Britty began to raise a family of her own. Maybe then she would learn how to see her parents as individuals, not as authority figures. Looking through the scope of hindsight, perhaps she'd appreciate the family she had enjoyed in her youth.

He closed his eyes as another bolt of remorse struck him. *Had* enjoyed? Why did he always find himself thinking in past tenses?

He stood, then crossed the foyer and went out the front door. Pausing on the front porch, he listened. A midnight silence enveloped the neighborhood, with no televisions, no music, no clattering skateboards to disturb it. Overhead, a wind whispered through the sheltering oak near the sidewalk, rustling like the silken swish of the black dress Diana used to wear on special evenings out.

The memory tugged at him, drew him onward. A light burned from the neighbor's front porch, and somewhere in the distance a dog barked. Steve stepped into the sultry darkness and began to walk, adding the quiet jingle of the change in his pocket to the night sounds.

He'd passed three houses when he saw Diana standing beneath the live oak. In the slanting silvery rays of moonlight she stood on the sidewalk, her shoulders bent, her head bowed, her hands pressed to her face . . . receiving, no doubt, her tears.

He quickened his pace to join her, and she looked up at the sounds of his steps on the sidewalk. When he opened his arms, she stepped into them willingly.

Without speaking he held her, all his loneliness and confusion fusing together in one surge of terrible yearning.

Forty-six

FEELING AS THOUGH DEVILISH HANDS WERE SLOWLY twisting the joy from my heart, I leaned against Steve's chest and cried out my anger, sorrow, and frustration.

"Why is God doing this to me? I'm not Job! But he's taken everything, beginning with Scott Daniel. He took my son, my job, my career, and now he's taking my daughter—"

Steve's hand, which had been stroking my shoulder, suddenly froze. "Your career?"

Pulling back, I palmed tears from my cheeks. "The network fired me when I announced my plans to proceed with the cloning. I'll be okay; my agent thinks I can get a TV show, but it couldn't have happened at a worse time."

He reached into his pocket, then offered me a handkerchief. "I'm sorry."

Grateful for his thoughtfulness, I took it and blew my nose. "Thanks. Really." Squinting, I looked up at him. "Is Britt okay?"

"She went up to bed. I imagine she'll cry herself to sleep, but this night has given her a lot to think about."

I pressed a hand to my temple, where I could already feel my veins warming up to a major migraine. "Me, too. I can't believe I never saw any signs of her feelings."

"We did see signs, Di. We misinterpreted them." Pausing, he looked at me, and I wondered at the speculation in his eyes. "What'd you say a minute ago about God doing this to you? I thought you had decided God had nothing to do with it."

I shook my head. "Maybe Pastor John had a point. All I know is that I really do feel like Job. It's like God decided to take everything I loved just to see if I'd curse him and die."

I paused to blow my nose, then dabbed at it with the handkerchief. My stomach writhed and knotted under Steve's compassionate gaze. I didn't know how to explain all the feelings storming my heart—I've always found it easier to verbalize thoughts than emotions—but I knew this man would listen without judging me too harshly.

"I tell you one thing—I'm ready to give up on advice-giving. I'm a fraud."

"Now, Diana—"

"It's true! I try to tell other people how to raise their children, and look at me! I can't raise a daughter, and I couldn't protect my son. I'm an utter failure, and—" Fresh tears choked my throat. "I can't even stay married!"

"Hush, now." His hands fell on my shoulders, then he lowered his head until his brow rested upon mine. "Diana, you're being too hard on yourself. I lost a son, too. My daughter's in trouble, too."

"But your entire life isn't falling apart. You still have your practice."

"That's crazy, Diana. I lost you, and *you* were my life. The practice is just busywork."

Amazed that he could still hold me with tenderness, I looked at him through a haze of tears.

"And you're forgetting something about Job. Job was a righteous believer, but he wasn't perfect. He was clinging to something even during all his trials, something God wiped away in the end."

Frowning, I pulled away. I thought I knew everything about Job, but I had no idea what Steve meant. "Job had nothing but his nagging wife, and who'd want to cling to her?"

Steve laughed. "I wasn't talking about his wife; I was referring to his pride. Even in his suffering, Job was proud of himself . . . until God showed him how small he was."

My husband—no, my friend—gave me a smile that gleamed in the moonlight. "What are you clinging to, Diana?"

Crickets chirped an accompaniment as I considered the question. What *did* I have left? I'd been stripped as thoroughly as an abandoned car. All I had now were dreams of the future and a desperate desire to hold my child again—

My thoughts came to an abrupt halt. The most important thing in my life since Scott Daniel's accident was the cloning. That hope kept me going, yet it had splintered my marriage and fractured my family.

I swallowed hard. Surely God wouldn't ask me to give up an opportunity he had provided.

Steve pressed through my silence. "Diana?"

"I know what you want me to say." I crossed my arms. "You want me to change my mind about the cloning. But I can't. It's my pearl of great price, the thing I am willing to give everything for."

Steve shook his head. "You've misunderstood the analogy."

Again, I had encountered stubborn stone. "I understand it fine! I know it's about salvation, but sometimes a verse can apply to more than one situation. And I really believe God sent the cloning opportunity our way. I think you're wrong to disagree with me. I think our divorce is wrong. I think Brittany's made wrong choices in her behavior. But most of all I think it'd be wrong to give up on my baby."

He looked at me then, and in his eyes I saw pity mingled with regret. "I should be getting back." He slid his hands into his pockets. "I've a full day tomorrow."

"Me, too," I answered, though I had absolutely nothing on my calendar. I'd probably sleep late and spend the afternoon sending out résumés.

"Before I go, though, I want to say this—you are doing your dead-level best to avoid facing reality, Diana. Scotty is gone, and there's nothing you can do about it. You can't bring him back. You can't replicate him. God brought him into our lives, yes, but God also took him away. And I have to believe he had a reason."

I resisted the childish impulse to throw my hands over my ears. "I don't want to hear this."

"Of course you don't. It's too painful. But in the last few months I've learned that grief is like standing in twilight. You can run west toward the setting sun, hoping to avoid the darkness, but the fastest way to see sunshine again is to walk east through the night. It's not easy, because grief is a lot darker than dusk. But it's the surest and least exhausting way to live in the sun again."

I stared at him, surprise mingling with indignation. Who was *he* to give me counsel? I had two degrees in psychology and one in biblical studies. He was a *dentist*.

Steve's face twisted in a small grimace, and I had the uncomfortable sense that he'd read my thoughts. "One thing I know," he said, featherlike lines crinkling around his eyes. "God is in the dark, too. I feel his presence every minute."

A wave of guilt slapped at my soul. How long had it been since I felt God's presence?

I raised my hand as if to ward away the question, then shook my head and turned toward home. We walked back together, then Steve got into his car while I walked into the dark house without him.

Forty-seven

STEVE WAITED UNTIL HE HEARD THE SLAM OF THE front door and the click of the deadbolt, then he started the car and pulled out into the street. With every yard he traveled, the emptiness in his soul seemed to expand.

He was driving away from the two women he loved most in the world, and both were in terrible pain. Both of them needed him.

Neither of them wanted him.

His fingers tightened around the steering wheel. Once he'd told his Sunday school class that he hadn't really understood the depths of God's love until he became a parent; tonight he was glimpsing the depths of God's forgiving mercy.

He loved them; he saw the error of their ways and the denial in their hearts. Brittany had been showered with love and affection from the moment they grafted her into their family, and nothing would ever make him stop loving her.

So why did she resist him? Why hadn't she broken down in remorse and fallen into his arms? Her feeble "I'm sorry" meant, "I'm sorry you caught me," nothing more. Defiance had still gleamed in her eyes when she raced up the stairs, and soon she would be away at school where they'd have no way to supervise her.

All they could do was pray.

He pulled up to a red light. A teenage couple sat in the car next to him, the girl draped over the boy, the boy energetically chewing something as he bounced in time to the throbbing rhythm of whatever was pounding through his speakers.

Looking away, Steve shook his head. Why were people so stubborn?

Diana was the worst. She could be as stubborn as a stuck door when she made up her mind to believe something. No amount of pushing or prying could shake her free of her convictions.

Yet he understood what drove her toward cloning. Her ability to love deeply was one of the things that had first attracted him to her. She brought passion to her projects, she threw herself headlong into whatever causes she felt led to undertake, and he'd always stood with her, supporting her.

This time, though, he couldn't follow her.

The light changed. He waited until the teenager in the next lane had roared ahead, then he eased down on the accelerator and turned the car toward Clearwater Beach.

He pressed his hand to his chest, where his heart literally ached.

Father . . . why does love have to hurt so much?

Forty-eight

I SLEPT THAT NIGHT IN A SHALLOW DOZE IN WHICH dreams mingled with inchoate fragments of memory. I sought my dream of Scott Daniel, but it was Brittany's face, pale and sorrowful, playing on the backs of my eyelids, followed by Steve's sad smile as he said good-bye on the front porch.

Waking was a relief. At seven o'clock I flung off the heavy comforter and padded down the hall, then quietly peeked into Brittany's bedroom. Something in me feared she had slipped away for good in the night, but her form lay beneath the covers, her red hair streamed across the pillow.

Closing the door, I breathed a prayer of thankfulness and climbed back into my big bed. After drawing the heavy comforter over my shoulders, I nestled into the warm space I had occupied all too short a time. But wakefulness had deposited remnants of reality upon my pillow, needling thoughts that weren't about to let me retreat into unconsciousness.

Unasked, my ex-husband had come when I needed him.

My daughter had been lying to us for months.

Steve still loved me.

My virtuous daughter wasn't virtuous.

Steve would come back if I could give up the most important thing in my life.

Brittany hated me with a passion.

If I didn't want Steve, some other woman would be happy to move into the space I had vacated. Steve was a good man, handsome, faithful, and a good provider. Furthermore, he was the marrying type. It wouldn't be long before some single woman caught him on her radar and flew in to intercept.

I had nearly lost my daughter—and I might lose her still.

Steve would not come back unless I gave up the cloned baby . . .

But I couldn't lose the baby, too. At the moment, the baby was the most certain thing in my future.

I lay with my eyes closed for fifteen minutes, then gave up the struggle to sleep. I climbed out of bed, showered, and went downstairs for my morning caffeine. Twenty minutes later I was sitting in my study with the yellow pages open.

I called the first three realtors listed, made appointments for them to see the house, and promised myself I'd sign an agreement with the first one to show up with an adequate marketing plan. Within seven weeks Brittany would be leaving for college, and even if the house sold tomorrow, it'd take at least six weeks for us to de-clutter, pack, and handle the paperwork required for closing.

I spent the rest of my Saturday interviewing real-estate agents. One dear lady hugged me three times when hearing of my sad situation (divorce, empty nest, job relocation); the second woman made regretful *tsk*ing noises as we toured the house.

I hired the third agent out of sheer weariness. He shook my hand, produced a listing agreement, and told me the sign guy would plant the "For Sale" sign first thing Monday morning.

Brittany and I avoided each other for the rest of the day. She did not go to Charisse's house, but stayed in her room. Something in me hoped she was tossing out trashy magazines and obscene CDs, but when I walked past her door, nothing in her room had changed.

After dinner I moved through the house with a notepad in one hand and a pencil behind my ear, making a list of all the cosmetic things I'd have to do to sell the house. The paint on my shower ceiling was peeling; the paintings in the stairwell would have to come down so I could patch the nail holes and repaint the wall. The carpets would have to be cleaned; the sod patched, fresh flowers planted in the pots beside the front door. Maybe geraniums, since they were bright and easy to grow . . .

Since I'd put all Scott Daniel's things in storage for the new baby, his room was pristine. Brittany's room—well, I'd just promise prospective buyers that I'd install new carpet and paint the walls in September. No sense in cleaning a room that would be a wreck again by nightfall.

On Sunday Britt and I went to church. We sat together in the service, not looking at each other and not speaking. The sermon was on God's sovereignty, and I found myself praying that Brittany would listen.

Our pastor talked about the media in today's society, and I found myself thinking of the terrible magazines I'd seen in Britt's bedroom. Then he read God's message to the prophet Isaiah: "I am the one who exposes the false prophets as liars by causing events to happen that are contrary to their predictions. I cause wise people to give bad advice, thus proving them to be fools."

I could only hope Britt would realize she'd been reading bad advice.

She spent all Sunday afternoon in her bedroom, venturing out only long enough to eat and dart into the bathroom. I tried talking to her about trivial things like the weather when she came into the kitchen, but my attempts at conversation fell flat.

Sunday night I went into her bedroom and stood in the doorway. Britt sat upon her bed, one leg crossed, the other dangling over the edge of the mattress.

"I love you, Britt"—tears weakened my voice—"I'm sorry for the times I wasn't there for you."

A shadow of annoyance crossed her face. "What are you apologizing to *me* for? I'm the one who messed up."

"We all mess up, honey. But just as the Lord forgives us, we need to forgive each other. I need you to forgive me, and I'll forgive you."

She lowered her gaze to the magazine on her bed, though the twitch of a muscle in her jaw told me she was upset. I waited for a response, but she said nothing.

"Britt? Do you forgive me?"

"Yes." The reply was sharp.

"I forgive you, too." I spoke in as gentle a tone as I could manage. "And tomorrow will be a new day, a new week. We can each start over with a clean slate."

She didn't answer, but I walked forward and drew her stiff body into my arms, holding her long enough to whisper again, "I love you, honey."

I wouldn't have been surprised if she were rolling her eyes while I hugged her.

She didn't dissolve, she didn't confess, she only remained silent. I left her sitting there, knowing I had done the best I could at the moment. What was it Charity had said? At some time every parent is the parent of the wandering prodigal . . . and prodigals had to *want* to come home.

I rose early on Monday morning. After a cup of coffee, a quick shower, and enough newspaper reading to convince me I wasn't the most miserable woman in the world, I went to my desk with a blank legal pad. I had never submitted a formal proposal—my radio career had begun almost accidentally after I accepted a six-week gig as a temporary host. Our ratings soared, my position became permanent, and my career blossomed when we were picked up by the network.

I wrote the word *staff*, then scrawled, *Gary Ripley, producer.* That much was easy; I couldn't imagine doing a show without Gary. We'd been together so long he could practically read my mind, and I was certain he would welcome a move to television. Radio had its perks, but the potential demographics of television made it look like small potatoes. Our earning potential would rise dramatically, too, and Gary certainly wouldn't mind making more money.

I grinned, thinking of him working on-camera like producer Michael Gelman, who had a huge on-screen presence on *Live with Regis and Kelly*. Gary was a handsome guy, young enough to draw the eighteen-to-thirty-four demographic, and the camera would eat him up. So would my audience.

I tapped the pencil against my cheek as I considered other possible staff members. Chad would probably get a kick out of being employed by a television network, but he worked for other radio shows, too, so I wasn't sure he would want to leave WFLZ.

Maybe I was putting the cart before the horse. We had to sell the concept of the show first; we could worry about staff later. And my agent would know what sorts of personnel perks were negotiable.

I had just fleshed out an introductory statement—*Dr. Diana Sheldon, renowned radio host and experienced counselor, offers moral and ethical perspectives on the latest medical technologies, with an emphasis on reproductive technologies*—when the phone rang, scattering my thoughts.

I picked it up. "Hello?"

The caller was Cynthia Somebody-or-Other, calling from the personnel office of WHGK in Fort Lauderdale. Her voice was warm and friendly.

My thoughts focused immediately. "WHGK? Are you a talk-radio format?"

"That's us." My heart did a double-beat. Could they have heard about my availability? I wasn't looking for a job at an independent station, but if this was the door God opened . . . Working in Florida might be a good option for Brittany's sake, since she would be going to Florida State.

I took care to match Cynthia's friendly tone. "What can I do for you?"

"I'm calling about Gary Ripley. He has applied for a position and listed you as a reference. Do you mind if I ask you a few questions about Mr. Ripley?"

My mouth went dry. "Um, sure." I took pains to sound cheerful as I assured her that Gary was a good worker, innovative, reliable, and visionary.

"He was my right hand," I said, uncomfortably aware that I was speaking of him in the past tense. "I don't know what I'll do without him."

Cynthia Whoever seemed oblivious to the note of desperation in my voice as she thanked me and hung up. Dropping the handset back to the phone, I clapped my hand to my cheek and considered the paper on the desk before me.

Gary, who'd been my shadow for the last five years, had decided not to hitch his wagon to a falling star. Obviously he hadn't believed my assurances that we'd find a spot in television, and he had wasted no time applying at another station—probably half a dozen. Gary never did a thing halfway, and with his credentials he'd be hired within the month. Which left me alone, with no producer to help me shape the program, no friend to help me pitch the idea.

At least I still had my agent. As long as I paid him, he wouldn't jump ship.

I ate a tasteless lunch of tomato soup and stale crackers, then went back to my study and tried to focus on my task. Six weeks of severance pay wouldn't last long, and I needed to pay my lawyer and set money aside for Project One's fee.

Time to type up the official proposal. I slid into my desk chair and rolled across the tile floor, then picked up the legal pad and propped it against the printer. I had no sooner clicked on the icon for my word processing program than the phone rang again.

I stared at it, wondering if this was yet another call from a personnel office. Gary would be thorough, and as much as I wanted to tell anyone who called to go jump in a lake, I couldn't do that to a friend.

Sighing, I picked up the phone. "Hello?"

"Dr. Diana Sheldon?"

Gritting my teeth, I glanced at the caller ID. No station call letters this time, just a private number with a Fort Lauderdale area code. Probably someone from WHGK wanting to know where to send Gary's first paycheck.

"Speaking."

"You don't know me, but I've been dying to talk to you."

Inwardly, I groaned. *This* was the reason I had an unlisted number. At work I took calls from the public all day; I did not want to do telephone counseling at home. Besides, hadn't this person heard I was out of the business?

"I'm sorry," I said, "but I really can't take counseling calls now. And how did you get this number?"

"Please, Dr. Diana—" The woman's voice wavered. "A friend gave me your number; she saw it somewhere in her office. I called because I have to know about cloning. I desperately want to do it, and no one here seems to understand why this is something I have to do."

I didn't hang up. Despite the intrusion, I leaned forward on the desk.

"Tell me your story."

"I have a son—his name is Tyler; he's three months old. He was perfectly healthy at birth, but he developed pneumonia when he swallowed some amniotic fluid. The doctors gave him a drug—too much, actually—and it severely damaged his lungs. We've filed a lawsuit and we'll soon have the money to do the cloning procedure. I've read about your situation in the paper, and my husband and I know our best answer is cloning."

"Really." I felt myself begin to relax. If Steve were here, I'd put him on the extension to hear this woman's perspective. Maybe then he'd begin to understand that it was perfectly rational to want to produce a twin who could continue when one child's life had been prematurely ended.

"Do you have access to Tyler's tissue samples?"

"Yes. He was genetically perfect at birth, but with his damaged lungs the doctors say he may not live past the age of three or four. So I want to have another baby—"

"Wait." A sudden chill touched my spine. "Your son is still living?"

"Of course. Our doctors all agree a lung transplant is Tyler's best chance at a normal life. And since he is still young and small for his age, there's a good chance the clone's lungs will grow quickly to catch up."

I felt a sudden coldness in my stomach, as though I had swallowed a fist-sized chunk of ice. "I'm sorry. I didn't catch your name."

"Glenda. Glenda Jones."

"Well, Glenda, let me see if I'm understanding the full picture— you want to conceive a child in order to use his body for spare parts? You want to give this new baby's lungs to your present son?"

"That's the idea." Her voice held a note of surprise. "I thought you understood."

"But . . . that's illegal." My mind flashed back to Andrew's reasoned defenses of the cloning procedure. "Cloned children are perfectly protected under existing American law. You're talking about infanticide."

"I'm talking about a late-term abortion." Glenda spoke in an eerily calm voice. "My doctors haven't exactly endorsed the plan, but I've done enough research to know it's perfectly feasible. I'll go overseas to have the clone implanted. Then when I'm full term, I'll have a late-term procedure and the doctors will use the fetal lungs for a transplant. You'll probably deliver first, so you'll get all the publicity while my husband and I quietly do what we must to save our son."

Stunned beyond words, I sat still as the full import of her words hit me. She was talking about a D&X, or partial-birth abortion, in which a surgeon delivers a late-term baby feetfirst. We had debated the issue on my show often enough that I could recite the horrific details verbatim. The surgeon used his fingers to deliver the baby's lower extremity, then the torso, the shoulders, and the neck. The skull, however, would become lodged at the opening to the uterus, for the mother's cervix would not have dilated enough for it to pass through. The baby would be turned upside down, his spine facing the ceiling. While his little arms and legs kicked, the surgeon would slide the fingers of his left hand along the baby's back and hook the shoulders with his index and ring fingers. Next the doctor would take a pair of blunt, curved Metzenbaum scissors in his right hand. He would carefully advance the tip, curved edge down, along the spine and under his middle finger until he felt it contact the base of the skull. He would then force the scissors into the baby's head. Once the blade had entered, he would spread the scissors to enlarge the opening, then remove the blade and insert a suction tube to draw out the infant's brain . . .

A tremor wriggled up the back of my neck. If this woman needed a healthy set of infant lungs, she would wait until the last possible moment to have the abortion, for the lungs developed only in the last stages of pregnancy.

With the phone in my hand, I trembled until I thought my teeth would chatter. I had assured Steve such monstrosities would not happen in this country. Yet they could, and desperate people like Glenda would be certain they *would*.

A quiet voice reminded me that desperate mothers could do unimaginable things.

"Glenda"—my voice sounded strangled to my own ears—"I can't endorse what you're planning."

"I didn't call for your endorsement." Her voice had gone chilly. "I called for a phone number. I'd like you to place me in touch with the group who does the cloning. I understand their main office is in France?"

I closed my eyes. "I can't give you that information."

Silence hummed over the phone line for a moment. "I can't believe you'd refuse me. What do you want? Glory? We aren't trying to steal your thunder."

"I don't want . . . thunder."

"Then why are you refusing to help? Of all people, I thought you'd understand."

"I do understand." I closed my eyes as a window in my mind began to open. "More than you know."

"Well?" She waited, and when I did not respond, she huffed in my ear. "I can get it somewhere else, you know. I'll find that number. I'd do *anything* to save my son."

"I know."

She drew an audible breath and pressed on. "I was real sorry to hear about what happened to your little boy. That's why I thought you'd understand—when your child is sick and dying, you'll do anything to save him."

Troubled by images of a lifeless infant in a doctor's hand, I opened my eyes. My gaze fell upon a photograph of Steve, Britt, Scott Daniel, and me on our last trip to Disney World. Things had been so happy then, so normal. What would I give to return to that time?

"Not anything," I said, then hung up the phone.

For three days Glenda's conversation haunted me. Every time the phone rang I worried that she had called back, each chime of the computer made me flinch in the fear that she or some other desperate woman had found my e-mail address.

When I went to bed and closed my eyes, I did not dream of Scott Daniel. Instead, the vision of a prone infant in a surgeon's gloved hand fluttered across my eyelids. I dreamed of dead babies, I heard their cries in the wail of the lovelorn cat next door.

Waking in the throes of a nightmare, I would roll over and doze again, only to see images of clustered cells dividing to line up beside a primitive streak. These roly-poly circles, each colored by a brilliant string of forty-six chromosomes, marched across the movie screen in my mind and jiggled to the funky musical riff from the *Dr. Sheldon Show*. Disney's *Fantasia* animators would have been hard-pressed to compete with my imaginative subconscious.

I woke every morning more tired than I'd been when I went to bed.

I tried to concentrate on my daily routine, but other thoughts intruded. Most persistent was my personal theory that the egg and sperm must somehow contain a divine spark of life. If I was right—and I still believed I was—then those invisible seeds of a soul had to be present in a morula and a blastocyst, too. The flame of divine life flickered in every cell, no matter how small or undeveloped. And since we legally protected the eggs of bald eagles—which could be fertile or infertile, but were certainly only *potential* eagles—should we not also protect potential babies?

Science seemed to indicate that human life began approximately two weeks after conception. But some questions could not be settled by science . . . some matters depended upon higher disciplines and spiritual wisdom.

When cleaning off my desk one afternoon, I saw a notepad covered in my own scrawlings. At the top of one page I had written, *How can we say a blastocyst is a person?*

Now I wondered how we could know a blastocyst was not two people, or even three. More to the point, how could I have imagined that these matters had nothing to do with me?

I wanted to discuss these thoughts with someone, but Brittany was rarely at home and I doubted she'd be interested. Steve might have listened if I called, but I'd given up the right to telephone him at any hour with random musings.

So I carried my thoughts to bed, where they churned and stewed in my weary psyche, then spilled out into my dreams.

The moment I opened the car door, I knew I had returned to the hospital in my recurrent dream. The steady whoosh of cars on the highway provided an accompaniment to the pounding of my heart, and Steve's greeting sent a thrill down every nerve of my body.

Despite the events of the last few days, Scott Daniel had not left me. In this hospital, at least, he still lived and breathed.

"This way," Steve called, and I ran after him, nearly passing him in my eagerness to reach Scott's room. I gave the old men at the receptionist's desk only a passing glance; the pregnant women in wheelchairs could have been mere wallpaper. Reaching the elevator before Steve, I slapped the call button with my palm, then leaned against the wall in order to avoid the flood of faceless folks who would pour out in only a moment.

The dream did not disappoint. The elevator chimed, the animated mannequins rushed forward, and I whirled into the elevator without so much as a backward glance. As I pressed the single button, I realized that this was what psychologist Frederik van Eeden had called a "lucid dream"—a dream in which the sleeper knows she is dreaming.

I knew it, all right, and I didn't care. Reality had become so difficult in the last few weeks that I couldn't wait to see Scott, to be his mother again.

When the elevator doors opened, I ran through the sea of mist to his room, then pushed the door open. Unlike the other times, Steve had not arrived before me. No one kept a vigil with my boy, but he was not completely alone. A dark-haired doctor in a white lab coat stood in the curtained shadows, his clipboard shining through the gloom.

Ignoring the physician, I hurried to Scott's bedside, then pressed my palm to his cheek. Thankfully, it was still warm.

"He's alive." I breathed the words as a prayer of gratitude.

"Of course he is," the doctor answered in a low voice that was at once powerful and gentle. "But he's not here, Diana."

"He will be when he wakes up." I trailed a fingertip down the length of Scott Daniel's nose. "Wake up, sweetie. The sun's come up and so should we, snugglebugs though we may be."

I waited, listening to the click and hiss of the respirator, but Scott did not respond.

"Diana." The doctor spoke again, his voice commanding my attention. "You have to let him go."

"No." Refusing even to look in his direction, I kept my gaze fastened to my son's sweet face. "He's only asleep. He'll come back to me; I'm trying so hard to bring him back—"

"Diana." The man's voice wasn't much above a whisper, but the effect was as great as if he'd shouted in my ear.

I cast an irritated look over my shoulder. "Don't you have someplace else to be?"

From the corner of my eye, I saw a smile light his face. "My place is with you and Scott. I've been with you both all along."

I shuddered and fought down the momentary unease that twisted my stomach. "You're a figment of my imagination—a fantasy physician, probably inserted by the part of my brain that insists on facing reality."

"Scott Daniel is happy in my Father's house . . . and you need to have faith in my promise."

Have faith in *what* promise? That was the trouble with dream doctors, they didn't have to make any sense.

Dropping my hands to the railing at the edge of the bed, I whirled to confront the meddlesome physician . . . and what I saw turned my knees to water.

The doctor's lab coat fairly shone with such brilliance my eyes began to sting. His hair gleamed like spun silk under the hospital lights while his eyes glowed with power, authority, and compassion.

When he spoke my name again, I understood how he had summoned the dead from Hades and calmed the stormy seas. Slowly, I released my grip on the bed railing and dropped to my knees, the floor tiles cold under my hands as my heart knocked in fear and dread.

Something—perhaps the instinctive drive for self-preservation—woke me. I lay flat on my back, my sweating palms pressed to the bedsheets, my eyes fixed on the spinning ceiling fan overhead. My heart felt as heavy as a stone within my chest, weighing me down so I could not move.

After a long while, I found my voice. "It was a dream. A lucid dream. That's all."

But I lay without turning until the rising sun fringed the window blinds and a mockingbird heralded my return to a new day.

Forty-nine

ON FRIDAY I MANAGED TO SHOVE TROUBLING thoughts about dreams and medical ethics aside long enough to input the final changes on my proposal for a televised *Dr. Sheldon Show*. My agent had been talking up the program since Monday, but I knew he'd need something polished in hand to seal the deal.

At 11:00 A.M. I was doing my best to nibble off the remaining vestiges of my right thumbnail when the phone rang. I glanced at the caller ID—the name was unavailable, but I recognized a New York area code.

I snatched up the phone. "Hello?"

"Diana Sheldon, please."

"Speaking."

"Dr. Sheldon, this is Les Phillips, director of programming at the WB Network. I talked to your agent this morning, and we're very excited about the possibility of hosting your new television show. We'd like to bring you to New York to discuss the possibilities. Would you be open next week?"

A rush of pleasure warmed my face as my hand flew to my desk calendar. "Any particular day?"

"How about Tuesday? I know that's short notice, but we have a morning slot we're trying to fill. Your agent has given me a brief synopsis of what you'd like to do, but we're anxious to talk to you personally. We'd like to get things started before you go to Europe to have the procedure done."

My fingers froze on the calendar pages. "You want the program to address cloning?"

"We want to follow your pregnancy from the first moment. We'll begin with a prime-time special covering your court battle for the tissue samples, and we'll be sure to mention the sacrifices you've made in order to follow this dream to its conclusion. We'd like to get some shots of your son and have you talk about him on camera."

"Oh." I couldn't come up with anything more profound; my brain was reeling.

Phillips laughed. "We are absolutely gonzo about this idea. Not since Katie Couric had her colonoscopy on live television has anyone done anything like this—and your ratings will leave Katie in the dust. The country's first cloned child—it's killer! And we'll be with you every step of the way." His voice lowered to a conspiratorial tone. "Your agent mentioned the matter of your expenses, of course, and I'm pleased to report that our network would be more than willing to cover all costs related to the procedure."

"You'll pay all the expenses? The fees, the travel—"

"Everything. After all, we'll be putting your life on public display. Your agent says you're okay with this."

I bit my lip. "To a point. Once the baby is born, I'd want to be left alone."

"No problem. It's the conception and delivery we're most interested in. If at a later date you want to show his picture on the air so viewers can see how he's growing up, that'd be great. By that time your show will have branched out into other areas, and I'm sure other reproductive technologies will be in the spotlight. We'll expect you to keep our viewers on the cutting edge of the reproductive revolution."

"I see." I would be the first, so the network wanted to capitalize on my opportunity. They'd pay for the privilege, though, which meant my financial worries would end.

I struggled to think of a question that would make me sound intelligent instead of dumbfounded. "Would the show be filmed in New York?"

"That's negotiable. It's possible we could film in Tampa, since that's your home base. We'll rent a studio, and you could have input in the hiring of capable staff. Sure, I think we could consider a satellite show. We're certainly willing to negotiate."

I leaned back in my chair. This offer would mean coast-to-coast coverage of my pregnancy, as well as national and international publicity . . . and both Steve and Brittany would despise that kind of attention. But Britt would be away at college, so she wouldn't be faced with it every day, and if Steve was determined to remain an ex-husband, he would be out of the picture.

That thought brought another in its wake, along with a chill that struck deep in the pit of my stomach. Steve might be out of the picture, but I'd be influencing hundreds of women like Glenda Jones, women who urgently wanted a child, and couples who were willing to work within existing laws to chase their desperate desires.

People like me.

Cold, clear reality swept over me in a terrible wave, one so powerful I struggled to breathe. For weeks—months—I had been focused on my desire to restore my son, but if I went on national television, the same women who went to their hairdressers to demand Jennifer Aniston haircuts could go to Project One to demand cloning for any number of reasons . . . and in this country those developing babies would not be protected until birth. What if pressure from those people caused American politicians to rethink their positions on cloning? Science would declare open season on morulas, blastocysts, and human embryos, all of which contained the seeds of eternal souls.

Project One wanted publicity; they would get it from me in spades if I went through with this.

"I can't." I heard myself say the words before I consciously gathered the courage to bend them to my will.

I heard the rustling of papers over the line. "You can't come next week?"

"No—" I closed my eyes, a sick feeling deep inside me. *Dear God, what was I thinking?* "I can't come at all. I can't do the show."

"If the lack of privacy concerns you, I promise we'll handle the matter in good taste." Phillips's tone suggested he was trying hard to speak clearly to a novice. "Your agent says you know how to handle the press—"

"It's not the publicity."

"The money, then. We're completely agreeable to a fair salary in addition to the fees we'll be paying. And nearly everything is open to negotiation."

I realized I was crying only when I tasted the salt of my tears running into the corners of my mouth. "You don't understand, Mr. Phillips. I can't take your job . . . because I can't go through with the cloning."

My refusal fell on the stony ground of his silence, but I lifted the family photo on my desk and held it against my heart. "I'm not sure I can explain my reasons in a way you'll understand, but my decision is irrevocable. It has taken me a long time to see things clearly—*Too long, Lord. I'm so sorry*—But I know one thing—what you're suggesting would cost too much."

"But we're paying for everything!"

"I'm talking about the currency of human life."

I thanked him for his time, then hung up. Moving on legs that felt like wooden stumps, I climbed the stairs and went into Scott Daniel's room, then sat on the edge of his bed as comprehension began to seep through my despair.

What had I done?

A few days ago I had been wondering why the Spirit of God hadn't knocked my daughter flat with conviction while I should have wondered the same thing about myself. Every parent at some time is the parent of the wandering prodigal, but in this situation *I* was the prodigal and God the parent . . . how long had he been waiting for me to understand? He had tried to speak to me through people, through his Word, even through my dreams, and I'd turned a deaf ear to every plea.

A snatch of Scripture from last Sunday's sermon drifted back to me on a current of memory: *I am the God who kills and gives life; I am the one who wounds and heals.*

I thought of how Britt had chafed against the rules I had instituted to protect her. She would say I was trying to wound her, when in fact I wanted only to love her.

God had led me to the valley of the shadow of death, and I had refused to walk through it. I had kicked and screamed and railed against his will, then I calmly plotted a course around the valley, thinking I could join my family on the other side unscathed.

What a fool I'd been. I had hurt all the people I loved most. By taking matters into my own hands, I had systematically destroyed my life.

I thought God was intent upon wounding me.

He wanted only to draw me closer.

I had been running from that severe love since Scott Daniel's accident, chasing the fading sunlight rather than stepping into the darkness and holding tight to my loved ones.

"God, forgive me. I've been so blind." Dredging the admission from a place beyond logic and reason, I closed my eyes. "Forgive me for being selfish, proud, and stubborn. Open my eyes now to the things that matter, to the things you'd have me do."

By the time I had finished unburdening my guilty heart, the shadows had shifted from the Tampa Bay Bucs wallpaper to the red-uniformed tin soldiers. I stood on trembling legs and crossed to the closet where I had stored Scott Daniel's toys.

Reaching up, I took the plastic-shrouded monkey from the top shelf, then pulled away the wrapping. Sinking onto the bed, I gathered the yellow-and-black monkey in a tight embrace and inhaled the scents of foam rubber, my beloved son, and love.

Bending over it, I bowed my head as the tears began in earnest.

Fifty

STEVE PULLED UP TO THE HOUSE AND PARKED ON THE curb, then got out and slipped his keys into his pocket. Diana had said she was going to hire someone to cut the grass, but obviously she hadn't gotten around to it. His once-beautiful lawn, which grew like a jungle in the rainy months of summer, was looking a little wild. The red-and-white For Sale sign in the center of the lawn sat in a tuft of grass six inches high.

He pressed his lips together as he walked to the door. No sense in ragging on Diana about the lawn, she'd obviously had a lot to do in trying to sell the house and find a new job. In addition to that, she still had to deal with Brittany.

Brittany was doing better, Diana had said in her call, but she wanted him to come over to discuss something important. No, she couldn't discuss it on the phone and no, it really couldn't wait.

So here he was on a lovely Saturday morning, a man who should have been playing golf or trying to forget about his problems instead of running homeward every time his wife—*ex*-wife—called for help.

He rang the bell, and a moment later Britty opened the door. She looked thin around the eyes and cheeks, but she smiled when she saw him. "Hi, Dad!"

"Hi, kiddo." He gave her a hug, then peered past her into the foyer. "Is your mom around?"

"She's in the study, probably gabbing on-line. You can go on in if you want."

"No—I'll wait in the living room. She'll come out when she's ready."

He moved toward the formal living area they had used more in the last month than in the ten years they'd lived in this house. But he wasn't about to go into her study as if he belonged there. Diana had set the rules; she had relegated him to the position of *Outsider*. And Outsiders didn't go into private areas unless they were invited.

Britty had followed him, and now she leaned against the wall, her eyes alight. "Want something to eat? Some cookies, maybe? I made some last night."

He sank onto the sofa. "You didn't go out?"

"No." Her face fell. "That wouldn't have been such a hot idea. But Mom dug out her old recipe for snickerdoodles and we made a batch. They're pretty good, if you want one."

"Sounds good to me."

He placed his hands on his knees, about to rise, but she whirled away. "I'll get them," she called over her shoulder, moving down the hall.

He leaned back as an odd sense of disappointment slapped at him. So . . . even Britty wanted to treat him like a guest.

A moment later a shadow fell across the carpet. Diana stood in the doorway, and at the sight of her frayed smile he had to fight an overwhelming desire to enfold her in his arms. "Thanks for coming, Steve."

"No problem." He tried to grin as if he hadn't a care in the world. "What's up? You having trouble with your car?"

"No."

"Britty need an application signed? You need a tax form?"

She drew a deep, audible breath. "I need some brawn."

He laughed. "Diana, you can't call me over here every time you need someone to open a pickle jar—"

"It's not a pickle jar. It's something bigger."

Her eyes were gleaming with some emotion he couldn't define. Fear, perhaps? Insecurity?

"I need you," she began again, "to help me pull up the sign out front. Because we're not moving. Because I'm not going anywhere, not even to France."

He stared at her, searching her face, probing for the meaning behind her words. "You mean—"

"I'm not going through with the cloning, Steve. I called off my lawyer. I can't afford it."

So money had prevailed where he could not.

Looking down to hide his disappointment, he rubbed a smear on the arm of the sofa. "I'm sure the house will sell, Diana. And you'll find a job."

"It's not the money, it's everything else." She caught his gaze and held it. "I can't afford to lose you or Brittany."

Warmth spread through his bloodstream as his reserve began to thaw. "What are you saying?"

She lifted one shoulder in a shrug he had once found charming . . . and still did.

"I'm saying you were right. I was afraid to go through the darkness of grief. But earlier this week I began to understand that my actions were not only destroying my family, but others, too—people I have never even met." Her gaze lowered. "The cloning opportunity is not of God. I thought it was, but it couldn't be. I should have listened to you."

As a feeling of glorious happiness sprang up in his heart, Steve took her hand, drawing her to his side. "I'll be with you in the dark, Diana. I've been feeling my way through it for the last several months . . . and I think I've found the way out."

Her chin trembled. Her lips parted as if she would speak, then she closed her eyes and nodded.

Steve drew his wife into his arms and held her as she wept.

He stroked Diana's cheek, felt her tears on his fingertips, then buried his face in her shoulder and went quietly and thoroughly to pieces.

"I'll be with you, darling," he whispered when he could speak again. He ran his fingers through the strands of her hair. "Every step of the way."

Fifty-one

Humming along with Alan Jackson, I pressed the live mike button as the strains of his latest hit drifted away.

"Hold on tight, darlin'," I murmured in my most velvety voice as the music faded. "Lovely tune, isn't it? Now we have Thomas on the line, calling from Largo. Thomas, you there? What's on your mind tonight?"

"Lynda, is that you?"

"I'm right here, Tom." I smiled, warmed by the reminder of how quickly the listeners of country music's WCTY had warmed to "Lynda Love," the golden-voiced gal who spun tunes and talked to callers during the lonely hours of nine to midnight every weekday night. The program director had correctly figured that an out-of-work psychologist with a gift for gab might be just the person to charm the lonely and lovelorn.

As for me, I couldn't have been happier. Steve listened every night, often calling in to keep me company on the air, and once or twice Brittany had called from Tallahassee, where a friend of hers sometimes picked us up on the Web broadcast.

Steve and I had remarried in mid-August. He restored my wedding ring to my finger only a few days before we drove Brittany to Tallahassee and deposited her in a freshman dorm. She seemed to be doing well in school, and surprised us now and then with calls "just to talk." It was, I told Steve, as if she was finally beginning to see us as something other than parents.

"But we'll always be her parents," he'd protested.

"That's true. But this past year she saw us as authority figures, not people. One day I'd like to be her friend."

After writing Andrew Norcross to say I would not be pursuing cloning, I received a short note in reply. My deposit, he informed me, was nonrefundable, as it had already been spent on research.

Regretfully, I chalked up the cost to the price one pays for experience.

I paid a lot during those tumultuous four months—personally and with the emotions of the people I love. But God was merciful to me, and, like Job, he restored my losses. My husband was back in my home and my heart; my daughter, though still independent and reserved, seemed more open to us now that she was away from our direct supervision.

And my sweet Scott Daniel, my son, waited for me in heaven. I look forward to joining him there one day.

I enjoyed my new job even more than the *Dr. Sheldon Show.* The pressure was gone, and as "Lynda Love" I was able to be sweet and sentimental as opposed to sharp and synthetic. Instead of doling out principles and witticisms, I listened, I commiserated, sometimes I even wept. I became a different person, a lot softer and more sympathetic.

Sometimes I was a little dumbfounded when I realized that even a professional counselor could be blindsided by grief, but the human mind is amazing. It can nurture delusions; it can rationalize the vilest of crimes. Those who operated the ovens at Auschwitz learned to think of their Jewish prisoners as dirt, not people. And so they sent thousands to their graves.

I shuddered to think how close I came to falling victim to a similar sort of tunnel vision. Only the prayers of my husband and the grace of God kept me from going down a path that could have resulted in disaster not only for me, but for thousands of deluded people who could not see the dangers inherent in the work of Project One.

I learned that God is sovereign over the tragedies and triumphs of life. He is never caught by surprise, never perplexed by the things that happen. And he is so loving and powerful that he orchestrates even the tragedies of our lives so that good results from them.

Rebirth. Restoration. Renewal.

I realized all these things and more after submitting myself to the sovereignty of God. By accepting Scott Daniel's death instead of trying to circumvent it, I finally found peace.

I still had dark days . . . and sometimes the sight of that rubber-faced monkey spurred fresh tears. But Steve was right. God walked with me in the darkness, too.

On line one, Thomas from Largo was saying his teenage son was being rebellious.

"You're not alone, Tom. How old is your son?"

"Seventeen."

"That's a tough age."

"I just don't know what to do with him. He doesn't listen, he rolls his eyes at everything I have to say, and when he loses his temper—man, look out. We nearly had a fistfight the other night. My wife and I are counting the months until we can send him off to join the armed services."

I laughed softly. "I hear what you're saying, Tom, and I'm also the parent of a teenager. I sent my child off to college a few months ago, and I have to admit I had mixed feelings. Part of me was glad to see her go—for some of the reasons you've expressed and because I think life itself can teach her things she won't accept from me right now. But another part of me was sad to see her leave. I'll miss her and I worry.

From this point forward, she'll start to make her own choices, and that scares me silly. What we see as loving concern, our kids see as overprotection."

"So . . . how do you get through it?"

I smiled at the question. I was a slow learner, but the Lord had reminded me that I loved Brittany more than life, and not because she was my only remaining child. I loved her because of who she was, and because her arrival in our family had been no less miraculous than Scott Daniel's.

I hoped she would forgive me one day for forgetting that.

"How do I get through it? I pray, Tom. Deeply, fervently, and with tears, I lift my daughter up to the Lord and trust him to take care of her. When she asks for my advice, I'll give it, but until then I'll pray."

"Well, we pray, too," Tom drawled, "but sometimes it seems like our prayers aren't goin' much higher than the ceiling."

"Oh, they're going all the way up." I laughed softly. "You know much about oysters, Tom?"

"I know I don't like to eat 'em."

"Me, either. But you should also know that oysters are one of God's most wonderful creations. When a grain of sand enters their shell, they don't even try to eject the irritation. Instead they embrace it, pull it close, and surround it with their very essence. In time, their ability to wrap beauty around trouble results in a pearl."

I clicked the next button, which sent a stream of soft music over the airwaves. "That's what you need to do with your son, Tom. When he irritates you, embrace him, pull him close, and tell him you love him more than anything. In time, my friend, you'll have a pearl."

As the Dixie Chicks began to sing "Doctor, Please Bypass This Heart," I settled back in my chair, picked up the phone, and joined Tom in praying that the love of God would touch his son.

Discussion Questions / Study Guide

1. Some of Diana's actions may seem far-fetched to you, but grief often drives individuals to behavioral extremes. Have you ever suffered extreme grief? How did it affect you?

2. Diana enters deep denial after Scotty's death, confusing her desires with God's leading. How was God directing her during this time? Why did she miss hearing his voice? Has there been a time you felt you were hearing God's voice only to find out later that you'd been listening instead to your own desires? How did God help you through this time? How can we ensure we're really hearing God's voice?

3. What was ironic about Diana's philosophy of wifely submission in a Christian marriage? How does submission relate to our relationship with Christ?

4. At certain points of the story, you may have wondered if Diana's commitment to Christ was genuine. But isn't it possible for

believers to step out of fellowship with God and stray from his intended path for us? What must we do to restore that fellowship?

5. How did you feel about Diana's early views on cloning? Her later views? Do you think science will ever be able to pinpoint the moment a soul is created? Why or why not?

6. What sort of mother is Diana? What could she have done differently in Brittany's situation? Have you ever had reason to doubt your ability to parent your child in difficult situations? Where do you find help in those times?

7. This story illustrates how one wrong decision can systematically destroy everything in our lives. As Diana says, "Hurt people, hurt people." If we do not find healing, or if we do not repent and turn back, we drift farther and farther from the place we should be. Has someone you know experienced a similar situation?

   Perhaps there's someone in your own life who has hurt you deeply—is it possible that person was acting out of his or her own pain? What, if anything, can you do to encourage reconciliation?

8. Since the beginning of recorded history, man has pondered the meaning of suffering. God is not the author of evil, but neither is he its victim. As novelist Randy Alcorn says, "God is not only more powerful than any evildoer, he can take the worst evil and use it for the highest good . . . We can't figure out how that works. (Why should we expect our finite minds to understand the workings of the infinite God? Isaiah 55:8–9.) Fortunately, our inability to understand how it works never diminishes the sovereignty of God." What does this story teach you about the power of God?

Author's Note

NO WRITER TRULY WRITES ALONE, AND I OWE MANY thanks to many people.

First, I must thank the guys at the *Glenn Beck* radio program at WFLA in Tampa for letting me pop in one morning to observe. Thanks also to friend, minister, and novelist Al Gansky for providing up-to-date information on cloning and teaching me the meaning of *traducianism*.

Thanks to Susan Richardson, Marilyn Meberg, and my secret pal for reading through rough drafts and providing expert comments. Marilyn's delightful book *The Zippered Heart* provided the basis for the bear-and-the-preacher story. Robin Jones Gunn contributed the parents-as-guardrails metaphor.

The statistics about the population of heaven come from Dr. Harold Willmington's wonderful book, *The King Is Coming* (Tyndale House), and he cites the following verses to assure us that young children go to heaven upon death: 2 Samuel 12:23; Matthew 18:1–6, 10; 19:14; Luke 18:15–17.

Thank you to the community of writers known as ChiLibris for providing fellowship and the answers to all sorts of odd questions.

And now, the disclaimers:

This book is a little unusual because the most far-out situations are based in truth and the most ordinary are completely fictional.

Yes, the Raelians do exist; yes, apparently they do believe aliens created human life; and yes, they are intent upon human cloning. I am afraid we may see the successful cloning of a human infant in the next few years. The information about ACT is true. You can find Dr. Michael West's interview with CNN at http://www.cnn.com/2001/TECH/science/11/25/cloning.west.cnna.

Yes, much to my chagrin, the state of Florida does allow on-line divorces.

And while my family does contain two teenagers and a husband, all of them would want you to know they have not been depicted in this book.

ABOUT the AUTHORS

Award-winning novelist and speaker **Patricia Hickman** has published fourteen novels, including her critically acclaimed *Fallen Angels* and *Nazareth's Song.* Her works have been praised in such publications as *Publishers Weekly, Romantic Times,* and *Library Journal.*

HOMETOWN: Huntersville, North Carolina

Lori Copeland is a member of the Missouri Writers Hall of Fame. Her works have won numerous honors, including the Romantic Times Reviewer's Choice Award, Walden's Books' Best Seller, and Holt Medallion Awards.

HOMETOWN: Springfield, Missouri

Christy-Award winner **Angela Hunt** writes books for everyone who wants to expect the unexpected. With more than three million copies of her books sold worldwide, she is the best-selling author of *Unspoken, The Awakening, The Debt, The Canopy, The Note, The Pearl,* and *The Justice.*

HOMETOWN: Tampa, Florida